The Complete Magazine Stories of F. Scott Fitzgerald, 1921–1924

The Complete Magazine Stories of F. Scott Fitzgerald, 1921–1924

F. Scott Fitzgerald

Edited by Alexandra Mitchell and Jennifer Nolan

EDINBURGH
University Press

Edinburgh University Press is one of the leading university presses in the UK. We publish academic books and journals in our selected subject areas across the humanities and social sciences, combining cutting-edge scholarship with high editorial and production values to produce academic works of lasting importance. For more information visit our website: edinburghuniversitypress.com

Grateful acknowledgement is made to the sources listed in the List of Illustrations for permission to reproduce material previously published elsewhere. Every effort has been made to trace the copyright holders, but if any have been inadvertently overlooked, the publisher will be pleased to make the necessary arrangements at the first opportunity.

Edinburgh University Press Ltd
The Tun – Holyrood Road
12(2f) Jackson's Entry
Edinburgh EH8 8PJ

Typeset in 11/13 Adobe Sabon by
IDSUK (DataConnection) Ltd, and
printed and bound in Great Britain

A CIP record for this book is available from the British Library

ISBN 978 1 3995 1221 3 (hardback)
ISBN 978 1 3995 1223 7 (webready PDF)
ISBN 978 1 3995 1224 4 (epub)

Contents

List of Figures

Acknowledgments

No project of this type is possible without the help of many librarians and library staff. Research for this project was conducted in the Manuscript Reading Room at the Library of Congress in Washington DC, the Irvin Department of Rare Books and Special Collections at the University of South Carolina, and at the British Library.

Special thanks go to Michael Weisenburg, Reference and Instruction Librarian in the Irvin Department of Rare Books and Special Collections at the University of South Carolina libraries, for his research assistance and support, and Matt Hodge, User Services Librarian at University of South Carolina libraries, for his unparalleled PDF-making abilities. This project also owes much to the help and support of the North Carolina State University libraries, and particularly for the Tripsaver department, which consistently goes above and beyond to provide often difficult-to-locate materials.

Illustrations for this volume from *Metropolitan*, *McCall's*, and *Hearst's International* are reproduced from issues held in the Matthew J. and Arlyn Bruccoli Collection of F. Scott Fitzgerald, Irvin Department of Rare Books and Special Collections, University of South Carolina libraries. Images from the *Smart Set* were made available through the Modernist Journals Project (www.modjourn.org), while images from the *Saturday Evening Post* are reproduced from the Internet Archive (archive.org).

We are also grateful to the F. Scott Fitzgerald Society and the scholarly community it supports, most especially to Kirk Curnutt, Executive Director of the Society, who brought us together on this project. For his friendship, editorial advice, and proofreading, Jennifer is also grateful to Bryant Mangum, Professor at Virginia Commonwealth University.

Thank you to the team at EUP – Emily Sharp, Susannah Butler, Caitlin Murphy, Fiona Conn, and Geraldine Lyons. Thank you to

Michelle Houston, for your unflagging belief in this project, and to Bryony Randall for the introduction.

Many thanks to those who generously shared their expertise on the cities Fitzgerald lived in, worked in, and wrote about in his fiction: Mark Taylor for illuminating Fitzgerald's St. Paul, Alaina Doten for invaluable detail about Zelda's Montgomery, and Mike Franch and Edward Papenfuse for their knowledge of antebellum Baltimore. Thanks too to John Collins and Mark Rossier of Elevator Repair Service, both for *Gatz* and their willingness to answer questions about it.

Alexandra would like to thank her husband, Matt D'Cruz, for his unwavering enthusiasm and support. Thanks to Charlotte Gill, Dan Griffiths, Ellis Saxey, Margo Howie, and Vicki Sunter for all the friendship and encouragement. Thank you to Jennifer Nolan for making this project more, and better, than I would ever have dreamed on my own.

Jennifer would also like to thank her husband, Bryan Gilmer, for his editorial skills and support, and Alexandra Mitchell for bringing me in and trusting me with her project.

Introduction

Jennifer Nolan

On the eve of the period that this volume addresses (1921–1924), F. Scott Fitzgerald was largely taking a break from writing short stories for the magazines after his initial spectacular success earlier in the year. As he would tell his literary agent Harold Ober in a letter dated 6 August 1920, Carl "Hovey, of the *Metropolitan* wrote me asking for more short stories but I'm embarked on my new novel now and tremendously interested."[1] Given the contract Fitzgerald had signed with *Metropolitan* for six stories in May,[2] the first of which ("The Jelly-Bean") he had promptly written that very month, Hovey's inquiry was understandable, and indeed the only story Fitzgerald would write and submit between August 1920 and August 1921 was "His Russet Witch," the second story published by *Metropolitan* under this contract, which appeared in the February 1921 issue.[3]

Yet while Fitzgerald's focus was on writing his second novel, the magazines were not far from his mind. From its outset in July 1920, the novel he had "embarked on," *The Beautiful and Damned*, was framed as a serial for *Metropolitan*, as revealed in letters sent that

---

[1] Matthew J. Bruccoli, ed., with the assistance of Jennifer McCabe Atkinson, *As Ever, Scott Fitz—: Letters Between F. Scott Fitzgerald and His Literary Agent Harold Ober, 1919–1940* (Philadelphia, Lippincott, 1972), 18.

[2] Bryant Mangum, *A Fortune Yet: Money in the Art of F. Scott Fitzgerald's Short Stories* (New York: Garland Publishing, 1991), 41.

[3] In an October 1920 letter to Hovey about "His Russet Witch," Fitzgerald notes that he paused writing his novel after finding his "account so distressingly not to say so alarmingly low that [he] had to do a short story at once." Matthew J. Bruccoli and Margaret M. Duggan, eds., with the assistance of Susan Walker, *Correspondence of F. Scott Fitzgerald* (New York: Random House, 1980), 70. "The Lees of Happiness" was written in July 1920 and published in December.

month to both Ober and his editor at Scribner's, Maxwell Perkins,[4] and on 12 August 1920 Fitzgerald sent a detailed reply to Hovey about how to navigate the publication of the serial and the stories Hovey had requested.[5] Also revealingly, as Kirk Curnutt explores, writing stories for the magazines shows up as "an unlikely plot twist" in *The Beautiful and Damned*, with the protagonist Anthony's unsuccessful attempt to "earn a fast buck writing popular fiction."[6] While ultimately Anthony proves unsuccessful due to his lack of dedication and ability, suggesting that such endeavors require some skill, there is still a hint of derision in Fitzgerald's description of the popular formula, and Curnutt argues that Fitzgerald's depiction of Anthony's processes demonstrate his own conflicted feelings: "'He offered, in his protagonists, the customary denizens of the pink-and-blue literary world, immersing them in a saccharine plot that would offend not a single stomach in Marietta.'"[7] Fitzgerald's satirical sketch, "This is a Magazine," which appeared in the December 1920 issue of *Vanity Fair*, likewise lampoons the "vast and soggy interior of a magazine" with all of its awkwardly juxtaposed stories and surrounding materials, like advertisements and political articles.[8] While somewhat contemptuous of popular magazines, "This is a Magazine" also reveals that it is clearly a world Fitzgerald deeply understands – the satire works, as all effective satire does, because of how well Fitzgerald has captured his subject – and the piece simultaneously demonstrates the extent that "the American Periodical World" was still very much at the forefront of his mind, as would be borne out over the next several years as he explored this market. Thus, our starting point finds Fitzgerald anything but removed from the popular magazines of his day, and this period is especially interesting because it demonstrates how he is figuring out this market and his place in it: in no other period did he publish his stories in so many different magazines.

[4] In a letter dated 7 July 1920, Fitzgerald tells Perkins that the novel "ought to be finished by Sept. 15th [and that] the Metropolitan will probably begin to serialize it right off" while shortly after, on 17 July 1920, he told Ober "I am starting on that novel for the Metropolitan Magazine." Jackson R. Bryer and John Kuehl, eds., *Dear Scott/Dear Max: The Fitzgerald-Perkins Correspondence* (London: Cassell & Company, 1971), 31; *As Ever*, 17.

[5] *Correspondence*, 65.

[6] Kirk Curnutt, "The Periodical World of *The Beautiful and Damned*," in *F. Scott Fitzgerald's* The Beautiful and Damned: *New Critical Essays*, eds. William Blazek, David W. Ullrich, and Kirk Curnutt (Baton Rouge: Louisiana State University Press, 2022), 73.

[7] Qtd in Curnutt, 74.

[8] F. Scott Fitzgerald, "This is a Magazine," *Vanity Fair*, December 1920, 71.

Exploring the American Periodical World, 1921–1924

As the United States finally recovered from the postwar recessions[9] and entered the economic prosperity of the Jazz Age in mid-1921, the American magazine market underwent a period of fluctuation. Established magazines, like *Metropolitan*, faced economic hardship from which they could not recover, or changed fundamentally in character, as the *Smart Set* did upon H. L. Mencken and George Jean Nathan's departure in 1923.[10] New challengers arose to unsettle the old stalwarts, as *Liberty* set out to do to the *Saturday Evening Post* in 1924 (albeit with limited initial success).[11] Fitzgerald's magazine career during this period both reflects these shifts and his insightful navigation through them as he set out to define himself and his career between his initial burst of success and the publication of *The Great Gatsby* in 1925.

In his 1915 introduction to the first of the (ongoing even today) yearly anthology series, *Best American Short Stories*, Edward O'Brien asserted that the true measure of American literary accomplishment resided in the short story,[12] and that "to undertake a study of the American short story" one must look to "the American periodicals which care most to develop its art and influences."[13] As Bryant Mangum has established in his book on the economics of Fitzgerald's magazine career, *A Fortune Yet*, from 1919–1924 Fitzgerald "shopped around for markets and published stories in most of the important periodicals

[9] The United States suffered a brief recession from August 1918–March 1919, followed by a more severe one, which lasted from January 1920–July 1921.

[10] Mencken and Nathan left the *Smart Set* in December of 1923 and by the following October it "consisted largely of pictures . . . sex and sensational fiction, mainly of the 'true story' type; sentiment . . . and a little cheap advertising," prompting a reader to ponder, "'Why couldn't she have died before she lost her good name?'" Frank Luther Mott, "*The Smart Set*," in *A History of American Magazines, Volume V: 1905–1930* (Cambridge, MA: Harvard University Press, 1968), 270–271.

[11] Such claims did not faze George Horace Lorimer, long-time editor of the *Post*, however, as this 4 January 1924 letter reveals: "I have been hearing for sometime that the new weekly was being planned to put the Saturday Evening Post out of business . . . [but] there is no good reason why there should not be a number of good weeklies in the field." Correspondence from George Horace Lorimer to Joseph H. Patterson, 4 January 1924, Wesley Winans Stout papers, 1913–1954, Library of Congress, Washington, DC.

[12] For more information on O'Brien and the *Best American Stories* anthology, see Kasia Boddy "Edward J. O'Brien's Prize Stories of the 'National Soul,'" *Critical Quarterly* 52, no. 2 (2010): 14–28.

[13] Edward O'Brien, introduction to *The Best American Short Stories of 1915 and the Yearbook of the American Short Story* (Boston, MA: Small, Maynard, and Company, 2016), 4.

of the times,"[14] which means that studying his career in this period offers insight into the broader magazine landscape as well. Setting aside for future consideration the early years where Fitzgerald was just starting out, this volume focuses on Fitzgerald's magazine career from 1921 to 1924, which can be roughly divided into three eras, loosely based on which magazine had the most financial power over Fitzgerald's career (contractually or not) at each stage:

- In the first, which lasted until the end of 1922, Fitzgerald's career and fortunes were largely intertwined with *Metropolitan*, where he published three stories under the aforementioned contract, as well as the serialization of *The Beautiful and Damned* from September 1921 to March 1922.
- The second era was dominated by his contract with Hearst's *Cosmopolitan* for an option on his output in 1923, which he signed in December 1922 when *Metropolitan* went into receivership.[15] Though ultimately only four of his stories were accepted and published in *Hearst's International* under this contract, every story he wrote in 1923 was written to fulfill its terms with the exception of "Absolution," which was initially part of an early draft of *Gatsby* and was eventually published in *American Mercury* in 1924.
- In the final era, Fitzgerald returned to the well-paying magazine that had helped bring him to national prominence, the *Saturday Evening Post*, and with which he would become almost exclusively affiliated toward the end of the decade. Though the *Post* prided itself on its "refus[al] to buy 'names' and to make contracts with authors,"[16] artists and authors who published elsewhere, especially in other popular magazines, were warned by Lorimer, the all-powerful editor, that "to maintain the individuality of the *Saturday Evening Post* . . . the writers that we feature, must not be contributors to other weeklies," as he told author Julian Street in a July 1924 letter[17] – the same month when two of Fitzgerald's stories were published by the *Post*.

---

[14] Mangum, *A Fortune Yet*, 6.
[15] *Correspondence*, 119; *As Ever*, 51.
[16] This internal communication was published in a booklet containing articles "prepared by the Editors of *The Saturday Evening Post* for the bi-weekly bulletin which is sent to representatives of the Advertising and Circulation Departments." *Saturday Evening Post* Editorial Staff, *Saturday Evening Post* (Philadelphia, PA: Curtis Publishing Company, Advertising Department, 1923), 13.
[17] Correspondence from George Horace Lorimer to Julian Street, 30 July 1924, Wesley Winans Stout papers.

Metropolitan (1921–1922)

In May 1920, Fitzgerald signed a contract with *Metropolitan* for an option on the next six stories he wrote at a price of $900 each, which offered him not only the largest amount he had earned for a single story to date, but which he also felt would help him secure

Figure I.1 *Metropolitan* cover for issue including "His Russet Witch" (February 1921). Yale Collection of American Literature, Beinecke Rare Book and Manuscript Library.

their interest in serializing *The Beautiful and Damned.*[18] Of the texts included in this volume, three were originally published in *Metropolitan* under this contract, "His Russet Witch," "Two for a Cent," and "Winter Dreams" (see Appendix 2 for more details). "The Curious Case of Benjamin Button" was rejected and instead published in *Collier's*, another popular magazine undergoing a period of editorial upheaval in this era.[19] Though both magazines were somewhat imperiled at this time, *Collier's* was evidently delighted with *Metropolitan*'s scraps, advertising Fitzgerald's upcoming story in both their 6 May and 20 May issues, which heralded it as "the most original tale in years; one you will never forget"[20] by "the most brilliant of our younger writers."[21]

As Bryant Mangum posits, "there is much to suggest . . . that the *Metropolitan* contract represented a rebellion against the restrictions that the *Post* placed on Fitzgerald" both in terms of length and subject matter, and, despite their differences, all three of these stories contain somber reflections on lost youth.[22] Of the three, his final publication in the magazine, "Winter Dreams" (December 1922) has had the most scholarly attention,[23] while "Two for a Cent" (April 1922) received the most attention when it was published, being chosen by

---

[18]   William Blazek, David W. Ullrich, and Kirk Curnutt, introduction to *F. Scott Fitzgerald's* The Beautiful and Damned: *New Critical Essays*, eds. William Blazek, David W. Ullrich, and Kirk Curnutt (Baton Rouge: Louisiana State University Press, 2022), 6.

[19]   *Collier's* had been on somewhat of a downhill slide for several years before its sale in 1919, after which it "passed though the darkest period in its life" and would not recover until William Ludlow Chenery became editor in 1925. Frank Luther Mott, "Collier's," in *A History of American Magazines, Volume IV: 1885–1905* (Cambridge, MA: Harvard University Press, 1957), 466–469. In 1922, weekly issues were substantially shorter than the *Post*'s, with the 27 May issue where "Benjamin Button" was published having only 34 pages to the *Post*'s 132 pages the same week (covers exclusive).

[20]   "Why, You're Growing Younger Every Year," advertisement, *Collier's*, 6 May 1922, 20.

[21]   "Was Mark Twain Right?," advertisement, *Collier's*, 20 May 1922, 30.

[22]   Mangum, *A Fortune Yet*, 42.

[23]   While listing all of the scholarly considerations of this story would be prohibitive given space limitations, the following explicitly discuss the publication of "Winter Dreams" in *Metropolitan*: Thomas E. Daniels, "The Texts of 'Winter Dreams,'" Fitzgerald/Hemingway Annual 9 (1977): 77–100; Bryant Mangum, "*Metropolitan*'s 'Winter Dreams' and *The Great Gatsby*," *F. Scott Fitzgerald Review* 19 (2021): 54–66; Jennifer Nolan, "Illustrating 'Winter Dreams,'" *F. Scott Fitzgerald Review* 19 (2021): 32–53. An image of the first page of "Winter Dreams" as it appeared in *Metropolitan* has been included in this volume.

Edward O'Brien as one of "The Best American Short Stories" of 1922 – despite Fitzgerald's lack of enthusiasm for it. As Fitzgerald explained to Ober in November of 1921, "it is a fair story with an O. Henry twist but it is niether [*sic*] 1st class nor popular . . . my heart wasn't in it so I know it lacks vitality."[24] Nor, despite its popular reception, was he alone in disliking the story. In his review of the 1922 *Best American Short Story* volume for the influential modernist magazine, *The Dial*, then-editor Gilbert Seldes went further, calling "Two for a Cent" "one of the trickiest and cheapest of F. Scott Fitzgerald's 'output.'"[25] In general, as Roy Simmonds argues in his book on O'Brien's legacy, as far as Fitzgerald's magazine stories were concerned O'Brien's collection frequently "mistook the not so good for the gold," completely ignoring "The Diamond as Big as the Ritz" in the 1922 volume for example, which prompted Fitzgerald to refer to him as "'the world's greatest admirer of mediocre short stories'"[26] (though he would continue to mark how many stars O'Brien awarded his stories in his Ledger – where he kept meticulous record of his works and their publication history).

Fitzgerald's hopes that the *Metropolitan* contract would ease his financial difficulties were somewhat frustrated by the magazine's own ongoing financial troubles. While their promised $900 per story far outstripped the $500 the *Post* had been offering, and he was ultimately paid $7,000 for the serialization of *The Beautiful and Damned*, the process of receiving this money was fraught, as evidenced by his correspondence with Harold Ober throughout 1921 and 1922. On 14 September 1921, Fitzgerald wrote to Ober suggesting that "the [*Metropolitan*] contract is certainly null and void if they are not willing to pay cash within the month for short stories whether they intend publishing them in one month or one year" and that "they can't keep buying my stories agreeing to pay when they've finished paying for the serial."[27] Thus, as the serialization of *The Beautiful and Damned* began that fall, he wrote three stories, which were all offered to the *Post* first despite his contract with *Metropolitan*. The first of these, "Two for a Cent," was turned down by the *Post* and ultimately sent to Hovey, presumably without him being

---

[24]   *As Ever*, 29.
[25]   Gilbert Seldes, "Shorter and Better Stories," *The Dial* 75 (August 1923), 186.
[26]   Roy S. Simmonds, *Edward J. O'Brien and his Role in the Rise of the American Short Story in the 1920s and 1930s* (Lewiston, NY: Edwin Mellen Press, 2001), 164–165.
[27]   *As Ever*, 26.

any the wiser.[28] The second, what would ultimately become "The Diamond as Big as the Ritz," was first refused by the *Post*, then heavily revised and offered around before being submitted to and accepted by the *Smart Set* for a price of $300 in February 1922.[29] And though Fitzgerald seemed to express some doubt about whether the terms of his *Metropolitan* contract would allow for it when he sent the story to Ober, "The Popular Girl," was written, submitted to, and accepted by the *Post* in November 1921 for his highest price yet of $1,500.[30] *Metropolitan* finally settled up with Fitzgerald in April 1922 when "Two for a Cent" was published, one month after the serial was completed and five months after the story was submitted.[31] Ultimately, the rumors Fitzgerald had been hearing about *Metropolitan* being "on the verge of failure"[32] proved true, and Fitzgerald was released from his contract in December 1922 when the magazine went into receivership, the same month "Winter Dreams," his final story to appear there, was published.

Promise and disenchantment at Hearst (1923)

Despite his delight at being released from his *Metropolitan* contract,[33] Fitzgerald's independence was short-lived as the offer he received later that month from Ray Long, the editor-in-chief of the Hearst magazine empire, was too good to pass up, and as of January 1923, Hearst held the option for six stories at $1,500 a story with a $1,500 signing bonus – or, as Fitzgerald put it to Ober, what "amounts to $1,750 a story" at a time when he had it on good authority that the *Post* was only paying $1,500.[34] Fitzgerald expressed a few reservations about the deal to Ober, largely over concern about his "ability to write popular fiction," especially as he felt that Norman Hapgood, the editor at *Hearst's International* where his stories

---

[28] *As Ever*, 26–29. On 22 November 1921, Fitzgerald alludes to this when he tells Ober he "shall not mention [the story's] history to [Hovey]," having referred to the *Post* refusing a story in early October, which could only be "Two for a Cent" as he had not sent "The Diamond as Big as the Ritz" yet.

[29] *As Ever*, 28–29, 31, 34–36, 39.

[30] *As Ever*, 29–32. Though Ober initially told Fitzgerald that the Post would "use it as a one part story" (31), the story ended up being published in two parts in the 11 February and 18 February issues.

[31] *As Ever*, 41.

[32] *As Ever*, 35.

[33] *Correspondence*, 119.

[34] The "good authority" being his friend Ring Lardner. *As Ever*, 51.

were to be published, was "positively hostile to my stuff," and that Long had been talked into offering him the deal by Hovey, who was soon to become managing editor at the magazine after having left *Metropolitan.*[35]

Whether there was any truth behind Fitzgerald's concerns about the editors' perception of him, the magazine began their relationship with great fanfare. The April 1923 Table of Contents proclaimed Fitzgerald "our youngest and most brilliant fiction star" in their advertisement for his upcoming debut of "Dice, Brassknuckles and Guitar" the following month,[36] and the contents of the May 1923 issue began with the famous Alfred Cheney Johnston photograph of Scott and Zelda to announce that "all of F. Scott Fitzgerald's new fiction will appear in *Hearst's International*" (see Figure I.2). Fitzgerald's status as the "best loved author of the younger generation" whose stories "are to the young people of *this generation* what O. Henry was to the last," is emphasized throughout the editorial commentary,[37] and the May 1923 issue suggests excitement about this pairing, with Fitzgerald's story leading off the content and Fitzgerald himself being one of the "Geniuses" featured in Ring Lardner's satirical article in the same issue about "the personal life and hobbies of some of the men and women whose name is on every tongue."[38]

Such excitement was not borne out, however, as Fitzgerald's concerns about his inability to "give them what they want" seemed to

[35] *As Ever*, 51. The announcement of Hovey's move was made in the 5 May 1923 issue of *The Editor: The Journal of Information for Literary Workers*: "Carl Hovey, who was managing editor of *The Metropolitan Magazine* for so many years, is now managing editor of *Hearst's International*" (II).

[36] *Hearst's International* (April 1923), 2. All mentions of this story in the magazine (i.e., in advertising, in the Table of Contents, in headings, as well as on the first page) spell "brassknuckles" as one word, which has been replicated here. On the other hand, while the first page of the story uses an ampersand in the title, "and" is spelled out every other time the title is mentioned, and thus this volume replicates the ampersand only on the first page of the story as was done in the magazine. (This is also the case for another story in this volume, "Hot and Cold Blood," published in the August 1923 issue of *Hearst's International*). Looking to other issues of the magazine and stories written by different authors reveals that using an ampersand to replace "and" on the first page of fiction titles was common practice for *Hearst's International* and is not particular to Fitzgerald – see, for example, the first page of "Paul and Ruth and Solomon" in the August 1922 issue, which is written "Paul & Ruth & Solomon" on the first page of the story (49), and otherwise with "and" spelled out.

[37] *Hearst's International* (May 1923), 5.

[38] Ring Lardner, "In Regards to Geniuses," *Hearst's International* (May 1923), 28.

Figure I.2 Alfred Cheney Johnston, photograph of Scott and Zelda for *Hearst's International* masthead (May 1923), 5. The Matthew J. & Arlyn Bruccoli Collection of F. Scott Fitzgerald, Irvin Department of Rare Books and Special Collections, University of South Carolina Libraries.

be well placed.[39] He spent most of 1923 preoccupied with his unsuccessful play, *The Vegetable*, and before the play's disastrous opening night in November 1923, wrote only one additional story for *Hearst's International*, "Hot and Cold Blood,"[40] which was buried in the August 1923 issue of the magazine on p. 82. Though he returned to short story writing with a renewed vigor at this point, completing ten stories by the end of March 1924,[41] only "Diamond Dick and the First Law of Woman" was eventually published in *Hearst's International*, while two – "The Sensible Thing"[42] and "Rags Martin-Jones and the Pr-nce of W-les" – were initially bought but returned to Fitzgerald after what he termed a "Grand fight with Hovey" in the autobiographical portion of his Ledger.[43]

Though *McCall's* and *Liberty* occupied different spaces in the mid-1920s American popular magazine market and were viewed differently by Fitzgerald, their editorial framing of the author and his work was similar and consistent with the image promoted by *Hearst's International*, with *McCall's* labeling him "the writer who discovered the flapper" in their headnote to "Rags Martin-Jones" and *Liberty* emphasizing his role as an interpreter of "youth" in their headnote on "The Sensible Thing." In 1924, *McCall's* was a well-established women's magazine that had hired Harry Payne Burton as editor in 1921 with "a mandate to bring famous and popular writers into *McCall's* pages."[44] For his part, one reason Fitzgerald had accepted the Hearst contract was that he was "not awfully keen about writing fiction for MCaulls" [*sic*],[45] though receiving $1,750 for a story Hearst would have paid $1,500 for must have somewhat softened the blow. *Liberty*, on the other hand, was a newcomer to the American magazine market in 1924 and Fitzgerald sent "The Sensible Thing" there because they were "evidently in the market for a little more serious

---

[39]   *As Ever*, 51.

[40]   For more on what Fitzgerald was doing during this period, see Matthew J. Bruccoli, *Some Sort of Epic Grandeur: The Life of F. Scott Fitzgerald*, 2nd revised edition (Columbia: University of South Carolina Press, 2002), chapters 23 and 24.

[41]   Bruccoli, *Some Sort*, 185.

[42]   Fitzgerald added quotation marks around this title for the publication of the story in *All the Sad Young Men*, which are included in most subsequent volumes. Our volume replicates the title as published in "Liberty," which did not include quotation marks.

[43]   See *As Ever*, 59 for the details of the exchange. F. Scott Fitzgerald, "Outline Chart of My Life," *Ledger 1919–1938*, 178.

[44]   Mott, "McCall's Magazine," in *A History of American Magazines, Volume IV*, 584.

[45]   *As Ever*, 51.

stuff."[46] *Liberty* also was Fitzgerald's preferred magazine for the serialization of *The Great Gatsby*, and the primary reason Fitzgerald did not submit more stories to them was the antagonism between *Liberty* and the *Post*, as he explained to Ober in November and December of 1924: "As to Wheeler [the editor of *Liberty*] – the only thing to do is to offer him the first thing Lorimer turns down. I can't risk my standing with Lorimer now" and "I don't want to be the goat of an inter-editorial row."[47] This antagonism was well-deserved, as *Liberty* had explicitly announced itself as a competitor of the *Post* and had set about pilfering as many *Post* writers and artists as would publish there, such that by October 1924 Lorimer described them as "hang[ing] on the flanks of the *Saturday Evening Post* and one or two other magazines and try[ing] to pick off their contributors who have definitely arrived."[48] Though for different reasons, Fitzgerald would not publish fiction in either magazine again until almost 11 years later, in June of 1935, when his relationship with the *Post* was faltering.

Return to the Saturday Evening Post and "Absolution" (1924)

Having fulfilled the terms of the Hearst contract by submitting the requisite six stories, in 1924, Fitzgerald returned to the magazine that would eventually become his primary market, the *Saturday Evening Post*.[49] By 1923, the *Post* had achieved a weekly readership of two and a half million people, and according to the editors, "in every number stories unite with the *Post*'s editorials and articles to portray American Life – its ideals, its struggles, its defeats and its successes in a way that has made it recognized as the dominant and representative American Publication, not only at home, but in every country abroad,"[50] to the extent that other magazines, like the aforementioned *Liberty*, were copying its style and raiding its authors and artists. As Jan Cohn described it "each big glossy issue presented a portrait of American success, lavish, powerful, abundant" and "in advertising and entertainment, in the lighter articles that appeared continually, two or three a week, the *Saturday Evening Post* was a temple to

---

[46] *As Ever*, 59.
[47] *As Ever*, 70–71.
[48] Correspondence from George Horace Lorimer to George Pattullo, 31 October 1924, Wesley Winans Stout papers.
[49] A copy of the first of these stories, "Gretchen's Forty Winks," as it appeared in the 15 March 1924 issue of the *Saturday Evening Post*, is available in Appendix 3.
[50] *Saturday Evening Post* Editorial Staff, 19–20.

consumerism."[51] Fitzgerald's own contributions to the magazine in 1924 included two of these articles, "How to Live on $36,000 a Year" and the follow-up "How to Live on Practically Nothing a Year."[52]

In keeping with this consumerist orientation, by the 1920s advertising made up over 50 percent of each issue, with the majority being full-page display ads,[53] and after a few pages, stories continued to the back of the magazine surrounded by this sea of advertising.[54] The advertisement pictured in Figure I.3, which appeared on the first page of the 26 July 1924 issue where "John Jackson's Arcady" was published, is representative of these values: according to the "True Story of the Rise of Jobadiah Scruggs, the Corkscrew Magnate" the way to become profitable is to look profitable by purchasing an appropriately expensive suit. As Leon Whipple would put it in 1928, "the text is like a teller of tales hired by the merchants in a bazaar; you come for the tales but en route you listen to the solicitations of the vendors."[55] And, as Bryant Mangum demonstrates, the four stories Fitzgerald published in the *Post* between March and July 1924 all reinforced and celebrated "success and American business."[56]

Of all of the stories published in 1924, "Absolution" is an outlier for many reasons. Written initially during the summer of 1923 not as a short story, but rather, as he told Perkins, as a prologue to an initial version of *The Great Gatsby*,[57] the story was the only one published in 1923–1924 that was offered neither to Hearst nor to the *Post* by Ober, but rather to H. L. Mencken and George Jean Nathan's new venture, *American Mercury*, directly by Fitzgerald himself.[58] In a December 1923 letter, Fitzgerald had heralded the "appearance in January of the *American Mercury*" as "the real [literary] event of the year,"[59] and thus it is not surprising that he would submit this

---

[51] Jan Cohn, *Creating America: George Horace Lorimer and the* Saturday Evening Post (Pittsburgh, PA: University of Pittsburgh Press, 1989), 166, 201.

[52] Published 5 April and 20 September 1924, respectively.

[53] Cohn, *Creating America*, 166.

[54] As explained below, this volume indicates the place in the texts where this break occurs with an asterisk.

[55] Leon Whipple, "SatEvePost: Mirror of These States," *The Survey* (1 March 1928), 714.

[56] Mangum, *A Fortune Yet*, 53.

[57] Bryer and Kuehl, *Dear Scott/Dear Max*, 72.

[58] This, in itself, was not unprecedented, as Fitzgerald had sold stories directly to the *Smart Set* due to his relationship with Nathan and Mencken, and had offered to do so in 1922 for "The Diamond as Big as the Ritz" if Ober would "rather not deal with" them. *As Ever*, 36.

[59] *Correspondence*, 138.

Figure I.3 Advertisement, Adler Collegian Clothes, *Saturday Evening Post* (26 July 1924), 1. First item in the issue where "John Jackson's Arcady" was published.

decidedly non-commercial story directly to them. There is evidence to suggest that the addition may have been somewhat last-minute, as Fitzgerald is not included on the list of "The American Mercury Authors" in the back of the magazine and he wrote in the $118 he was paid for the story at the bottom of his "Record for 1924" in his Ledger as an "ommission" [*sic*], though a letter to Perkins demonstrates that the deal was in place by 10 April 1924.[60] While this positioned the sale firmly in the midst of Fitzgerald's renewed relationship with the *Post*, the more highbrow *American Mercury* occupied a different enough position in the magazine market to not be viewed as one of the *Post*'s competitors, and this sale would have been unlikely to draw Lorimer's ire.[61]

Editorial Principles and the Magazine Context

While previous editions of Fitzgerald's stories, most notably James L. W. West III's unparalleled Cambridge editions, foreground authorial intent, this series foregrounds reception. By focusing on the magazines, we shift the authority from Fitzgerald to the contexts in which his short stories were published and read by his largest audiences. Thus, our volume reprints the magazine texts of the 18 short stories published in American magazines by Fitzgerald between 1921 and 1924 in the order that they appeared in the literary marketplace – that is, we replicate, as near as possible, the version of Fitzgerald's texts American audiences would have read, in the order that the stories would have been available to them. Like West, we have chosen to include every story, even those Fitzgerald chose not to reprint in his lifetime, because we agree that the value of having all of his published stories available provides an important resource that will help students, readers, and scholars to better understand his career and the popular print contexts that published and supported it.

Choosing to reprint the stories as they were available to Fitzgerald's original audiences means that textual errors printed in the magazines have been replicated in the texts in this volume as well, with the corrections relegated to the notes, a decision that is the inverse of what most careful editions do. At first this choice may seem odd, as surely these mistakes were intended by no one, but as part of the versions read by most of Fitzgerald's contemporary audiences, these mistakes are an important part of the reception history of his magazine stories. Revealingly, *Metropolitan* included

---

[60] *Ledger*, 56–57. Bryer and Kuehl, *Dear Scott/Dear Max*, 69.
[61] In contrast, Lorimer identified "*Colliers, Liberty*, [and] *The Cosmopolitan*" as particularly problematic. Correspondence from George Horace Lorimer to George Pattullo, 31 October 1924, Wesley Winans Stout papers.

far more errors in the Fitzgerald stories they published than any other magazine in this volume, even though he published just as many stories in *Hearst's International* and more in the *Post* during this time, which seems likely to be a reflection of their ongoing financial difficulties and therefore lack of resources for first-rate proofreading.

Arranging the stories chronologically in terms of when they were made available to the public accentuates elements of the magazine market that are downplayed or elided when Fitzgerald's stories are arranged by when he wrote them or the order of their subsequent publication in his short story collections. Favoring composition dates privileges Fitzgerald's experience as an author, rather than the reception of his works as this volume does, while arranging the stories as he chose to arrange them in later collections prioritizes their book publishing history rather than their magazine contexts. This is especially clear with the nine stories included in *All the Sad Young Men* (1926), which were originally published in seven different magazines between 1922 and 1926. Reuniting these stories with those Fitzgerald published in the same period foregrounds his place in the magazine market, while bringing back together stories written under the same contracts – i.e., "Winter Dreams" and the other *Metropolitan* stories, "Hot and Cold Blood," "Rags Martin-Jones and the Pr-nce of W-les," and "The Sensible Thing," with the other stories written for *Hearst's International*, and "Gretchen's Forty Winks" with the stories he wrote for the *Post* in 1924 – places them in different contexts and raises different questions about these stories than reading them in their revised forms as part of his 1926 collection, as addressed above. The sheer number of magazines included is also revealing both about Fitzgerald's career at this time, as it allows for side-by-side comparisons of what types of stories were published in each magazine, and about the size, scope, and power of the American magazine market as the Jazz Age began.

Ngram and magazine publication appendices

In addition to the paratextual features and image appendix discussed below, this volume includes two appendices that highlight different aspects of Fitzgerald's career. The first, compiled by Alexandra Mitchell, uses Google Ngram to map the ubiquity and usage of different phrases over time to demonstrate how finely tuned Fitzgerald's ear was to the vernacular, fashions, and trends of his day. While this ability was noticed almost immediately by his contemporaries[62] and has been lauded by scholars, Google Ngram provides quantifiable evidence of just how accurate he was, which was key in establishing his legitimacy as the voice of the younger generation with readers of popular magazines. The second appendix, compiled by Jennifer Nolan, provides a chart that gives an overview of the magazine placement of the stories included in this volume. In addition to listing the magazine, publication date, and price he was paid for each story, this chart contains a final column indicating how many stories Fitzgerald had published in that magazine up to that moment and how many he would eventually publish there over the course of his career, thereby providing both a snapshot of how often he had appeared in each magazine at the time each story was published and what role each magazine played in his career overall.

Textual variants

Of the 18 stories in this volume, evidence exists of significant post-publication revisions made by Fitzgerald to the magazine texts of 12, largely in preparation for their republication in his short story collections: five of them were included in *Tales of the Jazz Age* (1922)[63] and six in *All the Sad Young Men* (1926),[64] while unpublished "heavy revisions" of "Dice, Brassknuckles and Guitar" "survive in his papers at Princeton,"[65] and authoritative versions of all of these stories have been established by James L. W. West III. For the remaining six, "no manuscript or typescript versions appear to survive,"[66] and thus West's texts of these are largely based on the magazine versions, while Matthew J. Bruccoli relied upon the *Hearst's International* text of

---

[62] Comments of this sort run throughout reviews of his first novel, *This Side of Paradise*, for example. See Jackson Bryer, ed., *"This Side of Paradise,"* in *Scott Fitzgerald: The Critical Reception* (New York: Burt Franklin & Co, 1978), 1–32.

[63] In the order in which they appear in this volume, these include "Jemina, the Mountain Girl," "His Russet Witch" (renamed "O Russet Witch!"), "Tarquin of Cheapside," "The Curious Case of Benjamin Button," and "The Diamond as Big as the Ritz."

[64] In the order in which they appear in this volume, these include "Winter Dreams," "Hot and Cold Blood," "Rags Martin-Jones and the Pr-nce of W-les," "The Sensible Thing," "Gretchen's Forty Winks," and "Absolution."

[65] For more on this, see James L. W. West III, introduction to *Tales of the Jazz Age* by F. Scott Fitzgerald (New York: Cambridge University Press, 2002), xxiv.

[66] James L. W. West III, introduction to *Flappers and Philosophers* by F. Scott Fitzgerald (New York: Cambridge University Press, 2000), xxii.

"Dice, Brassknuckles and Guitar" in *The Short Stories of F. Scott Fitzgerald* (1989) and the *Metropolitan* text of "Winter Dreams" is available in Bryant Mangum's *Best Early Stories of F. Scott Fitzgerald* (2005). However, while Bruccoli does replicate the magazine publication dates for the stories he includes, and West's volumes include every story, our volume is the only one to do both – that is, to print every story Fitzgerald published in magazines during this era in the order they were published, as well as the only volume to do so without correction.

More relevant to the goals of this volume, evidence of pre-magazine publication versions also exist for four of the included stories. Three of these are discussed by West in his "Record of Variants" for *All the Sad Young Men*, the most intriguing perhaps being the holograph of "Rags Martin-Jones and the Pr-nce of W-les," which he argues differs so much "from the ASYM version that they constitute two separate versions," raising questions about its comparison to the *McCall's* version of the story.[67] A trace of the pre-publication version of "The Popular Girl" also exists, which provides evidence of the editorial processes at the magazine where Fitzgerald would ultimately find his home, the *Saturday Evening Post*. In his introduction to the Cambridge Edition of *All the Sad Young Men*, West reveals several significant excisions made to later stories by the editors at the *Post*, brought to light by comparing the typescripts of three stories published in 1927 and 1928 with their magazine versions, and suggests that "these verbal cleansings were designed to render the stories suitable for the broad, conventional, middle-class readership of the *Post*."[68] While West suggests that it is likely that Fitzgerald was unaware of "these expurgations [since] no evidence survives to show that he compared the *Post* texts" with the typescripts and that, in any case, "any objection from him would have been futile,"[69] a series of letters between associate editor Adelaide Neall and Fitzgerald written in December 1921 reveals that this was not the case with at least one textual change the *Post* made to "The Popular Girl." In the first letter, Neall related that Lorimer was concerned that Fitzgerald had tied the protagonist, Yanci's, heritage to a real historical figure and was requesting that Fitzgerald "change her name or change the

[67] The typescript for "Hot and Cold Blood" suggests only "a final round of light revision" and those from "Gretchen's Forty Winks" seem equally minor. James L. W. West III, ed., *All the Sad Young Men* (New York: Cambridge University Press, 2007), 439, 442–4.
[68] West, *ASYM*, xxv.
[69] West, *ASYM*, xxv–xxvi.

reference to her relationship to [the real] Governor Yancey."[70] When almost two weeks passed with no reply, Neall sent a follow-up letter indicating that a "sentence or so in the first installment of 'The Popular Girl,' in which the girl told of her direct relationship to the famous Yancey gentleman of historic fame" had been cut.[71] Aside from demonstrating the granular level of editorial oversight the *Post* was famous for, these letters are significant because no competing version of "The Popular Girl" exists. Fitzgerald begrudgingly agreed to the change, though not without pointing out that their reasons for requesting it were flawed:

> As to Yancey. He was never governor of Maryland. The girl's *father's* father was governor of Maryland and his name was Bowman – (this is fictitious). My wife's aunt was named Yancey (after her uncle, the celebrated one) and I'm sure the family wouldn't mind. However, your judgement [*sic*] is better than mine, so if you like, change the phrase.[72]

The timing of Fitzgerald's infamous exclamation to Ober, "by God + Lorimer, I'm going to make a fortune yet," is suggestive as well, which he wrote in a letter shortly after this exchange and the same month that "The Popular Girl" ran in the *Post*. While Neall's assessment that this change "does not hurt the story" seems accurate, this example offers a rare window into how the magazines shaped what version of Fitzgerald his audiences read.

Paratextual inclusions and exclusions

Aside from behind-the-scenes editing of Fitzgerald's texts, editorial interventions are also explicitly evident within the pages of the stories themselves, and all of these extratextual features positioning and interpreting the texts are what Gérard Genette calls "paratexts."[73] Some magazines used headnotes to provide direction to the reader as they began the story, such as the headnote from "Rags Martin-Jones and the Pr-nce of W-les" included in Figure I.4, which highlights Fitzgerald's reputation as the flapper's historian and assures *McCall's*

---

[70] Correspondence from Adelaide Neall to F. Scott Fitzgerald, 15 December 1921, Wesley Winans Stout papers.

[71] Correspondence from Adelaide Neall to F. Scott Fitzgerald, 28 December 1921, Wesley Winans Stout papers.

[72] Correspondence from F. Scott Fitzgerald to Adelaide Neall, undated, Wesley Winans Stout papers.

[73] Gérard Genette, "Introduction to the Paratext," translated by Marie Mclean, *New Literary History* 22, no. 2 (Spring 1991): 261–272.

Figure I.4 First page of "Rags Martin-Jones and the Pr-nce of W-les," *McCall's* (July 1924), 6. The Matthew J. & Arlyn Bruccoli Collection of F. Scott Fitzgerald, Irvin Department of Rare Books and Special Collections, University of South Carolina Libraries.

readers that this story will pay off as "one of the best love stories of the day." These types of editorial interventions created explicitly to shape a reader's expectations as they read the story have been replicated in this volume. Likewise, section or chapter breaks indicated by Roman numerals in the *Smart Set*, *Post*, and *American Mercury* stories have been reproduced. After printing a few continuous pages of a story near the front of the magazine, most popular magazines in Fitzgerald's day continued stories in the back (see "Gretchen's Forty Winks" in Appendix 3) to encourage readers to engage with other materials in the magazine, especially the advertising that paid for it all; this edition is the first to indicate where this break occurred, marked by an asterisk in each text with a note at the bottom of the page specifying how many contiguous pages were printed before the break and the page number where the story resumed. On the other hand, editorial framing that was purely navigational in purpose – such as subsequent indications of which pages the story continued on – is excluded because its meaning is lost in a book format making its inclusion distracting for modern readers.

Also excluded – with no small measure of regret – are most of the visual elements that framed each text, which most significantly means that most of the illustrations for these stories have not been included in this volume. As I have argued extensively elsewhere,[74] far from being incidental in the illustrated magazine, the pictorial and textual worked together to co-produce meaning for their audiences, and the omission of this visual element therefore removes a key element of the composite text Fitzgerald's readers would have encountered. To provide some sense of this, Appendix 3 includes several images to help modern readers experience how the stories would have looked in different magazines for Fitzgerald's original readers. To highlight the contrasts between the higher-brow smart magazines and the more popular illustrated magazines, Appendix 3 juxtaposes the cover and austere first page of "The Diamond as Big as the Ritz" from the June 1922 issue of the *Smart Set* with the cover and illustrated first page of "Winter Dreams" from the December 1922 issue

---

[74] For a consideration of the role of illustrations in framing one of the stories in this volume, see Nolan, "Illustrating 'Winter Dreams." See also "May Wilson Preston and the Birth of Fitzgerald's Flapper: Illustrating Social Transformation in 'Bernice Bobs Her Hair,'" *Journal of Modern Periodical Studies* 8, no. 1 (2017): 56–80; "Reading 'Babylon Revisited' as a *Post* Text: F. Scott Fitzgerald, George Horace Lorimer, and the *Saturday Evening Post* Audience," *Book History* 20 (2017): 351–373; and "Visualizing 'The Rich Boy:' F. Scott Fitzgerald, F. R. Gruger, and *Red Book Magazine*," *The F. Scott Fitzgerald Review* 15 (2017): 17–33.

of *Metropolitan*. And to demonstrate what one of Fitzgerald's stories would have looked like in the highly visual and commercial *Saturday Evening Post*, it includes "Gretchen's Forty Winks" with the facing advertisements from the 15 March 1924 issue.

The *Post* publication of "Gretchen's Forty Winks" pulls together many of the strands discussed in this introduction. In terms of formatting, it follows the typical popular magazine layout in this period, beginning with a two-page illustrated spread printed near the front of the magazine (pp. 14 and 15) and concluding with three verso (or left-hand) pages (pp. 128, 130, and 132), which each faced a full-page advertisement. Taken together, these visually emphasize the extent to which literature published in these types of magazines shared its space with extratextual materials that, as John K. Young has argued, "direct the terms under which the pieces of fiction can be processed."[75] Both the illustrations on the first two pages and the advertisements printed on the left half of pp. 128 and 130 take up as much space as the text itself (only a small portion of which is Fitzgerald's story on p. 128). Considered alongside the fact that pp. 128 and 130 each faced a full-page advertisement, the text seems almost secondary, framed and dwarfed as it is by the "merchants in [this] bazaar" whose "solicitations" seem impossible to ignore.[76] Thematically, the second illustration (p. 15) and the first advertisement (p. 128) exemplify the business focus of the *Post* discussed above. Also notably, the illustrator himself, Charles D. Mitchell, occupied the same professional world as Fitzgerald and had illustrated many of Fitzgerald's early stories, including his first story to appear in the *Post* in the 21 February 1920 issue, "Head and Shoulders," as well as three of the stories in this volume – "The Popular Girl,"[77] "Gretchen's Forty Winks," and "The Third Casket." Mitchell's work also appeared in the issue of *Metropolitan* where "His Russet Witch" was published, in two of the three *Hearst's International* issues featuring Fitzgerald's work, and in the issue of the *Post* that included "The Unspeakable Egg."[78] For all of these paratextual and contextual reasons, "Gretchen's Forty Winks" gives readers of this volume a useful glimpse into the magazine world of Fitzgerald's day.

[75]   John K. Young, "Pynchon in Popular Magazines," *Critique* 44, no. 4 (Summer 2003): 392.

[76]   Whipple, "SatEvePost," 714.

[77]   Of which Fitzgerald was a fan, as he said to Ober in a February 1922 letter: "I'm glad the *Post* gave me first place and good illustrations." *As Ever*, 37.

[78]   *Metropolitan*, February 1921. *Hearst's International*, May 1923 and August 1923. *Saturday Evening Post*, 12 July 1924.

These efforts aside, much of the reading experience for Fitzgerald's original audiences cannot be captured by reprinting the magazine texts in a bound volume. In addition to the illustrations, the other stories, editorials, articles, and advertising all played a role in how Fitzgerald's original readers understood his magazine stories, as well as material elements, like paper quality and size, which cannot be reproduced even if the impracticality of reproducing the magazine layouts in a single volume could be overcome (though enterprising readers could overcome these considerations by seeking out issues of the magazines themselves). Mentions of Fitzgerald or his work in advertising or articles in the same or previous issues could also shape how a reader approached his texts, as we saw at play in *Hearst's International* above. More broadly, magazines exist within the contexts of their own histories and reputations; as Travis Kurowski explains, unlike books "magazines are experienced as social texts" and "a single copy of a magazine represents one instance in a larger publishing conversation extending backward and forward in time."[79] While many of these elements are touched upon in this introduction, Appendix 2, and in some of the notes, we still must accept that large parts of this experience are simply not replicable.

By bringing the magazine texts together, however, this volume offers a gateway into the living textual history of Fitzgerald's work, warts and all, and how he was being framed by the magazines for his largest audiences. As Bryant Mangum has argued, "one conclusion to be drawn from a summary of Fitzgerald's professional career . . . is that he was at his best artistically in the years of his greatest popularity. During the composition of *The Great Gatsby* [that is, the years that this volume encompasses], Fitzgerald's commercial fiction was in such demand that the large magazines such as the *Post*, *Metropolitan*, and *Hearst's* competed for it."[80] This volume allows the reader to experience all of these stories in order, tells the story of how those magazines published and promoted his work in this era, and opens the door for students and scholars to consider what it means to put Fitzgerald back into his original context, the American magazine of the 1920s.

---

[79] Travis Kurowski, "The Literary in Theory," in *The Routledge Companion to the British and North American Literary Magazine*, ed. Tim Lanzendörfer (New York: Routledge, 2022), 29.

[80] Mangum, *A Fortune Yet*, 7.

Stories

Jemina, the Mountain Girl

Vanity Fair
January 1921
$100

One of Those Family Feud Stories of the Blue Ridge
Mountains—with Apologies to Stephen Leacock[1]

It was night in the mountains of Kentucky. Wild hills rose on all sides.
Swift mountain streams flowed rapidly up and down the mountains.

Jemina Tantrum was down at the stream, brewing whiskey at the
family still.

She was a typical mountain girl.

Her feet were bare. Her hands, large and powerful, hung down
below her knees. Her face showed the ravages of work. Although
but sixteen, she had for over a dozen years been supporting her aged
pappy and mappy by brewing mountain whiskey.

From time to time she would pause in her task, and, filling a
dipper full of the pure, invigorating liquid, would drain it off—then
pursue her work with renewed vigor.

She would place the rye in the vat, thresh it out with her feet and,
in twenty minutes, the completed product would be turned out.

A sudden cry made her pause in the act of draining a dipper and
look up.

"Hello," said a voice. It came from a man clad in hunting boots
reaching to his neck, who had emerged from the wood.

"Hi, thar," she answered sullenly.

"Can you tell me the way to the Tantrums' cabin?"

"Are you uns from the settlements down thar?"

She pointed her hand down to the bottom of the hill, where
Louisville lay. She had never been there; but once, before she was

born, her great-grandfather, old Gore Tantrum, had gone into the settlements in the company of two marshalls, and had never come back. So the Tantrums, from generation to generation, had learned to dread civilization.

The man was amused. He laughed a light tinkling laugh; the laugh of a Philadelphian. Something in the ring of it thrilled her. She drank off another dipper of whiskey.

"Where is Mr. Tantrum, little girl?" he asked not without kindness.

She raised her foot and pointed her big toe toward the woods. "Thar in the cabing behind those thar pines. Old Tantrum air my old man."

The man from the settlements thanked her and strode off. He was fairly vibrant with youth and personality. As he walked along he whistled and sang and turned handsprings and flapjacks, breathing in the fresh, cool air of the mountains.

The air around the still was like wine.

Jemina Tantrum watched him entranced. No one like him had ever come into her life before.

She sat down on the grass and counted her toes. She counted eleven. She had learned arithmetic in the mountain school.

A Mountain Feud

Ten years before a lady from the settlements had opened a school on the mountain. Jemina had no money, but she had paid her way in whiskey, bringing a pailful to school every morning and leaving it on Miss Lafarge's desk. Miss Lafarge had died of delirium tremens after a year's teaching, and so Jemina's education had stopped.

Across the stream there stood another still. It was that of the Doldrums. The Doldrums and the Tantrums never exchanged calls.

They hated each other.

Fifty years before old Jem Doldrum and old Jem Tantrum had quarreled in the Tantrum cabin over a game of slapjack.[2] Jem Doldrum had thrown the king of hearts in Jem Tantrum's face, and old Tantrum, enraged, had felled the old Doldrum with the nine of diamonds. Other Doldrums and Tantrums had joined in and the little cabin was soon filled with flying cards.[3] Harstrum Doldrum, one of the younger Doldrums, lay stretched on the floor writhing in agony, the ace of hearts crammed down his throat. Jem Tantrum, standing in the doorway, ran through suit after suit, his face alight with fiendish hatred. Old Mappy Tantrum stood on the table wetting down the

Doldrums with hot whiskey. Old Heck Doldrum, having finally run out of trumps, was backed out of the cabin, striking left and right with his tobacco pouch, and gathering around him the rest of his clan. Then they mounted their steers and galloped furiously home.

That night old man Doldrum and his sons, vowing vengeance, had returned, put a ticktock on the Tantrum window, stuck a pin in the doorbell, and beaten a retreat.

A week later the Tantrums had put Cod Liver Oil in the Doldrums' still, and so, from year to year, the feud had continued, first one family being entirely wiped out, then the other.

The Birth of Love

Every day little Jemina worked the still on her side of the stream, and Boscoe Doldrum worked the still on his side.

Sometimes, with automatic inherited hatred, the feudists would throw whiskey at each other, and Jemina would come home smelling like a French table d'hôte.

But now Jemina was too thoughtful to look across the stream.

How wonderful the stranger had been and how oddly he was dressed! In her innocent way she had never believed that there were any civilized settlements at all, and she had put the belief in them down to the credulity of the mountain people.

She turned to go up to the cabin, and, as she turned something struck her in the neck. It was a sponge, thrown by Boscoe Doldrum—a sponge soaked in whiskey from his still on the other side of the stream.

"Hi, thar, Boscoe Doldrum," she shouted in her deep bass voice.

"Yo! Jemina Tantrum. Gosh ding yo'!" he returned.

She continued her way to the cabin.

The stranger was talking to her father. Gold had been discovered on the Tantrum land, and the stranger, Edgar Edison, was trying to buy the land for a song. He was considering what song to offer.

She sat upon her hands and watched him.

He was wonderful. When he talked his lips moved.

She sat upon the stove and watched him.

Suddenly there came a blood-curdling scream. The Tantrums rushed to the windows.

It was the Doldrums.

They had hitched their steers to trees and concealed themselves behind the bushes and flowers, and soon a perfect rattle of stones and bricks beat against the windows, bending them inward.

"Father, father," shrieked Jemina.

Her father took down his slingshot from his slingshot rack on the wall and ran his hand lovingly over the elastic band. He stepped to a loophole. Old Mappy Tantrum stepped to the coalhole.

A Mountain Battle

The stranger was aroused at last. Furious to get at the Doldrums, he tried to escape from the house by crawling up the chimney. Then he thought there might be a door under the bed, but Jemina told him there was not. He hunted for doors under the beds and sofas, but each time Jemina pulled him out and told him there were no doors there. Furious with anger, he beat upon the door and hollered at the Doldrums. They did not answer him, but kept up their fusillade of bricks and stones against the window. Old Pappy Tantrum knew that as soon as they were able to effect an aperture they would pour in and the fight would be over.

Then old Heck Doldrum, foaming at the mouth and expectorating on the ground, left and right, led the attack.

The terrific slingshots of Pappy Tantrum had not been without their effect. A master shot had disabled one Doldrum, and another Doldrum, shot three times through the abdomen, fought feebly on.

Nearer and nearer they approached the house.

"We must fly," shouted the stranger to Jemina. "I will sacrifice myself and bear you away."

"No," shouted Pappy Tantrum, his face begrimed. "You stay here and fit on. I will bar Jemina away. I will bar Mappy away. I will bar myself away."

The man from the settlements, pale and trembling with anger, turned to Ham Tantrum, who stood at the door throwing loophole after loophole at the advancing Doldrums.

Soon smoke began to filter through the floor and ceiling. Shem Doldrum had come up and touched a match to old Japhet Tantrum's breath as he leaned from a loophole, and the alcoholic flames shot up on all sides.

The whiskey in the bathtub caught fire. The walls began to fall in.

Jemina and the man from the settlements looked at each other.

"Jemina," he whispered.

"Stranger," she answered.

"We will die together," he said. "If we had lived I would have taken you to the city and married you. With your ability to hold liquor, your social success would have been assured."

She caressed him idly for a moment, counting her toes softly to herself. The smoke grew thicker. Her left leg was on fire.

She was a human alcohol lamp.

Their lips met in one long kiss and then a wall fell on them and blotted them out.[4]

His Russet Witch

Metropolitan
February 1921
$900

Merlin Grainger was employed by the Moonlight Quill Bookshop, which you may have visited, just around the corner from the Ritz-Carlton[1] on Forty-seventh Street. The Moonlight Quill is a very romantic little store, considered radical and admitted dark. It is spotted interiorly with red and orange posters of breathless exotic intent, and lit no less by the shiny reflecting bindings of special editions than by the great squat lamp of crimson satin that, lighted through all the day, swings overhead. It is truly a mellow bookshop. The words "Moonlight Quill" are worked over the door in a sort of turpentine[2] embroidery. The windows seem always full of something that has passed the literary censors[3] with little to spare; things with covers of deep orange bearing the titles on little white paper squares. And above all there is the smell of musk, which the clever Mr. Moonlight Quill has ordered to be sprinkled about—the smell half of a curiosity shop located in Dickens' London and half of a coffee house on the shores of the Bosphorus.

From nine until five-thirty Merlin Grainger asked old ladies in black and young men with dark circles under their eyes if they "had seen that," if they "cared for this fellow," if they were interested in first editions. Did they buy novels with cowboys on the cover or books which gave Shakespeare's newest sonnets as dictated psychicly to Miss Sutton of South Dakota,[4] he sniffed. As a matter of fact, his own taste ran to these latter, but as an employee at the Moonlight Quill he assumed for the working day the attitude of a disillusioned connoisseur.

After he had crawled over the window display to pull down the front shade at five-thirty every afternoon and said good-bye to Mr. Moonlight Quill and the lady clerk, Miss McCracken, and the lady stenographer, Miss Masters, he went home to the girl, Caroline. He did not eat supper with Caroline. It is very doubtful if Caroline would have considered eating off his bureau with the collar buttons dangerously near the cottage cheese and the ends of his necktie just missing his glass of milk—he had never asked her to eat with him. He ate alone. He went into Braegdort's delicatessen on Sixth Avenue and bought a box of crackers, a tube of anchovy paste and some oranges, or else a little jar of sausages and some potato salad and a bottled soft drink, and with these in a big, brown package he went to his room at Fifty-something West Fifty-eighth Street and ate his supper and saw Caroline.

Caroline was a very young and gay person who lived with her mother and was quite possibly nineteen. She was like a ghost in that she never existed until evening. She sprang into life when the lights went on in her apartment at about six and disappeared at the latest about midnight. Her apartment was a very nice one, in a very nice building with a white stone front, opposite the south side of Central Park. The back of her apartment faced the single window of the single room occupied by the single Mr. Grainger.

He called her Caroline because there was a picture that looked like her on the jacket of a book of that name down at the Moonlight Quill.

Now, Merlin Grainger was a thin young man of twenty-five, with dark hair and no mustache or beard or anything, but Caroline was dazzlingly light, with a shimmering morass of russet waves to take the place of hair, and the sort of features that remind you of kisses— the sort of features you thought your first girl had but know now she didn't. She dressed in pink or blue usually, but of late she had sometimes put on a slender black gown that was evidently her especial pride, for whenever she wore it she would stand regarding herself before a certain place on the wall which Merlin thought must be either a picture of some lover killed in the war or else a mirror. She sat usually in the profile chair near the window, but sometimes honored the *chaise longue* by the lamp, and often she leaned 'way back and smoked a cigarette with conscious posturings of her arms and hands that Merlin considered very graceful.

At another time she had come to the window and stood in it magnificently, and looked out because the moon had somehow lost its way and was dripping the strangest and most transforming brilliance into the area-way between, turning the motif of ash cans and clothes-lines into a vivid impressionism of silver casks and gigantic gossamer cobwebs. Merlin was sitting in plain sight, eating cottage cheese with sugar and milk on it; and so quickly did he reach out for the window cord that he tipped the cottage cheese into his lap with his free hand—and the milk was cold and the sugar made spots on his trousers—and he wasn't sure that she hadn't seen him after all.

Sometimes there were callers—men in dinner coats, who stood and bowed, hat in hand and coat on arm, as they talked to Caroline's mother; then bowed some more and backed out of the light with her mother's daughter, obviously bound for a play or for a dance. Other young men came and sat and smoked cigarettes and seemed trying to tell Caroline something—she sitting either in the profile chair and watching them with eager intentness or else in the *chaise longue* by the lamp, looking very lovely and youthfully inscrutable indeed.

Merlin enjoyed these calls. Of some of the men he approved. Others won only his grudging toleration, one or two he loathed—especially a man with black hair and a black mustache and a pitch dark soul, who called twice and was seen no more.

Now, Merlin's whole life was not "bound up with this romance he had constructed"; it was not "the happiest hour of his day." He never arrived at a street corner in time to rescue her from an evil suitor's clutches; nor did he ever marry her. A very much stranger thing happened than any of these, and it is this strange thing that will presently be set down here. It began one October afternoon when she walked briskly into the mellow interior of the Moonlight Quill.

It was a dark afternoon, threatening rain, catastrophe and the end of the world, and done in that particularly gloomy gray that only New York afternoons affect. A breeze was crying down the streets, whisking along battered newspapers and pieces of things, and little lights were pricking out all the windows—it was so desolate that one was sorry for the tops of skyscrapers lost up there in the dark green and gray heaven, and felt that now surely the farce was to close, and presently all the buildings would collapse like card houses and pile in a dusty, sardonic heap upon all the millions who presumed to wind in and out of them.

At least these were the sort of musings that sat heavily upon the soul of Merlin Grainger as he stood by the window putting a dozen books back in a row after a cyclonic visit by a lady with ermine trimmings. He looked out of the window full of the most distressing thoughts—of the early novels of H. G. Wells,[5] of the book of Genesis, of how Thomas Edison had said that in thirty years there would be no dwelling houses upon the island, but only a vast and turbulent bazar; and then he put a novel by Mr. McGlucklin[6] next to a novel by Mr. MacMayne, turned around—and Caroline walked coolly into the shop.

She was dressed in a jaunty but quite conventional walking costume—he remembered this when he thought about it later. Her skirt
was plaid, pleated like a concertina; her jacket was a soft but brisk
tan; her shoes and spats were brown[7] and her hat, small and trim,
completed her like the top of a very expensive and beautifully fitted
candy box.

Merlin, breathless and startled, put an Elsie book[8] between a
dictionary and an encyclopedia and came slowly toward her.

"Good afternoon—" he said, and then stopped—why, he did not
know, except that it came to him that something very portentous in
his life was about to occur, and that it would need no furbishing but
silence, and the proper amount of expectant attention. And in that
minute before the thing began to happen he had the sense of a breathless second hanging pendent[9] in time: he saw through the glass partition that bounded off the little office of Mr. Moonlight Quill the bald,
conical head of his employer bent over his correspondence. He saw
Miss McCracken and Miss Masters as two patches of hair drooping
over piles of paper; he saw the crimson lamp overhead and noticed
with a touch of pleasure how really pleasant and romantic it made the
bookshop seem.

Then the thing happened, or rather it began to happen. Caroline
picked up a book lying loose upon a pile, fingered it absently with
her slender white hand, and suddenly, with an easy gesture, tossed it
upward toward the ceiling where it disappeared in the crimson lamp
and lodged there, seen through the illuminated silk as a dark, bulging
rectangle. This pleased her—she broke into young and very conta-
gious laughter, in which Merlin found himself presently joining.

"It stayed up!" she cried merrily. "It stayed up, didn't it." To both
of them this seemed the height of brilliant absurdity. Their laughter
mingled and filled the bookshop, and Merlin was glad to find that
her voice was rich and full of sorcery.

"Try another," he found himself suggesting—"try a red one."

At this her laughter increased, and she had to rest her hands upon
the stack to steady herself.

"Try another," she managed to articulate between spasms of mirth.
"Oh, golly, try another!"

"Try two."

"Yes, try two. Oh, I shall choke if I don't stop laughing. Here it
goes."

Suiting her action to the word, she picked up a red book and
sent it ceilingwards in a gentle hyperbole,[10] where it sank into place
beside the first. It was a few minutes before either of them could

do more than rock back and forth in helpless glee; but then by mutual agreement they took up the sport anew, this time in unison. Merlin seized a large, specially bound French classic and whirled it upward. Applauding his own accuracy, he took a best-seller in one hand and a book on barnacles in the other and waited breathlessly while she made her shot. Then business waxed fast and furious— sometimes they alternated, and, watching, he found how supple she was in every movement; sometimes one of them made shot after shot, picking up the nearest book, sending it off, merely taking time to follow it with a glance before reaching for another. Within three minutes they had cleared a little place on the table, and the lamp of crimson satin was bulging so with books that it was almost breaking.

"Silly game, basket-ball," she cried scornfully as a book left her hand. "High school girls play it in hideous bloomers."[11]

"Idiotic," he agreed.

She paused in the act of tossing a book, and replaced it suddenly in its position on the table.

"I think we've got room to sit down now," she said gravely.

They had; they had cleared an ample space for two. With a faint touch of nervousness Merlin glanced toward Mr. Moonlight Quill's glass partition, but the three heads were still bent earnestly over their work, and it was evident that they had not seen what had gone on in the shop. So when Caroline put her hands on the table and hoisted herself up, Merlin calmly imitated her, and they sat side by side looking very earnestly at each other.

"I had to see you," she began, with a rather pathetic expression in her brown eyes.

"I know."

"It was that last time," she continued, her voice trembling a little, though she tried to keep it steady. "I was frightened. I don't like you to eat off the dresser. I'm so afraid you'll—you'll swallow a collar button."

"I did once—almost," he confessed reluctantly, "but it's not so easy, you know. I mean you can swallow the flat part easy enough or else the other part—that is, separately—but for a whole collar button you'd have to have a specially made throat." He was astonishing himself by the debonnaire appropriateness of his remarks. Words seemed for the first time in his life to ran at him shrieking to be used, gathering themselves into carefully arranged squads and platoons and being presented to him by punctilious adjutants of paragraphs.

"That's what scared me," she said. "I knew you had to have a specially made throat—and I knew, at least I felt sure, that you didn't have one."

He nodded frankly.

"I haven't. It costs money to have one—more money than I unfortunately possess."

He felt no shame in saying this—rather a delight in making the admission—he knew that nothing he could say or do would be beyond her comprehension; least of all his poverty and the practical impossibility of ever extricating himself from it.

Caroline looked down at her wrist watch, and with a little cry slid from the table on to her feet.

"It's after five," she cried. "I didn't realize. I have to be at the Ritz-Carlton at five-thirty. Let's hurry and get this done."

With one accord they set to work. Caroline began the matter by seizing a book on insects and sending it whizzing, and finally crashing through the glass partition that housed Mr. Moonlight Quill. The proprietor glanced up with an aggravated look, impatiently brushed a few pieces of glass from his desk, and went on with his letters. Miss McCracken gave no sign of having heard—only Miss Masters started and gave a little frightened scream before she bent to her task again.

But to Merlin and Caroline it didn't matter. In a perfect orgy of energy they were hurling book after book in all directions until sometimes three or four were in the air at once, smashing against shelves, cracking the glass of pictures on the walls, falling in bruised and torn heaps upon the floor. It was fortunate that no customers happened to come in, for it is certain they would never have come in again—the noise was too tremendous, a noise of smashing and ripping and tearing, mixed now and then with the tinkling of glass, the quick breathing of the two throwers and the intermittent outbursts of laughter to which both of them periodically surrendered.

At five-thirty Caroline tossed a last book at the lamp, and so gave the final impetus to the load it carried. The weakened silk tore and dropped its cargo in one vast splattering of white and color to the already littered floor. Then with a sigh of relief she turned to Merlin and held out her hand.

"Good-bye," she said simply.

"Are you going?" He knew she was. His question was simply a lingering wile to detain her and extract for an extra moment that dazzling essence of light he drew from her presence by him, to continue his enormous satisfaction in her features, which were like kisses and, he thought, like the features of a girl he had known back in 1910. For a minute he pressed the softness of her hand—then she smiled and withdrew it and, before he could spring to open the door, she had done it herself and was gone out into the turbid and ominous twilight that brooded narrowly over Forty-seventh Street.

I would like to tell you how Merlin walked into the little partition of Mr. Moonlight Quill and gave up his job then and there; thence issuing out into the street a much finer and nobler and increasingly ironic man. But the truth is much more commonplace. Merlin Grainger stood up and surveyed the wreck of the bookshop, the ruined volumes, the torn silk remnants of the once beautiful crimson lamp, the crystalline sprinkling of broken glass which lay in iridescent dust over the whole interior—and then he went to a corner where a broom was kept and began cleaning up and rearranging and as far as he was able restoring the shop to its former condition. He found that, though some few of the books were uninjured, most of them had suffered in varying extents. The backs were off some, the pages were torn from others, still others were just slightly cracked in the front, which as all careless book returners know makes a book unsalable and therefore second hand.

Nevertheless by six o'clock he had done much to repair the damage. He had returned the books to their original places, swept the floor, put new lights in the sockets overhead—the red shade itself was ruined beyond redemption and Merlin thought with some regret that the money to replace it would have to come out of his salary. At six, therefore, having done the best he could, he crawled over the front window display to pull down the blind. As he was treading delicately back, he saw Mr. Moonlight Quill rise from his desk, put on his overcoat and hat and emerge into the shop. He nodded coldly at Merlin and went toward the door. With his hand on the knob he paused, turned around and in a voice curiously compounded of fierceness and uncertainty, he said:

"If that girl comes in here again, you tell her to behave."

With that he opened the door, drowning Merlin's meek "Yessir" in its creak, and went out.

Merlin stood there for a moment, deciding wisely not to worry about what was for the present only a possible futurity, and then he went into the back of the shop and invited Miss Masters to have supper with him at Pulpat's French Restaurant where one could still get red wine at dinner despite the Great Federal Government.[12] Miss Masters accepted.

"Wine makes me feel all tingly," she said.

Merlin laughed inwardly as he compared her to Caroline, or rather as he didn't compare her. There was no comparison.

Mr. Moonlight Quill though considered by his wife to be a very flighty gentleman, infinitely susceptible to unwarranted generosities, penurities, depressions and elations, was in the less nearsighted judgement of his employees a man of weight and decision. His weight—waiving its sheerly physical aspect of one hundred and eighteen pounds, the weight of a likely débutante—consisted of his bearing down upon a problem quickly, momentously and severely. And it was thus that he approached the problem of his wrecked shop. Unless he should make an outlay equal to the original cost of his entire stock—a step beyond his means—it would be impossible for him to continue in business with the Moonlight Quill as before. There was but one thing to do and he did it. He promptly turned his establishment from an up-to-the-minute book-store into a second-hand bookshop. The damaged books were marked down from twenty-five to fifty per cent, the name over the door whose turpentine embroidery had once shone so insolently and delightfully bright was allowed to grow dim and of the indescribably vague color of old paint, and, having a strong penchant for ceremonial, the proprietor even went so far as to buy two skull caps of shoddy red felt, one for himself and one for his clerk Merlin Grainger. Moreover, he let his goatee grow until it resembled the tail-feathers of an ancient sparrow and substituted for a once dapper business suit a reverence-inspiring affair of shiny alpaca.[13]

In fact within a year after Caroline's catastrophic visit to the bookshop the only thing in it that preserved any semblance of being up-to-date was Miss Masters. Miss McCracken had followed in the footsteps of Mr. Moonlight Quill and become an intolerable dowd.

Yes, Merlin too, from a feeling compounded of loyalty and listlessness had let his exterior take on the semblance of a deserted garden. He accepted the red felt skull cap as a symbol of his decay. Always a young man known as a "pusher,"[14] since the day of his graduation from the manual training department of a New York High School he had been an inveterate brusher of clothes, hair, teeth and even eyebrows[15] and had learned the value of laying all his clean socks toe upon toe and heel upon heel in a certain drawer of his bureau which would be known as the sock drawer.

These things, he felt, had won him his place in the greatest splendor of the Moonlight Quill. It was due to them that he was not still making "chests useful for keeping things," as he was taught with breathless practicality in High School, and selling them to whoever had use of such chests—possibly undertakers. Nevertheless when the progressant Moonlight Quill became the retrogressent[16] Moonlight Quill he preferred to sink with it, and so took to letting his suits gather undisturbed the wispy burdens of the air and to throwing his socks indiscriminately into the shirt drawer, the underwear drawer and even into no drawer at all. It was not uncommon in his new carelessness to let many of his clean* clothes go directly back to the laundry without having ever been worn, a frequent eccentricity among impoverished bachelors. And this in the face of his favorite magazines, which at that time were fairly staggering with articles by successful authors against the frightful extravagances of the poor, such as the buying of silk shirts and nice cuts of meat, and the fact that they preferred good investments in jewelry to respectable ones in four per cent saving banks.

It was indeed a strange state of affairs and a sorry one for many worthy and God-fearing men. For the first time in the history of the Republic almost any negro in the country could change a one-dollar bill. But as at this time the cent was rapidly approaching the purchasing power of zero and was only a thing you got back occasionally after paying for a soft drink and could use merely for getting your correct weight, this was perhaps not so strange a phenomenon as it at first seems.[17] It was too curious a state of things, however, for Merlin Grainger to take the step that he did take—the hazardous, almost involuntary step of proposing to Miss Masters. Stranger still that she accepted him,

It was at Pulpat's on Saturday night and over a $1.75 bottle of water diluted *vin ordinaire* that the proposal occurred.

"Wine makes me feel all tingly, doesn't it you?" chattered Miss Masters gayly.

"Yes," answered Merlin absently; and then, after a long and pregnant pause: "Miss Masters—Olive—I want to say something to you if you'll listen to me."

The tingliness of Miss Masters (who knew what was coming) increased until it seemed that she would shortly be electrocuted by her own nervous reactions. But her "Yes, Merlin" came without a sign or flicker of interior disturbance. Merlin swallowed a stray bit of air that he found in his mouth.

"I have no fortune," he said with the manner of making an announcement. "I have no fortune at all."

---

* *Metropolitan* broke the text at this point after three contiguous pages (pp. 11–13), continuing the story on p. 45.

Their eyes met, locked, became wistful and dreamy and beautiful.
"Olive," he told her, "I love you."

"I love you too, Merlin," she answered simply. "Shall we have another bottle of wine?"

"Yes," he cried, his heart beating at a great rate. "Do you mean——"

"To drink to our engagement," she interrupted bravely. "May it be a short one!"

"No!" he almost shouted, bringing his fist fiercely down upon the table. "May it last forever!"

"What?"

"I mean—oh, I see what you mean. You're right. May it be a short one." He laughed and added "My error," by which it may be perceived that he was not without his share of humor.

After the wine arrived they discussed the matter thoroughly.

"We'll have to take a small apartment at first," he said, "and I believe, yes, by golly, I know there's a small one in the house where I live, a big room and a sort of a dressing-room-kitchenette and the use of a bath on the same floor."

She clapped her hands happily and he thought how pretty she was really, that is the upper part of her face—from the bridge of the nose down she was somewhat out of true. She continued enthusiastically:

"And as soon as we can afford it we'll take a real swell apartment with an elevator and a telephone girl."

"And after that a place in the country—and a car."

"I can't imagine nothing more fun. Can you?"

Merlin fell silent a moment. He was thinking that he would have to give up his room, the fourth floor rear. Yet it mattered very little now. For the past year and a half, in fact from the very date of Caroline's visit to the Moonlight Quill, he had never seen her. For a week after that visit her lights had failed to go on—darkness brooded out into the area-way, seemed to grope blindly in at his expectant, uncurtained window. Then the lights had appeared at last and instead of Caroline and the men in black and white they showed a stodgy family—a little man with a bristly mustache and a full-bosomed woman who spent her evenings largely in patting her hips and rearranging bric-a-brac. After two days of them Merlin had callously pulled down his shade.

No, Merlin could think of nothing more fun than rising in the world with Olive. There would be a cottage in a suburb, a cottage painted blue, just one class below the sort of cottages that are of white stucco with a green roof. In the grass around the cottage would be rusty trowels and a broken green bench and a baby-carriage with a wicker body that sagged to the left. And around the grass and the baby-carriage and the cottage itself, around his whole world there would be the arms of Olive, a little stouter, the arms of her neo-Olivian period, when, as she walked, her cheeks would tremble up and down ever so slightly from too many face-massages. He could hear her voice now, two spoons' length away:

"I knew you were going to say this tonight, Merlin. I could see——"

She could see. Ah—suddenly he wondered how much she could see. Could she see that the girl who had come in with a party of three men and sat down at the next table was—was Caroline? Ah, could she see that? Could she see that the men carried liquor far more potent than Pulpat's red ink condensed three-fold . . .?

Merlin stared breathlessly, half-hearing through an auditory ether Olive's low soft monologue, as like a persistent honey-bee she sucked sweetness from her memorable hour. Merlin was listening to the clinking of glasses and the fine laughter of all four at some pleasantry—and that laughter of Caroline's that he knew so well lifted him, stirred him, called his heart imperiously over to her table, whither it obediently went. He could see her quite plainly and he fancied that in the last year and a half she had changed, if ever so slightly. Was it the light or were her cheeks a little thinner and her eyes less fresh, if more liquid, than of old? Yet the shadows were still purple in her russet hair; her mouth hinted yet of kisses as did the profile that came sometimes between his eyes and a row of books, when it was twilight in the bookshop where the crimson lamp presided no more.

And she had been drinking. The three-fold flush in her cheeks was compounded of youth and wine and fine cosmetic—that he could tell. She was making great amusement for the young man on her left and the portly person on her right and even for the old fellow opposite her for he uttered from time to time the shocked and mildly reproachful cackles of another generation. Merlin caught the words of a song she was intermittently singing—

"Just snap your fingers at care,
Don't cross the bridge 'till you're there—"[18]

The portly person filled her glass with chill amber. A waiter after several trips about the table, punctuated by helpless glances at Caroline who was maintaining a cheerful if futile questionnaire as to the succulence of this or that dish on the menu, managed to obtain the semblance of an order and hurried away . . .

Olive was speaking to Merlin—

"When, then?" she asked, her voice faintly shaded with disappointment. He realized that he had just answered no to some question she had asked him.

"Oh, sometime."

"Don't you—care?"

A rather pathetic poignancy in her question brought his eyes back to her.

"As soon as possible, dear," he replied with surprising tenderness. "In two months—in June."

"So soon?" Her delightful excitement quite took her breath away.

"Oh, yes, I think we'd better say June. No use waiting."

Olive began to pretend that two months was really too short a time for her to make preparations. Wasn't he a bad boy! Wasn't he impatient, though! Well, she'd show him he mustn't be too quick with *her*. Indeed he was so sudden she didn't exactly know whether she ought to marry him at all.

"June," he repeated sternly.

Olive sighed and smiled and drank her coffee, her little finger lifted high above the others in true refined fashion. A stray thought came to Merlin that he would like to buy five rings and throw at it.

"By gosh!" he exclaimed aloud. He was realizing that he was soon to do some such thing with rings on one of her fingers.

His eyes swung sharply to the right. The party of four had become so riotous that the head-waiter had spoken to them. Caroline was arguing with him in a raised voice, so clear and young that it seemed as though the whole restaurant would listen—the whole restaurant except Olive Masters, self-absorbed in her new secret.

"How-do-you-do," Caroline was saying. "Probably handsomest head-waiter in captivity. Too much noise? Very unfortunate. Something have to be done about it. Gerald"—she addressed the man on her right—"head-waiter says too much noise. Appeals to us to have it stopped. What'll I say?"

"Sh!" remonstrated Gerald, with laughter. "Sh!" and Merlin heard him add in an undertone: "All the bourgeoisie will be aroused. This is where the floorwalkers[19] bring their women."

Caroline sat up straight with a sort of unsteady alertness.

"Where's floorwalker?" she cried. "Show me floorwalker. One thing I hate's a floorwalker. If you must walk for a profession, why not choose a rope or a wire?" This seemed to amuse the party, for they all, including Caroline, burst into renewed laughter. The head-waiter, after a last conscientious but despairing admonition, became Gallic with his shoulders and retired into the background.

Pulpat's, as every one knows, has the unvarying respectability of the table d'hôte. It is not a gay place in the conventional sense. One comes, drinks the red wine, talks perhaps a little more and a little louder than usual under the low, smoky ceilings and then goes home. It closes up at nine-thirty, tight as a drum; the policeman, who waits to throw out revenue officers,[20] is paid off and given an extra bottle of wine for the Missus; the coat-room girl hands her tips to the collector, and then darkness crushes the little round tables out of sight and life. But excitement was prepared for Pulpat's this evening—excitement of no mean variety. A beautiful young girl with russet, purple-shadowed hair mounted to her table-top and began to dance thereon.

"*Sacre nom Dieu!* Come down off there!" cried the head-waiter; "stop that music!"

But the musicians were already playing so loud that they could pretend not to hear his order; having once been young they played louder and more gaily than ever, and Caroline danced with grace and vivacity unmatched for leagues around, her pink, filmy dress swirling about her, her agile arms playing in supple, tenuous gestures along the smoky air.

A group of Frenchmen at a table nearby broke into cries of applause, in which other parties joined—in a moment the room was full of clapping and shouting; half the diners were on their feet, crowding up, and on the outskirts the hastily summoned proprietor was giving indistinct vocal evidences of his desire to put an end to this thing as quickly as possible.

". . . Merlin!" cried Olive, awake, aroused at last; "she's such a wicked girl! Let's get out—now!"

The fascinated Merlin protested feebly that the check was not paid.

"It's all right. Lay three dollars on the table. I despise that girl. I can't *bear* to look at her." She was on her feet now, tugging at Merlin's arm.

Helplessly, listlessly, and then with what amounted to downright unwillingness, Merlin rose, followed Olive dumbly as she picked her way through the delirious clamor, now approaching its height and threatening to become a wild and memorable riot. Submissively he took his coat and stumbled up half a dozen steps into the moist April air outside, his ears still ringing with the sound of light feet on the table and of laughter all about and over the little world of the café. In silence they walked along toward Fifth Avenue and a bus.

It was not until next day that she told him about the wedding—how she had moved the date forward: it was much better that they should be married on the first of May.

And married they were, in a somewhat stuffy manner, under the chandelier of the flat where Olive lived with her mother. After marriage came elation, and then, with gradual revelation, the growth of weariness. Responsibility descended upon Merlin, the responsibility of making his thirty dollars a week and her twenty[21] suffice under the civilization of freedom to keep them respectably fat and to hide decently the fact that they were.

It was decided after several weeks of disastrous and well-nigh humiliating experiments with restaurants that they would join the great army of the delicatessen fed, so he took up his old way of life again, in that he stopped every evening at Braegdort's delicatessen and bought potatoes in salad, ham in slices, and sometimes even stuffed-tomatoes in bursts of extravagance.

Then he would trudge homeward, enter the dark hallway and climb three rickety flights of stairs covered by an ancient carpet of long obliterated design. The hall had an ancient smell—of the vegetables of 1880, of the furniture polish in vogue when Bryan ran against William McKinley,[22] of portières an ounce heavier with dust from worn-out shoes and lint from dresses turned long since into patch-work quilts. This smell would pursue him up the stairs, revivified and made poignant at each landing by the aura of contemporary cooking, and then, as he began the next flight, diminishing into the odor of the dead routine of a dead generation.

Eventually would occur the door of his room, which slipped open with indecent willingness and closed with almost a sniff upon his "Hello, dear! Got a treat for you tonight."

Olive, who always rode home on the bus to "get a morsel of air," would be making the bed and hanging up things. At his call she would come up to him and give him a quick kiss with wide-open eyes, while he held her upright like a ladder, his hands on her two arms, as though she were a thing without equilibrium, and would, once he relinquished hold, fall stiffly backward to the floor. This is the kiss that comes in with the second year of marriage,[23] succeeding the bridegroom kiss (which is rather stagey at best, say those who know about such things, and apt to be copied from the moving pictures).

Then came supper, and after that they went out for a walk, up two blocks and through Central Park, whose paper-littered grass was mercifully softened now by the gathered night, or sometimes to a moving picture,[24] which taught them patiently that they were the sort of people for whom life was ordered, and that something very grand and brave and beautiful would soon happen to them if they were docile and obedient to their rightful superiors and kept away from vampires, male and female.

Such was their day for three years. Then change came into their lives: Olive had a baby, and as a result Merlin had a new influx of material resources. In the third week of Olive's confinement, after an hour of nervous rehearsing, he went into the office of Mr. Moonlight Quill and demanded an enormous increase in salary.

"I've been here ten years," he said; "since I was nineteen. I've done good, honest work—tried to do my best in the interests of the business."

Mr. Moonlight Quill said that he would think it over. Next morning he announced, to Merlin's great delight, that he was going to put into effect a project long premeditated—he was going to retire from active work in the bookshop, confining himself to periodic visits and leaving Merlin as manager on a salary of fifty dollars[25] a week and one-tenth interest in the business. When the old man finished, Merlin's cheeks were glowing and his eyes full of tears. He seized his employer's hand and shook it violently, saying over and over again:

"It's very nice of you, sir. It's very white of you. It's very, very nice of you."

So after ten years of faithful work he had won out at last. Looking back, he saw his own progress toward this hill of elation no longer as a sometimes sordid and always gray decade of worry and failing enthusiasm and failing dreams, years when the moonlight had grown duller in the area-way and the youth had faded out of Olive's face, but as a glorious and triumphant climb over obstacles which he had determinedly surmounted by unconquerable will-power. The optimistic self-delusion that had kept him from misery was seen now in the golden garments of stern resolution. Half a dozen times he had taken steps to leave the Moonlight Quill and soar upward, but through sheer faint-heartedness he had stayed on and his design had feebly died. Strangely enough he now thought that those were times when he had exerted tremendous persistence and had "determined" to fight it out where he was.

At any rate, let us not for this moment begrudge Merlin his new and magnificent view of himself. He had arrived. At thirty he had reached a post of importance. He left the shop that evening fairly radiant, invested every penny in his pocket in the most tremendous feast that Braegdort's delicatessen offered, and staggered homeward with the great news and four gigantic paper bags. The fact that Olive was too sick to eat, that he made himself faintly but unmistakably ill by a struggle with four stuffed tomatoes, and that most of the food deteriorated rapidly in an iceless ice-box[26] all next day did not mar the occasion. For the first time since the week of his marriage Merlin Grainger lived under a sky of unclouded tranquillity.

The baby boy was christened Arthur, and life became dignified, significant and, at length, centered. Merlin and Olive resigned themselves to a somewhat secondary place in their own cosmos; but what they lost in personality they regained in a sort of vague primordial pride. The country house did not come, but a month in an Asbury Park[27] boarding-house each summer took its place; and during Merlin's two weeks' holiday this excursion assumed the air of a really merry jaunt—especially when, the baby being asleep in a wide room opening technically on the sea, Merlin strolled with Olive along the thronged board-walk puffing at his cigar with the assurance and weightiness of a retired revenue-agent.

With no alarm at the slowing up of the days and the accelerating of the years Merlin became thirty-one, thirty-two—then almost with a rush arrived at that age which, with all its washing and panning, can only muster a bare handful of that precious stuff called youth: he became thirty-five. And then one day on Fifth Avenue he saw Caroline.

It was Sunday, a radiant, flowerful Easter morning and the avenue was a pageant of lilies and cutaways[28] and happy April-colored bonnets. Twelve o'clock: the great churches were letting out their people—St. Simon's, St. Hilda's, The Church of the Epistles[29] opened their doors like wide mouths until the people pouring forth surely resembled happy laughter as they met and strolled and chattered, or else waved white bouquets at waiting chauffeurs.

In front of the Church of the Epistles stood the twelve vestrymen, carrying out the time-honored custom of giving away Easter eggs full of face-powder to the church-going débutantes of the year. Around them delightedly danced the two thousand miraculously groomed children of the very rich, correctly cute and curled, shining like sparkling little jewels upon their mothers' fingers. Speaks the sentimentalist for the children of the poor? Ah, but the children of the rich, laundried, sweet-smelling, complexioned of the country, and, above all, with soft, well-bred voices.

Little Arthur was five, child of the middle-class. Undistinguished, unnoticed, with a nose that forever marred what Grecian yearnings his features might have had, he held tightly to his mother's warm, sticky hand, and, with Merlin on his other side, moved upon the home-coming throng. At Fifty-third Street, where there were two churches, and the congestion was at its thickest, its richest, its most be-cutawayed and be-bonneted, their progress was of necessity retarded to such an extent that even little Arthur had not the slightest difficulty in keeping up. Then it was that Merlin perceived an open landaulet of deepest crimson, with the richest of nickel trimmings, glide slowly up to the curb and come to a stop. In it sat Caroline.

She was dressed in black, a tight-fitting gown trimmed with lavender, flowered at the waist with a corsage of orchids.[30] Merlin started violently, and then scrutinized her with care. Here for the first time since his marriage, he was encountering the girl again. But a girl no longer. Her figure was slim as ever—or perhaps not quite, for a certain boyish swagger, a sort of insolent adolescence, had gone the way of the first blooming of her cheeks. But she was beautiful; dignity was there now, and the charming lines of a fortuitous nine-and-twenty; and she sat in the car with such perfect appropriateness and self-possession that it made him breathless to watch her.

Suddenly she smiled—the smile of old, bright as that very Easter and its flowers, mellower than ever—yet somehow with not quite the radiance and infinite promise of that first smile back there in the bookshop nine years before. It was a harder smile, disillusioned, faintly sad.

But it was soft enough and smile enough to make a pair of young men in cutaway coats hurry over, to pull their high hats off their wetted, iridescent hair; to bring them, flustered and bowing, to the edge of her landaulet, where her lavender gloves gently touched their gray ones. And these two were presently joined by another, and then two more, until there was a rapidly swelling crowd around the landaulet, a group augmented more than frequently at the expense of a young and well-favored feminine stroller. Merlin would hear a young man beside him say:

"If you'll just pardon me a moment, there's some one I *have* to speak to. Walk right ahead. I'll catch up."

Within three minutes every inch of the landaulet, front, back and side, was occupied by a man—a man trying to construct a sentence clever enough to find its way to Caroline through the stream of conversation. Luckily for Merlin a portion of little Arthur's clothing had chosen this opportunity to threaten a collapse, and Olive had hurriedly rushed him over against a building for some extemporaneous repair work, so Merlin was able to watch, unhindered, the salon in the street.

The crowd swelled. A row formed in back of the first, two more behind that. In the midst, a tiger lily rising from a black bouquet, sat Caroline enthroned in her obliterated car, nodding and crying salutations and smiling with such true happiness that of a sudden a new influx of gentlemen who appeared to know her had left their wives and consorts and were striding toward her.

The crowd, now phalanx deep, began to be augmented by the merely curious; men of all ages who could not possibly have known Caroline jostled over and melted into the circle of ever-increasing diameter until the lady in lavender was the center of a vast impromptu auditorium.

All about her were faces—clean-shaven, bewhiskered, old, young and ageless, and now, here and there, a woman. The mass was rapidly spreading to the opposite curb, and, as St. Anthony's let out just around the corner, it overflowed to the side-walk and crushed up against the iron picket-fence of a millionaire just across the street. The motors speeding along the avenue were compelled to stop, and in a jiffy were piled three, four, five and six deep at the edge of the crowd; auto buses, top-heavy turtles of traffic, plunged into the jam, their passengers crowding to the edges of the roofs in wild excitement and peering down into the center of the mass, which presently could hardly be seen from the mass's edge.

The crush had become terrific. No fashionable audience at a Yale-Princeton football game, no damp mob at a world's series, could be compared with the panoply that talked, stared, laughed and honked about the lady in black and lavender. It was stupendous; it was terrible. A quarter mile down the block a half frantic policeman called his precinct; on the same corner a frightened civilian crashed in the glass of a fire-alarm and sent in a wild pæan for all the fire-engines of the city; up in an apartment high in one of the tall buildings a hysterical old maid telephoned in turn for the prohibition enforcement agent, the special deputies on Bolshevism[31] and the maternity ward of Bellevue Hospital.

The noise increased. The first fire-engine arrived, filling the Sunday air with smoke, clanging and crying a brazen, metallic message down the high resounding walls. In the notion that some terrible calamity had overtaken the city, two excited deacons ordered special services immediately and set tolling the great bells of St. Hilda's and St. Anthony's, presently joined by the jealous gongs of St. Simon's and the Church of the Epistles. Even far off in the Hudson and East River the sounds of the commotion were heard, and the ferry-boats and tugs and ocean liners set up sirens and whistles that sailed in melancholy cadence, now varied, now reiterated, across the whole diagonal width of the city from Riverside Drive to the gray water-fronts of the lower East Side . . .

In the center of her landaulet sat the lady in black and lavender, chatting pleasantly first with one, then with another of that fortunate few in cutaways who had found their way to speaking distance in the first rush. After a while she glanced around her and beside her with a look of growing annoyance that the inevitable psychologist[32] would have vaguely named professional jealousy—more especially when she sweetly remarked:

"Fire or something. Imagine! What a bother! I *knew* those silly traffic lights would never work on Fifth Avenue."[33]

Then she yawned and asked the man nearest her if he couldn't run in somewhere and get her a glass of water. The man apologized in some embarrassment. He could not have moved hand or foot. He could not have scratched his own ear . . .

As the first blast of the river sirens keened along the air, Olive fastened the last safety-pin in little Arthur's rompers and looked up. Merlin saw her start, stiffen slowly like hardening stucco, and then give a little gasp of surprise and disapproval.

"That woman," she cried suddenly. "Oh!"

She flashed a glance at Merlin that mingled reproach and pain, and without another word gathered up little Arthur with one hand, grasped her husband by the other and darted amazingly in a wind-ing, pushing, bumping canter through the crowd. Somehow people gave way before her; somehow she managed to retain her grasp on her son and husband; somehow she managed to emerge two blocks up, battered and dishevelled, into an open space, and, without slow-ing up her pace, darted down a side-street. Then at last, when the uproar had died away into a dim and distant clamor, did she come to a walk and set little Arthur upon his feet.

"And on Sunday, too! Hasn't she disgraced herself enough?" This was her only comment. She said it to Arthur, as she seemed to address her remarks to Arthur throughout the remainder of the day. For some curious and esoteric reason she had never once looked at her husband during the entire retreat.

The years between thirty-five and sixty-five resolve before the pas-sive mind as one unexplained, confusing merry-go-round. True, they are a merry-go-round of ill-gaited and wind-broken horses, painted first in pastel colors, then in dull grays and browns, but perplexing and intolerably dizzy the thing is, as never were the merry-go-rounds of childhood or adolescence, as never, surely, were the certain-coursed, dynamic roller-coasters of youth. For most men and women these thirty years are taken up with a gradual withdrawal from life, a retreat first from a front with many shelters, those myriad amusements and curiosities of youth, to a line with less, when we peel down our ambitions to one ambition, our recreations to one recreation, our friends to a few to whom we are anesthetic; ending up at last in a solitary, desolate strong-point where the shells now whistle abominably, now are but half-heard as by turns frightened and tired we sit waiting for death.

At forty, then, Merlin was no different from himself at thirty-five; a larger paunch, a gray twinkling near his ears, a more certain lack of vivacity in his walk. His forty-five differed from his forty by a like margin, unless one mention a slight deafness in his left ear. But at fifty-five the process had become a chemical change of immense rapidity. Yearly he was more and more an "old man" to his family—senile almost, so far as his wife was concerned. He was by this time complete owner of the bookshop. Mr. Moonlight Quill, dead some five years and not survived by his wife, had deeded the whole stock and store over to him, and there he still spent his days, conversant now by name with almost all that man has recorded for three thousand years, a human catalogue, an authority upon tooling and binding, upon folios and first editions, an accurate inventory of a thousand authors whom he could never have understood and had certainly never read.

At sixty-five he distinctly doddered. He had assumed the melancholy habits of the aged so often portrayed by the second old man in standard comedies. He consumed vast warehouses of time searching for mislaid spectacles. He "nagged" his wife and was nagged in turn. He gave his son weird, impossible directions and orations about life, and told the same jokes three or four times a year at the family table. Mentally and materially he was so entirely different from the Merlin Grainger of twenty-five that it seemed incongruous that he should bear the same name.

He worked still in the bookshop with the assistance of a youth, whom, of course, he considered very idle, indeed, and a new young woman, Miss Gaffney. Miss McCracken, ancient and unvenerable as himself, still kept the accounts. Young Arthur was gone into Wall Street to sell bonds, as all the young men seemed to be doing in that day.[34] This, of course, was as it should be. Let old Merlin get what magic he could from his books—the place of young King Arthur was in the counting house.

One afternoon at four when he had slipped noiselessly up to the front of the store on his soft-soled slippers, led by a newly-formed habit, that, to be fair, he was rather ashamed of, that of spying upon the young man clerk, he looked casually out of the front window, straining his faded eye-sight to reach the street. A limousine, large, portentous, impressive, had drawn to the curb and the chauffeur after dismounting and holding some sort of conversation with persons in the interior of the car turned about and advanced in a bewildered fashion toward the entrance of the Moonlight Quill. He opened the door, shuffled in and glancing uncertainly at the old man in the skull cap addressed him in a thick murky voice, as though his words came through a fog.

"Do you—do you sell additions?"

Merlin nodded.

"Oh, yes. The Arithmetic books are in the back of the store."

The chauffeur took off his cap and scratched a close-cropped fuzzy head.

"Oh, naw. This I want's a detecatif story," he jerked a thumb back toward the limousine. "She seen it in the paper. Firs' addition."

Merlin's interest quickened. Here was possibly a big sale.

"Oh, editions. I see. Yes, we've advertised some first editions but—detective stories, I—don't—believe—What was the title?"

"I forget. About a crime."

"About a crime. I have—Well, I have The Crimes of the Borgias[35]—full Morocco, London 1769, beautifully—"

"Naw," interrupted the chauffeur, "this was one fella did this crime. She seen you had it for sale in the paper."

Merlin racked his brains in vain. The chauffeur rejected several possible titles with the air of connoisseur.

"Silver Bones," announced the chauffeur suddenly out of a slight pause.

"What?" demanded Merlin, suspecting that the stiffness of his sinews were being commented on.

"Silver Bones. That was the guy that done the crime."

"Silver Bones?"

"Silver Bones. Indian maybe."

Merlin stroked his grizzly cheeks.

"Gee, Mister," went on the prospective purchaser, "if you wanna save me an'[36] awful ballin' out jes' try an' think. The old lady goes wil' if everythin' don't go smooth."

But Merlin's musings on the subject of crimes and Silver Bones was as unproductive of results as his obliging search through the shelves, and five minutes later a very dejected charioteer wound his way back to his mistress. Through the glass Merlin could see the visible symbols of a tremendous uproar going on in the interior of the limousine. The chauffeur made wild appealing gestures of his innocence, evidently to no avail, for when he turned around and climbed back into the driver's seat his face was a papyrus in dejection.

Then the door of the limousine opened and gave forth a very pale and slim young man of about twenty, dressed in the attenuation of fashion and carrying a wisp of a cane.[37] He entered the shop, walked past Merlin and proceeded to take out a cigarette and light it. Merlin approached him.

"Anything I can do for you, sir?"

"Old boy," said the youth coolly, "there are seveereal things. You can first let me smoke my ciggy in here out of sight of that old lady in the limousine who happens to be my grandmother. Her knowledge as to whether I smoke it or not happens to be a matter of five thousand dollars[38] to me. The second thing is that you should look up your first edition of the Crime of Sylvestre Bonnard[39] that you advertised in last Sunday's *Times*.[40] My grandmother there happens to want to take it off your hands."

Detecatif story! Crime of somebody! Silver Bones! All was explained. With a faint deprecatory chuckle, as if to say that he would have enjoyed this had life put him in the habit of enjoying anything, Merlin doddered away to the back of his shop where his treasures were kept, to get this latest investment which he had picked up rather cheaply at the sale of a big collection.

When he returned with it the young man was drawing on his cigarette and blowing out quantities of smoke with immense satisfaction.

"My God!" he said, "She keeps me so close to her the entire day running idiotic errands that this happens to be my first puff in six hours. What's the world coming to, I ask you, when a feeble old lady in the milk toast era can dictate to a man as to his personal vices? I happen to be unwilling to be so dictated to. Let's see the book."

Merlin passed it to him tenderly and the young man, after opening it with a carelessness that gave a momentary jump to the bookdealer's heart, ran through the pages with his thumb.

"No illustrations, eh?" he commented. "Well, old boy, what's it worth? Speak up! We're willing to give you a fair price, though why I don't know."

"Two hundred dollars,"[41] said Merlin with a frown.

The young man gave a startled whistle.

"Whew! Come on. You're not dealing with somebody from the cornbelt. I happen to be a city-bred man and my grandmother happens to be a city-bred woman, though I'll admit it'd take a special tax appropriation to keep her in repair. We'll give you twenty-five dollars, and let me tell you that's liberal. We've got books in our attic, up in our attic with my old playthings, that were written before the old boy that wrote this was born."

Merlin stiffened, expressing a rigid and meticulous horror.

"Did your grandmother give you twenty-five dollars to buy this with?"

"She did not. She gave me a hundred but she expects change. I know that old lady."

"You tell her," said Merlin with dignity, "that she has missed a very great bargain."

"Give you fifty," urged the young man. "Come on now—be reasonable and don't try to hold us up—"

Merlin had wheeled around with the precious volume under his arm and was about to return it to its special drawer in his office when there was a sudden interruption. With unheard of magnificence the front door burst rather than swung open and admitted into the dark interior a majestic apparition in black silk and fur which bore rapidly down upon him. The cigarette leaped from the fingers of the urban young man and he gave breath to an inadvertent "Damn!"—but it was upon Merlin that the entrance seemed to have the most remarkable and incongruous effect—so strong an effect that the greatest treasure of his shop slipped from his hand and joined the cigarette on the floor. There before him stood Caroline.

She was an old woman, an old woman remarkably preserved, unusually handsome, unusually erect, but still an old woman. Her hair was a soft and beautiful white, elaborately dressed and jewelled; her face, faintly rouged à la grande dame, showed webs of wrinkles at the edges of her eyes and two deeper lines in the form of stanchions connected her nose with the corners of her mouth. Her eyes were dim, ill-natured and querulous.

But it was Caroline without a doubt, Caroline's features though in decay, Caroline's figure, if brittle and stiff in movement, Caroline's manner, unmistakably compounded of a delightful insolence and an enviable self assurance, and, most of all, Caroline's voice, broken and shaky yet with a ring in it that still could and did make chauffeurs assume despondent expressions and cause cigarettes to fall from the fingers of urban grandsons.

She stood and sniffed. Her eyes found the cigarette upon the floor.

"What's that?" she cried. The words were not a question— they were an entire litany of suspicion, accusation, confirmation and decision. She tarried over them scarcely an instant. "Stand up!" she said to her grandson, "stand up and blow that nicotine out of your lungs!"

The young man looked at her in trepidation.

"Blow!" she commanded.

He pursed his lips feebly and blew into the air.

"Blow!" she repeated, more peremptorily than before.

He blew again, helplessly, ridiculously.

"Do you realize," she went on briskly, "that you've forfeited five thousand dollars in five minutes?"

Merlin momentarily expected the young man to fall pleading upon his knees but such is the nobility of human nature that he remained standing, even blew again into the air, partly from nervousness, partly, no doubt, from some vague hope of re-ingratiating himself.

"Young ass!" cried Caroline. "Once more, just once more and you leave college and go to work."

This threat had such an overwhelming effect upon the young man that he took on an even paler pallor than was natural to him. But Caroline was not through.

"Do you think I don't know what you and your brothers, yes and your precious rascal of a father too think of me? Well, I do. You think I'm senile. You think I'm soft. I'm not!" She struck herself with her fist as though to prove that she was a mass of muscle and sinew. "And I'll have more brains left when you've got me laid out in the drawing-room some bad day than you and the rest of them were born with."

"But Grandmother—"

"Be quiet. You, a little chit of a boy who if it weren't for my money might have risen to be a journeyman barber out in the Bronx—Let me see your hands. Ugh! The hands of a barber—*you* presume to be smart with *me* who once had three counts and a bona fide duke, not to mention half a dozen papal titles pursue me from the city of Rome to the city of New York." She paused, took breath. "Stand up! Blow!"

The young man obediently blew. Simultaneously the door opened and an excited gentleman of middle age who wore a coat and hat trimmed with fur (and seemed, moreover, to be trimmed with the same sort of fur himself on upper lip and chin) rushed into the store and up to Caroline.

"Found you at last," he cried. "Been looking for you all over town. Tried your house on the 'phone and your secretary told me he thought you'd gone to a bookshop called the Moonlight—"

Caroline turned to him irritably.

"Do I employ you for history or economics?" she snapped. "Are you my tutor or my broker?"

"Your broker," confessed the fur-trimmed man, taken somewhat aback.

"Then please refrain from paragraphs about the past."

"I beg your pardon. I came about that phonograph stock.[42] I can sell for a hundred and five."

"Then do it."

"Very well. I thought I'd better—"

"Go sell it. I'm talking to my grandson."

"Very well. I—"

"Good-bye."

"Good-bye, Madame." The fur trimmed man made a slight bow and hurried in some confusion from the shop.

"As for you," said Caroline, turning to her grandson. "You stay just where you are and be quiet."

She turned to Merlin and included his entire length in a not unfriendly survey. Then she smiled and he found himself smiling too. In an instant they had both broken into a cracked but none the less spontaneous chuckle. She seized his arm and hurried him to the other side of the store. There they stopped, faced each other and gave vent to another long fit of senile glee.

"It's the only way," she gasped in a sort of triumphant malignity. "The only thing that keeps old folks like me happy is the sense that they can make other people step around. To be old and rich and have poor descendants is almost as much fun as to be young, beautiful and have ugly sisters."

"Oh, yes," chuckled Merlin. "I know. I envy you."

She nodded blinking.

"The last time I was in here, forty years ago," she said, "you were a young man very anxious to kick up your heels."

"I was," he confessed.

"My visit must have meant a good deal to you," she mused aloud.

"You have all along," he exclaimed. "I thought—I used to think at first that you were a real person—human, I mean."

She laughed.

"Many men have thought me inhuman."

"But now," continued Merlin excitedly, "I understand. Understanding is allowed to us old people—after nothing much matters. I see now that on a certain night when you danced upon a table-top you were nothing but my primordial masculine yearning for a beautiful and perverse woman."

Her old eyes were far away, her voice no more than the echo of a forgotten dream.

"How I danced that night! I remember."

"You were making an attempt at me. Olive's arms were closing about me and you warned me to be free and keep my measure of youth and irresponsibility. But it seemed like an effect gotten up at the last moment. It came too late."

"You are very old," she said inscrutably, "I did not realize."

"I am old but I have not forgotten what you did to me when I was thirty-five. You shook me with that traffic tie-up. It was a magnificent effort. The beauty you radiated! The power it wielded! You became personified even to my wife and she feared you. For weeks I wanted to slip out of the house at dark and forget the stuffiness of life with music and cocktails and careless laughing women. But then—I no longer knew how."

"And now you are so very old." With a sort of awe she moved back and away from him.

"Yes, leave me!" he cried, "you are old also; the spirit withers with the skin. Have you come here only to tell me something I had best forget: that to be old and poor is perhaps more wretched than to be old and rich; to remind me that *my* son hurls my gray failure in my face?"

"Give me my book," she commanded harshly. "Be quick, old man!"

Merlin looked at her once more and then patiently obeyed. He picked up the book and handed it to her, shaking his head when she offered him a bill.

"Why go through the farce of paying me? Once you made me wreck this very premises."

"I did," she said in anger, "and I'm glad. Perhaps there had been enough done to ruin *me*."

"Poverty drove me to curb you in youth."

She gave him a glance, half of disdain, half of ill-concealed uneasiness, and with a brisk word to her urban grandson moved toward the door.

Then she was gone—out of his shop—out of his life. The door clicked. With a sigh he turned and walked brokenly back toward the glass partition that enclosed the yellowed accounts of many years as well as the mellowed, wrinkled Miss McCracken.

Merlin regarded her parched, cobwebbed face with an odd sort of pity. She, at any rate, had had less from life than he. No rebellious romantic spirit cropping out unbidden had in its unsought but memorable moments given life a zest and a glory.

Then Miss McCracken looked up and spoke to him:

"Still a spunky old piece, isn't she?"

Merlin started.

"Who?"

"Old Alicia Dare. Mrs. Thomas Allerdyce she is now, of course; has been these thirty years."

"What? I don't understand you." Merlin sat down suddenly in his swivel chair; his eyes were wide.

"Why, surely, Mr. Grainger, you can't tell me that you've forgotten her when for ten years she was the most notorious character in New York—why, one time when she was the corespondent in the Throckmorton divorce case she attracted so much attention on Fifth Avenue that there was a traffic tie-up. Didn't you read it in the papers."

"I never used to read the papers." His ancient brain was whirring.

"Well, you can't have forgotten the time she came in here and ruined the business. Let me tell you I came near asking Mr. Moonlight Quill for my salary and clearing out."

"Do you mean that—that you *saw* her?"

"Saw her! How could I help it with the racket that went on. Heaven knows Mr. Moonlight Quill didn't like it either but of course *he* couldn't say anything. He was paying for her apartment on 59th Street and the second he opposed one of her whims she'd threaten to make trouble for him. Served him right. She came in here in a fit of temper. The idea of that man falling for a pretty adventuress and keeping a double establishment! Of course she proved too expensive for him even though the shop paid well in those days."

"But when I saw her," stammered Merlin, "that is, when I thought I saw her, she lived with her mother."

"Mother, trash!" said Miss McCracken indignantly. "She had a woman there she called 'Aunty' who was no more related to her than I am. Oh, she was a bad one—but clever. Right after the Throckmorton divorce case she married Thomas Allerdyce and made herself secure for life."

"Who was she?" cried Merlin. "For God's sake what was she, a witch?"

"Why, she was Alicia Dare, the dancer, of course. In those days you couldn't pick up a paper without finding her picture."

Merlin sat very quiet, his brain suddenly fatigued and stilled. He was an old man now indeed, so old that it was impossible for him to dream of ever having been young, so old that the glamor was gone out of the world, passing not into the faces of children and the persistent comforts of warmth and life but passing out of the range of sight and feeling. He was never to smile again or sit in a long reverie when spring evenings wafted the cries of children in at his window until gradually they became the friends of his boyhood out there, urging him to come and play before the last dark came down. Even for those memories he was too old now.

That night he sat at supper with his wife and son who had used him for their blind purposes. Olive said:

"Don't sit there like a death's-head. Say something."

"Let him sit quiet," growled Arthur. "If you encourage him he'll tell us a story we've heard a hundred times before."

Merlin went upstairs very quietly at nine o'clock. When he was in his room and had closed the door tight he stood by it for a moment, his thin limbs trembling. He thought he was a fool.

Tarquin of Cheapside[1]

Smart Set
February 1921
$50

I

Running footsteps—light, soft-soled shoes made of curious leathery cloth brought from Ceylon[2] setting the pace; thick flowing boots, two pairs, dark blue and gilt, reflecting the moonlight in blunt gleams and splotches, following a stone's throw behind.

Soft Shoes flashes through a patch of moonlight, then darts into a blind labyrinth of alleys and becomes only an intermittent scuffle ahead somewhere in the enfolding darkness. In go Flowing Boots with short swords lurching and long plumes awry, finding a breath to curse God and the black lanes of London.

Soft Shoes leaps a shadowy gate and crackles through a hedgerow. Flowing Boots leap the gate and crackles through the hedgerow— and there, startlingly, is the watch ahead—two murderous pikemen[3] of ferocious cast of mouth acquired in Holland and the Spanish[4] marches.[5]

But there is no cry for help. The pursued does not fall panting at the feet of the watch, clutching a purse; neither do the pursuers raise a hue and cry. Soft Shoes goes by in a rush of air. The watch curse and hesitate, glance after the fugitive and then spread their pikes grimly across the road and wait for Flowing Boots. Darkness, like a great hand, cuts off the even flow of the moon.

The hand moves off the moon whose pale caress finds again the eaves and lintels, and the watch, wounded and tumbled in the dust. Up the street one of Flowery Boots leaves a black trail of spots until he binds himself clumsily as he runs, with fine lace caught from his throat.

It was no affair for the watch: Satan was out tonight and Satan seemed to be he who appeared dimly in front, heel over gate, knee over fence. Moreover the adversary was obviously traveling near home or at least in that section of London consecrated to his coarser whims, for the street narrowed like a road in a picture and the houses bent over further and further, cooping in natural ambushes suitable for murder and its histrionic sister, sudden death.

Down long and sinuous lanes twisted the hunted and the harriers, always in and out of the moon in a perpetual queen's move over a checker-board of glints and patches. Ahead, the quarry, minus his leather jerkin now and half blinded by drips of sweat, had taken to scanning his ground desperately on both sides. As a result he suddenly slowed down, and retracing his steps a bit scooted up an alley so dark that it seemed that here sun and moon had been in eclipse since the last glacier slipped roaring over the earth. Two hundred yards down he stopped short and crammed himself into a niche in the wall where he huddled and panted silently, a grotesque god without bulk or outline in the gloom.

Flowing Boots, two pairs, drew near, came up, went by, halted twenty yards beyond him, and spoke in breathless whispers:

"I was attune to that scuffle; it stopped."

"Within twenty paces."

"He's hid."

"Stay together now and we'll cut him up. This way."

The voice faded into a low crunch of a boot, nor did Soft Shoes wait to hear more—he sprang in three leaps across the alley, where he bounded up, flapped for a moment on the top of the wall like a huge bird, and disappeared, gulped down by the hungry night at a mouthful.

II

> *"He read at wine, he read in bed*
> *He read aloud, had he the breath,*
> *His every thought was with the dead*
> *And so he read himself to death."*

Any visitor to the old James the First graveyard near Peat's Hill may spell out this bit of doggerel, undoubtedly one of the worst recorded of an Elizabethan, on the tomb of Wessel Caxter.

This death of his, says the antiquary, occurred when he was thirty-seven, but as this story is concerned with the night of a certain chase through darkness, we find him still alive, still reading. His eyes were somewhat dim, his stomach somewhat obvious—he was a misbuilt man and a lazy one. But an era is an era and in the reign of Elizabeth,[6] by the grace of Luther,[7] Queen of England, no man could help but catch the spirit of excitement. Every loft in Cheapside published its *Magnum Folium* (or magazine) of the new blank verse; the Cheapside Players would produce anything on sight as long as it "got away from those reactionary miracle plays," and the English Bible had run through seven printings in as many months.[8]

So Wessel Caxter, who in his youth had gone to sea, was now an inveterate reader of all on which he could lay his hands—he read friends' manuscripts; he dined poets; he loitered about the shops where the *Magna Folia* were printed, and he listened tolerantly while the young playwrights wrangled and bickered among themselves and behind each other's backs made bitter and malicious charges of plagiarism or anything else they could think of.

Tonight he had a book, a piece of work which, tho inordinately versed, contained, he thought, some rather excellent political satire. *The Faery Queene* by Edmund Spencer[9] lay before him under the tremulous candle-light. He had finished a canto; he was beginning another:

> *The Legend of Britomartis or of Chastity.*
> *It falls me here to write of Chastity.*
> *The fayrest vertue, far above the rest . . .*[10]

A sudden rush of feet on the stairs, a rusty swing open of the thin door, and a man thrust himself into the room, a man without a jerkin, panting and sobbing and on the verge of collapse.

"Wessel," he choked out, "stick me away somewhere, for the love of Our Lady!"

Caxter rose, carefully closing his book, and bolted the door in some concern.

"I'm pursued," cried out Soft Shoes. "I vow there's two short-witted blades trying to make me into mince meat and near succeeding. They saw me jump the back wall!"

"It would need," said Wessel, looking at him curiously, "several battalions armed with arabesques and two or three Armadas to keep you reasonably secure from the revenges of the world."

Soft Shoes smiled with satisfaction. His sobbing gasps were giving way to quick precise breathing; his hunted air had faded to a faintly perturbed irony.

"I feel little surprise," continued Wessel.

"They were two such apes."

"Making a total of three."

"Only two unless you stick me away. Man, man, come alive; they'll be on the stairs in a spark's age."

Wessel took a dismantled pike-staff from the corner and raising it to the high ceiling dislodged a rough trap-door opening into a garret above.

"There's no ladder."

He moved a bench under the trap upon which Soft Shoes mounted, crouched, hesitated, crouched again and then leaped amazingly upward. He caught at the edge of the aperture and swung back and forth for a moment, shifting his hold; finally doubled up and disappeared into the darkness above. There was a scurry like a migration of rats as the trap door was replaced; then silence.

Wessel returned to his reading table, opened to the Legend of Britomartis or of Chastity—and waited. Almost a minute later there was a scramble on the stairs and an intolerable hammering at the door. Wessel sighed and, picking up his candle, rose.

"Who's there?"

"Open the door!"

"Who's there?"

A mighty blow shook the frail wood and splintered it around the edge. Wessel opened it a bare three inches and held the candle high. His was to play the timorous, the super-respectable citizen, disgracefully disturbed.

"One small hour of the night for rest. Is that too much to ask from every brawler and—"

"Quiet, gossip.[11] Have you seen a perspiring fellow?"

The shadows of the two gallants fell in immense wavering outlines over the narrow stairs; by the light Wessel scrutinized them closely. Gentlemen, they were, hastily but richly dressed—one of them wounded severely in the hand, both radiating a sort of furious horror. Waving aside Wessel's ready miscomprehension, they pushed by him into the room and with their swords went through the business of poking carefully into all suspected hiding places in the rooms, further extending their search to Wessel's bed-chamber.

"Is he hid here?" demanded the wounded man fiercely.

"Is who here?"

"Any man but you."

"Only two others that I know of."

For a second Wessel feared that he had spoken too much, for the gallants made as tho to run him through.

"I heard a man on the stairs," he said hastily, "full five minutes ago, it was. He most certainly failed to come up."

He went on to explain his absorption in the Faery Queene but, for the moment at least, his visitors were anæsthetic to culture.

"What's been done?" inquired Wessel.

"Violence!" said the man with the wounded hand. Wessel noticed that his eyes were quite wild. "My own sister. Oh, Christ in heaven, give us this man!"

Wessel winced.

"Who is the man?"

"God's word! We know not even that. What's that trap up there?" he added suddenly.

"It's nailed down. It's not been used for years." He thought of the pole in the corner and quailed inwardly, but the utter despair of the two men dulled their astuteness.

"It would take a ladder for anyone not a tumbler,"[12] said the wounded man listlessly.

His companion broke into hysterical laughter.

"A tumbler. Oh, a tumbler. Oh—"

Wessel stared at them in wonder.

"That, by chance, does appeal to my most ironic humor," cried the man, "that no one—oh, no one—could get up there but a tumbler."

The gallant with the wounded hand snapped his fingers impatiently.

"We must go next door—and then on—"

Helplessly they went as two walking under a dark and storm-swept sky.

Wessel closed and bolted the door and stood a moment by it, frowning in pity.

A low breath "Ha!" made him look up. Soft Shoes had already raised the trap and was looking down into the room, his rather elfish face squeezed into a grimace, half of distaste, half of sardonic amusement.

"They take off their heads with their helmets," he remarked in a whisper, "but as for you and me, Wessel, we are two cunning men."

"Now you be cursed," cried Wessel vehemently. "I knew you for a dog ever, but when I hear even the half of a tale like this I know you for such a dirty cur that I am minded to crack your skull."

Soft Shoes stared at him, blinking.

"At all events," he replied finally, "I find dignity impossible in this position."

With this he let his body through the trap, hung for an instant and dropped the seven feet to the floor.

"There was a rat considered my ear with the air of a gourmet," he continued, dusting his hands on his breeches. "I told him in the rat's peculiar idiom that I was deadly poison so he took himself off."

"Let's hear of this night's business!" insisted Wessel angrily.

Soft Shoes touched his thumb to his nose and wiggled the fingers derisively at Wessel.

"Street gamin!" muttered Wessel.

"Have you any paper?" demanded Soft Shoes irrelevantly, and then rudely added, "or can you write?"

"Why should I give you paper?"

"You wanted to hear of the night's business. So you shall and you give me pen, ink, a sheaf of paper and a room to myself."

Wessel hesitated.

"Get out!" he said finally.

"As you will. Yet you have missed a most intriguing story."

Wessel wavered, gave in. Soft Shoes went into the adjoining room with the begrudged writing materials and carefully closed the door. Wessel grunted and returned to the Faery Queene; so silence came once more upon the house.

III

Three o'clock went into four. The room paled, the dark outside was shot through with damp and chill, and Wessel, cupping his head in his hands bent low over his table, tracing through the pattern of knights and fairies and the harrowing distresses of many girls. There were dragons chortling along the narrow street outside; when the sleepy armourer's boy began his work at half past five the heavy clink and chank of plate and linked mail swelled to the echo of a marching cavalcade.

A fog shut down at the first flare of dawn and the room was grayish yellow at six when Wessel tiptoed to his cupboard bed-chamber and pulled open the door. His guest turned on him a face pale as parchment in which two distraught eyes burned like great red letters. He had drawn a chair close to Wessel's *prie-dieu*[13] which he was using as a desk; and on it was an amazing stack of closely written pages. With a long sigh Wessel withdrew and returned to his syren,[14] calling himself fool for not claiming his bed here at dawn.

The clump of boots outside, the croaking of old beldames[15] from attic to attic, the dull murmur of morning, unnerved him, and half dozing he slumped in his chair, his brain, overladen with sound and colour, working intolerably over the imagery that stacked it. In this restless dream of his he was one of a thousand groaning bodies crushed near the sun, a helpless bridge for the strong-eyed Apollo. The dream tore at him, scraped along his mind like a ragged knife. When a hot hand touched his shoulder, he awoke with what was nearly a scream to find the fog thick in the room and his guest, a gray ghost of misty stuff, beside him with a pile of paper in his hand.

"It should be a most intriguing tale, I believe, though it requires some going over. May I ask you to lock it away, and in God's name let me sleep?"

He waited for no answer, but thrust the pile at Wessel and literally poured himself like stuff from a suddenly inverted bottle upon a couch in the corner; slept, with his breathing regular but his brow wrinkled in a curious and somewhat uncanny manner.

Wessel yawned sleepily and, glancing at the scrawled, uncertain first page, he began reading aloud very softly:

The Rape of Lucrece

"From the besieged Ardea all in post,
Borne by the trustless wings of false desire,
Lust-breathing Tarquin leaves the Roman host—"[16]

The Popular Girl

Saturday Evening Post
11 and 18 February 1922
$1,500

Along about half past ten every Saturday night Yanci Bowman eluded her partner by some graceful subterfuge and from the dancing floor went to point of vantage overlooking the country-club bar. When she saw her father she would either beckon to him, if he chanced to be looking in her direction, or else she would dispatch a waiter to call attention to her impendent presence. If it were no later than half past ten—that is, if he had had no more than an hour of synthetic gin rickeys[1]—he would get up from his chair and suffer himself to be persuaded into the ballroom.

"Ballroom," for want of a better word. It was that room, filled by day with wicker furniture, which was always connoted in the phrase "Let's go in and dance." It was referred to as "inside" or "downstairs." It was that nameless chamber wherein occur the principal transactions of all the country clubs in America.

Yanci knew that if she could keep her father there for an hour, talking, watching her dance, or even on rare occasions dancing himself, she could safely release him at the end of that time. In the period that would elapse before midnight ended the dance he could scarcely become sufficiently stimulated to annoy anyone.

All this entailed considerable exertion on Yanci's part, and it was less for her father's sake than for her own that she went through with it. Several rather unpleasant experiences were scattered through this past summer. One night when she had been detained by the impassioned and impossible-to-interrupt speech of a young man from Chicago her father had appeared swaying gently in the ballroom doorway; in his ruddy handsome face two faded blue eyes were squinted half shut as he tried to focus them on the dancers, and he was obviously preparing to offer himself to the first dowager who caught his eye. He was ludicrously injured when Yanci insisted upon an immediate withdrawal.

After that night Yanci went through her Fabian[2] maneuver to the minute.

Yanci and her father were the handsomest two people in the Middle Western city where they lived. Tom Bowman's complexion was hearty from twenty years spent in the service of good whisky and bad golf. He kept an office downtown, where he was thought to transact some vague real-estate business; but in point of fact his chief concern in life was the exhibition of a handsome profile and an easy well-bred manner at the country club, where he had spent the greater part of the ten years that had elapsed since his wife's death.

Yanci was twenty, with a vague die-away manner which was partly the setting for her languid disposition and partly the effect of a visit she had paid to some Eastern relatives at an impressionable age. She was intelligent, in a flitting way, romantic under the moon and unable to decide whether to marry for sentiment or for comfort, the latter of these two abstractions being well enough personified by one of the most ardent among her admirers. Meanwhile she kept house, not without efficiency, for her father, and tried in a placid unruffled tempo to regulate his constant tippling to the sober side of inebriety.

She admired her father. She admired him for his fine appearance and for his charming manner. He had never quite lost the air of having been a popular Bones[3] man at Yale. This charm of his was a standard by which her susceptible temperament unconsciously judged the men she knew. Nevertheless, father and daughter were far from that sentimental family relationship which is a stock plant in fiction, but in life usually exists in the mind of only the older party to it. Yanci Bowman had decided to leave her home by marriage within the year. She was heartily bored.

Scott Kimberly, who saw her for the first time this November evening at the country club, agreed with the lady whose house guest he was that Yanci was an exquisite little beauty. With a sort of conscious sensuality surprising in such a young man—Scott was only twenty-five—he avoided an introduction that he might watch her undisturbed for a fanciful hour, and sip the pleasure or the disillusion of her conversation at the drowsy end of the evening.

"She never got over the disappointment of not meeting the Prince of Wales[4] when he was in this country," remarked Mrs. Orrin Rogers, following his gaze. "She said so, anyhow; whether she was serious or not I don't know. I hear that she has her walls simply plastered with pictures of him."

"Who?" asked Scott suddenly.

"Why, the Prince of Wales."

"Who has plaster pictures of him?"

"Why, Yanci Bowman, the girl you said you thought was so pretty."

"After a certain degree of prettiness, one pretty girl is as pretty as another," said Scott argumentatively.

"Yes, I suppose so."

Mrs. Rogers' voice drifted off on an indefinite note. She had never in her life compassed a generality until it had fallen familiarly on her ear from constant repetition.

"Let's talk her over," Scott suggested.

With a mock reproachful smile Mrs. Rogers lent herself agreeably to slander. An encore was just beginning. The orchestra trickled a light overflow of music into the pleasant green-latticed room and the two score couples who for the evening comprised the local younger set moved placidly into time with its beat. Only a few apathetic stags gathered one by one in the doorways, and to a close observer it was apparent that the scene did not attain the gayety which was its aspiration. These girls and men had known each other from childhood; and though there were marriages incipient upon the floor to-night, they were marriages of environment, of resignation, or even of boredom.

Their trappings lacked the sparkle of the seventeen-year-old affairs that took place through the short and radiant holidays. On such occasions as this, thought Scott as his eyes still sought casually for Yanci, occurred the matings of the left-overs, the plainer, the duller, the poorer of the social world; matings actuated by the same urge toward perhaps a more glamourous destiny, yet, for all that, less beautiful and less young. Scott himself was feeling very old.

But there was one face in the crowd to which his generalization did not apply. When his eyes found Yanci Bowman among the dancers he felt much younger. She was the incarnation of all in which the dance failed—graceful youth, arrogant, languid freshness and beauty that was sad and perishable as a memory in a dream. Her partner, a young man with one of those fresh red complexions ribbed with white streaks, as though he had been slapped on a cold day, did not appear to be holding her interest, and her glance fell here and there upon a group, a face, a garment, with a far-away and oblivious melancholy.

"Dark-blue eyes," said Scott to Mrs. Rogers. "I don't know that they mean anything except that they're beautiful, but that nose and upper lip and chin are certainly aristocratic—if there is any such thing," he added apologetically.

"Oh, she's very aristocratic," agreed Mrs. Rogers. "Her grandfather was a senator or governor or something in one of the Southern States.[5] Her father's very aristocratic looking too. Oh, yes, they're very aristocratic; they're aristocratic people."

"She looks lazy."

Scott was watching the yellow gown drift and submerge among the dancers.

"She doesn't like to move. It's a wonder she dances so well. Is she engaged? Who is the man who keeps cutting in on her, the one who tucks his tie under his collar so rakishly and affects the remarkable slanting pockets?"[6]

He was annoyed at the young man's persistence, and his sarcasm lacked the ring of detachment.

"Oh, that's"—Mrs. Rogers bent forward, the tip of her tongue just visible between her lips—"that's the O'Rourke boy. He's quite devoted, I believe."

"I believe," Scott said suddenly, "that I'll get you to introduce me if she's near when the music stops."

They arose and stood looking for Yanci—Mrs. Rogers, small, stoutening, nervous, and Scott Kimberly, her husband's cousin, dark and just below medium height. Scott was an orphan with half a million[7] of his own, and he was in this city for no more reason than that he had missed a train. They looked for several minutes, and in vain. Yanci, in her yellow dress, no longer moved with slow loveliness among the dancers.

The clock stood at half past ten.

II

"Good evening," her father was saying to her at that moment in syllables faintly slurred. "This seems to be getting to be a habit."

They were standing near a side stairs, and over his shoulder through a glass door Yanci could see a party of half a dozen men sitting in familiar joviality about a round table.

"Don't you want to come out and watch for a while?" she suggested, smiling and affecting a casualness she did not feel.

"Not to-night, thanks."

Her father's dignity was a bit too emphasized to be convincing.

"Just come out and take a look," she urged him. "Everybody's here, and I want to ask you what you think of somebody."

This was not so good, but it was the best that occurred to her.

"I doubt very strongly if I'd find anything to interest me out there," said Tom Bowman emphatically. "I observe that f'some insane reason I'm always taken out and aged on the wood for half an hour as though I was irresponsible."

"I only ask you to stay a little while."

"Very considerate, I'm sure. But to-night I happ'n be interested in a discussion that's taking place in here."

"Come on, father."

Yanci put her arm through his ingratiatingly; but he released it by the simple expedient of raising his own arm and letting hers drop.

"I'm afraid not."

"I'll tell you," she suggested lightly, concealing her annoyance at this unusually protracted argument, "you come in and look, just once, and then if it bores you you can go right back."

He shook his head.

"No, thanks."

Then without another word he turned suddenly and reëntered the bar. Yanci went back to the ballroom. She glanced easily at the stag line as she passed, and making a quick selection murmured to a man near her, "Dance with me, will you, Carty? I've lost my partner."

"Glad to," answered Carty truthfully.

"Awfully sweet of you."

"Sweet of me? Of you, you mean."

She looked up at him absently. She was furiously annoyed at her father. Next morning at breakfast she would radiate a consuming chill, but for to-night she could only wait, hoping that if the worst happened he would at least remain in the bar until the dance was over.

Mrs. Rogers, who lived next door to the Bowmans, appeared suddenly at her elbow with a strange young man.

"Yanci," Mrs. Rogers was saying with a social smile, "I want to introduce Mr. Kimberly. Mr. Kimberly's spending the week-end with us, and I particularly wanted him to meet you."

"How perfectly slick!" drawled Yanci with lazy formality.

Mr. Kimberly suggested to Miss Bowman that they dance, to which proposal Miss Bowman dispassionately acquiesced. They mingled their arms in the gesture prevalent and stepped into time with the beat of the drum. Simultaneously it seemed to Scott that the room and the couples who danced up and down upon it converted themselves into a background behind her. The commonplace lamps, the rhythm of the music playing some paraphrase of a paraphrase, the faces of many girls, pretty, undistinguished or absurd, assumed a certain solidity as though they had grouped themselves in a retinue for Yanci's languid eyes and dancing feet.

"I've been watching you," said Scott simply. "You look rather bored this evening."

"Do I?" Her dark-blue eyes exposed a borderland of fragile iris as they opened in a delicate burlesque of interest. "How perfectly kill-ing!" she added.

Scott laughed. She had used the exaggerated phrase without smiling, indeed without any attempt to give it verisimilitude. He had heard the adjectives of the year—"hectic," "marvelous" and "slick"—delivered casually, but never before without the faintest meaning. In this lacka-daisical young beauty it was inexpressibly charming.

The dance ended. Yanci and Scott strolled toward a lounge set against the wall, but before they could take possession there was a shriek of laughter and a brawny damsel dragging an embarrassed boy in her wake skidded by them and plumped down upon it.

"How rude!" observed Yanci.

"I suppose it's her privilege."

"A girl with ankles like that has no privileges."[8]

They seated themselves uncomfortably on two stiff chairs.

"Where do you come from?" she asked of Scott with polite disinterest.

"New York."

This having transpired, Yanci deigned to fix her eyes on him for the best part of ten seconds.

"Who was the gentleman with the invisible tie," Scott asked rudely, in order to make her look at him again, "who was giving you such a rush? I found it impossible to keep my eyes off him. Is his personality as diverting as his haberdashery?"

"I don't know," she drawled; "I've only been engaged to him for a week."

"My Lord!" exclaimed Scott, perspiring suddenly under his eyes.

"I beg your pardon. I didn't ——"

"I was only joking," she interrupted with a sighing laugh. "I thought I'd see what you'd say to that."

Then they both laughed, and Yanci continued, "I'm not engaged to anyone. I'm too horribly unpopular."[9] Still the same key, her lan-guorous voice humorously contradicting the content of her remark. "No one'll ever marry me."

"How pathetic!"

"Really," she murmured; "because I have to have compliments all the time, in order to live, and no one thinks I'm attractive any more, so no one ever gives them to me."

Seldom had Scott been so amused.

"Why, you beautiful child," he cried, "I'll bet you never hear anything else from morning till night!"

"Oh, yes I do," she responded, obviously pleased. "I never get compliments unless I fish for them."

"Everything's the same," she was thinking as she gazed around her in a peculiar mood of pessimism. Same boys sober and same boys tight; same old women sitting by the walls—and one or two girls sitting with them who were dancing this time last year.

Yanci had reached the stage where these country-club dances seemed little more than a display of sheer idiocy. From being an enchanted carnival where jeweled and immaculate maidens rouged to the pinkest propriety displayed themselves to strange and fascinating men, the picture had faded to a medium-sized hall where was an almost indecent display of unclothed motives and obvious failures. So much for several years! And the dance had changed scarcely by a ruffle in the fashions or a new flip in a figure of speech.

Yanci was ready to be married.

Meanwhile the dozen remarks rushing to Scott Kimberly's lips were interrupted by the apologetic appearance of Mrs. Rogers.

"Yanci," the older woman was saying, "the chauffeur's just telephoned to say that the car's broken down. I wonder if you and your father have room for us going home. If it's the slightest inconvenience don't hesitate to tell ——"

"I know he'll be terribly glad to. He's got loads of room, because I came out with someone else."

She was wondering if her father would be presentable at twelve.

He could always drive at any rate[10]—and, besides, people who asked for a lift could take what they got.

"That'll be lovely. Thank you so much," said Mrs. Rogers.

Then, as she had just passed the kittenish late thirties when women still think they are persona grata with the young and entered upon the early forties when their children convey to them tactfully that they no longer are, Mrs. Rogers obliterated herself from the scene. At that moment the music started and the unfortunate young man with white streaks in his red complexion appeared in front of Yanci.

Just before the end of the end of the next dance Scott Kimberly cut in on her again.

"I've come back," he began, "to tell you how beautiful you are."

"I'm not, really," she answered. "And, besides, you tell everyone that."

The music gathered gusto for its finale, and they sat down upon the comfortable lounge.

"I've told no one that for three years," said Scott.

There was no reason why he should have made it three years, yet somehow it sounded convincing to both of them. Her curiosity was stirred. She began finding out about him. She put him to a lazy questionnaire which began with his relationship to the Rogerses and ended, he knew not by what steps, with a detailed description of his apartment in New York.

"I want to live in New York," she told him; "on Park Avenue,[11] in one of those beautiful white buildings that have twelve big rooms in each apartment and cost a fortune to rent."

"That's what I'd want, too, if I were married. Park Avenue— it's one of the most beautiful streets in the world, I think, perhaps chiefly because it hasn't any leprous park trying to give it an artificial suburbanity."

"Whatever that is," agreed Yanci. "Anyway, father and I go to New York about three times a year. We always go to the Ritz."[12]

This was not precisely true. Once a year she generally pried her father from his placid and not unbeneficent existence that she might spend a week lolling by the Fifth Avenue shop windows, lunching or having tea with some former school friend from Farmover,[13] and occasionally going to dinner and the theater with boys who came up from Yale or Princeton for the occasion. These had been pleasant adventures—not one but was filled to the brim with colorful hours—dancing at Mont Martre,[14] dining at the Ritz, with some movie star or super-eminent society woman at the next table, or else dreaming of what she might buy at Hempel's or Waxe's or Thrumble's if her father's income had but one additional naught on the happy side of the decimal. She adored New York with a great impersonal affection—adored it as only a Middle Western or Southern girl can. In its gaudy bazaars she felt her soul transported with turbulent delight, for to her eyes it held nothing ugly, nothing sordid, nothing plain.

She had stayed once at the Ritz—once only. The Manhattan,[15] where they usually registered, had been torn down. She knew that she could never induce her father to afford the Ritz again.

After a moment she borrowed a pencil and paper and scribbled a notification "To Mr. Bowman in the grill" that he was expected to drive Mrs. Rogers and her guest home, "by request"—this last underlined. She hoped that he would be able to do so with dignity.

This note she sent by a waiter to her father. Before the next dance began it was returned to her with a scrawled O. K. and her father's initials.

The remainder of the evening passed quickly. Scott Kimberly cut in on her as often as time permitted, giving her those comforting assurances of her enduring beauty which not without a whimsical pathos she craved. He laughed at her also, and she was not so sure that she liked that. In common with all vague people, she was unaware that she was vague. She did not entirely comprehend when Scott Kimberly told her that her personality would endure long after she was too old to care whether it endured or not.

She liked best to talk about New York, and each of their interrupted conversations gave her a picture or a memory of the metropolis on which she speculated as she looked over the shoulder of Jerry O'Rourke or Carty Braden or some other beau, to whom, as to all of them, she was comfortably anæsthetic. At midnight she sent another note to her father, saying that Mrs. Rogers and Mrs. Rogers' guest would meet him immediately on the porch by the main driveway. Then, hoping for the best, she walked out into the starry night and was assisted by Jerry O'Rourke into his roadster.[16]

III

"Good night, Yanci." With her late escort she was standing on the curbstone in front of the rented stucco house where she lived. Mr. O'Rourke was attempting to put significance into his lingering rendition of her name. For weeks he had been straining to boost their relations almost forcibly onto a sentimental plane; but Yanci, with her vague impassivity, which was a defense against almost anything, had brought to naught his efforts. Jerry O'Rourke was an old story. His family had money; but he—he worked in a brokerage house along with most of the rest of his young generation. He sold bonds— bonds were now the thing; real estate was once the thing—in the days of the boom; then automobiles were the thing. Bonds were the thing now.[17] Young men sold them who had nothing else to go into.

"Don't bother to come up, please." Then as he put his car into gear, "Call me up soon!"

A minute later he turned the corner of the moonlit street and disappeared, his cut-out[18] resounding voluminously through the night as it declared that the rest of two dozen weary inhabitants was of no concern to his gay meanderings.

Yanci sat down thoughtfully upon the porch steps. She had no key and must wait for her father's arrival. Five minutes later a roadster turned into the street, and approaching with an exaggerated caution stopped in front of the Rogers' large house next door. Relieved, Yanci arose and strolled slowly down the walk. The door of the car had swung open and Mrs. Rogers, assisted by Scott Kimberly, had alighted safely upon the sidewalk; but to Yanci's surprise Scott Kimberly, after escorting Mrs. Rogers to her steps, returned to the car. Yanci was close enough to notice that he took the driver's seat. As he drew up at the Bowman's curbstone Yanci saw that her father was occupying the far corner, fighting with ludicrous dignity against a sleep that had come upon him. She groaned. The fatal last hour had done its work—Tom Bowman was once more *hors de combat.*

"Hello," cried Yanci as she reached the curb.

"Yanci," muttered her parent, simulating, unsuccessfully, a brisk welcome. His lips were curved in an ingratiating grin.

"Your father wasn't feeling quite fit, so he let me drive home," explained Scott cheerfully as he got himself out and came up to her.

"Nice little car. Had it long?"

Yanci laughed, but without humor.

"Is he paralyzed?"

"Is who paralyze'?" demanded the figure in the car with an offended sigh.

Scott was standing by the car.

"Can I help you out, sir?"

"I c'n get out. I c'n get out," insisted Mr. Bowman. "Just step a li'l' out my way. Someone must have given me some stremely bad whisk'."

"You mean a lot of people must have given you some," retorted Yanci in cold unsympathy.

Mr. Bowman reached the curb with astonishing ease; but this was a deceitful success, for almost immediately he clutched at a handle of air perceptible only to himself, and was saved by Scott's quickly proffered arm. Followed by the two men, Yanci walked toward the house in a furor of* embarrassment. Would the young man think that such scenes went on every night? It was chiefly her own presence that made it humiliating for Yanci. Had her father been carried to bed by two butlers each evening she might even have been proud of the fact that he could afford such dissipation; but to have it thought

---

* The *Saturday Evening Post* broke the text at this point after three contiguous pages (pp. 3–5), continuing the story on p. 82.

that she assisted, that she was burdened with the worry and the care! And finally she was annoyed with Scott Kimberly for being there, and for his officiousness in helping to bring her father into the house.

Reaching the low porch of tapestry brick, Yanci searched in Tom Bowman's vest for the key and unlocked the front door. A minute later the master of the house was deposited in an easy-chair.

"Thanks very much," he said, recovering for a moment. "Sit down. Like a drink? Yanci, get some crackers and cheese, if there's any, won't you, dear?"

At the unconscious coolness of this Scott and Yanci laughed.

"It's your bedtime, father," she said, her anger struggling with diplomacy.

"Give me my guitar," he suggested, "and I'll play you tune."

Except on such occasions as this, he had not touched his guitar for twenty years. Yanci turned to Scott.

"He'll be fine now. Thanks a lot. He'll fall asleep in a minute and when I wake him he'll go to bed like a lamb."

"Well ——"

They strolled together out the door.

"Sleepy?" he asked.

"No, not a bit."

"Then perhaps you'd better let me stay here with you a few minutes until you see if he's all right. Mrs. Rogers gave me a key so I can get in without disturbing her."

"It's quite all right," protested Yanci. "I don't mind a bit, and he won't be any trouble. He must have taken a glass too much, and this whisky we have out here—you know! This has happened once before—last year," she added.

Her words satisfied her; as an explanation it seemed to have a convincing ring.

"Can I sit down for a moment, anyway?" They sat side by side upon a wicker porch settee.

"I'm thinking of staying over a few days," Scott said.

"How lovely!" Her voice had resumed its die-away note.

"Cousin Pete Rogers wasn't well to-day, but to-morrow he's going duck shooting, and he wants me to go with him."

"Oh, how thrill-ing! I've always been mad to go, and father's always promised to take me, but he never has."

"We're going to be gone about three days, and then I thought I'd come back and stay over the next week-end ——" He broke off suddenly and bent forward in a listening attitude.

"Now what on earth is that?"

The sounds of music were proceeding brokenly from the room they had lately left—a ragged chord on a guitar and half a dozen feeble starts.

"It's father!" cried Yanci.

And now a voice drifted out to them, drunken and murmurous, taking the long notes with attempted melancholy:

> *Sing a song of cities,*
> > *Ridin' on a rail,*
> *A niggah's ne'er so happy*
> > *As when he's out-a jail.*

"How terrible!" exclaimed Yanci. "He'll wake up everybody in the block."

The chorus ended, the guitar jangled again, then gave out a last harsh spang! and was still. A moment later these disturbances were followed by a low but quite definite snore. Mr. Bowman, having indulged his musical proclivity, had dropped off to sleep.

"Let's go to ride," suggested Yanci impatiently. "This is too hectic for me."

Scott arose with alacrity and they walked down to the car.

"Where'll we go?" she wondered.

"I don't care."

"We might go up half a block to Crest Avenue[19]—that's our show street—and then ride out to the river boulevard."

IV

As they turned into Crest Avenue the new cathedral, immense and unfinished, in imitation of a cathedral left unfinished by accident in some little Flemish town,[20] squatted just across the way like a plump white bulldog on its haunches. The ghosts of four moonlit apostles looked down at them wanly from wall niches still littered with the white, dusty trash of the builders. The cathedral inaugurated Crest Avenue. After it came the great brownstone mass built by R. R. Comerford,[21] the flour king,[22] followed by a half mile of pretentious stone houses put up in the gloomy 90's.[23] These were adorned with monstrous driveways and porte-cochères[24] which had once echoed to the hoofs of good horses and with huge circular windows that corseted the second stories.

The continuity of these mausoleums was broken by a small park, a triangle of grass where Nathan Hale[25] stood ten feet tall with his hands bound behind his back by stone cord and stared over a great bluff at the slow Mississippi. Crest Avenue ran along the bluff, but neither faced it nor seemed aware of it, for all the houses fronted inward toward the street. Beyond the first half mile it became newer, essayed ventures in terraced lawns, in concoctions of stucco or in granite mansions which imitated through a variety of gradual refinements the marble contours of the Petit Trianon.[26] The houses of this phase rushed by the roadster for a succession of minutes; then the way turned and the car was headed directly into the moonlight which swept toward it like the lamp of some gigantic motorcycle far up the avenue.

Past the low Corinthian lines of the Christian Science[27] Temple, past a block of dark frame horrors, a deserted row of grim red brick—an unfortunate experiment of the late 90's—then new houses again, bright-red brick now, with trimmings of white, black iron fences and hedges binding flowery lawns. These swept by, faded, passed, enjoying their moment of grandeur; then waiting there in the moonlight to be outmoded as had the frame, cupolaed mansions of lower town[28] and the brownstone piles of older Crest Avenue in their turn.

The roofs lowered suddenly, the lots narrowed, the houses shrank up in size and shaded off into bungalows. These held the street for the last mile, to the bend in the river which terminated the prideful avenue at the statue of Chelsea Arbuthnot.[29] Arbuthnot was the first governor—and almost the last of Anglo-Saxon blood.

All the way thus far Yanci had not spoken, absorbed still in the annoyance of the evening, yet soothed somehow by the fresh air of Northern November that rushed by them. She must take her fur coat out of storage next day, she thought.

"Where are we now?"

As they slowed down Scott looked up curiously at the pompous stone figure, clear in the crisp moonlight, with one hand on a book and the forefinger of the other pointing, as though with reproachful symbolism, directly at some construction work going on in the street.

"This is the end of Crest Avenue," said Yanci, turning to him. "This is our show street."

"A museum of American architectural failures."

"What?"

"Nothing," he murmured.

"I should have explained it to you. I forgot. We can go along the river boulevard if you'd like—or are you tired?"

Scott assured her that he was not tired—not in the least.

Entering the boulevard, the cement road twisted under darkling trees.

"The Mississippi—how little it means to you now!" said Scott suddenly.

"What?" Yanci looked around. "Oh, the river."

"I guess it was once pretty important to your ancestors up here."

"My ancestors weren't up here then," said Yanci with some dignity. "My ancestors were from Maryland.[30] My father came out here when he left Yale."

"Oh!" Scott was politely impressed.

"My mother was from here.[31] My father came out here from Baltimore because of his health."

"Oh!"

"Of course we belong here now, I suppose"—this with faint condescension—"as much as anywhere else."

"Of course."

"Except that I want to live in the East and I can't persuade father to," she finished.

It was after one o'clock and the boulevard was almost deserted. Occasionally two yellow disks would top a rise ahead of them and take shape as a late-returning automobile. Except for that they were alone in a continual rushing dark. The moon had gone down.

"Next time the road goes near the river let's stop and watch it," he suggested.

Yanci smiled inwardly. This remark was obviously what one boy of her acquaintance had named an international petting cue, by which was meant a suggestion that aimed to create naturally a situation for a kiss. She considered the matter. As yet the man had made no particular impression on her. He was good-looking, apparently well-to-do and from New York. She had begun to like him during the dance, increasingly as the evening had drawn to a close; then the incident of her father's appalling arrival had thrown cold water upon this tentative warmth; and now—it was November, and the night was cold. Still ——

"All right," she agreed suddenly.

The road divided; she swerved around and brought the car to a stop in an open place high above the river.

"Well?" she demanded in the deep quiet that followed the shutting off of the engine.

"Thanks."

"Are you satisfied here?"

"Almost. Not quite."

"Why not?"

"I'll tell you in a minute," he answered. "Why is your name Yanci?"

"It's a family name."

"It's very pretty." He repeated it several times caressingly. "Yanci— it has all the grace of Nancy, and yet it isn't prim."

"What's your name?" she inquired.

"Scott."

"Scott what?"

"Kimberly. Didn't you know?"

"I wasn't sure. Mrs. Rogers introduced you in such a mumble."

There was a slight pause.

"Yanci," he repeated; "beautiful Yanci, with her dark-blue eyes and her lazy soul. Do you know why I'm not quite satisfied, Yanci?"

"Why?"

Imperceptibly she had moved her face nearer until as she waited for an answer with her lips faintly apart he knew that in asking she had granted.

Without haste he bent his head forward and touched her lips.

He sighed, and both of them felt a sort of relief—relief from the embarrassment of playing up to what conventions of this sort of thing remained.

"Thanks," he said as he had when she first stopped the car.

"Now are you satisfied?"

Her blue eyes regarded him unsmilingly in the darkness.

"After a fashion; of course, you can never say—definitely."

Again he bent toward her, but she stooped and started the motor. It was late and Yanci was beginning to be tired. What purpose there was in the experiment was accomplished. He had had what he asked. If he liked it he would want more, and that put her one move ahead in the game which she felt she was beginning.

"I'm hungry," she complained. "Let's go down and eat."

"Very well," he acquiesced sadly. "Just when I was so enjoying— the Mississippi."

"Do you think I'm beautiful?" she inquired almost plaintively as they backed out.

"What an absurd question!"

"But I like to hear people say so."

"I was just about to—when you started the engine."

Downtown in a deserted all-night lunch room they ate bacon and eggs. She was pale as ivory now. The night had drawn the lazy vitality and languid color out of her face. She encouraged him to talk to her of New York until he was beginning every sentence with, "Well, now, let's see ——"

The repast over, they drove home. Scott helped her put the car in the little garage, and just outside the front door she lent him her lips again for the faint brush of a kiss. Then she went in.

The long living room which ran the width of the small stucco house was reddened by a dying fire which had been high when Yanci left and now was faded to a steady undancing glow. She took a log from the fire box and threw it on the embers, then started as a voice came out of the half darkness at the other end of the room.

"Back so soon?"

It was her father's voice, not yet quite sober, but alert and intelligent.

"Yes. Went riding," she answered shortly, sitting down in a wicker chair before the fire. "Then went down and had something to eat."

"Oh!"

Her father left his place and moved to a chair nearer the fire, where he stretched himself out with a sigh. Glancing at him from the corner of her eye, for she was going to show an appropriate coldness, Yanci was fascinated by his complete recovery of dignity in the space of two hours. His graying hair was scarcely rumpled; his handsome face was ruddy as ever. Only his eyes, crisscrossed with tiny red lines, were evidence of his late dissipation.

"Have a good time?"

"Why should you care?" she answered rudely.

"Why shouldn't I?"

"You didn't seem to care earlier in the evening. I asked you to take two people home for me, and you weren't able to drive your own car."

"The deuce I wasn't!" he protested. "I could have driven in—in a race in an arana, areaena. That Mrs. Rogers insisted that her young admirer should drive, so what could I do?"

"That isn't her young admirer," retorted Yanci crisply. There was no drawl in her voice now. "She's as old as you are. That's her niece—I mean her nephew."

"Excuse me!"

"I think you owe me an apology." She found suddenly that she bore him no resentment. She was rather sorry for him, and it occurred to her that in asking him to take Mrs. Rogers home she had somehow imposed on his liberty. Nevertheless, discipline was necessary—there would be other Saturday nights. "Don't you?" she concluded.

"I apologize, Yanci."

"Very well, I accept your apology," she answered stiffly.

"What's more, I'll make it up to you."

Her blue eyes contracted. She hoped—she hardly dared to hope that he might take her to New York.

"Let's see," he said. "November, isn't it? What date?"

"The twenty-third."

"Well, I'll tell you what I'll do." He knocked the tips of his fingers together tentatively. "I'll give you a present. I've been meaning to let you have a trip all fall, but business has been bad." She almost smiled—as though business was of any consequence in his life. "But then you need a trip. I'll make you a present of it."

He rose again, and crossing over to his desk sat down.

"I've got a little money in a New York bank that's been lying there quite a while," he said as he fumbled in a drawer for a check book. "I've been intending to close out the account. Let—me—see. There's just ——" His pen scratched. "Where the devil's the blotter? Uh!"

He came back to the fire and a pink oblong paper fluttered into her lap.

"Why, father!"

It was a check for three hundred dollars.[32]

"But can you afford this?" she demanded.

"It's all right," he reassured her, nodding. "That can be a Christmas present, too, and you'll probably need a dress or a hat or something before you go."

"Why," she began uncertainly, "I hardly know whether I ought to take this much or not! I've got two hundred of my own downtown, you know. Are you sure ——"

"Oh, yes!" He waved his hand with magnificent carelessness. "You need a holiday. You've been talking about New York, and I want you to go down there. Tell some of your friends at Yale and the other colleges and they'll ask you to the prom or something. That'll be nice. You'll have a good time."

He sat down abruptly in his chair and gave vent to a long sigh. Yanci folded up the check and tucked it into the low bosom of her dress.

"Well," she drawled softly with a return to her usual manner, "you're a perfect lamb to be so sweet about it, but I don't want to be horribly extravagant."

Her father did not answer. He gave another little sigh and relaxed sleepily into his chair.

"Of course I do want to go," went on Yanci.

Still her father was silent. She wondered if he were asleep.

"Are you asleep?" she demanded, cheerfully now. She bent toward him; then she stood up and looked at him.

"Father," she said uncertainly.

Her father remained motionless; the ruddy color had melted suddenly out of his face.

"Father!"

It occurred to her—and at the thought she grew cold, and a brassière of iron clutched at her breast—that she was alone in the room. After a frantic instant she said to herself that her father was dead.

V

Yanci judged herself with inevitable gentleness—judged herself very much as a mother might judge a wild, spoiled child. She was not hard-minded, nor did she live by any ordered and considered philosophy of her own. To such a catastrophe as the death of her father her immediate reaction was a hysterical self-pity. The first three days were something of a nightmare; but sentimental civilization, being as infallible as Nature in healing the wounds of its more fortunate children, had inspired a certain Mrs. Oral, whom Yanci had always loathed, with a passionate interest in all such crises. To all intents and purposes Mrs. Oral buried Tom Bowman. The morning after his death Yanci had wired her maternal aunt in Chicago, but as yet that undemonstrative and well-to-do lady had sent no answer.

All day long, for four days, Yanci sat in her room upstairs, hearing steps come and go on the porch, and it merely increased her nervousness that the doorbell had been disconnected. This by order of Mrs. Oral! Doorbells were always disconnected! After the burial of the dead the strain relaxed. Yanci, dressed in her new black, regarded herself in the pier glass,[33] and then wept because she seemed to herself very sad and beautiful. She went downstairs and tried to read a moving-picture magazine, hoping that she would not be alone in the house when the winter dark came down just after four.

This afternoon Mrs. Oral had said *carpe diem* to the maid, and Yanci was just starting for the kitchen to see whether she had yet gone when the reconnected bell rang suddenly through the house. Yanci started. She waited a minute, then went to the door. It was Scott Kimberly.

"I was just going to inquire for you," he said.

"Oh! I'm much better, thank you," she responded with the quiet dignity that seemed suited to her rôle.

They stood there in the hall awkwardly, each reconstructing the half-facetious, half-sentimental occasion on which they had last met.

It seemed such an irreverent prelude to such a somber disaster. There was no common ground for them now, no gap that could be bridged by a slight reference to their mutual past, and there was no foundation on which he could adequately pretend to share her sorrow.

"Won't you come in?" she said, biting her lip nervously. He followed her to the sitting room and sat beside her on the lounge. In another minute, simply because he was there and alive and friendly, she was crying on his shoulder.

"There, there!" he said, putting his arm behind her and patting her shoulder idiotically. "There, there, there!"

He was wise enough to attribute no ulterior significance to her action. She was overstrained with grief and loneliness and sentiment; almost any shoulder would have done as well. For all the biological thrill to either of them he might have been a hundred years old. In a minute she sat up.

"I beg your pardon," she murmured brokenly. "But it's—it's so dismal in this house to-day."

"I know just how you feel, Yanci."

"Did I—did I—get—tears on your coat?"

In tribute to the tenseness of the incident they both laughed hysterically, and with the laughter she momentarily recovered her propriety.

"I don't know why I should have chosen you to collapse on," she wailed. "I really don't just go round doing it in-indiscriminately on anyone who comes in."

"I consider it a—a compliment," he responded soberly, "and I can understand the state you're in." Then, after a pause, "Have you any plans?"

She shook her head.

"Va-vague ones," she muttered between little gasps. "I tho-ought I'd go down and stay with my aunt in Chicago a while."

"I should think that'd be best—much the best thing." Then, because he could think of nothing else to say, he added, "Yes, very much the best thing."

"What are you doing—here in town?" she inquired, taking in her breath in minute gasps and dabbing at her eyes with a handkerchief.

"Oh, I'm here with—with the Rogerses. I've been here."

"Hunting?"

"No, I've just been here."

He did not tell her that he had stayed over on her account. She might think it fresh.

"I see," she said. She didn't see.

"I want to know if there's any possible thing I can do for you, Yanci. Perhaps go downtown for you, or do some errands—anything. Maybe you'd like to bundle up and get a bit of air. I could take you out to drive in your car some night, and no one would see you."

He clipped his last word short as the inadvertency of this suggestion dawned on him. They stared at each other with horror in their eyes.

"Oh, no, thank you!" she cried. "I really don't want to drive."

To his relief the outer door opened and an elderly lady came in. It was Mrs. Oral. Scott rose immediately and moved backward toward the door.

"If you're sure there isn't anything I can do ——"

Yanci introduced him to Mrs. Oral; then leaving the elder woman by the fire walked with him to the door. An idea had suddenly occurred to her.

"Wait a minute."

She ran up the front stairs and returned immediately with a slip of pink paper in her hand.

"Here's something I wish you'd do," she said. "Take this to the First National Bank and have it cashed for me. You can leave the money here for me any time."

Scott took out his wallet and opened it.

"Suppose I cash it for you now," he suggested.

"Oh, there's no hurry."

"But I may as well." He drew out three new one-hundred-dollar bills and gave them to her.

"That's awfully sweet of you," said Yanci.

"Not at all. May I come in and see you next time I come West?"

"I wish you would."

"Then I will. I'm going East to-night."

The door shut him out into the snowy dusk and Yanci returned to Mrs. Oral. Mrs. Oral had come to discuss plans.

"And now, my dear, just what do you plan to do? We ought to have some plan to go by, and I thought I'd find out if you had any definite plan in your mind."

Yanci tried to think. She seemed to herself to be horribly alone in the world.

"I haven't heard from my aunt. I wired her again this morning. She may be in Florida."

"In that case you'd go there?"

"I suppose so."

"Would you close this house?"

"I suppose so."

Mrs. Oral glanced around with placid practicality. It occurred to her that if Yanci gave the house up she might like it for herself.

"And now," she continued, "do you know where you stand financially?"

"All right, I guess," answered Yanci indifferently; and then with a rush of sentiment, "There was enough for t-two; there ought to be enough for o-one."

"I didn't mean that," said Mrs. Oral. "I mean, do you know the details?"

"No."

"Well, I thought you didn't know the details. And I thought you ought to know all the details—have a detailed account of what and where your money is. So I called up Mr. Haedge, who knew your father very well personally, to come up this afternoon and glance through his papers. He was going to stop in your father's bank, too, by the way, and get all the details there. I don't believe your father left any will."

Details! Details! Details!

"Thank you," said Yanci. "That'll be—nice."

Mrs. Oral gave three or four vigorous nods that were like heavy periods. Then she got up.

"And now if Hilma's gone out I'll make you some tea. Would you like some tea?"

"Sort of."

"All right, I'll make you some ni-ice tea."

Tea! Tea! Tea!

Mr. Haedge, who came from one of the best Swedish families in town,[34] arrived to see Yanci at five o'clock. He greeted her funereally; said that he had been several times to inquire for her; had organized the pallbearers and would now find out how she stood in no time. Did she have any idea whether or not there was a will? No? Well, there probably wasn't one.

There was one. He found it almost at once in Mr. Bowman's desk—but he worked there until eleven o'clock that night before he found much else. Next morning he arrived at eight, went down to the bank at ten, then to a certain brokerage firm, and came back to Yanci's house at noon. He had known Tom Bowman for some years, but he was utterly astounded when he discovered the condition in which that handsome gallant had left his affairs.

He consulted Mrs. Oral, and that afternoon he informed a frightened Yanci in measured language that she was practically penniless. In the midst of the conversation a telegram from Chicago told her that her aunt had sailed the week previous for a trip through the Orient and was not expected back until late spring.

The beautiful Yanci, so profuse, so debonair, so careless with her gorgeous adjectives, had no adjectives for this calamity. She crept upstairs like a hurt child and sat before a mirror, brushing her luxurious hair to comfort herself. One hundred and fifty strokes she gave it, as it said in the treatment, and then a hundred and fifty more—she was too distraught to stop the nervous motion. She brushed it until her arm ached, then she changed arms and went on brushing.

The maid found her next morning, asleep, sprawled across the toilet things on the dresser in a room that was heavy and sweet with the scent of spilled perfume.

(TO BE CONCLUDED)*

VI

To be precise, as Mr. Haedge was to a depressing degree, Tom Bowman left a bank balance that was more than ample—that is to say, more than ample to supply the post-mortem requirements of his own person. There was also twenty years' worth of furniture, a temperamental roadster with asthmatic cylinders and two one-thousand-dollar bonds of a chain of jewelry stores which yielded 7.5 per cent interest. Unfortunately these were not known in the bond market.[35]

When the car and the furniture had been sold and the stucco bungalow sublet, Yanci contemplated her resources with dismay. She had a bank balance of almost a thousand dollars. If she invested this she would increase her total income to about fifteen dollars a month. This, as Mrs. Oral cheerfully observed, would pay for the boarding-house room she had taken for Yanci as long as Yanci lived. Yanci was so encouraged by this news that she burst into tears.

So she acted as any beautiful girl would have acted in this emergency. With rare decision she told Mr. Haedge that she would leave her thousand dollars in a checking account, and then she walked out of his office and across the street to a beauty parlor to have her hair waved. This raised her morale astonishingly. Indeed, she moved that very day out of the boarding house and into a small room at the best hotel in town. If she must sink into poverty she would at least do so in the grand manner.

* The remainder of "The Popular Girl" was printed in the next issue of the *Saturday Evening Post*, beginning on p. 18.

Sewed into the lining of her best mourning hat were the three new one-hundred-dollar bills, her father's last present. What she expected of them, why she kept them in such a way, she did not know, unless perhaps because they had come to her under cheerful auspices and might through some gayety inherent in their crisp and virgin paper buy happier things than solitary meals and narrow hotel beds. They were hope and youth and luck and beauty; they began, somehow, to stand for all the things she had lost in that November night when Tom Bowman, having led her recklessly into space, had plunged off himself, leaving her to find the way back alone.

Yanci remained at the Hiawatha Hotel for three months, and she found that after the first visits of condolence her friends had happier things to do with their time than to spend it in her company. Jerry O'Rourke came to see her one day with a wild Celtic look in his eyes, and demanded that she marry him immediately. When she asked for time to consider he walked out in a rage. She heard later that he had been offered a position in Chicago and had left the same night.

She considered, frightened and uncertain. She had heard of people sinking out of place, out of life. Her father had once told her of a man in his class at college who had become a worker around saloons, polishing brass rails for the price of a can of beer; and she knew also that there were girls in this city with whose mothers her own mother had played as a little girl, but who were poor now and had grown common; who worked in stores and had married into the proletariat. But that such a fate should threaten her—how absurd! Why, she knew everyone! She had been invited everywhere; her great-grandfather had been governor of one of the Southern States!

She had written to her aunt in India and again in China, receiving no answer. She concluded that her aunt's itinerary had changed, and this was confirmed when a post card arrived from Honolulu which showed no knowledge of Tom Bowman's death, but announced that she was going with a party to the east coast of Africa. This was a last straw. The languorous and lackadaisical Yanci was on her own at last.

"Why not go to work for a while?" suggested Mr. Haedge with some irritation. "Lots of nice girls do nowadays, just for something to occupy themselves with. There's Elsie Prendergast, who does society news on the Bulletin,[36] and that Semple girl ——"

"I can't," said Yanci shortly with a glitter of tears in her eyes. "I'm going East in February."

"East? Oh, you're going to visit someone?"

She nodded.

"Yes, I'm going to visit," she lied, "so it'd hardly be worth while to go to work." She could have wept, but she managed a haughty look. "I'd like to try reporting sometime, though, just for the fun of it."

"Yes, it's quite a lot of fun," agreed Mr. Haedge with some irony. "Still, I suppose there's no hurry about it. You must have plenty of that thousand dollars left."

"Oh, plenty!"

There were a few hundred, she knew.

"Well, then I suppose a good rest, a change of scene would be the best thing for you."

"Yes," answered Yanci. Her lips were trembling and she rose, scarcely able to control herself. Mr. Haedge seemed so impersonally cold. "That's why I'm going. A good rest is what I need."

"I think you're wise."

What Mr. Haegde would have thought had he seen the dozen drafts she wrote that night of a certain letter is problematical. Here are two of the earlier ones. The bracketed words are proposed substitutions:

> *Dear Scott:* Not having seen you since that day I was such a silly ass and wept on your coat, I thought I'd write and tell you that I'm coming East pretty soon and would like you to have lunch [dinner] with me or something. I have been living in a room [suite] at the Hiawatha Hotel, intending to meet my aunt, with whom I am going to live [stay], and who is coming back from China this month [spring]. Meanwhile I have a lot of invitations to visit, etc., in the East, and I thought I would do it now. So I'd like to see you ——

This draft ended here and went into the wastebasket. After an hour's work she produced the following:

> *My dear Mr. Kimberly:* I have often [sometimes] wondered how you've been since I saw you. I am coming East next month before going to visit my aunt in Chicago, and you must come and see me. I have been going out very little, but my physician advises me that I need a change, so I expect to shock the proprieties by some very gay visits in the East ——

Finally in despondent abandon she wrote a simple note without explanation or subterfuge, tore it up and went to bed. Next morning she identified it in the wastebasket, decided it was the best one after all and sent him a fair copy. It ran:

> *Dear Scott:* Just a line to tell you I will be at the Ritz-Carlton Hotel from February seventh, probably for ten days. If you'll phone me some rainy afternoon I'll invite you to tea.

Sincerely,   YANCI BOWMAN.

VII

Yanci was going to the Ritz for no more reason than that she had once told Scott Kimberly that she always went there. When she reached New York—a cold New York, a strangely menacing New York, quite different from the gay city of theaters and hotel-corridor rendezvous that she had known—there was exactly two hundred dollars in her purse.

It had taken a large part of her bank account to live, and she had at last broken into her sacred three hundred dollars to substitute pretty and delicate quarter-mourning clothes for the heavy black she had laid away.

Walking into the hotel at the moment when its exquisitely dressed patrons were assembling for luncheon, it drained at her confidence to appear bored and at ease. Surely the clerks at the desk knew the contents of her pocketbook. She fancied even that the bell boys were snickering at the foreign labels she had steamed from an old trunk of her father's and pasted on her suitcase. This last thought horrified her. Perhaps the very hotels and steamers so grandly named had long since been out of commission!

As she stood drumming her fingers on the desk she was wondering whether if she were refused admittance she could muster a casual smile and stroll out coolly enough to deceive two richly dressed women standing near. It had not taken long for the confidence of twenty years to evaporate. Three months without security had made an ineffaceable mark on Yanci's soul.

"Twenty-four sixty-two," said the clerk callously.

Her heart settled back into place as she followed the bell boy to the elevator, meanwhile casting a nonchalant glance at the two fashionable women as she passed them. Were their skirts long or short?—longer, she noticed.[37]

She wondered how much the skirt of her new walking suit could be let out.

At luncheon her spirits soared. The head waiter bowed to her. The light rattle of conversation, the subdued hum of the music soothed her. She ordered supreme of melon, eggs Susette and an artichoke, and signed her room number to the check with scarcely a glance at it as it lay beside her plate. Up in her room, with the telephone directory open on the bed before her, she tried to locate her scattered metropolitan acquaintances. Yet even as the phone numbers, with their supercilious tags, Plaza, Circle and Rhinelander,[38] stared out at her, she could feel a cold wind blow at her unstable confidence. These girls, acquaintances of school, of a summer, of a house party, even of a week-end at a college prom—what claim or attraction could she, poor and friendless, exercise over them? They had their loves, their dates, their week's gayety planned in advance. They would almost resent her inconvenient memory.

Nevertheless, she called four girls. One of them was out, one at Palm Beach, one in California. The only one to whom she talked said in a hearty voice that she was in bed with grippe, but would phone Yanci as soon as she felt well enough to go out. Then Yanci gave up the girls. She would have to create the illusion of a good time in some other manner. The illusion must be created—that was part of her plan.

She looked at her watch and found that it was three o'clock. Scott Kimberly should have phoned before this, or at least left some word. Still, he was probably busy—at a club, she thought vaguely, or else buying some neckties. He would probably call at four.

Yanci was well aware that she must work quickly. She had figured to a nicety that one hundred and fifty dollars carefully expended would carry her through two weeks, no more. The idea of failure, the fear that at the end of that time she would be friendless and penniless had not begun to bother her.

It was not the first time that for amusement, for a coveted invitation or for curiosity she had deliberately set out to capture a man; but it was the first time she had laid her plans with necessity and desperation pressing in on her.

One of her strongest cards had always been her background, the impression she gave that she was popular and desired and happy. This she must create now, and apparently out of nothing. Scott must somehow be brought to think that a fair portion of New York was at her feet.

At four she went over to Park Avenue, where the sun was out walking and the February day was fresh and odorous of spring and the high apartments of her desire lined the street with radiant whiteness. Here she would live on a gay schedule of pleasure. In these smart not-to-be-entered-without-a-card women's shops she would spend the morning hours acquiring and acquiring, ceaselessly and without thought of expense; in these restaurants she would lunch at noon in company with other fashionable women, orchid-adorned[39] always, and perhaps bearing an absurdly dwarfed Pomeranian in her sleek arms.

In the summer—well, she would go to Tuxedo,[40] perhaps to an immaculate house perched high on a fashionable eminence, where she would emerge to visit a world of teas and balls, of horse shows and polo. Between the halves of the polo game the players would cluster around her in their white suits and helmets, admiringly, and when she swept away, bound for some new delight, she would be followed by the eyes of many envious but intimidated women.

Every other summer they would, of course, go abroad. She began to plan a typical year, distributing a few months here and a few months there until she—and Scott Kimberly, by implication—would become the very auguries of the season, shifting with the slightest stirring of the social barometer from rusticity to urbanity, from palm to pine.

She had two weeks, no more, in which to attain to this position. In an ecstasy of determined emotion she lifted up her head toward the tallest of the tall white apartments.

"It will be too marvelous!" she said to herself.

For almost the first time in her life her words were not too exaggerated to express the wonder shining in her eyes.

VIII

About five o'clock she hurried back to the hotel, demanding feverishly at the desk if there had been a telephone message for her. To her profound disappointment there was nothing. A minute after she had entered her room the phone rang.

"This is Scott Kimberly."

At the words a call to battle echoed in her heart.

"Oh, how do you do?"

Her tone implied that she had almost forgotten him. It was not frigid—it was merely casual.

As she answered the inevitable question as to the hour when she had arrived a warm glow spread over her. Now that, from a personification of all the riches and pleasure she craved, he had materialized as merely a male voice over the telephone, her confidence became strengthened. Male voices were male voices. They could be managed; they could be made to intone syllables of which the minds behind them had no approval. Male voices could be made sad or tender or despairing at her will. She rejoiced. The soft clay was ready to her hand.

"Won't you take dinner with me to-night?" Scott was suggesting.

"Why"—perhaps not, she thought; let him think of her to-night— "I don't believe I'll be able to," she said. "I've got an engagement for dinner and the theater. I'm terribly sorry."

Her voice did not sound sorry—it sounded polite. Then as though a happy thought had occurred to her as to a time and place where she could work him into her list of dates, "I'll tell you: Why don't you come around here this afternoon and have tea with me?"

He would be there immediately. He had been playing squash[41] and as soon as he took a plunge he would arrive. Yanci hung up the phone and turned with a quiet efficiency to the mirror, too tense to smile.

She regarded her lustrous eyes and dusky hair in critical approval. Then she took a lavender[42] tea gown from her trunk and began to dress.

She let him wait seven minutes in the lobby before she appeared; then she approached him with a friendly, lazy smile.

"How do you do?" she murmured. "It's marvelous to see you again. How are you?" And, with a long sigh, "I'm frightfully tired. I've been on the go ever since I got here this morning; shopping and then tearing off to luncheon and a matinée. I've bought everything I saw. I don't know how I'm going to pay for it all."

She remembered vividly that when they had first met she had told him, without expecting to be believed, how unpopular she was. She could not risk such a remark now, even in jest. He must think that she had been on the go every minute of the day.

They took a table and were served with olive sandwiches and tea. He was so good-looking, she thought, and marvelously dressed. His gray eyes regarded her with interest from under immaculate ash-blond hair. She wondered how he passed his days, how he liked her costume, what he was thinking of at that moment.

"How long will you be here?" he asked.

"Well, two weeks, off and on. I'm going down to Princeton for the February prom and then up to a house party in Westchester County[43] for a few days. Are you shocked at me for going out so soon? Father would have wanted me to, you know. He was very modern in all his ideas."

She had debated this remark on the train. She was not going to a house party. She was not invited to the Princeton prom. Such things, nevertheless, were necessary to create the illusion. That was everything—the illusion.

"And then," she continued, smiling, "two of my old beaus are in town, which makes it nice for me."

She saw Scott blink and she knew that he appreciated the significance of this.

"What are your plans for this winter?" he demanded. "Are you going back West?"

"No. You see, my aunt returns from India this week. She's going to open her Florida house, and we'll stay there until the middle of

March. Then we'll come up to Hot Springs[44] and we may go to Europe for the summer."

This was all the sheerest fiction. Her first letter to her aunt, which had given the bare details of Tom Bowman's death, had at last reached its destination. Her aunt had replied with a note of conventional sympathy and the announcement that she would be back in America within two years if she didn't decide to live in Italy.

"But you'll let me see something of you while you're here," urged Scott, after attending to this impressive program. "If you can't take dinner with me to-night, how about Wednesday—that's the day after to-morrow?"

"Wednesday? Let's see." Yanci's brow was knit with imitation thought. "I think I have a date for Wednesday, but I don't know for certain. How about phoning me to-morrow, and I'll let you know? Because I want to go with you, only I think I've made an engagement."

"Very well, I'll phone you."

"Do—about ten."*

"Try to be able to—then or any time."

"I'll tell you—if I can't go to dinner with you Wednesday I can go to lunch surely."

"All right," he agreed. "And we'll go to a matinée."

They danced several times. Never by word or sign did Yanci betray more than the most cursory interest in him until just at the end, when she offered her hand to say good-by.

"Good-by, Scott."

For just the fraction of a second—not long enough for him to be sure it had happened at all, but just enough so that he would be reminded, however faintly, of that night on the Mississippi boulevard—she looked into his eyes. Then she turned quickly and hurried away.

She took her dinner in a little tea room around the corner. It was an economical dinner which cost a dollar and a half. There was no date concerned in it at all, and no man—except an elderly person in spats[45] who tried to speak to her as she came out the door.

IX

Sitting alone in one of the magnificent moving-picture theaters—a luxury which she thought she could afford—Yanci watched Mae

---

* The *Saturday Evening Post* broke the text at this point after a two-page spread (pp. 18–19), continuing the story on p. 105.

Murray[46] swirl through splendidly imagined vistas, and meanwhile considered the progress of the first day. In retrospect it was a distinct success. She had given the correct impression both as to her material prosperity and as to her attitude toward Scott himself. It seemed best to avoid evening dates. Let him have the evenings to himself, to think of her, to imagine her with other men, even to spend a few lonely hours in his apartment, considering how much more cheerful it might be if —— Let time and absence work for her.

Engrossed for a while in the moving picture, she calculated the cost of the apartment in which its heroine endured her movie wrongs. She admired its slender Italian table, occupying only one side of the large dining room and flanked by a long bench which gave it an air of medieval luxury. She rejoiced in the beauty of Mae Murray's clothes and furs, her gorgeous hats, her short-seeming French shoes. Then after a moment her mind returned to her own drama; she wondered if Scott were already engaged, and her heart dipped at the thought. Yet it was unlikely. He had been too quick to phone her on her arrival, too lavish with his time, too responsive that afternoon.

After the picture she returned to the Ritz, where she slept deeply and happily for almost the first time in three months. The atmosphere around her no longer seemed cold. Even the floor clerk had smiled kindly and admiringly when Yanci asked for her key.

Next morning at ten Scott phoned. Yanci, who had been up for hours, pretended to be drowsy from her dissipation of the night before.

No, she could not take dinner with him on Wednesday. She was terribly sorry; she had an engagement, as she had feared. But she could have luncheon and go to a matinée if he would get her back in time for tea.

She spent the day roving the streets. On top of a bus, though not on the front seat, where Scott might possibly spy her, she sailed out Riverside Drive[47] and back along Fifth Avenue just at the winter twilight, and her feeling for New York and its gorgeous splendors deepened and redoubled. Here she must live and be rich, be nodded to by the traffic policemen at the corners as she sat in her limousine— with a small dog—and here she must stroll on Sunday to and from a stylish church, with Scott, handsome in his cutaway and tall hat, walking devotedly at her side.

At luncheon on Wednesday she described for Scott's benefit a fanciful two days. She told of a motoring trip up the Hudson and gave him her opinion of two plays she had seen with—it was implied— adoring gentlemen beside her. She had read up very carefully on the plays in the morning paper and chosen two concerning which she could garner the most information.

"Oh," he said in dismay, "you've seen *Dulcy?*[48] I have two seats for it—but you won't want to go again."

"Oh, no, I don't mind," she protested truthfully. "You see, we went late, and anyway I adored it."

But he wouldn't hear of her sitting through it again—besides, he had seen it himself. It was a play Yanci was mad to see, but she was compelled to watch him while he exchanged the tickets for others, and for the poor seats available at the last moment. The game seemed difficult at times.

"By the way," he said afterwards as they drove back to the hotel in a taxi, "you'll be going down to the Princeton prom to-morrow, won't you?"

She started. She had not realized that it would be so soon or that he would know of it.

"Yes," she answered coolly. "I'm going down to-morrow after-noon."

"On the 2:20, I suppose," Scott commented; and then, "Are you going to meet the boy who's taking you down—at Princeton?"

For an instant she was off her guard.

"Yes, he'll meet the train."

"Then I'll take you to the station," proposed Scott. "There'll be a crowd, and you may have trouble getting a porter."

She could think of nothing to say, no valid objection to make. She wished she had said that she was going by automobile, but she could conceive of no graceful and plausible way of amending her first admission.

"That's mighty sweet of you."

"You'll be at the Ritz when you come back?"

"Oh, yes," she answered. "I'm going to keep my rooms."

Her bedroom was the smallest and least expensive in the hotel.

She concluded to let him put her on the train for Princeton; in fact, she saw no alternative. Next day as she packed her suitcase after luncheon the situation had taken such hold of her imagination that she filled it with the very things she would have chosen had she really been going to the prom. Her intention was to get out at the first stop and take the train back to New York.

Scott called for her at half past one and they took a taxi to the Pennsylvania Station.[49] The train was crowded as he had expected, but he found her a seat and stowed her grip in the rack overhead.

"I'll call you Friday to see how you've behaved," he said.

"All right. I'll be good."

Their eyes met and in an instant, with an inexplicable, only half-conscious rush of emotion, they were in perfect communion. When Yanci came back, the glance seemed to say, ah, then ——

A voice startled her ear:

"Why, Yanci!"

Yanci looked around. To her horror she recognized a girl named Ellen Harley, one of those to whom she had phoned upon her arrival.

"Well, Yanci Bowman! You're the last person I ever expected to see. How are you?"

Yanci introduced Scott. Her heart was beating violently.

"Are you coming to the prom? How perfectly slick!" cried Ellen. "Can I sit here with you? I've been wanting to see you. Who are you going with?"

"No one you know."

"Maybe I do."

Her words, falling like sharp claws on Yanci's sensitive soul, were interrupted by an unintelligible outburst from the conductor. Scott bowed to Ellen, cast at Yanci one level glance and then hurried off.

The train started. As Ellen arranged her grip and threw off her fur coat Yanci looked around her. The car was gay with girls whose excited chatter filled the damp, rubbery air like smoke. Here and there sat a chaperon, a mass of decaying rock in a field of flowers, predicting with a mute and somber fatality the end of all gayety and all youth. How many times had Yanci herself been one of such a crowd, careless and happy, dreaming of the men she would meet, of the battered hacks waiting at the station, the snow-covered campus, the big open fires in the clubhouses, and the imported orchestra beating out defiant melody against the approach of morning.

And now—she was an intruder, uninvited, undesired. As at the Ritz on the day of her arrival, she felt that at any instant her mask would be torn from her and she would be exposed as a pretender to the gaze of all the car.

"Tell me everything!" Ellen was saying. "Tell me what you've been doing. I didn't see you at any of the football games last fall."

This was by way of letting Yanci know that she had attended them herself.

The conductor was bellowing from the rear of the car, "Manhattan Transfer[50] next stop!"

Yanci's cheeks burned with shame. She wondered what she had best do—meditating a confession, deciding against it, answering Ellen's chatter in frightened monosyllables—then, as with an ominous thunder of brakes the speed of the train began to slacken, she sprang on a despairing impulse to her feet.

"My heavens!" she cried. "I've forgotten my shoes! I've got to go back and get them."

Ellen reacted to this with annoying efficiency.

"I'll take your suitcase," she said quickly, "and you can call for it. I'll be at the Charter Club."[51]

"No!" Yanci almost shrieked. "It's got my dress in it!"

Ignoring the lack of logic in her own remark, she swung the suitcase off the rack with what seemed to her a superhuman effort and went reeling down the aisle, stared at curiously by the arrogant eyes of many girls. When she reached the platform just as the train came to a stop she felt weak and shaken. She stood on the hard cement which marks the quaint old village of Manhattan Transfer and tears were streaming down her cheeks as she watched the unfeeling cars speed off to Princeton with their burden of happy youth.

After half an hour's wait Yanci got on a train and returned to New York. In thirty minutes she had lost the confidence that a week had gained for her. She came back to her little room and lay down quietly upon the bed.

X

By Friday Yanci's spirits had partly recovered from their chill depression. Scott's voice over the telephone in mid-morning was like a tonic, and she told him of the delights of Princeton with convincing enthusiasm, drawing vicariously upon a prom she had attended there two years before. He was anxious to see her, he said. Would she come to dinner and the theater that night? Yanci considered, greatly tempted. Dinner—she had been economizing on meals, and a gorgeous dinner in some extravagant show place followed by a musical comedy appealed to her starved fancy, indeed; but instinct told her that the time was not yet right. Let him wait. Let him dream a little more, a little longer.

"I'm too tired, Scott," she said with an air of extreme frankness; "that's the whole truth of the matter. I've been out every night since I've been here, and I'm really half dead. I'll rest up on this house party over the week-end and then I'll go to dinner with you any day you want me."

There was a minute's silence while she held the phone expectantly.

"Lot of resting up you'll do on a house party," he replied; "and, anyway, next week is so far off. I'm awfully anxious to see you, Yanci."

"So am I, Scott."

She allowed the faintest caress to linger on his name. When she had hung up she felt happy again. Despite her humiliation on the train her plan had been a success. The illusion was still intact; it was nearly complete. And in three meetings and half a dozen telephone calls she had managed to create a tenser atmosphere between them than if he had seen her constantly in the moods and avowals and beguilements of an out-and-out flirtation.

When Monday came she paid her first week's hotel bill. The size of it did not alarm her—she was prepared for that—but the shock of seeing so much money go, of realizing that there remained only one hundred and twenty dollars of her father's present, gave her a peculiar sinking sensation in the pit of her stomach. She decided to bring guile to bear immediately, to tantalize Scott by a carefully planned incident, and then at the end of the week to show him simply and definitely that she loved him.

As a decoy for Scott's tantalization she located by telephone a certain Jimmy Long, a handsome boy with whom she had played as a little girl and who had recently come to New York to work. Jimmy Long was deftly maneuvered into asking her to go to a matinée with him on Wednesday afternoon. He was to meet her in the lobby at two.

On Wednesday she lunched with Scott. His eyes followed her every motion, and knowing this she felt a great rush of tenderness toward him. Desiring at first only what he represented, she had begun half unconsciously to desire him also. Nevertheless, she did not permit herself the slightest relaxation on that account. The time was too short and the odds too great. That she was beginning to love him only fortified her resolve.

"Where are you going this afternoon?" he demanded.

"To a matinée—with an annoying man."

"Why is he annoying?"

"Because he wants me to marry him and I don't believe I want to."

There was just the faintest emphasis on the word "believe." The implication was that she was not sure—that is, not quite.

"Don't marry him."

"I won't—probably."

"Yanci," he said in a low voice, "do you remember a night on that boulevard ——"

She changed the subject. It was noon and the room was full of sunlight. It was not quite the place, the time. When he spoke she must have every aspect of the situation in control. He must say only what she wanted said; nothing else would do.

"It's five minutes to two," she told him, looking at her wrist watch. "We'd better go. I've got to keep my date."

"Do you want to go?"

"No," she answered simply.

This seemed to satisfy him, and they walked out to the lobby. Then Yanci caught sight of a man waiting there, obviously ill at ease and dressed as no habitué of the Ritz ever was. The man was Jimmy Long, not long since a favored beau of his Western city. And now—his hat was green, actually! His coat, seasons old, was quite evidently the product of a well-known ready-made concern.[52] His shoes, long and narrow, turned up at the toes. From head to foot everything that could possibly be wrong about him was wrong. He was embarrassed by instinct only, unconscious of his *gaucherie*, an obscene specter, a Nemesis, a horror.

"Hello, Yanci!" he cried, starting toward her with evident relief.

With a heroic effort Yanci turned to Scott, trying to hold his glance to herself. In the very act of turning she noticed the impeccability of Scott's coat, his tie.

"Thanks for luncheon," she said with a radiant smile. "See you to-morrow."

Then she dived rather than ran for Jimmy Long, disposed of his outstretched hand and bundled him bumping through the revolving door with only a quick "Let's hurry!" to appease his somewhat sulky astonishment.

The incident worried her. She consoled herself by remembering that Scott had had only a momentary glance at the man, and that he had probably been looking at her anyhow. Nevertheless, she was horrified, and it is to be doubted whether Jimmy Long enjoyed her company enough to compensate for the cut-price, twentieth-row tickets he had obtained at Black's Drug Store.

But if Jimmy as a decoy had proved a lamentable failure, an occurrence of Thursday offered her considerable satisfaction and paid tribute to her quickness of mind. She had invented an engagement for luncheon, and Scott was going to meet her at two o'clock to take her to the Hippodrome.[53] She lunched alone somewhat imprudently in the Ritz dining room and sauntered out almost side by side with a good-looking young man who had been at the table next to her. She expected to meet Scott in the outer lobby, but as she reached the entrance to the restaurant she saw him standing not far away.

On a lightning impulse she turned to the good-looking man abreast of her, bowed sweetly and said in an audible, friendly voice, "Well, I'll see you later."

Then before he could even register astonishment she faced about quickly and joined Scott.

"Who was that?" he asked, frowning.

"Isn't he darling-looking?"

"If you like that sort of looks."

Scott's tone implied that the gentleman referred to was effete and overdressed. Yanci laughed, impersonally admiring the skillfulness of her ruse.

It was in preparation for that all-important Saturday night that on Thursday she went into a shop on Forty-second Street to buy some long gloves. She made her purchase and handed the clerk a fifty-dollar bill[54] so that her lightened pocketbook would feel heavier with the change she could put in. To her surprise the clerk tendered her the package and a twenty-five-cent piece.

"Is there anything else?"

"The rest of my change."

"You've got it. You gave me five dollars. Four-seventy-five for the gloves leaves twenty-five cents."

"I gave you fifty dollars."

"You must be mistaken."

Yanci searched her purse.

"I gave you fifty!" she repeated frantically.

"No, ma'am, I saw it myself."

They glared at each other in hot irritation. A cash girl was called to testify, then the floor manager; a small crowd gathered.

"Why, I'm perfectly sure!" cried Yanci, two angry tears trembling in her eyes. "I'm positive!"

The floor manager was sorry, but the lady really must have left it at home. There was no fifty-dollar bill in the cash drawer. The bottom was creaking out of Yanci's rickety world.

"If you'll leave your address," said the floor manager, "I'll let you know if anything turns up."

"Oh, you damn fools!" cried Yanci, losing control. "I'll get the police!"

And weeping like a child she left the shop. Outside, helplessness overpowered her. How could she prove anything? It was after six and the store was closing even as she left it. Whichever employe[55] had the fifty-dollar bill would be on her way home now before the police could arrive, and why should the New York police believe her, or even give her fair play?

In despair she returned to the Ritz, where she searched through her trunk for the bill with hopeless and mechanical gestures. It was not there. She had known it would not be there. She gathered every penny together and found that she had fifty-one dollars and thirty cents. Telephoning the office, she asked that her bill be made out up to the following noon—she was too dispirited to think of leaving before then.

She waited in her room, not daring even to send for ice water. Then the phone rang and she heard the room clerk's voice, cheerful and metallic.

"Miss Bowman?"

"Yes."

"Your bill, including to-night, is ex-act-ly fifty-one twenty."

"Fifty-one twenty?" Her voice was trembling.

"Yes, ma'am."

"Thank you very much."

Breathless, she sat there beside the telephone, too frightened now to cry. She had ten cents left in the world!

XI

Friday. She had scarcely slept. There were dark rings under her eyes, and even a hot bath followed by a cold one failed to arouse her from a despairing lethargy. She had never fully realized what it would mean to be without money in New York; her determination and vitality seemed to have vanished at last with her fifty-dollar bill. There was no help for it now—she must attain her desire to-day or never.

She was to meet Scott at the Plaza for tea. She wondered—was it her imagination, or had his manner been consciously cool the afternoon before? For the first time in several days she had needed to make no effort to keep the conversation from growing sentimental. Suppose he had decided that it must come to nothing—that she was too extravagant, too frivolous. A hundred eventualities presented themselves to her during the morning—a dreary morning, broken only by her purchase of a ten-cent bun at a grocery store.

It was her first food in twenty hours, but she self-consciously pretended to the grocer to be having an amusing and facetious time in buying one bun. She even asked to see his grapes, but told him, after looking at them appraisingly—and hungrily—that she didn't think she'd buy any. They didn't look ripe to her, she said. The store was full of prosperous women who, with thumb and first finger joined and held high in front of them, were inspecting food. Yanci would have liked to ask one of them for a bunch of grapes. Instead she went up to her room in the hotel and ate her bun.

When four o'clock came she found that she was thinking more about the sandwiches she would have for tea than of what else must occur there, and as she walked slowly up Fifth Avenue toward the Plaza she felt a sudden faintness which she took several deep breaths of air to overcome. She wondered vaguely where the bread line[56] was. That was where people in her condition should go—but where was it? How did one find out? She imagined fantastically that it was in the phone book under *B*, or perhaps under *N*, for New York Bread Line.

She reached the Plaza. Scott's figure, as he stood waiting for her in the crowded lobby, was a personification of solidity and hope.

"Let's hurry!" she cried with a tortured smile. "I feel rather punk[57] and I want some tea."

She ate a club sandwich, some chocolate ice cream and six tea biscuits. She could have eaten much more, but she dared not. The eventuality of her hunger having been disposed of, she must turn at bay now and face this business of life, represented by the handsome young man who sat opposite watching her with some emotion whose import she could not determine just behind his level eyes.

But the words, the glance, subtle, pervasive and sweet, that she had planned, failed somehow to come.

"Oh, Scott," she said in a low voice, "I'm so tired."

"Tired of what?" he asked coolly.

"Of—everything."

There was a silence.

"I'm afraid," she said uncertainly—"I'm afraid I won't be able to keep that date with you to-morrow."

There was no pretense in her voice now. The emotion was apparent in the waver of each word, without intention or control.

"I'm going away."

"Are you? Where?"

His tone showed a strong interest, but she winced as she saw that that was all.

"My aunt's come back. She wants me to join her in Florida right away."

"Isn't this rather unexpected?"

"Yes."

"You'll be coming back soon?" he said after a moment.

"I don't think so. I think we'll go to Europe from—from New Orleans."

"Oh!"

Again there was a pause. It lengthened. In the shadow of a moment it would become awkward, she knew. She had lost—well? Yet, she would go on to the end.

"Will you miss me?"

"Yes."

One word. She caught his eyes, wondered for a moment if she saw more there than that kindly interest; then she dropped her own again.

"I like it—here at the Plaza," she heard herself saying.

They spoke of things like that. Afterwards she could never remember what they said. They spoke—even of the tea, of the thaw that was ended and the cold coming down outside. She was sick at heart and she seemed to herself very old. She rose at last.

"I've got to tear," she said. "I'm going out to dinner."

To the last she would keep on—the illusion, that was the important thing. To hold her proud lies inviolate—there was only a moment now. They walked toward the door.

"Put me in a taxi," she said quietly. "I don't feel equal to walking."

He helped her in. They shook hands.

"Good-by, Scott," she said.

"Good-by, Yanci," he answered slowly.

"You've been awfully nice to me. I'll always remember what a good time you helped to give me this two weeks."

"The pleasure was mine. Shall I tell the driver the Ritz?"

"No. Just tell him to drive out Fifth. I'll tap on the glass when I want him to stop."

Out Fifth! He would think, perhaps, that she was dining on Fifth. What an appropriate finish that would be! She wondered if he were impressed. She could not see his face clearly, because the air was dark with the snow and her own eyes were blurred by tears.

"Good-by," he said simply.

He seemed to realize that any pretense of sorrow on his part would be transparent. She knew that he did not want her.

The door slammed, the car started, skidding in the snowy street.

Yanci leaned back dismally in the corner. Try as she might, she could not see where she had failed or what it was that had changed his attitude toward her. For the first time in her life she had ostensibly offered herself to a man—and he had not wanted her. The precariousness of her position paled beside the tragedy of her defeat.

She let the car go on—the cold air was what she needed, of course. Ten minutes had slipped away drearily before she realized that she had not a penny with which to pay the driver.

"It doesn't matter," she thought. "They'll just send me to jail, and that's a place to sleep."

She began thinking of the taxi driver.

"He'll be mad when he finds out, poor man. Maybe he's very poor, and he'll have to pay the fare himself." With a vague sentimentality she began to cry.

"Poor taxi man," she was saying half aloud. "Oh, people have such a hard time—such a hard time!"

She rapped on the window and when the car drew up at a curb she got out. She was at the end of Fifth Avenue and it was dark and cold.

"Send for the police!" she cried in a quick low voice. "I haven't any money!"

The taxi man scowled down at her.

"Then what'd you get in for?"

She had not noticed that another car had stopped about twenty-five feet behind them. She heard running footsteps in the snow and then a voice at her elbow.

"It's all right," someone was saying to the taxi man. "I've got it right here."

A bill was passed up. Yanci slumped sideways against Scott's overcoat.

Scott knew—he knew because he had gone to Princeton to surprise her, because the stranger she had spoken to in the Ritz had been his best friend, because the check of her father's for three hundred dollars had been returned to him marked "No funds." Scott knew—he had known for days.

But he said nothing; only stood there holding her with one arm as her taxi drove away.

"Oh, it's you," said Yanci faintly. "Lucky you came along. I left my purse back at the Ritz, like an awful fool. I do such ridiculous things ——"

Scott laughed with some enjoyment. There was a light snow falling, and lest she should slip in the damp he picked her up and carried her back toward his waiting taxi.

"Such ridiculous things," she repeated.

"Go to the Ritz first," he said to the driver. "I want to get a trunk."

Two for a Cent

Metropolitan
April 1922
$900

When the rain was over the sky became yellow in the west and the air was cool. Close to the street, which was of red dirt and lined with cheap bungalows dating from 1910,[1] a little boy was riding a big bicycle along the sidewalk. His plan afforded a monotonous fascination. He rode each time for about a hundred yards, dismounted, turned the bicycle around so that it adjoined a stone step and getting on again, not without toil or heat, retraced his course. At one end this was bounded by a colored girl of fourteen holding an anemic baby, and at the other by a scarred, ill-nourished kitten, squatting dismally on the curb. These four were the only souls in sight.

The little boy had accomplished an indefinite number of trips oblivious alike to the melancholy advances of the kitten at one end and to the admiring vacuousness of the colored girl at the other when he swerved dangerously to avoid a man who had turned the corner into the street and recovered his balance only after a moment of exaggerated panic.

But if the incident was a matter of gravity to the boy, it attracted scarcely an instant's notice from the newcomer, who turned suddenly from the sidewalk and stared with obvious and peculiar interest at the house before which he was standing. It was the oldest house in the street, built with clapboards and a shingled roof.[2] It was a *house*—in the barest sense of the word: the sort of house that a child would draw on a blackboard. It was of a period, but of no design, and its exterior had obviously been made only as a decent cloak for what was within. It antedated the stucco bungalows by about thirty years and except for the bungalows, which were reproducing their species with prodigious avidity as though by some monstrous affiliation with the guinea-pig, it was the most common type of house in the country. For thirty years such dwellings had satisfied the canons of the middle class; they had satisfied its financial canons by being cheap, they had satisfied its aesthetic canons by being hideous. It was a house built by a race whose more energetic complement hoped either to move up or move on, and it was the more remarkable that its instability had survived so many summers and retained its pristine hideousness and discomfort so obviously unimpaired.

The man was about as old as the house, that is to say, about forty-five. But unlike the house, he was neither hideous nor cheap. His clothes were too good to have been made outside of a metropolis—moreover, they were so good that it was impossible to tell in which metropolis they were made. His name was Abercrombie and the most important event of his life had taken place in the house before which he was standing. He had been born there.

It was one of the last places in the world where he should have been born. He had thought so within a very few years after the event and he thought so now—an ugly home in a third rate Southern town where his father had owned a partnership in a grocery store.[3] Since then Abercrombie had played golf with the President of the United States and sat between two duchesses at dinner. He had been bored with the President, he had been bored and not a little embarrassed with the duchesses—nevertheless, the two incidents had pleased him and still sat softly upon his naive vanity. It delighted him that he had gone far.

He had looked fixedly at the house for several minutes before he preceived[4] that no one lived there. Where the shutters were not closed it was because there were no shutters to be closed and in these vacancies, blind vacuous expanses of grey window looked unseeingly down at him. The grass had grown wantonly long in the yard and faint green mustaches were sprouting facetiously in the wide cracks of the walk. But it was evident that the property had been recently occupied for upon the porch lay half a dozen newspapers rolled into cylinders for quick delivery and as yet turned only to a faint resentful yellow.

They were not nearly so yellow as the sky when Abercrombie walked up on the porch and sat down upon an immemorial bench, for the sky was every shade of yellow, the color of tan, the color of gold, the color of peaches. Across the street and beyond a vacant lot rose a rampart of vivid red brick houses and it seemed to Abercrombie that the picture they rounded out was beautiful—the warm earthy brick and the sky fresh after the rain, changing and gray as a dream. All his life when he had wanted to rest his mind he had called up into it the image those two things had made for him when the air was clear just at this hour. So Abercrombie sat there thinking about his young days.

Ten minutes later another man turned the corner of the street, a different sort of man, both in the texture of his clothes and the texture of his soul. He was forty-six years old and he was a shabby drudge, married to a woman, who, as a girl, had known better days. This latter fact, in the republic, may be set down in the red italics of misery.

His name was Hemmick—Henry W. or George D. or John F.— the stock that produced him had had little imagination left to waste either upon his name or his design. He was a clerk in a factory which made ice for the long Southern Summer. He was responsible to the man who owned the patent for canning ice,[5] who, in his turn was responsible only to God. Never in his life had Henry W. Hemmick discovered a new way to advertise canned ice nor had it transpired that by taking a diligent correspondence course[6] in ice canning he had secretly been preparing himself for a partnership. Never had he rushed home to his wife, crying: "You can have that servant now, Nell, I have been made General Superintendent." You will have to take him as you take Abercrombie, for what he is and will always be. This is a story of the dead years.

When the second man reached the house he turned in and began to mount the tipsy steps, noticed Abercrombie, the stranger, with a tired surprise, and nodded to him.

"Good evening," he said.

Abercrombie voiced his agreement with the sentiment.

"Cool"—The newcomer covered his forefinger with his handkerchief and sent the swatched digit on a complete circuit of his collar band. "Have you rented this?" he asked.

"No, indeed, I'm just—resting. Sorry if I've intruded—I saw the house was vacant——"

"Oh, you're not intruding!" said Hemmick hastily. "I don't reckon anybody *could* intrude in this old barn. I got out two months ago. They're not ever goin' to rent it any more. I got a little girl about this high—" he held his hand parallel to the ground and at an indeterminate distance "—and she's mighty fond of an old doll that got left here when we moved. Began hollerin' for me to come over and look it up."

"You used to live here?" inquired Abercrombie with interest.

"Lived here eighteen years. Came here'n I was married, raised four children in this house. Yes, *sir*. I know this old fellow." He struck the door-post with the flat of his hand. "I know every leak in her roof and every loose board in her old floor."

Abercrombie had been good to look at for so many years that he knew if he kept a certain attentive expression on his face his companion would continue to talk—indefinitely.

"You from up North?" inquired Hemmick politely, choosing with habituated precision the one spot where the anemic wooden railing would support his weight. "I thought so," he resumed at Abercrombie's nod. "Don't take long to tell a Yankee."

"I'm from New York."

"So?" The man shook his head with inappropriate gravity. "Never have got up there, myself. Started to go a couple of times, before I was married, but never did get to go."

He made a second excursion with his finger and handkerchief and then, as though having come suddenly to a cordial decision, he replaced the handkerchief in one of his bumpy pockets and extended the hand toward his companion.

"My name's Hemmick."

"Glad to know you." Abercrombie took the hand without rising. "Abercrombie's mine."

"I'm mighty glad to know you, Mr. Abercrombie."

Then for a moment they both hesitated, their two faces assumed oddly similar expressions, their eyebrows drew together, their eyes looked far away. Each was straining to force into activity some minute cell long sealed and forgotten in his brain. Each made a little noise in his throat, looked away, looked back, laughed. Abercrombie spoke first.

"We've met."

"I know," agreed Hemmick, "but whereabouts? That's what's got me. You from New York you say?"

"Yes, but I was born and raised in this town. Lived in this house till I left here when I was about seventeen. As a matter of fact, I remember you—you were a couple of years older."

Again Hemmick considered.

"Well," he said vaguely, "I sort of remember, too. I *begin* to remember—I got your name all right and I guess maybe it was your daddy had this house before I rented it. But all I can recollect about you is, that there was a boy named Abercrombie and he went away."

In a few moments they were talking easily. It amused them both to have come from the same house—amused Abercrombie especially, for he was a vain man, rather absorbed, that evening, in his own early poverty. Though he was not given to immature impulses he found it necessary somehow to make it clear in a few sentences that five years after he had gone away from the house and the town he had been able to send for his father and mother to join him in New York.

Hemmick listened with that exaggerated attention which men who have not prospered generally render to men who have. He would have continued to listen had Abercrombie become more expansive, for he was beginning faintly to associate him with an Abercrombie who had figured in the newspapers for several years at the head of shipping boards and financial committees. But Abercrombie, after a moment, made the conversation less personal.

"I didn't realize you had so much heat here. I guess I've forgotten a lot in twenty-five years."

"Why, this is a *cool* day," boasted Hemmick, "this is *cool*. I was just sort of overheated from walking when I came up."

"It's too hot," insisted Abercrombie with a restless movement; then he added abruptly, "I don't like it here. It means nothing to me—nothing—I've wondered if I did, you know, that's why I came down. And I've decided.

"You see," he continued hesitantly, "up to recently the North was still full of professional Southerners, some real, some by sentiment, but all given to flowery monologues on the beauty of their old family plantations and all jumping up and howling when the band played Dixie.[7] You know what I mean"—he turned to Hemmick—"it got to be a sort of a national joke. Oh, I was in the game, too, I suppose, I used to stand up and perspire and cheer, and I've given young men positions for no particular reason except that they claimed to come from South Carolina or Virginia—" again he broke off and became suddenly abrupt—"but I'm through, I've been here six hours and I'm through!"

"Too hot for you?" inquired Hemmick, with mild surprise.

"Yes! I've felt the heat and I've seen the men—those two or three dozen loafers standing in front of the stores on Jackson Street—in thatched straw hats"—then he added, with a touch of humor, "they're what my son calls 'slash-pocket, belted-back boys.' Do you know the ones I mean?"

"Jelly-beans,"[8] Hemmick nodded gravely, "we call 'em Jelly-beans. No-account lot of boys all right. They got signs up in front of most of the stores asking 'em not to stand there."

"They ought to!" asserted Abercrombie, with a touch of irasci-bility. "That's my picture of the South now, you know—a skinny, dark-haired young man with a gun on his hip and a stomach full of corn liquor or Dope Dola,[9] leaning up against a drug store waiting for the next lynching."[10]

Hemmick objected, though with apology in his voice.

"You got to remember, Mr. Abercrombie, that we haven't had the money down here since the war—"

Abercrombie waved this impatiently aside.

"Oh, I've heard all that," he said, "and I'm tired of it. And I've heard the South lambasted till I'm tired of that, too. It's not taking France and Germany fifty years to get on their feet, and their war made your war look like a little fracas up an alley. And it's not your fault and it's not anybody's fault. It's just that this is too damn hot to be a white man's country and it always will be. I'd like to see 'em pack two or three of these states full of darkies and drop 'em out of the Union."

Hemmick nodded, thoughtfully, though without thought. He had never thought; for over twenty years he had seldom ever held opinions, save the opinions of the local press or of some majority made articulate through passion. There was a certain luxury in thinking that he had never been able to afford. When cases were set before him he either accepted them outright, if they were comprehensible to him or rejected them if they required a modicum of concentration. Yet he was not a stupid man. He was poor and busy and tired and there were no ideas at large in his community, even had he been capable of grasping them. The idea that he did not think would have been equally incomprehensible to him. He was a closed book, half full of badly printed, uncorrelated trash.

Just now, his reaction to Abercrombie's assertion was exceedingly simple. Since the remarks proceeded from a man who was a Southerner by birth, who was successful—moreover, who was confident and decisive and persuasive and suave—he was inclined to accept them without suspicion or resentment.

He took one of Abercrombie's cigars and pulling on it, still with a stern imitation of profundity upon his tired face, watched the color glide out of the sky and the grey veils come down. The little boy and his bicycle, the baby, the nursemaid, the forlorn kitten, all had departed. In the stucco bungalows pianos gave out hot weary notes that inspired the crickets to competitive sound, and squeaky graphophones[11] filled in the intervals with patches of whining ragtime[12] until the impression was created that each living room in the street opened directly out into the darkness.

"What *I* want to find out," Abercrombie was saying with a frown, "is why I didn't have sense enough to *know* that this was a worthless town. It was entirely an accident that I left here, an utterly blind chance, and as it happened, the very train that took me away was full of luck for me. The man I sat beside gave me my start in life." His tone became resentful. "But I thought this was all right. I'd have stayed except that I'd gotten into a scrape down at the High School—I got expelled and my daddy told me he didn't want me at home any more. Why didn't I know the place wasn't any good? Why didn't I *see?*"

"Well, you'd probably never known anything better?" suggested Hemmick mildly.

"That wasn't any excuse," insisted Abercrombie. "If I'd been any good I'd have known. As a matter of fact—as—a—matter—of—fact," he repeated slowly, "I think that at heart I was the sort of boy who'd have lived and died here happily and never known there was anything better." He turned to Hemmick with a look almost of distress. "It worries me to think that my—that what's happened to me can be ascribed to chance. But that's the sort of boy I think I was. I didn't start off with the Dick Whittington idea—I started off by accident."

After this confession, he stared out into the twilight with a dejected expression that Hemmick could not understand. It was impossible for the latter to share any sense of the importance of such a distinction—in fact from a man of Abercrombie's position it struck him as unnecessarily trivial. Still, he felt that some manifestation of acquiescence was only polite.

"Well," he offered, "it's just that some boys get the bee to get up and go North and some boys don't. I happened to have the bee to go North. But I didn't. That's the difference between you and me."

Abercrombie turned to him intently.

"You did?" he asked, with unexpected interest, "you wanted to get out?"

"At one time." At Abercrombie's eagerness Hemmick began to attach a new importance to the subject. "At one time," he repeated, as though the singleness of the occasion was a thing he had often mused upon.

"How old were you?"

"Oh—'bout twenty."

"What put it into your head?"

"Well, let me see—" Hemmick considered. "—I don't know whether I remember sure enough but it seems to me that when I was down to the University—I was there two years—one of the professors told me that a smart boy ought to go North. He said, business wasn't going to amount to much down here for the next fifty years. And I guessed he was right. My father died about then, so I got a job as runner in the bank here, and I didn't have much interest in anything except saving up enough money to go North. I was bound I'd go."

"Why didn't you? Why didn't you?" insisted Abercrombie in an aggrieved tone.

"Well," Hemmick hesitated. "Well, I right near did but—things didn't work out and I didn't get to go. It was a funny sort of business. It all started about the smallest thing you can think of. It all started about a penny."

"A penny?"

"That's what did it—one little penny. That's why I didn't go 'way from here and all, like I intended."

"Tell me about it, man," exclaimed his companion. He looked at his watch impatiently. "I'd like to hear the story."

Hemmick sat for a moment, distorting his mouth around the cigar.

"Well, to begin with," he said, at length, "I'm going to ask you if you remember a thing that happened here about twenty-five years ago. A fellow named Hoyt, the cashier of the Cotton National Bank, disappeared one night with about thirty thousand dollars in cash.[13] Say, man, they didn't talk about anything else down here at the time. The whole town was shaken up about it, and I reckin'[14] you can imagine the disturbance it caused down at all the banks and especially at the Cotton National."

"I remember."

"Well, they caught him, and they got most of the money back, and by and by the excitement died down, except in the bank where the thing had happened. Down there it seemed as if they'd never get used to it. Mr. Deems, the First Vice President, who'd always been pretty kind and decent, got to be a changed man. He was suspicious of the clerks, the tellers, the janitor, the watchman, most of the officers, and yes, by Golly, I guess he got so he kept an eye on the President himself.

"I don't mean he was just watchful—he was downright hipped on the subject. He'd come up and ask you funny questions when you were going about your business. He'd walk into the teller's cage on tip-toe and watch him without saying anything. If there was any mistake of any kind in the book-keeping, he'd not only fire a clerk or so, but he'd raise such a riot that he made you want to push him into a vault and slam the door on him.

"He was just about running the bank then, and he'd effected[15] the other officers, and—oh, you can imagine the havoc a thing like that could work on any sort of an organization. Everybody was so nervous that they made mistakes whether they were careful or not.

Clerks were staying downtown until eleven at night trying to account for a lost nickel. It was a thin year, anyhow, and everything financial was pretty rickety,[16] so one thing worked on another until the crowd of us were as near craziness as anybody can be and carry on the banking business at all.

"I was a runner—and all through the heat of one God-forsaken Summer I ran. I ran and I got mighty little money for it, and that was the time I hated that bank and this town, and all I wanted was to get out and go North. I was getting ten dollars a week, and I'd decided that when I'd saved fifty out of it I was going down to the depot and buy me a ticket to Cincinnati. I had an uncle in the banking business there, and he said he'd give me an opportunity with him. But he never offered to pay my way, and I guess he thought if I was worth having I'd manage to get up there by myself. Well, maybe I wasn't worth having because, anyhow, I never did.

"One morning on the hottest day of the hottest July I ever knew— and you know what that means down here—I left the bank to call on a man named Harlan and collect some money that'd come due on a note. Harlan had the cash waiting for me all right, and when I counted it I found it amounted to three hundred dollars and eighty-six cents, the change being in brand new coin that Harlan had drawn from another bank that morning. I put the three one hundred dollar bills in my wallet and the change in my vest pocket, signed a receipt and left. I was going straight back to the bank.

"Outside the heat was terrible. It was enough to make you dizzy, and I hadn't been feeling right for a couple of days, so, while I waited in the shade for a street car, I was congratulating myself that in a month or so I'd be out of this and up where it was some cooler. And then as I stood there it occurred to me all of a sudden that outside of the money which I'd just collected, which, of course, I couldn't touch, I didn't have a cent in my pocket. I'd have to walk back to the bank, and it was about fifteen blocks away. You see, on the night before, I'd found that my change came to just a dollar, and I'd traded it for a bill at the corner store and added it to the roll in the bottom of my trunk. So there was no help for it—I took off my coat and I stuck my handkerchief into my collar and struck off through the suffocating heat for the bank.

"Fifteen blocks—you can imagine what that was like, and I was sick when I started. From away up by Juniper Street—you remember where that is: the new Mieger Hospital's there now—all the way down to Jackson.[17] After about six blocks I began to stop and rest whenever I found a patch of shade wide enough to hold me, and as I got pretty near I could just keep going by thinking of the big glass of iced tea my mother'd have waiting beside my plate at lunch. But after that I began getting too sick to even want the iced tea—I wanted to get rid of that money and then lie down and die.

"When I was still about two blocks away from the bank I put my hand into my watch pocket and pulled out that change; was sort of jingling it in my hand; making myself believe that I was so close that it was convenient to have it ready. I happened to glance into my hand, and all of a sudden I stopped up short and reached down quick into my watch pocket. The pocket was empty. There was a little hole in the bottom, and my hand held only a half dollar, a quarter and a dime. I had lost one cent.

"Well, sir, I can't tell you, I can't express to you the feeling of discouragement that this gave me. One penny, mind you—but think: just the week before a runner had lost his job because he was a little bit shy twice. It was only carelessness; but there you were! They were all in a panic that they might get fired themselves, and the best thing to do was to fire some one else—first.

"So you can see that it was up to me to appear with that penny.

"Where I got the energy to care as much about it as I did is more than I can understand. I was sick and hot and weak as a kitten, but it never occurred to me that I could do anything except find or replace that penny, and immediately I began casting about for a way to do it. I looked into a couple of stores, hoping I'd see some one I knew, but while there were a few fellows loafing in front, just as you saw them today, there wasn't one that I felt like going up to and saying: 'Here! You got a penny?' I thought of a couple of offices where I could have gotten it without much trouble, but they were some distance off, and besides being pretty dizzy, I hated to go out of my route when I was carrying bank money, because it looked kind of strange.

"So what should I do but commence walking back along the street toward the Union Depot[18] where I last remembered having the penny. It was a brand new penny, and I thought maybe I'd see it shining where it dropped. So I kept walking, looking pretty carefully at the sidewalk and thinking what I'd better do. I laughed a little, because I felt sort of silly for worrying about a penny, but I didn't enjoy laughing, and it really didn't seem silly to me at all.

"Well, by and by I got back to the Union Depot without having either seen the old penny or* having thought what was the best

---

* *Metropolitan* broke the text at this point after four contiguous pages (pp. 23–26), continuing the story on p. 93.

way to get another. I hated to go all the way home, 'cause we lived a long distance out; but what else was I to do? So I found a piece of shade close to the depot, and stood there considering, thinking first one thing and then another, and not getting anywhere at all. One little penny, just *one*—something almost any man in sight would have given me; something even the nigger baggage-smashers were jingling around in their pockets. . . . I must have stood there about five minutes. I remember there was a line of about a dozen men in front of an army recruiting station they'd just opened, and a couple of them began to yell 'Join the Army!' at me. That woke me up, and I moved on back toward the bank, getting worried now, getting mixed up and sicker and sicker and knowing a million ways to find a penny and not one that seemed convenient or right. I was exaggerating the importance of losing it, and I was exaggerating the difficulty of finding another, but you just have to believe that it seemed about as important to me just then as though it were a hundred dollars.

"Then I saw a couple of men talking in front of Moody's soda place,[19] and recognized one of them—Mr. Burling—who'd been a friend of my father's. That was relief, I can tell you. Before I knew it I was chattering to him so quick that he couldn't follow what I was getting at.

"'Now', he said, 'you know I'm a little deaf and can't understand when you talk that fast! What is it you want, Henry? Tell me from the beginning.'

"'Have you got any change with you?' I asked him just as loud as I dared. 'I just want—' Then I stopped short; a man a few feet away had turned around and was looking at us. It was Mr. Deems, the first Vice-President[20] of the Cotton National Bank."

Hemmick paused, and it was still light enough for Abercrombie to see that he was shaking his head to and fro in a puzzled way. When he spoke his voice held a quality of pained surprise, a quality that it might have carried over twenty years.

"I never *could* understand what it was that came over me then. I must have been sort of crazy with the heat—that's all I can decide. Instead of just saying, 'Howdy' to Mr. Deems, in a natural way, and telling Mr. Burling I wanted to borrow a nickel for tobacco, because I'd left my purse at home, I turned away quick as a flash and began walking up the street at a great rate, feeling like a criminal who had come near being caught.

"Before I'd gone a block I was sorry. I could almost hear the conversation that must've been taking place between those two men:

"'What do you reckon's the matter with that young man?' Mr. Burling would say without meaning any harm. 'Came up to me all excited and wanted to know if I had any money, and then he saw you and rushed away like he was crazy.'

"And I could almost see Mr. Deems' big eyes get narrow with suspicion and watch him twist up his trousers and come strolling along after me. I was in a real panic now, and no mistake. Suddenly I saw a one-horse surrey[21] going by, and recognized Bill Kennedy, a friend of mine, driving it. I yelled at him, but he didn't hear me. Then I yelled again, but he didn't pay any attention, so I started after him at a run, swaying from side to side, I guess, like I was drunk, and calling his name every few minutes. He looked around once, but he didn't see me; he kept right on going and turned out of sight at the next corner. I stopped then because I was too weak to go any farther. I was just about to sit down on the curb and rest when I looked around, and the first thing I saw was Mr. Deems walking after me as fast as he could come. There wasn't any of my imagination about it this time—the look in his eyes showed he wanted to know what was the matter with *me!*

"Well, that's about all I remember clearly until about twenty minutes later, when I was at home trying to unlock my trunk with fingers that were trembling like a tuning fork. Before I could get it open, Mr. Deems and a policeman came in. I began talking all at once about not being a thief and trying to tell them what had happened, but I guess I was sort of hysterical, and the more I said the worse matters were. When I managed to get the story out it seemed sort of crazy, even to me—and it was true—it was true, true as I've told you—every word!—that one penny that I lost somewhere down by the station—" Hemmick broke off and began laughing grotesquely—as though the excitement that had come over him as he finished his tale was a weakness of which he was ashamed. When he resumed it was with an affectation of nonchalance.

"I'm not going into the details of what happened because nothing much did—at least not on the scale you judge events by up North. It cost me my job, and I changed a good name for a bad one. Somebody tattled and somebody lied, and the impression got around that I'd lost a lot of the bank's money and had been tryin' to cover it up.

"I had an awful time getting a job after that. Finally I got a statement out of the bank that contradicted the wildest of the stories that had started, but the people who were still interested said it was just because the bank didn't want any fuss or scandal—and the rest had forgotten: that is they'd forgotten what had happened, but they remembered that somehow I just wasn't a young fellow to be trusted——"

Hemmick paused and laughed again, still without enjoyment, but bitterly, uncomprehendingly, and with a profound helplessness.

"So, you see, that's why I didn't go to Cincinnati," he said slowly; "my mother was alive then, and this was a pretty bad blow to her. She had an idea—one of those old-fashioned Southern ideas that stick in people's heads down here—that somehow I ought to stay here in town and prove myself honest. She had it on her mind, and she wouldn't hear of my going. She said that the day I went'd be the day she'd die. So I sort of had to stay till I'd got back my—my reputation."

"How long did that take?" asked Abercrombie quietly.

"About—ten years."

"Oh——"

"Ten years," repeated Hemmick, staring out into the gathering darkness. "This is a little town, you see: I say ten years because it was about ten years when the last reference to it came to my ears. But I was married long before that; had a kid. Cincinnati was out of my mind by that time."

"Of course," agreed Abercrombie.

They were both silent for a moment—then Hemmick added apologetically:

"That was sort of a long story, and I don't know if it could have interested you much. But you asked me——"

"It *did* interest me," answered Abercrombie politely. "It interested me tremendously. It interested me much more than I thought it would."

It occurred to Hemmick that he himself had never realized what a curious, rounded tale it was. He saw dimly now that what had seemed to him only a fragment, a grotesque interlude, was really significant, complete. It was an interesting story; it was the story upon which turned the failure of his life. Abercrombie's voice broke in upon his thoughts.

"You see, it's so different from my story," Abercrombie was saying. "It was an accident that you stayed—and it was an accident that I went away. You deserve more actual—actual credit, if there is such a thing in the world, for your intention of getting out and getting on. You see, I'd more or less gone wrong at seventeen. I was—well, what you call a Jelly-bean. All I wanted was to take it easy through life—and one day I just happened to see a sign up above my head that had on it: 'Special rate to Atlanta, three dollars and forty-two cents.' So I took out my change and counted it——"

Hemmick nodded. Still absorbed in his own story, he had forgotten the importance, the comparative magnificence of Abercrombie. Then suddenly he found himself listening sharply:

"I had just three dollars and forty-one cents in my pocket. But, you see, I was standing in line with a lot of other young fellows down by the Union Depot about to enlist in the army for three years. And I saw that extra penny on the walk not three feet away. I saw it because it was brand new and shining in the sun like gold."

The Alabama night had settled over the street, and as the blue drew down upon the dust the outlines of the two men had become less distinct, so that it was not easy for any one who passed along the walk to tell that one of these men was of the few and the other of no importance. All the detail was gone—Abercrombie's fine gold wrist watch, his collar, that he ordered by the dozen from London,[22] the dignity that sat upon him in his chair—all faded and were engulfed with Hemmick's awkward suit and preposterous humped shoes into that pervasive depth of night that, like death, made nothing matter, nothing differentiate, nothing remain. And a little later on a passerby saw only the two glowing disks about the size of a penny that marked the rise and fall of their cigars.

The Curious Case of Benjamin Button

Collier's
27 May 1922
$1,000

As long ago as 1860 it was the proper thing to be born at home.[1] At present, so I am told, the high gods of medicine have decreed that the first cries of the young shall be uttered upon the anesthetic air of a hospital, preferably a fashionable one. So young Mr. and Mrs. Roger Button were fifty years ahead of style when they decided, one day in the summer of 1860, that their first baby should be born in a hospital. Whether this anachronism had any bearing upon the astonishing history I am about to set down will never be known.

I shall tell you what occurred and let you judge for yourself.

The Roger Buttons held an enviable position, both social and financial, in ante bellum Baltimore. They were related to the This Family and the That Family, which, as every Southerner knew, entitled them to membership in that enormous peerage which largely populated the Confederacy.[2] This was their first experience with the charming old custom of having babies—Mr. Button was naturally nervous. He hoped it would be a boy so that he could be sent to Yale College in Connecticut, at which institution Mr. Button himself had been known for four years by the somewhat obvious nickname of "Cuff."

On the September morning consecrated to the enormous event he arose nervously at six o'clock, dressed himself, adjusted an impeccable stock and hurried forth through the streets of Baltimore to the hospital, to determine whether the darkness of the night had borne in new life upon its bosom.

When he was approximately a hundred yards from the even then old-fashioned building known as the Maryland Private Hospital for Ladies and Gentlemen he saw Dr. Keene, the Buttons' family physician, descending the front steps, rubbing his hands together with a washing movement—as all doctors are required to do by the unwritten ethics of their profession.

Mr. Roger Button, the president of Roger Button & Co., Wholesale Hardware,[3] began to run toward Dr. Keene with much less dignity than was expected from a Southern gentleman of that picturesque period. "Dr. Keene!" he called. "Oh, Dr. Keene!"

The doctor heard him and stopped, faced around, and stood waiting, a curious expression settling on his harsh, medicinal face as Mr. Button drew near.

"What happened?" demanded Mr. Button, as he came up in a gasping rush. "What was it? How is she? A boy? Who is it? What—"

"Talk sense!" said Dr. Keene sharply. He appeared somewhat irritated.

"Is the child born?" begged Mr. Button, a trifle more calmly.

Dr. Keene frowned. "Why, yes, I suppose so—after a fashion." Again he threw a curious glance at Mr. Button.

"Is my wife all right?"

"Yes."

"Is it a boy or a girl?"

"Here now!" cried Dr. Keene in a perfect passion of irritation. "I'll ask you to go and see for yourself. Outrageous!" He snapped the last word out in almost one syllable, then he turned away muttering: "Do you imagine a case like this will help my professional reputation? One more would ruin me—ruin anybody."

"What's the matter?" demanded Mr. Button, appalled. "Triplets?"

"No, not triplets!" answered the doctor cuttingly. "What's more, you can go and see for yourself. And get another doctor. I brought you into the world, young man, and I've been physician to your family for forty years, but I'm through with you, do you understand? I don't want to see you or any of your relatives ever again! Good-by!"

Then he turned sharply, and without another word climbed into his phaeton,[4] which was waiting at the curbstone, and drove severely away.

Mr. Button stood there upon the sidewalk, stupefied and trembling from head to foot. What horrible mishap had occurred? He had suddenly lost all desire to go into the Maryland Private Hospital for Ladies and Gentlemen—it was with the greatest difficulty that, a moment later, he forced himself to mount the steps and enter the front door.

A nurse was sitting behind a desk in the opaque gloom of the hall. Swallowing his shame, Mr. Button approached her.

"Good morning," she remarked, looking up at him pleasantly.

"Good morning. I—I am Mr. Button."

At this a look of utter terror spread itself over the girl's face. She rose to her feet and seemed about to fly from the hall, restraining herself only with the most apparent difficulty.

"I want to see my child," said Mr. Button.

The nurse gave a little scream. "Oh—of course!" she cried hysterically. "Upstairs. Right upstairs. Go—*up!*"

She pointed the direction, and Mr. Button, bathed in cool perspiration, turned falteringly and began to mount to the second floor. In the upper hall he addressed a nurse who approached him, basin in hand. "I'm Mr. Button," he managed to articulate. "I want to see my—"

Clank! The basin clattered to the floor and rolled in the direction of the stairs. Clank! Clank! It began a methodical descent as if sharing in the general terror which this gentleman provoked.

"I want to see my child!" Mr. Button almost shrieked. He was on the verge of collapse.

Clank! The basin reached the first floor. The nurse regained control of herself and threw Mr. Button a look of hearty contempt.

"All *right*, Mr. Button," she agreed in a hushed voice. "Very *well!* But if you *knew* that state it's put us all in this morning! It's perfectly outrageous! The hospital will never have the ghost of a reputation after this—"

"Hurry!" he cried hoarsely. "I can't stand this!"

"Come this way, then, Mr. Button."

He dragged himself after her. At the end of a long hall they reached a room from which proceeded a variety of howls—indeed, a room which, in later parlance, would have been known as the "crying-room." They entered. Ranged around the walls were half a dozen white-enameled rolling cribs, in each of which lay a baby, identified by a tag printed with its parents' name and tied at the head of the crib.

"Well," gasped Mr. Button, "which is mine?"

"There!" said the nurse.

Mr. Button's eyes followed her pointing finger, and this is what he saw. Wrapped in a voluminous white blanket, and partially crammed into one of the cribs, there sat an old man apparently about seventy years of age. His sparse hair was almost white, and from his chin dripped a long smoke-colored beard, which waved absurdly back and forth, fanned by the breeze coming in at the window. He looked up at Mr. Button with dim, faded eyes in which lurked a curious, puzzled question.

"Am I mad?" thundered Mr. Button, his terror resolving into rage. "Is this some ghastly hospital joke?

"It doesn't seem like a joke to us," replied the nurse severely. "And I don't know whether you're mad or not—but that is most certainly your child."

The cool perspiration redoubled on Mr. Button's forehead. He closed his eyes, and then, opening them, looked again. There was no mistake—he was gazing at a man of threescore and ten—a *baby* of threescore and ten, a baby whose feet hung over the sides of the crib in which it was reposing.

The old man looked placidly from one to the other for a moment, and then suddenly spoke in a cracked and ancient voice. "Are you my father?" he demanded.

Mr. Button and the nurse started violently.

"Because if you are," went on the old man querulously, "I wish you'd get me out of this place—or, at least, get them to put a comfortable rocker in here,"

"Where in God's name did you come from? Who are you?" burst out Mr. Button frantically.

"I can't tell you *exactly* who I am," replied the querulous whine, "because I've only been born a few hours—but my last name is certainly Button."

"You lie! You're an impostor!"

The old man turned wearily to the nurse. "Nice way to welcome a new-born child," he complained in a weak voice. "Tell him he's wrong, why don't you?"

"You're wrong, Mr. Button," said the nurse severely. "This is your child, and you'll have to make the best of it. We're going to ask you to take him home with you as soon as possible—some time to-day."

"Home?" repeated Mr. Button incredulously.

"Yes, we can't have him here. We really can't, you know?"

"I'm right glad of it," whined the old man startlingly. "This is a fine place to keep a person of quiet tastes. With all this yelling and howling, I haven't been able to get a wink of sleep. I asked for something to eat"—here his voice rose to a shrill note of protest—"and they brought me a bottle of milk!"

Mr. Button sank down upon a chair near his son and concealed his face in his hands. "My heavens!" he murmured, in an ecstasy of horror. "What will people say? What must I do?"

"You'll have to take him home," insisted the nurse—"immediately!"

A grotesque picture formed itself with dreadful clarity before the eyes of the tortured man—a picture of himself walking through the crowded streets of the city with this appalling apparition stalking by his side. "I can't. I can't," he moaned.

People would stop to speak to him, and what was he going to say? He would have to introduce this—this septuagenarian: "This is my son, born early this morning." And then the old man would gather his blanket around him and they would plod on, past the bustling stores, the slave market⁵—for a dark instant Mr. Button wished passionately that his son was black—past the luxurious houses of the residential district, past the home for the aged. . . .*

"Come! Pull yourself together," commanded the nurse.

"See here," the old man announced suddenly. "If you think I'm going to walk home in this blanket, you're entirely mistaken."

"Babies always have blankets."

With a malicious cackle the old man held up a small white swaddling garment. "Look!" he quavered. "*This* is what they had ready for me."

"Babies always wear those," said the nurse primly.

"Well," said the old man, "this baby's not going to wear anything in about two minutes. This blanket itches. They might at least have given me a sheet."

"Keep it on! Keep it on!" said Mr. Button hurriedly. He turned to the nurse. "What'll I do?"

"Go downtown and buy your son some clothes."

Mr. Button went out the door; his son's voice followed him down into the hall: "And a cane, father. I want to have a cane."

Mr. Button banged the outer door savagely. . . .

"Good morning," Mr. Button said nervously to the clerk in the Chesapeake Dry Goods Company, "I want to buy some clothes."

"For who?" asked the clerk.

"For my child," replied Mr. Button.

"How old is your child, sir?"

"About six hours," answered Mr. Button, without due consideration.

"Babies' supply department in the rear."

"Why, I don't think—I'm not sure that's what I want. It's—he's an unusually large-size child. Exceptionally—ah—large."

"They have the largest child's sizes."

"Where is the boys' department?" inquired Mr. Button, shifting his ground desperately. He felt that the clerk must surely scent his shameful secret.

* *Collier's* broke the text at this point after two contiguous pages (pp. 5–6), continuing the story on p. 22.

"Right here."

"Well—" He hesitated. The notion of dressing his son in men's clothes was repugnant to him. If, say, he could only find a *very* large boy's suit, he might cut off that long and awful beard, dye the white hair brown, and thus manage to conceal the worst and to retain something of his own self-respect—not to mention his position in Baltimore society.

But a frantic inspection of the boys' department revealed no suits to fit the new-born Button. He blamed the store, of course—in such cases it is the thing to blame the store. One means nothing by it—one simply conforms to convention.

"How old did you say that boy of yours was?" demanded the clerk curiously.

"He's—sixteen."

"Oh, I beg your pardon. I thought you said six *hours*. You'll find the youths' department in the next aisle."

Mr. Button turned miserably away. Then he stopped, brightened, and pointed his finger toward a dressed dummy in the window display. "There!" he exclaimed. "I'll take that suit, out there on the dummy."

The clerk stared. "Why," he protested, "that's not a child's suit. At least it *is*, but it's for fancy dress. You could wear it yourself!"

"Wrap it up," insisted his customer nervously. "That's what I want."

The astonished clerk obeyed.

Back at the Maryland Private Hospital for Ladies and Gentlemen, Mr. Button entered the nursery and almost threw the package at his son. "Here's your clothes," he snapped out.

The old man untied the package and viewed the contents with a quizzical eye.

"They look sort of funny to me," he complained, "I don't want to be made a monkey of—"

"You've made a monkey of me!" retorted Mr. Button fiercely. "Never you mind how funny you look. Put them on—or I'll—or I'll *spank* you." He swallowed uneasily at the penultimate word, feeling nevertheless that it was the proper thing to say.

"All right, father"—this with a grotesque simulation of filial respect—"you've lived longer; you know best. Just as you say."

As before, the sound of the word "father" caused Mr. Button to start violently.

"And hurry."

"I'm hurrying, father."

When his son was dressed Mr. Button regarded him with depression. The costume consisted of dotted socks, pink pants, and a belted blouse with a wide white collar, and over the latter waved the long whitish beard, drooping almost to the waist. The effect was not good.

"Wait!"

Mr. Button seized a hospital shears and with three quick snaps amputated a large section of the beard. But even with this improvement the ensemble fell far short of perfection. The remaining brush of scraggly hair, the watery eyes, the ancient teeth, seemed oddly out of tone with the gayety of the costume. Mr. Button, however, was obdurate—he held out his hand. "Come along!" he said sternly.

His son took the hand trustingly. "What are you going to call me, dad?" he quavered as they walked from the nursery—"just 'baby' for a while? till you think of a better name?"

Mr. Button grunted. "I don't know," he answered harshly. "I think we'll call you Methuselah."[6]

Even after the new addition to the Button family had had his hair cut short and then dyed to a sparse unnatural black, had had his face shaved so close that it glistened, and had been attired in small-boy clothes made to order by a flabbergasted tailor, it was impossible for Mr. Button to ignore the fact that his son was a poor excuse for a first family baby. Despite his aged stoop, Benjamin Button—for it was by this name they called him instead of by the appropriate but invidious Methuselah—was five feet eight inches tall.

But Mr. Button persisted in his unwavering purpose. Benjamin was a baby, and a baby he should remain. At first he declared that if Benjamin didn't like warm milk he could go without food altogether, but he was finally prevailed upon to allow his son bread and butter and even oatmeal by way of a compromise.

One day he brought home a rattle and, giving it to Benjamin, insisted in no uncertain terms that he should "play with it," whereupon the old man took it with a weary expression and jingled it obediently at intervals throughout the day.

There can be no doubt, though, that the rattle bored him and that he found other and more soothing amusements when he was left alone. For instance, Mr. Button discovered one day that during the preceding week he had smoked more cigars than ever before—a phenomenon which was explained a few days later when, entering the nursery unexpectedly, he found the room full of faint blue haze and Benjamin with a guilty but contented expression on his face, trying to conceal the butt of a large and dark Havana. This, of course, called for a severe spanking, but Mr. Button found that he could not bring himself to administer it.

Nevertheless he persisted in his attitude. He brought home lead soldiers, he brought toy trains, he brought large pleasant animals made of cotton, and, to perfect the illusion which he was creating— for himself at least—he passionately demanded of the clerk in the toy store whether "the paint would come off the pink duck if the baby put it in his mouth." But, despite all his father's efforts, Benjamin refused to be interested. He would steal down the back stairs and return to the nursery with a volume of the "Encyclopædia Britannica," over which he would pore through an afternoon while his cotton cows and his Noah's ark were left neglected on the floor. Against such a stubbornness Mr. Button's efforts were of little avail.

The sensation created in Baltimore was, at first, prodigious. What the mishap would have cost the Buttons and their kinsfolk socially cannot be determined, for the outbreak of the Civil War[7] drew the city's attention to other things. A few people who were unfailingly polite racked their brains for compliments to give to the parents— and finally hit upon the ingenious device of declaring that the baby resembled the grandfather, a fact which, due to the state of decay common to all men of seventy, could not be denied. Mr. and Mrs. Roger Button were not pleased, and the grandfather himself was furiously insulted.

Benjamin, once he left the hospital, took life much as it came. He enjoyed himself—but not in the manner proper to a child of his age. Several small boys were brought to see him, and he spent an asthmatic afternoon trying to work up an interest in tops and marbles—he even managed, quite accidentally, to break a kitchen window with a stone from a sling shot, a feat which secretly delighted his father.

Thereafter Benjamin contrived to break something every day, but he did these things only because they were expected of him and because he was by nature obliging.

When his grandfather's initial antagonism wore off, Benjamin and that gentleman took enormous pleasure in one another's company. They would sit for hours, these two so far apart in age and experience, and, like old cronies, discuss with tireless monotony the slow events of the day. Benjamin felt more at ease in his grandfather's presence than in his parents'—they seemed always somewhat in awe of him.

He was as puzzled as anyone else at the apparently advanced age of his mind and body at birth. He read up on it in the medical journal, but found that no such case had been previously recorded. At his father's urging he made an honest attempt to play with other boys, and frequently he joined in the milder games—football shook him up too much, and he feared that in case of a fracture his ancient bones would refuse to knit.

When he was five he was sent to kindergarten, where he was initiated into the art of pasting green paper on orange paper, of weaving colored maps and manufacturing eternal cardboard necklaces. He was inclined to drowse off to sleep in the middle of these tasks, a habit which both irritated and frightened his young teacher. To his relief she complained to his parents, and he was removed from the school. The Roger Buttons told their friends that they felt he was too young.

By the time he was twelve years old his parents had grown used to him. Indeed, so strong is the force of custom that they no longer felt that he was different from any other child—except when some curious anomaly reminded them of the fact.

But one day a few weeks after his twelfth birthday, while looking in the mirror, Benjamin made, or thought he made, an astonishing discovery. Did his eyes deceive him, or had his hair turned in the dozen years of his life from white to iron-gray under its concealing dye? Was the network of wrinkles on his face becoming less pronounced? Was his skin healthier and firmer, with even a touch of ruddy winter color? He could not tell. He knew that he no longer stooped and that he had thus added two inches to his stature, and he was aware that his step was firmer and his physical condition improved since the early days of his life.

"Can it be—?" he thought to himself, or, rather, scarcely dared to think.

He went to his father. "I am grown," he announced determinedly. "I want to put on long trousers."[8]

His father hesitated. "Well," he said finally, "I don't know. Fourteen is the age for putting on long trousers—and you are only twelve."

"But you'll have to admit," protested Benjamin, "that I'm big for my age."

His father looked at him with illusory speculation. "Oh, I'm not so sure of that," he said. "I was as big as you when I was twelve."

This was not true—it was all part of Roger Button's silent agreement with himself to believe in his son's normality.

Finally a compromise was reached. Benjamin was to continue to dye his hair. He was to make a better attempt to play with boys of his own age. He was not to wear his spectacles or carry a cane in the street. In return for these concessions he was allowed his first suit of long trousers. . . .

Of the life of Benjamin Button between his twelfth and twenty-first year I intend to say little. Suffice to remark that they were years of normal growth—or rather, to use the word quite conventionally—of ungrowth. For the process that he had first noticed with astonishment when he was twelve seemed to continue. When Benjamin was eighteen he was erect as a man of fifty; he had more hair and it was of a dark gray; his step was firm, his voice had lost its cracked quaver and descended to a healthy baritone. So his father sent him up to Connecticut to take examinations for entrance to Yale College. Benjamin passed his examination and became a member of the freshman class.

On the third day following his matriculation he received a notification from Mr. Hart, the college registrar, to call at his office and arrange his schedule. Benjamin, glancing in the mirror, decided that his hair needed a new application of its brown dye, but an anxious inspection of his bureau drawer disclosed that the dye bottle was not there. Then he remembered—he had emptied it the day before and thrown it away.

He was in a dilemma. He was due at the registrar's in five minutes. There seemed to be no help for it—he must go as he was. He did.

"Good morning," said the registrar politely. "You've come to inquire about your son."

"Why, as a matter of fact, my name's Button—" began Benjamin, but Mr. Hart cut him off.

"I'm very glad to meet you, Mr. Button. I'm expecting your son here any minute."

"That's me!" burst out Benjamin. "I'm a freshman."

"What!"

"I'm a freshman."

"Surely you're joking."

"Not at all."

The registrar frowned and glanced at a card before him. "Why, I have Mr. Benjamin Button's age down here as eighteen."

"That's my age," asserted Benjamin, flushing slightly.

The registrar eyed him warily. "Now surely, Mr. Button, you don't expect me to believe that."

Benjamin smiled wearily. "I am eighteen," he repeated.

The registrar pointed sternly to the door. "Get out," he said. "Get out of college and get out of town. You are a dangerous lunatic."

"I am eighteen."

Mr. Hart opened the door. "The idea!" he shouted. "A man of your age trying to enter here as a freshman. Eighteen years old, are you? Well, I'll give you eighteen minutes to get out of town."

Benjamin Button walked with dignity from the room, and half a dozen undergraduates, who were waiting in the hall, followed him curiously with their eyes. When he had gone a little way he turned around, faced the infuriated registrar, who was still standing in the doorway, and repeated in a firm voice: "I am eighteen years old."

To a chorus of titters which went up from the group of undergraduates, Benjamin walked away.

But he was not fated to escape so easily. On his melancholy walk to the railroad station he found that he was being followed by a group, then by a swarm, and finally by a dense mass of undergraduates. The word had gone around that a lunatic had passed the entrance examinations for Yale and attempted to palm himself off as a youth of eighteen. A fever of excitement permeated the college. Men ran hatless out of classes, the football team abandoned its practice and joined the mob, professors' wives with bonnets awry and bustles[9] out of position ran shouting after the procession from which proceeded a continual succession of remarks aimed at the tender sensibilities of Benjamin Button.

"He must be the Wandering Jew!"[10]

"He ought to go to prep school at his age!"

"Look at the infant prodigy!"

"He thought this was the old men's home."

"Send your grandson in your place!"

"Go up to Harvard!"

Benjamin increased his gait, and soon he was running. He would show them! He *would* go to Harvard, and then they would regret these ill-considered taunts!

Safely on board the train for Baltimore, he put his head from the window. "You'll regret this!" he shouted.

"Ha-ha!" the undergraduates laughed. "Ha-ha-ha!" It was the biggest mistake that Yale College had ever made. . . .

In 1880 Benjamin Button was twenty years old, and he signalized his birthday by going to work for his father in Roger Button & Co., Wholesale Hardware. It was in that same year that he began "going out socially"—that is to say, his father insisted on taking him to several fashionable dances to which the family had received cards. Roger Button was now fifty, and the two were more and more companionable—in fact, since Benjamin had ceased to dye his hair (which was still grayish) they appeared about the same age, and could have passed for brothers.

One night in August they mounted into the phaeton attired in their full-dress suits and drove out to a dance at the Shevlins' country house, situated just outside of Baltimore. It was a gorgeous evening. A full moon drenched the road to the lusterless color of platinum, and late-blooming harvest flowers breathed into the motionless air aromas that were like low, half-heard laughter. The open country, carpeted for rods around with bright wheat, was translucent as in the day. It was almost impossible not to be affected by the sheer beauty of the sky—almost.

"There's a great future in the dry-goods business," Roger Button was saying thoughtfully. He was not a spiritual man—his esthetic sense was rudimentary.

"Old fellows like me can't learn new tricks," he observed profoundly. "It's you youngsters with energy and vitality that have the great future before you."

Far up the road the lights of the Shevlins' country house drifted into view, and presently there was a sighing sound that crept persistently toward them—it might have been the fine plaint of violins or the rustle of the silver wheat under the moon.

They pulled up behind a handsome brougham[11] whose passengers were disembarking at the door. A lady got out, then an elderly gentleman, then another young lady, beautiful as sin. Benjamin started; an almost chemical change seemed to dissolve and recompose the very elements of his body. A rigor passed over him, blood rose into his cheeks, his forehead, and there was a steady thumping in his ears. It was first love.

The girl was slender and frail, with hair that was ashen under the moon and honey-colored under the sputtering gas lamps of the porch. Over her shoulders was thrown a Spanish mantilla[12] of softest yellow, butterflied in black; her feet were glittering black buttons at the hem of her bustled dress.

Roger Button leaned over to his son. "That," he said, "is young Hildegarde Moncrief, the daughter of General Moncrief."

Benjamin nodded coldly. "Pretty little thing," he said indifferently.

When the negro boy had led the buggy away, and they were passing through the flower-hung front door, he added: "Dad, you might introduce me to her."

They approached a group of which Miss Moncrief was the center. Reared in the old tradition, she courtesied low before Benjamin. Yes, he might have a dance. He thanked her and walked away—staggered away.

The interval until the time for his turn should arrive dragged itself out interminably. He stood close to the wall, silent, inscrutable, watching with murderous eyes the young bloods of Baltimore as they eddied around Hildegarde Moncrief, passionate admiration in their eager faces. How obnoxious they seemed to Benjamin; how intolerably rosy! Their curling brown whiskers aroused in him a feeling equivalent to indigestion.

But when his own time came, and he drifted with her out upon the changing floor to the music of the latest waltz from Paris, his jealousies and anxieties melted from him like a mantle of snow. Blind with enchantment, he felt that life was just beginning.

"You and your brother got here just as we did, didn't you?" asked Hildegarde, looking up at him with eyes that were like bright blue enamel.

Benjamin hesitated. If she took him for his father's brother, would it be best to enlighten her? He remembered his experience at Yale, so he decided against it. It would be rude to contradict a lady; it would be criminal to mar this exquisite occasion with the grotesque story of his origin. Later, perhaps. So he nodded, smiled, listened, was happy.

"I like men of your age," Hildegarde told him. "Young boys are so idiotic. They tell me how much champagne they drink at college and how much money they lose playing cards. Men of your age know how to appreciate women."

Benjamin felt himself on the verge of a proposal—with an effort he choked back the impulse.

"You're just the romantic age," she continued—"fifty. Twenty-five is too wordly-wise; thirty is apt to be pale from overwork; forty is the age of long stories that take a whole cigar to tell; sixty is—oh, sixty is too near seventy; but fifty is the mellow age. I love fifty."

Fifty seemed to Benjamin a glorious age. He longed passionately to be fifty.

"I've always said," went on Hildegarde, "that I'd rather marry a man of fifty and be taken care of than marry a man of thirty and take care of *him*."

For Benjamin the rest of the evening was bathed in a honey-colored mist. Hildegarde gave him two more dances, and they discovered that they were marvelously in accord on all the questions of the day. She was to go driving with him on the following Sunday, and then they would discuss all these questions further.

Going home in the phaeton just before the crack of dawn, when the first bees were humming and the fading moon glimmered in the cool dew, Benjamin knew vaguely that his father was discussing wholesale hardware.

". . . And what do you think should merit our biggest attention after hammers and nails?" the elder Button was saying.

"Love," replied Benjamin absent-mindedly.

"Lugs?" exclaimed Roger Button. "Why, I've just covered the question of lugs."

Benjamin regarded him with dazed eyes just as the eastern sky was suddenly cracked with light and an oriole yawned piercingly in the quickening trees. . . .

When, six months later, the engagement of Miss Hildegarde Moncrief to Mr. Benjamin Button was made known (I say "made known," for General Moncrief declared he would rather fall upon his sword than announce it), the excitement in Baltimore society reached a feverish pitch.

The almost forgotten story of Benjamin's birth was remembered and sent out upon the winds of scandal in picaresque and incredible forms. It was said that Benjamin was really the father of Roger Button, that he was his brother who had been in prison for forty years, that he was John Wilkes Booth[13] in disguise—and, finally, that he had two small conical horns sprouting from his head.

The Sunday supplements of the New York papers played up the case with fascinating sketches which showed the head of Benjamin Button attached to a fish, to a snake, and, finally, to a body of solid brass. He became known, journalistically, as the Mystery Man of Maryland. But the true story, as is usually the case, had a very small circulation.

However, everyone agreed with General Moncrief that it was somehow criminal for a lovely girl who could have married any beau in Baltimore to throw herself into the arms of a man who was assuredly fifty. In vain Mr. Roger Button published his son's birth certificate in large type in the Baltimore "Blaze." No one believed it. Benjamin Button was fifty. You had only to look at him and see.

On the part of the two people most concerned there was no wavering. So many of the stories about her fiancé were false that Hildegarde refused stubbornly to believe even the true one. In vain General Moncrief invoked her filial affection. In vain he pointed out the high mortality among men of fifty—or, at least, among men who looked fifty; in vain he told her of the instability of the wholesale hardware business. Hildegarde had chosen to marry for mellowness—and marry she did. . . .

In one particular, at least, the friends of Hildegarde Moncrief were mistaken. The wholesale hardware business prospered amazingly. In the fifteen years between Benjamin Button's marriage in 1880 and his father's retirement in 1895, the family fortune was doubled—and this was due largely to the younger member of the firm.

Needless to say, Baltimore had long forgotten its spleen and received the couple to its bosom. Even old General Moncrief became reconciled to his daughter, and took a great fancy to his son-in-law when Benjamin gave him the money to bring out his "History of the Civil War" in twenty volumes, which had been refused by seventeen prominent publishers. In so far as the eye could see, all was merry and serene. The couple had vindicated the choice of their hearts and were basking in the sunshine of undeniable success.

In Benjamin himself fifteen years had wrought many changes. It seemed to him that his health improved day by day, the blood seemed to flow with new vigor through his veins. It began to be a pleasure to rise in the morning, to walk with an active step along the busy, sunny street, to work untiringly with his shipments of hammers and his cargoes of nails.

In addition, Benjamin began to discover that he was becoming more and more attracted by the gay and glittering things of life: trips to Europe, to New York, balls, dinners, and theatres. It was typical of his growing enthusiasm for pleasure that he was the first man in the city of Baltimore to own and run an automobile.[14] Meeting him on the street, his contemporaries would stare enviously at the picture he made of health and vitality.

"He seems to grow younger every year," they would remark, not knowing the truth they spoke.

And here we come to an unpleasant subject which it will be well to pass over as quickly as possible. There was only one thing that worried Benjamin Button; he discovered about this time, when he had been married fifteen years, that his wife had ceased to attract him.

At that time Hildegarde was a woman of thirty-five, with a son, Roscoe, fourteen years old. In the early days of their marriage Benjamin had worshiped her, and when she had presented him with the little boy he had been delighted. But, as the years passed, her honey-colored hair became an unexciting brown, she grew faintly stout, the blue enamel of her eyes assumed the aspect of cheap crockery—moreover, and most of all, she had become too settled in her ways, too placid, too content, too anemic in her excitements, and too sober in her taste.

When she had been a bride it was she who had "dragged" Benjamin to dances and dinners—now conditions were reversed. She went out socially with him and took trips with him, but without enthusiasm, devoured already by that eternal inertia which comes to live with each of us one day, and stays with us to the end. We are always blind to the things nearest us, and so Hildegarde, on her part, took no note of the change in her husband.

Benjamin's discontent waxed stronger. At the outbreak of the Spanish-American War in 1898[15] his home had for him so little charm that he decided to join the army. With his business influence he obtained a commission as captain, and proved so adaptable to the work that he was made a major, and finally a lieutenant colonel just in time to participate in the celebrated charge up San Juan Hill.[16] He was slightly wounded and received a medal.

Benjamin had become so attached to the activity and excitement of army life that he regretted to give it up, but his business required attention, so he resigned his commission and came home. He was met at the station by a brass band and escorted to his house.

Hildegarde, waving a large flag, greeted him on the porch, and even as he kissed her he felt with a sinking of the heart that these three years had taken their toll. She was a woman of forty now, and a faint squirmish[17] line of gray hairs was perceptible in her head. The sight depressed him.

Up in his room he saw his reflection in the familiar mirror—he went closer and examined his own face with anxiety, comparing it after a moment with a photograph of himself in uniform taken just before the war.

"Good Lord!" he said aloud. The process was continuing. There was no doubt of it—he looked now like a man of thirty; there was scarcely a wrinkle on his face. Instead of being delighted, he was thrilled by a curious and uneasy fear—he was growing younger. He had hitherto believed that once he reached a bodily age, equivalent to his age in years, the grotesque phenomenon which had marked his birth would cease to function, but this did not seem to be the case. He shuddered. His destiny seemed to him awful, incredible.

When he came downstairs Hildegarde was waiting for him in the drawing room. She appeared worried and annoyed, and he wondered if she had at last discovered that there was something amiss. It was with an effort to relieve the tension between them that he broached the matter at dinner in what he considered a delicate way.

"Well," he remarked lightly, "everybody says I look younger than ever."

Hildegarde regarded him with scorn. She sniffed. "Do you think it's anything to boast about?"

"I'm not boasting," he asserted uncomfortably.

She sniffed again. "The idea," she said, and after a moment: "I should think you'd have enough pride to stop it?"

"How can I?" he demanded.

"I'm not going to argue with you," she retorted. "But there's a right way of doing things and a wrong way. If you've made up your mind to be different from everybody else, I don't suppose I can stop you, but I really don't think it's very considerate."

"But, Hildegarde, I can't help it."

"Stuff and nonsense. You're simply stubborn. You think you don't want to be like anyone else. You always have been that way, and you always will be. But just think how it would be if everyone else looked at things as you do—what would the world do?"

As this is one of those inane and unanswerable arguments peculiar to stupid people, Benjamin made no answer, and from that time on a chasm began to widen between him and his wife. He wondered what possible fascination she had ever exercised over him.

To add to the breach, he found, as the new century gathered headway, that his thirst for gayety and excitement was growing stronger. Never a party of any kind in the city of Baltimore but he was there, dancing with the youngest and prettiest of the young married women, chatting with the most popular of the débutantes, and finding their company both seductive and charming, while his wife, a dowager of evil omen, sat among the chaperons, now in haughty disapproval, and now following him with solemn, puzzled, and reproachful eyes.

"Look!" people would remark. "What a pity! A young fellow that age tied to a woman of forty-five. He must be twenty years younger than his wife." They had forgotten—as people inevitably forget—that back in 1880 their mammas and papas had made a remark very much like that about this same ill-matched pair.

Benjamin's growing unhappiness at home was compensated for by the ecstatic sense of his own physical health that pervaded him. He took up golf and made a great success of it. He went in for dancing: in 1906 he was an expert at "The Boston," and in 1907 he experimented with "The Grizzly Bear"; in 1908 he was considered proficient at the "Maxixe," while in 1909 his "Castle Walk" was the envy of every young man in town.[18]

His social activities, of course, interfered to some extent with his business, but then he had worked hard at wholesale hardware for twenty-five years and felt that he could soon hand it on to his son, Roscoe, who had recently graduated from Harvard and was displaying himself as an efficient young man.

Benjamin and his son were, in fact, often mistaken for each other. This pleased Benjamin—he soon forgot the insidious fear which had come over him on his return from the Spanish-American War, and grew to take a naive pleasure in his appearance. There was only one fly in the delicious ointment—he hated to appear in public with his wife. Hildegarde was almost fifty, and the sight of her made him feel absurd. . . .

One September day in 1910—a few years after Roger Button & Co., Wholesale Hardware, had been handed over to young Roscoe Button—a man, apparently about twenty years old, entered himself as a freshman at Harvard University in Cambridge. He did not make the mistake of announcing that he would never see fifty again nor did he mention the fact that his son had been graduated from the same institution ten years before.

He was admitted, and almost immediately attained a prominent position in the class, partly because he seemed a little older than the other freshmen, whose average age was about eighteen.

But his success was largely due to the fact that in the football game with Yale[19] he played so brilliantly, with so much dash and with such a cold, remorseless anger that he scored seven touchdowns and fourteen field goals for Harvard, and caused one entire eleven of Yale men to be carried singly from the field, unconscious. In his sophomore year he repeated the performance with almost equal brilliance. He was the most celebrated man in college.

Strange to say, in his third or junior year he was scarcely able to "make" the team. The coaches said that he had lost weight, and it seemed to the more observant among them that he was not quite as tall as before. He made no touchdowns—indeed, he was retained on the team chiefly in hope that his enormous reputation would bring terror and disorganization to the Yale team.

In his senior year he did not "make" the team at all. He had grown so slight and frail that one day he was taken by some sophomores for a freshman, an incident which humiliated him terribly. He became known as something of a prodigy—a senior who was surely no more than sixteen—and he was often shocked at the worldliness of some of his classmates. His studies seemed harder to him—he felt that they were too advanced. He had heard his classmates speak of Hillkiss,[20] the famous preparatory school, at which so many of them had prepared for college, and he determined after his graduation to enter himself at Hillkiss, where he felt that the sheltered life among boys his own size would be more congenial to him.

Upon his graduation in 1914 he went home to Baltimore with his Harvard diploma in his pocket. Hildegarde was now residing in Italy, so Benjamin went to live with his son, Roscoe. But though he was welcomed in a general way, there was obviously no heartiness in Roscoe's feeling toward him—there was even perceptible a tendency on his son's part to think that Benjamin, as he moped about the house in adolescent mooniness, was somewhat in the way. Roscoe was married now and prominent in Baltimore life, and he wanted no scandal to creep out in connection with his family.

Benjamin, no longer persona grata with the débutantes and younger college set, found himself left much alone, except for the companionship of three or four fifteen-year-old boys picked up in the neighborhood. His idea of going to Hillkiss school recurred to him.

"Say," he said to Roscoe one day, "I've told you over and over that I want to go to prep school."

"Well, go, then," replied Roscoe shortly. The matter was distasteful to him and he wished to avoid a discussion.

"I can't go alone," said Benjamin helplessly. "You'll have to enter me and take me up there."

"I haven't got time," declared Roscoe abruptly. His eyes narrowed and he looked uneasily at his father. "As a matter of fact," he added, "you'd better not go on with this business much longer. You better pull up short. You better—you better"—he paused and his face crimsoned as he sought for words—"you better turn right around and start back the other way. This has gone too far to be a joke. It isn't funny any longer. You—you behave yourself!"

Benjamin looked at him, on the verge of tears.

"And another thing," continued Roscoe, "when visitors are in the house I want you to call me "Uncle"—not "Roscoe," but "Uncle," do you understand? It looks absurd for a boy of fifteen to call me by my first name. Perhaps you'd better call me "Uncle" *all* the time, so you'll get used to it."

And with a harsh look at his father, Roscoe turned away. . . .

At the termination of this interview Benjamin wandered dismally upstairs and stared at himself in the mirror. He had not shaved for three months, but he could find nothing on his face but a faint white down with which it seemed unnecessary to meddle. When he had first come home from Harvard, Roscoe had approached him with the proposition that he should wear eye-glasses and imitation whiskers glued to his cheeks, and it had seemed for a moment that the farce of his early years was to be repeated. But he was old and intolerant now. The whiskers had itched and made him ashamed. He wept and Roscoe had reluctantly relented.

Benjamin opened a book of boys' stories, "The Boy Scouts in Bimini Bay," and began to read. But he found himself thinking persistently about the war. America had joined the Allied cause during the preceding month,[21] and Benjamin wanted to enlist, but, alas, sixteen was the minimum age, and he did not look sixteen. His true age, which was fifty-seven, would have disqualified him, anyway.

There was a knock at his door, and the butler appeared with a letter, bearing a large official legend in the corner, and addressed to Mr. Benjamin Button. Benjamin tore it open eagerly, and as he read the inclosure a look of delight appeared on his face. It informed him that many reserve officers who had served in the Spanish-American War were being called back into service with a higher rank, and it inclosed his commission as brigadier general in the United States army with orders to report immediately.

Benjamin jumped to his feet fairly quivering with enthusiasm. This was what he had wanted. He seized his cap and ten minutes later he had entered a large tailoring establishment on Charles Street, and asked in his uncertain treble to be measured for a uniform.

"Want to play soldier, sonny?" demanded a clerk, casually.

Benjamin flushed. "Say! Never mind what I want!" he retorted angrily. "My name's Button and I live on Mt. Vernon Place, so you know I'm good for it."

"Well," admitted the clerk, hesitantly, "if you're not, I guess your daddy is, all right."

Benjamin was measured, and a week later his uniform was completed.

Without saying anything to Roscoe, he left the house one night and proceeded by train to Camp Mosby,[22] in South Carolina, where he was to command an infantry brigade. On a sultry April day he approached the entrance to the camp, paid off the taxicab which had brought him from the station and turned to the sentry on guard.

"Get some one to handle my luggage!" he said briskly.

The sentry eyed him reproachfully. "Say," he remarked, "where you goin' with the generals' duds, sonny?"

Benjamin, veteran of the Spanish-American War, whirled upon him with fire in his eye, but with, alas, a changing treble voice.

"Come to attention!" he tried to thunder, paused for breath—then suddenly he saw the sentry snap his heels together and bring his rifle to the present. Benjamin concealed a smile of gratification, but when he glanced around his smile faded. It was not he who had inspired obedience, but an imposing artillery colonel who was approaching on a large black horse.

"Colonel!" called Benjamin shrilly.

The colonel came up, drew rein, and looked coolly down at him with a twinkle in his eyes. "Whose little boy are you?" he demanded kindly.

"I'll soon darn well show you whose little boy I am!" retorted Benjamin in a ferocious voice. "Get down off that horse!"

The colonel roared with laughter.

"You want him, eh, general?"

"Here!" cried Benjamin desperately. "Read this." And he thrust his commission toward the colonel.

The colonel read it, his eyes popping from their sockets.

"Where'd you get this?" he demanded, slipping the document into his own pocket.

"I got it from the Government, as you'll soon find out!"

"You come along with me," said the colonel with a peculiar look. "We'll go up to headquarters and talk this over. Come along."

The colonel turned and began walking his horse in the direction of headquarters. There was nothing for Benjamin to do but follow with as much dignity as possible—meanwhile promising himself a sweet revenge.

But this revenge did not materialize. Two days later, however, his son Roscoe materialized from Baltimore, hot and cross from a hasty trip, and escorted the weeping general, *sans* uniform, back to his home. Benjamin's military hopes had ended in cruel disappointment.

In 1920 Roscoe Button's first child was born. During the attendant festivities, however, no one thought it "the thing" to mention that the little grubby boy, apparently about ten years of age who played around the house with lead soldiers and a miniature circus, was the new baby's own grandfather.

No one disliked the little boy, whose fresh, cheerful face was crossed with just a hint of sadness, but to Roscoe Button his presence was a source of almost torment. In the idiom of his generation Roscoe did not consider the matter "efficient."[23] It seemed to him that his father, in refusing to look sixty, had not behaved like a "red-blooded he-man"[24]—this was Roscoe's favorite expression—but in a curious and perverse manner.

If his father had been a business, Roscoe would have said that it "needed some new 100 per cent pep methods to speed up production."[25] As his father was a human being, he was unable to find words for him at all—indeed, to think about the matter for as much as a half an hour drove him to the edge of insanity. His father had behaved badly. Roscoe believed that "live wires"[26] should keep young, but carrying it out on such a scale was—was—was inefficient. And there Roscoe rested.

Five years later Roscoe's little boy had grown old enough to play childish games with little Benjamin under the supervision of the same nurse. Roscoe took them both to kindergarten on the same day and Benjamin found that playing with little strips of colored paper, making mats and chains and curious and beautiful designs, was the most fascinating game in the world. Once he was bad and had to stand in the corner—then he cried—but for the most part there were gay hours in the cheerful room with the sunlight coming in the windows and Miss Bailey's kind hand resting for a moment now and then in his tousled, curly hair.

The days flowed on in monotonous content. He went back a third year to the kindergarten, but he was too little now to understand what the bright shining strips of paper were for. He cried because the other boys were bigger than he and he was afraid of them. The teacher talked to him, but though he tried to understand he could not understand at all.

He was taken from the kindergarten. His nurse, Nana, in her starched gingham dress, became the center of his tiny world. On bright days they walked in the park; Nana would point at a great gray monster and say "elephant,"[27] and Benjamin would say it after her, and when he was being undressed for bed that night he would say it over and over aloud to her: "Elyphant, elyphant, elyphant." Sometimes Nana let him jump on the bed, which was fun because if you sat down exactly right it would bounce you up on your feet again, and if you said "Ah" for a long time while you jumped you got a very pleasing broken vocal effect.

He loved to take a big cane from the hatrack and go around hitting chairs and tables with it and saying: "Fight, fight, fight." When there were people there the old ladies would coo at him, which interested him, and the young ladies would try to kiss him, which he submitted to with mild boredom. And when the long day was done at five o'clock he would go upstairs with Nana and be fed oatmeal and nice soft mushy foods with a spoon.

There were no troublesome memories in his childish sleep; no token came to him of his brave days at college, of the glittering years when he flustered the hearts of many girls. There were only the white, safe walls of his crib and Nana and a man who came to see him sometimes, and a great big orange ball that Nana pointed at just before his twilight bed hour and called "sun." When the sun went his eyes were sleepy—there were no dreams, no dreams to haunt him.

The past—the wild charge at the head of his men up San Juan Hill; the first years of his marriage when he worked late into the summer dusk down in the busy city for young Hildegarde whom he loved; the days before that when he sat smoking far into the night in the gloomy old Button house on Monroe Street with his grandfather—all these had faded like unsubstantial dreams from his mind as though they had never been.

He did not remember. He did not remember clearly whether the milk was warm or cool at his last feeding or how the days passed—there was only his crib and Nana's familiar presence. And then he remembered nothing. When he was hungry he cried—that was all. Through the noons and nights he breathed and over him there were soft mumblings and murmurings that he scarcely heard, and faintly differentiated smells, and light and darkness.

Then it was all dark, and his white crib and the dim faces that moved above him, and the warm sweet aroma of the milk faded out altogether from his mind.

The Diamond as Big as the Ritz

Smart Set
June 1922
$300

[A Complete Novelette]

CHAPTER I

John T. Unger came from a family that had been well known in Hades—a small town on the Mississippi River—for several generations. John's father had held the amateur golf championship through many a heated contest; Mrs. Unger was known "from hot-box to hot-bed," as the local phrase went, for her coiffures and her public addresses; and young John T. Unger, who had just turned sixteen, had danced all the latest dances from New York almost before he put on long trousers. And now, for a certain time, he was to be away from home. That respect for a New England education which is the bane of all provincial places, which drains them yearly of their most promising young men, had seized upon his parents. Nothing would suit them but that he should go to St. Midas'[1] School near Boston. Their minds were made up—Hades was too small to hold their darling and gifted son. Now in Hades—as you must know if you ever have been there—the names of the more fashionable preparatory schools and colleges mean very little. The inhabitants have been so long out of the world that, though they make a great show of keeping up to date in dress and manners and literature, they depend to a great extent on hearsay, and a function that in Hades would be considered elaborate would doubtless be hailed by a Chicago beef-princess as "perhaps a little tacky."

John T. Unger was on the eve of departure. Mrs. Unger, with maternal fatuity, packed his trunks full of linen suits and electric fans, and Mr. Unger presented his son with a brand-new asbestos pocket-book stuffed with money.

"Remember, you are always welcome here," he said. "You can be sure, boy, that we'll keep the home fires burning."

"I know," answered John huskily.

"Don't forget who you are and where you come from," continued his father proudly, "and you can do nothing to harm you. You are an Unger—from Hades."

So the old man and the young shook hands and John walked away with tears streaming from his eyes. Ten minutes later he had passed outside the city limits and he stopped to look back for the last time. Over the gates the old-fashioned Victorian motto seemed strangely attractive to him. His father had tried time and time again to have it changed to something with a little more push and verve about it, such as "Hades—Home of Business Opportunity," or else a plain "Welcome" sign set over a hearty handshake pricked out in electric lights.[2] The old motto was a little depressing, Mr. Unger had thought.

So John took his last look and then set his face resolutely toward his destination. And yet, as he turned away, it seemed to him that the lights of Hades against the sky were full of a warm and passionate beauty.

St. Midas' School is half an hour from Boston in a Rols-Pearse[3] motor car. The actual distance will never be known, for no one, except John T. Unger, had ever arrived there save in a Rols-Pearse and probably no one ever will again. St. Midas' is the most expensive and most exclusive boys' preparatory school in the world.

John's first two years there passed pleasantly. The fathers of all the boys were great money-kings and John spent his summers visiting at all the fashionable resorts. While he was very fond of all the boys he visited, their fathers struck him as being much of a piece, and in his boyish way he often wondered at their exceeding sameness.

"How do you do, John?" they would say to him. "I'm always glad to meet a school friend of my son's—even though I've been pretty busy this Christmas speeding up production and installing a new triple efficiency system among our efficiency experts."[4]

When John told them where his home was they would ask jovially, "Pretty hot down there?" and John would muster a faint smile and answer, "It certainly is." His response would have been heartier had they not all made this same joke—at best varying it with, "Is it hot enough for you down there?" which he hated just as much.

In the middle of his second year at school, a quiet, handsome boy named Percy Washington had arrived at St. Midas' and been put in John's form. The newcomer was pleasant in his manner and exceedingly well-dressed even for St. Midas', but for some reason he kept himself aloof from the other boys. The only person with whom he was at all intimate was John T. Unger. John frankly admired him, but even to John, Percy was entirely uncommunicative concerning his home or his family. That he was wealthy went without saying, but beyond a few general deductions made from his habits and remarks, John knew very little of his friend, so it promised rich confectionery for his curiosity when Percy invited him to spend the summer at his home "in the West." He accepted without the faintest show of hesitation.

It was only when they were in the train bound westward that Percy became, for the first time, rather communicative. One day while they were eating lunch in the dining-car and discussing the imperfect characters of several of the boys at school, Percy suddenly changed his tone and made an abrupt remark.

"My father," he said, "is by far the richest man in the world."

"Oh," said John politely. He could think of no answer to make to this confidence. He considered "That's very nice," but it sounded a trifle hollow and was on the point of saying, "Really?" but refrained since it would seem to question Percy's statement. And such an astounding statement could scarcely be questioned.

"By far the richest," repeated Percy.

"I was reading in the *World Almanac,*" began John, "that there was one man in America with an income of over five million a year and four men with incomes of over three million a year,[5] and—"

"Oh, they're nothing." Percy's mouth was a half-moon of scorn. "Catch-penny capitalists, financial small-fry, petty merchants and money-lenders. My father could buy them out and not know he'd done it."

"But how does he—"

"Why haven't they put down *his* income tax?[6] Because he doesn't pay any. At least he pays a little one—but he doesn't pay any on his *real* income."

"He must be very rich," said John simply. "I'm glad. I like very rich people. I know that when men get very rich they never have to obey the laws, and I suppose it's logical that if they're rich enough they don't have to pay the income tax either."

"My father doesn't, anyhow."

"The richer a fella is, the better I like him," continued John, a look of passionate frankness upon his dark face. "I visited the Schnlitzer-Murphys last Easter. Vivian Schnlitzer-Murphy had rubies as big as hen's eggs, and sapphires that were like globes with lights inside them—"

"I love jewels," agreed Percy enthusiastically. "Of course I wouldn't want anyone at school to know about it, but I've got quite a collection myself. I used to collect them instead of stamps."

"And diamonds," continued John eagerly. "The Schnlitzer-Murphys had diamonds as big as walnuts—"

"That's nothing." Percy had leaned forward and sunk his voice to a low whisper. "That's nothing at all. My father has a diamond bigger than the Ritz-Carlton Hotel."[7]

CHAPTER II

The Montana sunset lay between two mountains like a gigantic bruise from which dark arteries spread themselves over a poisoned sky. An immense distance under the sky crouched the village of Fish, minute, dismal and forgotten. There were twelve men, so it was said, in the village of Fish, twelve somber and inexplicable souls who sucked a lean milk from the almost literally bare rock upon which a mysterious populatory force had begotten them. They had become a race apart, these twelve men of Fish, like some species developed by an early whim of nature, which on second thought had abandoned them to struggle and extermination.

Out of the blue-black bruise in the distance, far beneath the sky, crept a long line of moving lights upon the desolation of the land, and the twelve men of Fish gathered like ghosts at the shanty depot to watch the passing of the seven o'clock train, the Transcontinental Express from Chicago. Six times or so a year the Transcontinental Express, through some inconceivable jurisdiction, stopped at the village of Fish, and when this occurred a figure or so would disembark, mount into a buggy[8] that always appeared from out of the dusk and drive off toward the bruised sunset. The observation of this pointless and preposterous phenomenon had become a sort of cult among the men of Fish. To observe, that was all; there remained in them none of the vital quality of illusion which would make them wonder or speculate, else a religion might have grown up around these mysterious visitations. But the men of Fish were beyond all religion—the barest and most savage tenets of even Christianity could gain no foothold on that barren rock—so there was no altar, no priest, no sacrifice; only each night at seven the silent concourse by the shanty depot, a congregation who lifted up a prayer of dim, anæmic wonder.

On this June night, the Great Brakeman, whom, had they deified anyone, they might well have chosen as their celestial protagonist, had ordained that the seven o'clock train should leave its human (or inhuman) deposit at Fish. At two minutes after seven Percy Washington and John T. Unger disembarked, hurried past the spellbound, the agape, the fearsome eyes of the twelve men of Fish, mounted into a buggy which had obviously appeared from nowhere and drove away in the direction of the bruised sun.

After half an hour, when the twilight had coagulated into dark, the silent negro who was driving the buggy hailed an opaque body somewhere ahead of them in the gloom. As though in sudden response to his cry, it turned upon them a red, luminous disk which regarded them like a malign eye out of the unfathomable night. As they came closer, John saw that it was the tail of an immense automobile, larger and more magnificent than any he had ever seen. Its body was of some gleaming metal richer than nickel and lighter than silver, and the hubs of the wheels were studded with iridescent geometric figures of green and yellow—and John did not dare to guess whether they were of glass or of jewel.

Two negroes, dressed in glittering livery such as one sees in pictures of royal processions in London, were standing at attention beside the car and as the two young men dismounted from the buggy they were greeted in some language which the guest could not understand, but which seemed to be an extreme form of the Southern negro's dialect.

"Get in," said Percy to his friend, as their trunks were tossed to the ebony roof of the limousine. "Sorry we had to bring you this far in that ghastly buggy, but of course it wouldn't do for the people on the train or those God-forsaken fellas in Fish to see this automobile."

"Gosh! What a car!" This ejaculation was provoked by its interior. John saw that the upholstery consisted of a thousand minute and exquisite tapestries of silk, woven with jewels and fine embroideries and set upon a background of cloth of gold. The two armchair seats into which the boys sank luxuriously were covered with some stuff that resembled duvetyn[9] but seemed woven in numberless colors of the fine ends of ostrich feathers.

"What a car!" cried John again, in almost painful amazement.

"Nonsense!" Percy laughed. "Why, it's just an old thing we use for a station wagon."

By this time they were gliding along through the darkness toward the break between two mountains which had lately been occupied by the declining sun.

"We'll be there in an hour and a half," announced Percy, looking at the clock. "I may as well tell you it's not going to be like anything you ever saw before."

If the car was any indication of what John would see when they reached Percy's home, he was prepared to be astonished indeed. The simple piety prevalent in Hades has the earnest worship of and respect for riches as the first article of its creed—had John felt or thought otherwise than radiantly humble before it, his parents would have turned away in horror at the blasphemy.

They had now reached and were entering the break between the two mountains and almost immediately the way became much rougher.

"If the moon shone down here, you'd see that we're in a great big gulch," said Percy, trying to peer out of the window. He spoke a few words into the mouthpiece and immediately the footman turned on a tremendous searchlight and swept the hillsides with its immense beam.

"Rocky, you see. An ordinary car would be knocked to pieces in half an hour. In fact, it'd take a tank to navigate it unless you knew the way. You notice we're going uphill now. Pretty soon we'll show you a trick."

They were obviously ascending, and within a few minutes the car was crossing a high rise where they caught a glimpse of a pale green moon newly risen in the distance. The car stopped suddenly and several figures took shape out of the dark beside it—these were negroes also. Again the two young men were saluted in the same dimly recognizable dialect; then the negroes set to work and four immense cables dangling from overhead were attached with hooks to the hubs of the great jeweled wheels. At a gruff "Hey-yah!" John felt the car being lifted slowly from the ground—up and up—clear of the tallest rocks on both sides—then higher, until he could see a wavy, moonlit valley stretched out before him in sharp contrast to the uncharted quagmire of rocks that they had just left. Only on one side was there still rock—and then suddenly there was no rock beside them or anywhere around.

It was apparent that they had surmounted some immense knife-blade of stone, projecting perpendicularly into the air. In a moment they were going down again—down and down—finally with a soft bump they were landed once more upon the smooth earth.

"The worst is over," said Percy, squinting out the window. "It's only five miles from here, and our own road—tapestry brick—all the way. This belongs to us."

"I wish I could see."

"You'll be able to when we're out of the shadow of this cliff. This is where the United States ends, father says."

"What? Are we in Canada?"

"We are not. We're in the middle of the Montana Rockies. But you are now on the only five square miles of land in the country that's never been surveyed."

"Why hasn't it? Did they forget it?"

"No," said Percy, grinning, "they tried to do it three times. The first time my grandfather corrupted a whole department of the State survey; the second time he had the official maps of the United States tinkered with—that held them for fifteen years. The last time was harder. It was in 1916. My father fixed it so that their compasses were in the strongest magnetic field ever artificially set up. He had a whole set of surveying instruments made with a slight defection that would allow for this territory not to appear and he substituted them for the ones that were to be used. Then he had a river deflected and he had what looked like a village built up on its banks—so that they'd see it and think it was a town ten miles farther up the valley. There's only one thing my father's afraid of," he concluded, "only one thing in the world that could be used to find us out."

"What's that?"

Percy sank his voice to a whisper.

"Aeroplanes," he breathed. "We've got half a dozen anti-aircraft guns and we've arranged it so far—but there've been a few deaths and a great many prisoners. Not that we mind *that*, you know, father and I, but it upsets mother and the girls and there's always the chance that some time we won't be able to arrange it."

Shreds and tatters of chinchilla, courtesy clouds in the green moon's heaven, were passing the green moon like precious Eastern stuffs paraded for the inspection of some Tartar Khan. It seemed to John that it was day and that he was looking at some lads sailing above him in the air, showering down tracts and patent medicine circulars with their messages of hope for despairing, rockbound hamlets. It seemed to him that he could see them look down out of the clouds and stare—and stare at whatever there was to stare at in this place whither he was bound—What then? Were they induced to land by some insidious device there to be immured in a wretched dungeon far from patent medicines and from tracts until the judgment day—or, should they fail to fall into the trap, did a quick puff of smoke and the sharp round of a splitting shell bring them drooping to earth—and "upset" Percy's mother and sisters. John shook his head and the wraith of a hollow laugh issued silently from his parted lips. What desperate transaction lay hidden here? What a moral expedient of a bizarre Crœsus?[10] What terrible and golden mystery? . . .

The chinchilla clouds had drifted past now and outside the Montana night was bright as day. The tapestry brick of the road was smooth to the tread of the great tires as they rounded a still, moonlit lake; they passed into darkness for a moment, a pine grove, pungent and cool, then they came out into a broad avenue of lawn and John's exclamation of pleasure was simultaneous with Percy's taciturn "We're home."

Full in the light of the stars, an exquisite chateau rose from the borders of the lake, climbed in marble radiance half the height of an adjoining mountain, then melted in grace, in perfect symmetry, in translucent feminine languor, into the massed darkness of a forest of pine. The many towers, the slender tracery of the sloping parapets, the chiseled wonder of a thousand yellow windows with their oblongs and hectagons[11] and triangles of golden light, the shattered softness of the intersecting planes of star-shine and blue shade, all trembled on John's spirit like a chord of music. On one of the towers, the tallest, the blackest at its base, an arrangement of exterior lights at the top made a sort of floating fairyland—and as John gazed up in warm enchantment the faint acciaccare[12] sound of violins drifted down in a rococo harmony that was like nothing he had ever heard before. Then in a moment the car stopped before wide, high marble steps around which the night air was fragrant with a host of flowers. At the top of the steps two great doors swung silently open and amber light flooded out upon the darkness, silhouetting the figure of an exquisite lady with black, high-piled hair, who held out her arms toward them.

With a tranced step, as though walking in a dream, John dismounted from the car.

"Mother," Percy was saying, "this is my friend John Unger, from Hades."

Afterward John remembered that first night as a daze of many colors, of quick sensory impressions, of music soft as a voice in love and of the beauty of things, lights and shadows and motions and faces, such as he had never known. There was a white-haired man who stood drinking a many-hued cordial from a crystal thimble set on a golden stem. There was a girl with a flowery face, dressed like Titania[13] with braided sapphires in her hair. There was a room where the solid, soft gold of the walls yielded to the pressure of his hand and a room that was like a platonic conception of the ultimate prison—ceiling, floor, and all—it was lined with an unbroken mass of diamonds, diamonds of every size and shape, until, lit with tall violet lamps in the corners, it dazzled the eyes with a whiteness that could be compared only with itself, beyond human wish or dream.

Through a maze of these rooms the two boys wandered. Sometimes the floor under their feet would flame in brilliant patterns from concealed lighting below, patterns of barbarous clashing colors, of pastel delicacy, of sheer whiteness or of subtle and intricate mosaic, surely from some mosque on the Adriatic Sea. Sometimes beneath layers of thick crystal he would see blue or green water swirling, inhabited by vivid fish and growths of rainbow foliage. Then they would be treading on furs of every texture and color or along corridors of palest ivory, unbroken as though carved complete from the gigantic tusks of dinosaurs extinct before the age of man. . . .

Then a hazily remembered transition and they were at dinner— where each plate was of two almost imperceptible layers of solid diamond between which was curiously worked a filigree of emerald design, green air sliced from a shaving. Music, plangent and unobtrusive, drifted down through far corridors—his chair, feathered and curved treacherously to his back, seemed to engulf and overpower him as he drank his first glass of port. He tried drowsily to answer a question that had been asked him, but the honey luxury that clasped his body added to the illusion of sleep—jewels, fabrics, wines and metals blurred before his eyes into a sweet mist. . . .

"Yes," he replied with a polite effort, "it certainly is hot enough for me down there."

He managed to add a ghostly laugh; then, without movement, without resistance, he seemed to float off and away, leaving an iced dessert that was pink as a dream. . . . He fell asleep.

When he awoke he knew that several hours had passed. He was in a great quiet room with ebony walls and a dull illumination that was too faint, too subtle, to be called a light. His young host, clad in a dressing-gown of red brocade, was standing over him.

"You fell asleep at dinner," Percy was saying. "I nearly did, too— it was such a treat to be comfortable again after this year of school. Servants undressed and bathed you while you were sleeping."

"Is this a bed or a cloud?" sighed John. "Percy, Percy—before you go, I want to apologize."

"For what?"

"For doubting you when you said you had a diamond as big as the Ritz-Carlton Hotel."

Percy smiled.

"I thought you didn't believe me. It's that mountain, you know."

"What mountain?"

"The mountain the chateau rests on. It's not very big, for a mountain. But except about fifty feet of sod and gravel on top it's solid diamond. *One* diamond, one cubic mile without a flaw. Aren't you listening? Say—"

But John T. Unger had again fallen asleep.

CHAPTER III

Morning. As he awoke he perceived drowsily that the room had at the same moment become dense with sunlight. After a while he realized that the ebony panels of one wall had slid aside on a sort of track, leaving his chamber half open to the day. A large negro in a white flannel uniform stood beside his bed.

"Good evening," muttered John, summoning his brains from the wild places.

"Good morning, sir. Are you ready for your bath, sir? Oh, don't get up—I'll put you in, if you'll just unbutton your pajamas—there. Thank you, sir."

John lay quietly as his pajamas were removed—amused and delighted; he expected to be lifted like a child by this black Gargantua[14] who was tending him, but nothing of the sort happened; instead he felt the bed tilt up slowly on its side—he began to roll, startled at first, in the direction of the wall, but when he reached the wall its drapery gave way and sliding two yards farther down a fleecy incline he plumped gently into water the same temperature as his body.

He looked about him. The runway or rollway on which he had arrived had folded gently back into place. He had been projected into another chamber and was sitting in a sunken bath with his head just above the level of the floor. All about him, lining the walls of the room and the sides and bottom of the bath itself, was a blue aquarium, and gazing through the crystal surface on which he sat, he could see fishes swimming among amber lights and even gliding without curiosity past his outstretched toes, which were separated from them only by the thickness of the crystal. From overhead, sunlight came down through sea-green glass, making a colorful nautilus of the entire chamber.

"I suppose, sir, that you'd like hot rosewater and soapsuds this morning, sir—and perhaps cold salt water to finish."

The large negro in white flannel was standing beside him.

"Yes," agreed John, smiling inanely, "as you please." Any idea of ordering this bath according to his own meagre standards of living would have been priggish and not a little wicked.

The negro pressed a button and a warm rain began to fall, apparently from overhead, but really, so John discovered after a moment, from a fountain arrangement nearby. The water turned to a pale rose color and jets of liquid soap spurted into it from four miniature walrus heads at the corners of the bath. In a moment a dozen little paddle wheels, fixed to the sides, had churned the mixture into a radiant rainbow of pink foam which enveloped him softly with its delicious lightness and burst in shining, rosy bubbles here and there about him.

"Shall I turn on the moving-picture machine, sir?" suggested the negro deferentially. "There's a good one-reel comedy[15] in this machine today, or I can put in a serious piece in a moment if you prefer it."

"No, thanks," answered John, politely but firmly. He was enjoying his bath far too deeply to desire any distraction. But distraction came. In a moment he was listening intently to the sound of flutes from just outside, flutes dripping a melody that was like a waterfall, cool and green as the room itself, accompanying a frothy piccolo, in play more fragile than the lace of suds that covered and charmed him.

After a cold salt water bracer and a cold fresh finish, he stepped out and into a fleecy robe that dried him immediately, and upon a couch covered with the same material he was rubbed with oil, alcohol and spice. Later he sat in a voluptuous chair while he was shaved and his hair was trimmed.

"Mr. Percy is waiting in your sitting-room," said the negro when these operations were finished. He handed John a fresh suit of underwear and held up his dressing-gown. "My name is Gygsum,[16] Mr. Unger, sir. I am to see to Mr. Unger every morning."

John walked out into the brisk sunshine of his living-room, where he found breakfast waiting for him and Percy, dressed in white kid knickerbockers, smoking in an easy chair.

CHAPTER IV

This is a story of the Washington family as Percy sketched it for John during breakfast.

The father of the present Mr. Washington had been a Virginian, a direct descendant of George Washington, Lord Fairfax and Lord Baltimore.[17] At the close of the Civil War he was a twenty-five-year-old Colonel with tremendous ambition, a played-out plantation and about a thousand dollars in gold.

Fitz-Norman Culpepper[18] Washington, for that was the young Colonel's name, decided to present the Virginia estate to his younger brother and go West. He selected two dozen of the most faithful blacks, who, of course, worshipped him, and bought twenty-five tickets to Montana, where he intended to take out land in their names and start a sheep and cattle ranch.

When he had been in Montana for less than a month and things were going very poorly indeed, he stumbled on his great discovery. He had lost his way when riding by himself in the hills, and after a day and a night without food he began to grow exceedingly hungry. As he was without his rifle he was forced to pursue a gray squirrel, and in the course of the pursuit he noticed that it was carrying something shiny in its mouth. Just before it vanished into its hole—for Providence did not intend that this particular squirrel should alleviate his hunger—it dropped its burden. With a shout of wrath Fitz-Norman plunged his hand in after the rodent, but for reward received only a sharp bite on his finger. Then he gave up and sitting down to consider the situation his eye was caught by a gleam in the grass beside him. He put out his hand curiously—then he jumped to his feet. In ten seconds he had completely lost his appetite and gained one hundred thousand dollars. The squirrel, which had refused with annoying persistence to become food, had made him a present of a large and perfect diamond.

Late that night he found his way to camp and twelve hours later all the males among his darkies were back by the squirrel hole digging furiously at the side of the mountain. He told them he had discovered a rhinestone mine, and, as only one or two of them had ever seen even a small diamond before, they believed him, without a question.

When the magnitude of his discovery became apparent to him, he found himself in a quandary. The mountain was *a* diamond—it was literally nothing else but solid diamond. He filled four saddle bags full of glittering samples and started on horseback for far St. Paul. There he managed to dispose of half a dozen small stones—then he tried a larger one and a storekeeper fainted and Fitz-Norman was arrested as a public disturber. He escaped from jail and caught the train for New York, where he sold a few medium-sized diamonds and received in exchange about two hundred thousand dollars in gold. But he did not dare to produce any exceptional gens[19]—in fact he left New York just in time. Tremendous excitement had been created in jewelry circles, not so much by the size of his diamonds as by their appearance in the city from mysterious sources. Wild rumors became current that a diamond mine had been discovered in the Catskills, on the Jersey Coast, on Long Island, beneath Washington Square, and excursion trains, packed with men carrying picks and shovels, began to leave New York hourly, bound for various neighboring El Dorados.[20] But by that time young Fitz-Norman was on his way back to Montana.

By the end of a fortnight he had evolved a plan of campaign. He estimated that the diamond in the mountain was approximately equal in quantity to all the rest of the diamonds known to exist in the world. There was no valuing it by any regular computation, however, for it was *one solid diamond*—and if it were offered for sale not only would the bottom fall out of the market, but also, if the value should vary with its size in the usual arithmetical progression, there would not be enough gold in the world to buy a tenth part of it. And what could anyone do with a diamond that size?

It was an amazing predicament. He was, in one sense, the richest man that ever lived—and yet was he worth anything at all? If his secret should transpire there was no telling to what measures the Government might resort in order to prevent a panic, in gold as well as in jewels. They might take over the claim immediately and institute a monopoly.

There was no alternative—he must market his mountain in secret. It would be comparable to concealing a mammoth in a music room, but—there you were.

He sent South for his younger brother and put him in charge of his colored following—middle-aged, loyal and docile, all of them; Fitz-Norman was glad of that. They were darkeys who had never realized that slavery was abolished. To make sure of this, he read them a proclamation that he had composed, which announced that General Forrest[21] had reorganized the shattered Southern armies and defeated the North in one pitched battle. The negroes believed him implicitly. They passed a vote declaring it a good thing and held revival services immediately.

Fitz-Norman himself set out for foreign parts with one hundred thousand dollars and two trunks filled with rough diamonds of all sizes. He went to San Francisco and sailed for the South Sea Islands. There he chartered a Chinese junk and was landed in Russian territory just six months after his departure from Montana. Five weeks later he was in St. Petersburg.[22] He took obscure lodgings and called immediately upon the court jeweler, giving a false name and address and announcing that he had a diamond for the Czar. He remained in St. Petersburg for two weeks, in constant danger of being murdered, living from lodging to lodging and afraid to visit his trunks more than three or four times during the whole fortnight.

On his promise to return in a year with larger and finer stones, he was allowed to leave for India. Before he left, however, the Court Treasurers had deposited to his credit, in American banks, the sum of fifteen million dollars[23]—under four different aliases.

He returned to America in 1868, having been gone a little over two years. He had visited the Capitals of twenty-two countries and talked with five emperors, eleven kings, three princes, a shah, a khan and a sultan. At that time Fitz-Norman estimated his own wealth at one billion dollars.[24] One fact worked consistently against the disclosure of his secret. No one of his larger diamonds remained in the public eye for a week before being invested with a history of enough fatalities, amours, revolutions and wars to have occupied it from the days of the first Babylonian Empire.

From 1870 until his death in 1900, the history of Fitz-Norman Washington was a long epic in gold. There were side issues, of course—he evaded the surveys, he married a Virginia lady by whom he had a single son, and he was compelled, due to a series of unfortunate complications, to murder his brother, whose unfortunate habit of drinking himself into an indiscreet stupor had several times endangered their safety. But very few other murders stained these happy years of progress and expansion.

Just before he died he changed his policy and with all but a few million dollars of his outside wealth bought up platinum and other rare minerals in bulk which he deposited in the safety vaults of banks all over the world, marked as bric-à-brac. His son, Braddock Tarleton Washington,[25] followed this policy on an even more intensive scale. The platinum was converted into the rarest of all elements—radium[26]—so that the equivalent of a billion dollars in gold could be placed in a receptacle no bigger than a cigar box.

When Fitz-Norman had been dead three years, his son, Braddock, decided that the business had gone far enough. The amount of wealth that he and his father had taken out of the mountain was beyond all exact computation. He kept a note-book in cipher in which he set down the approximate quantity of radium in each of the thousand banks he patronized, and recorded the alias under which it was held. Then he did a very simple thing—he sealed up the mine.

He sealed up the mine. What had been taken out of it would support all the Washingtons yet to be born in unparalleled luxury for countless generations. His one care must be the protection of his secret lest in the possible panic attendant on its discovery he should be reduced with all the property holders in the world to utter poverty.

This was the family among whom John T. Unger was staying. This was the story he heard in his silver-walled living-room the morning after his arrival. It gave him a distinct feeling of uneasy fear.

CHAPTER V

When he had finished breakfast, John, realizing that Percy would want to see his parents alone, found his way out to the great marble entrance and looked curiously at the scene before him. The whole valley, from the diamond mountain against which the chateau reclined to the steep granite cliff five miles away over which they had been lowered the night before, still gave off a breath of golden haze which hovered idly above the fine sweep of lawns and marble lakes and brilliant gardens. Here and there clusters of elms and English oaks made delicate groves of patterned shade, contrasting strangely with the tough masses of pine forest that held fast the surrounding hills in a grip of dark blue-green. Even as John looked he saw three fawns in single file patter out from one clump about a half mile away and disappear in awkward gayety into the black-ribbed half-light of another. John would not have been surprised to see a goat-foot piping his way among the trees or to catch a glimpse of pink nymph-skin and flying yellow hair between the greenest of the green leaves.

In some such cool hope he descended the marble steps, disturbing faintly the sleep of two silky Russian wolfhounds at the bottom, and set off along a walk of white and blue brick that seemed to lead in no particular direction.

He was enjoying himself as much as he was able. It is youth's felicity as well as its insufficiency that it can never live in the present, but must always be measuring up the day against its own radiantly imagined future—flowers and gold, girls and stars, they are only prefigurations and prophecies of that incomparable, unattainable young dream.

John rounded a soft corner where the massed rosebushes filled the air with heavy scent, and struck off across a park toward a patch of moss under some trees. He had never lain upon moss and he wanted to see whether it was really soft enough to justify the use of its name as an adjective. Then he saw a girl coming toward him over the grass, and it occurred to him instantly that she was the most beautiful person he had ever seen.

She was dressed in a white little gown that came just below her knees, and a wreath of mignonettes clasped with blue slices of sapphire bound up her hair. Her pink bare feet scattered the dew before them as she came. She was younger than John—not more than sixteen.

"Hello," she cried softly, "I'm Kismine."

She was much more than that to John already. He advanced toward her, scarcely moving as he drew near lest he should tread on her bare toes.

"You haven't met me," said her soft voice. Her blue eyes added, "Oh, but you've missed a great deal!" . . . "You met my sister, Jasmine, last night. I was sick with lettuce poisoning," went on her soft voice, and her eyes continued, "and when I'm sick I'm sweet—and when I'm well."

"You have made an enormous impression on me," said John's eyes, "and I'm not so slow myself"—"How do you you[27] do?" said his voice. "I hope you're better this morning."—"You darling," added his eyes tremulously.

John observed that they had been walking along the path. On her suggestion they sat down together upon the moss, the softness of which he failed to determine.

He was critical about girls. A single defect—a thick ankle, a hoarse voice, a glass eye—was enough to make him utterly indifferent. And here for the first time in his life he was beside a maiden who seemed to him the incarnation of physical perfection.

"Are you from the East?" asked Kismine with unconcealed eager interest.

"No," said John simply. "I'm from Hades."

Either she had never heard of Hades or she could think of no pleasant comment to make upon it, for she did not discuss it further.

"I'm going East to school this fall," she said. "D'you think I'll like it? I'm going to New York to Miss Bulge's. It's very strict, but you see over the week-ends I'm going to live at home with the family in our New York house, because father heard that the girls had to go walking two by two. He said he would not have minded if we walked single file because many a good man—Indian or just unfortunate— had walked in single file, but no member of his family would ever walk in a pair."

"Your father wants you to be proud," observed John.

"We are," she answered, her eyes shining with dignity. "None of us has ever been punished. Father said we never should be. Once when my sister Jasmine was a little girl she pushed him downstairs and he just got up and limped away."

John was wishing that she would talk on forever—or at least until lunch time.

"Do you like mother?" she demanded. "Mother was—well, a little startled when she heard that you were from—from where you *are* from, you know. She said that when she was a young girl—but then, you see, she's a Spaniard and old-fashioned."

"Do you spend much time out here?" asked John, to conceal the fact that he was somewhat hurt by this remark. It seemed an unkind allusion to his provincialism.

"A few months of every year. Percy and Jasmine and I are here every summer, but next summer Jasmine is going to Newport.[28] She's coming out in London a year from this fall. She'll be presented at court."[29]

"Do you know," began John hesitantly, "you're a funny girl."

"Why?"

"You're much more sophisticated than I thought you were when I first saw you."

"Oh, no, I'm not," she exclaimed hurriedly. "Oh, I wouldn't think of being. I think that sophisticated young people are *terribly* common, don't you? I'm not at all, really. Truly I'm not. If you say I am I'm going to cry."

She was so distressed that her lip was trembling. John was impelled to say:

"I didn't mean that; I only said it to tease you."

"Because I wouldn't mind if I *were*," she persisted, "but I'm *not*. I'm very innocent and girlish. I never smoke or drink or read anything except poetry. I know scarcely any mathematics or chemistry. I dress *very* simply—in fact I scarcely dress at all. I think sophisticated is the last thing you can say about me. I believe that girls ought to enjoy their youths in a wholesome way."

"I do, too," said John heartily.

Kismine was cheerful again. She smiled at him and the tiniest stillborn tear dropped from the corner of one blue eye.

"I like you," she whispered intimately. "Are you going to spend all your time with Percy while you're here, or will you be nice to me? Just think—I'm absolutely fresh ground. I've never had a boy in love with me in all my life. I've never been allowed even to *see* boys alone—except Percy. I came all the way out here into this grove hoping to run into you where the family wouldn't be around."

Deeply flattered, John bowed from the hips as he had been taught at dancing school in Hades.

"We'd better go now," said Kismine sweetly. "I have to be with mother at eleven. You haven't asked me to kiss you once. I thought boys always did that nowadays."

John drew himself up proudly.

"Some of them do," he answered, "but not me. Girls don't do that sort of thing—in Hades."

Side by side they walked back toward the house.

CHAPTER VI

John stood facing Mr. Braddock Washington in the full sunlight. The elder man was about forty with a proud, vacuous face, intelligent eyes and a robust figure. In the mornings he smelt of horses—the best horses. He carried a plain walking-stick of gray willow with a single large opal for a grip. He and Percy were showing John around.

"The slaves' quarters are there." His walking-stick indicated a low cloister of marble on their left that ran in graceful Gothic along the side of the mountain. "In my youth I was distracted for a while from the business of life by a period of absurd idealism. During that time they lived in luxury. For instance, I equipped every one of their rooms with a tile bath."

"I suppose," ventured John, with an ingratiating laugh, "that they used the bathtub to keep coal in. Mr. Schnlitzer-Murphy told me that once he—"

"The opinions of Mr. Schnlitzer-Murphy are of little importance, I should imagine," interrupted Braddock Washington coldly. "My slaves did not keep coal in their bathtubs. They had orders to bathe every day, and they did. If they hadn't I might have ordered a sulphuric acid shampoo. I discontinued the baths for quite another reason. Several of them caught cold and died. Water is not good for certain races—except as a beverage."

John laughed and then nervously decided to nod his head in sober agreement. Braddock Washington made him inexplicably uncomfortable.

"All these negroes are descendants of the ones my father brought North with him. There are about two hundred and fifty now. You notice that they've lived so long apart from the world that their original dialect has become an almost indistinguishable patois. We bring a few of them up to speak English—my secretary and two or three of the house servants.

"This is the golf course," he continued as they strolled along the velvet winter grass. "It's all a green, you see—no fairway, no rough, no hazards."

He smiled pleasantly at John.

"Many men in the cage, father?" asked Percy suddenly.

Braddock Washington stumbled and let forth an involuntary curse.

"One less than there should be," he ejaculated darkly—and then added after a moment, "We've had difficulties."

"Mother was telling me," exclaimed Percy, "that Italian teacher—"

"A ghastly error," said Braddock Washington angrily. "But of course there's a good chance that we may have got him. Perhaps he fell somewhere in the woods or stumbled over a cliff. And then there's always the probability that if he did get away his story wouldn't be believed. They'd say it was too preposterous. Nevertheless, I've had two dozen men looking for him in different towns around here."

"And no luck?"

"Some. Fourteen of them reported to my agent that they'd killed a man answering to that description, but of course it was probably only the reward they were after—"

He broke off. They had come to a large cavity in the earth about the circumference of a merry-go-round and covered by a strong iron grating. Braddock Washington beckoned to John and pointed his cane down through the grating. John stepped to the edge and gazed. Immediately his ears were assailed by a wild clamor from below.

"Come on down to Hell!"

"Hello, kiddo, how's the air up there?"

"Hey! Throw us a rope!"

"Got an old doughnut, Buddy, or a couple of second-hand sandwiches?"

"Say, fella, if you'll push down that guy you're with we'll show you a quick disappearance scene."

"Paste him one for me, will you?"

It was too dark to see clearly into the pit below, but John could tell from the coarse optimism and rugged vitality of the remarks and voices that they proceeded from middle-class Americans of the more spirited type. Then Mr. Washington put out his cane and touched a button in the grass, and the scene below sprang into light.

"These are some adventurous mariners who had the misfortune to discover El Dorado," he remarked.

Below them there had appeared a large hollow in the earth shaped like the interior of a bowl. The sides were steep and apparently of polished glass, and on its slightly concave surface stood about two dozen men clad in the half costume, half uniform, of aviators. Their upturned faces lit with wrath, with malice, with despair, with cynical humor, were covered by long growths of beard; excepting a few who had pined perceptibly away, they seemed to be a well-fed and healthy lot.

Braddock Washington drew a wicker garden chair to the edge of the pit and sat down.

"Well, how are you, boys?" he inquired genially.

A chorus of execration in which all joined except a few too dispirited to cry out, rose up into the sunny air, but Braddock Washington heard it with unruffled composure. When its last echo had died away he spoke again.

"Have you thought up a way out of your difficulty?"

From here and there among them a remark floated up.

"We decided to stay here for love!"

"Bring us up there and we'll find us a way!"

Braddock Washington waited until they were again quiet. Then he said:

"I've told you the situation. I don't want you here. I wish to heaven I'd never seen you. Your own curiosity got you here and any time that you can think of a way out of the difficulty, one which protects me and my interests, I'll be glad to consider it. But so long as you confine your efforts to digging tunnels—yes, I know about the new one you've started—you won't get very far. This isn't as hard on you as you make it out, with all your howling for the loved ones at home. If you were the type who worried much about the loved ones at home you'd never have taken up aviation."[30]

A tall, dark-haired man moved apart from the others, and held up his hand to call his captor's attention to what he was about to say.

"Let me ask you a few questions!" he cried. "You pretend to be a fair-minded man."

"How absurd. How could a man of *my* position be fair-minded toward *you*? You might as well speak of a Spaniard being fair-minded toward a piece of steak."

At this harsh observation the faces of the two dozen steaks fell, but the tall dark-haired man continued:

"All right!" he cried. "We've argued this out before. You're not a humanitarian and you're not fair-minded, but you're human—at least you say you are—and you ought to be able to put yourself in our place for long enough to think how—how—how—"

"How what?" demanded Washington coldly.

"—how unnecessary—"

"Not to me."

"Well,—how cruel—"

"We've covered that. Cruelty doesn't exist where self-preservation is involved. You're soldiers; you know that. Try another."

"Well, then, how stupid."

"There," admitted Washington, "I grant you that. But try to think of an alternative. I've offered to have all or any of you painlessly executed if you wish. I've offered to have your wives, sweethearts, children and mothers kidnapped and brought out here. I'll enlarge your place down there and feed and clothe you the rest of your lives. If there was some method of producing permanent amnesia I'd have all of you operated on and released immediately, somewhere outside of my preserves. But that's as far as my ideas go."

"How about trusting us not to peach on you?" cried someone.

"You don't proffer that suggestion seriously," said Washington with an expression of scorn. "I did take out one man to teach my daughter Italian. Let me tell you what happened. Last week he got away."

A wild yell of jubilation went up suddenly from two dozen throats and a pandemonium of joy ensued. The prisoners danced and cheered and sang and wrestled with each other in a sudden uprush of animal spirits. They even ran up the glass sides of the bowl as far as they could, and slid back upon the natural cushions of their bodies. The black-haired man started a song in which they all joined—

> "*Oh, we'll hang the kaiser*
> *On a sour apple tree—*"[31]

Braddock Washington sat in inscrutable silence until the song was over.

"You see," he remarked when he could gain a modicum of attention. "I bear you no ill-will. I like to see you enjoying yourselves. That's why I didn't tell you all the story at once. The man—What was his name? Critchtichiello?—was shot by some of my agents in fourteen different places."

Not guessing that the places referred to were cities, the tumult of rejoicing subsided immediately.

"Nevertheless," cried Washington with a touch of anger, "he tried to run away. Do you expect me to take chances with any of you after an experience like that?"

Again a series of ejaculations went up.

"Sure!"

"Would your daughter like to learn Chinese?"

"Hey, I can speak Italian! My mother was a wop."

"Maybe she'd like t'learna speak N'Yawk!"

"If she's the little one with the big blue eyes I can teach her a lot of things better than Italian."

"I know some French songs—and I could hammer brass once't."

Mr. Washington reached forward suddenly with his cane and pushed the button in the grass so that the picture below went out instantly and there remained only that great dark mouth covered dismally with the black teeth of the grating.

"Hey!" called a single voice from below, "you ain't goin' away without givin' us your blessing?"

But Mr. Washington, followed by the two boys, was already strolling on toward the ninth hole on the golf course, as though the pit and its contents were no more than a hazard over which his facile iron had triumphed with ease.

CHAPTER VII

July under the lea[32] of the diamond mountain was a month of blanket nights and of warm, glowing days when John and Kismine walked clandestine paths together. Almost every morning they met in the grove of their first encounter and spent a halcyon hour. John neglected to confide anything of these meetings to Percy, perhaps from shyness, perhaps lest the cognizance of a third party should spoil a little the remembered freshness of this sylvan love affair. For John and Kismine were in first love. He did not know that the little gold football (inscribed with the words *St. Midas'* and the legend *Pro deum et patrium et St. Midam*) which he had given her rested on a platinum chain next to her bosom. But it did. And she for her part was not aware that a large sapphire which had dropped one day from her simple coiffure was stowed away tenderly in John's jewel box.

Late one afternoon when the ruby music room was quiet and dreamy, they spent an hour there together. He held her hand and she gave him such a look that he whispered her name aloud. She bent toward him—then hesitated.

"Did you say 'Kismine'," she asked softly, "or—"

She had wanted to be sure. She thought she might have misunderstood.

Neither of them had ever kissed before, but in the course of an hour it seemed to make little difference.

The afternoon drifted away. That night when the moon was green and a last breath of music drifted down from the highest tower, they each lay happily awake, reconstructing the separate minutes of the day. They had decided to be married as soon as possible.

CHAPTER VIII

Every day Mr. Washington and the two young men went hunting or fishing in the deep forests or played golf around the somnolent course—games in which John diplomatically allowed his host to win—or swam in the mountain coolness of the lake. John found Mr. Washington a pleasant if somewhat exacting personality—utterly uninterested in any ideas or opinions except his own. Mrs. Washington was aloof and reserved at all times. She was apparently indifferent to her two daughters and entirely absorbed in her son Percy with whom she held interminable conversations in rapid Spanish at dinner.

Jasmine, the elder daughter, who resembled Kismine in appearance—except that she was somewhat bow-legged, and terminated in large hands and feet—was utterly unlike her in temperament. She was enormously domestic. Her favorite books had to do with poor girls who kept house for widowed fathers. John learned from Kismine that Jasmine had never recovered from the shock and disappointment caused her by the termination of the World War, just as she was about to start for Europe as a canteen expert. She had even pined away for a time, and Braddock Washington had taken steps to promote a new war in the Balkans for her benefit[33]—but she had seen a photograph of some wounded Serbian soldiers and lost interest in the whole proceedings. But Percy and Kismine seemed to have inherited the arrogant attitude in all its harsh magnificence from their father. A chaste and consistent selfishness ran through their ideas and remarks.

John was ever enchanted by the wonders of the chateau and the valley. Braddock Washington, so Percy told him, had caused to be kidnapped a landscape gardener, an architect, a designer of state settings and a French decadent poet left over from the last century. He had put his entire force of negroes at their disposal, guaranteed to supply them with any materials that the world could offer, and left them to work out some ideas of their own. But one by one they had shown their uselessness. The decadent poet had at once begun wailing his separation from the boulevards in spring—he made some vague remarks about spices, apes and ivories, but said nothing that was of any practical value. The stage designer on his part wanted to make the whole valley a series of tricks and sensational effects—a state of things that the Washingtons would soon have got tired of. And as for the architect and the landscape gardener, they thought only in terms of convention. They must make this like this and that like that.

But they had, at least, solved the problem of what was to be done with them—they all went mad early one morning after spending the night in a single room trying to agree upon the location of a fountain, and were now confined very comfortably in an insane asylum at Westport, Connecticut.

"But," inquired John curiously, "who did plan all your wonderful reception rooms and halls and approaches and bathrooms—?"

"Well," answered Percy, "I blush to tell you, but it was a moving-picture fella. He was the only man we found who was used to playing with an unlimited amount of money, and though he tucked his napkin in his collar and couldn'[34] read or write, he did manage to brighten up the place considerably."

As August drew to a close John began to regret that he must soon go back to school. He and Kismine had decided to elope the following June.

"It would be nicer to be married here," Kismine confessed, "but of course I could never get father's permission to marry you at all. Next to that I'd rather elope. It's terrible for wealthy people to be married in America at present—they always have to send out bulletins to the press saying that they're going to be married in remnants, when what they mean is just a peck of old second-hand diamonds and some used lace worn once by the Empress Eugenie.[35] It would make me feel so hypocritical."

"I know," agreed John fervently. "When I was visiting the Schnlitzer-Murphys, the oldest daughter, Gwendolyn, married young Burton Hedge, whose father owns half of West Virginia. She wrote home saying what a tough struggle she was carrying on on his salary as a bank clerk—and then she ended up by saying that 'Thank God, I have four good maids anyhow, and that helps a little.'"

"It's absurd," commented Kismine. "Think of the millions and millions of people in the world, laborers and all, who get along with only two maids."

One afternoon late in August a chance remark of Kismine's changed the face of the entire situation and threw John in a state of utter terror.

They were in their favorite grove as usual, and between kisses John was indulging in some romantic forebodings which he fancied added poignancy to their relations.

"Sometimes I think we'll never marry," he said sadly. "You're too wealthy, too magnificent. No one as rich as you are can be like other girls. I should marry the daughter of some well-to-do whole-sale hardware[36] man from Omaha or Sioux City and be content with her half-million."

"I knew the daughter of a wholesale hardware man once," remarked Kismine. "I don't think you'd have been contented with her. She was a friend of my sister's. She visited here."

"Oh, then you've had other guests?" exclaimed John in surprise.

Kismine started and seemed to regret her words.

"Oh, yes," she said hurriedly, "we have had a few."

"But aren't you—wasn't your father afraid they'd talk outside?"

"Oh, to some extent, to some extent," she answered, "Let's talk about something pleasanter."

But John's curiosity was aroused.

"Something pleasanter!" he demanded. "What's unpleasant about that? Weren't they nice girls?"

To his great surprise Kismine began to weep.

"Yes—th-that's the—the whole t-trouble. I grew qu-quite attached to some of them. So did Jasmine, but she kept inv-viting them anyway. I couldn't under*stand* it."

A dark suspicion was born in John's heart.

"Do you mean that they *told*, and your father had them—removed?"

"Worse than that," she muttered brokenly. "Father took no chances—and Jasmine kept writing them to come, and they had *such* a good time!"

She was overcome by a paroxysm of grief.

Stunned with the horror of this revelation John sat there open-mouthed feeling the nerves of his body twitter like so many sparrows perched upon his spinal column.

"What?" he exclaimed.

"Now, I've told you, and I shouldn't have," she said, calming suddenly and drying her dark blue eyes.

"Do you mean to say that your father had them *murdered* before they left?"

She nodded.

"In August usually—or early in September. It's only natural for us to get all the pleasure out of them that we can first."

"Now[37] abominable! How—why, I must be going crazy! Did you really admit that—"

"I did," interrupted Kismine, shrugging her shoulders. "We can't very well imprison them like those aviators, where they'd be a continual reproach to us every day. And it's always been made easier for Jasmine and me, because father had it done sooner than we expected. In that way we avoided any farewell scene—"

"So you murdered them! Uh!" cried John.

"It was done very nicely. They were drugged while they were asleep—and their families were always told that they died of scarlet fever in Butte."

"But—I fail to understand why you kept on inviting them!"

"I didn't," burst out Kismine. "I never invited one. Jasmine did. And they always had a very good time. She'd give them the nicest presents toward the last. I shall probably have visitors too—I'll harden up to it. We can't let such an inevitable thing as death stand in the way of enjoying life while we have it. Think how lonesome it'd be out here if we never had *any* one. Why, father and mother have sacrificed some of their best friends just as we have."

"And so," asked John slowly and accusingly, "and so you were letting me make love to you and pretending to return it and talking about marriage, all the time knowing perfectly well that I'd never get out of here alive—"

"No," she protested passionately. "Not any more. I did at first. You were here. I couldn't help that and I thought your last days might as well be pleasant for both of us. But then I fell in love with you and—and I'm honestly sorry you're going to—going to be put away—though I'd rather you'd be put away than ever kiss another girl."

"Oh, you would, would you?" cried John ferociously.

"Much rather. Oh, why did I tell you? I've probably spoiled your whole good time now, and we were really enjoying things when you didn't know it. I knew it would make things sort of depressing for you. Besides, I've always heard that a girl can have more fun with a man whom she knows she can never marry."

"Oh, she can, can she?" John's voice trembled with anger. "Well, I've heard about enough of this. If you haven't any more pride and decency than to have an affair with a fellow that you know isn't much better than a corpse, well, I'll say that I don't want to have any more to do with you!"

"You're not a corpse!" she protested in horror. "You're not a corpse! I won't have you saying that I kissed a corpse!"

"I said nothing of the sort!"

"You did! You said I kissed a corpse!"

"I didn't!"

Their voices had risen, but upon a sudden interruption they both subsided into immediate silence. Footsteps were coming along the path in their direction and a moment later the rose bushes were parted displaying Braddock Washington, whose intelligent eyes set in his good-looking vacuous face were peering in at them.

"Who kissed a corpse?" he demanded in obvious disapproval.

"Nobody," answered Kismine quickly. "We were just joking."

"What are you two doing here, anyhow?" he demanded gruffly. "Kismine, you ought to be—to be reading or playing golf with your sister. Go read! Go play golf! Don't let me find you here when I come back!"

Then he bowed at John and went up the path.

"See?" said Kismine crossly, when he was out of hearing. "You've spoiled it all. We can never meet any more. He won't let me meet you. He'd have you poisoned if he thought we were in love."

"We're not, any more!" cried John fiercely, "so he can set his mind at rest upon that. Moreover, don't fool yourself that I'm going to stay around here. Inside of six hours I'll be over those mountains if I have to bite my way through them, and on my way East."

They had both got to their feet and at this remark Kismine came close to him and put her arm through his.

"I'm going, too."

"You must be crazy—"

"Of course I'm going," she interrupted impatiently.

"You most certainly are not. You—"

"Very well," she said quietly, "we'll catch up with father now and talk it over with him."

Defeated, John mustered a sickly smile.

"Very well, dearest," he agreed, with pale and unconvincing affection, "we'll go together."

His love for her returned and settled placidly on his heart. She was his—she would go with him to share his hardships and his dangers. He put his arms about her and kissed her fervent mouth. He must make the best of it—for after all she loved him and had done him no harm; she had saved him, in fact.

Discussing the matter they walked slowly back toward the chateau. They decided that since Braddock Washington had seen them together they had best depart the next night. Nevertheless, John's lips were unusually dry at dinner, and he nervously emptied a great spoonful of peacock soup into his left lung. He had to be carried into the turquoise music-room and pounded on the back by one of the under-butlers, which Percy considered a great joke.

CHAPTER IX

Long after midnight John felt his body give a nervous jerk, and he sat suddenly upright, staring into the veils of somnolence that draped the quiet room. Through the great squares of blue darkness that were his open windows he had heard a faint far-away sound that died upon a bed of wind before identifying itself upon his memory, clouded with uneasy dreams. But the sharp noise that had succeeded it was nearer, was just outside the room—the click of a turned knob, a footstep, a whisper, he did not know; a hard lump gathered in the pit of his stomach and his whole body ached in the moment that he strained agonizingly to hear. Then one of the veils seemed to dissolve before his eyes and he saw a vague figure standing by the door, a figure only faintly limned and blocked in upon the darkness, mingled so with the folds of the drapery as to seem distorted, like a reflection seen in a dirty pane of glass.

With a sudden half involuntary movement of fright or resolution John pressed the button by his bedside and the next moment he was sitting in the green sunken bath of the adjoining room, waked into alertness by the shock of the cold water which half filled it.

He sprang out, and, his wet pajamas scattering a heavy trickle of water behind him, ran for the aquamarine door which he knew led out onto the ivory landing of the second floor. The door opened noiselessly. A single crimson lamp burning in a great dome above lit the magnificent sweep of the carved stairways with a poignant beauty. For a moment John hesitated, appalled by the silent splendor massed about him, seeming to envelop in its gigantic folds and contours the solitary drenched little figure shivering upon the ivory floor. Then almost simultaneously two things happened. The door of his own sitting-room swung open, precipitating three almost naked negroes into the hall—and, as John swayed in wild terror toward the stairway, another door slid back in the wall on the other side of the corridor and John saw Braddock Washington standing in the lighted lift, wearing a fur coat and a pair of riding boots which reached to his knees and displayed above the glow of his rose-colored pajamas.

On the instant the three negroes—John had never seen any of them before and it flashed through his mind that they must be the professional executioners—paused in their movement toward John and turned expectantly to the man in the lift, who burst out with an imperious command.

"Get in here! All three of you! Quick as hell!"

Then, it seemed as though within the instant, three negroes darted into the cage, the oblong of light was blotted out as the lift door slid shut, and John was again alone in the hall. He slumped weakly down against an ivory stair.

It was apparent that something portentous had occurred, something which, for the moment at least, had postponed his own petty disaster. What was it? Had the negroes risen in revolt? Had the aviators forced aside the iron bars of the grating? Or had the men of Fish stumbled blindly through the hills and gazed with bleak, joyless eyes upon the gaudy valley? John did not know. He heard a faint whir of air as the lift whizzed up again, and then, a moment later, as it descended. It was probable that Percy was hurrying to his father's assistance, and it occurred to John that should this be so it was his opportunity to join Kismine and plan an immediate escape. He waited until the lift had been silent for several minutes and then, shivering a little with the night cool that whipped in through his wet pajamas, he returned to his room and dressed himself quickly. Then he mounted a long flight of stairs and turned down the corridor carpeted with Russian sable which led to Kismine's suite.

The door of her sitting-room was open and the lamps were lighted. Kismine, clad in a frail kimono of palest yellow, stood near the window of the room in a listening attitude, and as John entered almost noiselessly she started and turned toward him.

"Oh, it's you!" she whispered tensely, crossing the room toward him. "Did you hear them?"

I heard your father's slaves in my—"

"No," she interrupted excitedly. "Aeroplanes!"

"Aeroplanes? Perhaps that was the sound that woke me."

"There're at least a dozen. I saw one a few moments ago dead against the moon. The guard back by the cliff fired his rifle and that's what roused father. We're going to open on them right away."

"Are they here on purpose?"

"Yes—it's that Italian who got away—"

Simultaneously with her last word, a succession of sharp cracks tumbled in through the open window. Kismine uttered a little cry, took a penny with fumbling fingers from a box on her dresser, and ran to one of the electric lights. In an instant the entire house was in darkness—she had blown out the fuse.[38]

"Come on!" she cried to him "we'll go up to the roof garden and watch it from there!"

Drawing a cape about her she took his hand and they found their way out the door. It was only a step to the tower lift, and as she pressed the button that shot them upward he put his arms around her in the darkness and kissed her mouth. The spirit of romance had seized upon John Unger at last. A minute later they had stepped out upon the star-white platform and were gazing eagerly at the scene before them. Above, under the misty moon, sliding in and out of the patches of grey cloud that eddied below it, floated a dozen dark-winged bodies in a constant circling motion. From here and there in the valley flashes of fire leaped toward them, followed by sharp detonations. Kismine clapped her hands with pleasure, which, a moment later, turned to dismay as the aeroplanes at some pre-arranged signal, began to release their bombs and the whole of the valley became a panorama of deep reverberate sound and lurid light.

Before long the aim of the attackers became concentrated upon the points where the anti-aircraft guns[39] were situated, and although the latter responded vigorously, one of them was almost immediately reduced to a giant cinder and lay smoldering in a park of rose bushes.

"Kismine," begged John, "you'll be glad when I tell you that this attack came on the eve of my murder. If I hadn't heard that guard shoot off his gun back by the pass I should now be stone dead—"

"I can't hear you!" cried Kismine, intent on the scene before her. "You'll have to talk louder!"

"I simply said," shouted John, a little impatiently, "that we'd better get out before they begin to shell the chateau!"

"All right." She was leaning in entrancement over the parapet of the tower.

Suddenly the whole portico of the negro quarters cracked asunder, a geyser of flame shot up from under the colonnades and great fragments of jagged marble were hurled as far as the borders of the lake.

"There go fifty thousand dollars' worth of slaves," cried Kismine, "at pre-war prices. So few Americans have any respect for property."

John renewed his efforts to compel her to leave. The aim of the aeroplanes was becoming deadlier minute by minute, and only two of the anti-aircraft guns were still in commission. It was obvious that the garrison, encircled with a ring of fire, could not hold out much longer.

"Come on!" cried John, pulling at Kismine's arm, "we've got to go. Do you realize that those aviators would kill you without question if they find you?"

"Very well," she consented reluctantly, "perhaps we'd better."

"We'll have to wake Jasmine!" she said, as they hurried toward the lift. Then she added in a sort of childish delight, "We'll be poor, won't we? Like people in books. And I'll be an orphan and utterly free. Free and poor! What fun!" She stopped and raised her lips to him in a delighted kiss.

"It's impossible to be both together," said John grimly. "People have found that out. And I should choose to be free as preferable of the two. As an extra caution you'd better dump the contents of your jewel box into your pockets."

Ten minutes later the two girls met John in the dark corridor and they descended to the main floor of the chateau. Passing for the last time through the carved and jeweled magnificence of the splendid halls, they stood for a moment out on the terrace, watching the burning negro quarters and the flaming embers of two planes which had fallen on the other side of the lake. A solitary gun was still keeping up a sturdy popping, and the attackers seemed timorous about descending lower, but sent their thunderous fireworks in a circle around it until it seemed that any chance shot might annihilate its Nubian[40] crew.

John and the two sisters passed down the marble steps, he sedately and they sadly, turned sharply to the left and began to ascend a narrow path that wound like a garter about the diamond mountain. Kismine knew a heavily wooded spot half way up where they could lie concealed and yet be able to observe the wild night in the valley—finally to make an escape, when it should be necessary, along a secret path laid in a rocky gully.

CHAPTER X

It was three o'clock when they attained their destination. The obliging and phlegmatic Jasmine fell off to sleep immediately, leaning against the trunk of a large tree, while John and Kismine sat, his arm around her, and watched the desperate ebb and flow of the dying battle among the ruins of a vista that had been a garden spot that morning. Shortly after four o'clock the last remaining gun gave out a clanging sound and went out of action in a swift tongue of red smoke, and though the moon was down, they could distinctly perceive that the flying bodies were circling closer to the earth. When the planes had made certain that the beleaguered possessed no further resources, they would land and the dark but glittering reign of the Washingtons would be over.

With the cessation of the firing the valley grew very quiet. The embers of the two aeroplanes glowed like the eyes of some monster crouching in the grass. The chateau stood dark and silent, beautiful without light as it had been beautiful in the sun, while the woody rattles of Nemesis[41] filled the air above with a growing and receding complaint. Then John perceived that Kismine, like her sister, had fallen sound asleep.

It was long after four when he became aware of footsteps along the path they had lately followed, and he waited in breathless silence until the persons they belonged to had passed the vantage point he occupied. There was a faint stir in the air now that was not of human origin, and the dew was cold; he knew that the dawn would break soon. Yielding to an instinct of curiosity, John waited until the steps had gone a safe distance up the mountain and were inaudible. Then he followed. About half way to the steep summit the trees fell away and a hard saddle of rock spread itself over the diamond beneath. Just before he reached this point he slowed down his pace, warned by an animal sense that there was life just ahead of him. He progressed cautiously, and coming to a high boulder lifted his head gradually above its edge. His curiosity was rewarded; this is what he saw:

Braddock Washington was standing there motionless, silhouetted against the grey sky without sound or sign of life. As the dawn came up out of the east, lending a cold green color to the earth, it brought the solitary figure into insignificant contrast with the new day.

While John watched, his host remained for a few moments absorbed in some inscrutable contemplation; then he signaled to the two negroes who crouched at his feet to lift the burden which lay between them. As they struggled upright, the first yellow beam of the sun struck through the innumerable prisms of an immense and exquisitely chiseled diamond—and a white radiance was kindled that glowed upon the air like a fragment of the morning star. The bearers staggered beneath its weight for a moment—then their rippling muscles caught and hardened under the wet shine of the skins and the three figures were again motionless in their defiant impotency before the heavens.

After a while the white man lifted his head and slowly raised his arms in a gesture of attention as one who would call a great crowd to hear—but there was no crowd, only the vast silence of the mountain and the sky, broken by faint bird voices stirring down among the trees. The figure on the saddle of rock began to speak in nervous yet ponderous gravity with which was mingled an inextinguishable pride.

"You out there—" he cried in a trembling voice. "You—there—!" He paused, his arms still uplifted, his head held attentively as though he were expecting an answer. John strained his eyes to see whether there might be men coming down the mountain, but the mountain was bare of human life. There was only sky and mocking flute of wind along the tree tops. Could Washington be praying? For a moment John wondered. Then the illusion passed—there was something in the man's whole attitude antitethical[42] to prayer.

"O, you above there!"

The voice was become strong and confident. This was no forlorn supplication. If anything, there was in it a quality of monstrous condescension.

"You there—"

Words, too quickly uttered to be understood, flowing one into the other. . . . John listened breathlessly, catching a phrase here and there, while the voice broke off, resumed, broke off again—now strong and argumentative, now colored with a slow, puzzled impatience. Then a conviction commenced to dawn on the single listener, and as realization crept over him a spray of quick blood rushed through his arteries. Braddock Washington was offering a bribe to God!

That was it—there was no doubt. The diamond in the arms of his slaves was some advance sample, a promise of more to follow.

That, John perceived after a time, was the thread running through his sentences. Prometheus Enriched[43] was calling to witness forgotten sacrifices, forgotten rituals, prayers obsolete before the birth of

Christ. For a while his discourse took the form of reminding God of this gift or that which Divinity had deigned to accept from men—great churches if he would rescue cities from the plague, gifts of myrrh, incense and gold, of human lives and beautiful women and captive armies, of children and queens, of beasts of the forest and field, sheep and goats, harvests and cities, whole conquered lands that had been offered up in lust or blood for His appeasal, buying a meed's worth of alleviation from the Divine wrath—and now he, Braddock Washington, Emperor of Diamonds, king and priest of the age of gold, arbiter of splendor and luxury, would offer up a treasure such as princes before him had never dreamed of, offering it up not in suppliance, but in pride.

He would give to God, he continued, getting down to specifications, the greatest diamond in the world. This diamond would be cut with many more thousand facets than there were leaves on a tree, and yet the whole diamond would be shaped with the perfection of a stone no bigger than a fly. Many men would work upon it for many years. It would be set in a great dome of beaten gold, wonderfully carved and equipped with gates of opal and crusted sapphire. In the middle would be hollowed out a chapel presided over by an altar of iridescent, decomposing, ever-changing radium which would burn out the eyes of any worshipper who ever lifted up his head from prayer—and on this altar raised in its pristine depths there would be slain for the amusement of the Divine Benefactor any victim He should choose, even though it should be the greatest and most powerful man alive.

In return he asked only a simple thing, a thing that for God would be absurdly easy—only that matters should be as they were yesterday at this hour and that they should so remain. So very simple! Let but the heavens open, swallowing these men and their aeroplanes—and then close again. Let him have his slaves once more, restored to life and well.

There was no one else with whom he had ever needed to treat or bargain.

He doubted only whether he had made his bribe big enough. God had His price, of course. God was made in man's image, so it had been said; He must have His price. And the price would be rare—no cathedral whose building consumed many years, no pyramid constructed by ten thousand workmen would be like this cathedral, this pyramid.

He paused here. That was his proposition. Everything would be up to specifications and there was nothing vulgar in his assertion that it would be cheap at the price. He implied that Providence could take it or leave it.

As he approached the end his sentences became broken, became short and uncertain, and his body seemed tense, seemed strained to catch the slightest pressure or whisper of life in the spaces around him. His hair had turned gradually white as he talked and now he lifted his head high to the heavens like a prophet of old—magnificently mad.

Then, as John stared in giddy fascination, it seemed to him that a curious phenomenon took place somewhere around him. It was as though the sky had darkened for an instant, as though there had been a sudden murmur in a gust of wind, a sound of far-away trumpets, a sighing like the rustle of a great silken robe—for a time the whole of nature round about partook of this darkness; the birds' song ceased; the trees were still, and far over the mountain there was a mutter of dull, menacing thunder.

That was all. The wind died along the tall grasses of the valley. The dawn and the day resumed their place in a time, and the risen sun sent hot waves of yellow mist that made its path bright before it. The leaves laughed in the sun and their laughter shook the trees until each bough was like a girl's school in fairyland. God had refused to accept the bribe.

For another moment John watched the triumph of the day. Then, turning, he saw a flutter of brown down by the lake, then another flutter, then another, like the dance of great golden angels alighting from the clouds. The aeroplane fleet had come to earth.

John slid off the boulder and ran down the side of the mountain to the clump of trees where the two girls were awake and waiting for him. Kismine sprang to her feet, the jewels in her pockets jingling, a question on her breathless parted lips, but instinct told John that there was no time for words, they must get off the mountain without losing a moment. He seized a hand of each, and in silence they threaded the tree trunks, washed with light now and with the rising mist. Behind them from the diamond mountain and from the valley at its foot came no sound at all except the complaint of the peacocks far away and the pleasant undertone of morning.

When they had gone about half a mile, they avoided the park land and entered a narrow path that led over the next rise of ground. At the highest point of this John paused and turned around to see. The six eyes of the fugitives focused like one upon the mountain side they had just left—oppressed by some dark sense of tragic impendency.

Clear against the sky a broken white-haired man was slowly descending the steep slope, followed by two gigantic and emotionless negroes who carried a burden between them which still flashed and glittered in the sun. Half way down two other figures joined them—John could see that they were Mrs. Washington and her son, upon whose arm she leaned. The aviators had clambered from their machines to the sweeping lawn in front of the chateau, and with rifles in hand were starting up the diamond mountain in skirmishing formation.

But the little group of five which had formed farther up and was engrossing all the watchers' attention, had mounted upon a ledge of rock where the negroes stooped and pulled up what appeared to be a trap-door in the side of the mountain. Into this they all disappeared, the white-haired man first, then his wife and son, finally the two negroes, the glittering tips of whose jeweled headdresses caught the sun for a moment before the trap-door descended and engulfed them all.

Kismine clutched John's arm.

"Oh," she cried wildly, "where are they going? What are they going to do?"

"It must be some underground way of escape—"

A little scream from the two girls interrupted his sentence.

"Don't you see?" sobbed Kismine hysterically. "The mountain is wired!"

Even as she spoke, John put up his hands to shield his sight. Before their eyes the whole surface of the mountain had changed suddenly to a dazzling burning yellow which showed up through the jacket of turf as light shows through a human hand. For a moment the intolerable glow continued, and then like an extinguished filament it disappeared, revealing a black waste from which blue smoke arose slowly, carrying off with it what remained of vegetation and of human flesh. Of the aviators there was left neither blood nor bone—they were consumed as completely as the five souls who had gone inside.

Simultaneously, and with an immense concussion, the chateau seemed to throw itself into the air, bursting into flaming fragments as it rose and then tumbling back upon itself in a smoking pile that lay projecting half into the water of the lake. There was no fire—what smoke there was drifted off mingling with the sunshine and for a few minutes longer a powdery dust of marble drifted from the great featureless pile that had once been the house of jewels. There was no more sound and the three people were alone in the valley.

CHAPTER XI

At sunset John and his two companions reached the high cliff which had marked the boundaries of the Washingtons' dominion, and looking back they found the valley tranquil and lovely in the dusk. They sat down to finish the food that Jasmine had brought with her in a basket.

"There!" she said, as she spread the table-cloth and put the sandwiches in a neat pile upon it. "Don't they look tempting? I always think that food tastes better outdoors."

"With that remark," remarked Kismine, "Jasmine enters the middle class."

"Now," said John eagerly to Kismine, "turn out your pocket and let's see what jewels you brought along. If you made a good selection we three ought to live comfortably all the rest of our lives."

Obediently Kismine put her hand in her pocket and tossed two handfuls of glittering stones before him. "Not so bad," cried John, enthusiastically. "They aren't very big, but—Hello!" His expression changed as he held one of them up to the declining sun. "Why, these aren't diamonds! There's something the matter!

"By golly!" exclaimed Kismine, with a startled look. "What an idiot I am!"

"Why, these are rhinestones!" cried John.

"I know." She broke into a laugh. "I opened the wrong drawer. They belonged on the dress of a girl who visited Jasmine. I got her to give them to me in exchange for diamonds. I'd never seen anything but precious stones before."

"And this is what you brought?"

"I'm afraid so." She fingered the brilliants wistfully. "I think I like these better. I'm a little—a little tired of diamonds."

"Very well," said John gloomily. "We'll have to live in Hades. And you will grow old telling incredulous women that you got the wrong drawer. Unfortunately your father's bank-books were consumed with him."

"Well, what's the matter with Hades?"

"If I come home with a wife at my age my father is just as liable as not to cut me off with a hot coal, as they say down there."

Jasmine spoke up.

"I love washing," she said quietly. "I have always washed my own handkerchiefs. I'll take in laundry and support you both."

"Do they have washwomen in Hades?" asked Kismine innocently.

"Of course," answered John. "It's just like anywhere else."

"I thought—perhaps it was too hot to wear any clothes."

John laughed.

"Just try it!" he suggested. "They'll run you out before you're half started."

"Will father be there?" she asked.

John turned to her in astonishment.

"Your father is dead," he replied somberly. "Why should he go to Hades? They have enough dead ones along the Mississippi already. You have it confused with another place that was abolished long ago."

After supper they folded up the table-cloth and spread their blankets for the night.

"What a dream it was," Kismine sighed, gazing up at the stars. "How strange it seems to be here with one dress and a penniless fiancé!

"Under the stars," she repeated. "I never noticed the stars before. I always thought of them as great big diamonds that belonged to someone. Now they frighten me. They make me feel that it was all a dream, all my youth."

"It *was* a dream," said John quietly. "Everybody's youth is a dream, a form of chemical madness."

"How pleasant then to be insane!"

"So I'm told," said John gloomily. "I don't know any longer. At any rate let us love for awhile, for a year or so, you and me. That's a form of divine drunkenness that we can all try. There are only diamonds in the whole world, diamonds and perhaps the shabby gift of disillusion. Well, I have that last and I will make the usual nothing of it." He shivered. "Turn up your coat collar, little girl, the night's full of chill and you'll get pneumonia. His was a great sin who first invented consciousness. Let us lose it for a few hours."

So wrapping himself in his blanket, he fell off to sleep.

Winter Dreams

Metropolitan
December 1922
$900

Some of the caddies were poor as sin and lived in one-room houses with a neurasthenic cow in the front yard, but Dexter Green's father owned the second best grocery store[1] in Dillard—the best one was "The Hub," patronized by the wealthy people from Lake Erminie[2]— and Dexter caddied only for pocket-money.

In the fall when the days became crisp and grey and the long Minnesota winter shut down like the white lid of a box, Dexter's skis moved over the snow that hid the fairways of the golf course. At these times the country gave him a feeling of profound melancholy—it offended him that the links should lie in enforced gallowness,[3] haunted by ragged sparrows for the long season. It was dreary, too, that on the tees where the gay colors fluttered in summer there were now only the desolate sand-boxes knee-deep in crusted ice. When he crossed the hills the wind blew cold as misery, and if the sun was out he tramped with his eyes squinted up against the hard dimensionless glare.

In April the winter ceased abruptly. The snow ran down into Lake Erminie scarcely tarrying for the early golfers to brave the season with red and black balls. Without elation, without an interval of moist glory the cold was gone.

Dexter knew that there was something dismal about this northern spring, just as he knew there was something gorgeous about the fall. Fall made him clench his hands and tremble and repeat idiotic sentences to himself and make brisk abrupt gestures of command to imaginary audiences and armies. October filled him with hope which November raised to a sort of ecstatic triumph, and in this wood[4] the fleeting brilliant impressions of the summer at Lake Erminie were ready grist to his will.[5] He became a golf champion and defeated Mr. T. A. Hedrick in a marvelous match played over a hundred times in the fairways of his imagination, a match each detail of which he changed about untiringly—sometimes winning with almost laughable ease, sometimes coming up magnificently from behind. Again, stepping from a Pierce-Arrow automobile,[6] like Mr. Mortimer Jones, he strolled frigidly into the lounge of the Erminie Golf Club—or perhaps, surrounded by an admiring crowd, he gave an exhibition of fancy diving from the springboard of the Erminie Club raft. . . . Among those most impressed was Mr. Mortimer Jones.

And one day it came to pass that Mr. Jones, himself and not his ghost, came up to Dexter, almost with tears in his eyes and said that Dexter was the — — best caddy in the club and wouldn't he decide not to quit if Mr. Jones made it worth his while, because every other — — caddy in the club lost one ball a hole for him—regularly——

"No, sir," said Dexter, decisively, "I don't want to caddy any more." Then, after a pause, "I'm too old."

"You're—why, you're not more than fourteen. Why did you decide just this morning that you wanted to quit? You promised that next week you'd go over to the state tournament with me."

"I decided I was too old."

Dexter handed in his "A Class" badge,[7] collected what money was due him from the caddy master and caught the train for Dillard.

"The best — — caddy I ever saw," shouted Mr. Mortimer Jones over a drink that afternoon. "Never lost a ball! Willing! Intelligent! Quiet! Honest! Grateful!——"

The little girl who had done this was eleven—beautifully ugly as little girls are apt to be who are destined after a few years to be inexpressably[8] lovely and bring no end of misery to a great number of men. The spark, however, was perceptible. There was a general ungodliness in the way her lips twisted down at the corners when she smiled and in the—Heaven help us!—in the almost passionate quality of her eyes. Vitality is born early in such women. It was utterly in evidence now, shining through her thin frame in a sort of glow.

She had come eagerly out on to the course at nine o'clock with a white linen nurse and five small new golf clubs in a white canvas bag which the nurse was carrying. When Dexter first saw her she was standing by the caddy house, rather ill-at-ease and trying to conceal the fact by engaging her nurse in an obviously unnatural conversation illumined by startling and irrelevant smiles from herself.

"Well, it's certainly a nice day, Hilda," Dexter heard her say, then she drew down the corners of her mouth, smiled and glanced furtively around, her eyes in transit falling for an instant on Dexter.

Then to the nurse:

"Well, I guess there aren't very many people out here this morning, are there?"

The smile again radiant, blatantly artificial—convincing.

"I don't know what we're supposed to do now," said the nurse, looking nowhere in particular.

"Oh, that's all right"—the smile—"I'll fix it up."

Dexter stood perfectly still, his mouth faintly ajar. He knew that if he moved forward a step his stare would be in her line of vision—if he moved backward he would lose his full view of her face—For a moment he had not realized how young she was. Now he remembered having seen her several times the year before—in bloomers.

Suddenly, involuntarily, he laughed, a short abrupt laugh—then, startled by himself, he turned and began to walk quickly away.

"Boy!"

Dexter stopped.

"Boy——"

Beyond question he was addressed. Not only that, but he was treated to that absurd smile, that preposterous smile—the memory of which at least half a dozen men were to carry to the grave.

"Boy, do you know where the golf teacher is?"

"He's giving a lesson."

"Well, do you know where the caddy-master is?"

"He's not here yet this morning."

"Oh." For a moment this baffled her. She stood alternately on her right and left foot.

"We'd like to get a caddy," said the nurse, "Mrs. Mortimer Jones sent us out to play golf and we don't know how without we get a caddy."

Here she was stopped by an ominous glance from Miss Jones, followed immediately by the smile.

"There aren't any caddies here except me," said Dexter to the nurse, "and I got to stay here in charge until the caddy-master gets here."

"Oh."

Miss Jones and her retinue now withdrew and at a proper distance from Dexter became involved in a heated conversation. The conversation was concluded by Miss Jones taking one of the clubs and hitting it on the ground with violence. For further emphasis she raised it again and was about to bring it down smartly upon the nurse's bosom, when the nurse seized the club and twisted it from her hands.

"You darn *fool*!" cried Miss Jones wildly.

Another argument ensued. Realizing that the elements of the comedy were implied in the scene, Dexter several times began to smile but each time slew the smile before it reached maturity. He could not resist the monstrous conviction that the little girl was justified in beating the nurse.

The situation was resolved by the fortuitous appearance of the caddy-master who was appealed to immediately by the nurse.

"Miss Jones is to have a little caddy and this one says he can't go."

"Mr. McKenna said I was to wait here till you came," said Dexter quickly.

"Well, he's here now." Miss Jones smiled cheerfully at the caddy-master. Then she dropped her bag and set off at a haughty mince toward the first tee.

"Well?" The caddy-master turned to Dexter, "What you standing there like a dummy for? Go pick up the young lady's clubs."

"I don't think I'll go out today," said Dexter.

"You dont——"⁹

"I think I'll quit."

The enormity of his decision frightened him. He was a favorite caddy and the thirty dollars a month he earned through the summer were not to be made elsewhere in Dillard. But he had received a strong emotional shock and his perturbation required a violent and immediate outlet.

It is not so simple as that, either. As so frequently would be the case in the future, Dexter was unconsciously dictated to by his winter dreams.

Now, of course, the quality and the seasonability of these winter dreams varied, but the stuff of them remained. They persuaded Dexter several years later to pass up a business course at the State University—his father, prospering now, would have paid his way—for the precarious advantage of attending an older and more famous university in the East, where he was bothered by his scanty funds.¹⁰ But do not get the impression, because his winter dreams happened to be concerned at first with musings on the rich, that there was anything shoddy in the boy. He wanted not association with glittering things and glittering people—he wanted the glittering things themselves. Often he reached out for the best without knowing why he wanted it—and sometimes he ran up against the mysterious denials and prohibitions in which life indulges. It is with one of those denials and not with his career as a whole that this story deals.

He made money. It was rather amazing. After college he went to the city from which Lake Erminie draws its wealthy patrons.[11] When he was only twenty-three and had been there not quite two years, there were already people who liked to say, "Now *there's* a boy—" All about him rich men's sons were peddling bonds[12] precariously, or investing patrimonies precariously, or plodding through the two dozen volumes of canned rubbish in the "George Washington Commercial Course,"[13] but Dexter borrowed a thousand dollars on his college degree and his steady eyes, and bought a partnership in a *laundry*.

It was a small laundry when he went into it. Dexter made a specialty of learning how the English[14] washed fine woolen golf stockings without shrinking them. Inside of a year he was catering to the trade who wore knickerbockers.[15] Men were insisting that their shetland hose and sweaters go to his laundry just as they had insisted on a caddy who could find golf balls. A little later he was doing their wives' lingerie as well—and running five branches in different parts of the city. Before he was twenty-seven he owned the largest string of laundries in his section of the country. It was then that he sold out and went to New York. But the part of his story that concerns us here goes back to when he was making his first big success.

When he was twenty-three Mr. W. L. Hart—one of the grey-haired men who like to say "Now there's a boy"—gave him a guest card to the Lake Erminie Club for over a week-end. So he signed his name one day on the register, and that afternoon played golf in a foursome with Mr. Hart and Mr. Sandwood and Mr. T. A. Hedrick. He did not consider it necessary to remark that he had once carried Mr. Hart's bag over this same links and that he knew every trap and gully with his eyes shut—but he found himself glancing at the four caddies who trailed them, trying to catch a gleam or gesture that would remind him of himself, that would lessen the gap which lay between his past and his future.

It was a curious day, slashed abruptly with fleeting, familiar impressions. One minute he had the sense of being a trespasser—in the next he was impressed by the tremendous superiority he felt toward Mr. T. A. Hedrick, who was a bore and not even a good golfer any more.

Then, because of a ball Mr. Hart lost near the fifteenth green an enormous thing happened. While they were searching the stiff grasses of the rough there was a clear call of "Fore!" from behind a hill in their rear. And as they all turned abruptly from their search a bright new ball sliced abruptly over the hill and caught Mr. T. A. Hedrick rather neatly in the stomach.

Mr. T. A. Hedrick grunted and cursed.

"By Gad!" cried Mr. Hedrick. "They ought to put some of these crazy women off the course. It's getting to be outrageous."

A head and a voice came up together over the hill:

"Do you mind if we go through?"

"You hit me in the stomach!" thundered Mr. Hedrick.

"Did I?" The girl approached the group of men. "I'm sorry. I yelled 'Fore!'"

Her glance fell casually on each of the men. She nodded to Sandwood and then scanned the fairway for her ball.

"Did I bounce off into the rough?"

It was impossible to determine whether this question was ingenuous or malicious. In a moment, however, she left no doubt, for as her partner came up over the hill she called cheerfully.

"Here I am! I'd have gone on the green except that I hit something."

As she took her stance for a short mashie shot, Dexter looked at her closely. She wore a blue gingham dress, rimmed at throat and shoulders with a white edging that accentuated her tan. The quality of exaggeration, of thinness that had made her passionate eyes and down turning mouth absurd at eleven was gone now. She was arrestingly beautiful. The color in her cheeks was centered like the color in a picture—it was not a "high" color, but a sort of fluctuating and feverish warmth, so shaded that it seemed at any moment it would recede and disappear. This color and the mobility of her mouth gave a continual impression of flux, of intense life, of passionate vitality—balanced only partially by the sad luxury of her eyes.

She swung her mashie impatiently and without interest, pitching the ball into a sandpit on the other side of the green. With a quick insincere smile and a careless "Thank you!" she went on after it.

"That Judy Jones!" remarked Mr. Hedrick on the next tee, as they waited—some moments—for her to play on ahead, "All she needs is to be turned up and spanked for six months and then to be married off to an old-fashioned cavalry captain."

"Gosh, she's good-looking!" said Mr. Sandwood, who was just over thirty.

"Good-looking!" cried Mr. Hedrick contemptuously, "she always looks as if she wanted to be kissed! Turning those big cow-eyes on every young calf in town!"

It is doubtful if Mr. Hedrick intended a reference to the maternal instinct.

"She'd play pretty good golf if she'd try," said Mr. Sandwood.

"She has no form," said Mr. Hedrick solemnly.

"She has a nice figure," said Mr. Sandwood.

"Better thank the Lord she doesn't drive a swifter ball," said Mr. Hart, winking at Dexter. "Come on. Let's go."

Later in the afternoon the sun went down with a riotous swirl of gold and varying blues and scarlets, and left the dry rustling night of western summer. Dexter watched from the verandah of the Erminie Club, watched the even overlap of the waters in the little wind, silver molasses under the harvest moon. Then the moon held a finger to her lips and the lake became a clear pool, pale and quiet. Dexter put on his bathing suit and swam out to the farthest raft, where he stretched dripping on the wet canvas of the spring board.

There was a fish jumping and a star shining and the lights around the lake were gleaming. Over on a dark peninsula a piano was playing the songs of last summer and of summers before that—songs from "The Pink Lady" and "The Chocolate Soldier" and "Mlle. Modiste"[16]— and because the sound of a piano over a stretch of water had always seemed beautiful to Dexter he lay perfectly quiet and listened.

The tune the piano was playing at that moment had been gay and new five years before when Dexter was a sophmore[17] at college. They had played it at a prom once and because he could not afford the luxury of proms in those days he had stood outside the gymnasium and listened. The sound of the tune and the splash of the fish precipitated in him a sort of ecstasy and it was with that ecstasy he viewed what happened to him now. The ecstacy[18] was a gorgeous appreciation. It was his sense that, for once, he was magnificently atune[19] to life and that everything about him was radiating a brightness and a glamor he might never know again.

A low pale oblong detached itself suddenly from the darkness of the peninsula, spitting forth the reverberate sound of a racing motorboat. Two white streamers of cleft water rolled themselves out behind it and almost immediately the boat was beside him, drowning out the hot tinkle of the piano in the drone of its spray. Dexter raising himself on his arms was aware of a figure standing at the wheel, of two dark eyes regarding him over the lengthening space of water—then the boat had gone by and was sweeping in an immense and purposeless circle of spray round and round in the middle of the lake. With equal eccentricity one of the circles flattened out and headed back toward the raft.

"Who's that?" she called, shutting off her motor. She was so near now that Dexter could see her bathing suit, which consisted apparently of pink rompers. "Oh—you're one of the men I hit in the stomach."

The nose of the boat bumped the raft. After an inexpert struggle, Dexter managed to twist the line around a two-by-four. Then the raft tilted rakishly as she sprang on.

"Well, kidddo," she said huskily, "do you"—she broke off. She had sat herself upon the springboard, found it damp and jumped up quickly—"do you want to go surf-board riding?"[20]

He indicated that he would be delighted.

"The name is Judy Jones. Ghastly reputation but enormously popular." She favored him with an absurd smirk—rather, what tried to be a smirk, for, twist her mouth as she might, it was not grotesque, it was merely beautiful. "See that house over on the peninsula?"

"No."

"Well, there's a house there that I live in only you can't see it because it's too dark. And in that house there is a fella waiting for me. When he drove up by the door I drove out by the dock because he has watery eyes and asks me if I have an ideal."

There was a fish jumping and a star shining and the lights around the lake were gleaming. Dexter sat beside Judy Jones and she explained how her boat was driven. Then she was in the water, swimming to the floating surf-board with exquisite crawl. Watching her was as without effort to the eye as watching a branch waving or a sea-gull flying. Her arms, burned to butternut, moved sinuously among the dull platinum ripples, elbow appearing first, casting the forearm back with a cadence of falling water, then reaching out and down stabbing a path ahead.

They moved out into the lake and, turning, Dexter saw that she was kneeling on the low rear of the now up-tilted surf-board.

"Go faster," she called, "fast as it'll go."

Obediently he jammed the lever forward and the white spray mounted at the bow. When he looked around again the girl was standing up on the rushing board, her arms spread ecstatically, her eyes lifted toward the moon.

"It's awful cold, kiddo," she shouted, "What's your name anyways."

"The name is Dexter Green. Would it amuse you to know how good you look back there?"

"Yes," she shouted, "It would amuse me. Except that I'm too cold. Come to dinner tomorrow night." *

He kept thinking how glad he was that he had never caddied for this girl. The damp gingham clinging made her like a statue and turned her intense mobility to immobility at last.

---

* *Metropolitan* broke the text at this point after five contiguous pages (pp. 11–15), continuing the story on p. 98.

"—At seven o'clock," she shouted, "Judy Jones, Girl, who hit man in stomach. Better write it down."—and then, "Faster—oh, faster!"

Had he been as calm inwardly as he was in appearance, Dexter would have had time to examine his surroundings in detail. He received, however, an enduring impression that the house was the most elaborate he had ever seen. He had known for a long time that it was the finest on Lake Erminie, with a Pompeiian[21] swimming pool and twelve acres of lawn and garden. But what gave it an air of breathless intensity was the sense that it was inhabited by Judy Jones—that it was as casual a thing to her as the little house in the village had once been to Dexter. There was a feeling of mystery in it, of bedrooms upstairs more beautiful and strange than other bedrooms, of gay and radiant activities taking place through these deep corridors and of romances that were not musty and laid already in lavender, but were fresh and breathing and set forth in rich motor cars and in great dances whose flowers were scarcely withered. They were more real because he could feel them all about him, pervading the air with the shades and echoes of still vibrant emotion.[22]

And so while he waited for her to appear he peopled the soft deep summer room and the sun porch that opened from it with the men who had already loved Judy Jones. He knew the sort of men they were—the men who when he first went to college had entered from the great prep-schools with graceful clothes and the deep tan of healthy summer, who did nothing or anything with the same debonaire ease.

Dexter had seen that, in one sense, he was better than these men. He was newer and stronger. Yet in acknowledging to himself that he wished his children to be like them he was admitting that he was but the rough, strong stuff from which this graceful aristocracy eternally sprang.

When, a year before, the time had come when he could wear good clothes, he had known who were the best tailors in America, and the best tailor in America had made him the suit he wore this evening. He had acquired that particular reserve peculiar to his university, that set it off from other universities.[23] He recognized the value to him of such a mannerism and he had adopted it; he knew that to be careless in dress and manner required more confidence than to be careful. But carelessness was for his children. His mother's name had been Krimslich. She was a Bohemian of the peasant class and she had talked broken English to the end of her days.[24] Her son must keep to the set patterns.

He waited for Judy Jones in her house, and he saw these other young men around him. It excited him that many men had loved her. It increased her value in his eyes.[25]

At a little after seven Judy Jones came downstairs. She wore a blue silk afternoon dress. He was disappointed at first that she had not put on something more elaborate, and this feeling was accentuated when, after a brief greeting, she went to the door of a butler's pantry and pushing it open called: "You can have dinner, Martha." He had rather expected that a butler would announce dinner, that there would be a cocktail perhaps. It even offended him that she should know the maid's name.

Then he put these thoughts behind him as they sat down together on a chintz-covered lounge.

"Father and mother won't be here," she said.

"Ought I to be sorry?"

"They're really quite nice," she confessed, as if it had just occurred to her. "I think my father's the best looking man of his age I've ever seen. And mother looks about thirty."

He remembered the last time he had seen her father, and found he was glad the parents were not to be here tonight. They would wonder who he was. He had been born in Keeble, a Minnesota village fifty miles farther north and he always gave Keeble as his home instead of Dillard. Country towns were well enough to come from if they weren't inconveniently in sight and used as foot-stools by fashionable lakes.

Before dinner he found the conversation unsatisfactory. The beautiful Judy seemed faintly irritable—as much so as it was possible to be with a comparative stranger. They discussed Lake Erminie and its golf course, the surf-board riding of the night before and the cold she had caught, which made her voice more husky and charming than ever.[26] They talked of his university which she had visited frequently during the past two years, and of the nearby city which supplied Lake Erminie with its patrons and whither Dexter would return next day to his prospering laundries.

During dinner she slipped into a moody depression which gave Dexter a feeling of guilt. Whatever petulance she uttered in her throaty voice worried him. Whatever she smiled at—at him, at a silver fork, at nothing—, it disturbed him that her smile could have no root in mirth, or even in amusement. When the red corners of her lips curved down, it was less a smile than an invitation to a kiss.

Then, after dinner, she led him out on the dark sun-porch and deliberately changed the atmosphere.

"Do I seem gloomy?" she demanded.

"No, but I'm afraid I'm boring you," he answered quickly.

"You're not. I like you. But I've just had rather an unpleasant afternoon. There was a—man I cared about. He told me out of a clear sky that he was poor as a church-mouse. He'd never even hinted it before. Does this sound horribly mundane?"

"Perhaps he was afraid to tell you."

"I suppose he was," she answered thoughtfully. "He didn't start right. You see, if I'd thought of him as poor—well, I've been mad about loads of poor men, and fully intended to marry them all. But in this case, I hadn't thought of him that way and my interest in him wasn't strong enough to survive the shock."

"I know. As if a girl calmly informed her fiancé that she was a widow. He might not object to widows, but——"

"Let's start right," she suggested suddenly. "Who are you, anyhow?"

For a moment Dexter hesitated. There were two versions of his life that he could tell. There was Dillard and his caddying and his struggle through college, or——

"I'm nobody," he announced. "My career is largely a matter of futures."

"Are you poor?"

"No," he said frankly, "I'm probably making more money than any man my age in the northwest. I know that's an obnoxious remark, but you advised me to start right."

There was a pause. She smiled, and with a touch of amusement.

"You sound like a man in a play."

"It's your fault. You tempted me into being assertive."

Suddenly she turned her dark eyes directly upon him and the corners of her mouth drooped until her face seemed to open like a flower.[27] He dared scarcely to breathe, he had the sense that she was exerting some force upon him; making him overwhelmingly conscious of the youth and mystery that wealth imprisons and preserves, the freshness of many clothes, of cool rooms and gleaming things, safe and proud above the hot struggles of the poor.[28]

The porch was bright with the bought luxury of starshine. The wicker of the settee squeaked fashionably when he put his arm around her, commanded by her eyes.[29] He kissed her curious and lovely mouth and committed himself to the following of a grail.[30]

It began like that—and continued, with varying shades of intensity, on such a note right up to the dénoument.[31] Dexter surrendered a part of himself to the most direct and unprincipled personality with which he had ever come in contact. Whatever the beautiful Judy Jones desired, she went after with the full pressure of her charm. There was no divergence of method, no jockeying for position or premeditation of effects—there was very little mental quality in any of her affairs. She simply made men conscious to the highest degree of her physical loveliness.

Dexter had no desire to change her. Her deficiencies were knit up with a passionate energy that transcended and justified them.

When, as Judy's head lay against his shoulder that first night, she whispered:

"I don't know what's the matter with me. Last night I thought I was in love with a man and tonight I think I'm in love with you——"

——it seemed to him a beautiful and romantic thing to say. It was the exquisite excitability that for the moment he controlled and owned. But a week later he was compelled to view this same quality in a different light. She took him in her roadster[32] to a picnic supper and after supper she disappeared, likewise in her roadster, with another man. Dexter became enormously upset and was scarcely able to be decently civil to the other people present. When she assured him that she had not kissed the other man he knew she was lying—yet he was glad that she had taken the trouble to lie to him.

He was, as he found before the summer ended, one of a dozen, a varying dozen, who circulated about her. Each of them had at one time been favored above all others—about half of them still basked in the solace of occasional sentimental revivals. Whenever one showed signs of dropping out through long neglect she granted him a brief honeyed hour which encouraged him to tag along for a year or so longer. Judy made these forays upon the helpless and defeated without malice, indeed half unconscious that there was anything mischievous in what she did.

When a new man came to town everyone dropped out—dates were automatically cancelled.

The helpless part of trying to do anything about it was that she did it all herself. She was not a girl who could be "won" in the kinetic sense—she was proof against cleverness, she was proof against charm, if any of these assailed her too strongly she would immediately resolve the affair to a physical basis and under the magic of her physical splendor the strong as well as the brilliant played her game and not their own. She was entertained only by the gratification of her desires and by the direct exercise of her own charm. Perhaps from so much youthful love, so many youthful lovers she had come, in self defense, to nourish herself wholly from within.

Succeeding Dexter's first exhilaration came restlessness and dissatisfaction. The helpless ecstasy of losing himself in her charm was a powerful opiate rathen[33] than a tonic. It was fortunate for his work during the winter that those moments of ecstasy came infrequently. Early in their acquaintance it had seemed for a while that there was a deep and spontaneous mutual attraction—that first August for example—three days of long evenings on her dusky verandah, of strange wan kisses through the late afternoon, in shadowy alcoves or behind the protecting trellises of the garden arbors, of mornings when she was fresh as a dream and almost shy at meeting him in the clarity of the rising day. There was all the ecstasy of an engagement about it, sharpened by his realization that there was no engagement. It was during those three days that, for the first time, he had asked her to marry him. She said "maybe some day," she said "kiss me," she said "I'd like to marry you," she said "I love you,"—she said—nothing.

The three days were interrupted by the arrival of a New York man who visited the Jones' for half September. To Dexter's agony, rumor engaged them. The man was the son of the president of a great trust company. But at the end of a month it was reported that Judy was yawning. At a dance one night she sat all evening in a motor boat with an old beau, while the New Yorker searched the club for her frantically. She told the old beau that she was bored with her visitor and two days later he left. She was seen with him at the station and it was reported that he looked very mournful indeed.

On this note the summer ended. Dexter was twenty-four and he found himself increasingly in a position to do as he wished. He joined two clubs in the city and lived at one of them. Though he was by no means an integral part of the stag-lines[34] at these clubs he managed to be on hand at dances where Judy Jones was likely to appear. He could have gone out socially as much as he liked—he was an eligible young man, now, and popular with downtown fathers. His confessed devotion to Judy Jones had rather solidified his position. But he had no social aspirations and rather despised the dancing men who were always on tap for the Thursday or Saturday parties and who filled in at dinners with the younger married set. Already he was playing with the idea of going East to New York. He wanted to take Judy Jones with him. No disillusion as to the world in which she had grown up could cure his illusion as to her desirability.

Remember that—for only in the light of it can what he did for her be understood. Eighteen months after he first met Judy Jones he became engaged to another girl. Her name was Irene Scheerer and her father was one of the men who had always believed in Dexter. Irene was light haired and sweet and honorable and a little stout and she had two beaus whom she pleasantly relinquished when Dexter formally asked her to marry him.

Summer, fall, winter, spring, another summer, another fall—so much he had given of his active life to the curved lips of Judy Jones. She had treated him with interest, with encouragement, with malice, with indifference, with contempt. She had inflicted on him the innumerable little slights and indignities possible in such a case—as if in revenge for having ever cared for him at all. She had beckoned him and yawned at him and beckoned him again and he had responded often with bitterness and narrowed eyes. She had brought him ecstatic happiness and intolerable agony of spirit. She had caused him untold inconvenience and not a little trouble. She had insulted him and she had ridden over him and she had played his interest in her against his interest in his work—for fun. She had done everything to him except to criticise[35] him—this she had not done—it seemed to him only because it might have sullied the utter indifference she manifested and sincerely felt toward him.

When autumn had come and gone again it occurred to him that he could not have Judy Jones. He had to beat this into his mind but he convinced himself at last. He lay awake at night for a while and argued it over. He told himself the trouble and the pain she had caused him, he enumerated her glaring deficiencies as a wife. Then he said to himself that he loved her and after a while he fell asleep. For a week, lest he imagine her husky voice over the telephone or her eyes opposite him at lunch, he worked hard and late and at night he went to his office and plotted out his years.

At the end of a week he went to a dance and cut in on her once. For almost the first time since they had met he did not ask her to sit out with him or tell her that she was lovely. It hurt him that she did not miss these things—that was all. He was not jealous when he saw that there was a new man tonight. He had been hardened against jealousy long before.

He stayed late at the dance. He sat for an hour with Irene Scheerer and talked about books and about music. He knew very little about either. But he was beginning to be master of his own time now and

he had a rather priggish notion that he—the young and already fabu-
lously successful Dexter Green—should know more about such things.

That was in October when he was twenty-five. In January Dexter
and Irene became engaged. It was to be announced in June and they
were to be married three months later.

The Minnesota winter prolonged itself interminably and it was
almost May when the winds came soft and the snow ran down into
Lake Erminie at last. For the first time in over a year Dexter was
enjoying a certain tranquility of spirit. Judy Jones had been in Florida
and afterward in Hot Springs[36] and somewhere she had been engaged
and somewhere she had broken it off. At first, when Dexter had definitely given her up, it had made him sad that people still linked them
together and asked for news of her, but when he began to be placed
at dinner next to Irene Scheerer people didn't ask him about her any
more—they told him about her. He ceased to be an authority on her.

May at last. Dexter walked the streets at night when the darkness
was damp as rain, wondering that so soon, with so little done, so
much of ecstasy had gone from him. May, one year back had been
marked by Judy's poignant, unforgivable, yet forgiven turbulence—it
had been one of those rare times when he fancied she had grown to
care for him. That old penny's worth of happiness he had spent for
this bushel of content. He knew that Irene would be no more than a
curtain spread behind him, a hand moving among gleaming tea cups,
a voice calling to children . . . fire and loveliness were gone, magic of
night and the hushed wonder of the hours and seasons . . . slender
lips, down turning, dropping to his lips like poppy petals, bearing
him up into a heaven of eyes . . . a haunting gesture, light of a warm
lamp on her hair. The thing was deep in him. He was too strong, too
alive for it to die lightly.

In the middle of May when the weather balanced for a few days
on the thin bridge that led to deep summer he turned in one night
at Irene's house. Their engagement was to be announced in a week
now—no one would be surprised at it. And tonight they would sit
together on the lounge at the College Club[37] and look on for an hour
at the dancers. It gave him a sense of solidity to go with her—— She
was so sturdily popular, so intensely a "good egg."[38]

He mounted the steps of the brown stone house and stepped
inside.

"Irene," he called.

Mrs. Scheerer came out of the living room to meet him.

"Dexter," she said, "Irene's gone upstairs with a splitting headache.
She wanted to go with you but I made her go to bed."

"Nothing serious I——"

"Oh, no. She's going to play golf with you in the morning. You can spare her for just one night, can't you, Dexter?"

Her smile was kind. She and Dexter liked each other. In the living room he talked for a moment before he said goodnight.

Returning to the College Club, where he had rooms, he stood in the doorway for a moment and watched the dancers. He leaned against the door post, nodded at a man or two—yawned.

"Hello, kiddo."

The familiar voice at his elbow startled him. Judy Jones had left a man and crossed the room to him—Judy Jones, a slender enamelled doll in cloth of gold,[39] gold in a band at her head, gold in two slipper points at her dress's hem. The fragile glow of her face seemed to blossom as she smiled at him. A breeze of warmth and light blew through the room. His hands in the pockets of his dinner jacket tightened spasmodically. He was filled with a sudden excitement.

"When did you get back?" he asked casually.

"Come here and I'll tell you about it."

She turned and he followed her. She had been away—he could have wept at the wonder of her return. She had passed through enchanted streets, doing young things that were like plaintive music. All mysterious happenings, all fresh and quickening hopes, had gone away with her, come back with her now.

She turned in the doorway.

"Have you a car here? If you haven't I have."

"I have a coupé."[40]

In then, with a rustle of golden cloth. He slammed the door. Into so many cars she had stepped—like this—like that—her back against the leather, so—her elbow resting on the door—waiting. She would have been soiled long since had there been anything to soil her,—except herself—but these things were all her own outpouring.

With an effort he forced himself to start the car and avoiding her surprised glance backed into the street. This was nothing, he must remember. She had done this before and he had put her behind him, as he would have slashed a bad account from his books.

He drove slowly downtown and affecting a disinterested abstraction traversed the deserted streets of the business section, peopled here and there, where a movie was giving out its crowd or where consumptive or pugilistic youth lounged in front of pool halls. The clink of glasses and the slap of hands on the bars issued from saloons, cloisters of glazed glass and dirty yellow light.

She was watching him closely and the silence was embarrassing yet in this crisis he could find no casual word with which to profane the hour. At a convenient turning he began to zig-zag back toward the College Club.

"Have you missed me?" she asked suddenly.

"Everybody missed you."

He wondered if she knew of Irene Scheerer. She had been back only a day—her absence had been almost contemporaneous with his engagement.

"What a remark!" Judy laughed sadly—without sadness. She looked at him searchingly. He became absorbed for a moment in the dashboard.

"You're handsomer than you used to be," she said thoughtfully. "Dexter, you have the most rememberable eyes."

He could have laughed at this, but he did not laugh. It was the sort of thing that was said to sophomores. Yet it stabbed at him.

"I'm awfully tired of everything, kiddo." She called everyone kiddo, endowing the obsolete slang[41] with careless, individual com- radie.[42] "I wish you'd marry me."

The directness of this confused him. He should have told her now that he was going to marry another girl but he could not tell her. He could as easily have sworn that he had never loved her.[43]

"I think we'd get along," she continued, on the same note, "unless probably you've forgotten me and fallen in love with another girl."

Her confidence was obviously enormous. She had said, in effect, that she found such a thing impossible to believe, that if it were true he had merely committed a childish indiscretion—and probably to show off. She would forgive him, because it was not a matter of any moment but rather something to be brushed aside lightly.

"Of course you could never love anybody but me," she continued. "I like the way you love me. Oh, Dexter, have you forgotten last year?"

"No, I haven't forgotten."

"Neither have I!"

Was she sincerely moved—or was she carried along by the wave of her own acting?

"I wish we could be like that again," she said, and he forced himself to answer:

"I don't think we can."

"I suppose not. . . . I hear you're giving Irene Scheerer a violent rush."

There was not the faintest emphasis on the name, yet Dexter was suddenly ashamed.

"Oh, take me home," cried Judy suddenly. "I don't want to go back to that idiotic dance—with those children."

Then, as he turned up the street that led to the residence district, Judy began to cry quietly to herself. He had never seen her cry before.

The dark street lightened, the dwellings of the rich loomed up around them, he stopped his coupé in front of the great white bulk of the Mortimer Jones' house, somnolent, gorgeous, drenched with the splendor of the damp moonlight. Its solidity startled him. The strong walls, the fine steel of the girders, the breadth and beam and pomp of it were there only to bring out the contrast with the young beauty beside him. It was sturdy to accentuate her slightness—as if to show what a breeze could be generated by a butterfly's wing.

He sat perfectly quiet, his nerves in wild clamor, afraid that if he moved he would find her irresistibly in his arms. Two tears had rolled down her wet face and trembled on her upper lip.

"I'm more beautiful than anybody else," she said brokenly, "why can't I be happy?" Her moist eyes tore at his stability—mouth turned slowly downward with an exquisite sadness, "I'd like to marry you if you'll have me, Dexter. I suppose you think I'm not worth having but I'll be so beautiful for you, Dexter."

A million phrases of anger, of pride, of passion, of hatred, of tenderness fought on his lips. Then a perfect wave of emotion washed over him, carrying off with it a sediment of wisdom, of convention, of doubt, of honor. This was his girl who was speaking, his own, his beautiful, his pride.

"Won't you come in?" he heard her draw in her breath sharply.

Waiting.

"All right," his voice was trembling, "I'll come in."

It seems strange to say that neither when it was over nor a long time afterward did he regret that night. Looking at it from the perspective of ten years, the fact that Judy's flare for him endured just one month seemed of little importance. Nor did it matter that by his yielding he subjected himself to a deeper agony in the end and gave serious hurt to Irene Scheerer and to Irene's parents who had befriended him. There was nothing sufficiently pictorial about Irene's grief to stamp itself on his mind.

Dexter was at bottom hard-minded. The attitude of the city on his action was of no importance to him, not because he was going to leave the city, but because any outside attitude on the situation seemed superficial. He was completely indifferent to popular opinion.

Nor, when he had seen that it was no use, that he did not possess in himself the power to move fundamentally or to hold Judy Jones, did he bear any malice toward her. He loved her and he would love her until the day he was too old for loving—but he could not have her. So he tasted the deep pain that is reserved only for the strong, just as he had tasted for a little while the deep happiness.

Even the ultimate falsity of the grounds upon which Judy terminated the engagement that she did not want to "take him away" from Irene, that it was on her conscience—did not revolt him. He was beyond any revulsion or any amusement.

He went east in February with the intention of selling out his laundries and settling in New York—but the war came to America in March[44] and changed his plans. He returned to the west, handed over the management of the business to his partner and went into the first officers' training camp in late April. He was one of those young thousands who greeted the war with a certain amount of relief, welcoming the liberation from webs of tangled emotion.

This story is not his biography, remember, although things creep into it which have nothing to do with those dreams he had when he was young. We are almost done with them and with him now. There is only one more incident to be related here and it happens seven years farther on.

It took place in New York, where he had done well—so well that there were no barriers too high for him now. He was thirty-two years old, and, except for one flying trip immediately after the war, he had not been west in seven years. A man named Devlin from Detroit came into his office to see him in a business way, and then and there this incident occurred, and closed out, so to speak, this particular side of his life.

"So you're from the middle west," said the man Devlin with careless curiosity. "That's funny—I thought men like you were probably born and raised on Wall Street. You know—wife of one of my best friends in Detroit came from your city. I was an usher at the wedding."

Dexter waited with no apprehension of what was coming. There was a magic that his city would never lose for him. Just as Judy's house had always seemed to him more mysterious and gay than other houses, so his dream of the city itself, now that he had gone from it, was pervaded with a melancholy beauty.[45]

"Judy Simms," said Devlin with no particular interest. "Judy Jones she was once."

"Yes, I knew her." A dull impatience spread over him. He had heard, of course, that she was married,—perhaps deliberately he had heard no more.

"Awfully nice girl," brooded Devlin meaninglessly. "I'm sort of sorry for her."

"Why?" Something in Dexter was alert, receptive, at once.

"Oh, Joe Simms has gone to pieces in a way. I don't mean he beats her, you understand, or anything like that. But he drinks and runs around——"

"Doesn't she run around?"

"No. Stays at home with her kids."

"Oh."

"She's a little too old for him," said Devlin.

"Too old!" cried Dexter. "why man, she's only twenty-seven."

He was possessed with a wild notion of rushing out into the streets and taking a train to Detroit. He rose to his feet, spasmodically, involuntarily.

"I guess you're busy," Devlin apologized quickly. "I didn't realize——"

"No, I'm not busy," said Dexter, steadying his voice, "I'm not busy at all. Not busy at all. Did you say she was—twenty-seven. No, I said she was twenty-seven."

"Yes, you did," agreed Devlin drily.

"Go on, then. Go on."

"What do you mean?"

"About Judy Jones."

Devlin looked at him helplessly.

"Well, that's—I told you all there is to it. He treats her like the devil. Oh, they're not going to get divorced or anything. When he's particularly outrageous she forgives him. In fact, I'm inclined to think she loves him. She was a pretty girl when she first came to Detroit."

A pretty girl! The phrase struck Dexter as ludicrous.

"Isn't she—a pretty girl any more?"

"Oh, she's all right."

"Look here," said Dexter, sitting down suddenly, "I don't understand. You say she was a 'pretty girl' and now you say she's 'all right.' I don't understand what you mean—Judy Jones wasn't a pretty girl, at all. She was a great beauty. Why, I knew her, I knew her. She was——"

Devlin laughed pleasantly.

"I'm not trying to start a row," he said. "I think Judy's a nice girl and I like her. I can't understand how a man like Joe Simms could fall madly in love with her, but he did." Then he added, "Most of the women like her."

Dexter looked closely at Devlin, thinking wildly that there must be a reason for this, some insensitivity in the man or some private malice.

"Lots of women fade just-like-*that*," Devlin snapped his fingers. "You must have seen it happen. Perhaps I've forgotten how pretty she was at her wedding. I've seen her so much since then, you see. She has nice eyes."

A sort of dullness settled down upon Dexter. For the first time in his life he felt like getting very drunk. He knew that he was laughing loudly at something Devlin had said but he did not know what it was or why it was funny. When Devlin went, in a few minutes, he lay down on his lounge and looked out the window at the New York skyline into which the sun was sinking in dull lovely shades of pink and gold.

He had thought that having nothing else to lose he was invulnerable at last—but he knew that he had just lost something more, as surely as if he had married Judy Jones and seen her fade away before his eyes.

The dream was gone. Something had been taken from him. In a sort of panic he pushed the palms of his hands into his eyes and tried to bring up a picture of the waters lapping at Lake Erminie and the moonlit verandah, and gingham on the golf links and the dry sun and the gold color of her neck's soft down. And her mouth damp to his kisses and her eyes plaintive with melancholy and her freshness like new fine linen in the morning. Why these things were no longer in the world. They had existed and they existed no more.

For the first time in years the tears were streaming down his face. But they were for himself now. He did not care about mouth and eyes and moving hands. He wanted to care and he could not care. For he had gone away and he could never go back any more. The gates were closed, the sun was gone down and there was no beauty but the grey beauty of steel that withstands all time. Even the grief he could have borne was left behind in the country of illusion, of youth, of the richness of life, where his winter dreams had flourished.

"Long ago," he said, "long ago, there was something in me, but now that thing is gone. Now that thing is gone, that thing is gone. I cannot cry. I cannot care. That thing will come back no more."

Dice, Brassknuckles & Guitar

Hearst's International
May 1923
$1,500

A Typical Fitzgerald Story

Parts of New Jersey, as you know, are under water, and other parts are under continual surveillance by the authorities.[1] But here and there lie patches of garden country dotted with old-fashioned frame mansions, which have wide shady porches and a red swing on the lawn. And perhaps, on the widest and shadiest of the porches there is even a hammock left over from the hammock days, stirring gently in a mid-Victorian wind.

When tourists come to such last-century landmarks they stop their cars and gaze for a while and then mutter: "Well, thank God this age is joined on to *some*thing" or else they say: "Well, of course, that house is mostly halls and has a thousand rats and one bathroom, but there's an atmosphere about it——"

The tourist doesn't stay long. He drives on to his Elizabethan villa of pressed cardboard or his early Norman meat-market or his medieval Italian pigeon-coop[2]—because this is the twentieth century and Victorian houses are as unfashionable as the works of Humphry Ward.[3]

He can't see the hammock from the road—but sometimes there's a girl in the hammock. There was this afternoon. She was asleep in it and apparently unaware of the esthetic horrors which surrounded her, the stone statue of Diana,[4] for instance, which grinned idiotically under the sunlight on the lawn.

There was something enormously yellow about the whole scene— there was this sunlight, for instance, that was yellow, and the hammock was of the particularly hideous yellow peculiar to hammocks, and the girl's yellow hair was spread out upon the hammock in a sort of invidious comparison.

She slept with her lips closed and her hands clasped behind her head, as it is proper for young girls to sleep. Her breast rose and fell slightly with no more emphasis than the sway of the hammock's fringe.

Her name, Amanthis, was as old-fashioned as the house she lived in. I regret to say that her mid-Victorian connections ceased abruptly at this point.

Now if this were a moving picture (as, of course, I hope it will some day be)[5] I would take as many thousand feet of her as I was allowed— then I would move the camera up close and show the yellow down on the back of her neck where her hair stopped and the warm color of her cheeks and arms, because I like to think of her sleeping there, as you yourself might have slept, back in your young days. Then I would hire a man named Israel Glucose to write some idiotic line of transition, and switch thereby to another scene that was taking place at no particular spot far down the road.

In a moving automobile sat a southern gentleman accompanied by his body-servant.[6] He was on his way, after a fashion, to New York but he was somewhat hampered by the fact that the upper and lower portions of his automobile were no longer in exact juxtaposition. In fact from time to time the two riders would dismount, shove the body on to the chassis, corner to corner, and then continue onward, vibrating slightly in involuntary unison with the motor.

Except that it had no door in back the car might have been built early in the mechanical age. It was covered with the mud of eight states and adorned in front by an enormous but defunct motometer[7] and behind by a mangy pennant bearing the legend "Tarleton, Ga."[8] In the dim past someone had begun to paint the hood yellow but unfortunately had been called away when but half through the task.

As the gentleman and his body-servant were passing the house where Amanthis lay beautifully asleep in the hammock, something happened—the body fell off the car. My only apology for stating this so suddenly is that it happened very suddenly indeed. When the noise had died down and the dust had drifted away master and man arose and inspected the two halves.

"Look-a-there," said the gentleman in disgust, "the doggone thing got all separated that time."

"She bust in two," agreed the body-servant.

"Hugo," said the gentleman, after some consideration, "we got to get a hammer an' nails an' *tack* it on."

They glanced up at the Victorian house. On all sides faintly irregular fields stretched away to a faintly irregular unpopulated horizon.

There was no choice, so the black Hugo opened the gate and followed his master up a gravel walk, casting only the blasé glances of a confirmed traveler at the red swing and the stone statue of Diana which turned on them a storm-crazed stare.

At the exact moment when they reached the porch Amanthis awoke, sat up suddenly and looked them over.

The gentleman was young, perhaps twenty-four, and his name was Jim Powell.[9] He was dressed in a tight and dusty readymade suit which was evidently expected to take flight at a moment's notice for it was secured to his body by a line of six preposterous buttons.

There were supernumerary buttons upon the coat-sleeves also and Amanthis could not resist a glance to determine whether or not more buttons ran up the side of his trouser leg. But the trouser bottoms were distinguished only by their shape, which was that of a bell.[10] His vest was cut low, barely restraining an amazing necktie from fluttering in the wind.

He bowed formally, dusting his knees with a thatched straw hat. Simultaneously he smiled, half shutting his faded blue eyes and displaying white and beautifully symmetrical teeth.

"Good evenin'," he said in abandoned Georgian. "My automobile has met with an accident out yonder by your gate. I wondered if it wouldn't be too much to ask you if I could have the use of a hammer and some tacks—nails, for a little while."

Amanthis laughed. For a moment she laughed uncontrollably. Mr. Jim Powell laughed, politely and appreciatively, with her. His body-servant, deep in the throes of colored adolescence, alone preserved a dignified gravity.

"I better introduce who I am, maybe," said the visitor. "My name's Powell. I'm a resident of Tarleton, Georgia. This here nigger's my boy Hugo."

"Your *son!*" The girl stared from one to the other in wild fascination.

"No, he's my body-servant, I guess you'd call it. We call a nigger a boy down yonder."

At this reference to the finer customs of his native soil the boy Hugo put his hands behind his back and looked darkly and superciliously down the lawn.

"Yas'm," he muttered, "I'm a body-servant."

"Where you going in your automobile," demanded Amanthis.

"Goin' north for the summer."

"Where to?"

The tourist waved his hand with a careless gesture as if to indicate the Adirondacks, the Thousand Islands, Newport[11]—but he said:

"We're tryin' New York."

"Have you ever been there before?"

"Never have. But I been to Atlanta lots of times. An' we passed through all kinds of cities this trip. Man!"

He whistled to express the enormous spectacularity of his recent travels.

"Listen," said Amanthis intently, "you better have something to eat. Tell your—your body-servant to go 'round in back and ask the cook to send us out some sandwiches and lemonade. Or maybe you don't drink lemonade—very few people do any more."

Mr Powell by a circular motion of his finger sped Hugo on the designated mission. Then he seated himself gingerly in a rocking-chair and began revolving his thatched straw hat rapidly in his hands.

"You cer'nly are mighty kind," he told her. "An' if I wanted anything stronger than lemonade I got a bottle of good old corn[12] out in the car. I brought it along because I thought maybe I wouldn't be able to drink the whisky they got up here."

"Listen," she said, "my name's Powell too. Amanthis Powell."

"Say, is that right?" He laughed ecstatically. "Maybe we're kin to each other. I come from mighty good people," he went on. "Pore though. I got some money because my aunt she was using it to keep her in a sanitarium and she died." He paused, presumably out of respect to his late aunt. Then he concluded with brisk nonchalance, "I ain't touched the principal but I got a lot of the income all at once so I thought I'd come north for the summer."

At this point Hugo reappeared on the veranda steps and became audible.

"White lady back there she asked me don't I want eat some too. What I tell her?"

"You tell her yes ma'am if she be so kind," directed his master. And as Hugo retired he confided to Amanthis: "That boy's got no sense at all. He don't want to do nothing without I tell him he can. I brought him up," he added, not without pride.

When the sandwiches arrived Mr. Powell stood up. He was unaccustomed to white servants and obviously expected an introduction.

"Are you a married lady?" he inquired of Amanthis, when the servant was gone.

"No," she answered, and added from the security of eighteen, "I'm an old maid."

Again he laughed politely.

"You mean you're a society girl."

She shook her head. Mr. Powell noted with embarrassed enthusiasm the particular yellowness of her yellow hair.

"Does this old place look like it?" she said cheerfully. "No, you perceive in me a daughter of the countryside. Color—one hundred percent spontaneous—in the daytime anyhow. Suitors—promising young barbers from the neighboring village with somebody's late hair still clinging to their coat-sleeves."

"Your daddy oughtn't to let you go with a country barber," said the tourist disapprovingly. He considered—— "You ought to be a New York society girl."

"No." Amanthis shook her head sadly. "I'm too good-looking. To be a New York society girl you have to have a long nose and projecting teeth and dress like the actresses did three years ago."

Jim began to tap his foot rhythmically on the porch and in a moment Amanthis discovered that she was unconsciously doing the same thing.

"Stop!" she commanded, "Don't make me do that."

He looked down at his foot.

"Excuse me," he said humbly. "I don't know—it's just something I do."

This intense discussion was now interrupted by Hugo who appeared on the steps bearing a hammer and a handful of nails.

Mr. Powell arose unwillingly and looked at his watch.

"We got to go, daggone it," he said, frowning heavily. "See here. Wouldn't you *like* to be a New York society girl and go to those dances an' all, like you read about, where they throw gold pieces away?"

She looked at him with a curious expression.

"Don't your folks know some society people?" he went on.

"All I've got's my daddy—and, you see, he's a judge."[13]

"That's too bad," he agreed.

She got herself by some means from the hammock and they went down toward the road, side by side.

"Well, I'll keep my eyes open for you and let you know," he persisted. "A pretty girl like you ought to go round in society. We may be kin to each other, you see, and us Powells ought to stick together."

"What are you going to do in New York?"

They were now almost at the gate and the tourist pointed to the two depressing sectors of his automobile.

"I'm goin' to drive a taxi. This one right here. Only it's got so it busts in two all the time."

"You're going to drive *that* in New York?"

Jim looked at her uncertainly. Such a pretty girl should certainly control the habit of shaking all over upon no provocation at all.

"Yes mamm," he said with dignity.

Amanthis watched while they placed the upper half of the car upon the lower half and nailed it severely into place. Then Mr. Powell took the wheel and his body-servant climbed in beside him.

"I'm cer'nly very much obliged to you indeed for your hospitality. Convey my respects to your father."

"I will," she assured him. "Come back and see me, if you don't mind barbers in the room."

He dismissed this unpleasant thought with a gesture.

"Your company would always be charming." He put the car into gear as though to drown out the temerity of his parting speech. "You're the prettiest girl I've seen up north—by far."

Then with a groan and a rattle Mr. Powell of southern Georgia with his own car and his own body-servant and his own ambitions and his own private cloud of dust continued on North for the summer.

She thought she would never see him again. She lay in her hammock, slim and beautiful, opened her left eye slightly to see June come in and then closed it and retired contentedly back into her dreams.

But one day when the midsummer vines had climbed the precarious sides of the red swing on the lawn Mr. Jim Powell of Tarleton, Georgia, came vibrating back into her life. They sat on the wide porch as before.

"I've got a great scheme," he told her.

"Did you drive your taxi like you said?"

"Yes mamm, but the business was right bad. I waited around in front of all those hotels and theaters an' nobody ever got in."

"Nobody?"

"Well, one night there was some drunk fellas they got in, only just as I was gettin' started my automobile came apart. And another night it was rainin' and there wasn't no other taxis and a lady got in because she said she had to go a long ways. But before we got there she made me stop and she got out. She seemed kinda mad and she went walkin' off in the rain. Mighty proud lot of people they got up in New York."

"And so you're going home?" asked Amanthis sympathetically.

"No *mamm*. I got an idea." His blue eyes grew narrow. "Has that barber been around here—with hair on his sleeves?"

"No. He's—he's gone away."

"Well, then, first thing is I want to leave this car of mine here with you, if that's all right. It ain't the right color for a taxi. To pay for its keep I'd like to have you drive it just as much as you want. 'Long as you got a hammer an' nails with you there ain't much bad that can happen——"

"I'll take care of it," interrupted Amanthis, "but where are *you* going?"

"Southampton. It's about the most aristocratic watering trough—watering-place there is around here,[14] so that's where I'm going."

She sat up in amazement.

"What are you going to do there?"

"Listen." He leaned toward her confidentially. "Were you serious about wanting to be a New York society girl?"

"Deadly serious."

"That's all I wanted to know," he said inscrutably. "You just wait here on this porch a couple of weeks and—and sleep. And if any barbers come to see you with hair on their sleeves you tell 'em you're too sleepy to see 'em."

"What then?"

"Then you'll hear from me. Just tell your old daddy he can do all the judging he wants but you're goin' to do some *dancin'*. Mamm," he continued decisively, "you talk about society! Before one month I'm goin' to have you in more society than you ever saw."

Further than this he would say nothing. His manner conveyed that she was going to be suspended over a perfect pool of gaiety and violently immersed, to an accompaniment of: "Is it gay enough for you, mamm? Shall I let in a little more excitement, mamm?"

"Well," answered Amanthis, lazily considering, "there are few things for which I'd forego the luxury of sleeping through July and August—but if you'll write me a letter I'll—I'll run up to Southampton."

Jim snapped his fingers ecstatically.

"More society," he assured her with all the confidence at his command, "than anybody ever saw."

Three days later a young man wearing a straw hat that might have been cut from the thatched roof of an English cottage rang the doorbell of the enormous and astounding Madison Harlan house at Southampton. He asked the butler if there were any people in the house between the ages of sixteen and twenty. He was informed that Miss Genevieve Harlan and Mr. Ronald Harlan answered that description and thereupon he handed in a most peculiar card and requested in fetching Georgian that it be brought to their attention.

As a result he was closeted for almost an hour with Mr. Ronald Harlan (who was a student at the Hillkiss[15] School) and Miss Genevieve Harlan (who was not uncelebrated at Southampton dances). When he left he bore a short note in Miss Harlan's handwriting which he presented together with his peculiar card at the next large estate. It happened to be that of the Clifton Garneaus.[16] Here, as if by magic, the same audience was granted him.

He went on—it was a hot day, and men who could not afford to do so were carrying their coats on the public highway, but Jim, a native of southernmost Georgia was as fresh and cool at the last house as at the first. He visited ten houses that day. Anyone following him in his course might have taken him to be some curiously gifted book-agent with a much sought-after volume as his stock in trade.

There was something in his unexpected demand for the adolescent members of the family which made hardened butlers lose their critical acumen. As he left each house a close observer might have seen that fascinated eyes followed him to the door and excited voices whispered something which hinted at a future meeting.

The second day he visited twelve houses. Southampton has grown enormously—he might have kept on his round for a week and never seen the same butler twice—but it was only the palatial, the amazing houses which intrigued him.

On the third day he did a thing that many people have been told to do and few have done—he hired a hall. Perhaps the sixteen-to-twenty-year-old people in the enormous houses had told him to. The hall he hired had once been "Mr. Snorkey's Private Gymnasium for Gentlemen." It was situated over a garage on the south edge of Southampton and in the days of its prosperity had been, I regret to say, a place where gentlemen could, under Mr. Snorkey's direction, work off the effects of the night before. It was now abandoned— Mr. Snorkey had given up and gone away and died.

We will now skip three weeks during which time we may assume that the project which had to do with hiring a hall and visiting the two dozen largest houses in Southampton got under way.

The day to which we will skip was the July day on which Mr. James Powell sent a wire to Miss Amanthis Powell saying that if she still aspired to the gaiety of the highest society she should set out for Southampton by the earliest possible train. He himself would meet her at the station.

Jim was no longer a man of leisure so when she failed to arrive at the time her wire had promised he grew restless. He supposed she was coming on a later train, turned to go back to his—his project—and met her entering the station from the street side.

"Why, how did you———"

"Well," said Amanthis, "I arrived this morning instead, and I didn't want to bother you so I found a respectable, not to say dull, boarding-house on the Ocean Road."

She was quite different from the indolent Amanthis of the porch hammock, he thought. She wore a suit of robins' egg blue and a rakish young hat with a curling feather—she was attired not unlike those young ladies between sixteen and twenty who of late were absorbing his attention. Yes, she would do very well.

He bowed her profoundly into a taxicab and got in beside her.

"Isn't it about time you told me your scheme?" she suggested.

"Well, it's about these society girls up here." He waved his hand airily. "I know 'em all."

"Where are they?"

"Right now they're with Hugo. You remember—that's my body-servant."

"With Hugo!" Her eyes widened. "Why? What's it all about?"

"Well, I got—I got sort of a school, I guess you'd call it."

"A school?"

"It's a sort of Academy. And I'm the head of it. I invented it."

He flipped a card from his case as though he were shaking down a thermometer.

"Look."

She took the card. In large lettering it bore the legend

JAMES POWELL; J.M.
"Dice, Brassknuckles and Guitar"

She stared in amazement.

"Dice, Brassknuckles and Guitar?" she repeated in awe.

"Yes mamm."

"What does it mean? What———do you *sell* 'em?"

"No mamm, I teach 'em. It's a profession."

"Dice, Brassknuckles and Guitar? What's the J. M.?"

"That stands for Jazz Master."

"But what *is* it? What's it about?"

"Well, you see, it's like this. One night when I was in New York I got talkin' to a young fella who was drunk. He was one of my fares. And he'd taken some society girl somewhere and lost her."

"*Lost* her?"

"Yes mamm. He forgot her, I guess. And he was right worried. Well, I got to thinkin' that these girls nowadays—these society girls— they lead a sort of dangerous life and my course of study offers a means of protection against these dangers."

"You teach 'em to use brassknuckles?"

"Yes mamm, if necessary. Look here, you take a girl and she goes into some café where she's got no business to go. Well then, her escort he gets a little too much to drink an' he goes to sleep an' then some other fella comes up and says 'Hello, sweet mamma' or whatever one of those mashers[17] says up here. What does she do? She can't scream, on account of no real lady'll scream nowadays—no—She just reaches down in her pocket and slips her fingers into a pair of Powell's defensive brassknuckles, debutante's size, executes what I call the Society Hook, and *Wham!* that big fella's on his way to the cellar."

"Well—what—what's the guitar for?" whispered the awed Amanthis. "Do they have to knock somebody over with the guitar?"

"No, *mamm!*" exclaimed Jim in horror. "No mamm. In my course no lady would be taught to raise a guitar against anybody. I teach 'em to play. Shucks! you ought to hear 'em. Why, when I've given 'em two lessons you'd think some of 'em was colored."

"And the dice?"

"Dice? I'm related to a dice. My grandfather was a dice. I teach 'em how to make those dice perform. I protect pocketbook as well as person."[18]

"Did you——Have you got many pupils?"

"Mamm I got all the really nice, rich people in the place. What I told you ain't all. I teach lots of things. I teach 'em the jellyroll—and the Mississippi Sunrise.[19] Why, there was one girl she came to me and said she wanted to learn to snap her fingers. I mean *real*ly snap 'em—like they do. She said she never could snap her fingers since she was little. I gave her two lessons and now *Wham!* Her daddy says he's goin' to leave home."

"When do you have it?" demanded the weak and shaken Amanthis.

"Three times a week. We're goin' there right now."

"And where do I fit in?"

"Well, you'll just be one of the pupils. I got it fixed up that you come from very high-tone people down in New Jersey. I didn't tell 'em your daddy was a judge—I told 'em he was the man that had the patent on lump sugar."[20]

She gasped.

"So all you got to do," he went on, "is to pretend you never saw no barber."

They were now at the south end of the village and Amanthis saw a row of cars parked in front of a two-story building. The cars were all low, long, rakish and of a brilliant hue. They were the sort of car that is manufactured to solve the millionaire's problem on his son's eighteenth birthday.

Then Amanthis was ascending a narrow stairs to the second story. Here, painted on a door from which came the sounds of music and laughter were the words:

JAMES POWELL; J. M.
"Dice, Brassknuckles and Guitar"
Mon.—Wed.—Fri.
Hours 3–5 P.M.

"Now if you'll just step this way——" said the Principal, pushing open the door.

Amanthis found herself in a long, bright room, populated with girls and men of about her own age. The scene presented itself to her at first as a sort of animated afternoon tea but after a moment she began to see, here and there, a motive and a pattern to the proceedings.

The students were scattered into groups, sitting, kneeling, standing, but all rapaciously intent on the subjects which engrossed them. From six young ladies gathered in a ring around some indistinguishable objects came a medley of cries and exclamations—plaintive, pleading, supplicating, exhorting, imploring and lamenting—their voices serving as tenor to an undertone of mysterious clatters.

Next to this group, four young men were surrounding an adolescent black, who proved to be none other than Mr. Powell's late body-servant. The young men were roaring at Hugo apparently unrelated phrases, expressing a wide gamut of emotion. Now their voices rose to a sort of clamor, now they spoke softly and gently, with mellow implication. Every little while Hugo would answer them with words of approbation, correction or disapproval.

"What are they doing?" whispered Amanthis to Jim.

"That there's a course in southern accent. Lot of young men up here want to learn southern accent—so we teach it—Georgia, Florida, Alabama, Eastern Shore, Ole Virginian. Some of 'em even want straight nigger—for song purposes."

They walked around among the groups. Some girls with metal knuckles were furiously insulting two punching bags on each of which was painted the leering, winking face of a "masher." A mixed group, led by a banjo tom-tom, were rolling harmonic syllables from their guitars. There were couples dancing flat-footed in the corner to a phonograph record made by Rastus Muldoon's Savannah Band;[21] there were couples stalking a slow Chicago with a Memphis Side-swoop[22] solemnly around the room.

"Are there any rules?" asked Amanthis.

Jim considered.

"Well," he answered finally, "they can't smoke unless they're over sixteen, and the boys have got to shoot square dice and I don't let 'em bring liquor into the Academy."

"I see."

"And now, Miss Powell, if you're ready I'll ask you to take off your hat and go over and join Miss Genevieve Harlan at that punching bag in the corner." He* raised his voice. "Hugo," he called, "there's a new student here. Equip her with a pair of Powell's Defensive Brassknuckles—debutante size."

I regret to say that I never saw Jim Powell's famous Jazz School in action nor followed his personally conducted tours into the mysteries of Dice, Brassknuckles and Guitar. So I can give you only such details as were later reported to me by one of his admiring pupils. During all the discussion of it afterwards no one ever denied that it was an enormous success, and no pupil ever regretted having received its degree—Bachelor of Jazz.

The parents innocently assumed that it was a sort of musical and dancing academy, but its real curriculum was transmitted from Santa Barbara to Biddeford Pool by that underground associated press which links up the so-called younger generation. Invitations to visit Southampton were at a premium—and Southampton generally is almost as dull for young people as Newport.[23]

The Academy branched out with a small but well-groomed Jazz Orchestra.

"If I could keep it dark," Jim confided to Amanthis, "I'd have up Rastus Muldoon's Band from Savannah. That's the band I've always wanted to lead."

He was making money. His charges were not exorbitant—as a rule his pupils were not particularly flush—but he moved from his boarding-house to the Casino Hotel where he took a suite and had Hugo serve him his breakfast in bed.

* *Hearst's International* broke the text at this point after six contiguous pages (pp. 8–13), continuing the story on p. 145 where it resumed with the editorial gloss "F. Scott Fitzgerald Holds the Mirror up to Youth—From page 13."

The establishing of Amanthis as a member of Southampton's younger set was easier than he had expected. Within a week she was known to everyone in the school by her first name. Miss Genevieve Harlan took such a fancy to her that she was invited to a sub-deb[24] dance at the Harlan house—and evidently acquitted herself with tact, for thereafter she was invited to almost every such entertainment in Southampton.

Jim saw less of her than he would have liked. Not that her manner toward him changed—she walked with him often in the mornings, she was always willing to listen to his plans—but after she was taken up by the fashionable her evenings seemed to be monopolized. Several times Jim arrived at her boarding-house to find her out of breath as if she had just come in at a run, presumably from some festivity in which he had no share.

So as the summer waned he found that one thing was lacking to complete the triumph of his enterprise. Despite the hospitality shown to Amanthis, the doors of Southampton were closed to him. Polite to, or rather, fascinated by him as his pupils were from three to five, after that hour they moved in another world.

His was the position of a golf professional who, though he may fraternize, and even command, on the links, loses his privileges with the sun-down. He may look in the club window but he cannot dance. And, likewise, it was not given to Jim to see his teachings put into effect. He could hear the gossip of the morning after—that was all.

But while the golf professional, being English, holds himself proudly below his patrons, Jim Powell, who "came from a right good family down there—pore though," lay awake many nights in his hotel bed and heard the music drifting into his window from the Katzbys' house or the Beach Club, and turned over restlessly and wondered what was the matter. In the early days of his success he had bought himself a dress-suit, thinking that he would soon have a chance to wear it—but it still lay untouched in the box in which it had come from the tailor's.

Perhaps, he thought, there was some real gap which separated him from the rest. It worried him. One boy in particular, Martin Van Vleck, son of Van Vleck the ash-can King, made him conscious of the gap. Van Vleck was twenty-one, a tutoring-school product who still hoped to enter Yale. Several times Jim had heard him make remarks not intended for Jim's ear—once in regard to the suit with multiple buttons, again in reference to Jim's long, pointed shoes.[25] Jim had passed these over.

He knew that Van Vleck was attending the school chiefly to monopolize the time of little Martha Katzby, who was just sixteen and too young to have attention of a boy of twenty-one—especially the attention of Van Vleck, who was so spiritually exhausted by his educational failures that he drew on the rather exhaustible innocence of sixteen.

It was late in September, two days before the Harlan dance which was to be the last and biggest of the season for this younger crowd. Jim, as usual, was not invited. He had hoped that he would be. The two young Harlans, Ronald and Genevieve, had been his first patrons when he arrived at Southampton—and it was Genevieve who had taken such a fancy to Amanthis. To have been at their dance—the most magnificent dance of all—would have crowned and justified the success of the waning summer.

His class, gathering for the afternoon, was loudly anticipating the next day's revel with no more thought of him than if he had been the family butler. Hugo, standing beside Jim, chuckled suddenly and remarked:

"Look yonder that man Van Vleck. He paralyzed. He been havin' powerful lotta corn this evenin'."

Jim turned and stared at Van Vleck who had linked arms with little Martha Katzby and was saying something to her in a low voice. Jim saw her try to draw away.

He put his whistle to his mouth and blew it.

"All right," he cried, "Le's go! Group one tossin' the drumstick, high an' zig-zag, group two, test your mouth organs for the Riverfront Shuffle. Promise 'em sugar! Flatfoots this way! Orchestra—let's have the Florida Drag-Out played as a dirge."

There was an unaccustomed sharpness in his voice and the exercises began with a mutter of facetious protest.

With his smoldering grievance directing itself toward Van Vleck, Jim was walking here and there among the groups when Hugo tapped him suddenly on the arm. He looked around. Two participants had withdrawn from the mouth organ institute—one of them was Van Vleck and he was giving a drink out of his flask to fifteen-year-old Ronald Harlan.

Jim strode across the room. Van Vleck turned defiantly as he came up.

"All right," said Jim, trembling with anger, "you know the rules. You get out!"

The music died slowly away and there was a sudden drifting over in the direction of the trouble. Somebody snickered. An atmosphere of anticipation formed instantly. Despite the fact that they all liked Jim their sympathies were divided—Van Vleck was one of them.

"Get out!" repeated Jim, more quietly.

"Are you talking to me?" inquired Van Vleck coldly.

"Yes."

"Then you better say, sir."

"I wouldn't say, sir, to anybody that'd give a little boy whisky! You get out!"

"Look here!" said Van Vleck furiously. "You've butted in once too much. I've known Ronald since he was two years old. Ask *him* if he wants *you* to tell him what he can do!"

Ronald Harlan, his dignity offended, grew several years older and looked haughtily at Jim.

"Mind your own business!" he said defiantly, albeit a little guiltily.

"Hear that?" demanded Van Vleck. "My God, can't you see you're just a servant? Ronald here'd no more think of asking you to his party than he would his bootlegger."

"Youbettergetout!" cried Jim incoherently.

Van Vleck did not move. Reaching out suddenly Jim caught his wrist and jerking it behind his back forced his arm upward until Van Vleck bent forward in agony. Jim leaned and picked the flask from the floor with his free hand. Then he signed Hugo to open the hall-door, uttered an abrupt "You *step!*" and marched his helpless captive out into the hall where he literally *threw* him downstairs, head over heels bumping from wall to banister, and hurled his flask after him.

Then he reëntered his academy, closed the door behind him and stood with his back against it.

"It—it happens to be a rule that nobody drinks while in this Academy." He paused, looking from face to face, finding there sympathy, awe, disapproval, conflicting emotions. They stirred uneasily. He caught Amanthis's eye, fancied he saw a faint nod of encouragement and, with almost an effort, went on:

"I just *had* to throw that fella out an' you-all know it." Then he concluded with a transparent affectation of dismissing an unimportant matter——"All right, let's go! Orchestra——!"

But no one felt exactly like going on. The spontaneity of the proceedings had been violently disturbed. Someone made a run or two on the sliding guitar and several of the girls began whamming at the leer on the punching bags, but Ronald Harlan, followed by two other boys got their hats and went silently out the door.

Jim and Hugo moved among the groups as usual until a certain measure of routine activity was restored but the enthusiasm was unrecapturable and Jim, shaken and discouraged, considered discontinuing school for the day. But he dared not. If they went home in this mood they might not come back. The whole thing depended on a mood. He must recreate it, he thought frantically—now, at once!

But try as he might, there was little response. He himself was not happy—he could communicate no gaiety to them. They watched his efforts listlessly and, he thought, a little contemptuously.

Then the tension snapped when the door burst suddenly open, precipitating a brace of middle-aged and excited women into the room. No person over twenty-one had ever entered the Academy before—but Van Vleck had gone direct to headquarters. The women were Mrs. Clifton Garneau and Mrs. Poindexter Katzby, two of the most fashionable and, at present, two of the most flurried women in Southampton. They were in search of their daughters as, in these days, so many women continually are.[26]

The business was over in about three minutes.

"And as for you!" cried Mrs. Clifton Garneau in an awful voice, "your idea is to run a bar and—and *opium* den for children! You ghastly, horrible, unspeakable man! I can smell morphin fumes! Don't tell me I can't smell morphin fumes. I can smell morphin fumes!"

"And," bellowed Mrs. Poindexter Katzby, "you have colored men around! You have colored girls hidden![27] I'm going to the police!"

Not content with herding their own daughters from the room they insisted on the exodus of their friends' daughters. Jim was not a little touched when several of them—including even little Martha Katzby, before she was snatched fiercely away by her mother—came up and shook hands with him. But they were all going, haughtily, regretfully or with shamefaced mutters of apology.

"Good-by," he told them wistfully. "In the morning I'll send you the money that's due you."

And, after all, they were not sorry to go. Outside, the sound of their starting motors, the triumphant put-put of their cut-outs[28] cutting the warm September air, was a jubilant sound—a sound of youth and hopes high as the sun. Down to the ocean, to roll in the waves and forget—forget him and their discomfort at his humiliation.

They were gone—he was alone with Hugo in the room. He sat down suddenly with his face in his hands.

"Hugo," he said huskily. "They don't want us up here."

"Don't you care," said a voice.

He looked up to see Amanthis standing beside him.

"You better go with them," he told her. "You better not be seen here with me."

"Why?"

"Because you're in society now and I'm no better to those people than a servant. You're in society—I fixed that up. You better go or they won't invite you to any of their dances."

"They won't anyhow, Jim," she said gently. "They didn't invite me to the one tomorrow night."

He looked up indignantly.

"They *did*n't?"

She shook her head.

"I'll *make* 'em!" he said wildly, "I'll tell 'em they got to. I'll—I'll——"

She came close to him with shining eyes.

"Don't you mind, Jim," she soothed him. "Don't you mind. They don't matter. We'll have a party of our own tomorrow—just you and I."

"I come from right good folks," he said, defiantly. "Pore though."

She laid her hand softly on his shoulder.

"I understand. You're better than all of them put together, Jim."[29]

He got up and went to the window and stared out mournfully into the late afternoon.

"I reckon I should have let you sleep in that hammock."

She laughed.

"I'm awfully glad you didn't."

He turned and faced the room, and his face was dark.

"Sweep up and lock up, Hugo," he said, his voice trembling. "The summer's over and we're going down home."

Autumn had come early. Jim Powell woke next morning to find his room cool, and the phenomenon of frosted breath in September absorbed him for a moment to the exclusion of the day before. Then the lines of his face drooped with unhappiness as he remembered the humiliation which had washed the cheery glitter from the summer. There was nothing left for him except to go back where he was known, where under no provocation were such things said to white people as had been said to him here.

After breakfast a measure of his customary light-heartedness returned. He was a child of the South—brooding was alien to his nature. He could conjure up an injury only a certain number of times before it faded into the great vacancy of the past.

But when, from force of habit he strolled over to his defunct establishment, already as obsolete as Snorkey's late sanitarium, melancholy again dwelt in his heart. Hugo was there, a specter of despair, deep in the lugubrious blues amidst his master's broken hopes.

Usually a few words from Jim were enough to raise him to an inarticulate ecstasy but this morning there were no words to utter. For two months Hugo had lived on a pinnacle of which he had never dreamed. He had enjoyed his work simply and passionately, arriving before school hours and lingering long after Mr. Powell's pupils had gone.

The day dragged toward a not too promising night. Amanthis did not appear and Jim wondered forlornly if she had not changed her mind about dining with him that night. Perhaps it would be better if she were not seen with them. But then, he reflected dismally, no one would see them anyhow—everybody was going to the big dance at the Harlans' house.

When twilight threw unbearable shadows into the school hall he locked it up for the last time, took down the sign "James Powell, J. M., Dice, Brassknuckles and Guitar," and went back to his hotel. Looking over his scrawled accounts he saw that there was another month's rent to pay on his school and some bills for windows broken and new equipment that had hardly been used. Jim had lived in state, and he realized that financially he would have nothing to show for the summer after all.

When he had finished he took his new dress-suit out of its box and inspected it, running his hand over the satin of the lapels and lining. This, at least he owned and perhaps in Tarleton somebody would ask him to a party where he could wear it.

"Shucks!" he said scoffingly. "It was just a no account old academy, anyhow. Some of those boys round the garage down home could of beat it all hollow."

Whistling *Jeanne of Jelly-bean Town*[30] to a not dispirited rhythm Jim encased himself in his first dress-suit and walked downtown.

"Orchids," he said to the clerk. He surveyed his purchase with some pride. He knew that no girl at the Harlan dance would wear anything lovelier than these exotic blossoms that leaned languorously backward against green ferns.

In a taxi-cab, carefully selected to look like a private car, he drove to Amanthis's boarding-house. She came down wearing a rose-colored evening dress into which the orchids melted like colors into a sunset.

"I reckon we'll go to the Casino Hotel," he suggested, "unless you got some other place——"

At their table, looking out over the dark ocean, his mood became a contented sadness. The windows were shut against the cool but the orchestra played *Kalula* and *South Sea Moon*[31] and for awhile, with her young loveliness opposite him, he felt himself to be a romantic participant in the life around him. They did not dance, and he was glad—it would have reminded him of that other brighter and more radiant dance to which they could not go.

After dinner they took a taxi and followed the sandy roads for an hour, glimpsing the now starry ocean through the casual trees.

"I want to thank you," she said, "for all you've done for me, Jim."

"That's all right—we Powells ought to stick together."

"What are you going to do?"

"I'm going to Tarleton tomorrow."

"I'm sorry," she said softly. "Are you going to drive down?"

"I got to. I got to get the car south because I couldn't get what she was worth by sellin' it. You don't suppose anybody's stole my car out of your barn?" he asked in sudden alarm.

She repressed a smile.

"No."

"I'm sorry about this—about you," he went on huskily, "and—and I would like to have gone to just one of their dances. You shouldn't of stayed with me yesterday. Maybe it kept 'em from asking you."

"Jim," she suggested eagerly, "let's go and stand outside and listen to their old music. We don't care."

"They'll be coming out," he objected.

"No, it's too cold. Besides there's nothing they could do to you any more than they *have* done."

She gave the chauffeur a direction and a few minutes later they stopped in front of the heavy Georgian beauty of the Madison Harlan house whence the windows cast their gaiety in bright patches on the lawn. There was laughter inside and the plaintive wind of fashionable horns, and now and again the slow, mysterious shuffle of dancing feet.

"Let's go up close," whispered Amanthis in an ecstatic trance, "I want to hear."

They walked toward the house, keeping in the shadow of the great trees. Jim proceeded with awe—suddenly he stopped and seized Amanthis's arm.

"Man!" he cried in an excited whisper. "Do you know what that is?"

"A night watchman?" Amanthis cast a startled look around.

"It's Rastus Muldoon's Band from Savannah! Boy! I heard 'em once, an[32] I *know*. It's Rastus Muldoon's Band!"

They moved closer till they could see first pompadours, then slicked male heads, and high coiffures and finally even bobbed hair pressed under black ties. They could distinguish chatter below the ceaseless laughter. Two figures appeared on the porch, gulped something quickly from flasks and returned inside. But the music had bewitched Jim Powell. His eyes were fixed and he moved his feet like a blind man.

Pressed in close behind some dark bushes they listened. The number ended. A breeze from the ocean blew over them and Jim shivered slightly. Then, in a wistful whisper:

"I've always wanted to lead that band. Just once." His voice grew listless. "Come on. Let's go. I reckon I don't belong around here."

He held out his arm to her but instead of taking it she stepped suddenly out of the bushes and into a bright patch of light.

"Come on, Jim," she said startlingly, "Let's go inside."

"What——?"

She seized his arm and though he drew back in a sort of stupefied horror at her boldness she urged him persistently toward the great front door.

"Watch out!" he gasped. "Somebody's coming out of that house and see us."

"No, Jim," she said firmly, "Nobody's coming out of that house— but two people are going in."

"Why?" he demanded wildly, standing in full glare of the porte-cochére lamps.[33] "Why?"

"Why?" she mocked him, "Why, just because this dance happens to be given for me."

He thought she was mad.

"Come home before they see us," he begged her.

The great doors swung open and a gentleman stepped out on the porch. In horror Jim recognized Mr. Madison Harlan. He made a movement as though to break away and run. But the man walked down the steps holding out both hands to Amanthis.

"Hello at last," he cried "Where on earth have you two been? Cousin Amanthis——" He kissed her, and turned cordially to Jim. "And for you, Mr. Powell," he went on, "to make up for being late you've got to promise that for just one number you're going to lead that band."

New Jersey was warm, all except the part that was under water, and that mattered only to the fishes. All the tourists who rode through the long green miles stopped their cars in front of a spreading old-fashioned country house and looked at the red swing on the lawn and the wide, shady porch, and sighed and drove on—swerving a little to avoid a jet-black body-servant in the road. The body-servant was applying a hammer and nails to a decayed flivver[34] which flaunted from its rear the legend, "Tarleton, Ga."

A girl with yellow hair and a warm color to her face was lying in the hammock looking as though she could fall asleep any moment. Near her sat a gentleman in an extraordinarily tight suit. They had come down together the day before from the fashionable resort at Southampton.

"When you first appeared," she was explaining, "I never thought I'd see you again so I made that up about the barber and all. As a matter of fact I've been around quite a bit—with or without brassknuckles. I'm coming out[35] this autumn."

"I reckon I had a lot to learn," said Jim.

"And you see," went on Amanthis, looking at him rather anxiously, "I'd been invited up to Southampton to visit my cousins—and when you said you were going, I wanted to see what you'd do. I always slept at the Harlan's but I kept a room at the boarding-house so you wouldn't know. The reason I didn't get there on the right train was because I had to come early and warn a lot of people to pretend not to know me."

Jim got up, nodding his head in comprehension.

"I reckon I and Hugo had better be movin' along. We got to make Baltimore by night."

"That's a long way."

"I want to sleep south tonight," he said simply.

Together they walked down the path and past the idiotic statue of Diana on the lawn.

"You see," added Amanthis gently, "you don't have to be rich up here in order to—to go around, any more than you do in Georgia——" She broke off abruptly, "Won't you come back next year and start another Academy?"

"No mamm, not me. That Mr. Harlan told me I could go on with the one I had but I told him no."

"Haven't you——didn't you make money."

"No mamm," he answered. "I got enough of my own income to just get me home. I didn't have my principal along. One time I was way ahead but I was livin' high and there was my rent an' apparatus and those musicians. Besides, there at the end I had to pay back what they'd advanced me for their lessons."

"You shouldn't have done that!" cried Amanthis indignantly.

"They didn't want me to, but I told 'em they'd have to take it."

He didn't consider it necessary to mention that Mr. Harlan had tried to present him with a check.

They reached the automobile just as Hugo drove in his last nail. Jim opened a pocket of the door and took from it an unlabeled bottle containing a whitish-yellow liquid.

"I intended to get you a present," he told her awkwardly, "But my money got away before I could, so I thought I'd send you something from Georgia. This here's just a personal remembrance. It won't do for you to drink but maybe after you come out into society you might want to show some of those young fellas what good old corn tastes like."

She took the bottle.

"Thank you, Jim."

"That's all right." He turned to Hugo. "I reckon we'll go along now. Give the lady the hammer."

"Oh, you can have the hammer," said Amanthis tearfully. "Oh, won't you promise to come back?"

"Someday—maybe."

He looked for a moment at her yellow hair and her blue eyes misty with sleep and tears. Then he got into his car and as his foot found the clutch his whole manner underwent a change.

"I'll say good-by mamm," he announced with impressive dignity, "we're goin' south for the winter."

The gesture of his straw hat indicated Palm Beach, St. Augustine, Miami.[36] His body-servant spun the crank, gained his seat and became part of the intense vibration into which the automobile was thrown.

"South for the winter," repeated Jim, and then he added softly, "You're the prettiest girl I ever knew. You go back up there and lie down in that hammock, and sleep—sle-eep——"

It was almost a lullaby, as he said it. He bowed to her, magnificently, profoundly, including the whole North in the splendor of his obeisance——

Then they were gone down the road in quite a preposterous cloud of dust. Just before they reached the first bend Amanthis saw them come to a full stop, dismount and shove the top part of the car on to the bottom part. They took their seats again without looking around. Then the bend—and they were out of sight, leaving only a faint brown mist to show that they had passed.

Hot & Cold Blood

Hearst's International
August 1923
$1,500

What a wife learned who tried to improve her husband

Take the expression "cold-blooded" for instance—little shining pieces of ice circulating in the arteries, passing the heart every half hour and giving it a chill, flying through the brain like an express train through a prairie village and making warm decisions into cool ones. An unpleasant thought!

But there was nothing cold-blooded about young Coatesworth. He liked people—and that's much rarer than it sounds. Some are impelled to seek company by an inexhaustible curiosity, some are driven to it by sheer boredom with themselves and others congregate for no more reason than that the pithecanthropus erectus[1] huddled in groups a hundred thousand years ago. But young Coatesworth liked people. He had an almost blind eye for their imperfections, he knew how to keep his mouth shut and his blood was warm. He is what is often known among men as a "hell of a nice fellow." This was no casual compliment. As niceness goes in this somewhat unpleasant world, he *was*.

So in college he had been enormously popular—vice-president of his class and manager of some athletic team. Afterwards, in the army, his company were wildly sentimental about him, and when the war was over had a way of writing him from Kokomo, Indiana or Muscatine, Iowa, about their successes and their failures and the births of their male children. Coatesworth always answered their letters even when he was very busy—because he himself was somewhat sentimental. Besides, he was nice.

When he was twenty-seven he fell in love with Jaqueline James, who likewise lived in Indianapolis, and married her. She married him, of course, because he was such a nice fellow. Why he married her is a little harder to guess, because of all the young girls in the city she seemed the most completely selfish and the most exquisitely spoiled. People went around talking about the attraction of opposites for each other—and meant nothing complimentary to Jaqueline James.

After the Coatesworths had been married a year they came to themselves and began to look each other over with discerning eyes. There was a great deal of affection between them and neither found anything particularly alarming in the other, for a selfish person and an unselfish person usually get on together very well indeed. He liked her for being cool and clean and jaunty, for wearing her hardiness like a suit of armor against the world and being tender and warm for him only. She was like a silver cup. She was a plant from the high places sheathed with cool dew.[2]

She was like that when she came one day into his office where he carried on a wholesale grocery brokerage[3] with more than average success. Miss Clancy, the stenographer, nodded to her admiringly, as she passed breezily through the outer room.

At the open door of the inner office Jaqueline stopped and said: "Oh, excuse me——" She had interrupted an apparently trivial yet somehow intriguing scene. A young man named Bronson whom she knew slightly was standing with her husband, who had risen from his desk. Bronson had seized her husband's hand and was shaking it earnestly—something more than earnestly. When they heard Jaqueline's step in the doorway they turned and she saw that Bronson's eyes were red.

A moment later he came out, passing her with a somewhat embarrassed "How do you do?" She walked into her husband's office.

"What was Bronson doing here?" she demanded curiously, and at once.

Jim Coatesworth smiled at her, half shutting his gray eyes, and drew her quietly to a sitting position on his desk.

"He just dropped in for a minute," he answered easily. "How's everything at home?"

"All right." She looked at him with curiosity. "What did he want?" she insisted.

"Oh, he just wanted to see me about something."

"What?"

"Oh, just something. Business."

"Why were his eyes red?"

"Were they?" He looked at her innocently, and then suddenly they both began to laugh. Jaqueline rose and walked around the desk and plumped down into his swivel chair.

"You might as well tell me," she announced cheerfully, "because I'm going to stay right here till you do."

"Well——" he hesitated, frowning. "He wanted me to do him a little favor."

Then Jaqueline understood, or rather her mind leaped half accidentally to the truth.

"Oh." Her voice tightened a little. "You've been lending him some money."

"Only a little."

"How much?"

"Only three hundred."[4]

"*Only* three hundred." The voice was of the texture of Bessemer[5] cooled. "How much do we spend a month, Jim?"

"Why—why, about five or six hundred, I guess." He shifted uneasily. "Listen, Jack. Bronson'll pay that back. He's in a little trouble. He's—he's made a sort of mistake about a girl out in Woodmere——"

"And he knows you're famous for being an easy mark, so he comes to you," interrupted Jaqueline.

"No." He denied this formally.

"Don't you suppose I could use that three hundred dollars?" she demanded. "How about that trip to New York we couldn't afford last November?"

The lingering smile faded from Coatesworth's face. He went over and shut the door to the outer office.

"Listen, Jack," he began, "you don't understand this. Bronson's one of the men I eat lunch with almost every day. We used to play together when we were kids, we went to school together. Don't you see that I'm just the person he'd be right to come to in trouble? And that's just why I couldn't refuse."

Jaqueline gave her shoulders a twist as if to shake off this reasoning.

"Well," she answered decidedly, "all I know is that he's no good. He's always tight and if he doesn't choose to work he has no business living off the work you do."

They were sitting now on either side of the desk, each having adopted the attitude of one talking to a child. They began their sentences with "Listen!" and their faces wore expressions of rather tried patience.

"If you can't understand I can't tell you," Coatesworth concluded, at the end of fifteen minutes, on what was, for him, an irritated key. "Such obligations do happen to exist sometimes among men and they have to be met. It's more complicated than just refusing to lend money, especially in a business like mine where there's so much depends on the good will of men downtown."

Coatesworth was putting on his coat as he said this. He was going home with her on the street car to lunch. They were between automobiles—they had sold their old one and were going to get a new one in the Spring.

Now the street car, on this particular day, was distinctly unfortunate. The argument in the office might have been forgotten under other circumstances but what followed irritated the scratch until it became a serious temperamental infection.

They found a seat near the front of the car. It was late February and an eager, unpunctilious sun was turning the scrawny street snow into dirty, cheerful rivulets that echoed in the gutters. Because of this the car was less full than usual—there was no one standing. The motorman had even opened his window and a yellow breeze was blowing the late breath of Winter from the car.

It occurred pleasurably to Jaqueline that her husband sitting beside her was handsome and kind above other men. It was silly to try to change him. Perhaps Bronson might return the money after all and anyhow three hundred dollars wasn't a fortune. Of course he had no business doing it—but then——

Her musings were interrupted as an eddy of passengers pushed up the aisle. Jaqueline wished they'd put their hands over their mouths when they coughed, and she hoped that Jim would get a new machine pretty soon. You couldn't tell what disease you'd run into in these trolleys.

She turned to Jim to broach the subject—but emitted a gasp instead. Jim had stood up and was offering his seat to a woman who had been standing beside him in the aisle. The woman, without so much as a grunt, sat down. Jaqueline frowned.

The woman was about fifty, and enormous. When she first sat down she was content merely to fill the unoccupied part of the seat, but after a moment she began to expand and spread her great rolls of fat over a larger and larger area until the process took on the aspect of violent trespassing. When the car rocked in Jaqueline's direction the woman slid with it but when it rocked back she managed by some exercise of ingenuity to dig in and hold the ground won.

Jaqueline caught her husband's eye—he was swaying on a strap—and in an angry glance conveyed to him her entire disapproval of his action. He apologized mutely and became urgently engrossed in a row of car cards. The fat woman moved once more against Jaqueline—she was now practically overlapping her. Then she turned puffy, disagreeable eyes full on Mrs. James Coatesworth and coughed rousingly in her face.

With a smothered exclamation Jaqueline got to her feet, squeezed with brisk violence past the fleshy knees and made her way, pink with rage, toward the rear of the car. There she seized a strap and there she was presently joined by her husband in a state of considerable alarm.

They exchanged no word but stood silently side by side for ten minutes while a row of men sitting in front of them crackled their newspapers and kept their eyes fixed virtuously upon the day's cartoons.

When they left the car at last Jaqueline exploded.

"You big *fool!*" she cried wildly. "Did you see that horrible hog you gave your seat to? Why don't you consider *me* occasionally instead of every fat selfish washwoman you meet?"

"How should I know——"

But Jaqueline was as angry at him as she had ever been—it was unusual for anyone to get angry at him.

"You didn't see any of those men getting up for *me*, did you? No wonder you were too tired to go out last Monday night. You'd probably given your seat to some—to some horrible, Polish *wash*woman[6] that's strong as an ox and *likes* to stand up!"

They were walking along the slushy street stepping wildly into great pools of water. Confused and distressed Coatesworth could utter neither apology nor defense.

Jaqueline broke off and then turned to him with a steely light in her eyes. The words in which she couched her summary of the situation were probably the most disagreeable that had ever been addressed to him in his life.

"The trouble with you, Jim, the reason you're such an easy mark, is that you've got the ideas of a college freshman—you're a professional nice fellow."

The incident and the unpleasantness had been forgotten. Coatesworth's vast good nature had smoothed over the roughness within an hour. References to it fell with a dying cadence throughout the day—then ceased and tumbled into the limbo of oblivion. I say "limbo" for oblivion is, unfortunately, never quite oblivious. The subject was rather drowned out by the fact that Jaqueline with her customary spirit and coolness began the long, arduous, uphill business of bearing a child. Her natural traits and prejudices became intensified and she was less inclined to let things pass.

It was April now and as yet they had not bought a car. Coatesworth had discovered that he was saving practically nothing and that in another half year he was going to have a family on his hands. It worried him. A wrinkle—small, tentative, undisturbing—appeared for the first time as a shadow around his honest gray eyes. He worked far into the Spring twilight now and frequently brought home with him the overflow from his office day. The new car, he decided, would have to be postponed for a while.

April afternoon and all the city shopping on Washington Street. Jaqueline walked slowly past the shops brooding without fear or depression on the shape into which her life was now being arbitrarily forced. Dry summer dust was in the wind; the sun bounded cheerily from the plate glass windows and made radiant gasoline rainbows where automobile drippings had formed pools on the street.

Jaqueline stopped. Not six feet from her a bright new sport roadster[7] was parked at the curb. Beside it stood two men in conversation and at the moment when she identified one of them as young Bronson she heard him say to the other in a casual tone:

"Isn't it a beauty? I just bought it today."

Jaqueline turned abruptly and walked with quick tapping steps to her husband's office. With her usual curt nod to the stenographer she strode by her to the inner room. Coatesworth looked up from his desk in surprise.

"Jim," she began breathlessly, "did Bronson ever pay you that three hundred?"

"Why—no" he answered hesitantly, "not yet. He was in here last week and he explained that he was a little bit hard up."

Her eyes gleamed with angry triumph.

"Oh, he did?" she snapped out briskly. "Well, he's just bought a new sport roadster that must have cost anyhow twenty-five hundred dollars."[8]

He shook his head, unbelieving.

"I saw it," she insisted. "I heard him say he'd just bought it."

"He *told* me he was hard up," repeated Coatesworth helplessly.

Jaqueline audibly gave up by heaving a profound noise that may best be described as a sort of groanish sigh.

"He was *us*ing you! He knew you were easy and he was *us*ing you. Can't you see? He wanted *you* to buy him the car and you *did!*" She laughed bitterly. "He's probably roaring his sides out to think how easily he worked you."

"Oh, no," protested Coatesworth with a shocked expression, "you must have mistaken somebody for him———"

"We walk—and he rides on our money," she interrupted excitedly. "Oh, it's rich—it's rich. If it wasn't so maddening it'd be just absurd. Look here—!" Her voice grew sharper, more restrained—there was a touch of contempt in it now. "You spend half your time doing things for people who don't give a damn about you or what becomes of you. You give up your seat on the street car to *hogs* and come home too dead tired to even *move*. You're on all sorts of committees that take at least an hour a day out of your business and you don't get a cent out of them. You're—eternally—being *used!* I won't stand it! I thought I married a man—not a professional Samaritan who's going to fetch and carry for the world!"

As she finished her invective Jaqueline reeled suddenly and sank into a chair—nervously exhausted.

"Just at this time," she went on, brokenly now, "I need you. I need your strength and your health and your arms around me. And if you—if you just give it to *every*one, it's spread *so* when it reaches me——"

He knelt by her side, moving her tired young head until it lay against his shoulder.

"I'm sorry, Jaqueline," he said humbly, "I'll be more careful. I didn't realize what I was doing."

"You're the dearest person in the world," murmured Jaqueline huskily, "but I want all of you and the best of you for me."

He smoothed her hair over and over. For a few minutes they rested there silently having attained a sort of Nirvana of peace and understanding. Then Jaqueline reluctantly raised her head as they were interrupted by the voice of Miss Clancy in the doorway.

"Oh, I beg your pardon."

"What is it?"

"A boy's here with some boxes. It's C.O.D."

Coatesworth rose and followed Miss Clancy into the outer office.

"It's fifty dollars."[9]

He searched his wallet—remembered that he had forgotten to go to the bank that morning.

"Just a minute," he said abstractedly. His mind was on Jaqueline, Jaqueline who seemed forlorn in her trouble, waiting for him in the other room. He walked into the corridor and opening the door of "Clayton and Drake, Brokers' across the way, swung wide a low gate and went up to a man seated at a desk.

"Morning, Fred," said Coatesworth.

Drake, a little man of thirty with pince-nez and bald head, rose and shook hands.

"Morning, Jim. What can I do for you?"

"Just this. A boy's in my office with some stuff C.O.D. and I haven't a cent. Can you let me have fifty till this afternoon?"

Drake looked closely at Coatesworth. Then, slowly and startlingly, he shook his head—not up and down but from side to side.

"Sorry, Jim," he answered stiffly, "I've made a rule never to make a personal loan to anybody on any conditions. I've seen it break up too many friendships."

"What?"

Coatesworth had come out of his abstraction now and the mono-syllable held an undisguised quality of shock. Then his natural tact acted automatically, springing to his aid and dictating his words though his brain was suddenly numb. His immediate instinct was to put Drake at ease in his refusal.

"Oh, I see." He nodded his head as if in full agreement, as if he himself had often considered adopting just such a rule. "Oh, I see how you feel. Well—I just—I wouldn't have you break a rule like that for anything. It's—it's probably a good thing."

They talked for a minute longer. Drake justified his position easily; he had evidently rehearsed the part a great deal. He treated Coatesworth to an exquisitely frank smile.

Coatesworth went politely back to his office leaving Drake under the impression that he himself was the most tactful man in the city. Coatesworth had a way of leaving people with that impression. But when he entered his own office and saw his wife staring dismally out the window into the sunshine he clenched his hands and his mouth set in a hard, straight line.

"All right, Jack," he said slowly, "I guess you're right about most things and I'm wrong. I'm wrong as hell."

During the next three months Coatesworth thought back through many years. He had had an unusually happy life. Those frictions between man and man, between man and society, which harden most of us into a rough and cynical fighting trim had been conspicuous by their infrequency in his life. It had never occurred to him before that he had paid a price for this immunity, but now he perceived how here and there, and constantly, he had taken the rough side of the road to avoid enmity or argument, or even question.

There was, for instance, much money that he had lent privately, about thirteen hundred dollars[10] in all, which he realized, in his new enlightenment, he would never see again. It had taken Jaqueline's harder, feminine intelligence to know this. It was only now when he owed it to Jaqueline to have money in the bank that he missed these loans at all.

He realized too the truth of her assertions that he was continually doing favors—a little something here, a little something there, the sum total, in time and energy expended, was somewhat appalling. It had pleased him to do the favors. He reacted warmly to being thought well of, but he wondered now if he had not been merely indulging a selfish vanity of his own. In suspecting this, he was, as usual, not quite fair to himself. The truth was that Coatesworth was essentially and enormously romantic.

He decided that these expenditures of himself made him tired at night, less efficient in his work and less of a prop to Jaqueline, who, as the months passed, grew more heavy and bored, and sat through the long summer afternoons on the screened veranda waiting for his step at the end of the walk.

Lest that step falter Coatesworth gave up many things—among them the presidency of his college alumni association. He let slip other labors less prized. When he was put on a committee men had a habit of electing him chairman and retiring into a dim background where they were inconveniently hard to find. He was done with such things now. Also he avoided those who were prone to ask favors—fleeing a certain eager look that would be turned on him from some group up at his club.

The change in him came slowly. He was not exceptionally unworldly—under other circumstances Drake's refusal of money would not have surprised him. Had it come to him as a story he would scarcely have given it a thought. But it had broken in with harsh abruptness upon a situation existing in his own mind and the shock had given it a powerful and literal significance.

It was mid-August now and the last of a baking week. The curtains of his wide-open office windows had scarcely rippled all the day but lay like sails becalmed in warm juxtaposition with the smothering screens. Coatesworth was worried—Jaqueline had overtired herself and was paying for it by violent sick headaches, and business seemed to have come to an apathetic standstill. That morning he had been so irritable with Miss Clancy that she had looked at him in surprise. He had immediately apologized, wishing immediately afterwards that he hadn't. He was working at high speed through this heat—why shouldn't she?

She came to his door now and he looked up faintly frowning.

"Mr. Edward Lacy."

"All right," he answered listlessly. Old man Lacy—he knew him slightly. A melancholy figure—a brilliant start back in the eighties, and now one of the city's failures. He couldn't imagine what Lacy wanted unless it was soliciting.

"Good afternoon, Mr. Coatesworth."

A little, solemn, gray-haired man stood on the threshold. Coatesworth rose and greeted him politely.

"Are you busy?"

"Well, not so very." He stressed the qualifying word slightly.

Mr. Lacy sat down, obviously ill-at-ease. He kept his hat in his hands and clung to it tightly as he began to speak.

"Mr. Coatesworth, if you've got five minutes to spare I'm going to tell you something that—that I find at present it's necessary for me to tell you."

Coatesworth nodded. Some instinct warned him that there was a favor to be asked but he was tired and with a sort of lassitude he let his chin sink into his hand, welcoming any distraction from his more immediate cares.

"You see," went on Mr. Lacy—Coatesworth noticed that the hands which fingered at the hat were trembling—"back in eighty-four your father and I were very good friends. You've heard him speak of me no doubt."

Coatesworth nodded.

"I was asked to be one of the pallbearers. Once we were—very close. It's because of that that I come to you now. Never before in my life have I ever had to come to anyone as I've come to you now, Mr. Coatesworth—come to a stranger. But as you grow older your friends die or move away or some misunderstanding separates you. And your children die unless you're fortunate enough to go first—and pretty soon you get to be alone so that you don't have any friends at all. You're isolated." He smiled faintly. His hands were trembling violently now.

"Once upon a time almost forty years ago your father came to me and asked me for a thousand dollars.[11] I was a few years older than he was and though I knew him only slightly I had a high opinion of him. That was a lot of money in those days and he had no security— he had nothing but a plan in his head—but I liked the way he had of looking out of his eyes—you'll pardon me if I say you look not unlike him—so I gave it to him without security."

Mr. Lacy paused.

"Without security," he repeated. "I could afford it then. I didn't lose by it. He paid it back with interest at six percent before the year was up."

Coatesworth was looking down at his blotter, tapping out a series of triangles with his pencil. He knew what was coming now and his muscles physically tightened as he mustered his forces for the refusal he knew he would have to make.

"I'm now an old man, Mr. Coatesworth," the cracked voice went on. "I've made a failure—I *am* a failure—only we needn't go into that now. I have a daughter, an unmarried daughter who lives with me. She does stenographic work and has been very kind to me. We live together, you know, on Selby Avenue—we have an apartment, quite a nice apartment."

The old man sighed quaveringly. He was trying—and at the same time was afraid—to get to his request. It was insurance, it seemed. He had a ten-thousand-dollar[12] policy and he had borrowed on it up to the limit and to make a long story short he stood to lose the whole amount unless he could raise four hundred and fifty dollars.[13] He and his daughter had about seventy-five dollars[14] between them— that was all. They had no friends—he had explained that—and they had found it impossible to raise the money. . . .

Coatesworth could stand the miserable story no longer. He could not spare the money but he could at least relieve the old man of the blistered agony of asking for it.*

"I'm sorry, Mr. Lacy," he interrupted as gently as possible, "but I can't lend you that money."

"No?" The old man looked at him with faded, blinking eyes that were beyond all shock, almost, it seemed, beyond any human emotion except ceaseless care. The only change in his expression was that his mouth dropped slowly ajar.

Coatesworth fixed his eyes determinedly upon his blotter.

"We're going to have a baby in a few months and I've been saving for that. It wouldn't be fair to my wife to take anything from her—or the child—right now."

His voice sank to a sort of mumble. He found himself saying something about business being bad—saying it with revolting facility.

Mr. Lacy made no argument. He rose without visible signs of disappointment. Only his hands were still trembling and they worried Coatesworth. The old man was apologetic—he was sorry to have bothered Mr. Coatesworth at a time like this. Perhaps something would turn up. He had thought that if Mr. Coatesworth did happen to—to have a good deal extra—why, he might be the person to go to because he was the son of an old friend.

As he left the office he had trouble opening the outer door. Miss Clancy helped him. He went shabbily and unhappily down the corridor with his faded eyes blinking and his mouth still faintly ajar.

* *Hearst's International* broke the text at this point after five contiguous pages (pp. 80–84), continuing the story on p. 150 where it resumed with the editorial gloss "Fitzgerald's Story of a Good Fellow—From page 84."

Jim Coatesworth stood by his desk and put his hand over his face and shivered suddenly as if he were cold. But the five o'clock air outside was hot as a tropic noon.

The twilight was hotter still an hour later as he stood at the corner waiting for his car. The trolley ride to his house was twenty-five minutes and he bought a pink-jacketed newspaper to appetize his tired mind. Life had seemed less happy, less glamourous of late. Perhaps he had learned more of the world's ways—perhaps its glamor was evaporating little by little with the hurried years.

Nothing like this afternoon, for instance, had ever happened to him before. He could not dismiss the old man from his mind. He pictured him plodding home in the weary heat, on foot, probably, to save carfare, opening the door of a hot little flat, and confessing to his daughter that the son of his friend had not been able to help him out. All evening they would plan helplessly until they said good night to each other—father and daughter, isolated by chance in this world— and went to lie awake with a pathetic loneliness in their two beds.

Coatesworth's streetcar came along and he found a seat near the front, next to an old lady who looked at him grudgingly as she moved over. At the next block a crowd of girls from the department store district flowed up the aisle and Coatesworth unfolded his paper. Of late he had not indulged his habit of giving up his seat. He supposed Jaqueline was right—the average young girl was able to stand as well as he was. Giving up his seat was silly, a mere gesture, a sort of showing off. Nowadays not one woman in a dozen even bothered to thank him.

It was stifling hot in the car and he wiped the heavy damp from his forehead. The aisle was thickly packed now and a woman standing beside his seat was thrown momentarily against his shoulder as the car turned a corner. Coatesworth took a long breath of the hot foul air, which persistently refused to circulate, and tried to center his mind on a cartoon at the top of the sporting page.

"Move for'ard ina car, please!" The conductor's voice pierced the opaque column of humanity with raucous irritation, "Plen'y of room for'ard!"

The crowd made a feeble attempt to shove forward but the unfortunate fact that there was no space into which to move precluded any marked success. The car turned another corner and again the woman next to Coatesworth swayed against his shoulder. Ordinarily he would have given up his seat if only to avoid this reminder that she was there. It made him feel unpleasantly cold-blooded. And the car was horrible—horrible. They ought to put more of them on the line these sweltering days.

For the fifth time he looked at the pictures in the comic strip. There was a beggar in the second picture and the wavering image of Mr. Lacy persistently inserted itself in the beggar's place. God! Suppose the old man really did starve to death—suppose he threw himself into the river.

"Once," thought Coatesworth, "he helped my father. Perhaps if he hadn't my own life would have been different than it has been. But Lacy could afford it then—and I can't."

To force out the picture of Mr. Lacy Coatesworth tried to think of Jaqueline. He said to himself over and over that he would have been sacrificing Jaqueline to a played-out man who had had his chance and failed. Jaqueline needed her chance now as never before.

Coatesworth looked at his watch. He had been on the car ten minutes. Fifteen minutes still to ride, and the heat increasing with breathless intensity. The woman swayed against him once more and looking out the window he saw that they were turning the last downtown corner.

It occurred to him that perhaps he ought, after all, to give the woman his seat—her last sway toward him had been a particularly tired sway. If he were sure she was an older woman—but the texture of her dress as it brushed his hand gave somehow the impression that she was a young girl. He did not dare look up to see. He was afraid of the piteous appeal that might look out of her eyes if they were old eyes or the sharp contempt if they were young.

For the next five minutes his mind worked in a vague suffocated way on what now seemed to him the enormous problem of whether or not to give her the seat. He felt dimly that doing so would partially atone for his refusal to Mr. Lacy that afternoon. It would be rather terrible to have done those two cold-blooded things in succession—and on such a day.

He tried the cartoon again, but in vain. He must concentrate on Jaqueline. He was dead tired now and if he stood up he would be more tired. Jaqueline would be waiting for him, needing him. She would be depressed and she would want him to hold her quietly in his arms for an hour after dinner. When he was tired this was rather a strain. And afterwards when they went to bed she would ask him from time to time to get her her medicine or a glass of ice water.[15] He hated to show any weariness in doing these things. She might notice and, needing something, refrain from asking for it.

The girl in the aisle swayed against him once more—this time it was more like a sag. She was tired, too. Well, it was weary to work. The ends of many proverbs that had to do with toil and the long day floated fragmentarily through his mind. Everybody in the world was tired—this woman, for instance, whose body was sagging so wearily, so strangely against his. But his home came first and his girl that he loved was waiting for him there. He must keep his strength for her and he said to himself over and over that he would not give up his seat.

Then he heard a sort of long sigh followed by a sudden exclamation and he realized that the girl was no longer leaning against him. The exclamation multiplied into a clatter of voices—then came a pause—then a renewed clatter that traveled down the car in calls and little staccato cries to the conductor. The bell clanged violently and the hot car jolted to a sudden stop.

"Girl fainted up here!"

"Too hot for her!"

"Get back there! Get back there!"

"Just keeled right over!"

"Get back there! Gangway, you!"

"Pale as a ghost."

The crowd eddied apart. The passengers in front squeezed back and those on the rear platform temporarily disembarked. Curiosity and pity bubbled out of suddenly conversing groups. People tried to help, got in the way. Then the bell rang and voices rose stridently again.

"Get her out all right?"

"Say, did you see that?"

"This damn' company ought to——"

"Did you see the man that carried her out? He was pale as a ghost too."

"Yes, but did you hear——?"

"What?"

"That fella. That pale fella that carried her out. He was sittin' beside her an' he didn't know—he says she's his wife!"

The house was quiet. A breeze pressed back the dark vine leaves of the veranda letting in thin yellow rods of moonlight on the wicker chairs. The doctor was gone now and Jaqueline rested placidly on the long settee with her head in his arms. After awhile she stirred lazily; her hand reaching up patted his cheek.

"I think I'll go to bed now. I'm tired. I'm so tired. Will you help me up?"

He lifted her and laid her down among the pillows.

"I'll be with you in a minute," he said gently. "Can you wait for just a minute?"

"I can wait forever—for you."

He passed into the lighted living-room and she heard him thumbing the pages of a telephone directory. She listened idly as he called a number.

"Hello, is Mr. Lacy there? Why—yes, it *is* pretty important—if he hasn't gone to sleep."

A pause. Jaqueline could hear restless sparrows splattering through the leaves of the magnolia over the way. Then her husband's voice again at the telephone:

"Is this Mr. Lacy? Oh, this is Coatesworth, Mr. Lacy. Why—why, in regard to that matter we talked about this afternoon, I think—I guess I'll be able to fix that up somehow or other after all." He raised his voice a little as though someone at the other end found it difficult to hear. "James Coatesworth's son, I said—Coatesworth!"

When he came back to the veranda she said hesitantly, "You're tired too. Perhaps you'd better not try to carry me."

But he picked her up and, still holding her in his arms, he locked the door behind them and turned out the lights on the first floor and started up the stairs.[16]

"Put me down," she whispered. "You're—you're carrying a whole family now."

But he only laughed and told her that he wasn't tired at all. And she believed him because what he said was true.

Gretchen's Forty Winks

Saturday Evening Post
15 March 1924
$1,200

The sidewalks were scratched with brittle leaves and the wind blew the wet laundry stiff on the line. Snow before night, sure. Autumn was over. This, of course, raised the coal question and the Christmas question; but Roger Halsey, standing on his own front porch, announced to the dead suburban sky that he hadn't time for worrying about the weather. Then he let himself hurriedly into the house and left the subject out in the cold twilight.

The hall was dark, but from above he heard the voices of his wife and the nursemaid and the baby in one of their interminable conversations, which consisted chiefly of "Don't!" and "Look out, Maxy!" and "Oh, there he *goes!*" punctuated by wild threats and vague bumpings and the recurrent sound of small, venturing feet.

Roger turned on the hall light and walked into the living room and turned on the red silk lamp. He put his bulging portfolio on the table, and sitting down rested his intense young face in his hand for a few minutes, shading his eyes carefully from the light. Then he lit a cigarette, squashed it out, and going to the foot of the stairs called for his wife.

"Gretchen!"

"Hello, dear." Her voice was full of laughter. "Come see baby."[1]

He swore softly.

"I can't see baby now," he said aloud. "How long 'fore you'll be down?"

There was a mysterious pause and then a succession of Don'ts and Look out, Maxys, evidently meant to avert some threatened catastrophe.

"How long 'fore you'll be down?" repeated Roger, slightly irritated.

"Oh, I'll be right down."

"How soon?" he shouted.

He had trouble every day at this hour in adapting his voice from the urgent key of the city to the proper casualness for a model home. But tonight he was deliberately impatient. It almost disappointed him when Gretchen came running down the stairs, three at a time, crying "What is it?" in a rather surprised voice.

They kissed—lingered over it some moments. They had been married three years, and they were much more in love than that implies.[2] It was seldom that they hated each other with that violent hate of which only young couples are capable, for Roger was still actively sensitive to her beauty.

"Come in here," he said abruptly. "I want to talk to you."

His wife, a bright-colored, Titian-haired[3] girl, vivid as a French rag doll, followed him wonderingly into the living room.

"Listen, Gretchen"—he sat down at the end of the sofa—"beginning with tonight I'm going to —— What's the matter?"

"Nothing. I'm just looking for a cigarette. Go on."

She tiptoed breathlessly back to the sofa and settled at the other end.

"Gretchen ——" Again he broke off. Her hand, palm upward, was extended towards him. "Well, what is it?" he asked wildly.

"Matches."

"What?"

In his impatience it seemed incredible that she should ask for matches, but he fumbled automatically in his pocket.

"Thank you," she whispered. "I didn't mean to interrupt you. Go on."

"Gretch——"

Scratch! The match flared. They exchanged a tense look.

Her fawn's eyes apologized mutely this time and he laughed. After all, she had done no more than light a cigarette; but when he was in this mood her slightest positive action irritated him beyond measure.

"When you've got time to listen," he said crossly, "you might be interested in discussing the poorhouse question with me."

"What poorhouse?" Her eyes were wide, startled; she sat quiet as a mouse.

"That was just to get your attention. But, beginning tonight, I start on what'll probably be the most important six weeks of my life[4]—the six weeks that'll decide whether we're going on forever in this rotten little house in this rotten little suburban town."

Boredom replaced alarm in Gretchen's black eyes. She was a Southern girl[5] and any question that had to do with getting ahead in the world always tended to give her a headache.

"Six months ago I left the New York Lithographic Company," announced Roger, "and went in the advertising business for myself."[6]

"I know," interrupted Gretchen resentfully; "and now instead of getting six hundred a month sure, we're living on a risky five hundred."[7]

"Gretchen," said Roger sharply, "if you'll just believe in me as hard as you can for six weeks more we'll be rich. I've got a chance now to get some of the biggest accounts in the country." He hesitated. "And for these six weeks we won't go out at all and we won't have anyone here. I'm going to bring home work every night and we'll pull down all the blinds and if anyone rings the doorbell we won't answer."

He smiled airily as if it were a new game they were going to play. Then, as Gretchen was silent his smile faded, and he looked at her uncertainly.

"Well, what's the matter?" she broke out finally. "Do you expect me to jump up and sing? You do enough work as it is. If you try to do any more you'll end up with a nervous breakdown. I read about a ——"

"Don't worry about me," he interrupted; "I'm all right. But you're going to be bored to death sitting here every evening."

"No, I won't," she said without conviction—"except tonight."

"What about tonight?"

"George Tompkins asked us to dinner."

"Did you accept?"

"Of course I did," she said impatiently. "Why not? You're always talking about what a terrible neighborhood this is and I thought maybe you'd like to go to a nicer one for a change."

"When I go to a nicer neighborhood I want to go for good," he said grimly.

"Well, can we go?"

"I suppose we'll have to if you've accepted."

Somewhat to his annoyance the conversation abruptly ended. Gretchen jumped up and kissed him sketchily and rushed into the kitchen to light the hot water for a bath. With a sigh he carefully deposited his portfolio behind the bookcase—it contained only sketches and layouts for display advertising, but it seemed to him the first thing a burglar would look for. Then he went abstractedly upstairs, dropped into the baby's room for a casual moist kiss and began dressing for dinner.

They had no automobile, so George Tompkins called for them at 6:30. Tompkins was a successful interior decorator and his own house was a sort of intensification of all the houses he had ever designed. He was a broad, rosy man with a handsome mustache and a faint odor of imported perfume.[8] He and Roger had once roomed side by side in a boarding house in New York, but they had met only intermittently in the past five years.

"We ought to see each other more," he told Roger tonight. "You ought to go out more often, old boy. Here, have a cocktail."[9]

"No, thanks."

"No? Well, your beautiful wife will—won't you, Gretchen?"

"I love this house," she exclaimed, taking the glass and looking admiringly at the Chinese tapestry that took up one whole wall of the living room.

"I like it," said Tompkins with satisfaction. "I did it to please myself and I succeeded."

Roger stared moodily around the room.

"You look like the devil, Roger," said his host. "Have a cocktail and cheer up."

"Have one," urged Gretchen.

"What?" Roger turned around absently. "Oh, no, thanks. I've got to work after I get home."

"Work!" Tompkins smiled. "Listen, Roger, you'll kill yourself with work. Why don't you bring a little balance into your life—work a little, then play a little?"

"That's what I tell him," said Gretchen.

"Do you know an average business man's day?" demanded Tompkins as they went in to dinner. "Coffee in the morning, eight hours' work interrupted by a bolted luncheon and then home again with dyspepsia and a bad temper to give the wife a pleasant evening."

Roger laughed shortly.

"You've been going to the movies too much," he said dryly.

"What?" Tompkins looked at him with some irritation. "Movies? I've hardly ever been to the movies in my life. I think the movies are atrocious. My opinions on life are drawn from my own observations. I believe in a balanced life."

"What's that?" demanded Roger.

"Well"—he hesitated—"probably the best way to tell you would be to describe my own day. Would that seem horribly egotistic?"

"Oh, no!" Gretchen looked at him with interest. "I'd love to hear about it."

"Well, in the morning I get up and go through a series of exercises. I've got one room fitted up as a little gymnasium, and I punch the bag and do shadow boxing and weight pulling for an hour.[10] Then after a cold bath —— There's a thing now! Do you take a daily cold bath?"

"No," admitted Roger, "I take a hot bath in the evening three or four times a week."

A horrified silence fell. Tompkins and Gretchen exchanged a glance as if something obscene had been said.

"What's the matter?" broke out Roger, glancing from one to the other in some irritation. "You know I don't take a bath every day—I haven't got the time."

Tompkins gave a prolonged sigh.

"After my bath," he continued, "I have breakfast and drive to my office in New York, where I work until four. Then I lay off, and if it's summer I hurry out here for nine holes of golf,[11] or if it's winter I play squash for an hour at my club. Then a good snappy game of bridge until dinner. Dinner is liable to have something to do with business, but in a pleasant way. Perhaps I've just finished a house for some customer and he wants me to be on hand for his first party to see that the lighting is soft enough and all that sort of thing. Or maybe I sit down with a good book of poetry and spend the evening alone. At any rate, I do something every night to get me out of myself."

"It must be wonderful," said Gretchen enthusiastically. "I wish we lived like that."

Tompkins bent forward earnestly over the table.

"You can," he said impressively. "There's no reason why you shouldn't. Look here, if Roger'll play nine holes of golf every day it'll do wonders for him. He won't know himself. He'll do his work better, never get that tired, nervous feeling —— What's the matter?"

He broke off. Roger had perceptibly yawned.

"Roger," cried Gretchen sharply, "there's no need to be so rude. If you did what George said, you'd be a lot better off." She turned indignantly to their host. "The latest is that he's going to work at night for the next six weeks. He says he's going to pull down the blinds and shut us up like hermits in a cave. He's been doing it every Sunday for the last year; now he's going to do it every night for six weeks."

Tompkins shook his head sadly.

"At the end of six weeks," he remarked, "he'll be starting for the sanitarium. Let me tell you, every private hospital in New York is full of cases like yours. You just strain the human nervous system a little too far, and bang!—you've broken something. And in order to save sixty hours you're laid up sixty weeks for repairs."[12] He broke off, changed his tone and turned to Gretchen with a smile. "Not to mention what happens to you. It seems to me it's the wife rather than the husband who bears the brunt of these insane periods of overwork."

"I don't mind," protested Gretchen loyally.

"Yes, she does," said Roger grimly; "she minds like the devil. She's a short-sighted little egg and she thinks it's going to be forever until I get started and she can have some new clothes. But it can't be helped. The saddest thing about women is that, after all, their best trick is to sit down and fold their hands."

"Your ideas on women are about twenty years out of date," said Tompkins pityingly. "Women won't sit down and wait any more."

"Then they'd better marry men of forty,"[13] insisted Roger stubbornly. "If a girl marries a young man for love she ought to be willing to make any sacrifice within reason, so long as her husband keeps going ahead."

"Let's not talk about it," said Gretchen impatiently. "Please, Roger, let's have a good time just this once."

When Tompkins dropped them in front of their house at eleven Roger and Gretchen stood for a moment on the sidewalk looking at the winter moon. There was a fine, damp, dusty snow in the air and Roger drew a long breath of it and put his arm around Gretchen exultantly.

"I can make more money than he can," he said tensely. "And I'll be doing it in just forty days."

"Forty days," she sighed. "It seems such a long time—when everybody else is always having fun. If I could only sleep for forty days."

"Why don't you, honey? Just take forty winks, and when you wake up everything'll be fine."

She was silent for a moment.

"Roger," she asked thoughtfully, "do you think George meant what he said about taking me horseback riding on Sunday?"

Roger frowned.

"I don't know. Probably not—I hope to heaven he didn't." He hesitated. "As a matter of fact, he made me sort of sore tonight—all that junk about his cold bath."

With their arms about each other, they started up the walk to the house.

"I'll bet he doesn't take a cold bath every morning," continued Roger ruminatively; "or three times a week, either." He fumbled in his pocket for the key and inserted it in the lock with savage precision. Then he turned around defiantly. "I'll bet he hasn't had a bath for a month."

II

After a fortnight of intensive work, Roger Halsey's days blurred into each other and passed by in blocks of twos and threes and fours. From eight until 5:30 he was in his office. Then a half hour on the commuting train, where he scrawled notes on the backs of envelopes under the dull yellow light. By 7:30 his crayons, shears and* sheets of white cardboard[14] were spread over the living-room table and he labored there with much grunting and sighing until midnight, while Gretchen lay on the sofa with a book and the doorbell tinkled occasionally behind the drawn blinds. At twelve there was always an argument as to whether he would come to bed. He would agree to come after he had cleared up everything; but as he was invariably sidetracked by half a dozen new ideas he usually found Gretchen sound asleep when he tiptoed upstairs.

Sometimes it was three o'clock before Roger squashed his last cigarette into the overloaded ash tray, and he would undress in the darkness, hollow as a ghost, but with a sense of triumph that he had lasted out another day.

Christmas came and went and he scarcely noticed that it was gone. He remembered it afterwards as the day he completed the window cards for Garrod's shoes. This was one of the eight large accounts for which he was pointing in January—if he got half of them he was assured a quarter of a million dollars' worth of business during the year.[15]

But the world outside his business became a chaotic dream. He was aware that on three cool December Sundays George Tompkins had taken Gretchen horseback riding and that another time she had gone out with him in his automobile to spend the day skiing on the country-club hill. A picture of Tompkins, in an expensive frame, had appeared one morning on their bedroom wall. And one night he was shocked into a startled protest when Gretchen went to the theater with Tompkins in town.

But his work was almost done. Daily now his layouts arrived from the printers until seven of them were piled and docketed in his office safe. He knew how good they were.

Money alone couldn't buy such work; more than he realized himself, it had been a labor of love.[16]

December tumbled like a dead leaf from the calendar. There was an agonizing week when he had to give up coffee because it made

* The *Saturday Evening Post* broke the text at this point after a two-page spread (pp. 14–15), continuing the story on p. 128.

his heart pound so. If he could hold on now for four days—three days ——

On Thursday afternoon H. G. Garrod was to arrive in New York. On Wednesday evening Roger came home at seven to find Gretchen poring over the December bills with a strange expression in her eyes.

"What's the matter?"

She nodded at the bills. He ran through them, his brow wrinkling in a frown.

"Gosh!"

"I can't help it," she burst out suddenly. "They're terrible."

"Well, I didn't marry you because you were a wonderful housekeeper. I'll manage about the bills some way. Don't worry your pretty head about it."

She regarded him coldly.

"You talk as if I were a child."

"I have to," he said with sudden irritation.

"Well, at least I'm not a piece of bric-a-brac that you can just put somewhere and forget."

He knelt down by her quickly and took her arms in his hands.

"Gretchen, listen!" he said breathlessly. "For God's sake, don't go to pieces now! We're both all stored up with malice and reproach, and if we had a quarrel it'd be terrible. I love you, Gretchen. Say you love me—quick!"

"You know I love you."

The quarrel was averted, but there was an unnatural tenseness all through dinner. It came to a climax afterwards when he began to spread his working materials on the table.

"Oh, Roger," she protested, "I thought you didn't have to work tonight."

"I didn't think I'd have to, but something came up."

"I've invited George Tompkins over."

"Oh, gosh!" he exclaimed. "Well, I'm sorry, honey, but you'll have to phone him not to come."

"He's left," she said. "He's coming straight from town. He'll be here any minute now."

Roger groaned. It occurred to him to send them both to the movies, but somehow the suggestion stuck on his lips. He did not want her at the movies; he wanted her here, where he could look up and know she was by his side.

George Tompkins arrived breezily at eight o'clock.

"Aha!" he cried reprovingly, coming into the room. "Still at it."

Roger agreed coolly that he was.

"Better quit—better quit before you have to." He sat down with a long sigh of physical comfort and lit a cigarette. "Take it from a fellow who's looked into the question scientifically. We can stand so much, and then—bang!"

"If you'll excuse me"—Roger made his voice as polite as possible—"I'm going upstairs and finish this work."

"Just as you like, Roger." George waved his hand carelessly. "It isn't that I mind. I'm the friend of the family and I'd just as soon see the missus as the mister." He smiled playfully. "But if I were you, Roger, I'd put away my work and get a good night's sleep."

When Roger had spread out his materials on the bed upstairs he found that he could still hear the rumble and murmur of their voices through the thin floor. He began wondering what they found to talk about. As he plunged deeper into his work his mind had a tendency to revert sharply to his question, and several times he arose and paced nervously up and down the room.

The bed was ill adapted to his work. Several times the paper slipped from the board on which it rested and the pencil punched through. Everything was wrong tonight. Letters and figures blurred before his eyes, and as an accompaniment to the beating of his temples came those persistent murmuring voices.

At ten he realized that he had done nothing for more than an hour, and with a sudden exclamation he gathered together his papers, replaced them in his portfolio and went downstairs. They were sitting together on the sofa when he came in.

"Oh, hello!" cried Gretchen, rather unnecessarily, he thought. "We were just discussing you."

"Thank you," he answered ironically. "What particular part of my anatomy was under the scalpel?"

"Your health," said Tompkins jovially.

"My health's all right," answered Roger shortly.

"But you look at it so selfishly, old fella," cried Tompkins. "You only consider yourself in the matter. Don't you think Gretchen has any rights? If you were working on a wonderful sonnet or a—a portrait of some madonna or something"—he glanced at Gretchen's Titian hair—"why, then I'd say go ahead. But you're not. It's just some silly advertisement about how to sell Peptow's hair tonic, and if all the hair tonic ever made was dumped into the ocean tomorrow the world wouldn't be one bit the worse for it."

"Wait a minute," said Roger angrily; "that's not quite fair. I'm not kidding myself about the importance of my work—it's just as useless as the stuff you do.[17] But to Gretchen and me it's just about the most important thing in the world."

"Are you implying that my work is useless?" demanded Tompkins incredulously.

"No; not if it brings happiness to some poor sucker of a pants manufacturer who doesn't know how to spend his money."

Tompkins and Gretchen exchanged a glance.

"Oh-h-h!" exclaimed Tompkins ironically. "I didn't realize that all these years I've just been wasting my time."

"You're a loafer," said Roger rudely.

"Me?" cried Tompkins angrily. "You call me a loafer because I have a little balance in my life and find time to do interesting things? Because I play hard as well as work hard and do not let myself get to be a dull, tiresome drudge?"

Both men were angry now and their voices had risen, though on Tompkins' face there still remained the semblance of a smile.

"What I object to," said Roger steadily, "is that for the last six weeks you seem to have done all your playing around here."

"Roger!" cried Gretchen. "What do you mean by talking like that?"

"Just what I said."

"You've just lost your temper." Tompkins lit a cigarette with ostentatious coolness. "You're so nervous from overwork you don't know what you're saying. You're on the verge of a nervous break——"

"Shut up!" cried Roger fiercely.

"Calm down, yourself! If you took a cold bath every morning you wouldn't be so excitable."

"You get out of here!" Roger's voice was trembling. "You get out of here right now—before I throw you out!"

Tompkins got angrily to his feet.

"You—you throw me out?" he cried incredulously.

They were actually moving toward each other when Gretchen stepped between them, and grabbing Tompkins' arm urged him toward the door.

"He's acting like a fool, George, but you better get out," she cried, groping in the hall for his hat.

"He insulted me!" shouted Tompkins. "He threatened to throw me out!"

"Never mind, George," pleaded Gretchen. "He doesn't know what he's saying. Please go! I'll see you at ten o'clock tomorrow."

She opened the door.

"You won't see him at ten o'clock tomorrow," said Roger steadily. "He's not coming to this house any more."

Tompkins turned to Gretchen.

"It's his house," he suggested. "Perhaps we'd better meet at mine."

Then he was gone and Gretchen had shut the door behind him. Her eyes were full of angry tears.

"See what you've done!" she sobbed. "The only friend I had, the only person in the world who liked me enough to treat me decently is insulted by my husband in my own house."

She threw herself on the sofa and began to cry passionately into the pillows.

"He brought it on himself," said Roger stubbornly. "I've stood as much as my self-respect will allow. I don't want you going out with him any more."

"I will go out with him!" cried Gretchen wildly. "I'll go out with him all I want! Do you think it's any fun living here with you?"

"Gretchen," he said coldly, "get up and put on your hat and coat and go out that door and never come back!"

Her mouth fell slightly ajar.

"But I don't want to get out," she said dazedly.

"Well then, behave yourself," and he added in a gentler voice, "I thought you were going to sleep for this forty days."

"Oh, yes," she cried bitterly, "easy enough to say! But I'm tired of sleeping." She got up, faced him defiantly. "And what's more, I'm going riding with George Tompkins tomorrow."

"You won't go out with him if I have to take you to New York and sit you down in my office until I get through."

She looked at him with rage in her eyes.

"I hate you," she said slowly. "And I'd like to take all the work you've done and tear it up and throw it in the fire. And just to give you something to worry about tomorrow, I probably won't be here when you get back."

She got up from the sofa very deliberately, looked at her flushed, tear-stained face in the mirror. Then she ran upstairs and slammed herself into the bedroom.

Automatically Roger spread out his work on the living-room table. The bright colors of the designs, the vivid ladies—Gretchen had posed for one of them—holding orange ginger ale or glistening silk hosiery, dazzled his mind into a sort of coma. His restless crayon moved here and there over the pictures, shifting a block of letters half an inch to the right, trying a dozen blues for a cool blue, and eliminating the word that made a phrase anæmic and pale. Half an hour passed—he was deep in the work now; there was no sound in the room but the velvety scratch of the crayon over the glossy board.

After a long while he looked at his watch—it was after three. The wind had come up outside and was rushing by the house corners in loud, alarming swoops, like a heavy body falling through space. He stopped his work and listened. He was not tired now, but his head felt as if it was covered with bulging veins like those pictures that hang in doctors' offices showing a body stripped of decent skin. He put his hands to his head and felt it all over. It seemed to him that on his temple the veins were knotty and brittle around an old scar.

Suddenly he began to be afraid. A hundred warnings he had heard swept into his mind. People did wreck themselves with overwork, and his body and mind were of the same vulnerable and perishable stuff. For the first time he found himself envying George Tompkins' calm nerves and healthy body. He arose and began pacing the room in a panic.

"I've got to sleep," he whispered to himself tensely. "Otherwise I'm going crazy."

He rubbed his hand over his eyes and returned to the table to put up his work, but his fingers were shaking so that he could scarcely grasp the board. The sway of a bare branch against the window made him start and cry out. He sat down on the sofa and tried to think.

"Stop! Stop! Stop!" the clock said. "Stop! Stop! Stop!"

"I can't stop," he answered aloud. "I can't afford to stop."

Listen! Why, there was the wolf at the door now! He could hear its sharp claws scrape along the varnished woodwork. He jumped up, and running to the front door flung it open; then started back with a ghastly cry. An enormous wolf was standing on the porch, glaring at him with red, malignant eyes. As he watched it the hair bristled on its neck; it gave a low growl and disappeared in the darkness. Then Roger realized with a silent, mirthless laugh that it was the police dog from over the way.

Dragging his limbs wearily into the kitchen, he brought the alarm clock into the living room and set it for seven. Then he wrapped himself in his overcoat, lay down on the sofa and fell immediately into a heavy, dreamless sleep.

When he awoke the light was still shining feebly, but the room was the gray color of a winter morning. He got up, and looking anxiously at his hands found to his relief that they no longer trembled. He felt much better. Then he began to remember in detail the events of the night before, and his brow drew up again in three shallow wrinkles. There was work ahead of him, twenty-four hours of work; and Gretchen, whether she wanted to or not, must sleep for one more day.

Roger's mind glowed suddenly as if he had just thought of a new advertising idea. A few minutes later he was hurrying through the sharp morning air to Kingsley's drug store.

"Is Mr. Kingsley down yet?"

The druggist's head appeared around the corner of the prescription room.

"Here I am."

"Oh, I wonder if I can talk to you alone."

"Come right back here, Mr. Halsey."

At 7:30, Roger, back home again, walked into his own kitchen. The general housework girl had just arrived and was taking off her hat.

"Bebé"—he was not on familiar terms with her; this was her name—"I want you to cook Mrs. Halsey's breakfast right away. I'll take it up myself."

It struck Bebé that this was an unusual service for so busy a man to render his wife, but if she had seen his conduct when he had carried the tray from the kitchen she would have been even more surprised. For he set it down on the dining-room table and put into the coffee half a teaspoonful of a white substance that was not powdered sugar. Then he mounted the stairs and opened the door of the bedroom.

Gretchen woke up with a start, glanced at the twin bed[18] which had not been slept in and bent on Roger a glance of astonishment, which changed to contempt when she saw the breakfast in his hand. She thought he was bringing it as a capitulation.

"I don't want any breakfast," she said coldly, and his heart sank, "except some coffee."

"No breakfast?" Roger's voice expressed disappointment.

"I said I'd take some coffee."

Roger discreetly deposited the tray on a table beside the bed and returned quickly to the kitchen.

"We're going away until tomorrow afternoon," he told Bebé, "and I want to close up the house right now. So you just put on your hat and go home."

He looked at his watch. It was ten minutes to eight and he wanted to catch the 8:10 train. He waited five minutes and then tiptoed softly upstairs and into Gretchen's room. She was sound asleep. The coffee cup was empty save for black dregs and a film of thin brown paste on the bottom. He looked at her rather anxiously, but her breathing was regular and clear.

From the closet he took a suitcase and very quickly began filling it with her shoes—street shoes, evening slippers, rubber-soled oxfords[19]—he had not realized that she owned so many pairs. When he closed the suitcase it was bulging.

He hesitated a minute, took a pair of sewing scissors from a box and following the telephone wire until it went out of sight behind the dresser, severed it in one neat clip. He jumped as there was a soft knock at the door. It was the nursemaid. He had forgotten her existence.

"Mrs. Halsey and I are going up to the city till tomorrow," he said glibly.

Back in the room, a wave of pity passed over him. Gretchen seemed suddenly lovely and helpless, sleeping there. It was somehow terrible to rob her young life of a day. He touched her hair with his fingers, and as she murmured something in her dream he leaned over and kissed her bright cheek. Then he picked up the suitcase full of shoes, locked the door and ran briskly down the stairs.

III

By five o'clock that afternoon the last package of cards for Garrod's shoes had been sent by messenger to H. G. Garrod at the Biltmore Hotel.[20] He was to give some sort of decision by nine o'clock next morning. At 5:30 Roger's stenographer tapped him on the shoulder.

"Here's Mr. Golden, the superintendent of the building, to see you."

Roger turned around dazedly.

"Oh, how do?"

Mr. Golden came directly to the point. If Mr. Halsey intended to keep the office any longer the little oversight about the rent had better be remedied right away.

"Mr. Golden," said Roger wearily, "everything'll be all right tomorrow. If you worry me now maybe you'll never get your money. After tomorrow nothing'll matter."

Mr. Golden looked at the tenant uneasily. Young men sometimes did away with themselves when business went wrong. Then his eye fell unpleasantly on the initialed suitcase beside the desk.

"Going on a trip?" he asked pointedly.

"What? Oh, no. That's just some clothes."

"Clothes, eh? Well, Mr. Halsey, just to prove that you mean what you say, suppose you let me keep that suitcase until tomorrow noon."

"Help yourself."

Mr. Golden picked it up with a deprecatory gesture.

"Just a matter of form," he remarked.

"I understand," said Roger, swinging around to his desk. "Good afternoon."

Mr. Golden seemed to feel that the conversation should close on a softer key.

"And don't work too hard, Mr. Halsey. You don't want to have a nervous break——"

"No," shouted Roger, "I don't. But I will if you don't leave me alone."

As the door closed behind Mr. Golden, Roger's stenographer turned sympathetically around.

"You shouldn't have let him get away with that," she said. "What's in there? Clothes?"

"No," answered Roger absently. "Just all my wife's shoes."

He slept in the office that night on a sofa beside his desk. At dawn he awoke with a nervous start, rushed out into the street for coffee and returned in ten minutes in a panic—afraid that he might have missed Mr. Garrod's telephone call. It was then 6:30.

By eight o'clock his whole body seemed to be on fire. When his two artists arrived he was stretched on the couch in almost physical pain. The phone rang imperatively at 9:30 and he picked up the receiver with trembling hands.

"Hello."

"Is this the Halsey agency?"

"Yes, this is Mr. Halsey speaking."

"This is Mr. H. G. Garrod."

Roger's heart stopped beating.

"I called up, young fellow, to say that this is wonderful work you've given us here. We want all of it and as much more as your office can do."

"Oh, God!" cried Roger into the transmitter.

"What?" Mr. H. G. Garrod was considerably startled. "Say, wait a minute there!"

But he was talking to nobody. The phone had clattered to the floor and Roger, stretched full length on the couch, was sobbing as if his heart would break.

IV

Three hours later, his face somewhat pale, but his eyes calm as a child's, Roger opened the door of his wife's bedroom with the morning paper under his arm. At the sound of his footsteps she started awake.

"What time is it?" she demanded.

He looked at his watch.

"Twelve o'clock."

Suddenly she began to cry.

"Roger," she said brokenly, "I'm sorry I was so bad last night."

He nodded coolly.

"Everything's all right now," he said. Then, after a pause, "I've got the account—the first one."

She turned towards him quickly.

"You have?" Then, after a minute's silence, "Can I get a new dress?"[21]

"Dress?" He laughed shortly. "You can get a dozen. This account alone will bring us in forty thousand a year.[22] It's one of the biggest in the West."

She looked at him, startled.

"Forty thousand a year!"

"Yes."

"Gosh"—and then faintly—"I didn't know it'd really be anything like that." Again she thought a minute. "We can have a house like George Tompkins'."

"I want a home—not an interior-decoration shop."

"Forty thousand a year!" she repeated again, and then added softly, "Oh, Roger ——"

"Yes?"

"I'm not going out with George Tompkins."

"I wouldn't let you," he said shortly, "even if you wanted to."

She made a show of indignation.

"Why, I've had a date with him for this Thursday for weeks."

"It isn't Thursday."

"It is."

"It's Friday."

"Why, Roger, you must be crazy! Don't you think I know what day it is?"

"It isn't Thursday," he said stubbornly. "Look!" And he held out the morning paper.

"Friday!" she exclaimed. "Why, this is a mistake! This must be last week's paper. Today's Thursday."

She closed her eyes and thought for a moment.

"Yesterday was Wednesday," she said decisively. "The laundress came yesterday. I guess I know."

"Well," he said smugly, "look at the paper. There isn't any question about it."

With a bewildered look on her face she got out of bed and began searching for her clothes. Roger went into the bathroom to shave. A minute later he heard the springs creak again. Gretchen was getting back into bed.

"What's the matter?" he inquired, putting his head around the corner of the bathroom.

"I'm scared," she said in a trembling voice. "I think my nerves are giving away. I can't find any of my shoes."

"Your shoes? Why, the closet's full of them."[23]

"I know, but I can't see one." Her face was pale with fear. "Oh, Roger!"

Roger came to her bedside and put his arm around her.

"Oh, Roger," she cried, "what's the matter with me? First that newspaper and now all my shoes. Take care of me, Roger."

"I'll get the doctor," he said.

He walked remorselessly to the telephone and took up the receiver.

"Phone seems to be out of order," he remarked after a minute; "I'll send Bebé."

The doctor arrived in ten minutes.

"I think I'm on the verge of a collapse," Gretchen told him in a strained voice.

Doctor Gregory sat down on the edge of the bed and took her wrist in his hand.

"It seems to be in the air this morning."

"I got up," said Gretchen in an awed voice, "and I found that I'd lost a whole day. I had an engagement to go riding with George Tompkins ——"

"What?" exclaimed the doctor in surprise. Then he laughed.

"George Tompkins won't go riding with anyone for many days to come."

"Has he gone away?" asked Gretchen curiously.

"He's going West."

"Why?" demanded Roger. "Is he running away with somebody's wife?"

"No," said Doctor Gregory. "He's had a nervous breakdown."

"What?" they exclaimed in unison.

"He just collapsed like an opera hat[24] in his cold shower."

"But he was always talking about his—his balanced life," gasped Gretchen. "He was always warning Roger about overstrain. He had it on his mind."

"I know," said the doctor. "He's been babbling about it all morning. I think it's driven him a little mad. He worked pretty hard at it, you know."

"At what?" demanded Roger in bewilderment.

"At keeping his life balanced." He turned to Gretchen. "Now all I'll prescribe for this lady here is a good rest. If she'll just stay around the house for a few days and take forty winks of sleep she'll be as fit as ever. She's been under some strain."

"Doctor," exclaimed Roger hoarsely, "don't you think I'd better have a rest or something? I've been working pretty hard lately."

"You!" Doctor Gregory laughed, slapped him violently on the back. "My boy, I never saw you looking better in your life."

Roger turned around quickly to conceal his smile—winked forty times, or almost forty times, at the autographed picture of Mr. George Tompkins, which hung slightly askew on the bedroom wall.

Diamond Dick and the First Law of Woman

Hearst's International
April 1924
$1,500

When Diana Dickey came back from France in the spring of 1919, her parents considered that she had atoned for her nefarious past. She had served a year in the Red Cross[1] and she was presumably engaged to a young American ace of position and charm. They could ask no more; of Diana's former sins only her nickname survived——

Diamond Dick![2]—she had selected it herself, of all the names in the world, when she was a thin, black-eyed child of ten.

"Diamond Dick," she would insist, "that's my name. Anybody that won't call me that's a double darn fool."

"But that's not a nice name for a little lady," objected her governess. "If you want to have a boy's name why don't you call yourself George Washington?"[3]

"Be-cause my name's Diamond Dick," explained Diana patiently. "Can't you understand? I got to be named that be-cause if I don't I'll have a fit and upset the family, see?"

She ended by having the fit—a fine frenzy that brought a disgusted nerve specialist out from New York—and the nickname too. And once in possession she set about modeling her facial expression on that of a butcher boy who delivered meats at Greenwich[4] back doors. She stuck out her lower jaw and parted her lips on one side, exposing sections of her first teeth—and from this alarming aperture there issued the harsh voice of one far gone in crime.

"Miss Caruthers," she would sneer crisply, "what's the idea of no jam? Do you wanta whack the side of the head?"

"*Diana!* I'm going to call your mother *this minute!*"

"Look at here!" threatened Diana darkly, "If you call her you're liable to get a bullet the side of the head."

Miss Caruthers raised her hand uneasily to her bangs. She was somewhat awed.

"Very well," she said uncertainly, "if you want to act like a little ragamuffin——"

Diana did want to. The evolutions which she practiced daily on the sidewalk and which were thought by the neighbors to be some new form of hop-scotch were in reality the preliminary work on an Apache slouch. When it was perfected, Diana lurched forth into the streets of Greenwich, her face violently distorted and half obliterated by her father's slouch hat, her body reeling from side to side, jerked hither and yon by the shoulders, until to look at her long was to feel a faint dizziness rising to the brain.

At first it was merely absurd, but when Diana's conversation commenced to glow with weird rococo phrases, which she imagined to be the dialect of the underworld, it became alarming. And a few years later she further complicated the problem by turning into a beauty—a dark little beauty with tragedy eyes and a rich voice stirring in her throat.

Then America entered the war[5] and Diana on her eighteenth birthday sailed with a canteen unit to France.

The past was over; all was forgotten. Just before the armistice was signed, she was cited in orders for coolness under fire. And—this was the part that particularly pleased her mother—it was rumored that she was engaged to be married to Mr. Charley Abbot of Boston and Bar Harbor, "a young aviator of position and charm."

But Mrs. Dickey was scarcely prepared for the changed Diana who landed in New York. Seated in the limousine bound for Greenwich, she turned to her daughter with astonishment in her eyes.

"Why, everybody's proud of you, Diana," she cried, "the house is simply bursting with flowers. Think of all you've seen and done, at *nineteen!*"

Diana's face, under an incomparable saffron hat, stared out into Fifth Avenue, gay with banners for the returning divisions.

"The war's over," she said in a curious voice, as if it had just occurred to her this minute.

"Yes," agreed her mother cheerfully, "and we won. I knew we would all the time."

She wondered how to best introduce the subject of Mr. Abbot.

"You're quieter," she began tentatively. "You look as if you were more ready to settle down."

"I want to come out this fall."

"But I thought——" Mrs. Dickey stopped and coughed—"Rumors had led me to believe——"

"Well, go on, Mother. What did you hear?"

"It came to my ears that you were engaged to that young Charles Abbot."

Diana did not answer and her mother licked nervously at her veil. The silence in the car became oppressive. Mrs. Dickey had always stood somewhat in awe of Diana—and she began to wonder if she had gone too far.

"The Abbots are such nice people in Boston,"[6] she ventured uneasily. "I've met his mother several times—she told me how devoted——"

"Mother!" Diana's voice, cold as ice, broke in upon her loquacious dream. "I don't care what you heard or where you heard it, but I'm not engaged to Charley Abbot. And please don't ever mention the subject to me again."

In November Diana made her début in the ball room of the Ritz.[7] There was a touch of irony in this "introduction to life"—for at nineteen Diana had seen more of reality, of courage and terror and pain, than all the pompous dowagers who peopled the artificial world.

But she was young and the artificial world was redolent of orchids and pleasant, cheerful snobbery and orchestras which set the rhythm of the year, summing up the sadness and suggestiveness of life in new tunes. All night the saxophones wailed the hopeless comment of the Beale Street Blues,[8] while five hundred pairs of gold and silver slippers shuffled the shining dust. At the gray tea hour there were always rooms that throbbed incessantly with this low sweet fever, while fresh faces drifted here and there like rose petals blown by the sad horns around the floor.

In the center of this twilight universe Diana moved with the season, keeping half a dozen dates a day with half a dozen men, drowsing asleep at dawn with the beads and chiffon of an evening dress tangled among dying orchids on the floor beside her bed.[9]

The year melted into summer. The flapper craze startled New York, and skirts went absurdly high and the sad orchestras played new tunes. For a while Diana's beauty seemed to embody this new fashion as once it had seemed to embody the higher excitement of the war; but it was noticeable that she encouraged no lovers, that for all her popularity her name never became identified with that of any one man. She had had a hundred "chances," but when she felt an interest was becoming an infatuation she was at pains to end it once and for all.

A second year dissolved into long dancing nights and swimming trips to the warm south. The flapper movement scattered to the winds and was forgotten; skirts tumbled precipitously to the floor[10] and there were fresh songs from the saxophone for a new crop of girls. Most of those with whom she had come out were married now—some of them had babies. But Diana, in a changing world, danced on to newer tunes.

With a third year it was hard to look at her fresh and lovely face and realize she had once been in the war. To the young generation it was already a shadowy event that had absorbed their older brothers in the dim past—ages ago. And Diana felt that when its last echoes finally died away her youth, too, would be over. It was only occasionally now that anyone called her "Diamond Dick." When it happened, as it did sometimes, a curious, puzzled expression would come into her eyes as though she could never connect the two pieces of her life that were broken sharply asunder.

Then, when five years had past,[11] a brokerage house failed in Boston and Charley Abbot, the war hero, came back from Paris, wrecked and broken by drink and with scarcely a penny to his name.

Diana saw him first at the Restaurant Mont Mihiel, sitting at a side table with a plump, indiscriminate blonde from the half-world. She excused herself unceremoniously from her escort and made her way toward him. He looked up as she approached and she felt a sudden faintness, for he was worn to a shadow and his eyes, large and dark like her own, were burning in red rims of fire.

"Why, Charley——"

He got drunkenly to his feet and they shook hands in a dazed way. He murmured an introduction, but the girl at the table evinced her displeasure at the meeting by glaring at Diana with cold blue eyes.

"Why, Charley——" said Diana again, "you've come home, haven't you."

"I'm here for good."

"I want to see you, Charley. I—I want to see you as soon as possible. Will you come out to the country tomorrow?"

"Tomorrow?" He glanced with an apologetic expression at the blonde girl. "I've got a date. Don't know about tomorrow. Maybe later in the week——"

"Break your date."

His companion had been drumming with her fingers on the cloth and looking restlessly around the room. At this remark she wheeled sharply back to the table.

"Charley," she ejaculated, with a significant frown.

"Yes, I know," he said to her cheerfully, and turned to Diana. "I can't make it tomorrow. I've got a date."

"It's absolutely necessary that I see you tomorrow," went on Diana ruthlessly. "Stop looking at me in that idiotic way and say you'll come out to Greenwich."

"What's the idea?" cried the other girl in a slightly raised voice. "Why don't you stay at your own table? You must be tight."

"Now Elaine!" said Charley, turning to her reprovingly.

"I'll meet the train that gets to Greenwich at six," Diana went on coolly. "If you can't get rid of this—this woman——" she indicated his companion with a careless wave of her hand—"send her to the movies."

With an exclamation the other girl got to her feet and for a moment a scene was imminent. But nodding to Charley, Diana turned from the table, beckoned to her escort across the room and left the café.

"I don't like her," cried Elaine querulously when Diana was out of hearing, "who is she anyhow? Some old girl of yours?"

"That's right," he answered, frowning. "Old girl of mine. In fact, my only old girl."

"Oh, you've known her all your life."

"No." He shook his head. "When I first met her she was a canteen worker in the war."

"*She* was!" Elaine raised her brows in surprise. "Why she doesn't look——"

"Oh, she's not nineteen any more—she's nearly twenty-five." He laughed. "I saw her sitting on a box at an ammunition dump near Soissons[12] one day with enough lieutenants around her to officer a regiment. Three weeks after that we were engaged!"

"Then what?" demanded Elaine sharply.

"Usual thing," he answered with a touch of bitterness. "She broke it off. Only unusual part of it was that I never knew why. Said good-by to her one day and left for my squadron. I must have said something or done something then that started the big fuss. I'll never know. In fact I don't remember anything about it very clearly because a few hours later I had a crash and what happened just before has always been damn dim in my head. As soon as I was well enough to care about anything I saw that the situation was changed. Thought at first that there must be another man."

"Did she break the engagement?"

"She cern'ly did. While I was getting better she used to sit by my bed for hours looking at me with the funniest expression in her eyes. Finally I asked for a mirror—I thought I must be all cut up or something. But I wasn't. Then one day she began to cry. She said she'd been thinking it over and perhaps it was a mistake and all that sort of thing. Seemed to be referring to some quarrel we'd had when we said good-by just before I got hurt. But I was still a pretty sick man and the whole thing didn't seem to make any sense unless there was another man in it somewhere. She said that we both wanted our freedom, and then she looked at me as if she expected me to make some explanation or apology—and I couldn't think what I'd done. I remember leaning back in the bed and wishing I could die right then and there. Two months later I heard she'd sailed for home."

Elaine leaned anxiously over the table.

"Don't go to the country with her, Charley," she said. "Please don't go. She wants you back—I can tell by looking at her."

He shook his head and laughed.

"Yes she does," insisted Elaine, "I can tell. I hate her. She had you once and now she wants you back. I can see it in her eyes. I wish you'd stay in New York with me."

"No," he said stubbornly. "Going out and look her over. Diamond Dick's an old girl of mine."

Diana was standing on the station platform in the late afternoon, drenched with golden light. In the face of her immaculate freshness Charley Abbot felt ragged and old. He was only twenty-nine,[13] but four wild years had left many lines around his dark, handsome eyes. Even his walk was tired—it was no longer a demonstration of fitness and physical grace. It was a way of getting somewhere, failing other forms of locomotion; that was all.

"Charley," Diana cried, "where's your bag?"

"I only came out to dinner—I can't possibly spend the night."

He was sober, she saw, but he looked as if he needed a drink badly. She took his arm and guided him to a red-wheeled coupé[14] parked in the street.

"Get in and sit down," she commanded. "You walk as if you were about to fall down anyhow."

"Never felt better in my life."

She laughed scornfully.

"Why do you have to get back tonight?" she demanded.

"I promised—you see I had an engagement—"

"Oh, let her wait!" exclaimed Diana impatiently. "She didn't look as if she had much else to do. Who is she anyhow?"

"I don't see how that could possibly interest you, Diamond Dick."

She flushed at the familiar name.

"Everything about you interests me. Who is that girl?"

"Elaine Russel. She's in the movies—sort of."

"She looked pulpy," said Diana thoughtfully. "I keep thinking of her. You look pulpy too. What are you doing with yourself—waiting for another war?"

They turned into the drive of a big rambling house on the Sound.[15] Canvas was being stretched for dancing on the lawn.

"Look!" She was pointing at a figure in knickerbockers[16] on a side veranda. "That's my brother Breck. You've never met him. He's home from New Haven[17] for the Easter holidays and he's having a dance tonight."

A handsome boy of eighteen came down the veranda steps towards them.

"He thinks you're the greatest man in the world," whispered Diana. "Pretend you're wonderful."

There was an embarrassed introduction.

"Done any flying lately?" asked Breck immediately.

"Not for some years," admitted Charley.

"I was too young for the war myself," said Breck regretfully, "but I'm going to try for a pilot's license this summer. It's the only thing, isn't it—flying I mean."[18]

"Why, I suppose so," said Charley somewhat puzzled. "I hear you're having a dance tonight."

Breck waved his hand carelessly.

"Oh, just a lot of people from around here. I should think anything like that'd bore you to death—after all you've seen."

Charley turned helplessly to Diana.

"Come on," she said, laughing, "we'll go inside."

Mrs. Dickey met them in the hall and subjected Charley to a polite but somewhat breathless scrutiny. The whole household seemed to treat him with unusual respect, and the subject had a tendency to drift immediately to the war.

"What are you doing now?" asked Mr. Dickey. "Going into your father's business?"

"There isn't any business left," said Charley frankly. "I'm just about on my own."

Mr. Dickey considered for a moment.

"If you haven't made any plans why don't you come down and see me at my office some day this week. I've got a little proposition that may interest you."

It annoyed Charley to think that Diana had probably arranged all this. He needed no charity. He had not been crippled, and the war was over five years. People did not talk like this any more.

The whole first floor had been set with tables for the supper that would follow the dance, so Charley and Diana had dinner with Mr. and Mrs. Dickey in the library upstairs. It was an uncomfortable meal at which Mr. Dickey did the talking and Diana covered up the gaps with nervous gaiety. He was glad when it was over and he was standing with Diana on the veranda in the gathering darkness.

"Charley——" She leaned close to him and touched his arm gently. "Don't go to New York tonight. Spend a few days down here with me. I want to talk to you and I don't feel that I can talk tonight with this party going on."

"I'll come out again—later in the week," he said evasively.

"Why not stay tonight?"

"I promised I'd be back at eleven."

"At eleven?" She looked at him reproachfully. "Do you have to account to that girl for your evenings?"

"I like her," he said defiantly. "I'm not a child, Diamond Dick, and I rather resent your attitude. I thought you closed out your interest in my life five years ago."

"You won't stay?"

"No."

"All right—then we only have an hour. Let's walk out and sit on the wall by the Sound."

Side by side they started through the deep twilight where the air was heavy with salt and roses.

"Do you remember the last time we walked somewhere together?" she whispered.

"Why—no. I don't think I do. Where was it?"

"It doesn't matter—if you've forgotten."

When they reached the shore she swung herself up on the low wall that skirted the water.

"It's spring, Charley."

"Another spring."

"No—just spring. If you say 'another spring' it means you're getting old." She hesitated. "Charley——"

"Yes, Diamond Dick."

"I've been waiting to talk to you like this for five years."

Looking at him out of the corner of her eye she saw he was frowning and changed her tone.

"What kind of work are you going into, Charley?"

"I don't know. I've got a little money left and I won't have to do anything for awhile. I don't seem to fit into business very well."

"You mean like you fitted into war."

"Yes." He turned to her with a spark of interest. "I belonged to the war. It seems a funny thing to say but I think I'll always look back on those days as the happiest in my life."

"I know what you mean," she said slowly. "Nothing quite so intense or so dramatic will ever happen to our generation again."

They were silent for a moment. When he spoke again his voice was trembling a little.

"There are things lost in it—parts of me—that I can look for and never find. It was my war in a way, you see, and you can't quite hate what was your own." He turned to her suddenly. "Let's be frank, Diamond Dick—we loved each other once and it seems—seems rather silly to be stalling this way with you."

She caught her breath.

"Yes," she said faintly, "let's be frank."

"I know what you're up to and I know you're doing it to be kind. But life doesn't start all over again when a man talks to an old love on a spring night."

"I'm not doing it to be kind."

He looked at her closely.

"You lie, Diamond Dick. But—even if you loved me now it wouldn't matter. I'm not like I was five years ago—I'm a different person, can't you see? I'd rather have a drink this minute than all the moonlight in the world. I don't even think I could love a girl like you any more."

She nodded.

"I see."

"Why wouldn't you marry me five years ago, Diamond Dick?"

"I don't know," she said after a minute's hesitation, "I was wrong."

"Wrong!" he exclaimed bitterly. "You talk as if it had been guesswork, like betting on white or red."

"No, it wasn't guesswork."

There was a silence for a minute—then she turned to him with shining eyes.

"Won't you kiss me, Charley?" she asked simply.

He started.

"Would it be so hard to do?" she went on. "I've never asked a man to kiss me before."

With an exclamation he jumped off the wall.

"I'm going to the city," he said.

"Am I—such bad company as all that?"

"Diana." He came close to her and put his arms around her knees and looked into her eyes. "You know that if I kiss you I'll have to stay. I'm afraid of you—afraid of your kindness, afraid to remember anything about you at all. And I couldn't go from a kiss of yours to—another girl."

"Good-by," she said suddenly.

He hesitated for a moment then he protested helplessly.

"You put me in a terrible position."

"Good-by."

"Listen Diana——"

"Please go away."

He turned and walked quickly toward the house.

Diana sat without moving while the night breeze made cool puffs and ruffles on her chiffon dress. The moon had risen higher now, and floating in the Sound was a triangle of silver scales, trembling a little to the stiff, tinny drip of the banjos on the lawn.[19]

Alone at last—she was alone at last. There was not even a ghost left now to drift with through the years. She might stretch out her arms as far as they could reach into the night without fear that they would brush friendly cloth. The thin silver had worn off from all the stars.

She sat there for almost an hour, her eyes fixed upon the points of light on the other shore. Then the wind ran cold fingers along her silk stockings so she jumped off the wall, landing softly among the bright pebbles of the sand.

"Diana!"

Breck was coming toward her, flushed with the excitement of his party.

"Diana! I want you to meet a man in my class at New Haven. His brother took you to a prom three years ago."

She shook her head.

"I've got a headache; I'm going upstairs."

Coming closer Breck saw that her eyes were glittering with tears.

"Diana, what's the matter?"

"Nothing."

"Something's the matter."

"Nothing, Breck. But oh, take care, take care! Be careful who you love."

"Are you in love with—Charley Abbot?"

She gave a strange, hard little laugh.

"Me? Oh, God, no, Breck! I don't love anybody. I wasn't made for anything like love. I don't even love myself any more. It was you I was talking about. That was advice, don't you understand?"

She ran suddenly toward the house, holding her skirts high out of the dew. Reaching her own room she kicked off her slippers and threw herself on the bed in the darkness.

"I should have been careful," she whispered to herself. "All my life I'll be punished for not being more careful. I wrapped all my love up like a box of candy and gave it away."

Her window was open and outside on the lawn the sad, dissonant horns were telling a melancholy story. A blackamoor was two-timing the lady to whom he had pledged faith. The lady warned him, in so many words, to stop fooling 'round Sweet Jelly-Roll,[20] even though Sweet Jelly-Roll was the color of pale cinnamon——

The 'phone on the table by her bed rang imperatively. Diana took up the receiver.

"Yes."

"One minute please, New York calling."

It flashed through Diana's head that it was Charley—but that was impossible. He must be still on the train.

"Hello." A woman was speaking. "Is this the Dickey residence?"

"Yes."

"Well, is Mr. Charles Abbot there?"

Diana's heart seemed to stop beating as she recognized the voice— it was the blonde girl of the café.

"What?" she asked dazedly.

"I would like to speak to Mr. Abbot at once please."

"You—you can't speak to him. He's gone."

There was a pause. Then the girl's voice, suspiciously:

"He isn't gone."

Diana's hands tightened on the telephone.

"I know who's talking," went on the voice, rising to a hysterical note, "and I want to speak to Mr. Abbot. If you're not telling the truth, and he finds out, there'll be trouble."

"Be quiet!"

"If he's gone, where did he go?"

"I don't know."

"If he isn't at my apartment in half an hour I'll know you're lying and I'll——"

Diana hung up the receiver and tumbled back on the bed—too weary of life to think or care. Out on the lawn the orchestra was singing and the words drifted in her window on the breeze.

> "Lis–*sen* while I—get you tole:
> Stop foolin' 'roun' sweet—Jelly-Roll——"

She listened. The negro voices were wild and loud—life was in that key, so harsh a key. How abominably helpless she was! Her appeal was ghostly, impotent, absurd, before the barbaric urgency of this other girl's desire.

> "Just treat me pretty, just treat me sweet
> "Cause I possess a fo'ty-fo' that don't repeat."

The music sank to a weird, threatening minor. It reminded her of something—some mood in her own childhood—and a new atmosphere seemed to open up around her. It was not so much a definite memory as it was a current, a tide setting through her whole body.

Diana jumped suddenly to her feet and groped for her slippers in the darkness. The song was beating in her head and her little teeth set together in a click. She could feel the tense golf-muscles rippling and tightening along her arms.

Running into the hall she opened the door to her father's room, closed it cautiously behind her and went to the bureau. It was in the top drawer—black and shining among the pale anaemic collars. Her hand closed around the grip and she drew out the bullet clip with steady fingers. There were five shots in it.

Back in her room she called the garage.

"I want my roadster[21] at the side entrance right away!"

Wriggling hurriedly out of her evening dress to the sound of breaking snaps she let it drop in a soft pile on the floor, replacing it with a golf sweater, a checked sport-skirt and an old blue and white blazer which she pinned at the* collar with a diamond bar. Then she pulled a tam-o-shanter over her dark hair and looked once in the mirror before turning out the light.

"Come on, Diamond Dick!" she whispered aloud.

With a short exclamation she plunged the automatic into her blazer pocket and hurried from the room.

Diamond Dick! The name had jumped out at her once from a lurid cover, symbolizing her childish revolt against the softness of life. Diamond Dick was a law unto himself, making his own judgements with his back against the wall. If justice was slow he vaulted into his saddle and was off for the foothills, for in the unvarying rightness of his instincts he was higher and harder than the law. She had seen in him a sort of deity, infinitely resourceful, infinitely just. And the commandment he laid down for himself in the cheap, ill-written pages was first and foremost to keep what was his own.

---

* *Hearst's International* broke the text at this point after six contiguous pages (pp. 58–63), continuing the story on p. 134.

An hour and a half from the time when she had left Greenwich, Diana pulled up her roadster in front of the Restaurant Mont Mihiel. The theaters were already dumping their crowds into Broadway and half a dozen couples in evening dress looked at her curiously as she slouched through the door. A moment later she was talking to the head waiter.

"Do you know a girl named Elaine Russel?"

"Yes, Miss Dickey. She comes here quite often."

"I wonder if you can tell me where she lives."

The head waiter considered.

"Find out," she said sharply, "I'm in a hurry."

He bowed. Diana had come there many times with many men. She had never asked him a favor before.

His eyes roved hurriedly around the room.

"Sit down," he said.

"I'm all right. You hurry!"

He crossed the room and whispered to a man at a table—in a minute he was back with the address, an apartment on Forty-Ninth Street.

In her car again she looked at her wrist watch—it was almost midnight, the appropriate hour. A feeling of romance, of desperate and dangerous adventure thrilled her, seemed to flow out of the electric signs and the rushing cabs and the high stars. Perhaps she was only one out of a hundred people bound on such an adventure tonight—for her there had been nothing like this since the war.

Skidding the corner into East Forty-Ninth Street she scanned the apartments on both sides. There it was—"The Elkson"—a wide mouth of forbidding yellow light. In the hall a negro elevator boy asked her name.

"Tell her it's a girl with a package from the moving picture company."

He worked a plug noisily.

"Miss Russel? There's a lady here says she's got a package from the moving picture company."

A pause.

"That's what she says. . . . All right." He turned to Diana. "She wasn't expecting no package but you can bring it up." He looked at her, frowned suddenly. "You ain't got no package."

Without answering she walked into the elevator and he followed, shoving the gate closed with maddening languor. . . .

"First door to your right."

She waited until the elevator had started down again. Then she knocked, her fingers tightening on the automatic in her blazer pocket.

Running footsteps, a laugh; the door swung open and Diana stepped quickly into the room.

It was a small apartment, bedroom, bath and kitchenette, furnished in pink and white and heavy with last week's smoke. Elaine Russel had opened the door herself. She was dressed to go out and a green evening cape was over her arm. Charley Abbot sipping at a highball was stretched out in the room's only easy chair.

"What is it?" cried Elaine quickly.

With a sharp movement Diana slammed the door behind her and Elaine stepped back, her mouth falling ajar.

"Good evening," said Diana coldly, and then a line from a forgotten nickel novel[22] flashed into her head, "I hope I don't intrude."

"What do you want?" demanded Elaine. "You've got your nerve to come butting in here!"

Charley who had not said a word set down his glass heavily on the arm of the chair. The two girls looked at each other with unwavering eyes.

"Excuse me," said Diana slowly, "but I think you've got my man."

"I thought you were supposed to be a lady!" cried Elaine in rising anger. "What do you mean by forcing your way into this room?"

"I mean business. I've come for Charley Abbot."

Elaine gasped.

"Why, you must be crazy!"

"On the contrary, I've never been so sane in my life. I came here to get something that belongs to me."

Charley uttered an exclamation but with a simultaneous gesture the two women waved him silent.

"All right," cried Elaine, "we'll settle this right now."

"I'll settle it myself," said Diana sharply. "There's no question or argument about it. Under other circumstances I might feel a certain pity for you—in this case you happen to be in my way. What is there between you two? Has he promised to marry you?"

"That's none of your business!"

"You'd better answer," Diana warned her.

"I won't answer."

Diana took a sudden step forward, drew back her arm and with all the strength in her slim hard muscles, hit Elaine a smashing blow in the cheek with her open hand.[23]

Elaine staggered up against the wall. Charley uttered an exclamation and sprang forward to find himself looking into the muzzle of a forty-four held in a small determined hand.

"Help!" cried Elaine wildly. "Oh, she's hurt me! She's hurt me!"

"Shut up!" Diana's voice was hard as steel. "You're not hurt. You're just pulpy and soft. But if you start to raise a row I'll pump you full of tin as sure as you're alive. Sit down! Both of you. Sit *down!*"

Elaine sat down quickly, her face pale under her rouge. After an instant's hesitation Charley sank down again into his chair.

"Now," went on Diana, waving the gun in a constant arc that included them both. "I guess you know I'm in a serious mood. Understand this first of all. As far as I'm concerned neither of you have any rights whatsoever and I'd kill you both rather than leave this room without getting what I came for. I asked if he'd promised to marry you."

"Yes," said Elaine sullenly.

The gun moved towards Charley.

"Is that so?"

He licked his lips, nodded.

"My God!" said Diana in contempt. "And you admit it. Oh, it's funny, it's absurd—if I didn't care so much I'd laugh."

"Look here!" muttered Charley, "I'm not going to stand much of this, you know."

"Yes you are! You're soft enough to stand anything now." She turned to the girl, who was trembling. "Have you any letters of his?"

Elaine shook her head.

"You lie," said Diana. "Go and get them! I'll give you three. One——"

Elaine rose nervously and went into the other room. Diana edged along the table, keeping her constantly in sight.

"Hurry!"

Elaine returned with a small package in her hand which Diana took and slipped into her blazer pocket.

"Thanks. You had 'em all carefully preserved I see. Sit down again and we'll have a little talk."

Elaine sat down. Charley drained off his whisky and soda and leaned back stupidly in his chair.

"Now," said Diana, "I'm going to tell you a little story. It's about a girl who went to a war once and met a man who she thought was the finest and bravest man she had ever known. She fell in love with him and he with her and all the other men she had ever known became like pale shadows compared with this man that she loved. But one day he was shot down out of the air, and when he woke up into the world he'd changed. He didn't know it himself but he'd forgotten things and become a different man. The girl felt sad about this—she saw that she wasn't necessary to him any more, so there was nothing to do but say good-by.

"So she went away and every night for a while she cried herself to sleep but he never came back to her and five years went by. Finally word came to her that this same injury that had come between them was ruining his life. He didn't remember anything important any more—how proud and fine he had once been, and what dreams he had once had. And then the girl knew that she had the right to try and save what was left of his life because she was the only one who knew all the things he'd forgotten. But it was too late. She couldn't approach him any more—she wasn't coarse enough and gross enough to reach him now—he'd forgotten so much.

"So she took a revolver, very much like this one here, and she came after this man to the apartment of a poor, weak, harmless rat of a girl who had him in tow. She was going to either bring him to himself—or go back to the dust with him where nothing would matter any more."

She paused. Elaine shifted uneasily in her chair. Charley was leaning forward with his face in his hands.

"Charley!"

The word, sharp and distinct, startled him. He dropped his hands and looked up at her.

"Charley!" she repeated in a thin clear voice. "Do you remember Fontenay[24] in the late fall?"

A bewildered look passed over his face.

"Listen, Charley. Pay attention. Listen to every word I say. Do you remember the poplar trees at twilight, and a long column of French infantry going through the town? You had on your blue uniform, Charley, with the little numbers on the tabs and you were going to the front in an hour. Try and remember, Charley!"

He passed his hand over his eyes and gave a funny little sigh. Elaine sat bolt upright in her chair and gazed from one to the other of them with wide eyes.

"Do you remember the poplar trees?" went on Diana. "The sun was going down and the leaves were silver and there was a bell ringing. Do you remember, Charley? Do you remember?"

Again silence. Charley gave a curious little groan and lifted his head.

"I can't—understand," he muttered hoarsely. "There's something funny here."

"Can't you remember?" cried Diana. The tears were streaming from her eyes. "Oh God! Can't you remember? The brown road and the poplar trees and the yellow sky." She sprang suddenly to her feet.

"Can't you remember?" she cried wildly. "Think, think—there's time. The bells are ringing—the bells are ringing, Charley! And there's just one hour!"

Then he too was on his feet, reeling and swaying.

"Oh-h-h-h!" he cried.

"Charley," sobbed Diana, "remember, remember, remember!"

"I see!" he said wildly. "I can see now—I remember, oh, I remember!"

With a choking sob his whole body seemed to wilt under him and he pitched back senseless into his chair.

In a minute the two girls were beside him.

"He's fainted!" Diana cried—"get some water quick."

"You devil!" screamed Elaine, her face distorted. "Look what's happened! What right have you to do this? What right? What right?"

"What right?" Diana turned to her with black, shining eyes. "Every right in the world. I've been married to Charley Abbot for five years."

Charley and Diana were married again in Greenwich early in June. After the wedding her oldest friends stopped calling her Diamond Dick—it had been a most inappropriate name for some years, they said, and it was thought that the effect on her children might be unsettling, if not distinctly pernicious.

Yet perhaps if the occasion should arise Diamond Dick would come to life again from the colored cover and, with spurs shining and buckskin fringes fluttering in the breeze, ride into the lawless hills to protect her own. For under all her softness Diamond Dick was always hard as steel—so hard that the years knew it and stood still for her and the clouds rolled apart and a sick man, hearing those untiring hoofbeats in the night, rose up and shook off the dark burden of the war.

The Third Casket

Saturday Evening Post
31 May 1924
$1,750

When you come into Cyrus Girard's office suite on the thirty-second floor you think at first that there has been a mistake, that the elevator instead of bringing you upstairs has brought you uptown, and that you are walking into an apartment on Fifth Avenue where you have no business at all. What you take to be the sound of a stock ticker[1] is only a businesslike canary swinging in a silver cage overhead, and while the languid debutante at the mahogany table gets ready to ask you your name you can feast your eyes on etchings, tapestries, carved panels and fresh flowers.

Cyrus Girard does not, however, run an interior-decorating establishment, though he has, on occasion, run almost everything else. The lounging aspect of his ante-room is merely an elaborate camouflage for the wild clamor of affairs that goes on ceaselessly within. It is merely the padded glove over the mailed fist, the smile on the face of the prize fighter.

No one was more intensely aware of this than the three young men who were waiting there one April morning to see Mr. Girard. Whenever the door marked Private trembled with the pressure of enormous affairs they started nervously in unconscious union. All three of them were on the hopeful side of thirty, each of them had just got off the train, and they had never seen one another before. They had been waiting side by side on a Circassian leather lounge for the best part of an hour.

Once the young man with the pitch-black eyes and hair had pulled out a package of cigarettes and offered it hesitantly to the two others. But the two others had refused in such a politely alarmed way that the dark young man, after a quick look around, had returned the package unsampled to his pocket. Following this disrespectful incident a long silence had fallen, broken only by the clatter of the canary as it ticked off the bond market in bird land.

When the Louis XIII clock stood at noon the door marked Private swung open in a tense, embarrassed way, and a frantic secretary demanded that the three callers step inside. They stood up as one man.

"Do you mean—all together?" asked the tallest one in some embarrassment.

"All together."

Falling unwillingly into a sort of lock step and glancing neither left nor right, they passed through a series of embattled rooms and marched into the private office of Cyrus Girard, who filled the position of Telamonian Ajax[2] among the Homeric characters of Wall Street.

He was a thin, quiet-mannered man of sixty, with a fine, restless face and the clear, fresh, trusting eyes of a child. When the procession of young men walked in he stood up behind his desk with an expectant smile.

"Parrish?" he said eagerly.

The tall young man said "Yes, sir," and was shaken by the hand.

"Jones?"

This was the young man with the black eyes and hair. He smiled back at Cyrus Girard and announced in a slightly Southern accent that he was mighty glad to meet him.

"And so you must be Van Buren," said Girard, turning to the third. Van Buren acknowledged as much. He was obviously from a large city—unflustered and very spick-and-span.

"Sit down," said Girard, looking eagerly from one to the other. "I can't tell you the pleasure of this minute."

They all smiled nervously and sat down.

"Yes, sir," went on the older man, "if I'd had any boys of my own I don't know but what I'd have wanted them to look just like you three." He saw that they were all growing pink, and he broke off with a laugh. "All right, I won't embarrass you any more. Tell me about the health of your respective fathers and we'll get down to business."

Their fathers, it seemed, were very well; they had all sent congratulatory messages by their sons for Mr. Girard's sixtieth birthday.

"Thanks. Thanks. Now that's over." He leaned back suddenly in his chair. "Well, boys, here's what I have to say. I'm retiring from business next year. I've always intended to retire at sixty, and my wife's always counted on it, and the time's come. I can't put it off any longer. I haven't any sons and I haven't any nephews and I haven't any cousins and I have a brother who's fifty years old and in the same boat I am.

He'll perhaps hang on for ten years more down here; after that it looks as if the house, Cyrus Girard, Incorporated, would change its name.

"A month ago I wrote to the three best friends I had in college, the three best friends I ever had in my life, and asked them if they had any sons between twenty-five and thirty years old. I told them I had room for just one young man here in my business, but he had to be about the best in the market. And as all three of you arrived here this morning I guess your fathers think you are. There's nothing complicated about my proposition. It'll take me three months to find out what I want to know, and at the end of that time two of you'll be disappointed; the other one can have about everything they used to give away in fairy tales, half my kingdom and, if she wants him, my daughter's hand." He raised his head slightly. "Correct me, Lola, if I've said anything wrong."

At these words the three young men started violently, looked behind them, and then jumped precipitately to their feet. Reclining lazily in an armchair not two yards away sat a gold-and-ivory little beauty with dark eyes and a moving, childish smile that was like all the lost youth in the world. When she saw the startled expressions on their faces she gave vent to a suppressed chuckle in which the victims after a moment joined.

"This is my daughter," said Cyrus Girard, smiling innocently. "Don't be so alarmed. She has many suitors come from far and near—and all that sort of thing. Stop making these young men feel silly, Lola, and ask them if they'll come to dinner with us tonight."

Lola got to her feet gravely and her gray eyes fell on them one after another.

"I only know part of your names," she said.

"Easily arranged," said Van Buren. "Mine's George."

The tall young man bowed.

"I respond to John Hardwick Parrish," he confessed, "or anything of that general sound."

She turned to the dark-haired Southerner, who had volunteered no information. "How about Mr. Jones?"

"Oh, just—Jones," he answered uneasily.

She looked at him in surprise.

"Why, how partial!" she exclaimed, laughing. "How—I might even say how fragmentary."

Mr. Jones looked around him in a frightened way.

"Well, I tell you," he said finally, "I don't guess my first name is much suited to this sort of thing."

"What is it?"

"It's Rip."

"Rip!"

Eight eyes turned reproachfully upon him.

"Young man," exclaimed Girard, "you don't mean that my old friend in his senses named his son that!"

Jones shifted defiantly on his feet.

"No, he didn't," he admitted. "He named me Oswald."

There was a ripple of sympathetic laughter.

"Now you four go along," said Girard, sitting down at his desk. "Tomorrow at nine o'clock sharp you report to my general manager, Mr. Galt, and the tournament begins. Meanwhile if Lola has her coupé-sport-limousine-roadster-landaulet,[3] or whatever she drives now, she'll probably take you to your respective hotels."

After they had gone Girard's face grew restless again and he stared at nothing for a long time before he pressed the button that started the long-delayed stream of traffic through his mind.

"One of them's sure to be all right," he muttered, "but suppose it turned out to be the dark one. Rip Jones, Incorporated!"

II

As the three months drew to an end it began to appear that not one, but all of the young men were going to turn out all right. They were all industrious, they were all possessed of that mysterious ease known as personality and, moreover, they all had brains. If Parrish, the tall young man from the West, was a little the quicker in sizing up the market; if Jones, the Southerner, was a bit the most impressive in his relations with customers, then Van Buren made up for it by spending his nights in the study of investment securities. Cyrus Girard's mind was no sooner drawn to one of them by some exhibition of shrewdness or resourcefulness than a parallel talent appeared in one of the others. Instead of having to enforce upon himself a strict neutrality he found himself trying to concentrate upon the individual merits of first one and then another—but so far without success.

Every week-end they all came out to the Girard place at Tuxedo Park,[4] where they fraternized a little self-consciously with the young and lovely Lola, and on Sunday mornings tactlessly defeated her father at golf. On the last tense week-end before the decision was to be made Cyrus Girard asked them to meet in his study after dinner. On their respective merits as future partners in Cyrus Girard, Inc., he had been unable to decide, but his despair had evoked another plan, on which he intended to base his decision.

"Gentlemen," he said, when they had convoked in his study at the appointed hour, "I have brought you here to tell you that you're all fired."

Immediately the three young men were on their feet, with shocked, reproachful expressions in their eyes.

"Temporarily," he added, smiling good-humoredly. "So spare a decrepit old man your violence and sit down."

They sat down, with short relieved smiles.

"I like you all," he went on, "and I don't know which one I like better than the others. In fact—this thing hasn't come out right at all. So I'm going to extend the competition for two more weeks—but in an entirely different way."

They all sat forward eagerly in their chairs.

"Now my generation," he went on, "have made a failure of our leisure hours. We grew up in the most hard-boiled commercial age any country ever knew,[5] and when we retire we never know what to do with the rest of our lives. Here I am, getting out at sixty, and miserable about it. I haven't any resources—I've never been much of a reader, I can't stand golf except once a week, and I haven't got a hobby in the world. Now some day you're going to be sixty too. You'll see other men taking it easy and having a good time, and you'll want to do the same. I want to find out which one of you will be the best sort of man after his business days are over."

He looked from one to the other of them eagerly. Parrish and Van Buren nodded at him comprehendingly. Jones after a puzzled half moment nodded too.

"I want you each to take two weeks and spend them as you think you'll spend your time when you're too old to work. I want you to solve my problem for me. And whichever one I think has got the most out of his leisure—he'll be the man to carry on my business. I'll know it won't swamp him like it's swamped me."

"You mean you want us to enjoy ourselves?" inquired Rip Jones politely. "Just go out and have a big time?"

Cyrus Girard nodded.

"Anything you want to do."

"I take it Mr. Girard doesn't include dissipation," remarked Van Buren.

"Anything you want to do," repeated the older man. "I don't bar anything. When it's all done I'm going to judge of its merits."

"Two weeks of travel for me," said Parrish dreamily. "That's what I've always wanted to do. I'll ——"

"Travel!" interrupted Van Buren contemptuously. "When there's so much to do here at home? Travel, perhaps, if you had a year; but for two weeks—— I'm going to try and see how the retired business man can be of some use in the world."

"I said travel," repeated Parrish sharply. "I believe we're all to employ our leisure in the best ——"

"Wait a minute," interrupted Cyrus Girard. "Don't fight this out in talk. Meet me in the office at 10:30 on the morning of August first—that's two weeks from tomorrow—and then let's see what you've done." He turned to Rip Jones. "I suppose you've got a plan too."

"No, sir," admitted Rip Jones with a puzzled look; "I'll have to think this over."

But though he thought it over for the rest of the evening Rip Jones went to bed still uninspired. At midnight he got up, found a pencil and wrote out a list of all the good times he had ever had. But all his holidays now seemed unprofitable and stale, and when he fell asleep at five his mind still threshed disconsolately on the prospect of hollow useless hours.

Next morning as Lola Girard was backing her car out of the garage she saw him hurrying toward her over the lawn.

"Ride in town, Rip?" she asked cheerfully.

"I reckon so."

"Why do you only reckon so? Father and the others left on the nine-o'clock train."

He explained to her briefly that they had all temporarily lost their jobs and there was no necessity of getting to the office today.

"I'm kind of worried about it," he said gravely. "I sure hate to leave my work. I'm going to run in this afternoon and see if they'll let me finish up a few things I had started."

"But you better be thinking how you're going to amuse yourself."

He looked at her helplessly.

"All I can think of doing is maybe take to drink," he confessed. "I come from a little town, and when they say leisure they mean hanging round the corner store."[6] He shook his head. "I don't want any leisure. This is the first chance I ever had, and I want to make good."*

"Listen, Rip," said Lola on a sudden impulse. "After you finish up at the office this afternoon you meet me and we'll fix up something together."

---

* The *Saturday Evening Post* broke the text at this point after a two-page spread (pp. 8–9), continuing the story on p. 78.

He met her, as she suggested, at five o'clock, but the melancholy had deepened in his dark eyes.

"They wouldn't let me in," he said. "I met your father in there, and he told me I had to find some way to amuse myself or I'd be just a bored old man like him."

"Never mind. We'll go to a show," she said consolingly; "and after that we'll run up on some roof and dance."[7]

It was the first of a week of evenings they spent together. Sometimes they went to the theater, sometimes to a cabaret; once they spent most of an afternoon strolling in Central Park. But she saw that from having been the most light-hearted and gay of the three young men, he was now the most moody and depressed. Everything whispered to him of the work he was missing.

Even when they danced at teatime, the click of bracelets on a hundred women's arms only reminded him of the busy office sound on Monday morning. He seemed incapable of inaction.

"This is mighty sweet of you," he said to her one afternoon, "and if it was after business hours I can't tell you how I'd enjoy it. But my mind is on all the things I ought to be doing. I'm—I'm right sad."

He saw then that he had hurt her, that by his frankness he had rejected all she was trying to do for him. But he was incapable of feeling differently.

"Lola, I'm mighty sorry," he said softly, "and maybe some day it'll be after hours again, and I can come to you ——"

"I won't be interested," she said coldly. "And I see I was foolish ever to be interested at all."

He was standing beside her car when this conversation took place, and before he could reply she had thrown it into gear and started away.

He stood there looking after her sadly, thinking that perhaps he would never see her any more and that she would remember him always as ungrateful and unkind. But there was nothing he could have said. Something dynamic in him was incapable of any except a well-earned rest.

"If it was only after hours," he muttered to himself as he walked slowly away. "If it was only after hours."

III

At ten o'clock on the morning of August first a tall, bronzed young man presented himself at the office of Cyrus Girard, Inc., and sent in his card to the president. Less than five minutes later another young man arrived, less blatantly healthy, perhaps, but with the light of triumphant achievement blazing in his eyes. Word came out through the palpitating inner door that they were both to wait.

"Well, Parrish," said Van Buren condescendingly, "how did you like Niagara Falls?"

"I couldn't tell you," answered Parrish haughtily. "You can determine that on your honeymoon."

"My honeymoon!" Van Buren started. "How—what made you think I was contemplating a honeymoon?"

"I merely meant that when you do contemplate it you will probably choose Niagara Falls."[8]

They sat for a few minutes in stony silence.

"I suppose," remarked Parrish coolly, "that you've been making a serious study of the deserving poor."

"On the contrary, I have done nothing of the kind." Van Buren looked at his watch. "I'm afraid our competitor with the rakish name is going to be late. The time set was 10:30; it now lacks three minutes of the half hour."

The private door opened, and at a command from the frantic secretary they both arose eagerly and went inside. Cyrus Girard was standing behind his desk waiting for them, watch in hand.

"Hello!" he exclaimed in surprise. "Where's Jones?"

Parrish and Van Buren exchanged a smile. If Jones were snagged somewhere so much the better.

"I beg your pardon, sir," spoke up the secretary, who had been lingering near the door; "Mr. Jones is in Chicago."

"What's he doing there?" demanded Cyrus Girard in astonishment.

"He went out to handle the matter of those silver shipments. There wasn't anyone else who knew much about it, and Mr. Galt thought ——"

"Never mind what Mr. Galt thought," broke in Girard impatiently. "Mr. Jones is no longer employed by this concern. When he gets back from Chicago pay him off and let him go." He nodded curtly. "That's all."

The secretary bowed and went out. Girard turned to Parrish and Van Buren with an angry light in his eyes.

"Well, that finishes him," he said determinedly. "Any young man who won't even attempt to obey my orders doesn't deserve a good chance." He sat down and began drumming with his fingers on the arm of his chair.

"All right, Parrish, let's hear what you've been doing with your leisure hours."

Parrish smiled ingratiatingly.

"Mr. Girard," he began, "I've had a bully time. I've been traveling."

"Traveling where? The Adirondacks?⁹ Canada?"

"No, sir. I've been to Europe."

Cyrus Girard sat up.

"I spent five days going over and five days coming back.¹⁰ That left me two days in London and a run over to Paris by aëroplane to spend the night.¹¹ I saw Westminster Abbey, the Tower of London and the Louvre, and spent an afternoon at Versailles. On the boat I kept in wonderful condition—swam, played deck tennis, walked five miles every day, met some interesting people and found time to read. I came back after the greatest two weeks of my life, feeling fine and knowing more about my own country since I had something to compare it with. That, sir, is how I spent my leisure time and that's how I intend to spend my leisure time after I'm retired."

Girard leaned back thoughtfully in his chair.

"Well, Parrish, that isn't half bad," he said. "I don't know but what the idea appeals to me—take a run over there for the sea voyage and a glimpse of the London Stock Ex—— I mean the Tower of London. Yes, sir, you've put an idea in my head." He turned to the other young man, who during this recital had been shifting uneasily in his chair. "Now, Van Buren, let's hear how you took your ease."

"I thought over the travel idea," burst out Van Buren excitedly, "and I decided against it. A man of sixty doesn't want to spend his time running back and forth between the capitals of Europe. It might fill up a year or so, but that's all. No, sir, the main thing is to have some strong interest—and especially one that'll be for the public good, because when a man gets along in years he wants to feel that he's leaving the world better for having lived in it. So I worked out a plan—it's for a historical and archæological¹² endowment center, a thing that'd change the whole face of public education, a thing any man would be interested in giving his time and money to. I've spent my whole two weeks working out the plan in detail, and let me tell you it'd be nothing but play work—just suited to the last years of an active man's life. It's been fascinating, Mr. Girard. I've learned more from doing it than I ever knew before—and I don't think I ever had a happier two weeks in my life."

When he had finished, Cyrus Girard nodded his head up and down many times in an approving and yet somehow dissatisfied way.

"Found an institute, eh?" he muttered aloud. "Well, I've always thought that maybe I'd do that some day—but I never figured on running it myself. My talents aren't much in that line. Still, it's certainly worth thinking over."

He got restlessly to his feet and began walking up and down the carpet, the dissatisfied expression deepening on his face. Several times he took out his watch and looked at it as if hoping that perhaps Jones had not gone to Chicago after all, but would appear in a few moments with a plan nearer his heart.

"What's the matter with me?" he said to himself unhappily. "When I say a thing I'm used to going through with it. I must be getting old."

Try as he might, however, he found himself unable to decide. Several times he stopped in his walk and fixed his glance first on one and then on the other of the two young men, trying to pick out some attractive characteristic to which he could cling and make his choice. But after several of these glances their faces seemed to blur together and he couldn't tell one from the other. They were twins who had told him the same story—of carrying the stock exchange by aëroplane to London and making it into a moving-picture show.

"I'm sorry, boys," he said haltingly. "I promised I'd decide this morning, and I will, but it means a whole lot to me and you'll have to give me a little time."

They both nodded, fixing their glances on the carpet to avoid encountering his distraught eyes.

Suddenly he stopped by the table and picking up the telephone called the general manager's office.

"Say, Galt," he shouted into the mouthpiece, "you sure you sent Jones to Chicago?"

"Positive," said a voice on the other end. "He came in here couple of days ago and said he was half crazy for something to do. I told him it was against orders, but he said he was out of the competition anyhow—and we needed somebody who was competent to handle that silver. So I ——"

"Well, you shouldn't have done it, see? I wanted to talk to him about something, and you shouldn't have done it."

Clack! He hung up the receiver and resumed his endless pacing up and down the floor. Confound Jones, he thought. Most ungrateful thing he ever heard of after he'd gone to all this trouble for his father's sake. Outrageous! His mind went off on a tangent and he began to wonder whether Jones would handle that business out in Chicago. It was a complicated situation—but then, Jones was a trustworthy fellow. They were all trustworthy fellows. That was the whole trouble.

Again he picked up the telephone. He would call Lola; he felt vaguely that if she wanted to she could help him. The personal element had eluded him here; her opinion would be better than his own.

"I have to ask your pardon, boys," he said unhappily; "I didn't mean there to be all this fuss and delay. But it almost breaks my heart when I think of handing this shop over to anybody at all, and when I try to decide, it all gets dark in my mind." He hesitated. "Have either one of you asked my daughter to marry him?"

"I did," said Parrish; "three weeks ago."

"So did I," confessed Van Buren; "and I still have hopes that she'll change her mind."

Girard wondered if Jones had asked her also. Probably not; he never did anything he was expected to do. He even had the wrong name.

The phone in his hand rang shrilly and with an automatic gesture he picked up the receiver.

"Chicago calling, Mr. Girard."

"I don't want to talk to anybody."

"It's personal. It's Mr. Jones."

"All right," he said, his eyes narrowing. "Put him on."

A series of clicks—then Jones' faintly Southern voice over the wire.

"Mr. Girard?"

"Yeah."

"I've been trying to get you since ten o'clock in order to apologize."

"I should think you would!" exploded Girard. "Maybe you know you're fired."

"I knew I would be," said Jones gloomily. "I guess I must be pretty dumb, Mr. Girard, but I'll tell you the truth—I can't have a good time when I quit work."

"Of course you can't!" snapped Girard. "Nobody can ——" he corrected himself. "What I mean is, it isn't an easy matter."

There was a pause at the other end of the line.

"That's exactly the way I feel," came Jones' voice regretfully. "I guess we understand each other, and there's no use my saying any more."

"What do you mean—we understand each other?" shouted Girard. "That's an impertinent remark, young man. We don't understand each other at all."

"That's what I meant," amended Jones; "I don't understand you and you don't understand me. I don't want to quit working, and you—you do."

"Me quit work!" cried Girard, his face reddening. "Say, what are you talking about? Did you say I wanted to quit work?" He shook the telephone up and down violently. "Don't talk back to me, young man! Don't tell me I want to quit! Why—why, I'm not going to quit work at all! Do you hear that? I'm not going to quit work at all!"

The transmitter slipped from his grasp and bounced from the table to the floor. In a minute he was on his knees, groping for it wildly.

"Hello!" he cried. "Hello—hello! Say, get Chicago back! I wasn't through!"

The two young men were on their feet. He hung up the receiver and turned to them, his voice husky with emotion.

"I've been an idiot," he said brokenly. "Quit work at sixty! Why—I must have been an idiot! I'm a young man still—I've got twenty good years in front of me! I'd like to see anybody send me home to die!"

The phone rang again and he took up the receiver with fire blazing in his eyes.

"Is this Jones? No, I want Mr. Jones; Rip Jones. He's—he's my partner." There was a pause. "No, Chicago, that must be another party. I don't know any Mrs. Jones—I want Mr. ——"

He broke off and the expression on his face changed slowly. When he spoke again his husky voice had grown suddenly quiet.

"Why—why, Lola ——"

Absolution

American Mercury
June 1924
$118

There was once a priest with cold, watery eyes, who, in the still of the night, wept cold tears. He wept because the afternoons were warm and long and he was unable to attain a complete mystical union with our Lord. Sometimes, near four o'clock, there was a rustle of Swede girls along the path by his window and in their shrill laughter he found a terrible dissonance that made him pray aloud for the twilight to come. At twilight the laughter and the voices were quieter but several times he had walked past Romberg's Drug Store when it was dusk and the yellow lights shone inside and the nickel taps of the soda fountain were gleaming, and he had found the scent of cheap toilet soap desperately sweet upon the air. He passed that way when he returned from hearing confessions on Saturday nights and he grew careful to walk on the other side of the street so that the smell of the soap would float upward somewhere between its counter and his nostrils as it drifted, rather like incense, toward the Summer moon.

But there was no escape from the hot madness of four o'clock. From his window as far as he could see, the Dakota wheat thronged the valley of the Red River. The wheat was terrible to look upon and the carpet pattern to which in agony he bent his eyes sent his thought brooding through grotesque labyrinths, open always to the unavoidable sun.

One afternoon when he had reached the point where the mind runs down like an old clock, his housekeeper brought into his study a beautiful, intense little boy of eleven named Rudolph Miller. The little boy sat down in a patch of sunshine and the priest, at his walnut desk, pretended to be very busy. This was to conceal his relief that someone had come into his haunted room.

Presently he turned around and found himself staring into two enormous and staccato eyes, lit with gleaming points of cobalt light.

For a moment their expression startled him—then he saw that his visitor was in a state of abject fear.

"Your mouth is trembling," said Father Schwartz, in a haggard voice.

The little boy covered his quivering mouth with his hand.

"Are you in trouble?" asked Father Schwartz, sharply. "Take your hand away from your mouth and tell me what's the matter."

The boy—Father Schwartz recognized him now as the son of a parishioner, Mr. Miller, the freight agent—moved his hand reluctantly off his mouth and became articulate in a despairing whisper.

"Father Schwartz—I've committed a terrible sin."

"A sin against purity?"

"No, Father . . . worse."

Father Schwartz's body jerked sharply.

"Have you killed somebody?"

"No—but I'm afraid—" the voice rose to a shrill whimper.

"Do you want to go to confession?"

The little boy shook his head miserably. Father Schwartz cleared his throat so that he could make his voice soft and say some quiet, kind thing. In this moment he should forget his own agony and try to act like God. He repeated to himself a devotional phrase, hoping that in return God would help him to act correctly.

"Tell me what you've done," said his new soft voice.

The little boy looked at him through his tears and was reassured by the impression of moral resiliency which the distraught priest had created. Abandoning as much of himself as he was able to this man, Rudolph Miller began to tell his story.

"On Saturday, three days ago, my father he said I had to go to confession, because I hadn't been for a month and the family they go every week and I hadn't been. So I just as leave go, I didn't care. So I put it off till after supper because I was playing with a bunch of kids and father asked me if I went, and I said 'no,' and he took me by the neck and he said 'You go now,' so I said 'All right,' so I went over to church. And he yelled after me, 'Don't come back till you go.' . . ."

II

"On Saturday, Three Days Ago"

The plush curtain of the confessional rearranged its dismal creases leaving exposed only the bottom of an old man's old shoe. Behind the curtain an immortal soul was alone with God and the Reverend

Adolphus Schwartz, priest of the parish. Sound began, a labored whispering, sibilant and discreet, broken at intervals by the voice of the priest in audible question.

Rudolph Miller knelt in the pew beside the confessional and waited, straining nervously to hear and yet not to hear what was being said within. The fact that the priest was audible alarmed him. His own turn came next and the three or four others who waited might listen unscrupulously while he admitted his violations of the Sixth and Ninth Commandments.[1]

Rudolph had never committed adultery, nor even coveted his neighbor's wife—but it was the confession of the associate sins that was particularly hard to contemplate. In comparison he relished the less shameful fallings away—they formed a grayish background which relieved the ebony mark of sexual offenses upon his soul.

He had been covering his ears with his hands, hoping that his refusal to hear would be noticed and a like courtesy rendered to him in turn, when a sharp movement of the penitent in the confessional made him sink his face precipitately into the crook of his elbow. Fear assumed solid form and pressed out a lodging between his heart and his lungs. He must try now with all his might to be sorry for his sins—not because he was afraid, but because he had offended God. He must convince God that he was sorry and to do so he must first convince himself. After a tense emotional struggle he achieved a tremulous self-pity, and decided that he was now ready. If, by allowing no other thought to enter his head, he could preserve this state of emotion unimpaired until he went into that large coffin set on end, he would have survived another crisis in his religious life.

For sometime, however, a demoniac notion had partially possessed him. He could go home now, before his turn came, and tell his mother that he had arrived too late and found the priest gone. This, unfortunately, involved the risk of being caught in a lie. As an alternative he could say that he *had* gone to confession, but this meant that he must avoid communion next day, for communion taken upon an uncleansed soul would turn to poison in his mouth and he would crumple limp and damned from the altar rail.

Again Father Schwartz's voice became audible.

"And for your—"

The words blurred to a husky mumble and Rudolph got excitedly to his feet. He felt that it was impossible for him to go to confession this afternoon. He hesitated tensely. Then from the confessional came a tap, a creak and a sustained rustle. The slide had fallen and the plush curtain trembled. Temptation had come to him too late. . . .

"Bless me, Father, for I have sinned. . . . I confess to Almighty God and to you, Father, that I have sinned . . . Since my last confession it has been one month and three days . . . I accuse myself of—taking the Name of the Lord in vain . . ."

This was an easy sin. His curses had been but bravado—telling of them was little less than a brag.

". . . of being mean to an old lady."

The wan shadow moved a little on the latticed slat.

"How, my child?"

"Old lady Swenson," Rudolph's murmur soared jubilantly. "She got our baseball that we knocked in her window, and she wouldn't give it back, so we yelled 'Twenty-three, Skidoo'[2] at her all afternoon. Then about five o'clock she had a fit and they had to have the doctor."

"Go on, my child."

"Of—of not believing I was the son of my parents."

"What?" The interrogation was distinctly startled.

"Of not believing that I was the son of my parents."[3]

"Why not?"

"Oh, just pride," answered the penitent airily.

"You mean you thought you were too good to be the son of your parents?"

"Yes, Father." On a less jubilant note.

"Go on."

"Of being disobedient and calling my mother names. Of slandering people behind my back. Of smoking—"

Rudolph had now exhausted the minor offenses and was approaching the sins it was agony to tell. He held his fingers against his face like bars as if to press out between them the shame in his heart.

"Of dirty words and immodest thoughts and desires," he whispered very low.

"How often?"

"I don't know."

"Once a week? Twice a week?"

"Twice a week."

"Did you yield to these desires?"

"No, Father."

"Were you alone when you had them?"

"No, Father. I was with two boys and a girl."

"Don't you know, my child, that you should avoid the occasions of sin as well as the sin itself? Evil companionship leads to evil desires and evil desires to evil actions. Where were you when this happened?"

"In a barn in back of—"

"I don't want to hear any names," interrupted the priest sharply.

"Well, it was up in the loft of this barn and this girl and—a fella, they were saying things—saying immodest things and I stayed."

"You should have gone—you should have told the girl to go."

He should have gone! He could not tell Father Schwartz how his pulse had bumped in his wrist, how a strange, romantic excitement had possessed him when those curious things had been said. Perhaps in the houses of delinquency among the dull and hard-eyed incorrigible girls can be found those for whom has burned the whitest fire.

"Have you anything else to tell me?"

"I don't think so, Father."

Rudolph felt a great relief. Perspiration had broken out under his tight-pressed fingers.

"Have you told any lies?"

The question startled him. Like all those who habitually and instinctively lie he had an enormous respect and awe for the truth. Something almost exterior to himself dictated a quick, hurt answer.

"Oh, no, Father, I never tell lies."

For a moment, like the commoner in the king's chair, he tasted the pride of the situation. Then as the priest began to murmur conventional admonitions he realized that in heroically denying he had told lies, he had committed a terrible sin—he had told a lie in confession.

In automatic response to Father Schwartz's "Make an act of contrition," he began to repeat aloud meaninglessly:

"Oh, my God, I am heartily sorry for having offended Thee . . ."

He must fix this now—it was a bad mistake—but as his teeth shut on the last words of his prayer there was a sharp sound and the slat was closed.

A minute later when he emerged into the twilight the relief in coming from the muggy church into an open world of wheat and sky postponed the full realization of what he had done. Instead of worrying he took a deep breath of the crisp air and began to say over and over to himself the words "Blatchford Sarnemington, Blatchford Sarnemington!"

Blatchford Sarnemington was himself and these words were in effect a lyric. When he became Blatchford Sarnemington a suave nobility flowed from him. Blatchford Sarnemington lived in great sweeping triumphs. When Rudolph half-closed his eyes it meant that Blatchford had established dominance over him and, as he went by, there were envious mutters in the air: "Blatchford Sarnemington! There goes Blatchford Sarnemington."[4]

He was Blatchford now for awhile as he strutted homeward along the staggering road, but when the road braced itself in macadam in order to become the main street of Ludwig, Rudolph's exhilaration faded out and his mind cooled and he felt the horror of his lie. God, of course, already knew of it—but Rudolph reserved a corner of his mind where he was safe from God, where he prepared the subterfuges with which he often tricked God. Hiding now in this corner he considered how he could best avoid the consequences of his misstatement.

At all costs he must avoid communion next day. The risk of angering God to such an extent was too great. He would have to drink water "by accident" in the morning and thus, in accordance with a church law, render himself unfit to receive communion that day.[5] In spite of its flimsiness this subterfuge was the most feasible that occurred to him. He accepted its risks and was concentrating on how best to put it into effect, as he turned the corner by Romberg's Drug Store and came in sight of his father's house.

III

Rudolph's father, the local freight agent, had floated with the second wave of German and Irish stock to the Minnesota-Dakota country.[6] Theoretically, great opportunities lay ahead of a young man of energy in that day and place, but Carl Miller had been incapable of establishing either with his superiors or his subordinates the reputation for approximate immutability which is essential to success in a hierarchic industry. Somewhat gross and utterly deficient in curiosity, he was unable to take fundamental relationships for granted and this inability made him suspicious, unrestful and continually dismayed.

His two bonds with the colorful life were his faith in the Holy Roman Catholic Church and his mystical worship of the Empire Builder, James J. Hill.[7] Hill was the apotheosis of that quality in which Miller himself was deficient—the sense of things, the feel of things, the hint of rain in the wind on the cheek. Miller's mind worked late on the old decisions of other men and he had never in his life felt the balance of any single thing in his hands. His weary, sprightly, undersized body was growing old in Hill's gigantic shadow. For twenty years he had lived alone with Hill's name and God.

On Sunday morning Carl Miller awoke in the dustless quiet of six o'clock. Kneeling by the side of the bed he bent his yellow gray hair and the full dapple bangs of his moustache into the pillow, and prayed for several minutes. Then he drew off his night-shirt—like the

rest of his generation he had never been able to endure pajamas—
and clothed his thin, white, hairless body in woolen underwear.

He shaved. Silence in the other bedroom where his wife lay nervously asleep. Silence from the screened-off corner of the hall where
his son's cot stood, and his son slept among his Alger[8] books, his collection of cigar bands, his mothy pennants—"Cornell," "Hamlin"[9]
and "Greetings from Pueblo, New Mexico"—and the other possessions of his private life. From outside Miller could hear the shrill
birds and the whirring movement of the poultry and, as an undertone, the low, swelling click-a-tick of the six-fifteen through-train
for Montana and the green coast beyond. Then as the cold water
dripped from the washrag in his hand he raised his head suddenly—
he had heard a furtive sound from the kitchen below.

He dried his razor hastily, slipped his dangling suspenders to
his shoulder, and listened. Someone was walking in the kitchen,
and he knew by the light footfall that it was not his wife. With his
mouth faintly ajar he ran quickly down the stairs and opened the
kitchen door.

Standing by the sink, with one hand on the still dripping faucet and
the other clutching a full glass of water, stood his son. The boy's eyes,
still heavy with sleep, met his father's with a frightened, reproachful
beauty. He was barefooted and his pajamas were rolled up at the
knees and sleeves.

For a moment they both remained motionless—Carl Miller's
brow went down and his son's went up, as though they were striking
a balance between the extremes of emotion which filled them. Then
the bangs of the parent's moustache descended portentously until
they obscured his mouth and he gave a short glance around to see if
anything had been disturbed.

The kitchen was garnished with sunlight which beat on the panes
and made the smooth boards of the floor and table yellow and clean
as wheat. It was the centre of the house where the fire burned and
the tins fitted into tins like glittering toys and the steam whistled all
day on a thin pastel note. Nothing was moved, nothing touched—
except the faucet where beads of water still formed and dripped with
a white flash into the sink below.

"What are you doing?"

"I got awful thirsty, so I thought I'd just come down and get—"

"I thought you were going to communion."

A look of vehement astonishment spread over his son's face.

"I forgot all about it."

"Have you drunk any water?"

"No—"

As the word left his mouth Rudolph knew it was the wrong answer, but the faded indignant eyes facing him had signalled up the truth before the boy's will could act. He realized, too, that he should never have come downstairs; some vague necessity for verisimilitude had made him want to leave a wet glass as evidence by the sink; the honesty of his imagination had betrayed him.

"Pour it out," commanded his father, "that water!"

Rudolph despairingly inverted the tumbler.

"What's the matter with you, anyways?" demanded Miller angrily.

"Nothing."

"Did you go to confession yesterday?"

"Yes."

"Then why were you going to drink water?"

"I don't know—I forgot."

"Maybe you care more about being a little bit thirsty than you do about your religion."

"I forgot." Rudolph could feel the tears straining in his eyes.

"That's no answer."

"Well, I did."

"You better look out!" His father held to a high, persistent, inquisitory note, "If you're so forgetful that you can't remember your religion something better be done about it."

Rudolph filled a sharp pause with:

"I can remember it all right."

"First you begin to neglect your religion," cried his father, fanning his own fierceness, "the next thing you'll begin to lie and steal and the *next* thing is the *reform* school!"

Not even this familiar threat could deepen the abyss that Rudolph saw before him. He must either tell all now, offering his body for what he knew would be a ferocious beating, or else tempt the thunderbolts by receiving the Body and Blood of Christ with sacrilege upon his soul. And of the two the former seemed more terrible— it was not so much the beating he dreaded as the savage ferocity, typical of the ineffectual man, which would lie behind it.

"Put down that glass and go upstairs and dress!" his father ordered, "and when we get to church, before you go to communion, kneel down and ask God to forgive you for your carelessness."

Some accidental emphasis in the phrasing of this command acted like a catalytic agent on the confusion and terror of Rudolph's mind. A wild, proud anger rose in him and he dashed the tumbler passion- ately into the sink.

His father uttered a strained, husky sound and sprang for him. Rudolph dodged to the side, tipped over a chair and tried to get beyond the kitchen table. He cried out sharply when a hand grasped his pajama shoulder, then he felt the dull impact of a fist against the side of his head and glancing blows on the upper part of his body. As he slipped here and there in his father's grasp, dragged or lifted when he clung instinctively to an arm, aware of sharp smarts and strains, he made no sound except that he laughed hysterically several times. Then after less than a minute the blows abruptly ceased. After a lull during which Rudolph was tightly held and during which they both trembled violently and uttered strange, truncated words, Carl Miller half dragged, half threatened his son upstairs.

"Put on your clothes!"

Rudolph was now both hysterical and cold. His head hurt him and there was a long, shallow scratch on his neck from his father's finger nail and he sobbed and trembled as he dressed. He was aware of his mother standing at the doorway in a wrapper, her wrinkled face compressing and squeezing and opening out into new series of wrinkles which floated and eddied from neck to brow. Despising her nervous ineffectuality and avoiding her rudely when she tried to touch his neck with witch hazel, he made a hasty, choking toilet. Then he followed his father out of the house and along the road toward the Catholic church.

IV

They walked without speaking except when Carl Miller acknowledged automatically the existence of passers-by. Rudolph's uneven breathing alone ruffled the hot Sunday silence.

His father stopped decisively at the door of the church.

"I've decided you'd better go to confession again. Go in and tell Father Schwartz what you did and ask God's pardon."

"You lost your temper, too!" said Rudolph, quickly.

Carl Miller took a step toward his son, who moved cautiously backward.

"All right, I'll go."

"Are you going to do what I say?" cried his father in a hoarse whisper.

"All right."

Rudolph walked into the church and for the second time in two days entered the confessional and knelt down. The slat went up almost at once.

"I accuse myself of missing my morning prayers."

"Is that all?"

"That's all."

A maudlin exultation filled him. Not easily ever again would he be able to put an abstraction before the necessities of his ease and pride. An invisible line had been crossed and he had become aware of his isolation—aware that it applied not only to those moments when he was Blatchford Sarnemington but that it applied to all his inner life. Hitherto such phenomena as "crazy" ambitions and petty shames and fears had been but private reservations, unacknowledged before the throne of his official soul. Now he realized unconsciously that his private reservations were himself—and all the rest a garnished front and a conventional flag. The pressure of his environment had driven him into the lonely secret road of adolescence.

He knelt in the pew beside his father. Mass began. Rudolph knelt up—when he was alone he slumped his posterior back against the seat—and tasted the consciousness of a sharp, subtle revenge. Beside him his father prayed that God would forgive Rudolph, and asked also that his own outbreak of temper would be pardoned. He glanced sidewise at this son and was relieved to see that the strained, wild look had gone from his face and that he had ceased sobbing. The Grace of God, inherent in the Sacrament, would do the rest and perhaps after Mass everything would be better. He was proud of Rudolph in his heart and beginning to be truly as well as formally sorry for what he had done.

Usually, the passing of the collection box was a significant point for Rudolph in the services. If, as was often the case, he had no money to drop in he would be furiously ashamed and bow his head and pretend not to see the box, lest Jeanne Brady in the pew behind should take notice and suspect an acute family poverty. But today he glanced coldly into it as it skimmed under his eyes, noting with casual interest the large number of pennies it contained.

When the bell rang for communion, however, he quivered. There was no reason why God should not stop his heart. During the past twelve hours he had committed a series of mortal sins increasing in gravity, and he was now to crown them all with a blasphemous sacrilege.

"Domini, non sum dignus; ut interes sub tectum meum; sed tantum dic verbo, et sanabitur anima mea . . ."[10]

There was a rustle in the pews and the communicants worked their ways into the aisle with downcast eyes and joined hands. Those of exceptional piety pressed together their fingertips to form steeples. Among these latter was Carl Miller. Rudolph followed him toward the altar rail and knelt down, automatically taking up the napkin under his chin. The bell rang sharply and the priest turned from the altar with the white Host held above the chalice:

"Corpus Domini nostri Jesu Christi custodiat animam meam in vitam aeternam."[11]

A cold sweat broke out on Rudolph's forehead as the communion began. Along the line Father Schwartz moved and with gathering nausea Rudolph felt his heart valves weakening at the will of God. It seemed to him that the church was darker and that a great quiet had fallen, broken only by the inarticulate mumble which announced the approach of the Creator of Heaven and Earth. He dropped his head down between his shoulders and waited for the blow.

Then he felt a sharp nudge in his side. His father was poking him to sit up, not to slump against the rail; the priest was only two places away.

"Corpus Domini nostri Jesu Christi custodiat animam meam in vitam aeternam."

Rudolph opened his mouth. He felt the sticky wax taste of the wafer on his tongue. He remained motionless for what seemed an interminable period of time, his head still raised, the wafer undissolved in his mouth. Then again he started at the pressure of his father's elbow, and saw that the people were falling away from the altar like leaves and turning with blind downcast eyes to their pews, alone with God.

Rudolph was alone with himself, drenched with perspiration and deep in mortal sin. As he walked back to his pew the sharp taps of his cloven hoofs were loud on the floor. It was a dark poison that he carried in his heart.

V

"Sagitta Volante in Dei"[12]

The beautiful little boy with eyes like blue stones and lashes that sprayed open from them like flowers had finished telling his sin to Father Schwartz—and the square of sunshine in which he sat had moved forward half an hour into the room. Rudolph had become less frightened now; once eased of the story a reaction had set in. He knew that as long as he was in the room with this priest God would not stop his heart, so he sighed and sat quietly, waiting for the priest to speak.

Father Schwartz's cold watery eyes were fixed upon the carpet pattern on which the sun had brought out the swastikas[13] and the flat bloomless vines and the pale echoes of flowers. The hall clock ticked insistently toward sunset and from the ugly room and from the after-noon outside the window arose a stiff monotony, shattered now and then by the reverberate clapping of a faraway hammer on the dry air. The priest's nerves were strung thin and the beads of his rosary were crawling and squirming like snakes upon the green felt of his table top. He could not remember now what it was he should say.

Of all the things in this lost Swede town[14] he was most aware of this little boy's eyes—the beautiful eyes, with lashes that left them reluctantly and curved back as though to meet them once more.

For a moment longer the silence persisted while Rudolph waited and the priest struggled to remember something that was slipping farther and farther away from him and the clock ticked in the bro-ken house. Then Father Schwartz stared hard at the little boy and remarked in a peculiar voice—

"When a lot of people get together in the best places things go glimmering."

Rudolph started and looked quickly at Father Schwartz's face.

"I said—" began the priest, and paused, listening. "Do you hear the hammer and the clock ticking and the bees? Well, that's no good. The thing is to have a lot of people in the centre of the world, wher-ever that happens to be. Then—" his watery eyes widened knowingly, "things go glimmering."

"Yes, Father," agreed Rudolph, feeling a little frightened.

"What are you going to be when you grow up?"

"Well, I was going to be a baseball player for awhile," answered Rudolph, nervously, "but I don't think that's a very good ambition, so I think I'll be an actor or a Navy officer."

Again the priest stared at him.

"I see *exactly* what you mean," he said, with a fierce air.

Rudolph had not meant anything in particular and at the implica-tion that he had, he became more uneasy.

"This man is crazy," he thought, "and I'm scared of him. He wants me to help him out some way and I don't want to."

"You look as if things went glimmering," cried Father Schwartz, wildly. "Did you ever go to a party?"

"Yes, Father."

"And did you notice that everybody was properly dressed? That's what I mean. Just as you went into the party there was a moment when everybody was properly dressed. Maybe two little girls were standing by the door and some boys were leaning over the bannisters and there were bowls around full of flowers."

"I've been to a lot of parties," said Rudolph, rather relieved that the conversation had taken this turn.

"Of course," continued Father Schwartz triumphantly, "I knew you'd agree with me. But my theory is that when a whole lot of people get together in the best places things go glimmering all the time."

Rudolph found himself thinking of Blatchford Sarnemington.

"Please listen to me!" commanded the priest, impatiently. "Stop worrying about last Saturday. Apostasy implies an absolute damnation only on the supposition of a previous perfect faith. Does that fix it?"

Rudolph had not the faintest idea what Father Schwartz was talking about but he nodded and the priest nodded back at him and returned to his mysterious preoccupation.

"Why," he cried, "they have lights now as big as stars—do you realize that? I heard of one light they had in Paris or somewhere that was as big as a star.[15] A lot of people had it—a lot of gay people. They have all sorts of things now that you never dreamed of."

"Look here—" He came nearer to Rudolph, but the boy drew away, so Father Schwartz went back and sat down in his chair, his eyes dried out and hot. "Did you ever see an amusement park?"

"No, Father."

"Well, go and see an amusement park," the priest waved his hand vaguely. "It's a thing like a Fair, only much more glittering. Go to one at night and stand a little way off from it in a dark place—under dark trees. You'll see a big wheel made of lights turning in the air and a long slide shooting boats down into the water. A band playing somewhere and a hard smell of peanuts—and everything will twinkle. But it won't remind you of anything, you see. It will all just hang out there in the night like a colored balloon—like a big yellow lantern on a pole."

Father Schwartz frowned as he suddenly thought of something.

"But don't get up close," he warned Rudolph, "because if you do you'll only feel the heat and the sweat and the life."

All this talking seemed particularly strange and awful to Rudolph, because this man was a priest. He sat there, half terrified, his beautiful eyes open wide and staring at Father Schwartz. But underneath his terror he felt that his own inner convictions were confirmed. There was something ineffably gorgeous somewhere that had nothing to do with God. He no longer thought that God was angry at him about the original lie, because He must have understood that Rudolph had done it to make things finer in the confessional, brightening up the dinginess of his admissions by saying a thing radiant and proud. At the moment when he had affirmed immaculate honor a silver pennon had flapped out into the breeze somewhere and there had been the crunch of leather and the shine of silver spurs and a troop of horsemen waiting for dawn on a low green hill. The sun had made stars of light on their breastplates like the picture at home of the German cuirassiers at Sedan.[16]

But now the priest was muttering inarticulate and dim and terrible words and the boy became wildly afraid. Horror entered suddenly in at the open window and the atmosphere of the room changed. Father Schwartz collapsed precipitously down on his knees and let his body settle back against a chair.

"Oh, my God!" he cried out, in a strange voice, and wilted to the floor.

Then a human oppression rose from the priest's worn clothes and mingled with the faint smell of old food in the corners. Rudolph gave a sharp cry and ran in a panic from the house—while the collapsed man lay there quite still, filling his room, filling it with voices and faces until it was crowded with shadowy movements, and rang loud with a steady, shrill note of laughter.

*   *   *

Outside the window the blue sirocco trembled over the wheat, and girls with yellow hair walked sensuously along roads that bounded the fields, calling innocent, exciting things to the young men who were working in the lines between the grain. Legs were shaped under starchless gingham and rims of the necks of dresses were warm and damp. For five hours now hot fertile life had burned in the afternoon. It would be night in three hours and all along the land there would be these blonde Northern girls and the tall young men from the farms lying out beside the wheat, under the moon.

Rags Martin-Jones and the Pr-nce of W-les

McCall's
July 1924
$1,750

*The writer who discovered the flapper tells how one of them acts when
she meets a real prince—in this, one of the best love stories of the day*

The Majestic[1] came gliding into New York harbor on an April morning. She sniffed at the tug-boats and turtle-gaited ferries, winked at a
gaudy young yacht and ordered a cattle-boat out of her way with a
snarling whistle of steam. Then she parked at her private dock with
all the fuss of a stout lady sitting down, and announced complacently
that she had just come from Cherbourg and Southampton[2] with a
cargo of the very best people in the world.

The very best people in the world stood on the deck and waved
idiotically to their poor relations who were waiting on the dock for
gloves from Paris. Before long a great toboggan had connected the
Majestic with the North American continent and the ship began to
disgorge these very best people in the world—who turned out to be
movie queens, missionaries, retired jewellers, British authors, musical
comedy twins, the Duchess Mazzini (nee Goldberg)[3] and, needless to
add, Lord and Lady Thingumbob, of Thingumbob Manor.

The photographers worked wildly as the stream of passengers
flowed on to the dock. There was a burst of cheering at the appearance of a pair of stretchers laden with two middle-westerners who
had drunk themselves delirious on the last night out.[4]

The deck gradually emptied but when the last Poiret[5] Madonna
had reached shore the photographers still remained at their posts.
And the officer in charge of debarkation still stood at the foot of
the gangway, glancing first at his watch and then at the deck as if
some important part of the cargo was still on board. At last from the

watchers on the pier there arose a long-drawn "Ah-h-h!" as a final entourage began to stream down from deck B.

First came two French maids, one carrying a pair of minute dogs and the other bearing an enormous green parrot in an enormous red cage. After these marched a squad of porters, blind and invisible under innumerable bunches and bouquets of fresh flowers. Another maid followed, leading a sad-eyed orphan child of a French flavor and close upon its heels walked the second officer pulling along three neurasthenic wolfhounds much to their reluctance and his own.

A pause. Then the Captain, Sir Howard Deems Macdougall appeared at the rail, with something that might have been a pile of gorgeous silver fox fur standing by his side—

Rags Martin-Jones, after two years in the capitals of Europe, was returning to her native land! Rags Martin-Jones was not a dog. She was half a girl and half a flower and as she shook hands with Captain Sir Howard Deems Macdougall she smiled as if someone had told her the newest, freshest joke in the world. All the people who had not already left the pier felt that smile trembling on the April air and turned around to see. She came slowly down the gangway. Her hat, an expensive, inscrutable experiment was crushed under her arm so that her scant French-bobbed[6] hair tossed and flopped a little in the harbor wind. Her face was like seven o'clock on a summer morning save where she had slipped a preposterous monocle into an eye of clear childish blue. At every few steps her long lashes would tilt out the monocle and she would laugh, a bored, happy laugh, and replace the supercilious spectacle in the other eye.

Tap! Her one hundred and five pounds reached the pier and it seemed to sway and bend from the shock of her beauty. A few porters fainted. A large, sentimental shark which had followed the ship across made a despairing leap to see her once more, and then dove, broken-hearted, back into the deep sea. Rags Martin-Jones had come home.

There was no member of her family there to meet her for the simple reason that she was the only member of her family left alive. In 1913 her parents had gone down on the Titanic[7] together rather than be separated in this world, and so the Martin-Jones fortune of seventy-five millions[8] had been inherited by a very little girl on her tenth birthday. It was what the pessimists always refers to as a "shame." Rags Martin-Jones (everybody had forgotten her real name long ago) was now photographed from all sides. The monocle persistently fell out and she kept laughing and yawning and replacing it, so no very clear picture of her was taken, except by the motion picture camera.

All the photographs, however, included a flustered, handsome young man, with an almost ferocious love-light burning in his eyes, who had met her on the dock. His name was John M. Chestnut, he was already talked of as a risen star in Wall Street and he had been hopelessly in love with Rags ever since the time when she, like the tides, had come under the influence of the summer moon.

When Rags became really aware of his presence they were walking down the pier, and she looked at him blankly as though she had never seen him before in this world.

"Rags," he began, "Rags—"

"John M. Chestnut?" she inquired, inspecting him with interest.

"Of course!" he exclaimed angrily. "Are you trying to pretend you don't know me? That you didn't write me to meet you here?" She laughed. A chauffeur appeared at her elbow and she twisted out of her coat, revealing a dress made in great splashy checks of sea-blue and gray. She shook herself like a wet bird.

"I've got a lot of junk to declare," she remarked absently.

"So have I," said Chestnut anxiously, "and the first thing I want to declare is that I've loved you, Rags, every minute since you've been away." She stopped with a groan.

"Please! There were some young men on the boat. The subject's gotten to be a bore."

"My God!" cried Chestnut, "do you mean to say that you class *my* love with what a lot of insolent idiots said to you on a boat?" His voice had risen and several people in the vicinity turned to hear.

"Sh!" she warned him, "I'm not giving a circus. If you want me to even see you while I'm here you'll have to be less violent."

But John M. Chestnut seemed unable to control his voice. "Do you mean to say"—it trembled to a carrying pitch—"that you've forgotten what you said on this very pier just twenty-two months ago last Thursday?" Half the passengers from the ship were now watching the scene on the dock and another little eddy drifted out of the customs house to see.

"John," her displeasure was increasing, "if you raise your voice again I'll arrange it so you'll have plenty of chance to cool off. I'm going to the Ritz.⁹ Come and see me there this afternoon."

"But Rags—!" he protested hoarsely. "Listen to me. Twenty-two months ago—" Then the watchers on the dock were treated to a curious sight. A beautiful lady in a checkered dress of sea-blue and grey took a brisk step forward so that her hands came into contact with the excited young man by her side. The young man retreating instinctively reached back with his foot, but finding nothing relapsed gently off the thirty foot dock and plopped into the Hudson River. A shout of alarm went up and there was a rush to the edge just as his head appeared above water. He was swimming easily and, perceiving this, the young lady who had apparently been the cause of the accident leaned over the pier and made a megaphone of her hands.

"I'll be in at half past four," she cried. And with a cheerful wave of her hand, which the engulfed gentleman was unable to return, she adjusted her monocle, threw one haughty glance at the gathered crowd and walked leisurely from the scene.

The five dogs, the three maids, the parrot and the French orphan were installed in the largest suite at the Ritz and Rags tumbled lazily into a steaming bath where she dozed for the greater part of an hour. At the end of that time she received business calls from a masseuse, a manicure, a beauty doctor and finally from a Parisian hairdresser who restored the French-bob to its original perfection. When John M. Chestnut arrived at four he found half a dozen lawyers and bankers, the administrators of the Martin-Jones trust fund, waiting in the hall. They had been there since half past one and were now in a state of considerable agitation. After one of the maids had subjected him to a severe scrutiny, possibly to be sure that he was thoroughly dry, John was conducted immediately into the presence of M'selle. M'selle was in her bedroom reclining on the chaise longue among two dozen silk pillows that had accompanied her from the other side. John came into the room somewhat stiffly and greeted her with a formal bow.

"You look better," she said, raising herself from her pillows and staring at him appraisingly, "it gave you a color." He thanked her coldly for the compliment.

"You ought to go in every morning." And then she added irrelevantly, "I'm going back to Paris tomorrow." John Chestnut gasped.

"I wrote you that I didn't intend to* stay more than a week anyhow," she added.

"But Rags—"

"Why should I? There isn't an interesting man in New York."

"But listen Rags, won't you give me a chance? Won't you stay for say ten days and get to know me a little."

"Know you!" Her tone implied that he was already a far too open book.

---

* *McCall's* broke the text at this point after a two-page spread (pp. 6–7), continuing the story on p. 32.

"Well, what do you want me to be?" he demanded resentfully. "A cross between an English actor and an amusement park?"

"I want a man who's capable of a gallant gesture."

"Do you mean you want me to express myself entirely in pantomime?" Rags uttered a disgusted sigh.

"I mean you haven't any imagination," she explained patiently. "No Americans have any imagination. Paris is the only city where a civilized person can exist. Paris is the capital of the world."[10]

"Don't you care for me at all any more?"

"I wouldn't have crossed the Atlantic to see you if I didn't. But as soon as I looked over the Americans on the boat I knew I couldn't marry you. I'd just hate you, John, and the only fun I'd have out of it would be the fun of breaking your heart." She began to twist herself down among the cushions until she almost disappeared from view.

"I've lost my monocle," she explained. After an unsuccessful search in the silken depths she discovered the illusive[11] glass hanging down the back of her neck.

"I'd love to be in love," she went on, replacing the monocle in her childish eye. "Last spring in Rome I almost eloped with an Indian Rajah,[12] but he was half a shade too dark and I took an intense dislike to one of his other wives."

"Don't talk that rubbish!" cried John, sinking his face into his hands.

"Well, I didn't marry him," she protested. "But in one way he had a lot to offer. He was the third richest subject of the British Empire. That's another thing, are you rich?"

"Not as rich as you."

"There you are. What have you to offer me?"

"Love."

"Love!" She disappeared again among the cushions. "Listen, John. Life to me is a series of glistening bazaars with a merchant in front of each one rubbing his hands together and saying 'Patronize this place here. Best bazaar in the world.' So I go in with my purse full of beauty and money and youth, all prepared to buy. 'What have you got for sale,' I ask him, and he rubs his hands together and says: 'Well, Mademoiselle, today we have some perfectly be-*oo*-tiful[13] love.' Sometimes he hasn't even got that in stock but he sends out for it when he finds I have so much money to spend. Oh, he always gives that to me before I go, and for nothing. That's the one revenge I have." John Chestnut rose despairingly to his feet and took a step toward the window.

"Don't throw yourself out," Rags exclaimed quickly.

"I won't." He tossed his cigarette down into Madison Avenue.

"It isn't just you," she said in a softer voice. "Dull and uninspired as you are I care for you more than I can say. But life's so stupid here. Nothing ever happens."

"Loads of things happen," he insisted. "Why, today there was a bank robbed in Brooklyn and a triple suicide in Maine, two dozen oil swindles in New York City—"

"Yes," she said ironically, "and little Jimmy Groody's cat fell out the window and broke its spine. Fascinating! Why, John, last month I sat at a dinner table while two men planned to break up the Kingdom of Schwartzberg-Rhine-minster.[14] In Paris I knew a man named Fernduc who was going down to the Balkans and start a New War."[15]

"Well," he said doggedly, "just for a change you come out with me tonight."

"Where to?" demanded Rags with scorn. "Do you think I can get a thrill from a cabaret and a bottle of bootleg champagne?[16] I prefer my own gaudy dreams."

"I'll take you to the most amusing place in the city."

"What'll happen? You've got to tell me what'll happen." John Chestnut suddenly drew a long breath and looked cautiously around as if he were afraid of being overheard.

"Well, to tell you the truth," he said in a low worried tone, "if everything was known something pretty awful would be liable to happen to *me*."

She sat upright and the pillows tumbled about her like leaves. "Do you mean to imply that there's anything shady in your life?" she cried, with laughter in her voice. "Do you expect me to believe that? No, John, you'll have your fun by plugging ahead on the beaten path, just plugging ahead."

Her mouth, a small insolent rose, dropped the words on him like thorns. John took his hat and coat from the chair and picked up his cane.

"For the last time, will you come along with me tonight and see what we can see?"

"See what? See whom? Is there anything in this country worth seeing?"

"Well," he said, in a matter-of-fact tone, "for one thing you'll see the Prince of Wales."[17]

"What?" She left the chaise longue at a bound. "Is he in New York?"

"He will be tonight. Would you care to see him?"

"Would I? I'd give a year of my life to see him for an hour." Her voice trembled with excitement.

"He's been in Canada. He's down here incognito for the big prize fight this afternoon. And I happen to know where he's going to be tonight."

Rags gave a sharp ecstatic cry: "Felice! Louise! Nanine!"

The three maids came running. The room seemed to fill suddenly with vibrations of wild, startled light.

"Felice, the car!" cried Rags. "Louise, my gold dress and the slippers with the real gold heels![18] The big pearls too, all the pearls, and the egg diamond and the stockings with the sapphire clocks! Nanine, send for the hairdresser on the run. My bath again, ice cold and half full of almond cream! Felice, Tiffany's,[19] like lightning, before they close! Find me a bracelet, a brooch, a pendant, anything, it doesn't matter, with the arms of the House of Windsor!" She was fumbling at the buttons of her dress, and as John turned it was already sliding from her shoulders.

"Orchids, for the love of heaven! Four dozen, so I can choose four."[20]

And then maids flew here and there about the room like frightened birds. "Perfume, Louise, bring out all my perfume and my white sable and my diamond garters and the sweet oil for my hands! Here, take these things! This too, and this, Ouch! and this!" With becoming modesty John Chestnut closed the outside door. The six trustees in various postures of fatigue, of ennui, of resignation, of despair were still cluttering up the outer hall.

"Gentlemen," announced John Chestnut, "I fear that Miss Martin-Jones is much too weary from her trip to talk to you this afternoon."

"This place, for no particular reason, is called the Hole in the Sky." Rags looked around her. They were on a roof garden[21] wide open to the April night. Overhead the true stars winked cold and the moon was a sliver of ice in the dark west. But where they stood it was warm as June and the couples dining or dancing on the inevitable central floor were unconcerned with the forbidding sky.

"What makes it so warm?" she whispered as they moved toward a table.

"It's some new trick that keeps the warm air from rising. I don't know the principle of the thing, but I know it's open like this even in the middle of winter. Do you see that man at the corner table? That's the heavyweight champion of the world. He knocked out the challenger at five o'clock this afternoon."

"Where's the Prince of Wales?" she demanded tensely.

John looked around. "He hasn't arrived yet. He won't be here for about half an hour."

She sighed profoundly. "It's the first time I've been excited in four years." Four years, one less than he had loved her. He wondered if when she was sixteen, a wild lovely child, sitting up all night in restaurants with officers who were to leave for France next day, losing the glamor of life too soon in the old, sad, poignant days of war, she had ever been so lovely as under these amber lights and this dark sky. From her excited eyes to her tiny slipper heels which were striped with layers of real silver and gold, she was like one of those amazing ships that are carved complete in a bottle. She was finished with that delicacy, with that care; as though the long lifetime of some worker in fragility had been used to make her so. John Chestnut wanted to take her up in his hands, turn her this way and that, examine the tip of a slipper or the tip of an ear or squint closely at the fairy stuff from which her lashes were made.

Rags became suddenly aware of the sound of violins and drums but the music seemed to come from far away, seemed to float over the crisp night and on to the floor with the added remoteness of a dream.

"The orchestra's on another roof," explained John. "It's a new idea. Look, the entertainment's beginning."

A negro girl, thin as a reed, emerged suddenly from a masked entrance into a circle or[22] harsh barbaric light, startled the music to a wild minor and commenced to sing a rhythmic, tragic song. The pipe of her body broke abruptly and she began a slow incessant step, without progress and without hope, like the failure of a savage insufficient dream. She had lost Papa Jack,[23] she cried over and over with a hysterical monotony at once despairing and unreconciled. One by one the loud horns tried to force her from the steady beat of madness but she listened only to the mutter of the drums which were isolating her in some lost place in time among many thousand forgotten years. After the failure of the piccolo, she made herself again into a thin brown line, wailed once with a sharp and terrible intensity, then vanished into sudden darkness.

"If you lived in New York you wouldn't need to be told who she is," said John when the amber lights flashed on. "Every performer here has made an immense personal hit in some current revue. The next fella is a comedian of the fatuous, garrulous type. It seems to me that he's the funniest man in the world—"

He broke off. Just as the lights went down for the second number Rags had given a long sigh and leaned forward tensely in her chair. Her eyes were rigid like the eyes of a pointer dog and John saw that they were fixed on a party that had come through some side entrance and were arranging themselves around a table in the half darkness.

The table was shielded with palms and Rags at first made out only three dim forms. Then she distinguished a fourth who seemed to be placed well behind the other three, a pale oval of a face topped with a glimmer of dark yellow hair.

"Hello!" ejaculated John, "There's his majesty now."

Her breath seemed to die murmurously in her throat. She was dimly aware that the comedian was now standing in a glow of white light on the dancing floor, that he had been talking for some moments and that there was a constant ripple of laughter in the air. But her eyes remained motionless, enchanted. She saw one of the party bend and whisper to another, and after the low glitter of a match the bright button of a cigarette end gleamed in the background. How long it was before she moved she did not know. Then something seemed to happen to her eyes, something white, something terribly urgent and she wrenched about sharply to find herself full in the center of a baby spotlight from above.

"Sit still!" John was whispering across the table. "He picks some-body out for this every night." Then she realized—it was the comedian. He was talking to her, arguing with her, about something that seemed incredibly funny to everyone else, but came to her ears only as a blur of muddled sound.

"You'll admit I gave you the pass," he was saying. "It was a real pass, see? Because here you are. But was it much of a kiss. Be—practically honest with me. If I'd given you that kind of a *pass* it wouldn't have got you past the coat-room."

Instinctively she had composed her face at the first shock of the light and now she smiled. It was a gesture of rare self-possession. Into this smile she insinuated a vast impersonality as if she were uncon-scious of the light, unconscious of his attempt to play upon her love-liness—but amused at an infinitely removed *him*, whose darts might have been thrown just as successfully at the moon. She was no longer a "lady"—a lady would have been harsh or pitiful or absurd; Rags stripped her attitude to a sheer consciousness of her own impervious beauty, sat there glittering until the comedian began to feel alone as he had never felt alone before. At a signal from him the spotlight was switched suddenly out. The moment was over. The moment was over, the comedian left the floor and the faraway music began. John leaned toward her.

"I'm sorry. There really wasn't anything to do. You were wonder-ful." She dismissed the incident with a casual laugh, then she started, there were now only two men sitting at the table across the floor.

"He's gone!" she exclaimed in quick distress.

"Don't worry, he'll be back. He's got to be awful carefull,²⁴ you see, so he's probably waiting outside with one of his aides until it gets dark again. He's not supposed to be in New York. He's even in Canada under another name." The lights dimmed again and almost immediately a dark haired man appeared out of the darkness and was standing by their table.

"May I introduce myself," he said rapidly to John in a supercilious British voice. "Lord Charles Este, of Baron Marchbanks' party." He glanced at John closely as if to be sure that he appreciated the significance of the name. John nodded.

"That is of course between ourselves."

"Of course." Rags groped on the table for her untouched champagne and tipped the glassful down her throat.

"Baron Marchbanks begs that the lady join his party during this number." Both men looked at Rags. There was a moment's pause.

"Very well," she said, glanced back again interrogatively at John. Again he nodded. Then she rose and with her heart beating wildly threaded the tables, making the half circuit of the room; then melted, a slim figure in shimmering gold, into the table set in half darkness.

The number drew to a close and John Chestnut sat alone at his table, stirring auxiliary bubbles in his glass of champagne. Just as the lights went on there was a soft rasp of gold cloth and Rags, flushed and breathing quickly, sank into her chair. Her eyes were shining with tears.

John looked at her moodily.

"Well, what did he say?"

"He was very quiet."

"Didn't he say a word?" Her hand trembled as she took up her glass of champagne.

"He just—looked at me while it was dark. And we said a few things, conventional things. He was like his pictures, only he looks very bored and tired. He didn't even ask my name."

"Is he leaving New York tonight?"

"In half an hour. He and his aides have a car outside and they expect to be over the border before dawn."

"Did you find him fascinating?" She hesitated and then slowly nodded her head.

"That's what everybody says," admitted John glumly. "Do they expect you back there?"

"I don't know." She looked uncertainly across the floor but the celebrated personage had again withdrawn from his table to some retreat outside. Just as she turned back an utterly strange young man who had been standing for a moment in the main entrance came toward them with an air of hurry. He was a deathly pale person in a disheveled business suit and he laid a trembling hand on John Chestnut's shoulder.

"Monte!" exclaimed John, starting up so suddenly that he upset his champagne. "What is it? What's the matter?"

"They've picked up the trail!" said the young man in a shaken whisper. He looked around. "I've got to speak to you alone." John got to his feet and Rags noticed that his face too had become white as the napkin in his hand. He excused himself and they retreated to an unoccupied table a few feet away. Rags watched them curiously for a moment then she resumed her scrutiny of the table across the floor. Would she be asked to come back? The Prince had simply risen and bowed and gone outside. Perhaps she should have waited until he returned. The pale person named Monte disappeared and John returned to the table. Rags was startled to find that a tremendous change had come over him. He lurched into his chair like a drunken man.

"John! What's the matter?" Instead of answering he reached for the champagne bottle but his fingers were trembling.

"Are you sick?"

"Rags," he said unsteadily, "I'm all through."

"What do you mean?"

"I'm all through, I tell you." He managed a sickly smile. "There's been a warrant out for me for over an hour."

"What have you done?" she demanded in a frightened voice. "What's the warrant for?"

The lights went out for the next number and he collapsed suddenly over the table.

"What is it?" she insisted, with rising apprehension. She leaned forward, his answer was barely audible.

"Murder?" She could feel her body grow cold as ice. He nodded. She took hold of both arms and tried to shake him upright as one shakes a coat into place. His eyes were rolling in his head.

"Is it true? Have they got proof?" Again he nodded drunkenly.

"Then you've got to get out of the country now! Do you hear me, John? You've got to get out *now*, before they come looking for you here!" He loosed a wild glance of terror toward the entrance.

"Oh, God!" cried Rags. "Why don't you do something?" She looked distractedly around the roof. Her eyes strayed here and there in desperation, became suddenly rigid. She drew in her breath sharply, hesitated, and then whispered fiercely into John's ear.

"If I arrange it, will you go to Canada tonight?"

"How?"

"I'll fix it, if you'll pull yourself together a little. This is Rags talking to you, don't you understand, John? I want you to sit here and not move until I come back!" A minute later she had crossed the room under cover of the darkness.

"Baron Marchbanks," she whispered softly, standing just behind his chair. He half rose, motioned her to sit down.

"Have you room in your car for two more passengers tonight?" One of the aides turned around abruptly.

"His Lordship's car is full," he said shortly.

"It's terribly urgent." Her voice was trembling.

"Well," said the Prince hesitatingly. "I don't know." Lord Charles Este looked at him and shook his head.

"I don't think it'd do, sir. This is a risky matter anyhow, with contrary orders from home. You know we agreed there'd be no complications." The Prince frowned.

"This isn't a complication," he objected. Este turned frankly to Rags.

"Why is it urgent?" Rags hesitated.

"Why—" She flushed suddenly. "It's a runaway marriage." The Prince laughed.

"Right-o!" he exclaimed. "That settles it. Este here is just being official. Bring over the lucky man right away. We're leaving shortly, what?" Este looked at his watch.

"Right now!" Rags rushed away. She wanted to move the whole party from the roof while the lights were still down.

"Hurry!" she cried in John's ear. "We're going over the border with the Prince of Wales. You'll be safe by morning."

He looked up at her with dazed eyes. She hurriedly paid the check and seizing his arm piloted him as inconspicuously as possible to the other table, where she introduced him with a word. The Prince acknowledged his presence by shaking hands, the aides nodded, only faintly concealing their displeasure.

"We'd better start," said Este, looking impatiently at his watch. They were on their feet when suddenly an exclamation broke out from all of them at once, two policemen and a red-haired man in plain clothes had come in at the main door.

"Out we go," breathed Este impelling the party toward the side entrance. "There's going to be some kind of riot here." He gasped. Two more bluecoats barred the exit there. They paused uncertainly. The plain clothes man was beginning a careful inspection of the people at the tables. Este looked sharply at Rags and then at John who shrank back behind the palms.

"Is that a prohibition fella out there?"

"No," whispered Rags, "there's going to be trouble. Can't we get out this entrance?" The Prince with rising impatience sat down again in his chair.

"Let me know when you chaps are ready to go." He smiled at Rags. "Now just suppose we all get in trouble just for that jolly face of yours." Then suddenly the lights went up. The plain clothes man whirled around quickly and sprang to the middle of the cabaret floor.

"Nobody try to leave this room!" he shouted. "Sit down, that party behind the palms! Is John M. Chestnut in this room?" Rags gave a short involuntary cry.

"Here!" cried the detective to the policeman behind him. "Take a look at that bunch over there. Hands up, you men!"

"My God!" whispered Este, "We've got to get out of here!" He turned to the Prince. "This won't do, Ted. You can't be seen here. I'll try and stall them off while you get to the car." He took a step toward the side entrance.

"Hands up, there!" cried the plain clothes man. "And when I say hands up I mean it! Which one of you's Chestnut?"

"You're mad!" shouted Este. "We're British subjects. We're not involved in this affair in any way!" A woman screamed somewhere and there was a general movement toward the elevator, a movement which stopped short before the muzzles of two automatic pistols. A girl next to Rags collapsed in a dead faint to the floor and at the same moment the music on the other roof began to play.

"Stop that music!" bellowed the plain clothes man. "And get some handcuffs on that whole bunch—quick!" Two policemen advanced toward the party and simultaneously Este and the other aides drew their revolvers and shielding the Prince as best they could began to edge toward the side. A shot rang out and then another, followed by a crash of silver and china as half a dozen diners overturned their tables and dropped quickly behind.

The panic became general. There were three shots in quick succession and then a fusillade. Rags saw Este firing cooly at the eight amber lights which lit the roof and a thick fume of grey smoke began to fill the air. As a strange undertone to the shouting and screaming came the incessant clamor of the distant Jazz Band. Then in a moment it was all over. A shrill whistle rang out over the roof, and through the smoke Rags saw John Chestnut advancing toward the plain clothes man, his hands held out in a gesture of surrender. There was a last nervous cry, a chill clatter as someone inadvertently stepped into a pile of dishes, and then a heavy silence fell on the roof—Even the band seemed to have died away.

"It's all over!" John Chestnut's voice rang out wildly on the night air. "The party's over. Everybody who wants to can go home!" Still there was silence, Rags knew it was the silence of awe, the strain of guilt had driven John Chestnut insane.

"It was a great performance," he was shouting. "I want to thank you one and all. If you can find any tables still standing champagne will be served as long as you care to stay." It seemed to Rags that the roof and the high stars suddenly began to swim round and round. She saw John take the detective's hand and shake it heartily and she watched the detective grin and pocket his gun. The music had recommenced and the girl who had fainted was suddenly dancing with Lord Charles Este in the corner. John was running here and there patting people on the back, and laughing and shaking hands. Then he was coming toward her, fresh and innocent as a child.

"Wasn't it wonderful?" he cried. Rags felt a faintness stealing over her. She groped backward with her hand toward a chair.

"What was it?" she cried dazedly. "Am I dreaming?"

"Of course not! You're wide awake. I made it up, Rags, don't you see? I made up the whole thing for you. I had it invented! The only thing real about it was my name!" She collapsed suddenly against his coat, clung to his lapels and would have wilted to the floor if he had not caught her quickly in his arms.

"Some champagne, hurry!" he called, and then he shouted at the Prince of Wales who stood nearby. "Order my car quick as hell! Miss Rags Martin-Jones has fainted from excitement."

The skyscraper rose bulkily through thirty tiers of windows before it attenuated itself to a graceful sugarloaf of shining white.[25] Then it darted up again another hundred feet, thinned to a mere oblong tower in its last fragile aspiration toward the sky. At the highest of its high windows Rags Martin-Jones stood full in the stiff breeze, gazing down at the city.

"Mr. Chestnut wants to know if you'll come right in to his private office." It was a respectful voice at her elbow.

Obediently her slim feet moved along the carpet into a high cool chamber overlooking the harbor and the wide sea. John Chestnut sat at his desk, waiting, and Rags walked to him and put her arms around his shoulder. "Are you sure *you're* real?" she asked anxiously. "Are you absolutely *sure?*"

"You only wrote me a week before you came," he protested modestly, "or I could have arranged a revolution."

"Was the whole thing just *mine?*" she demanded. "Was it a perfectly useless, gorgeous thing, just for me?"

"Useless?" He considered. "Well, it started out to be. At the last minute I invited a big restaurant man to be there, and while you were at the other table I sold him the whole idea of the cabaret." He looked at his watch.

"I've got one more thing to do, and then we've got just time to be married before lunch." He picked up his telephone. "Jackson? Send a triplicated cable to Paris, Berlin, and Budapest and have those men who've been trying to break up Schwartzberg-Rhineminster chased over the Polish border.[26] If the Dutchy won't act, lower the rate of exchange. Also, that idiot Fernduc is in the Balkans again, trying to start a new war. Tell him to leave for New York on the first boat or else throw him into a Greek jail." He rang off, turned to the wild-eyed girl with a laugh.

"John," she asked him intently. "Who was the Prince of Wales?" He waited till they were in the elevator, dropping twenty floors at a swoop. Then he leaned forward and tapped the lift boy on the shoulder.

"Not so fast, Cedric. This lady isn't used to falls from high places." The elevator boy turned around, smiled. His face was pale, oval, framed in yellow hair. Rags blushed like fire.

"Cedric's from Wessex," explained John. "The resemblance is, to say the least, amazing."

Rags took the monocle from around her neck and threw the ribbon over Cedric's head.

"Thank you," she said simply, "for the second greatest thrill of my life."

Then John Chestnut began rubbing his hands together in a commercial gesture. "Patronize this place, lady," he besought her. "Best bazaar in the city!"

"What have you got for sale?"

"Well, M'selle, today we have some perfectly bee-*oo*-tiful love."

"Wrap it up, Mr. Merchant," cried Rags Martin-Jones. "It looks like a bargain to me."

The Sensible Thing

Liberty
5 July 1924
$1,750

Youth, its bitter and its sweet, its tragic partings and its glad reunions, its passion and its calculation—all these are in this warm, colorful, wholly human short story.

Should a marriage wait until a boy's Ship of Good Fortune reaches port?

At the Great American Lunch Hour young George Rollins straightened his desk with an assumed air of interest. No one in the office must know that he was in a hurry, for success is a matter of atmosphere, and it is not well to advertise the fact that your mind is separated from your work by a distance of seven hundred miles. Offices are unreasonable.

But, once out of the building, he set his teeth and began to run, glancing now and then at the gay noon of early spring, which filled Times Square and loitered less than twenty feet, it seemed, over the heads of the crowd. The crowd all looked slightly upward and took deep March breaths and the sun dazzled their eyes so that scarcely anyone saw anyone else but only his own reflection on the sky.

George Rollins, whose mind was over seven hundred miles away, thought that the whole outdoors was horrible. He rushed into the subway and for ninety-five blocks bent a frenzied glance on a car-card which showed vividly how he had only one chance in five of keeping his teeth for ten years. At 137th Street he broke off his study of commercial art, left the subway and began to run again, a tireless, anxious run that brought him this time to his home—one room in a high, horrible apartment house[1] in the middle of nowhere.

There it was on the bureau, the letter—in sacred ink, on blessed paper—all over the city people, if they listened, could hear the beating of George Rollins' heart. He read the commas, the blots, and the thumbsmudges—then he threw himself hopelessly upon his bed.

He was in a mess, one of those deplorable messes which are ordinary incidents in the life of the poor—which follow poverty like birds of prey. The poor go under or go up or go wrong or even go on, somehow, in a way the poor have—but George Rollins was so new to poverty that he thought his case was the only one in the world.

Less than two years ago he had been graduated with honors from the Massachusetts Institute of Technology[2] and had taken a position with a firm of construction engineers in southern Tennessee. All his life he had thought in terms of tunnels and skyscrapers[3] and great, squat dams and tall, three-towered bridges that were like dancers holding hands in a row, with heads as tall as cities and skirts of cable strand. It had seemed romantic to George Rollins to change the sweep of rivers and the shape of mountains so that life could flourish in the old bad lands of the world where it had never taken root before.

He loved steel, and there was always steel near him in his dreams, liquid steel, steel in bars and blocks and beams and formless plastic masses, waiting for him, as paint and canvas to his hand. Steel inexhaustible, to be made lovely and austere in his imaginative fire . . . and now he was an insurance clerk at forty dollars a week, with his dream behind him. The dark little girl who had made this mess, this intolerable mess, was waiting for him in a town in Tennessee.[4]

In fifteen minutes the woman from whom he sublet his room knocked and asked him with maddening kindness if, since he was home, he would have some lunch. He shook his head, but this interruption aroused him, and, getting up from the bed, he wrote a telegram:

"Letter depressed me.

Have you lost your nerve?

You are foolish and just upset to think of breaking off. Why not marry me immediately? Sure we can make it all right——"

He hesitated for a wild minute and then added in a hand that could scarcely be recognized as his own: "In any case, I will arrive tomorrow at six o'clock."

When he finished he ran to the telegraph office near the subway station. He possessed in this world not quite one hundred dollars, but the letter showed that she was "nervous,"[5] and this left him no choice. He knew what "nervous" meant—that she was emotionally depressed, that the prospect of marrying into a life of poverty and struggle was putting too much strain upon her love.[6]

George Rollins reached the insurance company at his usual run. He went straight to the manager.

"I want to see you, Mr. Chambers," he announced breathlessly.

"Well?" Two eyes, eyes like winter windows, glared at him with ruthless impersonality.

"I want to get four days' vacation."

"Why, you had a vacation just two weeks ago!"

"That's true," admitted the distraught clerk. "But now I've got to have another."

"Where'd you go last time? To your home?"

"No, I went to—a place in Tennessee."

"Well, where do you want to go this time?"

"Well—a place in Tennessee."

"You're consistent, anyhow," exploded Mr. Chambers. "But I didn't know you were employed here as a traveling salesman."

"I'm not," cried George desperately. "But I've got to go."

"All right," agreed Mr. Chambers. "But you don't have to come back. So don't!"

"I won't." And to his own astonishment, as well as that of the manager, George's face beamed with pleasure. He felt happy, exultant—for the first time in six months he was absolutely free.

"I want to thank you," he said with a rush of emotion. "I don't want to come back. I think I'd have gone crazy if you'd said I could come back. Only I couldn't quit myself, and I want to thank you for—for quitting for me."

He waved his hand magnanimously, shouted aloud, "You owe me three days' salary, but you can keep it!" and rushed from the office.

Jonquil Cary was her name, and she was at the station waiting, a yellow daisy, with dark young eyes. To George Rollins nothing had ever looked so fresh and pale as her face when she saw him and quickly fled to him. Her arms were raised to him, her mouth was half parted for a kiss, when she held him off suddenly and lightly and with a touch of embarrassment looked around. Two boys, somewhat younger than George, were standing in the background.

"This is Mr. Craddock and Mr. Holt," she said, cheerfully. "You met them when you were here before."

Disturbed by the transition of a kiss into an introduction and suspecting some hidden significance, George was more confused when he found that the automobile which was to carry them to Jonquil's house belonged to one of the two young men. It put him, somehow, at a disadvantage.[7]

When, after twenty minutes, they were deposited at Jonquil's house George felt that the first happiness of the meeting, the joy he had recognized so surely in her eyes back in the station, had been dissipated by the intrusion of the ride. He was brooding on this as he said good night stiffly to the two young men. Then his ill humor faded as Jonquil drew him into a familiar embrace under the dim hall light and told him in a dozen ways, of which the best was without words, how she had missed him. Her emotion reassured him, seemed to promise that everything would be all right.

They sat together on the sofa, overcome by each other's presence, beyond all except fragmentary words. The supper hour came. Jonquil's father and mother appeared and were glad to see George. They liked him. Mr. Cary had been interested in his engineering career when he had first come to Tennessee over a year before. They had been sorry when George had given it up and had gone to New York to look for something more immediately profitable.

He and his wife deplored the young man's choice and the curtailment of his career, yet they sympathized with his point of view and were ready to recognize the engagement.[8] During dinner they asked him about his progress in New York.

"Everything's going fine," he told them, with a pretense of enthusiasm. "I've been promoted—better salary."

"They must like you!" cried Mrs. Cary. "I can see that—or they wouldn't let you off twice in three weeks to come down here."

"I told them they had to," explained George, hastily. "I told them if they didn't I wouldn't work for them any more."

"But you ought to save your money," Mrs. Cary reproached him gently, "and not spend it all on this expensive trip."

Dinner was over at last—he and Jonquil were alone and she came into his arms again, filling the simple room with black and yellow beauty.

"So glad you're here," she sighed. "Wish you never were going away again, darling. I miss you. O, so much, so much!"

"Do you—do other men come to see you often? Like those two kids?"

The dark velvet eyes stared at him.

"Why, of course they do," she answered. "All the time. Why, I've told you in letters that they did, dearest."

This was true—when he had first gone to the city there had been already a dozen boys around her, all responding to her picturesque fragility with adolescent worship and a few of them perceiving that her beautiful eyes were also sane and kind.

"Do you expect me never to go anywhere," Jonquil demanded, "and just fold my hands and sit still—forever?"

"What do you mean?" he cried. "Do you mean you think I'll never have enough money to marry you?"

"O, don't jump at conclusions so, George."

"I'm not jumping at conclusions. That's what you said."

George decided suddenly that he was on dangerous ground. He had not intended to let anything spoil this night. He tried to take her again in his arms, but she resisted unexpectedly, saying:

"It's hot. I'm going to get the electric fan."

When the fan was adjusted they sat down again, but he was in a supersensitive mood, and involuntarily he plunged into the very subject he had intended to avoid.

"When will you marry me?"

"Are you ready for me to marry you?"

All at once his nerves gave way and he sprang to his feet.

"Let's shut off that damned fan," he cried. "It drives me wild. It's like a clock ticking away the time I'll be with you. I came here to be happy and forget everything about New York and time——"

He sank down on the sofa as suddenly as he had risen. Jonquil turned off the fan, and, drawing his head down into her lap, began stroking his hair.

"Let's sit like this," she said softly; "just sit quiet like this and I'll put you to sleep. You're all tired and nervous, and your sweetheart'll take care of you."

"But I don't want to sit like this," he complained, sitting up suddenly. "I don't want to sit like this at all. I want you to kiss me. That's the only thing that makes me rest. And, anyway, I'm not nervous—it's you that's nervous. I'm not nervous at all."

To prove that he wasn't nervous he left the couch and plumped himself into a rocking chair across the room.

"Just when I'm ready to marry you you write me the most nervous letters, as if you're going to back out, and I have to come rushing down here——"

"You don't have to if you don't want to."

"But I do want to!" insisted George.

It seemed to him that he was being very cool and logical and that she was putting him deliberately in the wrong. With every word they were drawing farther and farther apart—and he was unable to stop himself or to keep worry and pain out of his voice.

But in a minute Jonquil began to cry sorrowfully, and he came back to the sofa and put his arm around her. He was the comforter now, drawing her head close to his shoulder, murmuring old familiar things until she grew calmer and only trembled a little, spasmodically, in his arms.

In the heat of the next day the breaking point came. They had each guessed the truth about the other, but of the two she was the more ready to admit the situation.

"There's no use going on," she said miserably. "You know you hate the insurance business, and you'll never do well in it."

"That's not it," he insisted, stubbornly. "I hate it without you. If you'll marry me and come with me and take a chance with me I can make good right away, but I can't do anything up there while I'm worrying about you down here."

She was silent a long time before she answered, not thinking—for she had seen the end—but only waiting, because she knew that every word would seem more cruel than the last. Finally she spoke:

"George, I love you with all my heart, and I don't see how I can ever love any one else. If you'd been ready for me two months ago I'd have married you—now I can't, because it doesn't seem to be the sensible thing."

He made wild accusations—there was some one else; she was keeping something from him!

"No, there's no one else."

This was true. But reacting from the strain of this affair Jonquil had found relief in the company of young boys like "Mr." Craddock or "Mr." Holt—they had the advantage of meaning absolutely nothing in her life.[9] Still, she did not tell this to George.

George did not take the situation well at all. He seized her in his arms and tried literally to kiss her into marrying him at once. When this failed he broke into a long monologue of self-pity and ceased only when he saw that he was making himself despicable in her sight. He threatened to leave when he had no intention of leaving and refused to go when she told him it was best that he should.[10]

For a while she was sorry, then for another while she was merely kind.

"You'd better go now!" she cried at last, so loud that Mrs. Cary came downstairs.

"Is something the matter?"

"I'm going away, Mrs. Cary," said George, brokenly. Jonquil had rushed from the room.

"Don't feel so badly, George." Mrs. Cary blinked at him in helpless sympathy, sorry, and, in the same moment, glad that the little tragedy was almost over. "If I were you I'd go home to your mother for a week or so. Perhaps, after all, this is the sensible thing——"

"Please don't talk!" he cried. "Please don't say anything to me now!"

Jonquil came into the room again, dressed for the street, her sorrow and her nervousness alike tucked under powder and rouge and hat.

"I've ordered a taxicab," she said, coolly. "We can drive around until your train leaves."

The taxicab came, and for an hour these two that had been lovers rode along the less frequented streets. He held her hand and grew calmer in the sunshine.

"I'll come back," he told her.

"I'll never forget you, George."

They reached the station, and she went with him while he bought his ticket.

*   *   *

On a damp afternoon in September of the following year an astonishingly brown young man got off the New Orleans train at a city in Tennessee. He taxied to the best hotel, where he registered as "George Rollins, Cuzco, Peru."[11]

Up in his room he sat for a few minutes at the window, looking out at the city below. Then, with his hand trembling faintly, he took off the telephone receiver and called a number.

"Hello. Is Miss Cary in?"

"This is she."

"O!" His voice, after overcoming a faint tendency to waver, went on with friendly formality.

"This is George Rollins. Did you get my letter?"

"Yes. I thought you'd be in today."

Her voice, cool and unmoved, disturbed him, but not as he had expected. This was the voice of a stranger, unexcited, pleasantly glad to see him—that was all. He wanted to put down the telephone and catch his breath.

"I haven't seen you for—a long time." He succeeded in making this sound offhand. "Over a year."

He knew how long it had been—to the day.[12]

"It'll be awfully good to talk to you again."

"Well, I'll be there—in about an hour."

He hung up. During the long seasons past every minute of his leisure had been full of this hour, and now the hour was here. He had thought of finding her married, in love—he had only found her unstirred at his return.

There would never again in his life, he suspected, be another seventeen months like these he had just gone through. He had made a remarkable showing in his profession for a young engineer. He had stumbled into two golden opportunities, one in Peru, whence he had just returned, and another, consequent upon it, in New York, whither he was bound. He had risen from obscurity to a high position for one so young.

He looked at himself in the mirror. He was almost black with tan, but it was a romantic black, and in the last week, since he had had time to think about it, it had given him considerable pleasure. The hardiness of his frame, too, he appraised with a sort of fascination. He had lost part of an eyebrow somewhere, and he still wore a bandage on his arm, but he was too young not to realize that on the steamer many women had looked at him with unusual tributary interest.

George Rollins of Cuzco, Peru, waited an hour and a half in the hotel, until the sun had reached a midway position in the sky. Then, freshly shaven and powdered toward a somewhat more Caucasian hue, he engaged a taxicab and set out for the house he knew so well.

The house was smaller and it seemed shabbier than before—there was no cloud of magic hovering over its roof.[13] He rang the doorbell and a colored maid appeared. Miss Jonquil was expecting him. She would be down in a moment. He wet his lips nervously and walked into the sitting room, and the feeling of unreality increased.

After all, he saw, this was only a room and not the enchanted chamber where he had passed those poignant hours. He sat in a chair, amazed to find it only a chair, realizing that his imagination had distorted and colored all these simple, familiar things.

The door opened and Jonquil came into the room—and everything seemed to blur before his eyes. He had not remembered how beautiful she was, and he felt his face grow pale and his voice fall to a poor sigh.

Jonquil was dressed in pale green, and a gold ribbon bound back her dark, straight hair like a crown. The familiar velvet eyes caught his as she came through the door, and a spasm of fright went through him at her beauty's power of inflicting pain.

He said, "Hello," and they each took a few steps forward and shook hands. Then they sat in chairs quite far apart and looked at each other across the room.

"You've come back," she said, and he answered, just as tritely, "I wanted to stop in and see you as I came through."

He tried to neutralize the tremor in his voice by looking anywhere but at her face. The obligation to speak was on him, but, unless he immediately began to boast, it seemed that there was nothing to say. There had never been anything casual in their previous relations. Was it possible that folks in this position talked about the weather?

"This seems ridiculous," he broke out in sudden embarrassment. "I don't know exactly what to do. Does my being here bother you?"

"No." The answer was both reticent and impersonally sad. It depressed him.

"Are you in love with some one?"

She shook her head.

"O!" He leaned back in his chair. Another subject seemed exhausted and the interview was not taking at all the course he had intended.

"Jonquil," he began, this time in a softer key, "after all that has happened I had to come back and see you, because whatever I do in the future I'll never love another girl as I've loved you."

This was one of the speeches he had rehearsed. On the steamer it had seemed to have just the right note—a referenece[14] to the tenderness he would always feel for her, combined with a noncommittal attitude toward his present state of mind. Here, with the past around him, beside him, growing minute by minute more heavy, it seemed theatrical.

"You don't love me any more, do you?" he added in a level voice. "No."

When Mrs. Carey[15] came in a minute later and spoke to George about his success—there had been a half column about him in the local paper—he was a mixture of emotions. He knew now that he still wanted this girl and he knew that the past sometimes comes back—that was all.[16] For the rest, he must be strong and watchful.

"And now," Mrs. Cary was saying, "I want you two to go and see the lady who has the chrysanthemums. She particularly told me she wanted to see you."

So they went to see the lady with the chrysanthemums. They walked along the street and the sun came out and the leaves made a stiff, cheerful rustle in the trees. The chrysanthemums were large and extraordinarily beautiful. The garden was full of them, white and pink and yellow, so that to be among them was like going back into the heart of summer. There were two gardens really, with a gate between them, and when they strolled toward the second garden the chrysanthemum lady went first through the gate.

And then a curious and significant little incident happened. George stepped aside to let Jonquil pass, but instead of going through she stood still and stared at him for a minute. It was not so much the look, which was not a smile, as it was the moment of silence. They saw each other's eyes and both took a short, faintly quickened breath, and then they went into the second garden.

The afternoon waned. They thanked the lady and walked home slowly, thoughtfully, side by side. Through dinner, too, they were silent. George told Mr. Cary something of what had happened in South America and managed to let it be known that everything would be plain sailing for him in the future.

Dinner was over and he and Jonquil were alone in the room which had seen the beginning of their love affair and the end. It seemed to him long ago and inexpressibly sad. On that sofa he had felt agony and grief such as he would never feel again. He would never be so weak or so tired and miserable and poor. Yet he knew that that boy of seventeen months before had had something, a trust, a warmth, that was gone forever. The sensible thing—they had done the sensible thing. He had traded his first youth for strength and carved success out of despair. But, with his youth, life had carried away the freshness of his love.

"You won't marry me, will you?" he said, quietly.

Jonquil shook her dark head.

"I'm never going to marry," she answered.

He nodded.

"I'm leaving for Washington in the morning," he said.

"O——"

"I have to go. I've got to be in New York by the first, and meanwhile I want to stop off in Washington."

"Business?"

"No-o," he said, as if reluctantly. "There's some one there I must see who was very kind to me when I seemed down and out."

There was no one in Washington for him to see—he had invented this—but he was watching her narrowly, and he was sure that she winced a little; that her eyes closed and then opened wide again.

"But before I go I want to tell you the things that happened to me since I saw you, and, as maybe we won't meet again, I wonder if—if just this once you'd sit in my lap like you used to. I wouldn't ask, except, since there's no one else—yet—perhaps it doesn't matter."

She nodded and in a moment was sitting in his lap as she had sat so often in that vanished spring. The feel of her head against his shoulder, of her body, sent a shock of emotion over him. His arms holding her had a tendency to tighten around her, so he leaned back and began to talk thoughtfully into the air.

He told her of a despairing two weeks in New York which had terminated with an attractive if not very profitable job in a construction plant in Jersey City. When the Peru business had first presented itself it had not seemed an extraordinary opportunity. He was to be third assistant engineer on the expedition, but only ten of the American party, including eight rod men and surveyors, had ever reached Cuzco. Ten days later the chief of the expedition was dead of yellow fever. That had been his chance, a chance for anybody but a fool, a gorgeous chance——

"A chance for anybody but a fool?" she interrupted, innocently.

"Even for a lunatic," he insisted. "It was wonderful. Well, I wired New York——"

"And so," she interrupted again, "they wired that you ought to take a chance?"

"Ought to!" he exclaimed, still leaning back. "That I *had* to! There was no time to lose——"

"Not a minute?"

"Not a minute."

"Not even time for——" She paused.

"For what?"

"Look!"

He bent his head forward suddenly, and she drew herself to him in the same moment, her mouth half open like a flower.[17]

"Yes," he whispered into her lips, "there's all the time in the world . . ."

All the time in the world—his life and hers. But for an instant as he kissed her he knew that though he search through eternity he could never recapture those lost April hours. He might press her close now till the muscles knotted on his arms—she was something desirable and rare that he had fought for and made his own—but never again an intangible whisper in the dusk or on the breeze of night . . .

Well, let it pass, he thought; April is over, April is over. There are all kinds of love in the world, but never the same love twice.

The Unspeakable Egg

Saturday Evening Post
12 July 1924
$1,750

When Fifi visited her Long Island[1] aunts the first time she was only ten years old, but after she went back to New York the man who worked around the place said that the sand dunes would never be the same again. She had spoiled them. When she left, everything on Montauk Point[2] seemed sad and futile and broken and old. Even the gulls wheeled about less enthusiastically, as if they missed the brown, hardy little girl with big eyes who played barefoot in the sand.

The years bleached out Fifi's tan and turned her a pale-pink color, but she still managed to spoil many places and plans for many hopeful men. So when at last it was announced in the best newspapers that she had concentrated on a gentleman named Van Tyne everyone was rather glad that all the sadness and longing that followed in her wake should become the responsibility of one self-sacrificing individual; not better for the individual, but for Fifi's little world very much better indeed.

The engagement was not announced on the sporting page, nor even in the help-wanted column, because Fifi's family belonged to the Society for the Preservation of Large Fortunes; and Mr. Van Tyne was descended from the man who accidentally founded that society, back before the Civil War.[3] It appeared on the page of great names and was illustrated by a picture of a cross-eyed young lady holding the hand of a savage gentleman with four rows of teeth. That was how their pictures came out, anyhow, and the public was pleased to know that they were ugly monsters for all their money, and everyone was satisfied all around. The society editor set up a column telling how Mrs. Van Tyne started off in the Aquitania[4] wearing a blue traveling dress of starched felt with a round square hat to match; and so far as human events can be prophesied, Fifi was as good as married; or, as not a few young men considered, as bad as married.

"An exceptionally brilliant match," remarked Aunt Cal on the eve of the wedding, as she sat in her house on Montauk Point and clipped the notice for the cousins in Scotland, and then she added abstractedly, "All is forgiven."

"Why, Cal!" cried Aunt Josephine. "What do you mean when you say all is forgiven? Fifi has never injured you in any way."

"In the past nine years she has not seen fit to visit us here at Montauk Point, though we have invited her over and over again."

"But I don't blame her," said Aunt Josephine, who was only thirty-one herself. "What would a young pretty girl do down here with all this sand?"

"We like the sand, Jo."

"But we're old maids, Cal, with no vices except cigarettes and double-dummy mah-jongg.[5] Now Fifi, being young, naturally likes exciting, vicious things—late hours, dice playing,[6] all the diversions we read about in these books."

She waved her hand vaguely.

"I don't blame her for not coming down here. If I were in her place ——"

What unnatural ambitions lurked in Aunt Jo's head were never disclosed, for the sentence remained unfinished. The front door of the house opened in an abrupt, startled way, and a young lady walked into the room in a dress marked "Paris, France."

"Good evening, dear ladies," she cried, smiling radiantly from one to the other. "I've come down here for an indefinite time in order to play in the sand."

"Fifi!"

"Fifi!"

"Aunts!"

"But, my dear child," cried Aunt Jo, "I thought this was the night of the bridal dinner."

"It is," admitted Fifi cheerfully. "But I didn't go. I'm not going to the wedding either. I sent in my regrets today."

It was all very vague; but it seemed, as far as her aunts could gather, that young Van Tyne was too perfect—whatever that meant. After much urging Fifi finally explained that he reminded her of an advertisement for a new car.[7]

"A new car?" inquired Aunt Cal, wide eyed. "What new car?"

"Any new car."

"Do you mean ——"

Aunt Cal blushed.

"I don't understand this new slang, but isn't there some part of a car that's called the—the clutch?"

"Oh, I like him physically," remarked Fifi coolly. Her aunts started in unison. "But he was just —— Oh, too perfect, too new; as if they'd fooled over him at the factory for a long time and put special curtains on him ——"

Aunt Jo had visions of a black-leather sheik.[8]

"——and balloon tires and a permanent shave. He was too civilized for me, Aunt Cal." She sighed. "I must be one of the rougher girls, after all."

She was as immaculate and dainty sitting there as though she were the portrait of a young lady and about to be hung on the wall. But underneath her cheerfulness her aunts saw that she was in a state of hysterical excitement, and they persisted in suspecting that something more definite and shameful was the matter.

"But it isn't," insisted Fifi. "Our engagement was announced three months ago, and not a single chorus girl has sued George for breach of promise. Not one! He doesn't use alcohol in any form except as hair tonic. Why, we've never even quarreled until today!"

"You've made a serious mistake," said Aunt Cal.

Fifi nodded.

"I'm afraid I've broken the heart of the nicest man I ever met in my life, but it can't be helped. Immaculate! Why, what's the use of being immaculate when, no matter how hard you try, you can't be half so immaculate as your husband? And tactful? George could introduce Mr. Trotzky to Mr. Rockefeller[9] and there wouldn't be a single blow. But after a certain point, I want to have all the tact in my family, and I told him so. I've never left a man practically at the church door before, so I'm going to stay here until everyone has had a chance to forget."

And stay she did—rather to the surprise of her aunts, who expected that next morning she would rush wildly and remorsefully back to New York. She appeared at breakfast very calm and fresh and cool, and as though she had slept soundly all night, and spent the day reclining under a red parasol beside the sunny dunes, watching the Atlantic roll in from the east. Her aunts intercepted the evening paper and burnt it unseen in the open fire, under the impression that Fifi's flight would be recorded in red headlines across the front page. They accepted the fact that Fifi was here, and except that Aunt Jo was inclined to go mah-jongg without a pair when she speculated on the too perfect man, their lives went along very much the same. But not quite the same.

"What's the matter with that niece of yourn?" demanded the yardman gloomily of Aunt Josephine. "What's a young pretty girl want to come and hide herself down here for?"

"My niece is resting," declared Aunt Josephine stiffly.

"Them dunes ain't good for wore-out people," objected the yardman, soothing his head with his fingers. "There's a monotoness about them. I seen her yesterday take her parasol and like to beat one down, she got so mad at it. Some day she's going to notice how many of them there are, and all of a sudden go loony." He sniffed. "And then what kind of a proposition we going to have on our hands?"

"That will do, Percy," snapped Aunt Jo. "Go about your business. I want ten pounds of broken-up shells rolled into the front walk."

"What'll I do with that parasol?" he demanded. "I picked up the pieces."

"It's not my parasol," said Aunt Jo tartly. "You can take the pieces and roll them into the front walk too."

And so the June of Fifi's abandoned honeymoon drifted away, and every morning her rubber shoes left wet footprints along a desolate shore at the end of nowhere. For a while she seemed to thrive on the isolation, and the sea wind blew her cheeks scarlet with health; but after a week had passed, her aunts saw that she was noticeably restless and less cheerful even than when she came.

"I'm afraid it's getting on your nerves, my dear," said Aunt Cal one particularly wild and windy afternoon. "We love to have you here, but we hate to see you looking so sad. Why don't you ask your mother to take you to Europe for the summer?"

"Europe's too dressed up," objected Fifi wearily. "I like it here where everything's rugged and harsh and rude, like the end of the world. If you don't mind, I'd like to stay longer."

She stayed longer, and seemed to grow more and more melancholy as the days slipped by to the raucous calls of the gulls and the flashing tumult of the waves along the shore. Then one afternoon she returned at twilight from the longest of her long walks with a strange derelict of a man. And after one look at him her aunts thought that the gardener's prophecy had come true and that solitude had driven Fifi mad at last.

II

He was a very ragged wreck of a man as he stood in the doorway on that summer evening, blinking into Aunt Cal's eyes; rather like a beach comber who had wandered accidentally out of a movie of the South Seas.[10] In his hands he carried a knotted stick of a brutal, treacherous shape. It was a murderous-looking stick, and the sight of it caused Aunt Cal to shrink back a little into the room.

Fifi shut the door behind them and turned to her aunts as if this were the most natural occasion in the world.

"This is Mr. Hopkins," she announced, and then turned to her companion for corroboration. "Or is it Hopwood?"

"Hopkins," said the man hoarsely. "Hopkins."

Fifi nodded cheerfully.

"I've asked Mr. Hopkins to dinner," she said.

There was some dignity which Aunt Cal and Aunt Josephine had acquired, living here beside the proud sea, that would not let them show surprise. The man was a guest now; that was enough. But in their hearts all was turmoil and confusion. They would have been no more surprised had Fifi brought in a many-headed monster out of the Atlantic.

"Won't you—won't you sit down, Mr. Hopkins?" said Aunt Cal nervously.

Mr. Hopkins looked at her blankly for a moment, and then made a loud clicking sound in the back of his mouth. He took a step toward a chair and sank down on its gilt frailty as though he meant to annihilate it immediately. Aunt Cal and Aunt Josephine collapsed rather weakly on the sofa.

"Mr. Hopkins and I struck up an acquaintance on the beach," explained Fifi. "He's been spending the summer down here for his health."

Mr. Hopkins fixed his eyes glassily on the two aunts.

"I come down for my health," he said.

Aunt Cal made some small sound; but recovering herself quickly, joined Aunt Jo in nodding eagerly at the visitor, as if they deeply sympathized.

"Yeah," he repeated cheerfully.

"He thought the sea air would make him well and strong again," said Fifi eagerly. "That's why he came down here. Isn't that it, Mr. Hopkins?"

"You said it, sister," agreed Mr. Hopkins, nodding.

"So you see, Aunt Cal," smiled Fifi, "you and Aunt Jo aren't the only two people who believe in the medicinal quality of this location."

"No," agreed Aunt Cal faintly. "There are—there are three of us now."

Dinner was announced.

"Would you—would you"—Aunt Cal braced herself and looked Mr. Hopkins in the eye—"would you like to wash your hands before dinner?"

"Don't mention it." Mr. Hopkins waved his fingers at her carelessly.

They went in to dinner, and after some furtive backing and bumping due to the two aunts trying to keep as far as possible from Mr. Hopkins, sat down at table.

"Mr. Hopkins lives in the woods," said Fifi. "He has a little house all by himself, where he cooks his own meals and does his own washing week in and week out."

"How fascinating!" said Aunt Jo, looking searchingly at their guest for some signs of the scholarly recluse. "Have you been living near here for some time?"

"Not so long," he answered with a leer. "But I'm stuck on it, see? I'll maybe stay here till I rot."

"Are you—do you live far away?" Aunt Cal was wondering what price she could get for the house at a forced sale, and how she and her sister could ever bear to move.

"Just a mile down the line. . . . This is a pretty gal you got here," he added, indicating their niece with his spoon.

"Why—yes." The two ladies glanced uneasily at Fifi.

"Some day I'm going to pick her up and run away with her," he added pleasantly.

Aunt Cal, with a heroic effort, switched the subject away from their niece. They discussed Mr. Hopkins' shack in the woods. Mr. Hopkins liked it well enough, he confessed, except for the presence of minute animal life, a small fault in an otherwise excellent habitat.

After dinner Fifi and Mr. Hopkins went out to the porch, while her aunts sat side by side on the sofa turning over the pages of magazines and from time to time glancing at each other with stricken eyes. That a savage had a few minutes since been sitting at their dinner table, that he was now alone with their niece on the dark veranda—no such terrible adventure had ever been allotted to their prim, quiet lives before.

Aunt Cal determined that at nine, whatever the consequences, she would call Fifi inside; but she was saved this necessity, for after half an hour the young lady strolled in calmly and announced that Mr. Hopkins had gone home. They looked at her, speechless.

"Fifi!" groaned Aunt Cal. "My poor child! Sorrow and loneliness have driven you insane!"

"We understand, my dear," said Aunt Jo, touching her handkerchief to her eyes. "It's our fault for letting you stay. A few weeks in one of those rest-cure places, or perhaps even a good cabaret, will ——"

"What do you mean?" Fifi looked from one to the other in surprise. "Do you mean you object to my bringing Mr. Hopkins here?"

Aunt Cal flushed a dull red and her lips shut tight together.

"'Object' is not the word. You find some horrible, brutal roust-about along the beach ——"

She broke off and gave a little cry. The door had swung open suddenly and a hairy face was peering into the room.

"I left my stick."

Mr. Hopkins discovered the unpleasant weapon leaning in the corner and withdrew as unceremoniously as he had come, banging the door shut behind him. Fifi's aunt sat motionless until his footsteps left the porch. Then Aunt Cal went swiftly to the door and pulled down the latch.

"I don't suppose he'll try to rob us tonight," she said grimly, "because he must know we'll be prepared. But I'll* warn Percy to go around the yard several times during the night."

"Rob you!" cried Fifi incredulously.

"Don't excite yourself, Fifi," commanded Aunt Cal. "Just rest quietly in that chair while I call up your mother."

"I don't want you to call up my mother."

"Sit calmly and close your eyes and try to—try to count sheep jumping over a fence."

"Am I never to see another man unless he has a cutaway coat[11] on?" exclaimed Fifi with flashing eyes. "Is this the Dark Ages, or the century of—of illumination? Mr. Hopkins is one of the most attractive eggs[12] I've ever met in my life."

"Mr. Hopkins is a savage!" said Aunt Cal succinctly.

"Mr. Hopkins is a very attractive egg."

"A very attractive what?"

"A very attractive egg."

"Mr. Hopkins is a—a—an unspeakable egg," proclaimed Aunt Cal, adopting Fifi's locution.

"Just because he's natural," cried Fifi impatiently. "All right, I don't care; he's good enough for me."

The situation, it seemed, was even worse than they thought. This was no temporary aberration; evidently Fifi, in the reaction from her recent fiancé, was interested in this outrageous man. She had met him several days ago, she confessed, and she intended to see him tomorrow. They had a date to go walking.

---

* The *Saturday Evening Post* broke the text at this point after a two-page spread (pp. 12–13), continuing the story on p. 125.

The worst of it was that after Fifi had gone scornfully to bed, Aunt Cal called up her mother—and found that her mother was not at home; her mother had gone to White Sulphur Springs[13] and wouldn't be home for a week. It left the situation definitely in the hands of Aunt Cal and Aunt Jo, and the situation came to a head the next afternoon at teatime, when Percy rushed in upon them excitedly through the kitchen door.

"Miss Marsden," he exclaimed in a shocked, offended voice, "I want to give up my position!"

"Why, Percy!"

"I can't help it. I lived here on the Point for more'n forty-five years, and I never seen such a sight as I seen just now."

"What's the matter?" cried the two ladies, springing up in wild alarm.

"Go to the window and look for yourself. Miss Fifi is kissing a tramp in broad daylight, down on the beach!"

III

Five minutes later two maiden ladies were making their way across the sand toward a couple who stood close together on the shore, sharply outlined against the bright afternoon sky. As they came closer Fifi and Mr. Hopkins, absorbed in the contemplation of each other, perceived them and drew lingeringly apart. Aunt Cal began to speak when they were still thirty yards away.

"Go into the house, Fifi!" she cried.

Fifi looked at Mr. Hopkins, who touched her hand reassuringly and nodded. As if under the influence of a charm, Fifi turned away from him, and with her head lowered walked with slender grace toward the house.

"Now, my man," said Aunt Cal, folding her arms, "what are your intentions?"

Mr. Hopkins returned her glare rudely. Then he gave a low hoarse laugh.

"What's that to you?" he demanded.

"It's everything to us. Miss Marsden is our niece, and your attentions are unwelcome—not to say obnoxious."

Mr. Hopkins turned half away.

"Aw, go on and blab your mouth out!" he advised her.

Aunt Cal tried a new approach.

"What if I were to tell you that Miss Marsden were mentally deranged?"

"What's that?"

"She's—she's a little crazy."

He smiled contemptuously.

"What's the idea? Crazy 'cause she likes me?"

"That merely indicates it," answered Aunt Cal bravely. "She's had an unfortunate love affair and it's affected her mind. Look here!" She opened the purse that swung at her waist. "If I give you fifty—a hundred dollars right now in cash, will you promise to move yourself ten miles up the beach?"

"Ah-h-h-h!" he exclaimed, so venomously that the two ladies swayed together.

"Two hundred!" cried Aunt Cal, with a catch in her voice.

He shook his finger at them.

"You can't buy me!" he growled. "I'm as good as anybody. There's chauffeurs and such that marry millionaires' daughters every day in the week.[14] This is Umerica, a free country, see?"

"You won't give her up?" Aunt Cal swallowed hard on the words. "You won't stop bothering her and go away?"

He bent over suddenly and scooped up a large double handful of sand, which he threw in a high parabola so that it scattered down upon the horrified ladies, enveloping them for a moment in a thick mist. Then laughing once again in his hoarse, boorish way, he turned and set off at a loping run along the sand.

In a daze the two women brushed the casual sand from their shoulders and walked stiffly toward the house.

"I'm younger than you are," said Aunt Jo firmly when they reached the living room. "I want a chance now to see what I can do."

She went to the telephone and called a New York number.

"Dr. Roswell Gallup's office? Is Doctor Gallup there?" Aunt Cal sat down on the sofa and gazed tragically at the ceiling. "Doctor Gallup? This is Miss Josephine Marsden, of Montauk Point. . . . Doctor Gallup, a very curious state of affairs has arisen concerning my niece. She has become entangled with a—a—an unspeakable egg." She gasped as she said this, and went on to explain in a few words the uncanny nature of the situation.

"And I think that perhaps psychoanalysis[15] might clear up what my sister and I have been unable to handle."

Doctor Gallup was interested. It appeared to be exactly his sort of a case.

"There's a train in half an hour that will get you here at nine o'clock," said Aunt Jo. "We can give you dinner and accommodate you overnight."

She hung up the receiver.

"There! Except for our change from bridge to mah-jongg,[16] this will be the first really modern step we've ever taken in our lives."

The hours passed slowly. At seven Fifi came down to dinner, as unperturbed as though nothing had happened; and her aunts played up bravely to her calmness, determined to say nothing until the doctor had actually arrived. After dinner Aunt Jo suggested mah-jongg, but Fifi declared that she would rather read, and settled on the sofa with a volume of the encyclopedia.[17] Looking over her shoulder, Aunt Cal noted with alarm that she had turned to the article on the Australian bush.

It was very quiet in the room. Several times Fifi raised her head as if listening, and once she got up and went to the door and stared out for a long time into the night. Her aunts were both poised in their chairs to rush after her if she showed signs of bolting, but after a moment she closed the door with a sigh and returned to her chair. It was with relief that a little after nine they heard the sound of automobile wheels on the shell drive and knew that Doctor Gallup had arrived at last.

He was a short, stoutish man, with alert black eyes and an intense manner. He came in, glancing eagerly about him, and his eye brightened as it fell on Fifi like the eye of a hungry man when he sees prospective food. Fifi returned his gaze curiously, evidently unaware that his arrival had anything to do with herself.

"Is this the lady?" he cried, dismissing her aunts with a perfunctory handshake and approaching Fifi at a lively hop.

"This gentleman is Doctor Gallup, dear," beamed Aunt Jo, expectant and reassured. "He's an old friend of mine who's going to help you."

"Of course I am!" insisted Doctor Gallup, jumping around her cordially. "I'm going to fix her up just fine."

"He understands everything about the human mind," said Aunt Jo.

"Not everything," admitted Doctor Gallup, smiling modestly. "But we often make the regular doctors wonder." He turned roguishly to Fifi. "Yes, young lady, we often make the regular doctors wonder."

Clapping his hands together decisively, he drew up a chair in front of Fifi.

"Come," he cried, "let us see what can be the matter. We'll start by having you tell me the whole story in your own way. Begin."

"The story," remarked Fifi, with a slight yawn, "happens to be none of your business."

"None of my business!" he exclaimed incredulously. "Why, my girl, I'm trying to help you! Come now, tell old Doctor Gallup the whole story."

"Let my aunts tell you," said Fifi coldly. "They seem to know more about it than I do."

Doctor Gallup frowned.

"They've already outlined the situation. Perhaps I'd better begin by asking you questions."

"You'll answer the doctor's questions, won't you, dear?" coaxed Aunt Jo. "Doctor Gallup is one of the most modern doctors in New York."

"I'm an old-fashioned girl," objected Fifi maliciously. "And I think it's immoral to pry into people's affairs. But go ahead and I'll try to think up a comeback for everything you say."

Doctor Gallup overlooked the unnecessary rudeness of this remark and mustered a professional smile.

"Now, Miss Marsden, I understand that about a month ago you came out here for a rest."

Fifi shook her head.

"No, I came out to hide my face."

"You were ashamed because you had broken your engagement?"

"Terribly. If you desert a man at the altar you brand him for the rest of his life."

"Why?" he demanded sharply.

"Why not?"

"You're not asking me. I'm asking you. . . . However, let that pass. Now, when you arrived here, how did you pass your time?"

"I walked mostly—walked along the beach."

"It was on one of these walks that you met the—ah—person your aunt told me of over the telephone?"

Fifi pinkened slightly.

"Yes."

"What was he doing when you first saw him?"

"He was looking down at me out of a tree."

There was a general exclamation from her aunts, in which the word "monkey" figured.

"Did he attract you immediately?" demanded Doctor Gallup.

"Why, not especially. At first I only laughed."

"I see. Now, as I understand, this man was very—ah—very originally clad."

"Yes," agreed Fifi.

"He was unshaven?"

"Yes."

"Ah!" Doctor Gallup seemed to go through a sort of convolution like a medium coming out of a trance. "Miss Fifi," he cried out triumphantly, "did you ever read The Sheik?"[18]

"Never heard of it."

"Did you ever read any book in which a girl was wooed by a so-called sheik or cave man?"

"Not that I remember."

"What, then, was your favorite book when you were a girl?"

"Little Lord Fauntleroy."[19]

Doctor Gallup was considerably disappointed. He decided to approach the case from a new angle.

"Miss Fifi, won't you admit that there's nothing behind this but some fancy in your head?"

"On the contrary," said Fifi startlingly, "there's a great deal more behind it than any of you suspect. He's changed my entire attitude on life."

"What do you mean?"

She seemed on the point of making some declaration, but after a moment her lovely eyes narrowed obstinately and she remained silent.

"Miss Fifi"—Doctor Gallup raised his voice sharply—"the daughter of C. T. J. Calhoun, the biscuit man, ran away with a taxi driver. Do you know what she's doing now?"

"No."

"She's working in a laundry on the East Side, trying to keep her child's body and soul together."

He looked at her keenly; there were signs of agitation in her face.

"Estelle Holliday ran away in 1920 with her father's second man!" he cried. "Shall I tell you where I heard of her last? She stumbled into a charity hospital, bruised from head to foot, because her drunken husband had beaten her to within an inch of her life!"

Fifi was breathing hard. Her aunts leaned forward. Doctor Gallup sprang suddenly to his feet.

"But they were playing safe compared to you!" he shouted. "They didn't woo an ex-convict with blood on his hands."

And now Fifi was on her feet, too, her eyes flashing fire.

"Be careful!" she cried. "Don't go too far!"

"I can't go too far!" He reached in his pocket, plucked out a folded evening paper and slapped it down on the table.

"Read that, Miss Fifi!" he shouted. "It'll tell you how four man-killers entered a bank in West Crampton three weeks ago. It'll tell you how they shot down the cashier in cold blood, and how one of them, the most brutal, the most ferocious, the most inhuman, got away. And it will tell you that that human gorilla is now supposed to be hiding in the neighborhood of Montauk Point!"

There was a short stifled sound as Aunt Jo and Aunt Cal, who had always done everything in complete unison, fainted away together. At the same moment there was loud, violent knocking, like the knocking of a heavy club, upon the barred front door.

IV

"Who's there?" cried Doctor Gallup, starting. "Who's there—or I'll shoot!"

His eyes roved quickly about the room, looking for a possible weapon.

"Who are you?" shouted a voice from the porch. "You better open up or I'll blow a hole through the door."

"What'll we do?" exclaimed Doctor Gallup, perspiring freely.

Fifi, who had been sprinkling water impartially upon her aunts, turned around with a scornful smile.

"It's just Percy, the yardman," she explained. "He probably thinks that you're a burglar."

She went to the door and lifted the latch. Percy, gun in hand, peered cautiously into the room.

"It's all right, Percy. This is just an insane specialist from New York."

"Everything's a little insane tonight," announced Percy in a frightened voice. "For the last hour I've been hearing the sound of oars."

The eyes of Aunt Jo and Aunt Cal fluttered open simultaneously.

"There's a fog all over the Point," went on Percy dazedly, "and it's got voices in it. I couldn't see a foot before my face, but I could swear there was boats offshore, and I heard a dozen people talkin' and callin' to each other, just as if a lot of ghosts was havin' a picnic supper on the beach."

"What was that noise?" cried Aunt Jo, sitting upright.

"The door was locked," explained Percy, "so I knocked on it with my gun."

"No, I mean now!"

They listened. Through the open door came a low, groaning sound, issuing out of the dark mist which covered shore and sea alike.

"We'll go right down and find out!" cried Doctor Gallup, who had recovered his shattered equilibrium; and, as the moaning sound drifted in again, like the last agony of some monster from the deep, he added, "I think you needed more than a psychoanalyst here tonight. Is there another gun in the house?"

Aunt Cal got up and took a small pearl-mounted revolver from the desk drawer.

"You can't leave us in this house alone," she declared emphatically. "Wherever you go we're going too!"

Keeping close together, the four of them, for Fifi had suddenly disappeared, made their way outdoors and down the porch steps, where they hesitated a moment, peering into the impenetrable haze, more mysterious than darkness upon their eyes.

"It's out there," whispered Percy, facing the sea.

"Forward we go!" muttered Doctor Gallup tensely. "I'm inclined to think this is all a question of nerves."

They moved slowly and silently along the sand, until suddenly Percy caught hold of the doctor's arm.

"Listen!" he whispered sharply.

They all became motionless. Out of the neighboring darkness a dim, indistinguishable figure had materialized, walking with unnatural rigidity along the shore. Pressed against his body he carried some long, dark drape that hung almost to the sand. Immediately he disappeared into the mist, to be succeeded by another phantom walking at the same military gait, this one with something white and faintly terrible dangling from his arm. A moment later, not ten yards away from them, in the direction in which the figure had gone, a faint dull glow sprang into life, proceeding apparently from behind the largest of the dunes.

Huddled together, they advanced toward the dune, hesitated, and then, following Doctor Gallup's example, dropped to their knees and began to crawl cautiously up its shoreward side. The glow became stronger as they reached the top, and at the same moment their heads popped up over the crest. This is what they saw:

In the light of four strong pocket flash lights, borne by four sailors in spotless white, a gentleman was shaving himself, standing clad only in athletic underwear upon the sand. Before his eyes an irreproachable valet held a silver mirror which gave back the soapy reflection of his face. To right and left stood two additional men-servants, one with a dinner coat and trousers hanging from his arm and the other bearing a white stiff shirt whose studs glistened in the glow of the electric lamps. There was not a sound except the dull scrape of the razor along its wielder's face and the intermittent groaning sound that blew in out of the sea.

But it was not the bizarre nature of the ceremony, with its dim, weird surroundings under the unsteady light, that drew from the two women a short, involuntary sigh. It was the fact that the face in the mirror, the unshaven half of it, was terribly familiar, and in a moment they knew to whom that half face belonged—it was the countenance of their niece's savage wooer who had lately prowled half naked along the beach.

Even as they looked he completed one side of his face, whereupon a valet stepped forward and with a scissors sheared off the exterior growth on the other, disclosing, in its entirety now, the symmetrical visage of a young, somewhat haggard but not unhandsome man. He lathered the bearded side, pulled the razor quickly over it and then applied a lotion to the whole surface, and inspected himself with considerable interest in the mirror. The sight seemed to please him, for he smiled. At a word one of the valets held forth the trousers in which he now incased his likely legs. Diving into his open shirt, he procured the collar, flipped a proper black bow with a practiced hand and slipped into the waiting dinner coat. After a transformation which had taken place before their very eyes, Aunt Cal and Aunt Jo found themselves gazing upon as immaculate and impeccable a young man as they had ever seen.

"Walters!" he said suddenly, in a clear, cultured voice.

One of the white-clad sailors stepped forward and saluted.

"You can take the boats back to the yacht. You ought to be able to find it all right by the foghorn."

"Yes, sir."

"When the fog lifts you'd better stand out to sea. Meanwhile, wireless[20] New York to send down my car. It's to call for me at the Marsden house on Montauk Point."

As the sailor turned away, his torch flashed upward accidentally wavering upon the four amazed faces which were peering down at the curious scene.

"Look there, sir!" he exclaimed.

The four torches picked out the eavesdropping party at the top of the hill.

"Hands up, there!" cried Percy, pointing his rifle down into the glare of light.

"Miss Marsden!" called the young man eagerly. "I was just coming to call."

"Don't move!" shouted Percy; and then to the doctor, "Had I better fire?"

"Certainly not!" cried Doctor Gallup. "Young man, does your name happen to be what I think it is?"

The young man bowed politely.

"My name is George Van Tyne."

A few minutes later the immaculate young man and two completely bewildered ladies were shaking hands. "I owe you more apologies than I can ever make," he confessed, "for having sacrificed you to the strange whim of a young girl."

"What whim?" demanded Aunt Cal.

"Why"—he hesitated—"you see, all my life I have devoted much attention to the so-called niceties of conduct; niceties of dress, of manners, of behavior ——"

He broke off apologetically.

"Go on," commanded Aunt Cal.

"And your niece has too. She always considered herself rather a model of—of civilized behavior"—he flushed—"until she met me."

"I see," Doctor Gallup nodded. "She couldn't bear to marry anyone who was more of a—shall we say, a dandy?—than herself."

"Exactly," said George Van Tyne, with a perfect eighteenth-century bow. "It was necessary to show her what a—what an——"

"—— unspeakable egg," supplied Aunt Josephine.

"—— what an unspeakable egg I could be. It was difficult, but not impossible. If you know what's correct, you must necessarily know what's incorrect; and my aim was to be as ferociously incorrect as possible. My one hope is that some day you'll be able to forgive me for throwing the sand—I'm afraid that my impersonation ran away with me."

A moment later they were all walking toward the house.

"But I still can't believe that a gentleman could be so—so unspeakable," gasped Aunt Jo. "And what will Fifi say?"

"Nothing," answered Van Tyne cheerfully. "You see, Fifi knew about it all along. She even recognized me in the tree that first day. She begged me to—to desist until this afternoon; but I refused until she had kissed me tenderly, beard and all."

Aunt Cal stopped suddenly.

"This is all very well, young man," she said sternly; "but since you have so many sides to you, how do we know that in one of your off moments you aren't the murderer who's hiding on the Point?"

"The murderer?" asked Van Tyne blankly. "What murderer?"

"Ah, I can explain that, Miss Marsden." Doctor Gallup smiled apologetically. "As a matter of fact, there wasn't any murderer."

"No murderer?" Aunt Cal looked at him sharply.

"No, I invented the bank robbery and the escaped murderer and all. I was merely applying a form of strong medicine to your niece."

Aunt Cal looked at him scornfully and turned to her sister. "All your modern ideas are not so successful as mah-jongg," she remarked significantly.

The fog had blown back to sea, and as they came in sight of the house the lamps were glowing out into the darkness. On the porch waited an immaculate girl in a gleaming white dress, strung with beads which glistened in the new moonlight.

"The perfect man," murmured Aunt Jo, flushing, "is, of course, he who will make any sacrifice."

Van Tyne did not answer; he was engaged in removing some imperceptible flaw, less visible than a hair, from his elbow, and when he had finished he smiled. There was now not the faintest imperfection anywhere about him, except where the strong beating of his heart disturbed faintly the satin facing of his coat.

John Jackson's Arcady

Saturday Evening Post
26 July 1924
$1,750

The first letter, crumpled into an emotional ball, lay at his elbow, and it did not matter faintly now what this second letter contained. For a long time after he had stripped off the envelope, he still gazed up at the oil painting of slain grouse over the sideboard, just as though he had not faced it every morning at breakfast for the past twelve years. Finally he lowered his eyes and began to read:

> "*Dear Mr. Jackson:* This is just a reminder that you have consented to speak at our annual meeting Thursday. We don't want to dictate your choice of a topic, but it has occurred to me that it would be interesting to hear from you on What Have I Got Out of Life. Coming from you this should be an inspiration to everyone.
>
> "We are delighted to have you anyhow, and we appreciate the honor that you confer on us by coming at all.
>
> > "Most cordially yours,
> > > "ANTHONY ROREBACK,
> > > > "Sec. Civic Welfare League."

"What have I got out of life?" repeated John Jackson aloud, raising up his head.

He wanted no more breakfast, so he picked up both letters and went out on his wide front porch to smoke a cigar and lie about for a lazy half hour before he went downtown. He had done this each morning for ten years—ever since his wife ran off one windy night and gave him back the custody of his leisure hours. He loved to rest on this porch in the fresh warm mornings and through a porthole in the green vines watch the automobiles pass along the street, the widest, shadiest, pleasantest street in town.

"What have I got out of life?" he said again, sitting down on a creeping wicker chair; and then, after a long pause, he whispered, "Nothing."

The word frightened him. In all his forty-five years he had never said such a thing before. His greatest tragedies had not embittered him, only made him sad. But here beside the warm friendly rain that tumbled from his eaves onto the familiar lawn, he knew at last that life had stripped him clean of all happiness and all illusion.

He knew this because of the crumpled ball which closed out his hope in his only son. It told him what a hundred hints and indication had told him before; that his son was weak and vicious, and the language in which it was conveyed was no less emphatic for being polite. The letter was from the dean of the college at New Haven,[1] a gentleman who said exactly what he meant in every word:

> "*Dear Mr. Jackson:* It is with much regret that I write to tell you that your son, Ellery Hamil Jackson, has been requested to withdraw from the university. Last year largely, I am afraid, out of personal feeling toward you, I yielded to your request that he be allowed another chance. I see now that this was a mistake, and I should be failing in my duty if I did not tell you that he is not the sort of boy we want here. His conduct at the sophomore dance was such that several undergraduates took it upon themselves to administer violent correction.
>
> "It grieves me to write you this, but I see no advantage in presenting the case otherwise than as it is. I have requested that he leave New Haven by the day after tomorrow. I am, sir,
>
> "Yours very sincerely,
>
> "AUSTIN SCHEMMERHORN,
>
> "Dean of the College."

What particularly disgraceful thing his son had done John Jackson did not care to imagine. He knew without any question that what the dean said was true. Why, there were houses already in this town where his son, John Jackson's son, was no longer welcome! For a while Ellery had been forgiven because of his father, and he had been more than forgiven at home, because John Jackson was one of those rare men who can forgive even their own families. But he would never be forgiven any more. Sitting on his porch this morning beside the gentle April rain, something had happened in his father's heart.

"What have I had out of life?" John Jackson shook his head from side to side with quiet, tired despair. "Nothing!"

He picked up the second letter, the civic-welfare letter, and read it over; and then helpless, dazed laughter shook him physically until he trembled in his chair. On Wednesday, at the hour when his delinquent boy would arrive at the motherless home, John Jackson would be standing on a platform downtown, delivering one hundred resounding platitudes of inspiration and cheer. "Members of the association"—their faces, eager, optimistic, impressed, would look up at him like hollow moons—"I have been requested to try to tell you in a few words what I have had from life ——"

Many people would be there to hear, for the clever young secretary had hit upon a topic with the personal note—what John Jackson, successful, able and popular, had found for himself in the tumultuous grab bag. They would listen with wistful attention, hoping that he would disclose some secret formula that would make their lives as popular and successful and happy as his own. They believed in rules; all the young men in the city believed in hard-and-fast rules, and many of them clipped coupons and sent away for little booklets that promised them the riches and good fortune they desired.[2]

"Members of the association, to begin with, let me say that there is so much in life that if we don't find it, it is not the fault of life, but of ourselves."

The ring of the stale, dull words mingled with the patter of the rain went on and on endlessly, but John Jackson knew that he would never make that speech, or any speeches ever again. He had dreamed his last dream too long, but he was awake at last.

"I shall not go on flattering a world that I have found unkind," he whispered to the rain. "Instead, I shall go out of this house and out of this town and somewhere find again the happiness that I possessed when I was young."

Nodding his head, he tore both letters into small fragments and dropped them on the table beside him. For half an hour longer he sat there, rocking a little and smoking his cigar slowly and blowing the blue smoke out into the rain.

II

Down at his office, his chief clerk, Mr. Fowler, approached him with his morning smile.

"Looking fine, Mr. Jackson. Nice day if it hadn't rained."

"Yeah," agreed John Jackson cheerfully. "Clear up in an hour. Anybody outside?"

"A lady named Mrs. Ralston."

Mr. Fowler raised his grizzled eyebrows in facetious mournfulness.

"Tell her I can't see her," said John Jackson, rather to his clerk's surprise. "And let me have a pencil memorandum of the money I've given away through her these twenty years."

"Why—yes, sir."

Mr. Fowler had always urged John Jackson to look more closely into his promiscuous charities; but now, after these two decades, it rather alarmed him.

When the list arrived—its preparation took an hour of burrowing through old ledgers and check stubs—John Jackson studied it for a long time in silence.

"That woman's got more money than you have," grumbled Fowler at his elbow. "Every time she comes in she's wearing a new hat. I bet she never hands out a cent herself—just goes around asking other people."

John Jackson did not answer. He was thinking that Mrs. Ralston had been one of the first women in town to bar Ellery Jackson from her house. She did quite right, of course; and yet perhaps back there when Ellery was sixteen, if he had cared for some nice girl ——

"Thomas J. MacDowell's outside. Do you want to see him? I said I didn't think you were in, because on second thoughts, Mr. Jackson, you look tired this morning ——"

"I'll see him," interrupted John Jackson.

He watched Fowler's retreating figure with an unfamiliar expression in his eyes. All that cordial diffuseness of Fowler's—he wondered what it covered in the man's heart. Several times, without Fowler's knowledge, Jackson had seen him giving imitations of the boss for the benefit of the other employees; imitations with a touch of malice in them that John Jackson had smiled at then, but that now crept insinuatingly into his mind.

"Doubtless he considers me a good deal of a fool," murmured John Jackson thoughtfully, "because I've kept him long after his usefulness was over. It's a way men have, I suppose, to despise anyone they can impose on."

Thomas J. MacDowell, a big barn door of a man with huge white hands, came boisterously into the office. If John Jackson had gone in for enemies he must have started with Tom MacDowell. For twenty years they had fought over every question of municipal affairs, and back in 1908 they had once stood facing each other with clenched hands on a public platform, because Jackson had said in print what everyone knew—that MacDowell was the worst political influence that the town had ever known. That was forgotten now; all that was remembered of it went into a peculiar flash of the eye that passed between them when they met.

"Hello, Mr. Jackson," said MacDowell with full, elaborate cordiality. "We need your help and we need your money."

"How so?"

"Tomorrow morning, in the Eagle, you'll see the plan for the new Union Station. The only thing that'll stand in the way is the question of location. We want your land."

"My land?"

"The railroad wants to build on the twenty acres just this side of the river, where your warehouse stands. If you'll let them have it cheap we get our station; if not, we can just whistle into the air."

Jackson nodded.

"I see."

"What price?" asked MacDowell mildly.

"No price."

His visitor's mouth dropped open in surprise.

"That from you?" he demanded.

John Jackson got to his feet.

"I've decided not to be the local goat any more," he announced steadily. "You threw out the only fair, decent plan because it interfered with some private reservations of your own. And now that there's a snag, you'd like the punishment to fall on me. I tear down my warehouse and hand over some of the best property in the city for a song because you made a little 'mistake' last year!"

"But last year's over now," protested MacDowell. "Whatever happened then doesn't change the situation now. The city needs the station, and so"—there was a faint touch of irony in his voice—"and so naturally I come to its leading citizen, counting on his well-known public spirit."

"Go out of my office, MacDowell," said John Jackson suddenly. "I'm tired."

MacDowell scrutinized him severely.

"What's come over you today?"

Jackson closed his eyes.

"I don't want to argue," he said after a while.

MacDowell slapped his fat upper leg and got to his feet.

"This is a funny attitude from you," he remarked. "You better think it over."

"Good-by."

Perceiving, to his astonishment, that John Jackson meant what he said, MacDowell took his monstrous body to the door.

"Well, well," he said, turning and shaking his finger at Jackson as if he were a bad boy, "who'd have thought it from you after all?"

When he had gone Jackson rang again for his clerk.

"I'm going away," he remarked casually. "I may be gone for some time—perhaps a week, perhaps longer. I want you to cancel every engagement I have and pay off my servants at home and close up my house."

Mr. Fowler could hardly believe his ears.

"Close up your house?"

Jackson nodded.

"But why—why is it?" demanded Fowler in amazement.

Jackson looked out the high window upon the gray little city drenched now by slanting, slapping rain—his city, he felt sometimes, in those rare moments when life had lent him time to be happy. That flash of green trees running up the main boulevard—he had made that possible, and Children's Park, and the white dripping buildings around Courthouse Square over the way.

"I don't know," he answered, "but I think I ought to get a breath of spring."

When Fowler had gone he put on his hat and raincoat and, to avoid anyone who might be waiting, went through an unused filing room that gave access to the elevator. The filing room was actively inhabited this morning, however; and, rather to his surprise, by a young boy about nine years old, who was laboriously writing his initials in chalk on the steel files.

"Hello!" exclaimed John Jackson.

He was accustomed to speak to children in a tone of interested equality.

"I didn't know this office was occupied this morning."

The little boy looked at him steadily.

"My name's John Jackson Fowler," he announced.

"What?"

"My name's John Jackson Fowler."

"Oh, I see. You're—you're Mr. Fowler's son?"

"Yeah, he's my father."

"I see." John Jackson's eyes narrowed a little. "Well, I bid you good morning."

He passed on out the door, wondering cynically what particular ax Fowler hoped to grind by this unwarranted compliment. John

Jackson Fowler! It was one of his few sources of relief that his own son did not bear his name.

A few minutes later he was writing on a yellow blank in the telegraph office[3] below:

"ELLERY JACKSON,

    "Chapel Street,

        "New Haven,

            "Connecticut.

"There is not the slightest reason for coming home, because you have no home to come to any more. The Mammoth Trust Company of New York will pay you fifty dollars a month for the rest of your life, or for as long as you can keep yourself out of jail.

                  "JOHN JACKSON."

"That's—that's a long message, sir," gasped the dispatcher, startled. "Do you want it to go straight?"[4]

"Straight," said John Jackson, nodding.

III

He rode seventy miles that afternoon, while the rain dried up into rills of dust on the windows of the train and the country became green with vivid spring. When the sun was growing definitely crimson in the west he disembarked at a little lost town named Florence, just over the border of the next state. John Jackson had been born in this town; he had not been back here for twenty years.

The taxi driver, whom he recognized, silently, as a certain George Stirling, playmate of his youth, drove him to a battered hotel, where, to the surprise of the delighted landlord, he engaged a room. Leaving his raincoat on the sagging bed, he strolled out through a deserted lobby into the street.

It was a bright, warm afternoon, and the silver sliver of a moon riding already in the east promised a clear, brilliant night. John Jackson walked along a somnolent Main Street, where every shop* and hitching post and horse fountain made some strange thing

---

* The *Saturday Evening Post* broke the text at this point after a two-page spread (pp. 8–9), continuing the story on p. 100.

happen inside him, because he had known these things for more than inanimate objects as a little boy. At one shop, catching a glimpse of a familiar face through the glass, he hesitated; but changing his mind, continued along the street, turning off at a wide road at the corner. The road was lined sparsely by a row of battered houses, some of them repainted a pale unhealthy blue and all of them set far back in large plots of shaggy and unkempt land.

He walked along the road for a sunny half mile—a half mile shrunk up now into a short green aisle crowded with memories. Here, for example, a careless mule had stamped permanently on his thigh the mark of an iron shoe. In that cottage had lived two gentle old maids, who gave brown raisin cakes every Thursday to John Jackson and his little brother—the brother who had died as a child.

As he neared the end of his pilgrimage his breath came faster and the house where he was born seemed to run up to him on living feet. It was a collapsed house, a retired house, set far back from the road and sunned and washed to the dull color of old wood.

One glance told him it was no longer a dwelling. The shutters that remained were closed tight, and from the tangled vines arose, as a single chord, a rich shrill sound of a hundred birds. John Jackson left the road and stalked across the yard knee-deep in abandoned grass. When he came near, something choked up his throat. He paused and sat down on a stone in a patch of welcome shade.

This was his own house, as no other house would ever be; within these plain walls he had been incomparably happy. Here he had known and learned that kindness which he had carried into life. Here he had found the secret of those few simple decencies, so often invoked, so inimitable and so rare, which in the turmoil of competitive industry had made him to coarser men a source of half-scoffing, half-admiring surprise. This was his house, because his honor had been born and nourished here; he had known every hardship of the country poor, but no preventable regret.

And yet another memory, a memory more haunting than any other, and grown strong at this crisis in his life, had really drawn him back. In this yard, on this battered porch, in the very tree over his head, he seemed still to catch the glint of yellow hair and the glow of bright childish eyes that had belonged to his first love, the girl who had lived in the long-vanished house across the way. It was her ghost who was most alive here, after all.

He got up suddenly, stumbling through the shrubbery, and followed an almost obliterated path to the house, starting at the whirring sound of a blackbird which rose out of the grass close by. The front porch sagged dangerously at his step as he pushed open the door. There was no sound inside, except the steady slow throb of silence; but as he stepped in a word came to him, involuntary as his breath, and he uttered it aloud, as if he were calling to someone in the empty house.

"Alice," he cried; and then louder, "Alice!"

From a room at the left came a short, small, frightened cry. Startled, John Jackson paused in the door, convinced that his own imagination had evoked the reality of the cry.

"Alice!" he called doubtfully.

"Who's there?"

There was no mistake this time. The voice, frightened, strange, and yet familiar, came from what had once been the parlor, and as he listened John Jackson was aware of a nervous step within. Trembling a little, he pushed open the parlor door.

A woman with alarmed bright eyes and reddish gold hair was standing in the center of the bare room. She was of that age that trembles between the enduring youth of a fine, unworried life and the imperative call of forty years, and there was that indefinable loveliness in her face that youth gives sometimes just before it leaves a dwelling it has possessed for long. Her figure, just outside of slenderness, leaned with dignified grace against the old mantel on which her white hand rested, and through a rift in the shutter a shaft of late sunshine fell through upon her gleaming hair.

When John Jackson came in the doorway her large gray eyes closed and then opened again, and she gave another little cry. Then a curious thing happened; they stared at each other for a moment without a word, her hand dropped from the mantel and she took a swaying step toward him. And, as if it were the most natural thing in the world, John Jackson came forward, too, and took her into his arms and kissed her as if she were a little child.

"Alice!" he said huskily.

She drew a long breath and pushed herself away from him.

"I've come back here," he muttered unsteadily, "and find you waiting in this room where we used to sit, just as if I'd never been away."

"I only dropped in for a minute," she said, as if that was the most important thing in the world. "And now, naturally, I'm going to cry."

"Don't cry."

"I've got to cry. You don't think"—she smiled through wet eyes—"you don't think that things like this hap—happen to a person every day."

John Jackson walked in wild excitement to the window and threw it open to the afternoon.

"What were you doing here?" he cried, turning around. "Did you just come by accident today?"

"I come every week. I bring the children sometimes, but usually I come alone."

"The children!" he exclaimed. "Have you got children?"

She nodded.

"I've been married for years and years."

They stood there looking at each other for a moment; then they both laughed and glanced away.

"I kissed you," she said.

"Are you sorry?"

She shook her head.

"And the last time I kissed you was down by that gate ten thousand years ago."

He took her hand, and they went out and sat side by side on the broken stoop. The sun was painting the west with sweeping bands of peach bloom and pigeon blood and golden yellow.

"You're married," she said. "I saw in the paper—years ago."

He nodded.

"Yes, I've been married," he answered gravely. "My wife went away with someone she cared for many years ago."

"Ah, I'm sorry." And after another long silence—"It's a gorgeous evening, John Jackson."

"It's a long time since I've been so happy."

There was so much to say and to tell that neither of them tried to talk, but only sat there holding hands, like two children who had wandered for a long time through a wood and now came upon each other with unimaginable happiness in an accidental glade. Her husband was poor, she said; he knew that from the worn, unfashionable dress which she wore with such an air. He was George Harland—he kept a garage in the village.

"George Harland—a red-headed boy?" he asked wonderingly.

She nodded.

"We were engaged for years. Sometimes I thought we'd never marry. Twice I postponed it, but it was getting late to just be a girl—I was twenty-five, so finally we did. After that I was in love with him for over a year."

When the sunset fell together in a jumbled heap of color in the bottom of the sky, they strolled back along the quiet road, still hand in hand.

"Will you come to dinner? I want you to see the children. My oldest boy is just fifteen."

She lived in a plain frame house two doors from the garage, where two little girls were playing around a battered and ancient but occupied baby carriage in the yard.

"Mother! Oh, mother!" they cried.

Small brown arms swirled around her neck as she knelt beside them on the walk.

"Sister says Anna didn't come, so we can't have any dinner."

"Mother'll cook dinner. What's the matter with Anna?"

"Anna's father's sick. She couldn't come."

A tall, tired man of fifty, who was reading a paper on the porch, rose and slipped a coat over his suspenders as they mounted the steps.

"Anna didn't come," he said in a noncommittal voice.

"I know. I'm going to cook dinner. Who do you suppose this is here?"

The two men shook hands in a friendly way, and with a certain deference to John Jackson's clothes and his prosperous manner, Harland went inside for another chair.

"We've heard about you a great deal, Mr. Jackson," he said as Alice disappeared into the kitchen. "We heard about a lot of ways you made them sit up and take notice over yonder."

John nodded politely, but at the mention of the city he had just left a wave of distaste went over him.

"I'm sorry I ever left here," he answered frankly. "And I'm not just saying that either. Tell me what the years have done for you, Harland. I hear you've got a garage."

"Yeah—down the road a ways. I'm doing right well, matter of fact. Nothing you'd call well in the city," he added in hasty depreciation.

"You know, Harland," said John Jackson, after a moment, "I'm very much in love with your wife."

"Yeah?" Harland laughed. "Well, she's a pretty nice lady, I find."

"I think I always have been in love with her, all these years."

"Yeah?" Harland laughed again. That someone should be in love with his wife seemed the most casual pleasantry. "You better tell her about it. She don't get so many nice compliments as she used to in her young days."

Six of them sat down at table, including an awkward boy of fifteen, who looked like his father, and two little girls whose faces shone from a hasty toilet. Many things had happened in the town, John discovered; the factitious prosperity which had promised to descend upon it in the late 90's had vanished when two factories had closed up and moved away, and the population was smaller now by a few hundred than it had been a quarter of a century ago.

After a plentiful plain dinner they all went to the porch, where the children silhouetted themselves in silent balance on the railing and unrecognizable people called greeting as they passed along the dark, dusty street. After a while the younger children went to bed, and the boy and his father arose and put on their coats.

"I guess I'll run up to the garage," said Harland. "I always go up about this time every night. You two just sit here and talk about old times."

As father and son moved out of sight along the dim street John Jackson turned to Alice and slipped his arm about her shoulder and looked into her eyes.

"I love you, Alice."

"I love you."

Never since his marriage had he said that to any woman except his wife. But this was a new world tonight, with spring all about him in the air, and he felt as if he were holding his own lost youth in his arms.

"I've always loved you," she murmured. "Just before I go to sleep every night, I've always been able to see your face. Why didn't you come back?"

Tenderly he smoothed her hair. He had never known such happiness before. He felt that he had established dominance over time itself, so that it rolled away for him, yielding up one vanished springtime after another to the mastery of his overwhelming emotion.

"We're still young, we two people," he said exultantly. "We made a silly mistake a long, long time ago, but we found out in time."

"Tell me about it," she whispered.

"This morning, in the rain, I heard your voice."

"What did my voice say?"

"It said, 'Come home.'"

"And here you are, my dear."

"Here I am."

Suddenly he got to his feet.

"You and I are going away," he said. "Do you understand that?"

"I always knew that when you came for me I'd go."

Later, when the moon had risen, she walked with him to the gate.

"Tomorrow!" he whispered.

"Tomorrow!"

His heart was going like mad, and he stood carefully away from her to let footsteps across the way approach, pass and fade out down the dim street. With a sort of wild innocence he kissed her once more and held her close to his heart under the April moon.

IV

When he awoke it was eleven o'clock, and he drew himself a cool bath, splashing around in it with much of the exultation of the night before.

"I have thought too much these twenty years," he said to himself. "It's thinking that makes people old."

It was hotter than it had been the day before, and as he looked out the window the dust in the street seemed more tangible than on the night before. He breakfasted alone downstairs, wondering with the incessant wonder of the city man why fresh cream is almost unobtainable in the country. Word had spread already that he was home, and several men rose to greet him as he came into the lobby. Asked if he had a wife and children, he said no, in a careless way, and after he had said it he had a vague feeling of discomfort.

"I'm all alone," he went on, with forced jocularity. "I wanted to come back and see the old town again."

"Stay long?" They looked at him curiously.

"Just a day or so."

He wondered what they would think tomorrow. There would be excited little groups of them here and there along the street with the startling and audacious news.

"See here," he wanted to say, "you think I've had a wonderful life over there in the city, but I haven't. I came down here because life had beaten me, and if there's any brightness in my eyes this morning it's because last night I found a part of my lost youth tucked away in this little town."

At noon, as he walked towards Alice's house, the heat increased and several times he stopped to wipe the sweat from his forehead. When he turned in at the gate he saw her waiting on the porch, wearing what was apparently a Sunday dress and moving herself gently back and forth in a rocking-chair in a way that he remembered her doing as a girl.

"Alice!" he exclaimed happily.

Her finger rose swiftly and touched her lips.

"Look out!" she said in a low voice.

He sat down beside her and took her hand, but she replaced it on the arm of her chair and resumed her gentle rocking.

"Be careful. The children are inside."

"But I can't be careful. Now that life's begun all over again, I've forgotten all the caution that I learned in the other life, the one that's past."

"Sh-h-h!"

Somewhat irritated, he glanced at her closely. Her face, unmoved and unresponsive, seemed vaguely older than it had yesterday; she was white and tired. But he dismissed the impression with a low, exultant laugh.

"Alice, I haven't slept as I slept last night since I was a little boy, except that several times I woke up just for the joy of seeing the same moon we once knew together. I'd got it back."

"I didn't sleep at all."

"I'm sorry."

"I realized about two o'clock or three o'clock that I could never go away from my children—even with you."

He was struck dumb. He looked at her blankly for a moment, and then he laughed—a short, incredulous laugh.

"Never, never!" she went on, shaking her head passionately. "Never, never, never! When I thought of it I began to tremble all over, right in my bed." She hesitated. "I don't know what came over me yesterday evening, John. When I'm with you, you can always make me do or feel or think just exactly what you like. But this is too late, I guess. It doesn't seem real at all; it just seems sort of crazy to me, as if I'd dreamed it, that's all."

John Jackson laughed again, not incredulously this time, but on a menacing note.

"What do you mean?" he demanded.

She began to cry and hid her eyes behind her hand because some people were passing along the road.

"You've got to tell me more than that," cried John Jackson, his voice rising a little. "I can't just take that and go away."

"Please don't talk so loud," she implored him. "It's so hot and I'm so confused.[5] I guess I'm just a small-town woman, after all. It seems somehow awful to be talking here with you, when my husband's working all day in the dust and heat."

"Awful to be talking here?" he repeated.

"Don't look that way!" she cried miserably. "I can't bear to hurt you so. You have children, too, to think of—you said you had a son."

"A son." The fact seemed so far away that he looked at her, startled. "Oh, yes, I have a son."

A sort of craziness, a wild illogic in the situation had communicated itself to him; and yet he fought blindly against it as he felt his own mood of ecstasy slipping away. For twenty hours he had recaptured the power of seeing things through a mist of hope—hope in some vague, happy destiny that lay just over the hill—and now with every word she uttered the mist was passing, the hope, the town, the memory, the very face of this woman before his eyes.

"Never again in this world," he cried with a last despairing effort, "will you and I have a chance at happiness!"

But he knew, even as he said this, that it had never been a chance; simply a wild, desperate sortie from two long-beleaguered fortresses by night.

He looked up to see that George Harland had turned in at the gate.

"Lunch is ready," called Alice, raising her head with an expression of relief. "John's going to be with us too."

"I can't," said John Jackson quickly. "You're both very kind."

"Better stay." Harland, in oily overalls, sank down wearily on the steps and with a large handkerchief polished the hot space beneath his thin gray hair. "We can give you some iced tea." He looked up at John. "I don't know whether these hot days make you feel your age like I feel mine."

"I guess—it affects all of us alike," said John Jackson with an effort. "The awful part of it is that I've got to go back to the city this afternoon."

"Really?" Harland nodded with polite regret.

"Why, yes. The fact is I promised to make a speech."

"Is that so? Speak on some city problem, I suppose."

"No; the fact is"—the words, forming in his mind to a senseless rhythm, pushed themselves out—"I'm going to speak on What Have I Got Out of Life."

Then he became conscious of the heat indeed; and still wearing that smile he knew so well how to muster, he felt himself sway dizzily against the porch rail. After a minute they were walking with him toward the gate,

"I'm sorry you're leaving," said Alice, with frightened eyes. "Come back and visit your old town again."

"I will."

Blind with unhappiness, he set off up the street at what he felt must be a stumble; but some dim necessity made him turn after he had gone a little way and smile back at them and wave his hand. They were still standing there, and they waved at him and he saw them turn and walk together into their house.

"I must go back and make my speech," he said to himself as he walked on, swaying slightly, down the street. "I shall get up and ask aloud 'What have I got out of life?' And there before them all I shall answer, 'Nothing.' I shall tell them the truth; that life has beaten me at every turning and used me for its own obscure purposes over and over; that everything I have loved has turned to ashes, and that every time I have stooped to pat a dog I have felt his teeth in my hand. And so at last they will learn the truth about one man's heart."

V

The meeting was at four, but it was nearly five when he dismounted from the sweltering train and walked toward the Civic Club hall. Numerous cars were parked along the surrounding streets, promising an unusually large crowd. He was surprised to find that even the rear of the hall was thronged with standing people, and that there were recurrent outbursts of applause at some speech which was being delivered upon the platform.

"Can you find me a seat near the rear?" he whispered to an attendant. "I'm going to speak later, but I don't—I don't want to go upon the platform just now."

"Certainly, Mr. Jackson."

The only vacant chair was half behind a pillar in a far corner of the hall, but he welcomed its privacy with relief; and settling himself, looked curiously around him. Yes, the gathering was large, and apparently enthusiastic. Catching a glimpse of a face here and there, he saw that he knew most of them, even by name; faces of men he had lived beside and worked with for twenty years. All the better. These were the ones he must reach now, as soon as that figure on the platform there ceased mouthing his hollow cheer.

His eyes swung back to the platform, and as there was another ripple of applause he leaned his face around the corner to see. Then he uttered a low exclamation—the speaker was Thomas MacDowell. They had not been asked to speak together in several years.

"I've had many enemies in my life," boomed the loud voice over the hall, "and don't think I've had a change of heart, now that I'm fifty and a little gray. I'll go on making enemies to the end. This is just a little lull when I want to take off my armor and pay a tribute to an enemy—because that enemy happens to be the finest man I ever knew."

John Jackson wondered what candidate or protégé of MacDowell's was in question. It was typical of the man to seize any opportunity to make his own hay.

"Perhaps I wouldn't have said what I've said," went on the booming voice, "were he here today. But if all the young men in this city came up to me and asked me 'What is being honorable?' I'd answer them, 'Go up to that man and look into his eyes.' They're not happy eyes. I've often sat and looked at him and wondered what went on back of them that made those eyes so sad. Perhaps the fine, simple hearts that spend their hours smoothing other people's troubles never find time for happiness of their own. It's like the man at the soda fountain who never makes an ice-cream soda for himself."

There was a faint ripple of laughter here, but John Jackson saw wonderingly that a woman he knew just across the aisle was dabbing with a handkerchief at her eyes.

His curiosity increased.

"He's gone away now," said the man on the platform, bending his head and staring down for a minute at the floor; "gone away suddenly, I understand. He seemed a little strange when I saw him yesterday; perhaps he gave in at last under the strain of trying to do many things for many men. Perhaps this meeting we're holding here comes a little too late now. But we'll all feel better for having said our say about him.

"I'm almost through. A lot of you will think it's funny that I feel this way about a man who, in fairness to him, I must call an enemy. But I'm going to say one thing more"—his voice rose defiantly— "and it's a stranger thing still. Here, at fifty, there's one honor I'd like to have more than any honor this city ever gave me, or ever had in its power to give. I'd like to be able to stand up here before you and call John Jackson my friend."

He turned away and a storm of applause rose like thunder through the hall. John Jackson half rose to his feet, and then sank back again in a stupefied way, shrinking behind the pillar. The applause continued until a young man arose on the platform and waved them silent.

"Mrs. Ralston," he called, and sat down.

A woman rose from the line of chairs and came forward to the edge of the stage and began to speak in a quiet voice. She told a story about a man whom—so it seemed to John Jackson—he had known once, but whose actions, repeated here, seemed utterly unreal, like something that had happened in a dream. It appeared that every year many hundreds of babies in the city owed their lives to something this man had done five years before; he had put a mortgage upon his own house to assure the children's hospital on the edge of town. It told how this had been kept secret at the man's own request, because he wanted the city to take pride in the hospital as a community affair, when but for the man's effort, made after the community attempt had failed, the hospital would never have existed at all.

Then Mrs. Ralston began to talk about the parks; how the town had baked for many years under the midland heat; and how this man, not a very rich man, had given up land and time and money for many months that a green line of shade might skirt the boulevards, and that the poor children could leave the streets and play in fresh grass in the center of town.

That was only the beginning, she said; and she went on to tell how, when any such plan tottered, or the public interest lagged, word was brought to John Jackson, and somehow he made it go and seemed to give it life out of his own body, until there was scarcely anything in this city that didn't have a little of John Jackson's heart in it, just as there were few people in this city that didn't have a little of their hearts for John Jackson.

Mrs. Ralston's speech stopped abruptly at this point. She had been crying a little for several moments, but there must have been many people there in the audience who understood what she meant—a mother or a child here and there who had been the recipients of some of that kindness—because the applause seemed to fill the whole room like an ocean, and echoed back and forth from wall to wall.

Only a few people recognized the short grizzled man who now got up from his chair in the rear of the platform, but when he began to speak silence settled gradually over the house.

"You didn't hear my name," he said in a voice which trembled a little, "and when they first planned this surprise meeting I wasn't expected to speak at all. I'm John Jackson's head clerk. Fowler's my name, and when they decided they were going to hold the meeting, anyhow, even though John Jackson had gone away, I thought perhaps I'd like to say a few words"—those who were closest saw his hands clench tighter—"say a few words that I couldn't say if John Jackson was here.

"I've been with him twenty years. That's a long time. Neither of us had gray hair when I walked into his office one day just fired from somewhere and asked him for a job. Since then I can't tell you, gentlemen, I can't tell you what his—his presence on this earth has meant to me. When he told me yesterday, suddenly, that he was going away, I thought to myself that if he never came back I didn't—I didn't want to go on living. That man makes everything in the world seem all right. If you knew how we felt around the office——" He paused and shook his head wordlessly. "Why, there's three of us there—the janitor and one of the other clerks and me—that have sons named after John Jackson. Yes, sir. Because none of us could think of anything better than for a boy to have that name or that example before him through life. But would we tell him? Not a chance. He wouldn't even know what it was all about. Why"—he sank his voice to a hushed whisper—"he'd just look at you in a puzzled way and say, 'What did you wish that on the poor kid for?'"

He broke off, for there was a sudden and growing interruption. An epidemic of head turning had broken out and was spreading rapidly from one corner of the hall until it had affected the whole assemblage. Someone had discovered John Jackson behind the post in the corner, and first an exclamation and then a growing mumble that mounted to a cheer swept over the auditorium.

Suddenly two men had taken him by the arms and set him on his feet, and then he was pushed and pulled and carried toward the platform, arriving somehow in a standing position after having been lifted over many heads.

They were all standing now, arms waving wildly, voices filling the hall with tumultuous clamor. Someone in the back of the hall began to sing "For he's a jolly good fellow," and five hundred voices took up the air and sang it with such feeling, with such swelling emotion, that all eyes were wet and the song assumed a significance far beyond the spoken words.

This was John Jackson's chance now to say to these people that he had got so little out of life. He stretched out his arms in a sudden gesture and they were quiet, listening, every man and woman and child.

"I have been asked ——" His voice faltered. "My dear friends, I have been asked to—to tell you what I have got out of life ——"

Five hundred faces, touched and smiling, every one of them full of encouragement and love and faith, turned up to him.

"What have I got out of life?"

He stretched out his arms wide, as if to include them all, as if to take to his breast all the men and women and children of this city. His voice rang in the hushed silence.

"Everything!"

At six o'clock, when he walked up his street alone, the air was already cool with evening. Approaching his house, he raised his head and saw that someone was sitting on the outer doorstep, resting his face in his hands. When John Jackson came up the walk, the caller—he was a young man with dark, frightened eyes—saw him and sprang to his feet.

"Father," he said quickly, "I got your telegram, but I—I came home."

John Jackson looked at him and nodded.

"The house was locked," said the young man in an uneasy way.

"I've got the key."

John Jackson unlocked the front door and preceded his son inside.

"Father," cried Ellery Jackson quickly, "I haven't any excuse to make—anything to say. I'll tell you all about it if you're still interested—if you can stand to hear ——"

John Jackson rested his hand on the young man's shoulder.

"Don't feel too badly," he said in his kind voice. "I guess I can always stand anything my son does."

This was an understatement. For John Jackson could stand anything now forever—anything that came, anything at all.

Explanatory Notes

Alexandra Mitchell

These notes were compiled by Alexandra Mitchell. Additions written by Jennifer Nolan are indicated in italics.

James L. W. West III's Cambridge Editions have been used as the authoritative texts for all versions of Fitzgerald's novels and volumes of short stories collected during Fitzgerald's lifetime. Abbreviations for these volumes follow the formatting used in *The F. Scott Fitzgerald Review*, and are as follows: *The Basil, Josephine and Gwen Stories (BJG), All the Sad Young Men (ASYM), The Beautiful and Damned (B&D), Flappers and Philosophers (F&P), Spires and Gargoyles (S&G), The Great Gatsby: A Variorum Edition (GG Var), Tales of the Jazz Age (TJA),* and *This Side of Paradise (TSOP).* All short stories cited that are not included in this volume are from West's volumes. Although it may seem more consonant with the project of this volume to cite the magazine texts, we have chosen to use West's volumes for their authority and wide availability.

These notes use issues of *Vanity Fair* and *Harper's Bazar* as contemporary sources for fashions in clothing, travel, and leisure activities, as both magazines reported on the activities of the society elite Fitzgerald described and satirized. As George Douglas described the former in its heyday, "*Vanity Fair* was the magazine people talked about, included in their conversations, displayed at their parties [because] . . . it mirrored to perfection its time and place" (*The Smart Magazines*, 101–102).

Estimations of the relative purchasing power of dollar amounts referred to in the stories have been calculated using the US Bureau of Labor Statistics' CPI Inflation Calculator at https://www.bls.gov/data/inflation_calculator.htm. For the few references to years before 1913, the calculation has been made using https://www.in2013dollars.com/.

Jemina, the Mountain Girl

Vanity Fair, January 1921, 44

Jennifer Nolan: *"Jemina" was first published in Princeton University's* Nassau Literary Magazine *in December 1916 as "Jemima A Story of the Blue Ridge Mountains by John Phlox, Jr." There is some debate about how to classify this piece. Though Fitzgerald includes it in his list of "fiction" in his Ledger, he labels it a "burlesque" rather than a "short story" (the label he uses for all of the other works featured in this volume) and lists it under "other writings" rather than stories on his record of earnings for 1921 in the Ledger. Likewise, in both the final and early "dummy" Table of Contents for* Tales of the Jazz Age *(1922), Fitzgerald referred to "Jemina" as a "sketch" (see West, TJA, for a copy of the dummy version).*

1. Stephen Leacock (1869–1944) was an English-Canadian humourist. When this story appeared in *Vanity Fair*, a satirical piece by Stephen Leacock appeared on the prior page. Stephen Leacock's PhD supervisor, Thorsten Veblen, coined the phrase "conspicuous consumption" in *The Theory of the Leisure Class*, published in 1899.
2. Slapjack is a simple card game whose aim is to gain all the cards in the deck; players put their cards face up in sequence and the first player to slap the pile when a jack is played wins the stack.
3. In *Gatz*, Elevator Repair Service's production of *The Great Gatsby*, the actors throw cards around the stage as Myrtle Wilson's party reaches its height. John Collins, the group's Artistic Director, confirms that this is a coincidence; "Ben Williams, who does the sound and sits at the side, could do that trick where you flick the cards. There was also a card deck on the stage and I think Bob Cucuzza (who originally played Tom) also just sort of spontaneously picked up the deck and started making a mess with it when we were rehearsing. The idea with that scene, when we staged it, was just to make a big mess. So the cards got pulled in to that chaos." Email to Alexandra Mitchell, 21 September 2021.
4. Jennifer Nolan: *As West discusses in his introduction to TJA, in order to "fit on a single page"* Vanity Fair *"dropped two paragraphs near the end of the story and omitted the entire final section." In keeping with our editorial policies, our text replicates these omissions. West, TJA, xxii.*

His Russet Witch

Metropolitan, February 1921, 11–13, 46–51

1. The Ritz-Carlton Hotel in New York was established in 1911, five years after the London Ritz and thirteen years after the Paris Ritz.

2. When this story was collected (as "O Russet Witch!") in *Tales of the Jazz Age* (1922), this was corrected to "serpentine" embroidery. Turpentine was commonly used as a paint thinner.

3. Literary censors had asserted their power in 1920, the year "His Russet Witch" was written. In the summer of 1920 John Sumner, head of the New York Society for the Suppression of Vice (NYSSV), brought action against both *The Little Review* and the Washington Square Book Shop for respectively selling and publishing the "Nausicaa" episode of James Joyce's *Ulysses*. John Sumner succeeded Anthony Comstock, who Fitzgerald mocked in 1922's *The Beautiful and Damned*, as head of the NYSSV. Fitzgerald, *Ledger*, 4 and Birmingham, *The Most Dangerous Book*, 162.

4. Compare to "The I. O. U.," also written in 1920 but published posthumously; the plot concerns a book which has been "psychically dictated" and accepted by a publisher who also accepts "long novels about young love written by old maids in South Dakota." "Psychicly" is preserved as printed in *Metropolitan*. Fitzgerald, *I'd Die for You and Other Lost Stories*, 3.

5. Herbert George Wells (1866–1946) was an English novelist and early influence on Fitzgerald. In book one, chapter four of *This Side of Paradise* (1920), Amory Blaine and Thomas Parke D'Invillers read aloud to one another from his 1911 novel *The New Machiavelli*. Fitzgerald, *TSOP*, 114.

6. Luke McLuke (or McGlook, or McGluke) were names used to conjure the idea of an everyman; in a 1923 interview with *Picture-Play* magazine Fitzgerald talked about "Minne McGluke" as the presumed audience for movies. Churchwell, *Careless People*, 270.

7. Spats covered the insteps and ankles of shoes (more usually men's shoes) to protect the shoes from the dirt of the street. They fell out of favor during the 1920s.

8. Series of novels for children by Martha Finley (1828–1909) about the young, pious Elsie Dinsmore.

9. "Pendent," rather than "pendant," reproduced as printed in *Metropolitan*.

10. Hyperbole is exaggeration for emphasis or effect. When this story was collected in *Tales of the Jazz Age*, Caroline is described as throwing the book in "gentle hyperbola." A hyperbola is a conic section formed by the intersection of a plane and a double cone. It is likely that Fitzgerald intended the reader to imagine the book travelling in a U-shaped curve – a parabola.

11. Basketball was created in 1891 and introduced to women's athletics in 1892. It was widely played in high schools across America. In 1905, the year it was officially recognized as a winter sport, *The Minneapolis Journal* reported that "Minnesota was the pioneer in the introduction of basket-ball in the west." *The Minneapolis Journal*, 10 December 1905, 2.

12. The Eighteenth Amendment, which prohibited the manufacture and sale of alcoholic beverages, was ratified in January 1919. Prohibition began a year later, on 17 January 1920. Behr, *Prohibition*, 80.

13. The material, as well as the shininess, of Mr. Midnight Quill's suit indicates its age. On 15 June 1922, *Vogue* described alpaca as "an old-time material"; presumably it had been for some time, as a satirical 1918 *Vanity Fair* article depicts an incompetent (and presumably unfashionable) government employee wearing "a black alpaca coat." *Vogue*, 15 June 1922, 47 and *Vanity Fair*, February 1918, 52.

14. Merlin, who is twenty-five at this point in the story, would have finished high school in the mid-1910s. Google Ngram shows the word "pusher" climbing in popularity throughout the early twentieth century to peak in 1916. See Appendix 1, Ngram Language Analysis, for more detail on this approach to textual analysis.

15. In a 1915 letter, Fitzgerald advised his sister Annabel that "with such splendid eyebrows as yours you should brush them or wet them and train them every morning and night"; this advice was repurposed in "Bernice Bobs Her Hair," with Marjorie telling Bernice that her eyebrows would "'be beautiful if you'd take care of them in one-tenth the time you take doing nothing.'" Fitzgerald, *A Life in Letters*, 10 and Fitzgerald, *F&P*, 119.

16. "Progressant" and "retrogressant" were corrected to "progressive" and "retrogressive" when reprinted in *Tales of the Jazz Age*.

17. The US economy was in a deflationary depression from January 1920 to July 1921. Total industrial production fell by 30 percent, wholesale prices fell by 37 percent, and unemployment rose sharply. Fitzgerald, whose 1920 earnings of $18,850 were 5.8 times higher than the average net income reported to the Treasury department ($3,269), describes here the effects of inflation. Fitzgerald, *Ledger*, 52 and Commissioner of Internal Revenue, *Statistics of Income from Returns of Net Income for 1920*, 2.

18. This is the refrain of "Just Snap Your Fingers at Care," composed by Louis Silvers with lyrics by B. G. DeSylva. This was introduced in the Greenwich Village Follies of 1920. The Paul Whiteman Orchestra's recording of this song was released in February 1921, the same month as *Metropolitan* published "His Russet Witch."

19. A floorwalker is a senior employee in a department store who serves customers and supervises other sales staff.

20. The Treasury Department's Bureau of Internal Revenue was responsible for enforcing Prohibition.

21. In 1921 $30 would have the purchasing power of approximately $460, and $20 the purchasing power of approximately $300, in 2022.

22. William Jennings Bryan (1860–1925) and William McKinley (1843–1901) were respectively the Democratic and Republican candidates in the 1896 presidential election. McKinley won with 271 Electoral College votes to Bryan's 176.

23. F. Scott and Zelda Fitzgerald were married on Saturday, 3 April 1920, and would begin their second year of marriage two months after *Metropolitan* published "His Russet Witch." Bruccoli, *Some Sort of Epic Grandeur*, 128.

24. Both production and consumption of movies increased significantly throughout the 1920s. In 1921, when "His Russet Witch" was published, box-office receipts from 1921 were $301 million from tickets that cost between ten and fifty cents. The top-grossing film of the year was D. W. Griffith's *Way Down East*, adapted from Lottie Blair Parker's melodramatic play of the same name and starring Lillian Gish. Currell, *American Culture in the 1920s*, 105.

25. In 1921 $50 would have the purchasing power of approximately $760 in 2022.

26. An ice box is a non-mechanical refrigerator; a large block of ice, placed at the top of the box and replenished as often as necessary, kept food cool. The first electric refrigerators were produced in 1913.

27. Asbury Park is a seaside community on New Jersey's central coast, which established itself as a holiday location from the 1890s.

28. A cutaway is a formal frock coat, worn in the 1920s with a waistcoat, standing collar, and dress trousers. Edwards, *How to Read a Suit*, 139.

29. These are fictionalized churches; West identifies their life analogues as St. Thomas Church on Fifty-third Street, St. Patrick's on Fifth Avenue, and the Collegiate Church of St. Nicholas at Fifth and Forty-eighth. The later named St. Anthony's is analogous to St. Bartholemew's at Park and Fiftieth. West, *TJA*, 517.

30. Lavender was a fashionable color and orchids a fashionable flower at the time. In a September 1920 feature on Paris fashions, *The Ladies' Home Journal* reported that "deep lavender is the fashionable color of the moment." In May of the same year, *Vanity Fair* asked "why is an orchid smart and not a tulip?" *The Ladies' Home Journal*, September 1920, 121 and *Vanity Fair*, May 1920, 120.

31. The Bolshevik Party seized power in Petrograd in 1917, precipitating a civil war that was still ongoing when "His Russet Witch" was written and published. The Soviet Union was established in 1923.

32. Sigmund Freud's *A General Introduction to Psychoanalysis* was published in English by Boni and Liveright in 1920.

33. The first traffic lights in New York were installed in the middle of Fifth Avenue in 1920, a gift from the millionaire New York commissioner of traffic, John A. Harriss. On 6 February 1920, the *New-York Tribune* reported that "[t]raffic police stationed in the signal towers now in course of erection on Fifth Avenue at Fifty-seventh, Fiftieth, Forty-second, Thirty-eighth and Thirty-fourth streets, will flash red, yellow, or green lights in directing the maze of vehicle and pedestrian traffic." *New-York Tribune*, 6 February 1920, 13.

34. Google Ngram shows 1920 as the year when use of the phrase "sell bonds" peaked. Fitzgerald was alive to these changing fashions; in

"The Popular Girl" (1922) a character "sold bonds – bonds were now the thing," (51) and in "Winter Dreams" (1922) the hero sees that "rich men's sons were peddling bonds precariously" (161). In chapter 1 of *The Great Gatsby*, which is set in 1922, Nick Carraway decides that "Everybody I knew was in the bond business so I supposed it could support one more single man." Fitzgerald, *GG Var*, 3–4. See Appendix 1, Ngram Language Analysis, for more detail on both this example and this approach to textual analysis.

35. *The Crimes of the Borgias* is part of the *Celebrated Crimes* collection by Alexandre Dumas *père* (1802–1870). This collection was compiled between 1839 and 1841; the 1769 date given by Merlin is spurious.

36 Reproduced as printed in *Metropolitan*.

37. With the rise of the car as a means of transportation canes fell out of everyday use after the First World War. Edwards, *How to Read a Suit*, 139.

38. In 1921 $5,000 would have the purchasing power of around $76,000 in 2022.

39. *The Crime of Sylvestre Bonnard* is an 1881 novel by Anatole France (1844–1924). Fitzgerald depicts his heroine reading *The Revolt of the Angels*, another Anatole France novel, in his short story "The Offshore Pirate" (1920) and in July 1921 Fitzgerald wrote to Edmund Wilson that "[w]hen Anatole France dies French literature will be a silly jealous rehashing of technical quarrels." Fitzgerald, *A Life in Letters*, 47.

40. The influence of *The New York Times* expanded in the early twentieth century; the paper won its first Pulitzer Prize in 1918. *The New York Times*, 4 June 1918, 11.

41. In 1921 $200 would have the purchasing power of around $3,040 in 2022.

42. The phonograph was the first means of recording and reproducing sound; it used cylinders rather than discs, and was patented by Thomas Edison (1847–1931) in 1877. Emile Berliner (1851–1929) developed his more practical disc-based gramophone between 1887 and 1893.

Tarquin of Cheapside

Smart Set, February 1921, 43–46

This story was first published as "Tarquin of Cheepside" in the April 1917 *Nassau Literary Magazine*.

1. Cheapside is an area in the City of London, England. The Mermaid Tavern in Cheapside was known to host the leading lights of Elizabethan literature including John Donne, Ben Johnson and – by tradition, although probably not in fact – William Shakespeare.

2. Ceylon is now known as Sri Lanka. The Portuguese arrived on the island in 1505 and established a fort there in 1517.

3. Pikemen are soldiers armed with pikes. The first recorded use of the word pikeman was in 1566.

4. These soldiers would have acquired their ferocity in the Eighty Years' War, fought in what is now the Netherlands between 1566 and 1809, and the Anglo-Spanish War, fought intermittently and across several territories between 1585 and 1604.

5. "Spanish marches" is a typographical error, reproduced as printed in *Smart Set*. The phrase is "Spanish marshes" in both the *Nassau Lit* and the *Tales of the Jazz Age* (1922) versions of the story.

6. Elizabeth I (1533–1603) was Queen of England and Ireland from 1588 to 1603. "Tarquin of Cheapside" highlights Fitzgerald's lifelong interest in English history; later in his life, he would teach his daughter mnemonics he created to remember the names of the kings and queens of England. Smith, *Bits of Paradise*, 12.

7. "[B]y the Grace of Luther" parodies "by the Grace of God," a reference to Martin Luther (1483–1546), critical figure in the Protestant Reformation. Henry VIII initiated the English Reformation, in which the Church of England broke away from the Catholic Church, in 1532. The Protestant Queen Elizabeth signed the death warrant of the Catholic Mary, Queen of Scots in 1587.

8. This paragraph mocks the little magazines and little theatre movement of the modernist era. Little magazines (including Margaret Anderson's *Little Review*, Schofield Thayer's *The Dial*, and Alfred Kreymbourg's *Others*) were low-budget, small-circulation magazines known for printing experimental prose, poetry, and in some cases art. Many of Fitzgerald's contemporaries, including Gertrude Stein, John Dos Passos, and Carl Van Vechten, published their work in little magazines. The little theatre movement, similarly, rejected commercially lucrative works in favor of formally innovative and socially significant works. The reference to the Bible going through "seven printings in as many months" is made the year after Fitzgerald had seen his debut novel, *This Side of Paradise*, go through nine printings between April and October 1920.

9. Edmund Spenser (1552/1553–1599) was an English poet now best known for *The Faerie Queene*, an epic poem written in praise of Elizabeth I. The first three books of *The Faerie Queene* were published in 1590. "Spencer" was corrected to "Spenser" when "Tarquin of Cheapside" was republished in *Tales of the Jazz Age*.

10. The first two lines of Canto I, Book III of *The Faerie Queene*.

11. In this case, gossip is used a noun meaning one who engages in familiar or idle talk. This usage appeared in the 1560s.

12. A tumbler is an acrobat; this is also a double entendre, as in "a tumble in the hay."

13. Literally "pray-God," a prie-dieu is a small desk with a sloping shelf for a book, intended for use in private prayer.
14. Syren was the preferred spelling of 'siren' before the 1850s (https://bit.ly/tarquinsyren).
15. Beldame is an archaic term for an old woman, which Shakespeare used in *Lucrece* (1594) (see next note); "beldam|beldame, n.," *OED Online*, June 2022. Oxford University Press.
16. The first three lines of "The Rape of Lucrece," a narrative poem by William Shakespeare (1564–1616), which was published in 1594 and dedicated to his patron Henry Wriothesley, Third Earl of Southampton (1573–1624). Duncan-Jones and Woudhuysen, *Shakespeare's Poems: Venus and Adonis, The Rape of Lucrece and the Shorter Poems*, 14. The Folger Shakespeare Library provides a link to the poem with commentary here: https://shakespeare.folger.edu/shakespeares-works/lucrece/

The Popular Girl

Saturday Evening Post, 11 February 1922, 3–5, 82, 84, 86, 89 and 18 February 1922, 18–19, 105–106, 109–110

Jennifer Nolan: *Though Fitzgerald wrote several novellas, "The Popular Girl" was one of only two of his stories to be published serially in a popular magazine, the other being "The Rich Boy" in the January and February 1926 issues of* Red Book Magazine. *While not a big fan of the story itself, Fitzgerald was pleased that the first installment of "The Popular Girl" was the first item in the magazine (As Ever 37).*

1. Synthetic gin was grain alcohol, flavored and sweetened to taste like the real thing. A recipe for synthetic gin in Fitzgerald's hand lists "80 drops juniper berry oil; 40 drops coriander oil; 3 drops aniseed oil [. . .] 40% alcohol; 60% distilled H2O [. . .] liquid rock candy syrup" as its ingredients. A gin rickey is a highball made from gin, lime and soda water. Churchwell, *Careless People*, 148.
2. Named for the Roman general Quintus Fabius Maximus Verrucosus, a Fabian strategy is one that focuses on wearing the enemy down by occupying them in minor skirmishes and disrupting their access to supplies.
3. The Skull and Bones is a prestigious secret senior society at Yale.
4. Edward, Prince of Wales from 1911 to 1936, visited America frequently throughout the 1920s. He was considered the world's most eligible bachelor, a theme Fitzgerald would visit in more detail in his 1924 short story "Rags Martin-Jones and the Pr-nce of W-les." See Appendix 1, Ngram Language Analysis, for more detail on this example.

5. Zelda Sayre's maternal grandfather, Willis B. Machen, was a Kentucky Senator.

6. By Scott's standards, Yanci's prospective suitor is dressed too informally for the occasion. In February 1921, *Vanity Fair* told its readers that a "turn down collar is permissible only with a jacket such as the double breasted one . . . otherwise a turn-down collar is not correct any more than it is when worn with a dinner jacket," and noted slanting pockets as a feature of a "very smart sports suit" in April 1922. *Vanity Fair*, February 1921, 74 and *Vanity Fair*, April 1922, 80.

7. In 1922 $500,000 would have the purchasing power of around $8.5 million in 2022.

8. *Vogue*'s 1 April 1922 issue carried an advertisement for Van Raalte silk stockings which reminded its readers that "Charming ankles are still in style." *Vogue*, 1 April 1922, 19.

9. In a 1915 letter to his sister Annabel, Fitzgerald noted that she should "Never try to give a boy the affect that you're popular – Ginevra [King] always starts by saying shes [*sic*] a poor unpopular woman without any beause [*sic*]." Fitzgerald, *A Life in Letters*, 8.

10. Minnesota outlawed drunken driving in 1911, although the definition of intoxication was left to the discretion of the arresting officer. *St. Paul Star Tribune*, 7 April 1911, 12.

11. In 1922 as now, Park Avenue was prime New York real estate. The 1920s saw extensive construction of apartment buildings on Park Avenue between Forty-second and Fifty-third Streets, and by 1927 *The Literary Digest* commented on "apartment houses with sixty millionaires under a single roof! Along the whole stretch of the Avenue, perhaps 3,000 are on exhibition, while another thousand have the spending of the income on a million – $50,000 and upward a year." *The Literary Digest*, 2 July 1927, 44.

12. The Ritz-Carlton Hotel in New York was established in 1911, five years after the London Ritz and thirteen years after the Paris Ritz.

13. "Farmover" is a combination of Farmington and Westover, a reference to two elite girl's prep schools in Connecticut: Miss Porter's School in Farmington and Westover School in Middlebury. Fitzgerald had used this conflation before, in *The Beautiful and Damned* (1922); in chapter 3 of book one, Richard Caramel "is torn between his innate cordiality and the fact that he considers these girls quite common – not at all the Farmover type." Richard's cousin, Gloria, had attended Farmover. Fitzgerald, *B&D*, 75.

14. Mont Martre was a nightclub on the second floor of a three-story nightclub space on Broadway and Fiftieth. West notes that it had an orchestra and a dancefloor, but no cabaret. West, *F&P*, 376.

15. The Manhattan, a "railroad hotel," was considerably less fashionable than the Ritz. Landau and Condit, *Rise of the New York Skyscraper 1865–1913*, 340.

16. A roadster is an open-top car for up to two passengers.

17. Google Ngram shows 1920 as the year in which the phrase "sell bonds" surpasses the phrase "sell real estate" and selling bonds is a common occupation for young men in Fitzgerald's earlier work. In "His Russet Witch" (1921), a young man goes to "Wall Street to sell bonds, as all the young men seemed to be doing in that day," and in "Winter Dreams" (1922) the hero notes that "rich men's sons were peddling bonds precariously." In *The Great Gatsby*, Nick Carraway decides that "Everybody I knew was in the bond business so I supposed it could support one more single man." Fitzgerald, *GG Var*, 3–4. See Appendix 1, Ngram Language Analysis, for more detail on both this example and this approach to textual analysis.

18. A cut-out switch lets the engine exhaust bypass the muffler, increasing both the power and the noisiness of the car.

19. Crest Avenue stands for Summit Avenue in St. Paul, where the Fitzgerald family lived from 1908. Crest Avenue is also mentioned in *The Vegetable* (1923), the ill-fated play upon which Fitzgerald embarked in the spring of 1922. Fitzgerald, *The Vegetable*, 32.

20. The Cathedral of St. Paul at 201 Summit Avenue held its first services in 1915 a decade after the ground was broken; work on the interior continued throughout the 1920s and 1930s. The cathedral's Beaux Arts architecture was inspired by the cathedrals of France. *St. Paul Star Tribune*, 29 March 1915, 1.

21. R. R. Comerford stands for James J. Hill (1838–1916), the railroad baron, whose Romanesque mansion still stands at 240 Summit Avenue. James J. Hill looms large in the imaginations of several of Fitzgerald's Midwestern characters; Basil Lee in "The Perfect Life" finds it "thrilling and romantic that a foothold on this island [Manhattan] was more precious than the whole rambling sweep of the James J. Hill house at home." In *The Great Gatsby* (1925) Hill is a man who "helped build up the country" to Gatsby's father, Henry Gatz, and an object of "mystical worship" (267) to his antecedent, Carl Miller in "Absolution" (1924). Fitzgerald, *GG Var*, 202 and Fitzgerald, *BJG*, 127.

22. Neighbouring Minneapolis was known as the "Flour Milling Capital of the World" between 1882 and 1930. *St. Paul Star Tribune*, 13 October 1948, 17.

23. "90's" rather than "90s" reproduced as printed in the *Saturday Evening Post* here and below.

24. A porte-cochére is a covered porch, giving sheltered access to a building from a car or carriage.

25. Nathan Hale (1755–1776) was a spy for the Continental Army during the American Revolutionary War. Nathan Hale Park, and the statue of Nathan Hale, is at 401 Summit Avenue.

26. The Petit Trianon is a Neoclassical chateau in the grounds of the Palace of Versailles, built during the reign of Louis XV. There are several houses

in the Neoclassical style on Summit Avenue; examples can be found at 340 and 808 Summit Avenue today.

27. Christian Science is a metaphysical Christian sect founded by Mary Baker Eddy (1821–1910) in 1879. Fitzgerald wrote a satire of its belief in the power of prayer to end all physical pain in his 1915 story, "Pain and the Scientist," for the Newman School's newsletter.

28. The lower town of St. Paul was where Fitzgerald's grandfather, Philip F. McQuillan (1834–1877) had his mansion before moving to Summit Avenue. Lower town was a fashionable location in the 1860s and 1870s, but by 1910 Summit Avenue had eclipsed it, with the *St. Paul Globe* noting on 21 February 1904 that "everybody used to live in lower town [. . .] Summit avenue [*sic*] would be a fine street one day, no doubt." *St. Paul Globe*, 21 February 1904, 26.

29. Minnesota's first governor was Henry H. Sibley (1811–1891); Chelsea Arbuthnot is apparently fictious. There is no statue of Sibley by the river. West, *F&P*, 377.

30. Edward Fitzgerald (1853–1931), F. Scott Fitzgerald's father, could trace his Maryland ancestry back to the seventeenth century.

31. Mollie McQuillan Fitzgerald (1859–1936), F. Scott Fitzgerald's mother, was born and raised in St. Paul, Minnesota.

32. In 1922 $300 would have the purchasing power of around $5,100 in 2022.

33. A pier glass is a large mirror, typically designed to occupy the space between two windows.

34. In the 1920 story "The Ice Palace," Fitzgerald uses Harry Bellamy to explain the social dynamics of Midwestern towns in the early twentieth century: "'this is a three-generation town. Everybody has a father and about half of us have grandfathers. Back of that we don't go.'" Fitzgerald, *F&P*, 46.

35. Compare to Fitzgerald's satirical autobiographical essay of 1924, "How to Live on $36,000 a Year," in which a broker "finally selected a bond for me that paid 7 per cent and wasn't listed on the market." *Saturday Evening Post*, 5 April 1924, 22.

36. Zelda Sayre's sister, Rosalind, was Society Editor of the *Montgomery Journal* between 1911 and 1912. *The Montgomery Advertiser*, 24 October 1912, 6.

37. A report on Paris fashions in the February 1922 issue of *Harper's Bazar* told its readers that "happily, one is coming back to the line of yesterday in lengthening the skirts and in draping the garments." *Harper's Bazar*, February 1922, 43.

38. Plaza, Circle, and Rhinelander were all fashionable areas of New York City. West writes that telephone numbers in 1922 were represented by a set of initials indicating location followed by three digits, so Yanci would have a sense of where her friends lived having looked them up in the phone book. West, *F&P*, 378.

39. Yanci potentially betrays her provincial imagination when she dreams of orchids. In January 1922, *Vanity Fair* declared that "orchids have become suburban, bad taste. Field flowers, which have always been considered to belong to country lanes, have come into their own in the smartest shops." *Vanity Fair*, January 1922, 16.

40. Tuxedo Park, originally developed as a hunting resort, was by the 1920s a playground for affluent New Yorkers. On 15 May 1921, the *New York Herald* told its readers that "the late Pierre Lorillard and his associates [. . .] founded Tuxedo Park about thirty years ago. It took the Tuxedo idea ten years to take root in New York Society." *New York Herald*, 15 May 1921, 37.

41. Squash was a relatively new sport in 1922; the National Squash Tennis Association ran the first open national handicap tournament in 1912. *The New York Times*, 7 January 1912, 69.

42. On 1 April 1922, *Vogue* noted that "Lavender and the bright blues have appeared in all shades." In *The Great Gatsby*, published in 1925 but set in 1922, Myrtle Wilson rejects several cabs in order to travel in a lavender car. *Vogue*, 1 April 1922, 65 and Fitzgerald, *GG Var*, 32.

43. Westchester County is an affluent county in New York State, in the Hudson Valley to the north of the city.

44. Hot Springs, Virginia, and specifically its luxury resort, The Homestead, hosted the rich and influential. *Harper's Bazar*'s June 1921 report on women's sportswear fashion features "Miss Gertrude Russell of Boston at Hot Springs." *Harper's Bazar*, June 1921, 55.

45. Spats covered the insteps and ankles of men's shoes to protect the shoes from the dirt of the street. They fell out of favor during the 1920s. The February 1922 issue of *Vanity Fair* informed its readers that "solid, coloured and patterned woolen socks worn with low shoes has replaced that of high boots or low shoes worn with spats." *Vanity Fair*, February 1922, 73.

46. Mae Murray (1885–1965) was an American actress of the silent era at the peak of her popularity in the early 1920s.

47. Riverside Drive is a north-south thoroughfare in Manhattan, designed by Frederick Law Olmstead and running from 72nd to 181st Street.

48. *Dulcy*, a play by George S. Kaufman and Marc Connelly, opened on Broadway in August 1921. In January 1923, Fitzgerald wrote to Maxwell Perkins, his editor at Scribner's, that he wanted his play *The Vegetable* to be printed "rather as 'Dulcy' was printed." Bryer and Kuehl, *Dear Scott/ Dear Max*, 66.

49. Pennsylvania Station, completed in 1910, gave direct rail access to New York from the South for the first time.

50. Manhattan Transfer was a transfer-only station in New Jersey, allowing passengers to change from the steam locomotives that served New Jersey to the electric locomotives that ran through the tunnel under the river to New York.

51. Charter Club was a Princeton undergraduate eating club, founded in 1901. Edmund Wilson, Fitzgerald's friend and "literary conscience" was a member. West notes that Ellen would not have been staying at Charter Club, but that she could be contacted through the club. West, *F&P*, 379.

52. *Vanity Fair* of January 1921 opined that "the ready-to-wear suits and coats are now excellent in cut and an entirely satisfactory investment." Jimmy Long presumably bought his coat before this became the case, his clothing indicating that he was relatively poor as well as unfashionable. *Vanity Fair*, January 1921, 82.

53. The Hippodrome was New York's largest and most successful theatre in the early 1920s. At the time "The Popular Girl" is set, the musical extravaganza *Better Times*, with book and lyrics by R. H. Burnside, would have been close to the end of its run at the Hippodrome.

54. In 1922 $50 would have the purchasing power of approximately $850 in 2022.

55. "[E]mploye" rather than "employee" reproduced as printed in the *Saturday Evening Post*.

56. The bread line – a line of poverty-stricken men queuing for free bread – was a New York philanthropic institution. Fleischmann's bakery at Broadway and Tenth Street would, from midnight, give away half a loaf of leftover bread to every man in the line.

57. Jennifer Nolan: *According to the* Oxford English Dictionary, *"Punk" in this sense means "in poor health" or "out of sorts," as used in Sinclair Lewis' 1922 novel* Babbitt. *"punk, adj.1." OED Online. June 2022. Oxford University Press.*

Two for a Cent

Metropolitan, April 1922, 23–26, 93–95

1. The area around Pleasant Avenue in Montgomery, Zelda Sayre Fitzgerald's home town, had newer bungalows amongst the older homes such as the one where Zelda and her family lived. In Fitzgerald's initial proposal for his 1922 short story collection *Tales of the Jazz Age*, which included "Two for a Cent" though ultimately it was not included, he described it as "my third story of Jelly-Bean Town – or rather, of Tarleton, Georgia." Tarleton is directly identified with Montgomery, Alabama; the other Tarleton stories are "The Ice Palace" (1920), "The Jelly-Bean" (1920), and "The Last of the Belles" (1929). Fitzgerald, "Appendix 1: Dummy Table of Contents and Promotional Copy," *TJA*, 536.

2. The Sayre house at 6 Pleasant Avenue, where Fitzgerald first courted Zelda, was a clapboard house with a shingled roof. *The Montgomery Advertiser*, 29 April 1973, 84.

3. In his biography of F. Scott Fitzgerald, Andrew Turnbull writes that P. F. McQuillan – Fitzgerald's maternal grandfather – "had been in wholesale rather than trade and that was considered 'all right.'" Here, Fitzgerald uses trade grocery to indicate shabbiness and limited opportunity. Turnbull, *Scott Fitzgerald*, 13.

4. This typographical error ("preceived" rather than "perceived") is preserved as printed in *Metropolitan*.

5. Ice was widely used in ice boxes, the main means of home refrigeration in the early 1920s. Canned ice was mechanically chilled distilled water, which became increasingly popular as opposed to natural ice over the first two decades of the twentieth century.

6. Correspondence courses were widely advertised in popular magazines; an advertisement for the School of Applied Art, placed in *Metropolitan* next to "Two for a Cent," claimed that "We can teach you drawing in your own home during your spare time." *Metropolitan Magazine*, April 1922, 95.

7. "Dixie," originally written by Daniel Decatur Emmettt for a blackface minstrel show, was widely adopted as an anthem by the Southern states during the Civil War. In "The Ice Palace," when Sally Carroll Happer hears "Dixie," she feels "something stronger and more enduring than her tears and smiles of the day brim up inside her." Fitzgerald, *F&P*, 54.

8. "Jelly Bean" was a Southern term for a shiftless young man. The word was used in this sense as early as 1909, and its use became widespread across the South in the 1920s. The 24 January 1920 issue of the *Richaland Beacon-News* of Rayville, Louisiana, described the Jelly Bean as "a peculiar creature, inhabiting nearly all climes of North America where there are soda fountains [. . .] The Jelly Bean is strictly a twentieth-century animal, its origin dating from the advent of prohibition and other reforms." On 3 October 1920, *The Montgomery Advertiser* reported on "war on the 'jelly-bean' and 'masher' who insist on parking themselves on downtown street corners." F. Scott Fitzgerald's 1920 short story, "The Jelly Bean," was published in *Metropolitan* magazine and widely syndicated, bringing the term to a national audience. *The Richaland Beacon-News*, 24 January 1920, 1 and *The Montgomery Advertiser*, 3 October 1920, 35.

9. Corn liquor is a form of whiskey, made with corn using a traditional mash process in which no sugar is added. Milford notes that during Zelda Sayre's school years "dope [. . .] was a concoction of Coca-Cola spiked with aromatic spirits of ammonia to give it a slight kick." Milford, *Zelda*, 12.

10. According to the Archives at Tuskegee Institute, fifty-nine Black people were lynched in the United States in 1921 and fifty-one in 1922. The Anti-Lynching Bill introduced by Leonidas Dyer (1877–1957) was passed by the House of Representatives on 26 January 1922, but a filibuster in the Senate by Southern Democrats halted its passage.

11. Volta Laboratory's graphophone was an early attempt at reproducing recorded music, improving on the phonograph Thomas Edison (1847–1931) patented in 1877. The cylinder-based graphophone had been superseded, at the time "Two for a Cent" was written, by the more practical disc-based gramophone patented by Emile Berliner (1847–1931).

12. Ragtime has its origins in African American communities, and is characterized by syncopated rhythms with melodic accents between metrical beats. Its popularity was at its peak between 1895 and 1919, with Google Ngram showing use of the word "ragtime" peaking in 1915. See Appendix 1, Ngram Language Analysis, for more detail on this approach to textual analysis.

13. In 1896 $30,000 would have the purchasing power of approximately $1 million in 2022.

14. The misplaced inverted comma is reproduced as printed in *Metropolitan*.

15. "Effected" (rather than "affected") is reproduced as printed in *Metropolitan*.

16. Hemmick's age at the time of his narrative places these events during the Panic of 1896, when the deflation of commodity prices drove the stock market to new lows.

17. Building began on St. Margaret's Hospital in Montgomery in 1902, several years after the story Hemmick tells. The building was on Adams Street, east of downtown and on a hill. The area around St. Margaret's is approximately twelve blocks downhill from Dexter Avenue and Court Square, where the banks would have been. *The Montgomery Advertiser*, 21 May 1902, 5.

18. Montgomery Union Station was built in 1898 by the Louisville and National Railroad, and remained operational until 1979. *The Montgomery Advertiser*, 5 May 1898, 5.

19. Hamrick's, on the corner of Dexter Avenue and Perry Street, was a Montgomery drug store, soda shop, and social center for Zelda and her friends. A 1917 advertisement for Hamrick's invited readers to "Meet Your Friends at Hamrick's – it's a most central location and the surroundings are full of life and impetus." *The Montgomery Advertiser*, 7 October 1917, 23.

20. Vice President is hyphenated in its second but not its first occurrence in "Two for a Cent."

21. A surrey is an open, four-wheeled carriage.

22. London was still considered the center of men's fashion; in March 1922 *Vanity Fair* told its readers that "Men's fashions, acclaimed originally in London, are exploited by New York." In *The Great Gatsby* (1925), Gatsby alludes to this prestige when he tells Daisy and Nick about his "'man in England who buys me clothes.'" *Vanity Fair*, March 1922, 12 and Fitzgerald, *GG Var*, 111.

The Curious Case of Benjamin Button

Collier's, 27 May 1922, 5–6, 22–28

Jennifer Nolan: *Despite having been rejected by* Metropolitan, Collier's *was evidently pleased by this story, which was given first position in this issue, appearing under the masthead.*

1. "The Curious Case of Benjamin Button" was published in 1922, less than a year after the Fitzgeralds' daughter, Scottie, was born at St. Paul's Miller Hospital. Between the late nineteenth century and the 1920s, expectations around childbirth had been in transition, between the home-based event attended by a midwife that Fitzgerald accurately describes as the norm in the 1860s and the hospital-based event attended by a doctor that he and Zelda experienced. Bruccoli, *Some Sort of Epic Grandeur*, 156 and Dye, "History of Childbirth in America," 98.
2. F. Scott Fitzgerald's father, Edward Fitzgerald (1853–1931), could trace his family back to the seventeenth century. He and his family were sympathetic to the Confederacy; Mary Surrat (1820 or 1823–1865), his first cousin, was hanged for conspiring in Lincoln's assassination. Brown, *Paradise Lost*, 21.
3. Compare to Nick Carraway's claim in chapter 1 of *The Great Gatsby* (1925) that "the actual founder of my line was my grandfather's brother, who came here in fifty-one, sent a substitute to the Civil War, and started the wholesale hardware business that my father carries on today." Fitzgerald, *GG Var*, 3.
4. A phaeton was an open-bodied carriage with large wheels. They were known for being fast and dangerous.
5. Slavery and the slave trade were legal in Maryland in 1860. Although there were no open auctions of enslaved people in the city, several slave dealers operated in Baltimore.
6. The name Methuselah is shorthand for extreme age; Genesis 5, verse 27 states that "all the days of Methuselah were nine hundred sixty and nine years," the oldest named in any of the Bible's genealogies.
7. The American Civil War began on 12 April 1861 and ended on 9 May 1865. Maryland, a slave state, fought for the Union, although Marylanders could also cross the Potomac River into secessionist Virginia to fight for the Confederacy. As a young native of Maryland, Edward Fitzgerald guided Confederate spies during the Civil War. Bruccoli, *Some Sort of Epic Grandeur*, 11.
8. Boys would traditionally wear knickerbockers between the ages of five and fourteen. In 1872, *Harper's Bazar* asked its readers to "recall a late picture of the family of the Prince of Wales, in which are two handsome boys [then aged twelve and eleven] in sailor suits of [. . .] dark blue

twilled flannel, consist[ing] of a shirt and knee-pantaloons." *Harper's Bazar*, 30 March 1872, 219.

9.   Bustles – structures worn around the waist to push the back of the skirt out – were worn with fashionable dresses between 1870 and 1875 and again between 1883 and 1889. Although 1878, the year in which Button is chased by professors' wives in bustles, falls outside of these time periods, the backs of skirts between 1876 and 1882 would have been considerably more pronounced than in 1922. Edwards, *How to Read a Dress*, 94.˙

10. By legend, the Wandering Jew was cursed to walk the earth until the Second Coming as a punishment for mocking Jesus on the road to Calvary.

11. A brougham was a light carriage with an enclosed body and a glazed front window which allowed travelers to see forwards.

12. A mantilla is a traditional Spanish shawl, made with silk or lace and worn over the head and shoulders. They were fashionable in the 1880s; in May 1880, *Godey's Lady's Book and Magazine* told its readers that the "favorite style of mantle this spring is the mantilla." *Godey's Lady's Book and Magazine*, May 1880, 476.

13. John Wilkes Booth (1838–1865) assassinated Abraham Lincoln (1809–1865) in Washington, DC in 1865. In 1907, Finis L. Bates' book, *Escape and Suicide of John Wilkes Booth*, contended that Booth was not killed in 1865, but eluded capture, committing suicide in 1903. Fitzgerald wrote about the possibility that Booth escaped with his life in "The Room with the Green Blinds," his 1911 story for his school magazine, the *St. Paul Academy Now and Then*.

14. The United States' first marketable automobile with a gasoline engine was developed by the Duryea brothers between 1893 and 1895. This part of the narrative is set in 1895, marking Benjamin as particularly early to the technology. Roberts, *The History of the Automobile*, 47.

15. The Spanish-American War of 1898, a US intervention in the Cuban War of Independence, resulted in Spain losing the last of its colonies. Cuba was put under control of a provisional military government, and Spain ceded ownership of Puerto Rico, Guam, and the Philippines to the United States.

16. The Battle of San Juan Hill on 1 July 1898 was a decisive battle of the Spanish-American War in which the numerically superior American forces dispersed the Spanish from the strategically valuable San Juan Heights. Fitzgerald refers to this battle again in his 1926 story "Presumption," the hero of which is named San Juan Chandler.

17. Reproduced as printed in *Collier's*; "squirmish" was changed to "skirmish" when "The Curious Case of Benjamin Button" was collected in *Tales of the Jazz Age*.

18. Reporting on a dance in 1906, *The Pittsburgh Press* identified "the Boston 'dip', [as] the very latest thing on the cards" and the *New Castle Herald* described the dance as a "very expressive combination of waltz

and push done languidly." The Grizzly Bear was a ragtime dance with "swayings of the body, steps with feet apart and a bear-like embrace," introduced to Broadway audiences in 1910 at the *Ziegfeld Follies*. The influential Vernon and Irene Castle described it as "ugly, ungraceful and out of fashion" in their 1914 book *Modern Dancing*, whereas the Maxixe, a tango, met their approval as a "development of the most attractive kind of folk-dancing." The Castles' original contribution to dancing was the Castle Walk, a one-step dance with the instructions to dancers that they should not "stand too close together or far apart" or "shuffle, [. . .] bob up and down or trot. Simply *walk*." The Maxixe, Grizzly Bear and Castle Walk all attained popularity some years after those given by Fitzgerald. *The Pittsburgh Press*, 21 October 1906, 20; *The New Castle Herald*, 20 October 1911; Castle, *Modern Dancing*, 189, 20–21 and 44.

19. By 1914, college football was an established sport, although still relatively new; its latest significant rule changes were made in 1905. Fitzgerald had entered Princeton in 1913 with hopes of playing football for the university, but he was too small and light to be invited to a second day of practice. Brown, *Paradise Lost*, 33 and 48.

20. Hillkiss School (an invention of Fitzgerald's) recurs in 1923's "Dice, Brassknuckles and Guitar"; "Mr. Ronald Harlan [. . .] was a student at the Hillkiss School" (185). In the version of "The Curious Case of Benjamin Button" collected in *Tales of the Jazz Age* (1922), Benjamin aspires to go to St. Midas, the school attended by John T. Unger in "The Diamond as Big as the Ritz" (1922).

21. The United States joined the Allied powers in the First World War on 6 April 1917.

22. John S. Mosby (1833–1916) was a battalion commander for the Confederacy during the Civil War.

23. Fitzgerald has Roscoe talk almost exclusively in the business cliches of his day; see also notes 24, 25, and 26. The rise of mass production, combined with war production, drove the use of the word "efficient" in the years from 1900 to 1919, as seen in Google Ngram. Eversharp advertised "the pencil of business efficiency" in *Collier's*, next to "The Curious Case of Benjamin Button." *Collier's*, 27 May 1922, 23. See Appendix 1, Ngram Language Analysis, for more detail on both this example and this approach to textual analysis.

24. Google Ngram shows use of the phrase "red blooded" reaching its peak in 1920; use of the phrase "he-man" would peak in 1926, but began its rise with the advent of the First World War in 1914. A half-page advertisement for Durham-Duplex razors in *Collier's*, placed next to "The Curious Case of Benjamin Button," promised readers "The Razor for He-Men." *Collier's*, May 27 1922, 25. See Appendix 1, Ngram Language Analysis, for more detail on both this example and this approach to textual analysis.

25. The popularity of the word "pep" began to increase in the early 1910s, reaching its peak in 1921. The imperatives of war production increased use of the phase "speed up production" between 1914 and 1919. See Appendix 1, Ngram Language Analysis, for more detail on this approach to textual analysis.
26. Use of the phrase "live wire" began to rise in 1884, two years after the Edison Illuminating Company built the first commercial power plant in the United States at Pearl Street in Manhattan. Use of the phrase peaked in 1918. See Appendix 1, Ngram Language Analysis, for more detail on this approach to textual analysis.
27. Baltimore Zoo opened in Druid Hill Park in 1876. Between 1921 and 1923, Raymond S. Tompkins, as the "Jungle Editor" of the *Baltimore Sun*, campaigned vigorously for an elephant for the Zoo. On 27 May 1922, the day "The Curious Case of Benjamin Button" was published in *Colliers*, the *Sun* announced that the "Elephant fund" had reached $630. Mary Ann the elephant was admitted to the Zoo in 1923. *The Baltimore Sun*, 27 May 1922, 6.

The Diamond as Big as the Ritz

Smart Set, June 1922, 5–29

Reproductions of the cover of this issue and first page of Fitzgerald's story are available in Appendix 3.

1. King Midas is known in Greek mythology for his ability to turn anything he touched to gold. In *The Great Gatsby* (1925), Nick Carraway "bought a dozen volumes on banking and credit and investment securities, and they stood on my shelf in red and gold like new money from the mint, promising to unfold the shining secrets that only Midas and Morgan and Maecenas knew." Fitzgerald, *GGVar*, 5.
2. West identifies the inscription above the gates of Hell in Dante's *Inferno* – "Abandon all hope ye who enter here" – as a possible motto for the city of Hades. West, *TJA*, 511.
3. The Rolls-Royce and the Pierce-Arrow were luxury cars of the time. In 1921, Rolls-Royce established its first factory in the United States, and a Pierce-Arrow carried Warren G. Harding to his inauguration.
4. Google Ngram shows that use of the phrase "efficiency expert" peaked in American English in 1917, with the phrase "speed up production" peaking in 1920; the fathers of John's friends are using the business cliches of their day. See Appendix 1, Ngram Language Analysis, for more detail on this approach to textual analysis.
5. On 25 July 1921, *The New York Times* reported that the 1918 income tax returns "showed the 67 individuals with net incomes of $1,000,000

or more to have included 1 with a net income of $5,000,000 or more, 2 with net incomes of $4,000,000 to $5,000,000, [and] 4 with net incomes of $3,000,000 to $4,000,000." *The New York Times*, 25 July 1921, 3.

6. The Sixteenth Amendment, passed by Congress in 1909 and ratified on 3 February 1913, allowed Congress to impose a federal income tax. The Revenue Act of 1913 established a tax of between 1 percent and 7 percent on the incomes of individuals.

7. The Ritz-Carlton Hotel in New York was established in 1911, five years after the London Ritz and thirteen years after the Paris Ritz.

8. A buggy is a light horse-drawn carriage for two passengers.

9. Duveytn is a twill fabric, usually made from cotton or wool, popular for clothing in the 1920s. *Harper's Bazar*, in a report on "How to Know the Winter Hat of 1921," notes duvetyn alongside velvet, plush, and fur as a fashionable material for winter hats. *Harper's Bazar*, October 1921, 59.

10. Croesus (born 595 BC) was the legendarily rich king of Lydia, credited with issuing the first gold coins of standard purity. Herodotus, *The Histories*, 15.

11. Reproducing the word "hectagons" as printed in *Smart Set*. It is likely that Fitzgerald meant hexagons, the six-sided polygons.

12. Reproducing "acciaccare" as printed in *Smart Set*. Acciaccare is an Italian verb, meaning to crush or to weaken. It is likely that Fitzgerald intended to refer to the "acciaccatura sound of violins"; acciaccatura is a note a half-step below the principal note, sounded with the principal note to build dissonance into the harmony.

13. Titiana is the Queen of the Fairies in Shakespeare's *A Midsummer Night's Dream*. Under Puck's enchantment, she falls in love with Bottom. As a weaver, Bottom is considerably below Titania in the social hierarchy. He also – thanks to another of Puck's spells – has the head of a donkey.

14. Gargantua is a giant of vast appetite in *The Life of Gargantua and Pantagruel* by François Rabelais (born between 1483 and 1494, died 1553). The adjective "gargantuan" is derived from his name.

15. One reel of film produces a short between ten and sixteen minutes in length.

16. "Jig" is a racial slur for Black Americans. Interestingly, the *OED* cites the first print usage as 1924. "jig, n.2." *OED Online*, June 2022, Oxford University Press.

17. This establishes the Washingtons as specifically Southern aristocracy, who can trace their ancestry back to colonial administrators in Virginia and Maryland. George Washington (1732–1799) was a Founding Father and first President of the United States between 1789 and 1797, as well as Surveyor of Culpeper County, Virginia, between 1749 and 1750. Thomas Fairfax, Sixth Lord Fairfax of Cameron (1693–1781), inherited substantial property in Virginia from his mother, Catherine

Colepeper, whose father, Thomas Colepeper, was the Colonial Governor of Virginia from 1677 to 1683. Cecil Calvert, the Second Baron Baltimore (1605–1675), was the first Proprietor of the Province of Maryland. The city of Baltimore was named for him.

18. Between 1066 and 1154, the kings of England were dukes from the house of Normandy. "Fitz" is a Norman prefix meaning "son of"; Brown notes that "[f]or centuries, the English and British royal families used 'Fitz' in surnames, often in cases of illegitimacy." Fitzgerald, who had a keen interest in history, would have been aware of the implications inherent in his own surname. Thomas Colepeper, Second Baron Colepeper of Thoresway (1635–1689), was granted over 20,000 square kilometres of land in Virginia's Northern Neck as the Colonial Governor of Virginia between 1677 and 1683. Brown, *Paradise Lost*, 27 and Campbell, *History of the Colony and Ancient Dominion of Virginia*, 248.

19. The word "gens" was corrected to "gems" when "The Diamond as Big as the Ritz" was collected in *Tales of the Jazz Age*.

20. El Dorado is a mythical city of gold in South America, for which the conquistadors launched unsuccessful searches throughout the early modern era.

21. Nathan Bedford Forrest (1821–1877) was a Confederate general and the first Grand Wizard of the Ku Klux Klan between 1867 and 1869. Martinez, *Terrorist Attacks on American Soil: From the Civil War Era to the Present*, 193.

22. St. Petersburg was home of the Imperial Russian court. The House of Bolin was the Romanov court jeweler in 1868; the House of Fabergé made its first jeweled egg in 1885.

23. In 1868 $15 million would have the purchasing power of approximately $305 million in 2022.

24. In 1868 $1 billion would have the purchasing power of approximately $20 billion in 2022.

25. Major General Edward Braddock (1695–1755), to whom George Washington served as an aide, was known for his rash decision making and for his defeat by the French at Fort Dusquesne. Sir Banastre Tarleton, First Baronet, GCB (1754–1833) was a British Lieutenant Colonel in the American War of Independence. His family was prominent in Liverpool's slave trade, and his later political career was marked by his opposition to abolition. Fitzgerald's fictionalized Montgomery (in "The Ice Palace" (1920), "The Jelly-Bean" (1920), and 1929's "The Last of the Belles") is named Tarleton.

26. Radium was discovered by Pierre and Marie Curie in 1898. In the 1920s, radioluminescent paint containing radium was widely used on watch faces and instrument dials.

27. The repeated "you" was removed when "The Diamond as Big as the Ritz" was collected in *Tales of the Jazz Age*.

28. Newport, Rhode Island was a fashionable summer resort for the rich. A 1921 advertisement for *Harper's Bazar* promised that subscribers would receive "[i]ntimate society gossip from Paris and New York, the Riviera, Palm Beach, Newport, Southampton." *Harper's Bazar*, December 1921, 16.

29. Until 1958, debutantes in the United Kingdom were presented to the king or queen at Buckingham Palace at the start of the social season. This was an honor open only to the well-connected; debutantes had to be presented by someone who had herself been presented at Court.

30. During the First World War, aviation was considered the most glamourous area of service; in book one, chapter 4 of *This Side of Paradise* (1920) Tom D'Invilliers asserts that "aviation sounds like the romantic side of the war, of course – like cavalry used to be." Fitzgerald, *TSOP*, 142.

31. An adaptation of "John Brown's Body," the Civil War marching song sung by Union soldiers, repurposed by American troops during the First World War to refer to hanging the Kaiser.

32. A lea is an area of flat grassland. The word "lea" was corrected to "lee" when "The Diamond as Big as the Ritz" was collected in *Tales of the Jazz Age*.

33. Compare to "Rags Martin-Jones and the Pr-nce of W-les" (1924): "In Paris I knew a man named Fernduc who was going down to the Balkans and start a New War" (281).

34. The word "couldn'" was corrected to "couldn't" when "The Diamond as Big as the Ritz" was collected in *Tales of the Jazz Age* in 1922.

35. Eugénie de Montijo (1826–1920) was Empress of France from her marriage to Napoleon III in 1853 to the overthrow of the Second Empire in 1870. Interest in the Empress Eugénie had been high in 1921, the year Fitzgerald wrote "The Diamond as Big as the Ritz"; in November 1921 *The New York Times'* "The Year in Books" remarked that "[e]arly in the Spring a number of books about the Empress Eugenie, who had just died, appeared. They had a transient vogue and then disappeared from view." *The New York Times*, 27 November 1921, 41.

36. Wholesale hardware was used by Fitzgerald to indicate unglamourous prosperity. Nick Carraway claims in chapter 1 of *The Great Gatsby* (1925) that "the actual founder of my line was my grandfather's brother, who came here in fifty-one, sent a substitute to the Civil War, and started the wholesale hardware business that my father carries on today." In 1922's "The Curious Case of Benjamin Button" the elder Button, also in wholesale hardware, is "not a spiritual man – his esthetic sense was rudimentary." (108) The same could be said of the somewhat oafish Harold Piper in "The Cut-Glass Bowl" (1920). Fitzgerald, *GGVar*, 3, Fitzgerald, *TJA*, 182, and Fitzgerald, *F&P*, 94.

37. "Now" was corrected to "How" when "The Diamond as Big as the Ritz" was collected in *Tales of the Jazz Age*.

38. West notes Kismine would have blown the fuse by screwing a copper penny into the light socket and turning the power on. West, *TJA*, 513.
39. The First World War saw the first military aircraft shot down by ground-to-air fire.
40. Nubians are the people of Northern Sudan and Southern Egypt. The term "Nubian" was commonly used to refer to Black servants in the 1920s; in *The Sheik*, E. M. Hull's popular romance novel of 1919, the heroine "walked slowly to the curtain and nodded to the Nubian to draw it aside." Hull, *The Sheik*, 218.
41. In Greek mythology, Nemesis was the goddess who delivered retribution against those who show arrogance before the gods.
42. Reproduced as printed in *Smart Set*; "antitethical" was corrected to "antithetical" when "The Diamond as Big as the Ritz" was collected in *Tales of the Jazz Age*.
43. In Greek mythology, Prometheus stole fire from the gods and gave it to humanity. His punishment for this crime was to be bound to a rock; every day, an eagle would eat his liver, which would grow back every night. "Prometheus Enriched" plays on *Prometheus Unbound*, an 1820 lyrical drama by Percy Bysshe Shelley (1792–1822).

Winter Dreams

Metropolitan, December 1922, 11–15, 98, 100–102, 104–107

Jennifer Nolan: *Reproductions of the cover of this issue and first page of Fitzgerald's story, with illustrations by Arthur William Brown, are available in Appendix 3. As with "His Russet Witch," "The Popular Girl," and "The Curious Case of Benjamin Button," "Winter Dreams" received first position in the magazine under the masthead, which serves as an indication of the perceived selling power of his stories in the popular magazine market. For more on Brown, see Nolan "Illustrating 'Winter Dreams.'"*

1. In his biography of F. Scott Fitzgerald, Andrew Turnbull writes that P. F. McQuillan – Fitzgerald's maternal grandfather – "had been in wholesale rather than trade and that was considered 'all right.'" Dexter's father's trade grocery indicates Dexter's circumscribed place in the social hierarchy. Turnbull, *Scott Fitzgerald*, 13.
2. Lake Erminie is an analogue for White Bear Lake outside St. Paul, Minnesota. The name of the lake was changed to Black Bear Lake when "Winter Dreams" was collected in 1926's *All the Sad Young Men*. In several of Fitzgerald's later Basil stories ("He Thinks He's Wonderful" (1928), "The Perfect Life," "Forging Ahead," and "Basil and Cleopatra," all 1929) the St. Paul-based hero pursues a girl named Erminie Bibble.

3. Reproduced as printed in *Metropolitan*; this was corrected to "fallowness" when "Winter Dreams" was collected in *All the Sad Young Men*.
4. Reproduced as printed in *Metropolitan*; this was corrected to "mood" when "Winter Dreams" was collected in *All the Sad Young Men*.
5. Reproduced as printed in *Metropolitan*; this was corrected to "mill" when "Winter Dreams" was collected in *All the Sad Young Men*.
6. The Pierce-Arrow was a luxury car of the time. In 1921 a Pierce-Arrow carried Warren G. Harding to his inauguration.
7. A badge indicating that Dexter, as a caddy, was allowed on the country club's golf course. The "A Class" signified that he was a first-rate caddy.
8. Reproduced as printed in *Metropolitan*.
9. Reproduced as printed in *Metropolitan*.
10. In "Forging Ahead" (1929) Basil proposes something similar to his mother on her suggestion that he go to the State University rather than Yale; when she asks what he would work at, he answers that he would "Take care of furnaces [. . . a]nd shovel snow off sidewalks. I think they mostly do that – and tutor people. You could let me have as much money as it would take to go to the State University?'" Bruccoli notes that for Fitzgerald himself "[t]he idea that he might be sent to the University of Minnesota to save money had filled [him] with dismay [. . . i]t was Princeton or nothing." Fitzgerald, *BJG*, 148 and Bruccoli, *Some Sort of Epic Grandeur*, 37.
11. This city is an analogue for St. Paul, where Fitzgerald was born and where he and Zelda lived between August 1921 and October 1922.
12. Google Ngram shows 1920 as the year in which use of the phrase 'sell bonds' peaked. Fitzgerald notes this cultural shift in several of his works of the time. In "The Popular Girl" (1921), he states that "[y]oung men sold them who had nothing else to go into" (51) and in "His Russet Witch" (1921), a young man goes to "Wall Street to sell bonds, as all the young men seemed to be doing in that day" (27). In *The Great Gatsby*, published in 1925 but set in 1922, Nick Carraway decides that "Everybody I knew was in the bond business so I supposed it could support one more single man." Fitzgerald, *GG Var*, 3–4. See Appendix 1, Ngram Language Analysis, for more detail on both this example and this approach to textual analysis.
13. Correspondence courses were widely advertised in popular magazines; an advertisement for the School of Applied Art, placed in *Metropolitan* next to "Winter Dreams," claimed that readers could "learn at home quickly" to "[b]ecome an artist." *Metropolitan Magazine*, December 1922, 101.
14. London was still considered the center of men's fashion; in March 1922 *Vanity Fair* told its readers that "Men's fashions, acclaimed originally in London, are exploited by New York." In *The Great Gatsby* (1925), Gatsby alludes to this prestige when he tells Daisy and Nick about his

"'man in England who buys me clothes.'" *Vanity Fair*, March 1922, 12 and Fitzgerald, *GGVar*, 111.

15. Knickerbockers were part of the golf costume of the early twentieth century. Before its mass popularity in the 1920s, golf was popular mainly with the business and political elite. In the June 1922 issue of *Vanity Fair*, Charles Evans Jr. wrote that "for a delightful period it was a very different and very exclusive game. To say that you played golf, however badly [. . .] was in a manner of declaring yourself a member of the best American society." Dexter focusing his laundry business on knickerbockers and other golf accoutrements in the early 1910s demonstrates his affiliation with this prosperity. *Vanity Fair*, June 1922, 77.

16. "The Pink Lady" was a musical comedy composed by Ivan Caryll (1861–1921) which ran on Broadway in 1911 and 1912. "The Chocolate Soldier," an operetta composed by Oscar Straus (1870–1954), premiered on Broadway in 1909 and was revived in 1910 and 1921. "Mlle. Modiste" was an operetta composed by Victor Herbert (1859–1924); it premiered on Broadway in 1905, with revivals in 1906, 1907, and 1913.

17. Spelling error (sophmore rather than sophomore) reproduced as printed in *Metropolitan*.

18. Spelling error (ecstacy rather than ecstasy) reproduced as printed in *Metropolitan*.

19. Spelling error (atune rather than attune) reproduced as printed in *Metropolitan*.

20. Aquaplaning, inspired by Hawaiian surfing and developed in the mid-1910s, was a direct predecessor of water-skiing. On 3 September 1916, *The Minneapolis Sunday Tribune* reported that the "Younger Society Set Takes to Aquaplaning as Late Summer Amusement," noting that "Girls Rival Boys in Mastery of Swimming Art." *The Minneapolis Sunday Tribune*, 3 September 1916, 1.

21. Early twentieth-century excavations at Pompeii were interrupted by the First World War and resumed in the 1920s.

22. Reused in chapter 8 of *The Great Gatsby*: "But what gave it an air of breathless intensity was that Daisy lived there – it was as casual a thing to her as his tent out at camp was to him. There was a ripe mystery about it, a hint of bedrooms upstairs more beautiful and cool than other bedrooms, of gay and radiant activities taking place through its corridors, and of romances that were not musty and laid away already in lavender but fresh and breathing and redolent of this year's shining motor-cars and of dances whose flowers were scarcely withered [. . .] He felt their presence all about the house, pervading the air with the shades and echoes of still vibrant emotions." See Bryant Mangum's 2021 article for *The F. Scott Fitzgerald Review* for a thorough discussion of the close ties between *Gatsby* and the *Metropolitan* version of "Winter Dreams." Fitzgerald, *GGVar*, 177–178.

23. Compare to Amory's characterization of Princeton in book one, chapter 1 of *This Side of Paradise* (1920): "I think of Princeton as being lazy and good-looking and aristocratic [. . .] Harvard seems sort of indoors." His interlocutor, Monsignor Darcy, characterizes Yale as "crisp and energetic." Fitzgerald, *TSOP*, 31.

24. The 1920 census showed that slightly under half (48 percent) of immigrants from Bohemia and Moravia (the modern-day Czech Republic) arrived in the United States in 1900 or earlier. Only German, Irish, and Scandinavian immigrants were more established immigrant groups at the turn of the century. Carpenter, *Immigrants and Their Children*, 62.

25. Reused in chapter 8 of *The Great Gatsby*: "It excited him, too, that many men had already loved Daisy – it increased her value in his eyes." See also note 22. Fitzgerald, *GGVar*, 177–178.

26. Reused in chapter 8 of *The Great Gatsby*: "She had caught a cold, and it made her voice huskier and more charming than ever." See also note 22. Fitzgerald, *GGVar*, 179.

27. Compare to chapter 6 of *The Great Gatsby*: "At his lips' touch she blossomed for him like a flower and the incarnation was complete." See also note 22. Fitzgerald, *GGVar*, 134.

28. Reused in chapter 8 of *The Great Gatsby*: "Gatsby was overwhelmingly aware of the youth and mystery that wealth imprisons and preserves, of the freshness of many clothes, and of Daisy, gleaming like silver, safe and proud above the hot struggles of the poor." See also note 22. Fitzgerald, *GGVar*, 179.

29. Reused in chapter 8 of *The Great Gatsby*: "Her porch was bright with the bought luxury of star-shine; the wicker of the settee squeaked fashionably as she turned toward him and he kissed her curious and lovely mouth." See also note 22. Fitzgerald, *GGVar*, 179.

30. Reused in chapter 8 of *The Great Gatsby*: "he found that he had committed himself to the following of a grail." See also note 22. Fitzgerald, *GGVar*, 179.

31. The word "dénoument" rather than "dénouement" is reproduced as printed in *Metropolitan*.

32. A roadster is an open-top car for up to two passengers.

33. Reproduced as printed in *Metropolitan*; "rathen" was corrected to "rather" when "Winter Dreams" was collected in *All the Sad Young Men*.

34. Stag lines were groups of young men attending a dance or social function without a partner. *Harper's Bazar* of November 1922 told its readers that "[t]he original purpose of a 'stag line' was to provide a place where unattached young men might stand while searching for a partner, but the institution has come to be a form of Supreme Court, passing life or death sentence on the various debutantes who pass before it." *Harper's Bazar*, November 1922, 130.

35. The English spelling, "criticise," reproduced as printed in Metropolitan.

36. Hot Springs, Virginia, and specifically its luxury resort, The Homestead, hosted the rich and influential. It was a popular honeymoon destination;

in June 1922, *Harper's Bazar* told its readers that "the spring find[s] White Sulphur and Hot Springs the proper Mecca for the smart young couple." *Harper's Bazar*, June 1922, 112.

37. College Club is an analogue for the St. Paul University Club, of which Fitzgerald was a member. Members were required to have attended a university accredited by the club. Bruccoli et al., *The Romantic Egoists*, 71.

38. In *Careless People*, Churchwell notes that the slang term "egg" had particular resonance for Fitzgerald, and it also appears in the 1924 story "The Unspeakable Egg" and the West Egg of *The Great Gatsby*. Churchwell, *Careless People*, 73.

39. Light gold and beige were popular colors for women's fashion in the 1920s; in her April 1922 review of *The Beautiful and Damned* (1922), Zelda Fitzgerald wrote that "everyone must buy this book for the following aesthetic reasons: First, because I know where there is the cutest cloth-of-gold dress for only $300." Edwards, *How to Read a Dress*, 148 and Sayre, *F. Scott Fitzgerald in His Own Time*, 332.

40. A coupé is a two-door car, usually for two passengers.

41. Google Ngram shows use of the word "kiddo" reaching its peak in 1916 and declining steadily thereafter. It was closer to obsolescence at the time of writing (1922) than the time of the setting; this conversation between Judy and Dexter takes place in late 1916. When "Winter Dreams" was collected in *All the Sad Young Men*, the reference to obsolescence was removed and Judy calls Dexter "darling." See Appendix 1, Ngram Language Analysis, for more detail on this approach to textual analysis.

42. Reproduced as printed in *Metropolitan*; this was corrected to camaraderie when "Winter Dreams" was collected in *All the Sad Young Men*.

43. In chapter 7 of *The Great Gatsby*, Daisy is unable to swear that she never loved Tom; "'Even alone I can't say I never loved Tom,' she admitted in a pitiful voice. 'It wouldn't be true.'" See also note 22. Fitzgerald, *GGVar*, 159–160.

44. The United States joined the Allied powers in the First World War on 6 April 1917.

45. Reused in chapter 8 of *The Great Gatsby*: "Just as Daisy's house had always seemed to him more mysterious and gay than other houses, so his idea of the city itself, even though she was gone from it, was pervaded with a melancholy beauty." See also note 22. Fitzgerald, *GGVar*, 183.

Dice, Brassknuckles and Guitar

Hearst's International, May 1923, 8–13, 145–149

1. The docks at Atlantic City, New Jersey, were a popular point of ingress for "rum-runners" bringing alcohol to America during Prohibition.

2. Compare to chapter 1 of *The Great Gatsby* (1925): "a factual imitation of some Hôtel de Ville in Normandy, with a tower on one side, spanking new under a thin beard of raw ivy." Fitzgerald, *GG Var*, 6.
3. Mary Augusta Ward (1851–1920), who wrote under the name Mrs. Humphrey Ward, was a novelist, frequently on religious themes. Her works and life exemplified Victorian morality; she was a social reformer, pioneering play centers for poor children, and a campaigner against women's suffrage.
4. In Ovid's *Metamorphoses*, Actaeon accidentally sees Diana, goddess of the hunt, bathing. She turns him into a stag, and his own dogs hunt and kill him. Ovid, *Metamorphoses*, 99–104.
5. When he wrote "Dice, Brassknuckles and Guitar," three of Fitzgerald's short stories, all published in the *Saturday Evening Post* in 1920, had been made into films; "Head and Shoulders," "Myra Meets His Family," and "The Offshore Pirate." Despite Fitzgerald's hints, "Dice, Brassknuckles and Guitar" was not sold to a production studio.
6. A body-servant is a valet.
7. A motometer was a cap-mounted temperature gauge which allowed the driver to monitor the temperature of the engine's radiator.
8. Tarleton, Georgia stands for Montgomery, Alabama, Zelda Sayre Fitzgerald's birthplace and home town. Three of Fitzgerald's short stories are set or partially set in Tarleton; "The Ice Palace" (1920), "The Jelly-Bean" (1920), and "The Last of the Belles" (1929).
9. Jim Powell is also the protagonist of "The Jelly-Bean" (1920).
10. Jim's clothes – old, unfashionable and readymade – mark him out as poor. The fashion by 1923 was for wider trousers that tapered toward the ankle; Jim wears tight trousers that flare around his ankles. Edwards, *How to Read a Suit*, 126.
11. The Adirondacks are a mountain range in New York state, and the Thousand Islands are an archipelago of islands between Canada and the United States. Both were attracting increasing numbers of visitors in the 1920s as the rise of the car made them more easily accessible. They were not society resorts, however; an advertisement in *Vanity Fair* for "The Nast International Travel Bureau" stated of the Adirondacks and the Thousand Islands that "[a]t some of the larger hotels you may see a man in evening clothes, but he looks lonesome." In contrast, Newport, Rhode Island, was a fashionable summer resort for the rich; in May 1922, *Harper's Bazar* informed its readers that "Newport will be up to its best this year. The leaders of Newport society, who have been in Europe for the past few years, are returning, ready and anxious to make the season one to remember." *Vanity Fair*, June 1922, 25 and *Harper's Bazar*, May 1922, 32–33.
12. Corn liquor is a form of whiskey, made with corn using a traditional mash process in which no sugar is added.
13. Zelda Fitzgerald's father, Anthony Dickinson Sayre, was a judge.

14. Southampton is a fashionable resort town on Long Island, New York. In June 1922, *Harper's Bazar* noted that "Bazar representatives have already been to Lake Placid, Palm Beach and now they are at White Sulphur Springs and Virginia Hot Springs. Newport and Southampton will follow. What the smartest women are wearing at the smartest resorts of fashion is therefore always accurately reported in Harper's Bazar." *Harper's Bazar*, June 1922, 127.

15. Hillkiss School, an invention of Fitzgerald's, is first mentioned in "The Curious Case of Benjamin Button" (1922): Benjamin "had heard his classmates speak of Hillkiss, the famous preparatory school," (115) and asks to attend himself.

16. Fitzgerald's 1926 short story "Presumption" features a similarly privileged, and unwelcoming, Garneau family.

17. A "masher" is a man who makes unwelcome advances to women. The term was dated in 1922; Google Ngram shows that its popularity peaked in 1887, and its unchecked decline began in 1917. Green, *Chambers Slang Dictionary*, 842. See Appendix 1, Ngram Language Analysis, for more detail on both this example and this approach to textual analysis.

18. In "The Jelly-Bean" Jim boasts to his friend Clark Darrow that "'Maybe you don't recollect I'm about the champion crap-shooter of this town. They make me shoot from a cup now because once I get the feel of a pair of dice they just roll for me.'" Fitzgerald, *TJA*, 17.

19. In December 1919, Fred Dabney's Novelty Band released the foxtrot "I Ain't Gonna Give None o' This Jelly Roll." While "jelly roll" was slang for female genitalia or sexual intercourse, here he seems to mean the dance itself; "jelly, n.1." *OED Online*, June 2022, Oxford University Press.

20. Sugar was produced in cubes from the mid-nineteenth century; the first patent was filed by Jakob Christof Rad (1799–1871) in 1841, and another process was developed and patented by Eugen Langen (1833–1895) in 1872.

21. Adams notes that "[t]he name Rastus Muldoon combines a common Irish surname with a reference to the racist portrayal of an African American character named Rastus, who is lazy and unreliable, in a series of films from 1910 to 1917." Adams, *F. Scott Fitzgerald's Short Fiction: From Ragtime to Swing Time*, 31.

22. The Chicago Waltz was a slow waltz. On 11 December 1922, *The San Francisco Examiner* reported that it was being abolished in New York dancehalls, and that "Mrs. George W. Loft, deputy police commissioner, has declared that 'slow dancing,' as practiced almost exclusively in Europe, and which is gaining strong footholds in this country, is 'disgusting.'" Adams describes the Memphis Side-swoop as "a kick and dip step which originated in New Orleans." *The San Francisco Examiner*, 11 December 1922, 8 and Adams, *F. Scott Fitzgerald's Short Fiction*, 31.

23. Santa Barbara is a coastal city in California favored by the rich and fashionable. An advertisement in *Harper's Bazar* of June 1922 claimed that "probably there is no place in America where quality and correctness count more and price counts less than at this world-famous watering hole of the rich." Biddeford Pool is a popular summer resort in Maine. Newport, Rhode Island, was also a fashionable summer resort for the rich; see note 14. *Harper's Bazar*, June 1922, 90.

24. A sub-deb is a girl in her mid-teens, who is not yet old enough to come out as a debutante.

25. As more comfortable, sporty clothing became popular throughout the early 1920s, pointed shoes became less fashionable. By way of illustration, *Vanity Fair's* 1920 guide, "For the Well Dressed Man," shows a man wearing pointed shoes on the beach. In 1923, the equivalent feature noted that "[t]his model of a stout tan walking shoe reflects the smart last with its semi-blunt toe." *Vanity Fair*, July 1920, 76 and *Vanity Fair*, October 1923, 86.

26. Compare to this description of the "Popular Daughter" in chapter 2 of *This Side of Paradise* (1920): "Try to find the P. D. between dances, just *try* to find her. The same girl . . . deep in an atmosphere of jungle music and the questioning of moral codes." Fitzgerald, *TSOP*, 62.

27. This concern with racial intermixing is mirrored by Tom Buchanan's anxiety in chapter 8 of *The Great Gatsby* that "they'll throw everything overboard and have intermarriage between black and white." Fitzgerald, *GG Var*, 156.

28. A cut-out switch let the engine exhaust bypass the muffler, increasing both the power and the noisiness of the car.

29. Compare to chapter 8 of *The Great Gatsby*: "'They're a rotten crowd,' I shouted across the lawn. 'You're worth the whole damn bunch put together.'" Fitzgerald, *GG Var*, 185.

30. Jim sings "Jeanne of Jelly-Bean Town" in "The Jelly Bean." The song is an invention of Fitzgerald's, and the lyrics given in "The Jelly Bean" are: "One mile from home in Jelly-bean town, / Lives Jeanne, the Jelly-bean Queen. / She loves her dice and treats 'em nice; / No dice would treat her mean. / Her Jelly Roll can twist your soul, / Her eyes are big and brown, / She's the Queen of the Queens of the Jelly-beans – / My Jeanne of Jelly-bean Town." Fitzgerald, *TJA*, 15–16.

31. "Ka-lu-a" was composed by Jerome Kern (1885–1945) for the 1922 musical *Good Morning, Dearie*. "'Neath the South Sea Moon" was composed by Victor Herbert (1859–1924) and used for a Gilda Gray number in the 1922 *Ziegfeld Follies*. Shaw, *The Jazz Age*, 131.

32. The word "an," without the terminal apostrophe to indicate a missing letter, is preserved as printed in *Metropolitan*.

33. A porte-cochére is a covered porch, giving sheltered access to a building from a car or carriage.

34. Flivver was slang for a small, cheap, old automobile. According to Google Ngram, the term's popularity peaked in 1923, the year "Dice,

Brassknuckles and Guitar" was published. See Appendix 1, Ngram Language Analysis, for more detail on both this example and this approach to textual analysis.

35. A debutante would "come out" – make her debut in society – at a debutante ball.

36. Palm Beach, St. Augustine, and Miami are all resorts in Florida. Palm Beach became increasingly popular with the wealthy and fashionable in the early 1920s; on 1 April 1922, *Vogue* noted that "[m]iles and miles of what, so late as 1919, were fields of wild, luxuriant vegetation now form parts of highly civilized estates, dominated by houses that in architectural beauty rival the famous Mediterranean resorts." *Vogue*, 1 April 1922, 68.

Hot and Cold Blood

Hearst's International, August 1923, 80–84, 150–151

1. *Pithecanthropus erectus* (now known as *Homo erectus erectus*) is an early human fossil, discovered in 1891 and 1892 by Eugène Dubois, who argued, controversially, that it represented a "missing link" between apes and humans.

2. In chapter 3 of *The Great Gatsby* (1925), Nick Carraway says of Jordan Baker that "there was a jauntiness about her movements as if she had first learned to walk upon golf courses on clean, crisp mornings." In chapter 8, her voice is described as "fresh and cool, as if a divot from a green golf-links had come sailing in at the office window." Fitzgerald, *GGVar*, 61 and 186.

3. In his biography of F. Scott Fitzgerald, Andrew Turnbull writes that P. F. McQuillan – Fitzgerald's maternal grandfather – "had been in wholesale rather than trade and that was considered 'all right.'" Fitzgerald uses the wholesale grocery brokerage here to indicate that the Coatesworth's financial and social position is stable, but not first-rate. Turnbull, *Scott Fitzgerald*, 13.

4. In 1923 $300 would have the purchasing power of approximately $5,200 in 2022.

5. The Bessemer process produces steel from iron quickly and on an industrial scale.

6. The 1920 census showed that over half of Polish immigrants to the United States arrived after 1905. The majority of men (61 percent) worked in coal mines and the majority of women (50 percent) worked in cotton factories. Carpenter, *Immigrants and Their Children*, 62 and 292.

7. A roadster is an open-top car for up to two passengers.

8. In 1923 $2,500 would have the purchasing power of approximately $43,000 in 2022. For comparison, a Ford Model T would cost $393

in 1923 (approximately $6,800 in 2022). *The Wall Street Journal*, 5 February 1923, 1.

9. In 1923 $50 would have the purchasing power of approximately $860 in 2022.

10. In 1923 $1,300 would have the purchasing power of approximately $22,400 in 2022.

11. In 1884 $1,000 would have the purchasing power of approximately $1,700 in 1923 and $29,500 in 2022.

12. In 1923 $10,000 would have the purchasing power of approximately $172,000 in 2022.

13. In 1923 $450 would have the purchasing power of approximately $7,700 in 2022.

14. In 1923 $75 would have the purchasing power of approximately $1,300 in 2022.

15. In book two, chapter 1 of *The Beautiful and Damned* (1922), Gloria asks Anthony to leave the bed and get her a water "with just a *little* piece of ice." Fitzgerald, *B&D*, 156.

16. In Fitzgerald's 1926 story "The Rich Boy," Hagerty carries a pregnant Paula up the stairs in the "'family gymnastic stunt.'" Fitzgerald, *ASYM*, 39.

Gretchen's Forty Winks

Saturday Evening Post, 15 March 1924, 14–15, 128, 130, 132

See Appendix 3 for a reproduction of this story as it appeared in the magazine.

1. Fitzgerald's daughter, Scottie, was two-and-a-half years old at the time of this story's publication, around the same age as Maxy. Bruccoli, *Some Sort of Epic Grandeur*, 156.

2. F. Scott Fitzgerald and Zelda Sayre Fitzgerald married on 3 April 1920, so had been married four years when the *Saturday Evening Post* published "Gretchen's Forty Winks." Bruccoli, *Some Sort of Epic Grandeur*, 128.

3. Reference to the golden-brown hair associated with the painter Tiziano Vecelli (1488–1576), known as Titian. Zelda Fitzgerald's hair was frequently described as golden.

4. "Gretchen's Forty Winks" was itself written in a similar period of intense work. Following the failure of his play, *The Vegetable* (1923), Fitzgerald wrote ten short stories, including this one, between late 1923 and early March 1924. Bruccoli, *Some Sort of Epic Grandeur*, 185.

5. Zelda Sayre Fitzgerald grew up in the South, in Montgomery, Alabama.

6. Fitzgerald worked for Barron Collier, an advertising firm in New York, between February and July 1919. Although Fitzgerald remembers his

boss telling him "it's plain there's a future for you in this business," he described himself as "mediocre at advertising." Mizener, *The Far Side of Paradise*, 86.

7. In 1924 $500 had the purchasing power of $8,400 in 2022, and $600 of $10,000. It was in April 1924 that the *Saturday Evening Post* published "How to Live on $36,000 a Year," Fitzgerald's satirical essay about his money troubles in the midst of his success. "Gretchen's Forty Winks," published in March of the same year, is a more serious consideration of how those troubles felt. *Saturday Evening Post*, 5 April 1924, 22.

8. Scent for men was limited to eau de cologne in the early 1920s. It was 1934 before Caron would create "Pour Un Homme," the first fragrance intended solely for men.

9. Tompkins is demonstrating his status to the Halseys in this offer. Compare to book three, chapter 2 of *The Beautiful and Damned* (1922): "when prohibition came in July he found that, among those who could afford it, there was more drinking than ever before. One's host now brought out a bottle upon the slightest pretext. The tendency to display liquor was a manifestation of the same instinct that led a man to deck his wife with jewels. To have liquor was a boast, almost a badge of respectability." Fitzgerald, *B&D*, 321.

10. Weightlifting was admitted to the Olympics as an event in its own right in 1920.

11. Golf experienced an explosion in popularity in the 1920s. Walter Hagen (1892–1969) became the first American-born winner of the British Open Championship in 1922, and in June of that year *Vanity Fair* reported that "[g]ently and quietly the game [of golf] has insinuated itself into the affections of the American people." The implication throughout Tompkins' picture of the "balanced life" is that he will take up any fashion he encounters. *Vanity Fair*, June 1922, 104.

12. In a letter to Edmund Wilson, Fitzgerald characterized the period in which he wrote "Gretchen's Forty Winks" as follows: "I really worked hard as hell last winter [. . .] and it nearly broke my heart as well as my iron constitution." Fitzgerald, *A Life in Letters*, 77.

13. Compare to "The Curious Case of Benjamin Button" (1922), in which the young woman who marries the eponymous hero says that she would "'rather marry a man of fifty and be taken care of than marry a man of thirty and take care of *him*.'" (109).

14. The crayons and cardboard were for advertising mock-ups.

15. In 1924 $250,000 had the purchasing power of $4.2 million in 2022. Fitzgerald was familiar with his own fantasies about large sums of money around the time he wrote "Gretchen's Forty Winks," having spent 1923 expecting his play, *The Vegetable*, to be a Broadway hit; on 5 February 1922 he wrote to his agent, Harold Ober, that his "play [. . .] is a wonder, I think, and should make a great deal of money." Bruccoli, *As Ever*, 35.

16. In his 1933 essay, "One Hundred False Starts," Fitzgerald writes that "I must start out with an emotion; one that's close to me and that I can understand." His own work – even that which, like "Gretchen's Forty Winks," he produced quickly and for money – was a "labour of love," drawing heavily on his own emotions and experiences. Fitzgerald, *My Lost City*, 87.

17. Fitzgerald's ambivalence about his own work is on display here. He described the ten stories he wrote between late 1923 to early 1924, including "Gretchen's Forty Winks," as "trash" in the aforementioned letter to Edmund Wilson (see note 12). Fitzgerald, *A Life in Letters*, 77.

18. Affluent Victorian couples would sleep in separate, possibly interconnected, bedrooms, a tradition modified to twin beds by the 1920s. In book two, chapter 1 of *The Beautiful and Damned*, Gloria cries for "Our two little beds here – side by side – they'll be always waiting for us." Fagan and Durrani, *What We Did in Bed*, 169 and Fitzgerald, *B&D*, 145.

19. Oxfords are formal shoes with closed lacing.

20. The Biltmore was a luxury hotel in New York, established in 1913; the Fitzgeralds honeymooned there in 1920. Bruccoli, *Some Sort of Epic Grandeur*, 128.

21. Compare to Zelda Fitzgerald's review of *The Beautiful and Damned* for the *New York Tribune* in 1922; "everyone must buy this book for the following aesthetic reasons; First, because I know there is the cutest cloth-of-gold dress for only $300 in a store on Forty-second Street." Sayre, *F. Scott Fitzgerald in His Own Time*, 332.

22. In 1924 $40,000 had the purchasing power of $670,000 in 2022. This number is slightly higher than the $36,000 (with the purchasing power of $620,000 in 2022) that Fitzgerald claims he and Zelda spent in 1923.

23. The *Saturday Evening Post* published "Gretchen's Forty Winks" in 1924; in 1938 *Gas Light*, the Patrick Hamilton play that now gives its name to this behavior, was performed at the Richmond Theatre for the first time.

24. A collapsible version of the standard top hat, allowing for easy storage in a theatre. The spring mechanism, patented by Gabriel Gibus in 1837, let the wearer collapse their hat at the touch of a button.

Diamond Dick and the First Law of Woman

Hearst's International, April 1924, 58–63, 134, 136

1. The American Red Cross installed 551 stations and spent almost $31 million in France from the start of the war to March 1918.

2. Diamond Dick was the hero of a series of novels and stories published under the name W. B. Lawson between 1878 and 1911; Richard

Wade, the Diamond Dick of the title, wore diamond studded clothes. Theodore Dreiser (1871–1945), the American naturalist writer much admired by Fitzgerald, may have been one of the writers behind the W. B. Lawson pseudonym. Cox, *Dashing Diamond Dick and Other Classic Dime Novels*, xxv.

3. George Washington (1732–1799), Founding Father and first President of the United States. Google Ngram shows that from 1890 Washington was the most frequently referenced Founding Father, overtaking John Adams who held sway over most of the Victorian age. Diana's nurse is suggesting that Diana emulate a historical figure whose popularity and perceived relevance was on the rise. See Appendix 1, Ngram Language Analysis, for more detail on this approach to textual analysis.

4. Greenwich is an affluent town on the Connecticut side of the New York State and Connecticut border.

5. The United States joined the Allied powers in the First World War on 6 April 1917.

6. Abbot is possibly a reference to the Cabot family, a part of Boston's traditional upper class.

7. Diana's debut was in not only a glamourous hotel but a new one. The Ritz-Carlton Hotel in New York was established in 1911, five years after the London Ritz and thirteen years after the Paris Ritz.

8. Blues song by W. C. Handy, published in 1917 and popularised in 1919 by Gilda Gray in the Broadway revue *Schubert's Gaieties*.

9. This paragraph and the one preceding it are reused in chapter 8 of *The Great Gatsby* (1925): "For Daisy was young and her artificial world was redolent of orchids and pleasant, cheerful snobbery and orchestras which set the rhythm of the year, summing up the sadness and suggestiveness of life in new tunes. All night the saxophones wailed the hopeless comment of the 'Beale Street Blues' while a hundred pairs of golden and silver slippers shuffled the shining dust. At the grey tea hour there were always rooms that throbbed incessantly with this low, sweet fever, while fresh faces drifted here and there like rose petals blown by the sad horns around the floor.

   Through this twilight universe Daisy began to move again with the season; suddenly she was again keeping half a dozen dates a day with half a dozen men, and drowsing asleep at dawn with the beads and chiffon of an evening dress tangled among dying orchids on the floor beside her bed." Fitzgerald, *GG Var*, 181.

10. A report on Paris fashions in the February 1919 issue of *Harper's Bazar* opined that "[w]e are far too happy in short skirts to willingly put on long, dragging draperies." By 1922, *Harper's Bazar*'s February report on Paris fashions told its readers that "happily, one is coming back to the line of yesterday in lengthening the skirts and in draping the garments." *Harper's Bazar*, February 1919, 33, and *Harper's Bazar*, February 1922, 43.

11. The word "past" rather than "passed" is reproduced as printed in *Hearst's International*.

12. Soissons is a city in the Aisne department in Northern France. It was on the Western Front and heavily bombarded during the First World War.

13. Thirty was a dangerous age in Fitzgerald's personal mythology. In December 1925, eighteen months after *Hearst's International* published "Diamond Dick and the First Law of Woman," he wrote to his publisher, Maxwell Perkins; "I used to say I wanted to die at thirty – well, now I'm twenty-nine and the prospect is still welcome." Bryer and Kuehl, *Dear Scott/Dear Max*, 126.

14. A coupé is a two-door car, usually for two passengers.

15. The Long Island Sound, bordering Greenwich, Connecticut to the south.

16. Knickerbockers were baggy-kneed short trousers popular in the 1920s and particularly associated with golf, where they live on as plus-fours.

17. Yale University in New Haven, Connecticut.

18. During the First World War, aviation was considered the most glamourous area of service; in book one, chapter 4 of *This Side of Paradise* (1920) Tom D'Invilliers asserts that "aviation sounds like the romantic side of the war, of course – like cavalry used to be." Fitzgerald, *TSOP*, 142.

19. Reused in chapter 3 of *The Great Gatsby*: "The moon had risen higher, and floating in the Sound was a triangle of silver scales, trembling a little to the stiff, tinny drip of the banjos on the lawn." Fitzgerald, *GGVar*, 57.

20. These lyrics and those that follow are from "Aggravatin' Papa: Don't You Try To Two-Time Me" by J. Russel Robinson and Roy Turk, published in 1922.

21. Her coupé, a roadster, is an open-top car for two passengers.

22. Inexpensively bound popular fiction, also known as dime novels. The term encompasses cheap paperbacks, story papers aimed at children and teenagers, and early pulp magazines. In all cases, these stories aimed for sensation rather than lasting literary value.

23. Compare to chapter 2 of *The Great Gatsby*: "Making a short deft movement, Tom Buchanan broke her nose with his open hand." Fitzgerald, *GGVar*, 45.

24. Fontenay appears to be a misspelling of Fontenoy, a commune in the Aisne department in Northern France. Fontenoy is approximately seven miles west of Soissons, where Charley and Diana met (see note 12).

The Third Casket

Saturday Evening Post, 31 May 1924, 8–9, 78

1. Stock tickers kept businesses updated on price movements in the market throughout the day. Prices were transmitted telegraphically to the ticker, which then printed them on thin strips of paper.

2. Ajax from *The Iliad* of Homer, introduced with the words "[o]f the men by far the best was Aias [Ajax], Telamon's son, as long as Achilleus kept up his anger – because he was by far the strongest." Homer, *The Iliad*, 37.

3. Girard lists these models and names of cars in roughly descending order of fashionableness. A coupé is a two-door car, usually for two passengers; its popularity as a term climbed steadily between 1916 and 1931. A limousine, usually driven by a chauffeur, has separate compartments for the driver and the passenger. Use of the term peaked in 1919. A roadster is an open-top car for up to two passengers, with the term reaching the height of its popularity in 1918. In a landaulet, the passengers at the rear are covered by a convertible top. Use of the term peaked in 1908. See Appendix 1, Ngram Language Analysis, for more detail on this approach to textual analysis.

4. Tuxedo Park, originally developed as a hunting resort, was by the 1920s a playground for affluent New Yorkers. On 6 September 1922, the *New York Tribune* referred to "members of society [who] will return or have returned, to the city for a few days before opening their estates on Long Island, in Westchester County, in New Jersey and at Tuxedo Park." *New York Tribune*, 6 September 1922, 11.

5. Girard, who is approaching sixty in 1923, would have entered business during the Gilded Age of the 1880s. A decade earlier, *The Atlantic Monthly* coined the term "robber barons" to describe the industrialists of the era, opining that "the old robber barons of the Middle Ages, who plundered sword in hand and lance in rest, were more honest than this new aristocracy of swindling millionaires." *The Atlantic Monthly*, August 1870, 199.

6. Jones refers obliquely to "jelly beans," then a Southern term for shiftless young men. On 3 October 1920, *The Montgomery Advertiser* reported on "war on the 'jelly-bean' and 'masher' who insist on parking themselves on downtown street corners." *The Montgomery Advertiser*, 3 October 1920, 35.

7. In 1915, Fitzgerald and Ginevra King saw *The Midnight Frolic* on the roof garden of the New Amsterdam Theater. He recalled this in his essay "My Lost City" as "one night when She made luminous the Ritz Roof," and in his 1924 short story "Rags Martin-Jones and the Pr-nce of W-les," which is largely set "on a roof garden wide open to the April night" (282). West, *The Perfect Hour*, 40, and Fitzgerald, *My Lost City*, 107.

8. Niagara Falls had been a popular honeymoon destination but was falling out of favor with fashionable society. In June 1922, *Harper's Bazar* published an article called "When the Honeymoon is A-Shining" in which it informed its readers that "[t]hen, bridal couples stood still and watched the panorama of sights flow by – from the thundering waters of Niagara to the Blue Room of the White House [. . .] But now the trip

is merely a piece of machinery that is carrying us to places where sports are done; from winter skiing in Quebec to surf bathing at Palm Beach." *Harper's Bazar*, June 1922, 51.

9. The Adirondacks is a mountain range in New York State, which attracted increasing numbers of visitors in the 1920s as the rise of the car made it more easily accessible. It would have been an adventurous rather than a fashionable choice; an advertisement in *Vanity Fair* for "The Nast International Travel Bureau" stated of the Adirondacks that "[a]t some of the larger hotels you may see a man in evening clothes, but he looks lonesome." *Vanity Fair*, June 1922, 25.

10. In 1907 the Cunard line's RMS *Mauretania* crossed the Atlantic in four and a half days, a record she held for twenty-two years. Hugill, *World Trade since 1431*, 128.

11. From April 1922 the Daimler Airway flew passengers from Croydon (near London) to Paris.

12. The tomb of Tutankhamun was discovered in November 1922 and was unsealed in February 1923. Popular interest in Egyptology, and in archaeology, was high; an advertisement for Cook's Mediterranean De Luxe Cruise promised "a long stay in Egypt" in the July 1923 issue of *Vanity Fair*, and a month later the same magazine showed a photograph of the dancer Gilda Gray "as Queen Tut-ankh-amen, in which character she is appearing at the Rendez-Vous." *Vanity Fair*, June 1923, 25 and August 1923, 43.

Absolution

American Mercury, June 1924, 141–149

Jennifer Nolan: *As discussed in the introduction, "Absolution" was written initially during the summer of 1923 as a part of* The Great Gatsby, *which Fitzgerald referred to in a June 1924 letter to Maxwell Perkins: "I'm glad you liked* Absolution. *As you know it was to have been the prologue of the novel but it interfered with the neatness of the plan"* (Dear Scott/Dear Max, *72).*

1. The Sixth and Ninth Commandments forbid, respectively, fornication and coveting one's neighbor's wife.
2. "Twenty-three" and "skidoo" were both slang terms meaning "get out." *The St. Louis Post-Dispatch* recorded twenty-three as a "new slang phrase" in 1899, noting that it is "a signal to clear out, run, get away." George M. Cohan's 1904 musical *Little Johnny Jones* used both "twenty-three" and "skidoo" in this sense. Google Ngram shows that the word "skidoo" rose in popularity at the turn of the century, then declined quickly after 1908. *The St. Louis Post-Dispatch*, 3 December

1899, 37. See Appendix 1, Ngram Language Analysis, for more detail on both this example and this approach to textual analysis.

3. Compare to chapter 6 of *The Great Gatsby* (1925): "His parents were shiftless and unsuccessful farm people – his imagination had never really accepted them as his parents at all." Fitzgerald, *GGVar*, 118.

4. The hero of Fitzgerald's 1917 short story, "Sentiment – and the Use of Rouge" is Clay Syneforth, son of Lord Blachford. Fitzgerald, *S&G*, 199.

5. The 1917 Code of Canon Law required Catholics to fast from all food and drink from midnight of the evening before receiving the Eucharist, a rule with only two exceptions: danger of death, and to prevent desecration of the Sacrament.

6. German and Irish immigration to the United States peaked in the years 1850–1859 (when 976,072 German and 1,029,486 Irish immigrants obtained legal permanent resident status) and 1880–1889 (when 1,445,181 German and 674,061 Irish immigrants obtained legal permanent resident status). In 1920 Germans made up 10–20 percent, and Irish people 5–10 percent, of Minnesota and South Dakota's foreign-born population. Fitzgerald's maternal grandfather, Philip F. McQuillan (1834–1877), arrived in Illinois from Ireland in 1843. Carpenter, *Immigrants and Their Children*, 123 and 125, and Turnbull, *Scott Fitzgerald*, 3.

7. James J. Hill (1838–1916), the railroad baron who lived in St. Paul and built his home on Summit Avenue. Gatsby's father, Henry Gatz, describes Hill as a man who "helped build up the country." Fitzgerald, *GGVar*, 202.

8. Horatio Alger (1832–1899) wrote inspiring, if formulaic, novels for young adults, in which a working-class young man (and occasionally young woman) attains an elevated social position through virtue, determination, and hard work.

9. Cornell is an Ivy League university in Ithaca, New York; Hamline is a private liberal arts college in St. Paul. Compare Rudolph Miller's college ambitions to those of Dexter Green in "Winter Dreams" (1922), who chose the "precarious advantage of attending an older and more famous university in the East," (150) and Jay Gatsby, who spent two weeks at St. Olaf's, another private liberal arts college in Minnesota, and was "dismayed at its ferocious indifference to the drums of his destiny." Fitzgerald, *GGVar*, 119.

10. From the Catholic Mass, translating as "Lord, I am not worthy that you should enter under my roof, but only say the word and my soul shall be healed."

11. From the Catholic Mass, translating as "May the Body of Jesus Christ bring your soul to everlasting life."

12. From Psalm 90:6; "a sagitta volante in die, a negotio perambulante in tenebris, ab incursu, et dæmonio meridian," translated as "Of the arrow that flieth in the day, of the business that walketh about in the dark: of

invasion, or of the noonday devil" in the Douay translation. As a Catholic, Fitzgerald would not have used the King James Version, where it is translated in Psalms 91:5–6 as "Thou shalt not be afraid for the terror by night; Nor for the arrow that flieth by day; Nor for the pestilence that walketh in darkness; Nor for the destruction that wasteth at noonday". "Dei," rather than "die," is a transcription error that persisted in the version of "Absolution" collected in *All the Sad Young Men*. West notes that the verse had particular resonance for Fitzgerald, who also referred to it in "Sleeping and Waking," his 1934 essay on insomnia. West, *ASYM*, 468, and Fitzgerald, *My Lost City*, 163.

13. The swastika was adopted by the Nazi Party of Germany in 1920, thirteen years before Hitler took power, but was not yet exclusively connected to them and was still used frequently as decoration in other spaces. In his essay "The Swastika" in the *Proceedings of the United States National Museum, Volume XVII, 1894*, Professor Thomas Wilson writes that "[w]hat seems to have been at all times an attribute of the Swastika is its character as a charm or amulet, as a sign of blessing, benediction, long life, good fortune, good luck [. . .] However many meanings it may have had, it was always ornamental." *Report of National Museum, 1894*, 771.

14. Compare to chapter 9 of *The Great Gatsby*: "That's my Middle West – not the wheat or the prairies or the lost Swede towns, but the thrilling returning trains of my youth." Fitzgerald, *GG Var*, 176.

15. This may be a reference to the Palace of Electricity at the Paris Exposition of 1900. *The Washington Times* of 15 April 1900 reported that "[t]he Palace of Electricity is illuminated by 5,000 incandescent lamps of various colors; by eight arc lights, with projectors, using colored glasses, and four arc lamps with reflectors [. . .] the visitor receives an ineffaceable impression of splendor and beauty." *The Washington Times*, 15 April 1900, 19.

16. Cuirassiers were cavalry; the cuirass is a piece of armor covering the torso. The Battle of Sedan, fought in 1870, tipped the balance of the Franco-Prussian War toward Prussia.

Rags Martin-Jones and the Pr-nce of W-les

McCall's, July 1924, 6–7, 32, 48, 50

1. An advertisement for the White Star Line, published in *Vanity Fair* in May 1924, proclaimed that the *Majestic* was the "world's largest ship, [and] holder of the speed record to Continental Europe." *Vanity Fair*, May 1924, 23.

2. Cherbourg and Southampton were the main tourist ports in France and the UK respectively in 1924. An advertisement in *Vanity Fair* notes that

the *Majestic* "maintain[ed] regular Saturday sailings to Cherbourg and Southampton." *Vanity Fair*, May 1924, 23.

3. *Titled Americans*, published in 1890, noted the "increasing frequency of marriages between American ladies, and foreigners possessed of either official or social rank in Europe." Of Italy, it informs its readers that "[t]here are more titles in Italy than in any other country of Europe [. . .] due to the fact that up to the year 1859 every petty sovereign, and even certain cities and towns, possessed the privilege of conferring titles." The most notable Mazzini at the time that "Rags Martin-Jones and the Pr-nce of W-les" was published was Guiseppe Mazzini (1805–1872), one of the architects of the unified Italian state and an ardent republican. *Titled Americans*, March 1890, 9 and 19.

4. Used light-heartedly here, the image of the anonymous drunk person on a stretcher recurs in chapter 9 of *The Great Gatsby* (1925): "In the foreground four solemn men in dress suits are walking along the sidewalk with a stretcher on which lies a drunken woman in a white evening dress. Her hand, which dangles over the side, sparkles cold with jewels. Gravely the men turn in at a house – the wrong house. But no one knows the woman's name, and no one cares." Fitzgerald, *GGVar*, 212–213.

5. Paul Poiret (1879–1944) was a French fashion designer. His clothes, influenced by Eastern and Near-Eastern styles, fell from favor throughout the 1920s as the simplicity exemplified by Chanel and Patou gained in popularity. This reference was removed when "Rags Martin-Jones and the Pr-nce of W-les" was collected in *All the Sad Young Men*.

6. An advertisement in the 21 January 1924 *Times Union* of Brooklyn, New York describes "the French bob that shingles smoothly up the back and frames the face with two flat waves in front." Google Ngram shows that the popularity of the term "French bob" increased by a factor of ten between 1920 and 1921 and continued to rise until its peak in 1926. *Times Union*, 21 January 1924, 7. See Appendix 1, Ngram Language Analysis, for more detail on both this example and this approach to textual analysis.

7. The *Titanic*, operated by the White Star Line, sank on 15 April 1912, resulting in the deaths of over 1,500 passengers and crew. Fitzgerald's error in placing this event in 1913 was reproduced when "Rags Martin-Jones and the Pr-nce of W-les" was collected in *AYSM*.

8. In 1924 $75 million would have the purchasing power of approximately $2.5 billion in 2022.

9. The Ritz-Carlton Hotel in New York was established in 1911, five years after the London Ritz and thirteen years after the Paris Ritz.

10. Paris was attractive to American expats in the 1920s; between 1919 and 1924 the franc fell by 30 percent, from 5.18 francs to the dollar in 1919 to 20 francs to the dollar in 1924. Major modernist works with their origins in Paris included James Joyce's *Ulysses*, published by

Shakespeare and Company in 1922, and T. S. Eliot's *The Waste Land*, which Eliot and Ezra Pound revised in Paris in 1922. The Fitzgeralds sailed for France in May 1924, two months before the publication of "Rags Martin-Jones and the Pr-nce of W-les." Tooze, *The Deluge*, 456, Rainey, *The Cambridge Companion to Modernism*, 44, and Bruccoli, *Some Sort of Epic Grandeur*, 192.

11. The word "illusive," rather than "elusive," is reproduced as printed in *McCall's*.

12. Compare to chapter 4 of *The Great Gatsby*: "After that I lived like a young rajah in all the capitals of Europe – Paris, Venice, Rome." The Fitzgeralds visited Rome on their first trip to Europe in 1921. Fitzgerald, *GG Var*, 79, and Bruccoli, *Some Sort of Epic Grandeur*, 147.

13. In February 1920, Zelda thanked Fitzgerald for the "be-au-ti-ful" platinum and diamond watch he bought her with proceeds from the sale of "Head and Shoulders" (1920) to Metro Films. Bryer and Barks, *Dear Scott, Dearest Zelda*, 43.

14. Schwartzberg-Rhine-minster is an invention of Fitzgerald's. Control over several formerly Russian territories, including Belarus, Ukraine, Latvia, and Lithuania, was ceded to Germany when Russia formally ended its participation in the First World War with the Treaty of Brest-Litovsk. After Germany's defeat, the Treaty of Versailles granted independence to these protectorates. Political stability proved elusive at the start of the 1920s, and Fitzgerald and his contemporaries would have had ample opportunity to read reports of revolutions and annexations of countries they had not previously heard of. These countries are approximately 1,000 miles from the Rhine; this is possibly a reference to Alsace-Lorraine, a border region between the Rhine and the Vosges mountains. A German territory since 1871, Alsace-Lorraine returned to France after the First World War.

15. Compare to "The Diamond as Big as the Ritz" (1922), in which "Braddock Washington had taken steps to promote a new war in the Balkans" (142).

16. The term "bootleg" had referred to illicit liquor from the 1880s. Google Ngram shows that use of the term increased drastically during Prohibition, between 1920 and 1933. See Appendix 1, Ngram Language Analysis, for more detail on this approach to textual analysis.

17. Edward, Prince of Wales from 1911 to 1936, visited America frequently throughout the 1920s. He was considered the world's most eligible bachelor and a leader in men's fashion; in the January 1924 issue of *Vanity Fair*, Aldous Huxley opined that "the Prince of Wales is no more than the type and model of Vanity Fair's Well Dressed Man." In "The Popular Girl" (1921), the heroine, Yanci, "never got over the disappointment of not meeting the Prince of Wales when he was in this country" (44). *Vanity Fair*, January 1924, 40. See Appendix 1, Ngram Language Analysis, for more detail on his popularity in the US and this approach to textual analysis.

18. Light gold and beige were popular colors for women's fashion in the 1920s. The January 1924 issue of *Harper's Bazar* told its readers that "[j]ust now many frocks are made of gold lace" and that "[f]or shoes, cut-out work gives way to appliques, metal cords, hand-painted bands, pipings of gold kid, and inserts of color in the heel." In her April 1922 review of *B&D* (1922), Zelda Fitzgerald wrote that "everyone must buy this book for the following aesthetic reasons: First, because I know where there is the cutest cloth-of-gold dress for only $300." Edwards, *How to Read a Dress*, 148, *Harper's Bazar*, January 1924, 104 and 51, and Sayre, *F. Scott Fitzgerald in His Own Time*, 332. See Appendix 1, Ngram Language Analysis, for more detail on both this example and this approach to textual analysis.

19. Founded in 1837, Tiffany & Co. established itself as a high-quality jeweler throughout the late 1800s; on 24 May 1887, *The New York Times* quoted a Tiffany & Co. representative who claimed that "our house was the largest buyer at the sale of the French Crown jewels." *The New York Times*, 24 May 1887, 14.

20. In June 1924, *Vanity Fair* referred to "the orchid, the rarest of our flowers, for which the most fabulous prices are paid." In discarding over 80 percent of the orchids she buys, Rags is being extravagantly wasteful. *Vanity Fair*, June 1924, 56.

21. In 1915, Fitzgerald and Ginevra King saw *The Midnight Frolic* on the roof garden of the New Amsterdam Theater. He recalled this in his essay "My Lost City" as "one night when She made luminous the Ritz Roof." In "The Third Casket" (1924), Lola Girard suggests that she and the hero "run up on some roof and dance" (256). West, *The Perfect Hour*, 40, and Fitzgerald, *My Lost City*, 107.

22. The word "or" rather than "of" reproduced as printed in *McCall's*.

23. The song appears to be an invention of Fitzgerald's. The name Papa Jack was possibly influenced by "Aggravatin' Papa," which appears in 1924's "Diamond Dick and the First Law of Woman" (243).

24. The word "carefull" rather than "careful" reproduced as printed in *McCall's*.

25. The Woolworth Building at 233 Broadway, designed by Cass Gilbert (1859–1934), was the tallest building in the world between 1913 and 1930. Its thirty floors are topped by a thirty-story tower.

26. Belarus, Ukraine, Latvia, and Lithuania all shared borders with Poland in 1924.

The Sensible Thing

Liberty, 5 July 1924, 10–14

Jennifer Nolan: *Unlike the* Saturday Evening Post *and other competitors,* Liberty *printed short stories on continuous pages, which they marketed as a selling point to authors, though this practice was clearly less compelling to advertisers.*

1. Churchwell links George's "high, horrible apartment-house in the middle of nowhere" to the boarding-house on Claremont and 125th, "where Fitzgerald had lived for four dreary months in 1919 while he worked in advertising and tried, with assurances of future literary glory, to convince a sceptical Zelda to marry him." Churchwell, *Careless People*, 82.
2. The Massachusetts Institute of Technology (MIT) was established in 1861. The curriculum initially emphasized applied science and engineering, after the European polytechnic model. Unlike the Ivy League universities, which were funded mostly through endowments, MIT was funded mostly through tuition fees in the first decades of the twentieth century. George, with his vocationally relevant (if prestigious) degree, is established as middle class and without the backing of family money. Geiger, *To Advance Knowledge*, 12.
3. In 1924, New York City had been home to the tallest buildings in the world for over a decade. The Singer Building, in 1908 the tallest building in the world at 612 feet, was superseded in 1909 by the Metropolitan Life Insurance Company Tower (700 feet), which was in turn surpassed in 1913 by the 792-foot Woolworth Building. See also note 25 to "Rags Martin-Jones and the Pr-nce of W-les."
4. Throughout 1919, Fitzgerald traveled between New York and Montgomery, Alabama to visit Zelda. Neither she nor her family were confident in his ability to support her with his salary as an advertising copywriter.
5. In April 1919 Fitzgerald telegrammed Zelda that she had "BETTER GIVE LETTER TO YOUR FATHER [a letter Fitzgerald had written to Anthony Sayre in March, asking to marry Zelda] IM SORRY YOURE NERVOUS." He had already sent her his mother's engagement ring. On 30 March 1919, less than a month before they were married, it was Fitzgerald who expressed nervousness, telegramming Zelda that "WE WILL BE AWFULLY NERVOUS UNTIL IT [their wedding] IS OVER." Bryer and Barks, *Dear Scott, Dearest Zelda*, 23 and 46.
6. In March 1919, Zelda wrote to Fitzgerald that "All the material things are nothing. I'd just hate to live a sordid, colorless existence – because you'd soon love me less – and less –." Rosalind, in *This Side of Paradise* (1920), used a similar argument when she told Amory that "I can't be shut away from the trees and flowers, cooped up in a little flat, waiting for you. You'd hate me in a narrow atmosphere. I'd make you hate me." Bryer and Barks, *Dear Scott, Dearest Zelda*, 15, and Fitzgerald, *TSOP*, 182.
7. Zelda continued to date other men in Montgomery while Fitzgerald was in New York. In May 1919, she wrote to him that "'Red' said last

night that I was the pinkest-whitest person he ever saw, so I went to sleep in his lap. Of cource [*sic*], you don't mind because it was really very fraternal, and we were chaperoned by three girls." There is no evidence that Fitzgerald "didn't mind," and some evidence that he did; see note 9. Bryer and Barks, *Dear Scott, Dearest Zelda*, 32.

8. Zelda Sayre's parents were considerably less enthusiastic than Jonquil Cary's. In March 1919, Zelda wrote to Fitzgerald that "Mamma knows that we are going to be married some day – but she keeps leaving stories of young authors, turned out on a dark and stormy night, on my pillow – I wonder if you hadn't better write to my Daddy [. . .] I'm not exactly *scared* of 'em, but they *could* be so unpleasant about what I'm going to do –." Bryer and Barks, *Dear Scott, Dearest Zelda*, 15.

9. In April 1919 Zelda wrote to Fitzgerald – who had evidently expressed concern about her other suitors – that "[i]n the first place, I haven't kissed anybody good-bye [. . .] But s'pose I did – Don't you know it'd just be absolutely *nothing*." Bryer and Barks, *Dear Scott, Dearest Zelda*, 24.

10. Milford writes that after Fitzgerald received a letter from Zelda intended for another man, he visited her in Montgomery having "decided that Zelda had to marry him immediately [. . .] Zelda refused. Both cried, and Scott stormed and tried to force her into marrying him with wild kisses and frantic arguments. He began to beseech Zelda, which was not at all the right tactic, for it demeaned him in her eyes, and she more resolutely than ever shied away from accepting his proposal. He became self-pitying and would not leave the house." Milford, *Zelda*, 52.

11. Now more usually spelled Cusco, this is a city in southeastern Peru, famous for the remains of Inca structures.

12. Compare to chapter 5 of *The Great Gatsby* (1925), in which Gatsby notes with a high degree of accuracy the last time he saw Daisy; "'We haven't met for many years,' said Daisy, her voice as matter-of-fact as it could ever be. / 'Five years next November.' / The automatic quality of Gatsby's answer set us all back at least another minute." Fitzgerald, *GGVar*, 105.

13. Compare to chapter 5 of *The Great Gatsby*, when Gatsby realizes that his relationship to Daisy's home has changed as his relationship to Daisy had changed: "the colossal significance of that light had now vanished forever [. . .] Now it was again a green light on a dock. His count of enchanted objects had diminished by one." Fitzgerald, *GGVar*, 112–113.

14. The word "referenece" rather that "reference" is reproduced as printed in *Liberty*.

15. The name "Carey" rather than "Cary" (the surname in the rest of the story) is reproduced as printed in *Liberty*.

16. George is more aware than Gatsby that his possibility to repeat the past might end in failure. Compare to chapter 6 of *The Great Gatsby*:

"after she was free, they were to go back to Louisville and be married from her house – just as if it were five years ago [. . .] / 'I wouldn't ask too much of her,' I ventured. 'You can't repeat the past.' / 'Can't repeat the past?' he cried incredulously. 'Why of course you can!'" Fitzgerald, *GG Var*, 133.

17. Compare to chapter 6 of *The Great Gatsby*: "At his lips' touch she blossomed for him like a flower and the incarnation was complete." Fitzgerald, *GG Var*, 134.

The Unspeakable Egg

Saturday Evening Post, 12 July 1924, 12–13, 125–126, 29

1. Long Island, east of Manhattan, is also the setting for *The Great Gatsby* (1925).
2. Montauk Point is the easternmost point on Long Island; West notes that it would have been remote and largely uninhabited in the early 1920s. In chapter 2 of *The Great Gatsby* the photographer McKee claims to have "done some nice things out on Long Island [. . .] Two studies. One of them I call *Montauk Point – The Gulls*, and the other I call *Montauk Point – The Sea*." West, *TJA*, 526, and Fitzgerald, *GG Var*, 38.
3. F. Scott Fitzgerald took a degree of pride in the fact that, through his father's family, he could trace his family back to the seventeenth century. In a letter to John O'Hara in 1933, he described himself as "half old American stock with the usual exaggerated ancestral pretentions." Fitzgerald, *A Life in Letters*, 233.
4. The *Aquitania* was the Cunard Line ocean liner on which the Fitzgeralds sailed to Europe in May 1921. Bruccoli, *Some Sort of Epic Grandeur*, 147.
5. Mah-jongg is a four-player game, originating in China in the nineteenth century. It gained popularity in the 1920s, with an advertisement in the March 1923 issue of *Vanity Fair* describing it as "the astonishing Chinese game that is literally sweeping the country" and noting that "[i]t has already replaced auction bridge in many of the smartest houses and clubs in the East and on the Pacific coast." *Vanity Fair*, March 1923, 11.
6. Fitzgerald depicted society girls learning to play dice in 1923's "Dice, Brassknuckles and Guitar"; it was unlikely to be a real vice for an upper-class young woman in 1924.
7. Compare to Daisy in chapter 7 of *The Great Gatsby*, who tells Gatsby that "'You resemble the advertisement of the man,' she went on innocently. 'You know the advertisement of the man –.'" Fitzgerald, *GG Var*, 142.
8. *The Sheik* was a wildly successful romance novel by E. M. Hull (1880–1947). First published in the US in 1921, it was reprinted forty-one times

within ten months. By the time "The Unspeakable Egg" was published the novel been adapted as a motion picture (*The Sheik*, 1921) starring Rudolph Valentino (1895–1926) in the title role that defined his career. The "sheik" was the male counterpart to the "flapper," and in 1925 Fitzgerald wrote an article for McCall's titled "What Became of Our Flappers and Sheiks." Regis, *A Natural History of the Romance Novel*, 117, and Fitzgerald, *F. Scott Fitzgerald in His Own Time*, 202.

9. Leon Trotsky (1879–1940) led the Red Army to victory in the Russian Civil War of 1918–1920, and remained prominent in the Bolshevik leadership until 1925. John D. Rockefeller (1839–1937) founded the Standard Oil Company; by 1880 his company refined 95 percent of all oil produced in the United States, and by 1912 he was established as the richest man in the world. Coffey, *John D. Rockefeller*, 73, and Chernow, *Titan*, 557.

10. South Sea movies were a popular genre in early cinema. Set in the islands of the Southern Pacific, they tended to portray the men of the Pacific islands as "savages." Examples roughly contemporary to "The Unspeakable Egg" include *The Idol Dancer* (1920), *Ebb Tide* (1922), and *The Ragged Edge* (1923).

11. A cutaway is a formal frock coat, worn in the 1920s with a waistcoat, standing collar, and dress trousers. Edwards, *How to Read a Suit*, 139.

12. In *Careless People*, Churchwell notes that the slang term "egg" had particular resonance for Fitzgerald. Churchwell, *Careless People*, 73.

13. The Greenbrier at White Sulphur Springs, West Virginia, was a luxury resort. In a June 1923 article on "Where Smart America Goes with Its Becoming Palm Beach Tan Still upon It," *Harper's Bazar* reported on the "young married set at White Sulphur." *Harper's Bazar*, June 1923, 56–57.

14. There were several stories of heiresses marrying chauffeurs in the early 1920s. On 31 March 1920, *The New York Times* reported that "Miss Emma Whitman Knapp, who inherited a fortune from her father [. . .] was married at 4 o'clock yesterday afternoon [. . .] to Claron George Soule. Mr. Soule was said last night to have been employed by Miss Knapp's aunt [. . .] as a chauffeur." By 1922, the New York *Daily News* was weary enough of the theme to refer to the "old, old story of the heiress's love fro [*sic*] her father's chauffeur." *The New York Times*, 31 March 1920, 11, and *Daily News*, 5 September 1922, 3.

15. Sigmund Freud's *A General Introduction to Psychoanalysis* was published in English by Boni and Liveright in 1920. Google Ngram shows that use of the term "psychoanalysis" in American English rose steadily between 1906 and 1923. See Appendix 1, Ngram Language Analysis, for more detail on this approach to textual analysis.

16. Although bridge was more a popular game than mah-jongg until 1938, mah-jongg was more fashionable. In June 1924, *Harper's Bazar* reported that "at present a distraction other than the dance dominates fashionable

gatherings: it is Mah-Jongg. It is a necessity now to know the game if you do not wish to bore your companions with your presence." *Harper's Bazar*, June 1924, 79.

17. In May 1924, two months before the publication of "The Unspeakable Egg," the Fitzgeralds sailed for Europe with an *Encyclopedia Britannica* that Fitzgerald intended to read in full. Bruccoli, *Some Sort of Epic Grandeur*, 192.

18. The heroine of E. M. Hull's *The Sheik* is kidnapped and raped by the eponymous sheik. For more on the novel and its impact on popular culture, see note 8.

19. *Little Lord Fauntleroy,* by Frances Hodgson Burnett (1849–1924), was serialized between 1885 and 1886 in *St. Nicholas Magazine* and published as a book in 1886. It is hard to imagine a character in fiction more distant from E. M. Hull's sheik. The word "innocent" is applied to the hero, Cedric, Lord Fauntleroy, nineteen times in the text; in describing the hero meeting his grandfather for the first time, Hodgson Burnett writes that "[i]f the Castle was like the palace in a fairy story, it must be owned that little Lord Fauntleroy was himself rather like a small copy of the fairy prince." Google Ngram shows that the popularity of the term "Little Lord Fauntleroy" peaked in 1889, before Fifi, in her early twenties in 1924, would have been born. Hodgson Burnett, *Little Lord Fauntleroy*, 97. See Appendix 1, Ngram Language Analysis, for more detail on this approach to textual analysis.

20. West notes that to wireless meant to send a message via radio telegraph, and that "[o]nly a person of means would have access to a private wireless." West, *TJA*, 527.

John Jackson's Arcady

Saturday Evening Post, 26 July 1924, 8–9, 100, 102, 105

Jennifer Nolan: *Bryant Mangum's fascinating 2006 F. Scott Fitzgerald Review article, "Echoes of Arcady: F. Scott Fitzgerald and It's a Wonderful Life," uses the publishing history of this story to convincingly demonstrate its connection to Frank Capra's 1946 film* It's a Wonderful Life. *For more on this and other aspects of the story, see also Kurk Curnutt and Robert Trogden's podcast,* Master the 40 *(April 2021).*

1. Yale University in New Haven, Connecticut.
2. Next to the table of contents in the *Saturday Evening Post* where "John Jackson's Arcady" first appeared are several advertisements inviting readers to send for information on making extra money as sales representatives. In one testimonial, an L. D. Payne attested that "I Averaged $20.77 profit per day for 217 Days" selling fire extinguishers. Readers could also clip and mail a coupon to sell subscriptions to the *Saturday*

Evening Post, The Ladies' Home Journal, and *The Country Gentleman*; the headline asked, "Want to be One of Our $50.00 a Week Men?" *Saturday Evening Post,* 26 July 1924, 126.

3. Page identifies the city in "John Jackson's Arcady" as St. Paul, and John Jackson's office as the New York Life Building where Fitzgerald had rented an office in October 1921: "Saint Paul's Old Courthouse Square could have been seen from offices on the back of the New York Life Building [. . . which] held one of only two telegraph offices in the city." Page and Koblas, *F. Scott Fitzgerald in Minnesota,* 223.

4. Telegrams were charged at a flat rate for the first ten words and per word thereafter, a pricing structure that remained in place to 1960. Over half of messages sent used ten or fewer words; only 4 percent of telegrams had over twenty-five words. At fifty-three words, John Jackson's telegram could easily have been the longest ever sent from his town. Hochfelder, *The Telegraph in America, 1832–1920,* 79.

5. Compare to chapter 7 of *The Great Gatsby* (1925): "'But it's so hot,' insisted Daisy, on the verge of tears, 'and everything's so confused. Let's all go to town!'" Fitzgerald, *GG Var,* 142.

Appendix 1:
Ngram Language Analysis

Alexandra Mitchell

From the very beginning of his career, critics and audiences alike were notably impressed by the authenticity of F. Scott Fitzgerald's work. A review of his first novel, *This Side of Paradise*, which appeared on 1 April 1920 in the *St. Louis Post-Dispatch*, noted that "Mr. Fitzgerald has all the small talk of undergraduates and the 'flapper' at his fingers' ends,"[1] and as Jackson Bryer has noted, reviews of the novel in college newspapers at the time "all provided ample evidence that Fitzgerald was reaching his own generation by depicting it accurately."[2] In the words of Matthew J. Bruccoli, "acutely sensitive to the moods and values of his time, [Fitzgerald] was a master of selective detail."[3]

Thanks to modern technology, we can now quantify just how accurately Fitzgerald depicted his generation. Google Ngram provides a searchable corpus of texts – magazines, books, and journal articles – from 1500 to the present day. The search results show how the concentration of a given word or phrase change over time within the corpus. Figure A.1 gives an example, showing the emergence and decline of the word "flapper" in American English throughout Fitzgerald's lifetime; its concentration in printed texts reached a peak in 1923 before beginning a virtually unchecked decline from the mid-1920s.

Using this technique gives us an indication of how widely used a word or phrase was over a period of time. However, Ngram is not perfect. Most obviously, it tracks only the written and not the

---

[1] "Good Afternoon! Have you a Little P.D. in Your Home?" review of *This Side of Paradise*, by F. Scott Fitzgerald, *St. Louis Post-Dispatch*, 1 April 1920, 29.

[2] Jackson Bryer, ed., introduction to *F. Scott Fitzgerald: The Critical Reception* (New York: Burt Franklin & Co, 1978), xiii.

[3] Matthew J. Bruccoli, "On F. Scott Fitzgerald and 'Bernice Bobs Her Hair,'" in *The American Short Story*, ed. Calvin Skaggs (New York: Dell, 1977), 221.

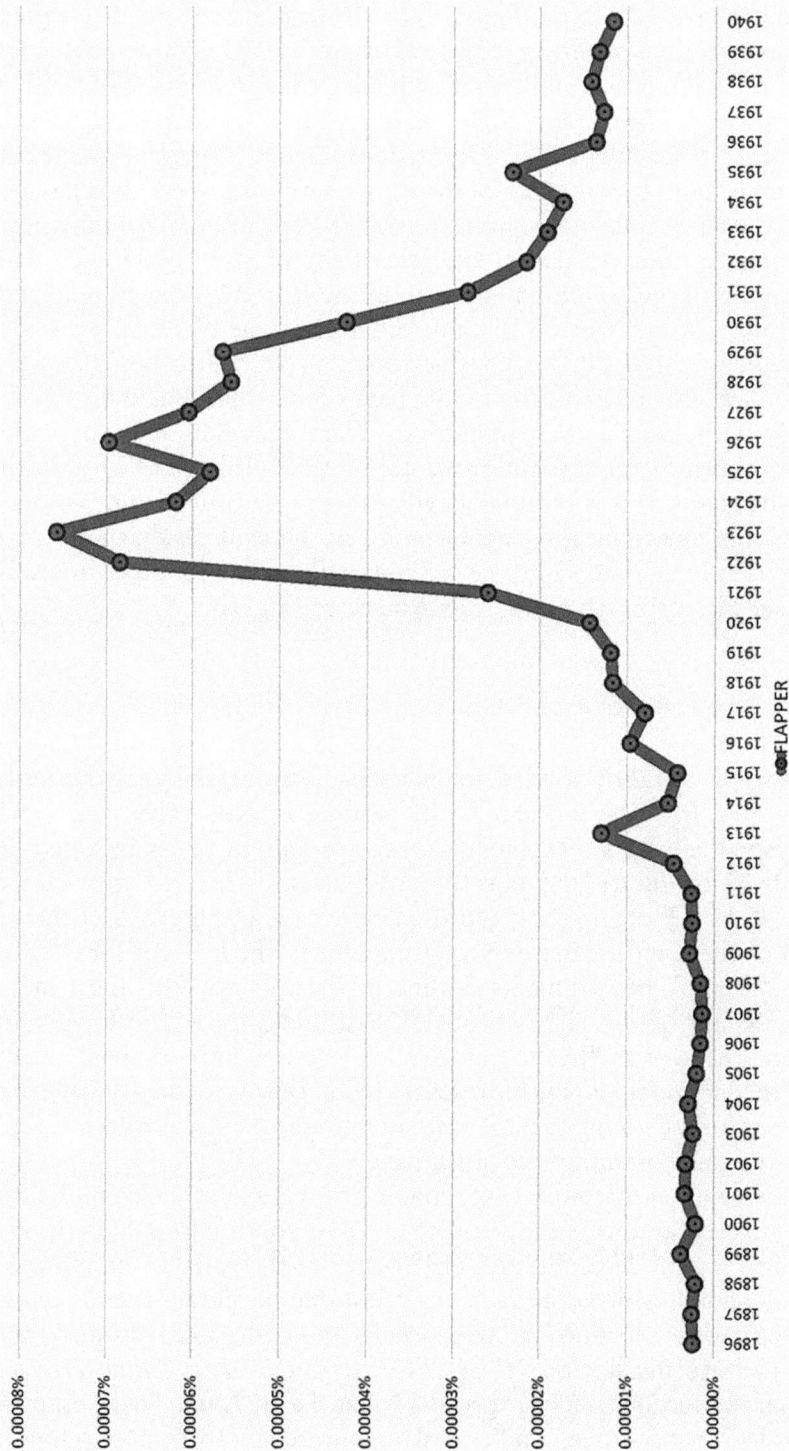

Figure A1.1 Flapper Ngram from the American English corpus (1896–1940)

spoken word – the "small talk" – that Fitzgerald recorded. Further, the texts in the corpus are digitized using Optical Character Recognition (OCR), a technique that produces consistent and predictable errors – e.g., the word "close" is likely to be rendered as "dose" and "morn" as "mom." The consistency of OCR errors means that Ngram is more useful as a tool showing relative numbers and changes over time than absolute numbers. More seriously, it is impossible to separate homonyms. An analysis of the phrase "good egg" will include both the colloquial use seen in the stories in this volume and advice to poultry farmers. Finally, the texts in the Ngram corpus are overwhelmingly from Anglo-American sources, which limits its utility for scholars of literature in languages other than English.

Notwithstanding these limitations, Ngram gives us a new perspective on both Fitzgerald and his time. In 1921–1924, the period this volume spans, this is especially evident with youthful slang, business argot, and emerging Jazz Age fashions. In the analysis that follows, I have used Fitzgerald's lifetime (1896–1940) as the period of analysis and set the corpus to exclusively American English.

The Language of Youth

Fitzgerald is rightly lauded for his sensitivity to changing patterns of speech. In "The Popular Girl," written in November 1921 and published February 1922, he writes directly about newly fashionable words, referring to "the adjectives of the year – 'hectic,' 'marvelous' and 'slick.'" Plotting these words together (as in Figure A.2) shows each of these words increasing in popularity throughout the 1920s, with "hectic" beginning its decline in the 1930s. With the benefit of hindsight (and a large corpus of data) we can see that Fitzgerald caught the words "hectic" and "slick" at the start of their ascent into the language of youth. In 1921–1922, they would have been the preserve of the young and the fashionable – as the decade progressed, they became commonplace adjectives.

Not only a chronicler of contemporary slang, Fitzgerald also remembered and used the slang of his own youth with a high degree of accuracy. In "Absolution" (1924), set in the early twentieth century, Rudolph Miller confesses to a priest that he and his friends yelled "Twenty three, skidoo" at an old lady until "she had a fit and they had to have the doctor." (265) "Twenty-three" and "skidoo" were both slang terms meaning "get out," and the *St. Louis Post-Dispatch* recorded twenty-three as a "new slang phrase" in 1899, noting that it

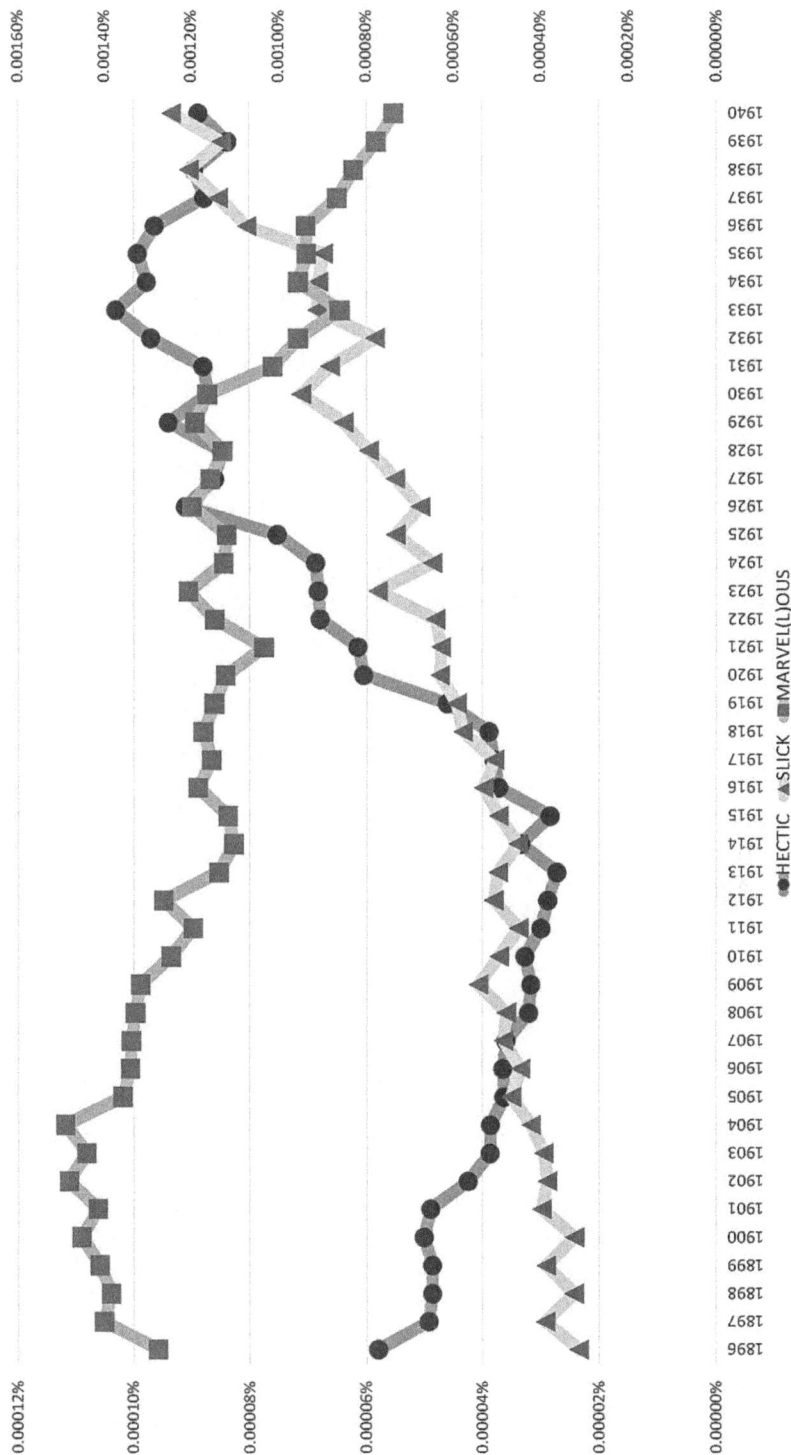

Figure A1.2 Hectic, Slick, Marvellous Ngram from the American English corpus (1896–1940). Hectic and slick are plotted on the primary axis and both Fitzgerald's spelling, marvelous, and the modern spelling, marvellous, are plotted on the secondary axis

is "a signal to clear out, run, get away."[4] Rudolph, eleven years old at the time of the story's action, uses the language that Fitzgerald, born in 1896, would have heard and used in his eleventh year, which is borne out by searching the term using Ngram. As Figure A.3 demonstrates, the word "skidoo" rose in popularity at the turn of the century, then declined quickly after 1908. On the other hand, "twenty-three" reveals one of the previously noted limitations of Ngram, which struggles to usefully track homonyms.

The examples so far have dealt with characters who used the language of their time to illustrate their social competency, but Fitzgerald also used old-fashioned language to mark characters as outsiders. In 1923's "Dice, Brassknuckles and Guitar," Jim Powell uses the word "masher" to mean a sexually predatory man. Jim is a character out of his milieu in this story; a Southerner in the North, and a poor man amongst the social set at Southampton. As Figure A.4 demonstrates, the use of the word "masher" peaked in 1887 and had begun its irrevocable decline by 1917. For the reader in 1923, Jim's use of such an unfashionable word would have firmly placed him as a man out of step with his surroundings. This is further emphasized by the narrator's use of "flivver" to describe Jim's car. Referring again to Figure A.4, "flivver," meaning a small, cheap, old automobile, grew in popularity from 1912 to reach its peak in 1923, the year of the story's publication. The narrator's use of it contrasts with Jim's antiquated language and reinforces how unfashionable Jim is: the up-to-the-minute slang of the narrator offers a sharp contrast to Jim's old car and old words.

Business Speak

Although Fitzgerald's own experience of office work was limited to three months of copywriting for the Barron Collier agency,[5] he was an accurate mimic and satirist of the business slang of his day. In a scene in "The Curious Case of Benjamin Button" set in the early 1920s, the hero's bumptious son thinks almost exclusively in the business cliches of his day; "in the idiom of his generation Roscoe did not consider the matter 'efficient.' It seemed to him that his father,

---

[4] *St Louis Post-Dispatch*, 3 December 1899.
[5] Matthew J. Bruccoli, *Some Sort of Epic Grandeur: The Life of F. Scott Fitzgerald*, 2nd revised edition (Columbia: University of South Carolina Press, 2002), 93–96.

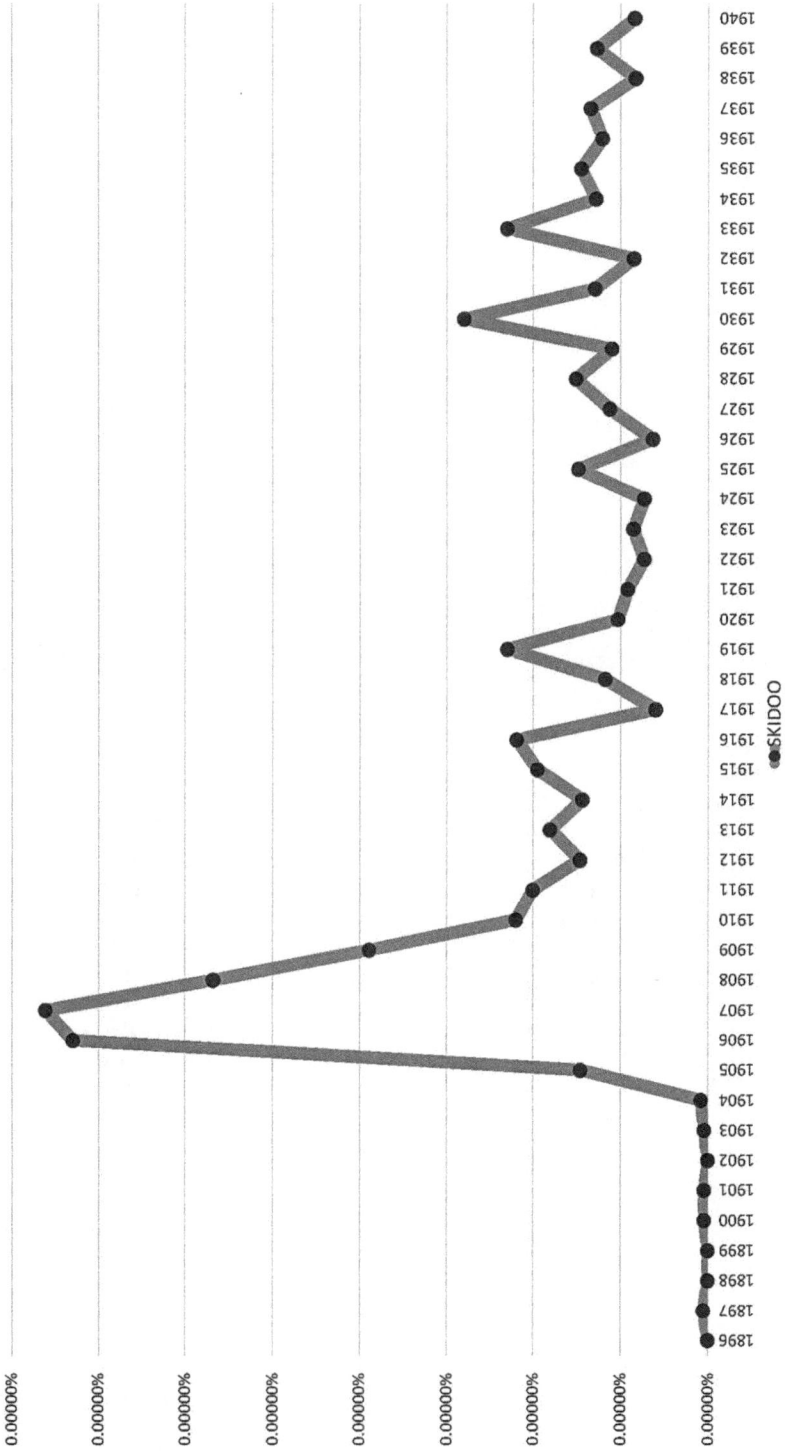

Figure A1.3 Skidoo Ngram from the American English corpus (1896–1940)

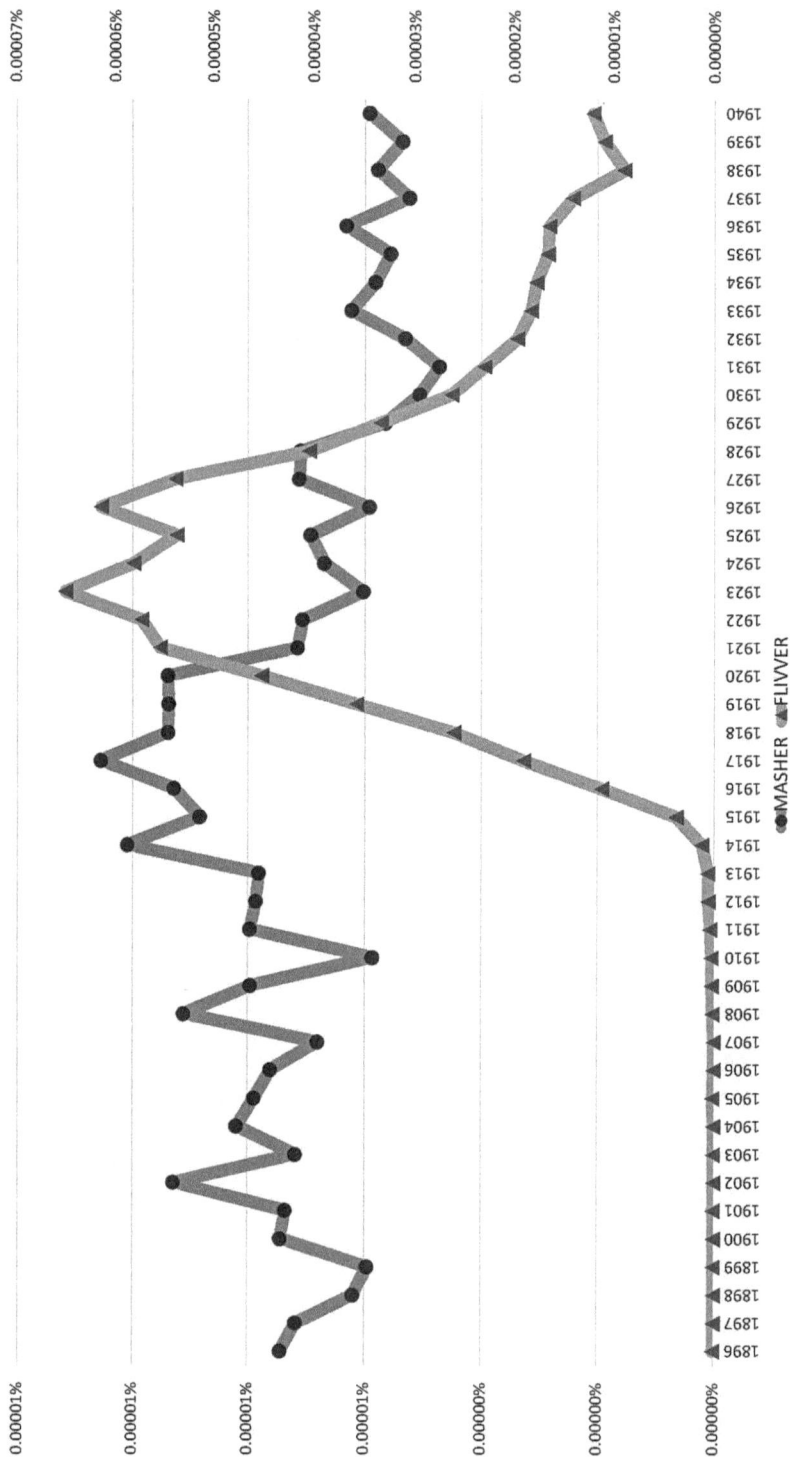

Figure A1.4 Masher, Flivver Ngram from the American English corpus (1896–1940). Masher is plotted on the primary axis and flivver on the secondary axis

in refusing to look sixty, had not behaved like a 'red-blooded he-man'" (118). Figure A.5 shows all of these words reaching or moving towards the peak of their popularity in the early 1920s. Studies on efficiency, including the time and motion studies of the Gilbreths from 1909, drove the use of the word "efficient" in the years from 1900 to 1919. Use of the phrase "red blooded" reached its peak in 1921. The phrase "he-man" would peak in 1928, but began its rise with the advent of the First World War in 1914. Delightfully further emphasizing the point, these words and phrases were used in half-page advertisements printed alongside Fitzgerald's text in *Collier's*: Eversharp advertised "the pencil of business efficiency"[6] alongside the fifth page of the story, while an advertisement for Durham-Duplex razors running alongside the seventh page promised readers "The Razor for He-Men."[7]

Fitzgerald was also a sharp observer of the changing trends in business itself. In 1922's "The Popular Girl," he writes that an unremarkable young man "sold bonds—bonds were now the thing; real estate was once the thing" (51). From the vantage point of 1921, the year the story was written, this was exactly what had just happened; Figure A.6 shows that, after a steady climb, 1920 was the year use of the phrase "sell bonds" surpassed the phrase "sell real estate" for the first time. After a brief reversal in 1922, bonds continued to be "the thing." Fitzgerald made multiple references to selling bonds as the new business activity in the earlier period covered by this volume. In "His Russet Witch" (1921), a young man goes to "Wall Street to sell bonds, as all the young men seemed to be doing in that day" (27) and in "Winter Dreams" (1922) the hero sees that "rich men's sons were peddling bonds precariously" (161). And famously, in *The Great Gatsby*, which was published in 1925 but set in 1922, Nick Carraway decides that "everybody I knew was in the bond business so I supposed it could support one more single man."[8]

Social Trends and Celebrity

Ngram analysis also demonstrates how well Fitzgerald captured the zeitgeist of the early Jazz Age. For example, in 1924's "Rags Martin-Jones and the Pr-nce of W-les" the eponymous heroine

[6] Eversharp, advertisement, *Collier's*, 27 May 1922, 23.
[7] Durham Duplex Razor Company, advertisement, *Collier's*, 27 May 1922, 25.
[8] Fitzgerald, *GG Var*, 3–4.

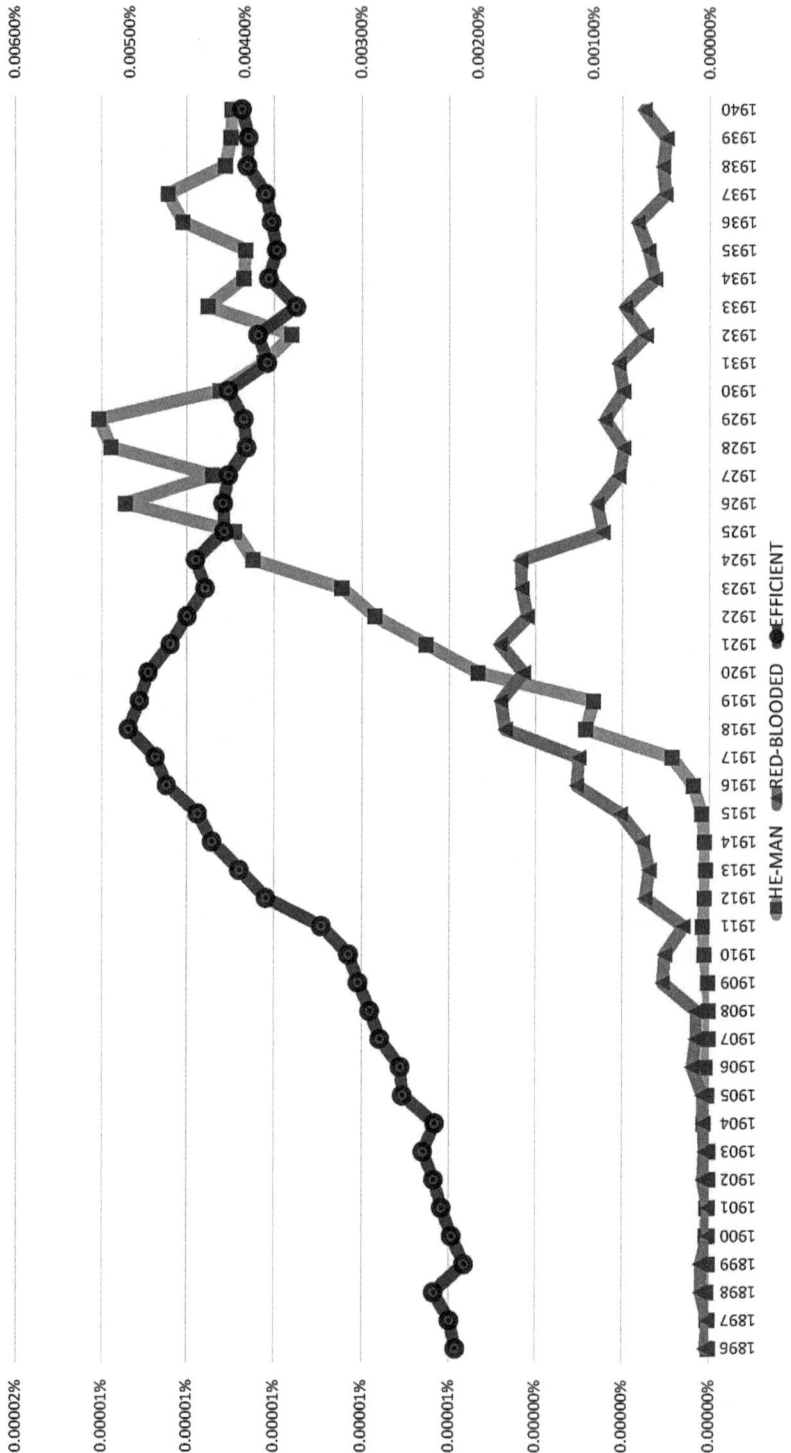

Figure A1.5 Early 1920s business speak: Efficient, Red Blooded, He-Man Ngram from the American English corpus (1896–1940). Red blooded and he-man are plotted on the primary axis and efficient on the secondary axis

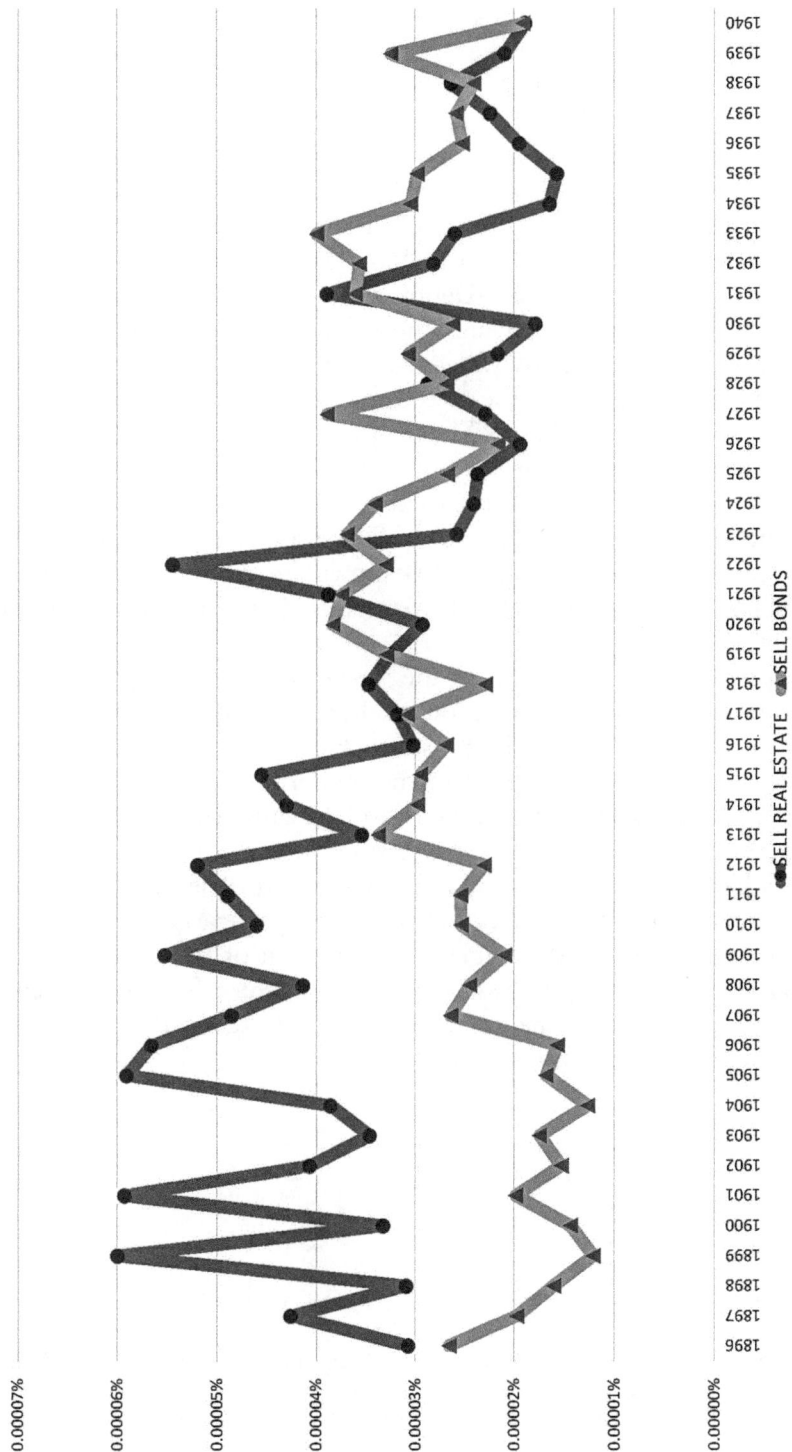

Figure A1.6 Sell Bonds, Sell Real Estate Ngram from the American English corpus (1896–1940)

perfectly exemplifies the styles of her day. Her "scant French-bobbed hair" (277) is noted when she is introduced; Figure A.7 shows that the popularity of the term "bobbed hair" increased by 281 percent between 1920 and 1924, the year it peaked. When she believes she is going to meet the Prince of Wales, she calls for her "'gold dress and the slippers with the real gold heels'" (282). Like Zelda in her desire for "the cutest cloth-of-gold dress,"[9] Rags wants increasingly fashionable clothes; Figure A.7 shows "gold dress" growing in popularity from 1921, to reach a pre-Depression peak in 1929.

Interest in the Prince of Wales himself can also be tracked through Ngram. Edward, Prince of Wales from 1911 to 1936, visited America frequently throughout the 1920s and was considered the world's most eligible bachelor.[10] Rags Martin-Jones claims she would "give a year of [her] life to see him for an hour" (281) and Yanci, in 1922's "The Popular Girl," is reported to have "'her walls simply plastered with pictures of him'" (44). Both of Fitzgerald's heroines were relatively early devotees; as Figure A.8 shows, interest in the Prince of Wales began to climb steeply in American English from 1918, to peak in 1926.

Fitzgerald's incisive grasp of the words and topics of his day is reflected in his deft manipulation of these to reflect his characters' social status. Jim, in "Dice, Brassknuckles and Guitar," is out of his element in New York and in the modern age. For Fitzgerald's contemporary readers, Jim's use of obsolete slang would have been a character detail that built that impression. By contrast, Rags Martin-Jones's hairstyle, clothes, and celebrity crush revealed that she was at the peak of fashion, indicating that she wasn't a generic flapper, but the ideal of the fashionable young woman of her time. Ngram analysis restores the fullness of these characters for the modern reader, and brings us a new appreciation of Fitzgerald's mastery of the cliches, fashions, and trends of his day.

[9] Zelda Sayre, "*The Beautiful and Damned*: Friend Husband's Latest," review of *The Beautiful and Damned* by F. Scott Fitzgerald [1922], in *F. Scott Fitzgerald in His Own Time*, eds. Matthew J. Bruccoli and Jackson R. Bryer (New York: Popular Library, 1971), 332.

[10] H. R. H. Edward, Duke of Windsor, *A King's Story: The Memoirs of the Duke of Windsor* (New York: G. P. Putnam's Sons, 1951), 203.

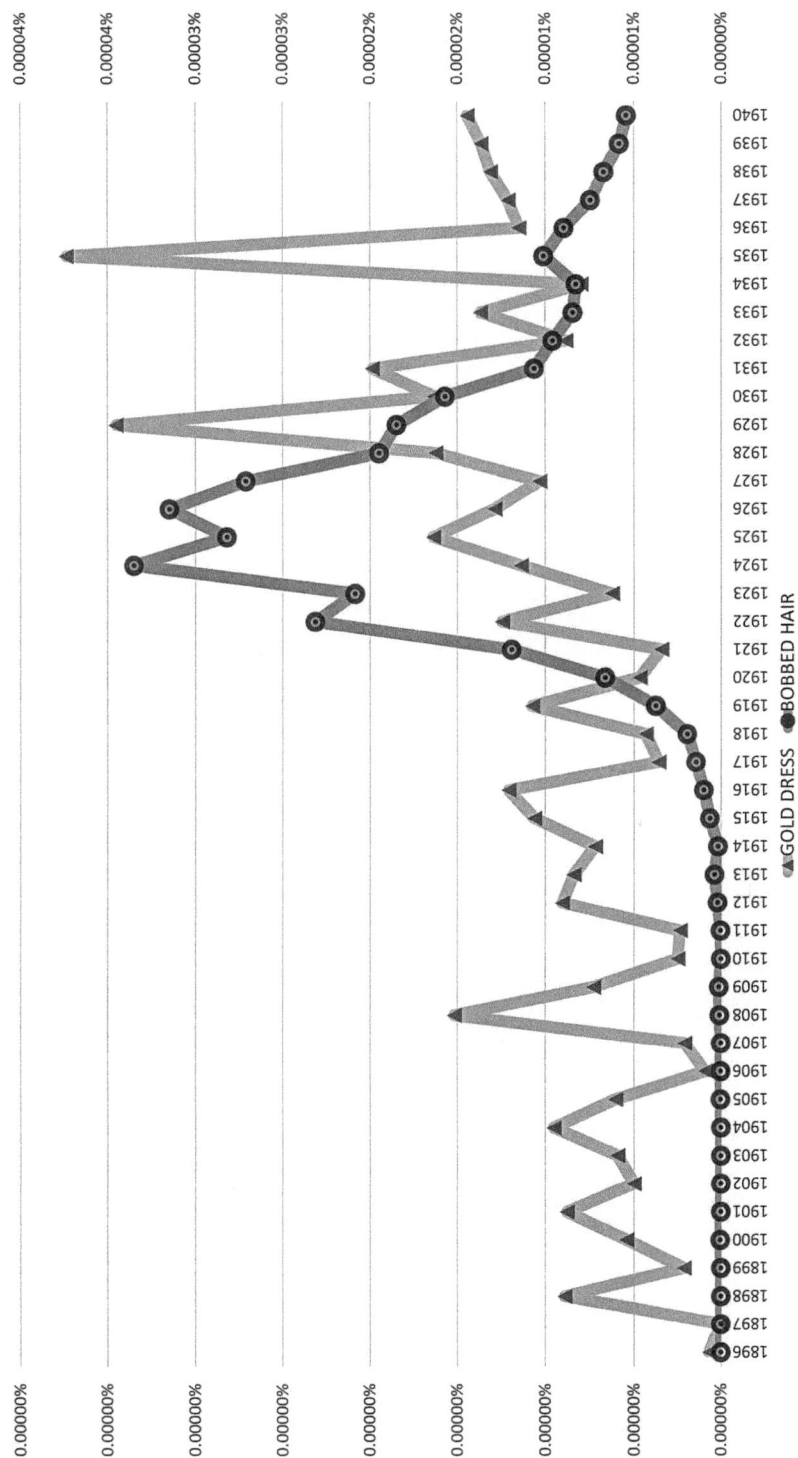

Figure A1.7 Early 1920s fashions: Bobbed Hair and Gold Dress Ngram from the American English corpus (1896–1940). Gold dress is plotted on the primary axis and bobbed hair on the secondary axis

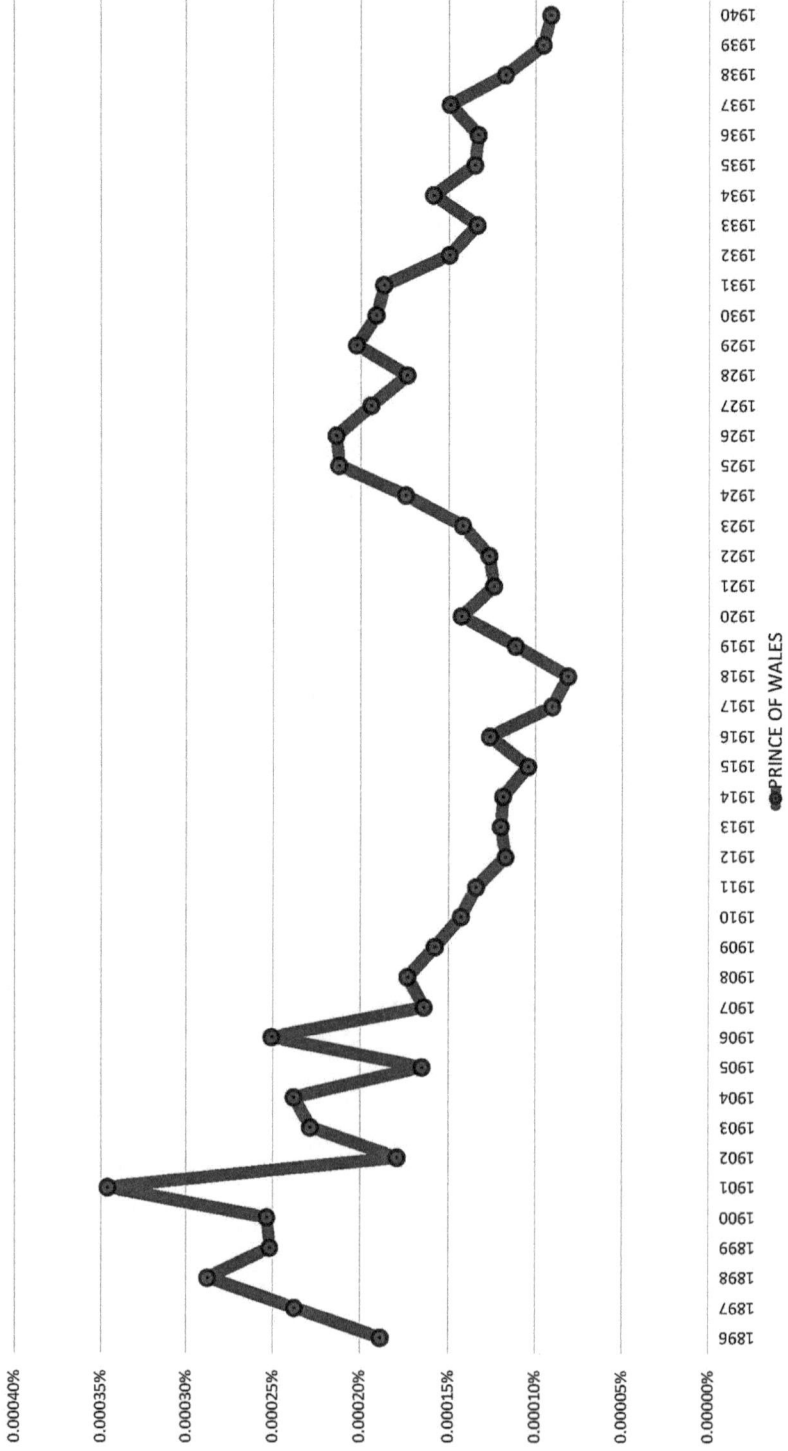

Figure A1.8 Prince of Wales Ngram from the American English corpus (1896–1940)

Appendix 2:
Magazine Publication Details

Jennifer Nolan

The chart below foregrounds the role of American magazines in the publication of the stories included in this volume. As such, it lists the magazine in which and date on which each story was published during this era in Fitzgerald's career, as well as how much each magazine paid for the story. While not a subject of this volume, the serialization of *The Beautiful and Damned* is also included because its exclusion gives a misleading picture of Fitzgerald's presence in the American periodical market during this period.[1]

The final column indicates how many times Fitzgerald had published in each magazine at the time each story appeared, as well as the total number of stories Fitzgerald published during his lifetime in each of the magazines, which provides insight into what role each magazine played at various points in his career. Because the focus of this volume is on the impact of the magazine market during Fitzgerald's life, posthumous publications have not been included in this tabulation. Non-fiction works, plays, book excerpts, and reprints have also been excluded (though they are referenced in the notes below, where relevant).

Most of the information in this chart is included in Appendix A of Bryant Mangum's *A Fortune Yet*, and it has also been checked against Fitzgerald's *Ledger*. Information for the final column was calculated from both sources. The notes below provide further information about each magazine.

---

[1] An argument could be made along the same lines that as an excerpt from *The Beautiful and Damned*, "The Far-Seeing Skeptics" (*Smart Set*, February 1922) should also be included in this list, but its brevity and placement in the magazine do not give it the same weight as the seven months that Fitzgerald's fiction consistently appeared in *Metropolitan* while the novel was serialized.

Title	Date published	Magazine	Price	Magazine stories
Jemina, the Mountain Girl	January 1921	*Vanity Fair*[2]	$100	1/1
His Russet Witch	February 1921	*Metropolitan*[3]	$900	2/4
Tarquin of Cheapside	February 1921	*Smart Set*[4]	$50	6/7
The Beautiful and Damned (serial)	September 1921– March 1922	*Metropolitan*	$7000	–
The Popular Girl	11 & 18 February 1922	*Saturday Evening Post*[5]	$1500	7/65
Two for a Cent	April 1922	*Metropolitan*	$900	3/4
The Curious Case of Benjamin Button	27 May 1922	*Collier's*[6]	$1000	1/2
The Diamond as Big as the Ritz	June 1922	*Smart Set*	$300	7/7
Winter Dreams	December 1922	*Metropolitan*	$900	4/4

[2] The difficulties with categorizing this piece are mentioned in the notes. As a humorous work, it fits in with the two other pieces Fitzgerald published in *Vanity Fair*, including "This is a Magazine" published the month before (December 1920).

[3] In May 1920, Fitzgerald signed a contract with *Metropolitan* granting them the right of first refusal on his next six stories, which ended in December 1922 when the magazine went into receivership after having accepted and published four of the five stories he submitted. For more details about this contract, see *As Ever*, 14 and *A Fortune Yet*, 41.

[4] The *Smart Set* was the magazine in which Fitzgerald had his first national commercial publication ("Babes in the Woods," September 1919) and was essential to his early career under editors H. L. Mencken and George Jean Nathan, who left in 1924 to start the *American Mercury*. In addition to the seven stories that appeared in the magazine during their tenure, *Smart Set* also published two of his one-act plays and an excerpt from *The Beautiful and Damned*, thus featuring his work ten times between 1919–1922. Fitzgerald never returned to the magazine after Mencken and Nathan's departure and it eventually ceased publication in 1930.

[5] "The Popular Girl" was sold in November 1921 to the *Post* and appeared in February 1922 while *Metropolitan* was serializing *The Beautiful and Damned* (September 1921–March 1922). Though Fitzgerald was still under contract with *Metropolitan* at this time, he'd become increasingly frustrated with the arrangement over their slow payments and on 14 September 1921 he wrote to Ober suggesting that "the contract is certainly null and void if they are not willing to pay cash within the month for short stories whether they intend publishing them in one month or one year" and that "they can't keep buying my stories agreeing to pay when they've finished paying for the serial" (*As Ever*, 26). As if to prove his point, *Metropolitan* accepted "Two for a Cent" in November 1921, the same month he sold "The Popular Girl" to the *Post*, which was published in February while *Metropolitan* was still paying off *The Beautiful and Damned* and had yet to pay for "Two for a Cent" (*As Ever*, 37).

[6] Ober submitted this story to *Collier's* (which was in a period of editorial upheaval) upon its rejection by *Metropolitan* in the spring of 1922. Fitzgerald would not be published in *Collier's* again until 1940 when "The End of Hate" was finally accepted in 1939 after a protracted period of revision that began in 1937.

Dice, Brassknuckles and Guitar[7]	May 1923	*Hearst's International*[8]	$1500	1/4
Hot and Cold Blood	August 1923	*Hearst's International*	$1500	2/4
Gretchen's Forty Winks	15 March 1924	*Saturday Evening Post*[9]	$1200	8/65
Diamond Dick and the First Law of Woman	April 1924	*Hearst's International*	$1500	3/4
The Third Casket	31 May 1924	*Saturday Evening Post*	$1750	9/65
Absolution	June 1924	*American Mercury*[10]	$118	1/2
Rags Martin-Jones and the Pr-nce of W-les	July 1924	*McCall's*[11]	$1750	1/3
The Sensible Thing[12]	5 July 1924	*Liberty*[13]	$1750	1/3
The Unspeakable Egg	12 July 1924	*Saturday Evening Post*	$1750	10/65
John Jackson's Arcady	26 July 1924	*Saturday Evening Post*	$1750	11/65

[7] *Hearst's International* consistently spells "brassknuckles" as one word, which is replicated throughout this volume.

[8] After his *Metropolitan* contract ended, Fitzgerald signed a contract with Hearst's *Cosmopolitan* in December 1922 for an option on his stories written in 1923, which were to appear in *Hearst's International*. Four stories were ultimately accepted under this contract, with his final appearance being "The Baby Party" (February 1925) (*As Ever*, 51). See introduction for further details.

[9] Though still early in his career with the *Post* (as the numbers indicate), with the publication of this story the magazine surpassed the *Smart Set* to become the place where Fitzgerald had most frequently published his stories, never to be supplanted.

[10] The *American Mercury* was started in 1924 when Alfred A. Knopf "offered to set up a monthly review" with Mencken and Nathan at the helm as editors after they parted with the *Smart Set* (Mott, *A History of American Magazines*, V, 4). "Absolution" was originally written as a portion of an early draft of *The Great Gatsby* during the summer of 1923 and, as he had often done with stories offered to the *Smart Set*, Fitzgerald sold it directly to Mencken rather than using Ober as his intermediary during the spring of 1924 (West, *All the Smart Young Men*, Appendix 2; Bryer and Kuehl, *Dear Scott/Dear Max*, 69). The story does not appear with the other stories in his list of earnings for 1924 in his *Ledger*, but rather is appended below the total for 1924 with the label "ommission" [*sic*] (*Ledger*, 55–56).

[11] Though this story was originally accepted as part of his contract with Hearst, it was returned, along with "The Sensible Thing," in January 1924 in exchange for "Diamond Dick and the First Law of Woman" and "The Baby Party." As he explained in a December 1922 letter, Fitzgerald was generally "not awfully keen about writing fiction for McCaulls," [*sic*] though he did publish two non-fiction articles there in 1924 and 1925 (*As Ever*, 51). He would not publish fiction again in *McCall's* until he was looking for a new market after his relationship with the *Post* soured in the early 1930s.

[12] Fitzgerald added quotation marks around this title for the publication of this story in *All the Sad Young Men*, which are included in most subsequent volumes. However, the title did not include quotation marks when the story was published in *Liberty*, and thus they are also not used in this volume.

[13] In 1924, *Liberty* was a new magazine explicitly positioning itself as a competitor to the *Saturday Evening Post* and Fitzgerald suggested that Ober send this story there after getting it back from Hearst because they're "evidently in the market for a little more serious stuff" (*As Ever*, 59). Though for different reasons, as with *McCall's*, Fitzgerald would not publish another short story in *Liberty* until he could no longer rely on the *Post* as a reliable source of income in the mid-1930s, though he did publish one article there in 1930, "Girls Believe in Girls."

Appendix 3:
Visual Contexts of Fitzgerald's Magazine Market

Jennifer Nolan

As described in the introduction to this volume, this appendix includes three sets of materials.

To demonstrate the visual contrasts between the two different ends of Fitzgerald's market – that is, the higher-brow, lower-circulation, lower-paying smart magazines and the lower-brow, higher-circulation, higher-paying popular magazines – this appendix includes the covers and opening pages of two of Fitzgerald's stories published in 1922. The first set features the June 1922 cover of the *Smart Set* where "The Diamond as Big as the Ritz" was published and the unadorned first page of the story, while the second set features the cover of the December 1922 issue of *Metropolitan* and the illustrated first page of "Winter Dreams." Gabrielle Dean has usefully suggested that "cover design serves the *prima facie* purpose of marking basic divisions in the periodical taxonomy,"[1] which is evident in the contrast between these two covers. As she argues, in the early 1920s, "to reinforce the reader's culturally elite, modern credentials, [*Smart Set*] cover images had to be genuinely startling, intriguing, lively, or mischievous,"[2] as seen in A. G. L's modishly angular dancers, while, as I have argued, Frederick Duncan's cover girl is part of *Metropolitan*'s "attempt to position itself as an authority on young women" to save itself from financial ruin.[3] The visual differences between the austere first page of "The Diamond as Big as the Ritz" and the expressiveness of Arthur William Brown's

---

[1] Gabrielle Dean, "Cover Story: The *Smart Set's* Clever Packaging, 1908–1923," *The Journal of Modern Periodical Studies* 4, no. 1 (2013): 3.

[2] Dean, 25.

[3] Jennifer Nolan, "Illustrating 'Winter Dreams,'" *F. Scott Fitzgerald Review* 19 (2021): 39.

dominating opening illustration for "Winter Dreams" are also striking representations of how differently each magazine was presenting itself and the work it published.

The final set of images reproduces the entirety of "Gretchen's Forty Winks" from the 15 March 1924 issue of the *Saturday Evening Post*, along with the facing advertisements, to provide modern readers with a sense of what Fitzgerald's stories looked like embedded within these highly visual and commercial spaces. As I have argued elsewhere,[4] readers of Fitzgerald's stories in the *Post* encountered the text within a nexus of other materials that shaped and directed how the stories were read and understood. In this case – which is discussed in greater detail in the introduction – the illustrations and surrounding advertisements reinforce the commercial values of the magazine and seeing them together vividly emphasizes the interrelationship between literature and commerce in these spaces.

---

[4]   Jennifer Nolan, "Reading 'Babylon Revisited' as a *Post* Text: F. Scott Fitzgerald, George Horace Lorimer, and the *Saturday Evening Post* Audience," *Book History* 20 (2017): 353.

Figure A3.1 Cover, *Smart Set* (June 1922). Cover art by A.G.L.

The Diamond as Big as the Ritz

[*A Complete Novelette*]

By F. Scott Fitzgerald

(Author of "This Side of Paradise," "The Beautiful and Damned," etc.)

CHAPTER I

JOHN T. UNGER came from a family that had been well known in Hades—a small town on the Mississippi River—for several generations. John's father had held the amateur golf championship through many a heated contest; Mrs. Unger was known "from hot-box to hot-bed," as the local phrase went, for her coiffures and her public addresses; and young John T. Unger, who had just turned sixteen, had danced all the latest dances from New York almost before he put on long trousers. And now, for a certain time, he was to be away from home. That respect for a New England education which is the bane of all provincial places, which drains them yearly of their most promising young men, had seized upon his parents. Nothing would suit them but that he should go to St. Midas' School near Boston. Their minds were made up—Hades was too small to hold their darling and gifted son. Now in Hades—as you must know if you ever have been there—the names of the more fashionable preparatory schools and colleges mean very little. The inhabitants have been so long out of the world that, though they make a great show of keeping up to date in dress and manners and literature, they depend to a great extent on hearsay, and a function that in Hades would be considered elaborate would doubtless be hailed by a Chicago beef-princess as "perhaps a little tacky."

John T. Unger was on the eve of departure. Mrs. Unger, with maternal fatuity, packed his trunks full of linen suits and electric fans, and Mr. Unger presented his son with a brand-new asbestos pocket-book stuffed with money.

"Remember, you are always welcome here," he said. "You can be sure, boy, that we'll keep the home fires burning."

"I know," answered John huskily.

"Don't forget who you are and where you come from," continued his father proudly, "and you can do nothing to harm you. You are an Unger—from Hades."

So the old man and the young shook hands and John walked away with tears streaming from his eyes. Ten minutes later he had passed outside the city limits and he stopped to look back for the last time. Over the gates the old-fashioned Victorian motto seemed strangely attractive to him. His father had tried time and time again to have it changed to something with a little more push and verve about it, such as "Hades—Home of Business Opportunity," or else a plain "Welcome" sign set over a hearty handshake pricked out in electric lights. The old motto was a little depressing, Mr. Unger had thought.

So John took his last look and then set his face resolutely toward his destination. And yet, as he turned away, it seemed to him that the lights of Hades against the sky were full of a warm and passionate beauty.

St. Midas' School is half an hour from Boston in a Rols-Pearse motor

5

Figure A3.2 Opening page of "The Diamond as Big as the Ritz," *Smart Set* (June 1922), 5.

Figure A3.3 Cover, *Metropolitan* (December 1922). Cover art by Frederick Duncan. The Matthew J. & Arlyn Bruccoli Collection of F. Scott Fitzgerald, Irvin Department of Rare Books and Special Collections, University of South Carolina Libraries.

METROPOLITAN

Winter Dreams

by
F. Scott
Fitzgerald

Illustrations
by
Arthur
William
Brown

"I don't know what's the matter with me. Last night I thought I was in love with a man and to-night I think I'm in love with you—"

ARTHUR WILLIAM BROWN

SOME of the caddies were poor as sin and lived in one-room houses with a neurasthenic cow in the front yard, but Dexter Green's father owned the second best grocery store in Dillard—the best one was " The Hub," patronized by the wealthy people from Lake Erminie—and Dexter caddied only for pocket-money.

In the fall when the days became crisp and grey and the long Minnesota winter shut down like the white lid of a box, Dexter's skis moved over the snow that hid the fairways of the golf course. At these times the country gave him a feeling of profound melancholy —it offended him that the links should lie in enforced gallowness, haunted by ragged sparrows for the long season. It was dreary, too, that on the tees where the gay colors fluttered in summer there were now only the desolate sand-boxes knee-deep in crusted ice. When he crossed the hills the wind blew cold as misery, and if the sun was out he tramped with his eyes squinted up against the hard dimensionless glare.

In April the winter ceased abruptly. The snow ran down into Lake Erminie scarcely tarrying for the early golfers to brave the season with red and black balls. Without elation,

Figure A3.4 Opening page of "Winter Dreams," *Metropolitan* (December 1922), 11. Illustration by Arthur William Brown. The Matthew J. & Arlyn Bruccoli Collection of F. Scott Fitzgerald, Irvin Department of Rare Books and Special Collections, University of South Carolina Libraries.

Figure A3.5 "Gretchen's Forty Winks" and facing pages. *Saturday Evening Post* (15 March 1924), 14–15, 128–133. Illustrations on pp. 14 and 15 by Charles D. Mitchell.

"You've been going to the movies too much," he said dryly.

"What?" Tompkins looked at him with some irritation. "Movies? I've hardly ever been to the movies in my life. I think the movies are atrocious. My opinions on life are drawn from my own observations. I believe in a balanced life."

"What's that?" demanded Roger.

"Well—" he hesitated—"probably the best way to tell you would be to describe my own day. Would that seem horribly egoistic?"

"Oh, no!" Gretchen looked at him with interest. "I'd love to hear about it."

"Well, in the morning I get up and go through a series of exercises. I've got one room fitted up as a little gymnasium, and I punch the bag and do shadow boxing and weight pulling for an hour. Then after a cold bath—There's a thing now! Do you take a daily cold bath?"

"No," admitted Roger, "I take a hot bath in the evening three or four times a week."

A horrified silence fell. Tompkins and Gretchen exchanged a glance as if something obscene had been said.

"What's the matter?" broke out Roger, glancing from one to the other in some irritation. "You know I don't take a bath every day—I haven't got the time."

Tompkins gave a prolonged sigh.

"After my bath," he continued, "I have breakfast and drive to my office in New York, where I work until four. Then I lay off, and if it's summer I hurry out here for nine holes of golf, or if it's winter I play squash for an hour at my club. Then a good snappy game of bridge until dinner. Dinner is liable to have something to do with business, but in a pleasant way. Perhaps I've just finished a house for some customer and he wants me to be on hand for his first party to see that the lighting is soft enough and all that sort of thing. Or maybe I sit down with a good book of poetry and spend the evening alone. At any rate, I do something every night to get me out of myself."

"It must be wonderful," said Gretchen enthusiastically. "I wish we lived like that."

Tompkins bent forward earnestly over the table.

"You can," he said impressively. "There's no reason why you shouldn't. Look here, if Roger'll play nine holes of golf every day it'll do wonders for him. He won't know himself. He'll do his work better, never get that tired, nervous feeling —— What's the matter?"

He broke off. Roger had perceptibly yawned.

"Roger," cried Gretchen sharply, "there's no need to be so rude. If you did what George said, you'd be a lot better off." She turned indignantly to their host. "The latest is that he's going to work at night for the next six weeks. He says he's going to pull down the blinds and shut us up like hermits in a cave. He's been doing it every Sunday for the last year; now he's going to do it every night for six weeks."

Tompkins shook his head sadly.

"At the end of six weeks," he remarked, "he'll be starting for the sanitarium. Let me tell you, every private hospital in New York is full of cases like yours. You just strain the human nervous system a little too far, and bang!—you've broken something. And in order to save sixty hours you're laid up sixty weeks for repairs." He broke off, changed his tone and turned to Gretchen with a smile. "Not to mention what happens to you. It seems to me it's the wife rather than the husband who bears the brunt of these insane periods of overwork."

"I don't mind," protested Gretchen loyally.

"Yes, she does," said Roger grimly; "she minds like the devil. She's a shortsighted little egg and she thinks it's going to be forever until I get started and she can have some new clothes. But it can't be helped. The saddest thing about women is that, after all, their best trick is to sit down and fold their hands."

"Your ideas on women are about twenty years out of date," said Tompkins pityingly. "Women won't sit down and wait any more."

"Then they'd better marry men of forty," insisted Roger stubbornly. "If a girl marries a young man for love she ought to be willing to make any sacrifice within reason, so long as her husband keeps going ahead."

"Let's not talk about it," said Gretchen impatiently. "Please, Roger, let's have a good time just this once."

When Tompkins dropped them in front of their house at eleven Roger and Gretchen stood for a moment on the sidewalk looking at the winter moon. There was a fine, damp, dusty snow in the air and Roger drew a long breath of it and put his arm around Gretchen exultantly.

"I can make more money than he can," he said tensely. "And I'll be doing it in just forty days."

"Forty days," she sighed. "It seems such a long time—when everybody else is always having fun. If I could only sleep for forty days."

"Why don't you, honey? Just take forty winks, and when you wake up everything'll be fine."

She was silent for a moment.

"Roger," she asked thoughtfully, "do you think George meant what he said about taking me horseback riding on Sunday?"

Roger frowned.

"I don't know. Probably not—I hope to heaven he didn't." He hesitated. "As a matter of fact, he made me sort of sore tonight—all that junk about his cold bath."

With their arms about each other, they started up the walk to the house.

"I'll bet he doesn't take a cold bath every morning," continued Roger ruminatively; "or three times a week, either." He fumbled in his pocket for the key and inserted it in the lock with savage precision. Then he turned around defiantly. "I'll bet he hasn't had a bath for a month."

II

AFTER a fortnight of intensive work, Roger Halsey's days blurred into each other and passed by in blocks of twos and threes and fours. From eight until 5:30 he was in his office. Then a half hour on the commuting train, where he scrawled notes on the backs of envelopes under the dull yellow light. By 7:30 his crayons, shears and

(Continued on Page 128)

"I'm the Friend of the Family and I'd Just as Soon Joy the Missus as the Mister." He Smiled Playfully. "But if I Were You, Roger, I'd Put Away My Work and Get a Good Night's Sleep"

128   THE SATURDAY EVENING POST   March 15, 1924

(Continued from Page 125)

My principal worry usually related to the success of the corporations we were financing. Try as you will, you cannot give absolute assurance, and yet that is what one is really promising to most of those who buy. The promise may be expressed or implied, but it is usually taken for granted. The buyer thinks it is there. These were speculative stocks and, of course, had the additional handicap of not being listed anywhere. When someone wanted to sell in an emergency, there wasn't any particular place to offer them, and no established market. This often resulted in very low prices being accepted even when the value was there. In short, they were just about the kind of stocks that investors with one thousand dollars or less ought to let alone—and those were the investors we principally interested. Nearly everyone knows something about how to make money, probably less than half know how to save, but when it comes to investing, very few know anything at all. Yet all these hurdles stand between a man and his comfortable old age.

My belated awakening, for which I am indebted to that bricklayer, was hurried along by an accidental meeting with a competitor. He was a cynical person, and his comments quickly opened my eyes to the fact that his appeals for men were consciously leveled to attract the type of Ralph Peters. He supposed that I had also taken a general survey of my business and knew what I was doing. But I had been too busy. In fact, I was on the job every morning between eight and nine o'clock and often remained until ten at night. My competitor didn't. He rarely showed his face. He was a legend to his men, just as I was, but an aloof sort of Olympian creature about whom they heard interesting fiction; they didn't see him often. When they did he was silent. That was his pose. He spent an hour or two in his office during the afternoon, remained up late every night and usually slept until nearly noon. But he knew all about my business and confessed that he had copied some of my methods. That interested me and left me incredulous, because I didn't think it possible for such a cold person to copy anything I had done.

All Worked by Formula

The next day I visited his establishment and the scales fell from my eyes. He had copied my formula, and I saw at once that it was fairly easy. The only difference was that I put myself into my efforts, and he hired other men who did just as well. After all, it is merely a formula. A crew to do the inspiring is easily recruited, and many of them will be just as sincere as I was. He had some sort of master of ceremonies, or yell leader, or whatever you might call him, whose voice had a peculiar metallic quality and astounding volume. When that man flooded a room with sound everyone was galvanized into attention. In fact, looking him over calmly I thought he was probably more effective than I.

Up to that time I had supposed there was no business institution similar to mine. The idea was original with me and grew out of my experience, but I soon found out that there were large numbers of them; some were much more ably managed than mine, while several were out-and-out frauds dealing only in worthless stocks. The latter would have a brief but prosperous career in some city, then move to another as soon as the volume of business declined.

The process of awakening, thus begun, was hurried along by an illness which removed me from the pressing details of the business. Lying on my bed in the hospital I had time to do a lot of thinking. First of all, I realized that I hadn't done any real thinking for several years. I hadn't viewed life as a whole or my business from any better position of vantage than the center of it, which, I should say, is the worst possible position for a general survey. For one thing, I hadn't asked myself honestly

and frankly whether I was doing what I wanted to do or just grabbing around wildly, very much as on the day I rushed into the restaurant to get a job as dishwasher. It occurred to me as a new thought, while I was lying there staring at the ceiling, that I wasn't going to live forever, and if there really was anything I'd like to do it was time to be doing it.

I began with the business and after half a day of thought on the subject decided that I never had done with it what I started out to do and that probably the need for my original great mission existed mainly in my imagination. Next I faced the fact that I had joined hands with that crew of preachers of discontent who prescribe more money as a cure for all ills. "Executive positions," I read in big letters in my advertisement in the newspaper; and then I rolled over to enjoy a good laugh. Yes, executive positions. I had one, and this was what it did to me. Perhaps if we were better executives it wouldn't lay so many of us on our backs, but the fact remains that executive positions are pretty good business getters for hospitals. And there was I, holding them out as bait to be nibbled at principally by men trying to dodge work. The whole thing became ridiculous, and I realized that I was through with my business. About the best I could say for it was that it was entirely legal, and we had financed some worthy enterprises.

Back to the Farm

What next, then? Did I wish to practice law? Decidedly not. In fact, I never had wanted to. I was in a frame of mind to examine life with more calmness than ever before. When a man is physically weak, but with a clear mind, and no telephones are attacking him, he throws overboard a lot of junk that has previously seemed important. At that moment ten thousand a year or any other sum had none of the bugle-call effect I used to put into it.

A new realization of the importance of contentment came over me. Checking back over the thousands of men I had known, I realized that a lot of them must have found their real pleasure in some simple activity in life to which no particular glamour attaches. I realized that men could *enjoy* running trains or repairing automobiles or putting engines together or setting type. The fanatic who attacks them with a standard of happiness based upon "How much do you make?" is their enemy. But that standard has terrific force in this country. Five have the nerve to face it without quailing. There was my father, a good farmer, a happy man, but with an urge to lift me out of farming, as though it were not so good as some occupation which enabled one to handle more money. Thinking of my father brought to my mind like a flash of recollection from some forgotten previous existence, that the one thing I would really like to do was fix up that farm, plant an apple orchard, put a dam in the creek and get some fish from the government hatchery. The more I thought of it the longer grew the list of things I had always wanted to do on that farm. The new inspiration actually helped my recovery. I had found my real self and I was a farmer boy who wanted to see the sun come up again, and wander down the pasture lane looking for rabbits. I had been chased away from that life by fear of not earning an imposing sum of money.

When I left the hospital I retired from the business and went to the only home I had ever known, the farm. I didn't wreck the business; no use doing that. My retiring isn't going to remove that sort of enterprise from the world, and I've reached the point where I'm not so certain about everything as I once was. There may be something to be said for those enterprises, and since there are now a lot of them, mine one's. I turned it over to the men who had helped me build it.

GRETCHEN'S FORTY WINKS

(Continued from Page 15)

sheets of white cardboard were spread over the living-room table and he labored there with much grunting and sighing until midnight, while Gretchen lay on the sofa with a book and the doorbell tinkled occasionally behind the drawn blinds. At twelve there was always an argument as to whether he would come to bed. He would

agree to come after he had cleared up everything; but as he was invariably sidetracked by half a dozen new ideas he usually found Gretchen sound asleep when he tiptoed upstairs.

Sometimes it was three o'clock before Roger squashed his last cigarette into the

(Continued on Page 130)

THE SATURDAY EVENING POST

129

To the Million or More Members of the Radio Broadcasting Public Elgin Makes This Announcement—

THROUGH the coöperation of the Chicago Board of Trade Broadcasting Station WDAP at the Drake Hotel, Chicago, and the Elgin Time Observatory of the Elgin National Watch Company—a new and forward-looking time-broadcasting service has been put into effect.

It has already demonstrated its place in the practical life of a busy nation.

Three times daily, Central Standard Time, the precise time supplied over direct wire from the Elgin Time Observatory, is broadcast through Station WDAP (360 meters, 833 kilocycles) by the Chicago Board of Trade.

As a practical step in using this service, please note that the time-broadcasting begins at 3:12, 5:57 and 10:57 p.m.—extends over three minutes each period—and the final signal is given at 3:15, 6:00 and 11:00 p.m. precisely.

Starting at 3:12 p.m., for instance, a dot is heard each second for 29 seconds. The 30th second is silent. Then again a dot each second for 25 seconds. Then 5 seconds of silence. This completes one minute of broadcasting.

The second minute duplicates the first.

The third minute also—29 dots, 1 second silence; 25 dots, 5 seconds silence.

Then a long dash is heard at exactly 3:15 p.m. This is Central Standard Time.

Listeners in the Eastern Time Zone will receive

Elgin "Streamline" in 25-year green or white Gold filled engraved case. $40.

Elgin Time at 4:12, 6:57 and 11:57 p.m. precisely.

In the Mountain Time Zone, at 2:12, 4:57 and 9:57 p.m. In the Pacific Time Zone, at 1:12, 3:57 and 8:57 p.m.

The Elgin Time Observatory is the source of the precise time standards of the Elgin work shops and timing rooms. It takes the time from the stars, and transmits it to all departments of the Elgin factories, thereby facilitating the production of dependable watches.

Now, with this time-broadcasting service, the Elgin Time Observatory assumes a new and broader significance than ever before.

Located in the heart of the great Central States, it serves thousands of short-distance receivers with precise time direct thrice daily. This service is also available to owners of long-distance radio sets anywhere in the country.

The day seems near at hand, when the owner of any watch of any make, anywhere in the United States, may check daily with the precise Elgin time.

It will bring home to him, too, the professional timekeeping standards embodied in the Elgin Watch.

ELGIN
The Professional Timekeeper

ELGIN NATIONAL WATCH COMPANY · ELGIN, U.S.A.

(Continued from Page 128)

overloaded ash tray, and he would undress in the darkness, hollow as a ghost, but with a sense of triumph that he had lasted out another day.

Christmas came and went and he scarcely noticed that it was gone. He remembered it afterwards as the day he completed the window cards for Garrod's shoes. This was one of the eight large accounts for which he was pointing in January—if he got half of them he was assured a quarter of a million dollars' worth of business during the year.

But the world outside his business became a chaotic dream. He was aware that on three cool December Sundays George Tompkins had taken Gretchen horseback riding and that another time she had gone out with him in his automobile to spend the day skiing on the country-club hill. A picture of Tompkins, in an expensive frame, had appeared one morning on their bedroom wall. And one night he was shocked into a startled protest when Gretchen went to the theater with Tompkins in town.

But his work was almost done. Daily now his layouts arrived from the printers until seven of them were piled and docketed in his office safe. He knew how good they were.

Money alone couldn't buy such work; more than he realized himself, it had been a labor of love.

December tumbled like a dead leaf from the calendar. There was an agonizing week when he had to give up coffee because it made his heart pound so. If he could hold on now for four days—three days——

On Thursday afternoon H. G. Garrod was to arrive in New York. On Wednesday evening Roger came home at seven to find Gretchen poring over the December bills with a strange expression in her eyes.

"What's the matter?"

She nodded at the bills. He ran through them, his brow wrinkling in a frown.

"Gosh!"

"I can't help it," she burst out suddenly. "They're terrible."

"Well, I didn't marry you because you were a wonderful housekeeper. I'll manage about the bills some way. Don't worry your pretty head about it."

She regarded him coldly.

"You talk as if I were a child."

"I have to," he said with sudden irritation.

"Well, at least I'm not a piece of bric-a-brac that you can just put somewhere and forget."

He knelt down by her quickly and took her arms in his hands.

"Gretchen, listen!" he said breathlessly. "For God's sake, don't go to pieces now! We're both all stored up with malice and reproach, and if we had a quarrel it'd be terrible. I love you, Gretchen. Say you love me—quick!"

"You know I love you."

The quarrel was averted, but there was an unnatural tenseness all through dinner. It came to a climax afterwards when he began to spread his working materials on the table.

"Oh, Roger," she protested, "I thought you didn't have to work tonight."

"I didn't think I'd have to, but something came up."

"I've invited George Tompkins over."

"Oh, gosh!" he exclaimed. "Well, I'm sorry, honey, but you'll have to phone him not to come."

"He's left," she said. "He's coming straight from town. He'll be here any minute now."

Roger groaned. It occurred to him to send them both to the movies, but somehow the suggestion stuck on his lips. He did not want her at the movies; he wanted her here, where he could look up and know she was by his side.

George Tompkins arrived breezily at eight o'clock.

"Aha!" he cried reprovingly, coming into the room. "Still at it."

Roger agreed coolly that he was.

"Better quit—better quit before you have to." He sat down with a long sigh of physical comfort and lit a cigarette. "Take it from a fellow who's looked into the question scientifically. We can stand so much, and then—bang!"

"If you'll excuse me—" Roger made his voice as polite as possible—"I'm going upstairs and finish this work."

"Just as you like, Roger." George waved his hand carelessly. "It isn't that I mind. I'm the friend of the family and I'd just as soon see the missus as the mister." He smiled playfully. "But if I were you,

Roger, I'd put away my work and get a good night's sleep."

When Roger had spread out his materials on the bed upstairs he found that he could still hear the rumble and murmur of their voices through the thin floor. He began wondering what they found to talk about. As he plunged deeper into his work his mind had a tendency to revert sharply to his question, and several times he arose and paced nervously up and down the room.

The bed was ill adapted to his work. Several times the paper slipped from the board on which it rested and the pencil punched through. Everything was wrong tonight. Letters and figures blurred before his eyes, and as an accompaniment to the beating of his temples came those persistent murmuring voices.

At ten he realized that he had done nothing for more than an hour, and with a sudden exclamation he gathered together his papers, replaced them in his portfolio and went downstairs. They were sitting together on the sofa when he came in.

"Oh, hello!" cried Gretchen, rather unnecessarily, he thought. "We were just discussing you."

"Thank you," he answered ironically. "What particular part of my anatomy was under the scalpel?"

"Your health," said Tompkins jovially.

"My health's all right," answered Roger shortly.

"But you look at it so selfishly, old fella," cried Tompkins. "You only consider yourself in the matter. Don't you think Gretchen has any rights? If you were working on a wonderful sonnet or a portrait of some madonna or something"—he glanced at Gretchen's Titian hair—"why, then I'd say go ahead. But you're not. It's just some silly advertisement about how to sell Peptone's hair tonic, and if all the hair tonic ever made was dumped into the ocean tomorrow the world wouldn't be one bit the worse for it."

"Wait a minute," said Roger angrily; "that's not quite fair. I'm not kidding myself about the importance of my work—it's just as useless as the stuff you do. But to Gretchen and me it's just about the most important thing in the world."

"Are you implying that my work is useless?" demanded Tompkins incredulously.

"No; not if it brings happiness to some poor marker of a paste manufacturer who doesn't know how to spend his money."

Tompkins and Gretchen exchanged a glance.

"Oh-h-h!" exclaimed Tompkins ironically. "I didn't realize that all these years I've just been wasting my time."

"You're a loafer," said Roger hotly.

"Me?" cried Tompkins angrily. "You call me a loafer because I have a little balance in my life and find time to do interesting things? Because I play hard as well as work hard and don't let myself get to be a dull, tiresome drudge?"

Both men were angry now and their voices had risen, though on Tompkins' face there still remained the semblance of a smile.

"What I object to," said Roger steadily, "is that for the last six weeks you seem to have done all your playing around here."

"Roger!" cried Gretchen. "What do you mean by talking like that?"

"Just what I said."

"You've just lost your temper." Tompkins lit a cigarette with ostentatious coolness. "You're so nervous from overwork you don't know what you're saying. You're on the verge of a nervous break——"

"Shut up!" cried Roger fiercely.

"Calm down, yourself! If you took a cold bath every morning you wouldn't be so excitable."

"You get out of here!" Roger's voice was trembling. "You get out of here right now—before I throw you out!"

Tompkins got angrily to his feet.

"You—you throw me out?" he cried incredulously.

They were actually moving toward each other when Gretchen stepped between them, and grabbing Tompkins' arm urged him toward the door.

"He's acting like a fool, George, but you better get out," she cried, groping in the hall for his hat.

"He insulted me!" shouted Tompkins. "He threatened to throw me out!"

"Never mind, George," pleaded Gretchen. "He doesn't know what he's saying. Please go! I'll see you at ten o'clock tomorrow."

She opened the door.

(Continued on Page 132)

He never knew why

ALMOST the first thing that greeted him on his return to town was a newspaper announcement telling him that the girl he had hoped to marry was engaged to another man. And, moreover, to a man he had never heard of before.

This accounted for her silence during his absence—not a single letter all the time he was away.

And he never found the real reason why his courtship had been so complete a failure.

* * * *

That's the insidious thing about halitosis (unpleasant breath). You, yourself, rarely know when you have it. And even your closest friends won't tell you.

Sometimes, of course, halitosis comes from some deep-seated organic disorder that requires professional advice. But usually—and fortunately—halitosis is only a local condition that yields to the regular use of Listerine as a mouth wash and gargle. It is an interesting thing that this well-known antiseptic that has been in use for years for surgical dressings, possesses those unusual properties as a breath deodorant.

It halts fasid fermentation in the mouth and leaves the breath sweet, fresh and clean. Not by substituting some other odor but by really removing the old one. The Listerine odor itself quickly disappears. So the systematic use of Listerine puts you on the safe and polite side.

Your druggist will supply you with Listerine. He sells lots of it. It has dozens of different uses as a safe antiseptic and has been trusted as such for half a century. Read the interesting little booklet that comes with every bottle. —*Lambert Pharmacal Company, Saint Louis, U. S. A.*

(Continued from Page 130)

"You won't see him at ten o'clock tomorrow," said Roger steadily. "He's not coming to this house any more."

Tompkins turned to Gretchen.

"It's his house," he suggested. "Perhaps we'd better meet at mine."

Then he was gone and Gretchen had shut the door behind him. Her eyes were full of angry tears.

"See what you've done!" she sobbed. "The only friend I had, the only person in the world who liked me enough to treat me decently is insulted by my husband in my own house."

She threw herself on the sofa and began to cry passionately into the pillows.

"He brought it on himself," said Roger stubbornly. "I've stood as much as my self-respect will allow. I don't want you going out with him any more."

"I will go out with him!" cried Gretchen wildly. "I'll go out with him all I want! Do you think it's any fun living here with you?"

"Gretchen," he said coldly, "get up and put on your hat and coat and go out that door and never come back!"

Her mouth fell slightly ajar.

"But I don't want to get out," she said dazedly.

"Well then, behave yourself," and he added in a gentler voice, "I thought you were going to sleep for this forty days."

"Oh, yes," she cried bitterly, "easy enough to say! But I'm tired of sleeping." She got up, faced him defiantly. "And what's more, I'm going riding with George Tompkins tomorrow."

"You won't go out with him if I have to take you to New York and sit you down in my office until I get through."

She looked at him with rage in her eyes.

"I hate you," she said slowly. "And I'd like to take all the work you've done and tear it up and throw it in the fire. And just to give you something to worry about tomorrow, I probably won't be here when you get back."

She got up from the sofa very deliberately, looked at her flushed, tear-stained face in the mirror. Then she ran upstairs and slammed herself into the bedroom.

Automatically Roger spread out his work on the living-room table. The bright colors of the designs, the vivid ladies—Gretchen had posed for one of them—holding orange ginger ale or glistening silk hosiery, dazzled his mind into a sort of coma. His restless crayon moved here and there over the pictures, shifting a block of letters half an inch to the right, trying a dozen blues for a cool blue, and eliminating the word that made a phrase anæmic and pale. Half an hour passed—he was deep in the work now; there was no sound in the room but the velvety scratch of the crayon over the glossy board.

After a long while he looked at his watch—it was after three. The wind had come up outside and was rushing by the house corners in loud, alarming swoops, like a heavy body falling through space. He stopped his work and listened. He was not tired now, but his head felt as if it was covered with bulging veins like those pictures that hang in doctors' offices showing a body stripped of decent skin. He put his hands to his head and felt it all over. It seemed to him that on his temple the veins were knotty and brittle around an old scar.

Suddenly he began to be afraid. A hundred warnings he had heard swept into his mind. People did wreck themselves with overwork, and his body and mind were of the same vulnerable and perishable stuff. For the first time he found himself envying George Tompkins' calm nerves and healthy body. He arose and began pacing the room in a panic.

"I've got to sleep," he whispered to himself tensely. "Otherwise I'm going crazy."

He rubbed his hand over his eyes and returned to the table to put up his work, but his fingers were shaking so that he could scarcely grasp the board. The sway of a bare branch against the window made him start and cry out. He sat down on the sofa and tried to think.

"Stop! Stop! Stop!" the clock said. "Stop! Stop! Stop!"

"I can't stop," he answered aloud. "I can't afford to stop."

Listen! Why, there was the wolf at the door now! He could hear its sharp claws scrape along the varnished woodwork. He jumped up, and running to the front door flung it open; then started back with a ghastly cry. An enormous wolf was standing on the porch, glaring at him with red, malignant eyes. As he watched it the hair bristled on its neck; it gave a low growl and disappeared in the darkness. Then Roger realized with a silent, mirthless laugh that it was the police dog from over the way.

Dragging his limbs wearily into the kitchen, he brought the alarm clock into the living room and set it for seven. Then he wrapped himself in his overcoat, lay down on the sofa and fell immediately into a heavy, dreamless sleep.

When he awoke the light was still shining feebly, but the room was the gray color of a winter morning. He got up, and looking anxiously at his hands found to his relief that they no longer trembled. He felt much better. Then he began to remember in detail the events of the night before, and his brow drew up again in three shallow wrinkles. There was work ahead of him, twenty-four hours of work; and Gretchen, whether she wanted to or not, must sleep for one more day.

Roger's mind glowed suddenly as if he had just thought of a new advertising idea. A few minutes later he was hurrying through the sharp morning air to Kingsley's drug store.

"Is Mr. Kingsley down yet?"

The druggist's head appeared around the corner of the prescription room.

"Here I am."

"Oh, I wonder if I can talk to you alone."

"Come right back here, Mr. Halsey."

At 7:30, Roger, back home again, walked into his own kitchen. The general housework girl had just arrived and was taking off her hat.

"Bebé"—he was not on familiar terms with her; this was her name—"I want you to cook Mrs. Halsey's breakfast right away. I'll take it up myself."

It struck Bebé that this was an unusual service for so busy a man to render his wife, but if she had seen his conduct when he had carried the tray from the kitchen she would have been even more surprised. For he set it down on the dining-room table and put into the coffee half a teaspoonful of a white substance that was not powdered sugar. Then he mounted the stairs and opened the door of the bedroom.

Gretchen woke up with a start, glanced at the twin bed which had not been slept in and bent on Roger a glance of astonishment, which changed to contempt when she saw the breakfast in his hand. She thought he was bringing it as a capitulation.

"I don't want any breakfast," she said coldly, and his heart sank, "except some coffee."

"No breakfast?" Roger's voice expressed disappointment.

"I said I'd take some coffee."

Roger discreetly deposited the tray on a table beside the bed and returned quickly to the kitchen.

"We're going away until tomorrow afternoon," he told Bebé, "and I want to close up the house right now. So you just put on your hat and go home."

He looked at his watch. It was ten minutes to eight and he wanted to catch the 8:10 train. He waited five minutes and then tiptoed softly upstairs and into Gretchen's room. She was sound asleep. The coffee cup was empty save for black dregs and a film of thin brown paste on the bottom. He looked at her rather anxiously, but her breathing was regular and clear.

From the closet he took a suitcase and very quickly began filling it with her shoes—street shoes, evening slippers, rubber-soled oxfords—he had not realized that she owned so many pairs. When he closed the suitcase it was bulging.

He hesitated a minute, took a pair of sewing scissors from a box and following the telephone wire until it went out of sight behind the dresser, severed it in one neat clip. He jumped as there was a soft knock at the door. It was the nursemaid. He had forgotten her existence.

"Mrs. Halsey and I are going up to the city till tomorrow," he said glibly.

Back in the room, a wave of pity passed over him. Gretchen seemed suddenly lovely and helpless, sleeping there. It was somehow terrible to rob her young life of a day. He touched her hair with his fingers, and as she murmured something in her dream he leaned over and kissed her bright cheek. Then he picked up the suitcase full of shoes, locked the door and ran briskly down the stairs.

III

BY FIVE o'clock that afternoon the last package of cards for Garrod's shoes had been sent by messenger to H. G. Garrod at the Biltmore Hotel. He was to give some sort of decision by nine o'clock next morning. At 5:30 Roger's stenographer tapped him on the shoulder.

"Here's Mr. Golden, the superintendent of the building, to see you."

Roger turned around dazedly.

"Oh, how do?"

Mr. Golden came directly to the point. If Mr. Halsey intended to keep the office any longer the little oversight about the rent had better be remedied right away.

"Mr. Golden," said Roger wearily, "everything'll be all right tomorrow. If you worry me now maybe you'll never get your money. After tomorrow nothing'll matter."

Mr. Golden looked at the tenant uneasily. Young men sometimes did away with themselves when business went wrong. Then his eye fell unpleasantly on the initialed suitcase beside the desk.

"Going on a trip?" he asked pointedly.

"What? Oh, no. That's just some clothes."

"Clothes, eh? Well, Mr. Halsey, just to prove that you mean what you say, suppose you let me keep that suitcase until tomorrow noon."

"Help yourself."

Mr. Golden picked it up with a deprecatory gesture.

"Just a matter of form," he remarked.

"I understand," said Roger, swinging around to his desk. "Good afternoon."

Mr. Golden seemed to feel that the conversation should close on a softer key.

"And don't work too hard, Mr. Halsey. You don't want to have a nervous break——"

"No," shouted Roger, "I don't. But I will if you don't leave me alone."

As the door closed behind Mr. Golden, Roger's stenographer turned sympathetically around.

"You shouldn't have let him get away with that," she said. "What's in there? Clothes?"

"No," answered Roger absently. "Just all my wife's shoes."

He slept in the office that night on a sofa beside his desk. At dawn he awoke with a nervous start, rushed out into the street for coffee and returned in ten minutes in a panic—afraid that he might have missed Mr. Garrod's telephone call. It was then 6:30.

By eight o'clock his whole body seemed to be on fire. When his two artists arrived he was stretched on the couch in almost physical pain. The phone rang imperatively at 9:30 and he picked up the receiver with trembling hands.

"Hello."

"Is this the Halsey agency?"

"Yes, this is Mr. Halsey speaking."

"This is Mr. H. G. Garrod."

Roger's heart stopped beating.

"I called up, young fellow, to say that this is wonderful work you've given us here. We want all of it and as much more as your office can do."

"Oh, God!" cried Roger into the transmitter.

"What?" Mr. H. G. Garrod was considerably startled. "Say, wait a minute there!"

But he was talking to nobody. The phone had clattered to the floor and Roger, stretched full length on the couch, was sobbing as if his heart would break.

IV

THREE hours later, his face somewhat pale, but his eyes calm as a child's, Roger opened the door of his wife's bedroom with the morning paper under his arm. At the sound of his footsteps she started awake.

"What time is it?" she demanded.

He looked at his watch.

"Twelve o'clock."

Suddenly she began to cry.

"Roger," she said brokenly, "I'm sorry I was so bad last night."

He nodded coolly.

"Everything's all right now," he said. Then, after a pause, "I've got the account—the first one."

She turned toward him quickly.

"You have?" Then, after a minute's silence, "Can I get a new dress?"

"Dress?" He laughed shortly. "You can get a dozen. This account alone will bring us in forty thousand a year. It's one of the biggest in the West."

She looked at him, startled.

"Forty thousand a year!"

"Yes."

"Gosh"—and then faintly—"I didn't know it'd really be anything like that." Again she thought a minute. "We can have a house like George Tompkins'."

"I want a home—not an interior-decoration shop."

"Forty thousand a year!" she repeated again, and then added softly, "Oh, Roger ——"

"Yes?"

"I'm not going out with George Tompkins."

"I wouldn't let you," he said shortly, "even if you wanted to."

She made a show of indignation.

"Why, I've had a date with him for this Thursday for weeks."

"It isn't Thursday."

"It is."

"It's Friday."

"Why, Roger, you must be crazy! Don't you think I know what day it is?"

"It isn't Thursday," he said stubbornly. "Look!" And he held out the morning paper.

"Friday!" she exclaimed. "Why, this is a mistake! This must be last week's paper. Today's Thursday."

She closed her eyes and thought for a moment.

"Yesterday was Wednesday," she said decisively. "The laundress came yesterday. I guess I know."

"Well," he said smugly, "look at the paper. There isn't any question about it."

With a bewildered look on her face she got out of bed and began searching for her clothes. Roger went into the bathroom to shave. A minute later he heard the springs creak again. Gretchen was getting back into bed.

"What's the matter?" he inquired, putting his head around the corner of the bathroom.

"I'm scared," she said in a trembling voice. "I think my nerves are giving away. I can't find any of my shoes."

"Your shoes? Why, the closet's full of them."

"I know, but I can't see one." Her face was pale with fear. "Oh, Roger!"

Roger came to her bedside and put his arm around her.

"Oh, Roger," she cried, "what's the matter with me? First that newspaper and now all my shoes. Take care of me, Roger."

"I'll get the doctor," he said.

He walked remorselessly to the telephone and took up the receiver.

"Phone seems to be out of order," he remarked after a minute; "I'll send Bebé."

The doctor arrived in ten minutes.

"I think I'm on the verge of a collapse," Gretchen told him in a strained voice.

Doctor Gregory sat down on the edge of the bed and took her wrist in his hand.

"It seems to be in the air this morning."

"I got up," said Gretchen in an awed voice, "and I found that I'd lost a whole day. I had an engagement to go riding with George Tompkins ——"

"What?" exclaimed the doctor in surprise. Then he laughed.

"George Tompkins won't go riding with anyone for many days to come."

"Has he gone away?" asked Gretchen curiously.

"He's going West."

"Why?" demanded Roger. "Is he running away with somebody's wife?"

"No," said Doctor Gregory. "He's had a nervous breakdown."

"What?" they exclaimed in unison.

"He just collapsed like an opera hat in his cold shower."

"But he was always talking about his—his balanced life," gasped Gretchen. "He was always warning Roger about overstrain. He had it on his mind."

"I know," said the doctor. "He's been babbling about it all morning. I think it's driven him a little mad. He worked pretty hard at it, you know."

"At what?" demanded Roger in bewilderment.

"At keeping his life balanced." He turned to Gretchen. "Now all I'll prescribe for this lady here is a good rest. If she'll just stay around the house for a few days and take forty winks of sleep she'll be as fit as ever. She's been under some strain."

"Doctor," exclaimed Roger hoarsely, "don't you think I'd better have a rest or something? I've been working pretty hard lately."

"You!" Doctor Gregory laughed, slapped him violently on the back. "My boy, I never saw you looking better in your life."

Roger turned around quickly to conceal his smile—winked forty times, or almost forty times, at the autographed picture of Mr. George Tompkins, which hung slightly askew on the bedroom wall.

Works Cited

Section 1: Works by F. Scott Fitzgerald

Due to the difficulties of obtaining the magazine texts for many of Fitzgerald's works as discussed in the introduction to this volume, we cite James L. W. West III's Cambridge Editions for Fitzgerald's works not included in this volume. When available, the paperback editions have been cited.

Short story collections

All the Sad Young Men. Edited by James L. W. West, III. New York: Cambridge University Press, 2007.

The Basil, Josephine, and Gwen Stories. Edited by James L. W. West III. New York: Cambridge University Press, 2009.

Best Early Stories of F. Scott Fitzgerald. Edited by Bryant Mangum. New York: The Modern Library, 2005.

Bits of Paradise. Edited by Matthew J. Bruccoli. Harmondsworth: Penguin, 1976.

Flappers and Philosophers. Edited by James L. W. West, III. New York: Cambridge University Press, 2012.

I'd Die for You and Other Lost Stories. Edited by Anne Margaret Daniel. London: Simon & Schuster UK, 2017.

The Short Stories of F. Scott Fitzgerald: A New Collection. Edited by Matthew J. Bruccoli. New York: Scribner, 1989.

Spires and Gargoyles. Edited by James L. W. West, III. New York: Cambridge University Press, 2010.

Tales of the Jazz Age. Edited by James L. W. West, III. New York: Cambridge University Press, 2012.

Fitzgerald's novels

The Beautiful and Damned. Edited by James L. W. West, III. New York: Cambridge University Press, 2014.

The Great Gatsby: A Variorum Edition. Edited by James L. W. West, III. New York: Cambridge University Press, 2019.
This Side of Paradise. Edited by James L. W. West, III. New York: Cambridge University Press, 2012.

Other works by Fitzgerald

Bruccoli, Matthew J. and Jackson R. Bryer, eds. *F. Scott Fitzgerald in His Own Time: A Miscellany.* Kent, OH: The Kent State University Press, 1971.
Bruccoli, Matthew J., Scottie Fitzgerald Smith, and Joan Kerr, eds. *The Romantic Egoists: A Pictorial Autobiography from the Scrapbooks and Albums of F. Scott and Zelda Fitzgerald.* Columbia: The University of South Carolina Press, 2003.
F. Scott Fitzgerald's Ledger, 1919–1938. The Matthew J. and Arlyn Bruccoli Collection of F. Scott Fitzgerald, University of South Carolina Library. https://digital.library.sc.edu/collections/f-scott-fitzgeralds-ledger-1919-1938/
"How to Live on $36,000 a Year." *Saturday Evening Post,* 5 April 1924.
My Lost City: Personal Essays, 1920–1940. Edited by James L. W. West, III. New York: Cambridge University Press, 2005.
"This is a Magazine." *Vanity Fair,* December 1920.
The Vegetable: Or from President to Postman. Clifton, NJ: Augustus M. Kelley, 1972.

Collections of letters

Bruccoli, Matthew J., ed. *F. Scott Fitzgerald: A Life in Letters.* New York: Touchstone, 1995.
Bruccoli, Matthew J., ed., with the assistance of Jennifer McCabe Atkinson. *As Ever, Scott Fitz—: Letters Between F. Scott Fitzgerald and His Literary Agent Harold Ober, 1919–1940.* Philadelphia, PA: Lippincott, 1972.
Bruccoli, Matthew J. and Margaret M. Duggan, eds., with the assistance of Susan Walker. *Correspondence of F. Scott Fitzgerald.* New York: Random House, 1980.
Bryer, Jackson R. and Cathy W. Barks, eds. *Dear Scott, Dearest Zelda: The Love Letters of F. Scott and Zelda Fitzgerald.* London: Bloomsbury, 2003.
Bryer, Jackson R. and John Kuehl, eds. *Dear Scott/Dear Max: The Fitzgerald-Perkins Correspondence.* London: Cassell & Company, 1971.

Section 2: Scholarly Sources

Adams, Jade Broughton. *F. Scott Fitzgerald's Short Fiction: From Ragtime to Swing Time*. Edinburgh: Edinburgh University Press, 2019.

Behr, Edward. *Prohibition: Thirteen Years That Changed America*. New York: Arcade Publishing, 1996.

Birmingham, Kevin. *The Most Dangerous Book: The Battle for James Joyce's* Ulysses. London: Head of Zeus, 2014.

Blazek, William, David W. Ullrich, and Kirk Curnutt. Introduction to *F. Scott Fitzgerald's* The Beautiful and Damned: *New Critical Essays*, 1–22. Edited by William Blazek, David W. Ullrich, and Kirk Curnutt. Baton Rouge: Louisiana State University Press, 2022.

Boddy, Kasia. "Edward J. O'Brien's Prize Stories of the 'National Soul.'" *Critical Quarterly* 52, no. 2 (2010): 14–28.

Brown, David S. *Paradise Lost: A Life of F. Scott Fitzgerald*. Cambridge, MA: The Belknap Press of Harvard University Press, 2017.

Bruccoli, Matthew J. "On F. Scott Fitzgerald and 'Bernice Bobs her Hair.'" In *The American Short Story*, edited by Calvin Skaggs, 219–223. New York: Dell, 1977.

Bruccoli, Matthew J. *Some Sort of Epic Grandeur: The Life of F. Scott Fitzgerald*, 2nd revised edition. Columbia: University of South Carolina Press, 2002.

Bryer, Jackson R., ed. *F. Scott Fitzgerald: The Critical Reception*. New York: Burt Franklin & Co, 1978.

Campbell, Charles. *History of the Colony and Ancient Dominion of Virginia*. Philadelphia, PA: J. B. Lippincott and Co, 1860.

Chernow, Ron. *Titan: The Life of John D. Rockefeller, Sr*. New York: Random House, 1998.

Churchwell, Sarah. *Careless People: Murder, Mayhem and the Invention of* The Great Gatsby. London: Virago, 2013.

Coffey, Ellen Greenman. *John D. Rockefeller: Empire Builder*. Englewood Cliffs, NJ: Silver Burdett Press, 1989.

Cohn, Jan. *Creating America: George Horace Lorimer and the* Saturday Evening Post. Pittsburgh, PA: University of Pittsburgh Press, 1989.

Cox, J. Randolph, ed. Introduction to *Dashing Diamond Dick and Other Classic Dime Novels,* ix–xxvi. London: Penguin Books, 2007.

Curnutt, Kirk. "The Periodical World of *The Beautiful and Damned*." In *F. Scott Fitzgerald's* The Beautiful and Damned: *New Critical Essays*, edited by William Blazek, David W. Ullrich, and Kirk Curnutt, 67–90. Baton Rouge: Louisiana State University Press, 2022.

Curnutt, Kirk and Robert Trogdon. "John Jackson's Arcady." *Master the 40: The Stories of F. Scott Fitzgerald*. Podcast audio. 22 April 2021. https://masterthe40.buzzsprout.com/

Currell, Susan. *American Culture in the 1920s*. Edinburgh: Edinburgh University Press, 2009.

Daniels, Thomas E. "The Texts of 'Winter Dreams.'" Fitzgerald/Hemingway Annual 9 (1977): 77–100.

Dean, Gabrielle. "Cover Story: The *Smart Set's* Clever Packaging, 1908–1923." *The Journal of Modern Periodical Studies* 4, no. 1 (2013): 1–29.

Douglas, George H. *The Smart Magazines: 50 Years of Literary Revelry and High Jinks at* Vanity Fair, The New Yorker, Life, Esquire, *and* The Smart Set. Hamden, CT: Archon Books, 1991.

Duncan-Jones, Katharine and H. R. Woudhuysen, eds. Introduction to *Shakespeare's Poems: Venus and Adonis, The Rape of Lucrece and the Shorter Poems*, 1–124. London: Bloomsbury, 2018.

Dye, Nancy Schrom. "History of Childbirth in America." *Signs* 6, no. 1 (1980): 97–108.

Edwards, Lydia. *How to Read a Dress*. London: Bloomsbury Academic, 2017.

Edwards, Lydia. *How to Read a Suit*. London: Bloomsbury, 2020.

Fagan, Brian and Nadia Durrani. *What We Did in Bed: A Horizontal History*. New Haven, CT: Yale University Press, 2019.

Geiger, Roger L. *To Advance Knowledge: The Growth of American Research Universities, 1900–1940*. New Brunswick, NJ: Transaction Publishers, 2004.

Genette, Gérard. "Introduction to the Paratext," translated by Marie Mclean. *New Literary History* 22, no. 2 (Spring 1991): 261–272.

Green, Jonathon. *Chambers Slang Dictionary*. Edinburgh: Chambers, 2009.

Herodotus. *The Histories*. Translated by Aubrey de Sélincourt. London: Penguin Books, 2003.

Hochfelder, David. *The Telegraph in America, 1832–1920*. Baltimore, MD: The Johns Hopkins University Press, 2012.

Homer. *The Iliad*. Translated by Martin Hammond. London: Penguin Books, 1987.

Hugill, Peter J. *World Trade Since 1431: Geography, Technology and Capitalism*. Baltimore, MD: The Johns Hopkins University Press, 1993.

Kurowski, Travis. "The Literary in Theory." In *The Routledge Companion to the British and North American Literary Magazine*, edited by Tim Lanzendörfer, 27–35. New York: Routledge, 2022.

Landau, Sarah Bradford and Carl W. Condit. *Rise of the New York Skyscraper, 1865–1913*. New Haven, CT: Yale University Press, 1996.

Mangum, Bryant. *A Fortune Yet: Money in the Art of F. Scott Fitzgerald's Short Stories*. New York: Garland Publishing, 1991.

Mangum, Bryant. "Echoes of Arcady: F. Scott Fitzgerald and *It's a Wonderful Life*." *F. Scott Fitzgerald Review* 5 (2006): 54–64.

Mangum, Bryant. "*Metropolitan's* 'Winter Dreams' and *The Great Gatsby*." *F. Scott Fitzgerald Review* 19 (2021): 54–66.

Martinez, J. Michael. *Terrorist Attacks on American Soil: From the Civil War Era to the Present*. Plymouth, MA: Rowman and Littlefield Publishers, 2012.

Milford, Nancy. *Zelda: A Biography*. New York: HarperCollins Publishers, 2011.

Mizener, Arthur. *The Far Side of Paradise: A Biography of F. Scott Fitzgerald*. London: William Heinemann, 1969.

Mott, Frank Luther. *A History of American Magazines, Volume IV: 1885–1905*. Cambridge, MA: Harvard University Press, 1957.

Mott, Frank Luther. *A History of American Magazines, Volume V: 1905–1930*. Cambridge, MA: Harvard University Press, 1968.

Nolan, Jennifer. "Illustrating 'Winter Dreams.'" *F. Scott Fitzgerald Review* 19 (2021): 32–53.

Nolan, Jennifer. "May Wilson Preston and the Birth of Fitzgerald's Flapper: Illustrating Social Transformation in 'Bernice Bobs Her Hair.'" *Journal of Modern Periodical Studies* 8, no. 1 (2017): 56–80.

Nolan, Jennifer. "Reading 'Babylon Revisited' as a *Post* Text: F. Scott Fitzgerald, George Horace Lorimer, and the *Saturday Evening Post* Audience." *Book History* 20 (2017): 351–373.

Nolan, Jennifer. "Visualizing 'The Rich Boy:' F. Scott Fitzgerald, F. R. Gruger, and *Red Book Magazine*. *The F. Scott Fitzgerald Review* 15 (2017): 17–33.

Ovid, *Metamorphoses: A New Verse Translation*. Translated by David Raeburn. London: Penguin Books, 2004.

Page, Dave and John Koblas. *F. Scott Fitzgerald in Minnesota: Toward the Summit*. Clearwater, MN: North Star Press of St. Cloud, 1996.

Rainey, Lawrence. "The Cultural Economy of Modernism." In *The Cambridge Companion to Modernism*, 2nd edition, edited by Michael Levenson, 33–62. Cambridge: Cambridge University Press, 2011.

Regis, Pamela. *A Natural History of the Romance Novel*. Philadelphia: University of Pennsylvania Press, 2007.

Roberts, Peter. *The History of the Automobile*. New York: Simon & Schuster, 1984.

Shaw, Arnold. *The Jazz Age: Popular Music in the 1920s*. New York: Oxford University Press, 1987.

Simmonds, Roy S. *Edward J. O'Brien and his Role in the Rise of the American Short Story in the 1920s and 1930s*. Lewiston, NY: Edwin Mellen Press, 2001.

Street & Smith. *Titled Americans: A List of American Ladies Who Have Married Foreigners of Rank*. New York: Street & Smith, 1890.

Tooze, Adam. *The Deluge: The Great War and the Remaking of Global Order*. London: Penguin Books, 2015.

Turnbull, Andrew. *Scott Fitzgerald*. Harmondsworth: Pelican Books, 1970.

Wesley Winans Stout Papers, 1913–1954. Library of Congress, Washington, DC.

West, James L. W. III. Introduction to *Flappers and Philosophers* by F. Scott Fitzgerald, xi–xxxi. New York: Cambridge University Press, 2000.

West, James L. W. III. Introduction to *Tales of the Jazz Age* by F. Scott Fitzgerald, xi–xxviii. New York: Cambridge University Press, 2002.

West, James L. W. III. *The Perfect Hour: The Romance of F. Scott Fitzgerald and Ginevra King, His First Love*. New York: Random House, 2005.

Young, John K. "Pynchon in Popular Magazines." *Critique* 44, no. 4 (Summer 2003): 389–404.

Section 3: Popular Sources

"$25 from Owl Club Swells Jungle Fund." *The Baltimore Sun*, 27 May 1922.

"16,000 Attend Masses in St. Paul Cathedral." *Star Tribune*, 29 March 1915.

"A. & S. Furniture Sale is only six days off—wait for it!" Advertisement. *Times Union*, 21 January 1924.

"All the World Returns to Paris." *Harper's Bazar*, June 1924.

"Any Time is 'Meadowbrook Time' at Aristocratic Santa Barbara." Advertisement. *Harper's Bazar*, July 1922.

"Be an Artist." Advertisement. *Metropolitan Magazine*, April 1922.

"Become an Artist!" Advertisement. *Metropolitan Magazine*, December 1922.

Benchley, Robert C. "Government Ownership of the Movies." *Vanity Fair*, February 1918.

Byrne, Donn. "Paul and Ruth and Solomon." *Hearst's International*, August 1922.

Carpenter, Niles. *Immigrants and Their Children: A Study Based on Census Statistics Relative to the Foreign Born and the Native White of Foreign or Mixed Parentage*. Washington: Government Printing Office, 1927.

Carstairs, J. Elbert. "How Can We Make America Support Its Artists?" *Vanity Fair*, June 1924.

Castle, Vernon. *Modern Dancing*. New York: The World Syndicate Co, 1914.

"Chauffeur Tells of His Love for Heiress." *Daily News*, 5 September 1922.

"'Chicago Dance' Too Slow for New York." *The San Francisco Examiner*, 11 December 1922.

"City Drops in Flour Race." *Star Tribune*, 13 October 1948.

Commissioner of Internal Revenue. *Statistics of Income from Returns of Net Income for 1920*. Washington: Government Printing Office, 1922.

"Cook's Mediterranean De Luxe Cruise." Advertisement. *Vanity Fair*, July 1923.

"The Crown Jewel Sale Ended." *The New York Times*, 24 May 1887.

"Curtain Down Soon in East." *The Pittsburgh Press*, 21 October 1906.

Durham Duplex Razor Company. Advertisement. *Collier's*, 27 May 1922.

"Erté Discusses Art in General and the Art of the Cinema in Particular." *Harper's Bazar*, February 1922.

Evans, Charles Jr. "The Royal and Ancient Game." *Vanity Fair*, June 1922.

Eversharp. Advertisement. *Collier's*, 27 May 1922.

"Extent of Ford Motor Parts Profit Revealed." *The Wall Street Journal*, 5 February 1923.

"Fashions." *Godey's Lady's Book and Magazine*, May 1880.

"The Fashions and Pleasures of New York." *Vanity Fair*, January 1922.

"Fashions and Pleasures of New York." *Vanity Fair*, March 1922.

"Footprints on the Sands of Palm Beach." *Vogue*, 1 April 1922.

"For the Well Dressed Man." *Vanity Fair*, July 1920.

"For the Well Dressed Man." *Vanity Fair*, January 1921.

"For the Well Dressed Man." *Vanity Fair*, February 1921.

"For the Well Dressed Man." *Vanity Fair*, February 1922.

"For the Well Dressed Man." *Vanity Fair*, October 1923.

"George Ade Explains 'Twenty-Three,' a New Slang Phrase." *The St. Louis Post-Dispatch*, 3 December 1899.

"Gilda Gray, an Exotic Reincarnation." *Vanity Fair*, August 1923.

"Good Afternoon! Have you a Little P.D. in Your Home?" Review of *This Side of Paradise*, by F. Scott Fitzgerald. *St. Louis Post-Dispatch*, 1 April 1920.

"Gophers are after Championship in Western Basket-ball Circles." *The Minneapolis Journal*, 10 December 1905.

"The Great Paris Show." *The Washington Times*, 15 April 1900.

Harper's Bazar. Advertisement. *Harper's Bazar*, December 1921.

Harr, L. L. "Pung-Chow." Advertisement. *Vanity Fair*, March 1923.

"Heiress is Wedded Despite Relatives." *The New York Times*, 31 March 1920.

Hibbard, George. "The Quality of Smartness." *Vanity Fair*, May 1920.

Higgins, Rosalie Armistead. "Women and Society." *The Montgomery Advertiser*, 24 October 1912.

Hodgson Burnett, Frances. *Little Lord Fauntleroy*. New York: Charles Scribner's Sons, 1897.

"How Harper's Bazar Gathers Its Fashion Information." *Harper's Bazar*, June 1922.

"How Our Plutocrats Roost in Park Avenue." *The Literary Digest*, 2 July 1927.

"How to Know the Winter Hat of 1921." *Harper's Bazar*, October 1921.

H.R.H. Edward, Duke of Windsor. *A King's Story: The Memoirs of the Duke of Windsor*. New York: G. P. Putnam's Sons, 1951.

Hull, E. M. *The Sheik*. Boston, MA: Small, Maynard and Company, 1921.

Huxley, Aldous. "Follow My Leader." *Vanity Fair*, January 1924.

"The Jelly Bean." *The Richaland Beacon-News*, 24 January 1920.

"'Jelly Beans' Must Stay Off Corners." *The Montgomery Advertiser*, 3 October 1920.

Lardner, Ring. "In Regards to Geniuses." *Hearst's International*, May 1923.

"The Literary Market." *The Editor: The Journal of Information for Literary Workers* 61, no. 5 (5 May 1922): I–IV.

"Little Bits of Local News." *The Montgomery Advertiser*, 5 May 1898.

"Long Boston Dance Is with Us at Last." *The New Castle Herald*, 20 October 1911.

Lowry, Helen Bullitt. "'When the Honeymoon is A-Shining.'" *Harper's Bazar*, June 1922.

Lyons, Marie. "From Head to Heel." *Harper's Bazar*, January 1924.

"Medieval History of Tenth Street and Its Mansards." *St. Paul Globe*, 21 February 1904.

"Mr. Hardhack on the Sensational in Literature and in Life." *The Atlantic Monthly*, August 1870.

The Nast International Travel Bureau. Advertisement. *Vanity Fair*, June 1922.

"Nation's Income Tax $1,269,630,104 in '19." *The New York Times*, 25 July 1921.

"New York Fashions." *Harper's Bazar*, 30 March 1872.

"Notes of the Legislature." *Star Tribune*, 7 April 1911.

O'Brien, Edward. Introduction to *The Best American Short Stories of 1915 and the Yearbook of the American Short Story*, 3–11. Boston, MA: Small, Maynard, and Company, 1916.

"Ohioans Mobilize Here." Advertisement. *The Montgomery Advertiser*, 7 October 1917.

"Paris Plans its Wardrobe for as Far South as Africa." *Harper's Bazar*, January 1924.

"Plan to Check 5th Av. Traffic Jam Approved." *New-York Tribune*, 6 February 1920.

"Pulitzer Medal Given to the Times." *The New York Times*, 4 June 1918.

"Ready-to-wear Sport Models for Spring and Summer." *Vanity Fair*, April 1922.

Saturday Evening Post Editorial Staff (George Horace Lorimer et al.). *The Saturday Evening Post*. Philadelphia, PA: Curtis Publishing Company, Advertising Department, 1923.

Sayre, Zelda. "*The Beautiful and Damned*: Friend Husband's Latest." Review of *The Beautiful and Damned* [1922]. In *F. Scott Fitzgerald in His Own Time*, edited by Matthew J. Bruccoli and Jackson R. Bryer, 332–334. New York: Popular Library, 1971.

Seldes, Gilbert. "Shorter and Better Stories." *The Dial* 75, August 1923.

Silk Stockings by Van Raalte. Advertisement. *Vogue*, 1 April 1922.

"Society Exodus from Summer Resorts Begins." *New York Tribune*, 6 September 1922.

"Society Turns to Out Door Life." *New York Herald*, 15 May 1921.

"The Sportswoman Costumes Her Many Rôles." *Harper's Bazar*, June 1921.

"St. Margaret's Hospital Dedicated by Bishop Edward P. Allen of Mobile in the Prescence of a Great Crowd." *The Montgomery Advertiser*, 21 May 1902.

Steward, Donald Ogden. "A Nonsense Book of Etiquette." *Harper's Bazar*, November 1922.

"Sumptuous Stuffs and Livelier Colors Mark the New Paris Mode." *Harper's Bazar*, February 1919.

Table of Contents. *Hearst's International*, April 1923.

"These Models Assure Fair Days for the Traveller." *Vogue*, 15 June 1922.

"The Truth About Newport." *Harper's Bazar*, May 1922.

"Want to be One of Our $50.00 a Week Men?" Advertisement. *Saturday Evening Post*, 26 July 1924.

"Was Mark Twain Right?" Advertisement. *Collier's*, 20 May 1922.

Wenglin, Barbara. "Zelda's Montgomery." *The Montgomery Advertiser*, 29 April 1973.

"Where Smart America Goes with Its Becoming Palm Beach Tan Still upon It." *Harper's Bazar*, June 1923.

Whipple, Leon. "SatEvePost: Mirror of These States." *The Survey*, 1 March 1928.

White Star Line. Advertisement. *Vanity Fair*, May 1924.

"Whitney Wins at Squash." *The New York Times*, 7 January 1912.

"Why, You're Growing Younger Every Year." Advertisement. *Collier's*, 6 May 1922.

Williams, Mary Brush. "Hemstitched Lingerie from Paris." *The Ladies' Home Journal*, September 1920.

Wilson, Thomas. "The Swastika, The Earliest Known Symbol, and Its Migrations: With Observations on the Migration of Certain Industries in Prehistoric Times." In *Proceedings of the United States National Museum, Volume XVII, 1894*. Washington: Government Printing Office, 1895.

"The Year in Books." *The New York Times*, 27 November 1921.

"Younger Society Set Takes to Aquaplaning as Late Summer Amusement at Minnetonka." *The Minneapolis Sunday Tribune*, 3 September 1916.